THE NIGHT WITCHES

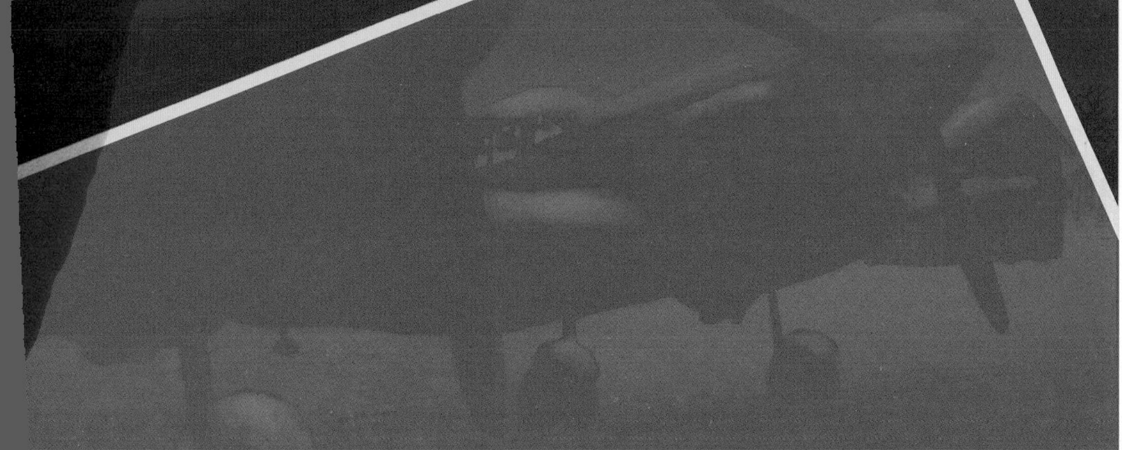

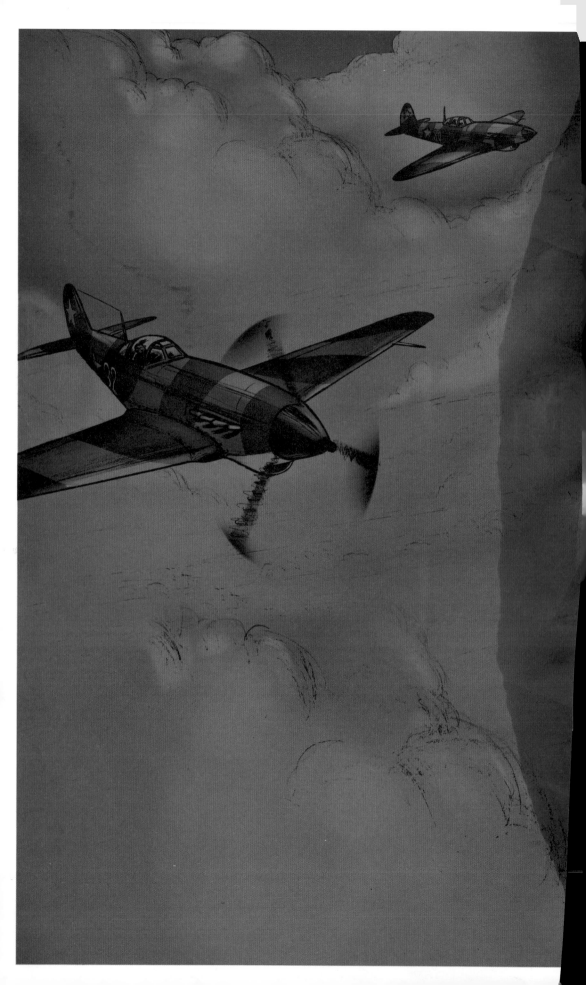

THE NIGHT WITCHES

Written by **GARTH ENNIS**
Penciled by **RUSS BRAUN**
Colored by **TONY AVIÑA**
Lettered by **SIMON BOWLAND**

Annapolis, Maryland

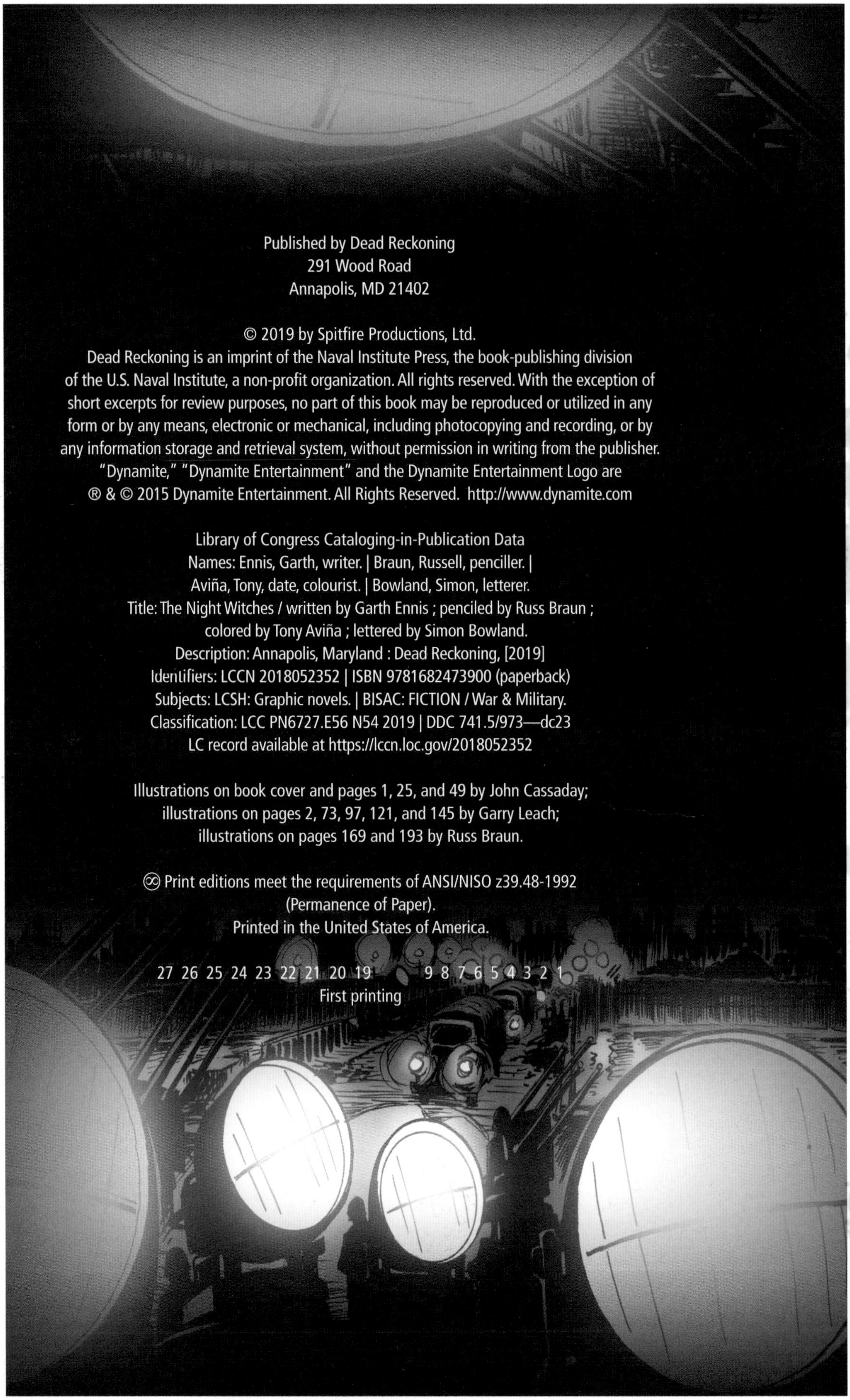

Published by Dead Reckoning
291 Wood Road
Annapolis, MD 21402

Library of Congress Cataloging-in-Publication Data
Names: Ennis, Garth, writer. | Braun, Russell, penciller. |
Aviña, Tony, date, colourist. | Bowland, Simon, letterer.
Title: The Night Witches / written by Garth Ennis ; penciled by Russ Braun ;
colored by Tony Aviña ; lettered by Simon Bowland.
Description: Annapolis, Maryland : Dead Reckoning, [2019]
Identifiers: LCCN 2018052352 | ISBN 9781682473900 (paperback)
Subjects: LCSH: Graphic novels. | BISAC: FICTION / War & Military.
Classification: LCC PN6727.E56 N54 2019 | DDC 741.5/973—dc23
LC record available at https://lccn.loc.gov/2018052352

Illustrations on book cover and pages 1, 25, and 49 by John Cassaday;
illustrations on pages 2, 73, 97, 121, and 145 by Garry Leach;
illustrations on pages 169 and 193 by Russ Braun.

♾ Print editions meet the requirements of ANSI/NISO z39.48-1992
(Permanence of Paper).
Printed in the United States of America.

27 26 25 24 23 22 21 20 19 9 8 7 6 5 4 3 2 1
First printing

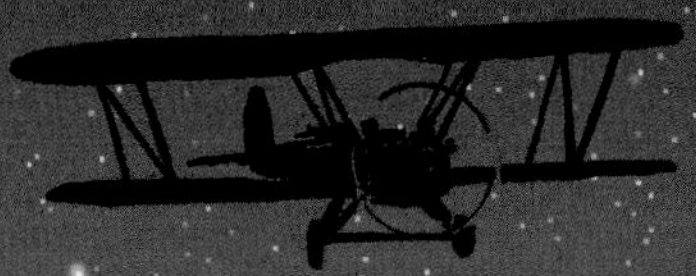

CONTENTS

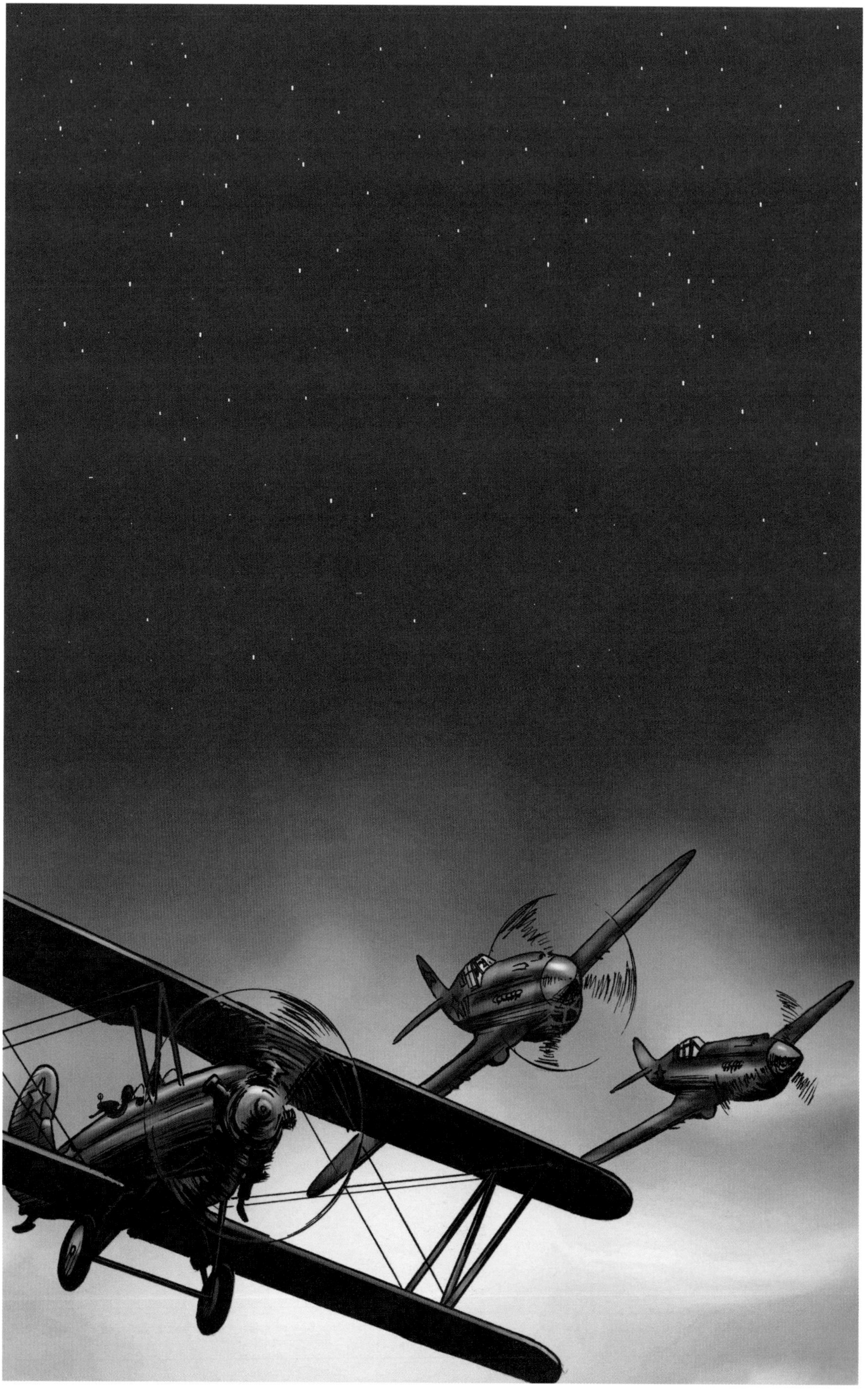

THE NIGHT WITCHES

Chapter 1

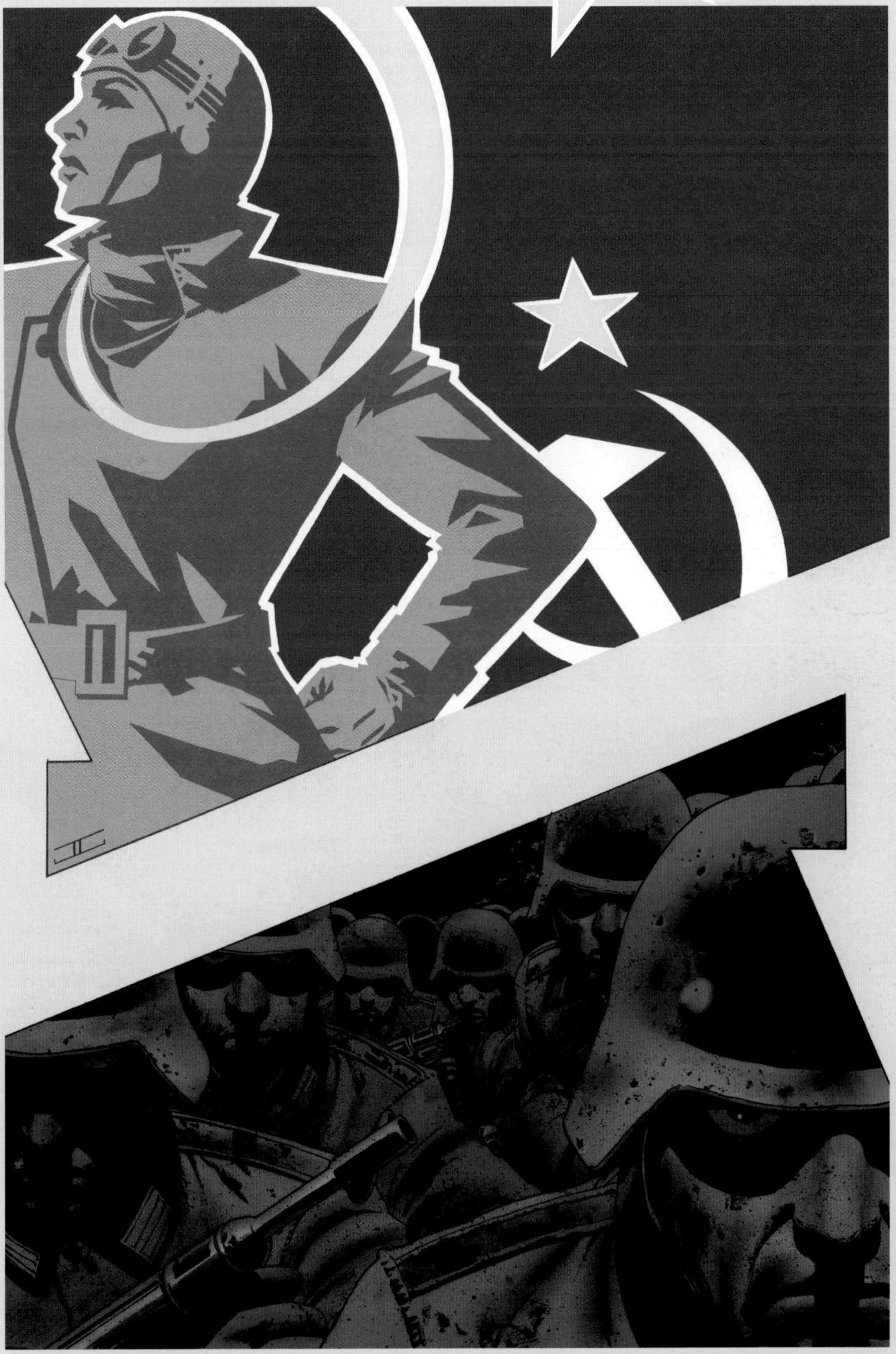

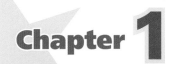

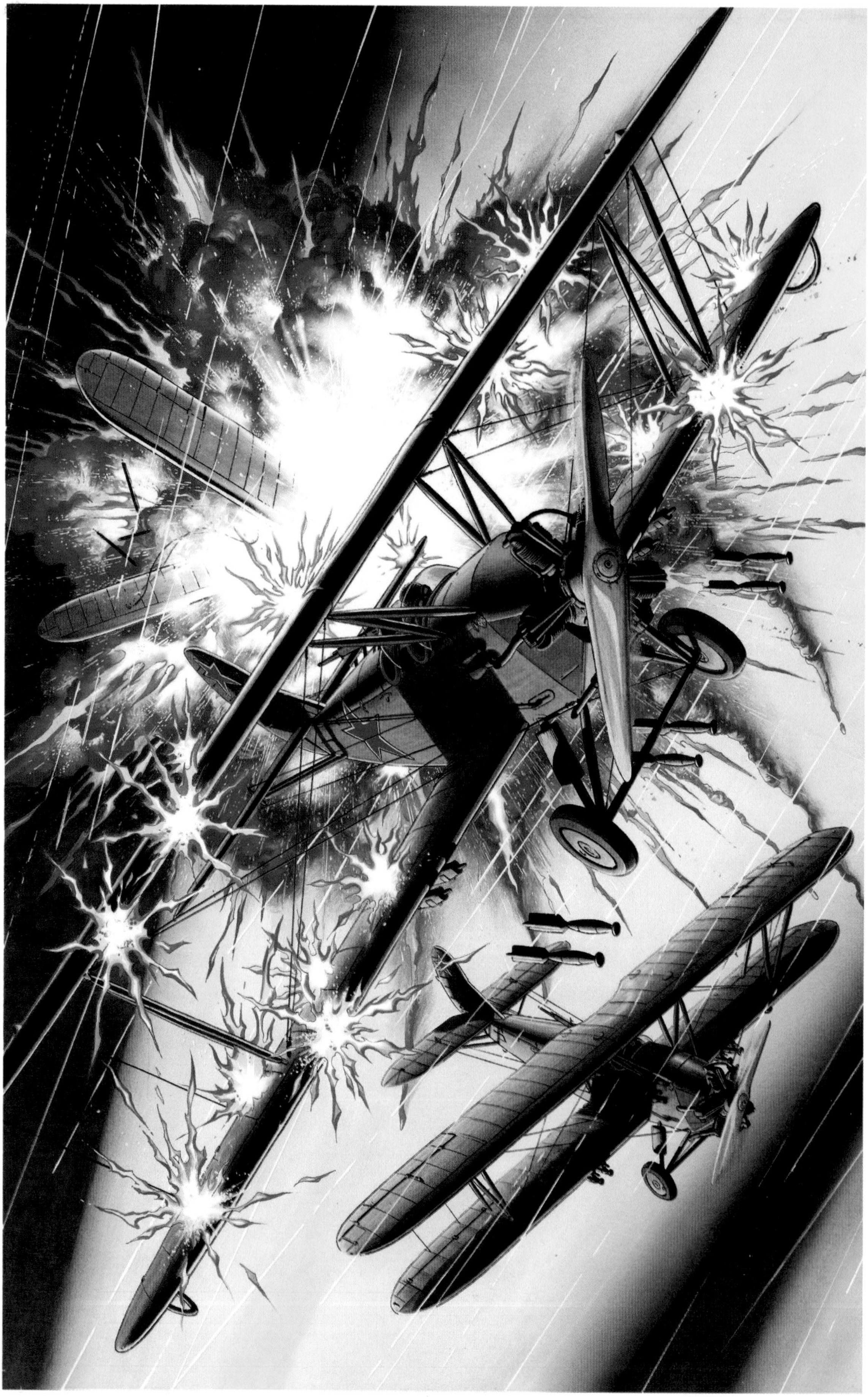

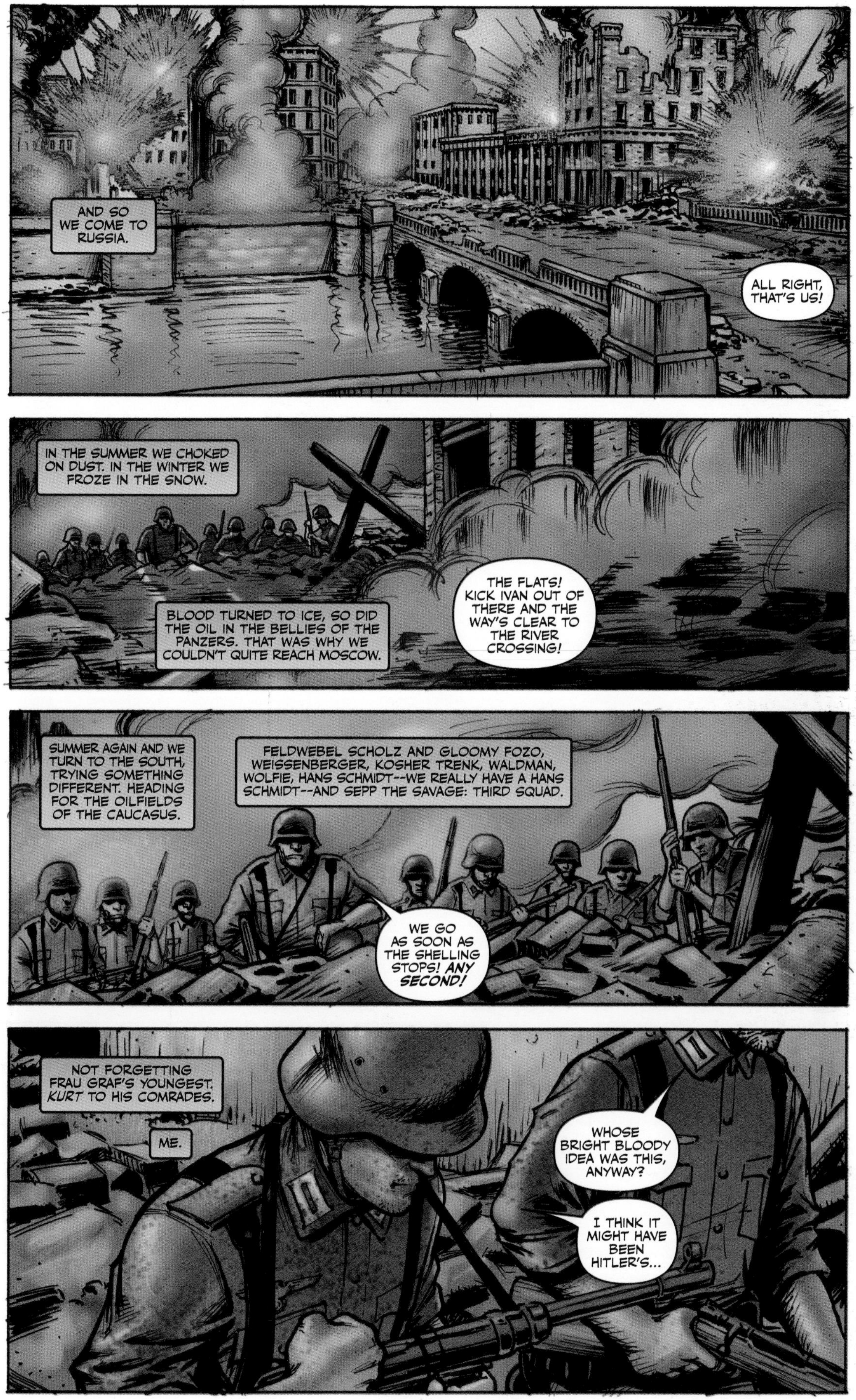
AND SO WE COME TO RUSSIA.
ALL RIGHT, THAT'S US!
IN THE SUMMER WE CHOKED ON DUST. IN THE WINTER WE FROZE IN THE SNOW.
BLOOD TURNED TO ICE, SO DID THE OIL IN THE BELLIES OF THE PANZERS. THAT WAS WHY WE COULDN'T QUITE REACH MOSCOW.
THE FLATS! KICK IVAN OUT OF THERE AND THE WAY'S CLEAR TO THE RIVER CROSSING!
SUMMER AGAIN AND WE TURN TO THE SOUTH, TRYING SOMETHING DIFFERENT. HEADING FOR THE OILFIELDS OF THE CAUCASUS.
FELDWEBEL SCHOLZ AND GLOOMY FOZO, WEISSENBERGER, KOSHER TRENK, WALDMAN, WOLFIE, HANS SCHMIDT--WE REALLY HAVE A HANS SCHMIDT--AND SEPP THE SAVAGE: THIRD SQUAD.
WE GO AS SOON AS THE SHELLING STOPS! *ANY SECOND!*
NOT FORGETTING FRAU GRAF'S YOUNGEST. *KURT* TO HIS COMRADES.
ME.
WHOSE BRIGHT BLOODY IDEA WAS THIS, ANYWAY?
I THINK IT MIGHT HAVE BEEN HITLER'S...

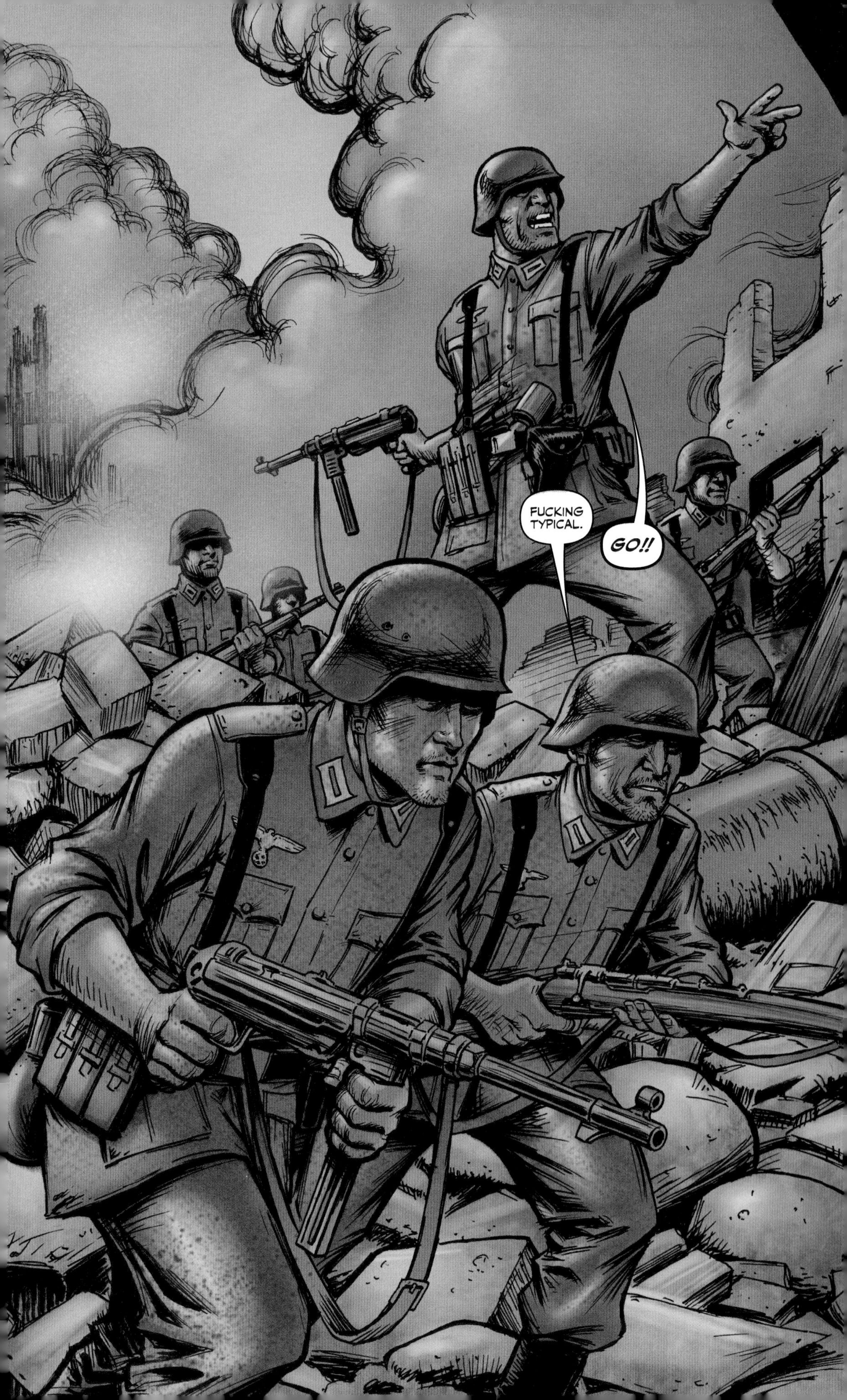
FUCKING TYPICAL.
GO!!

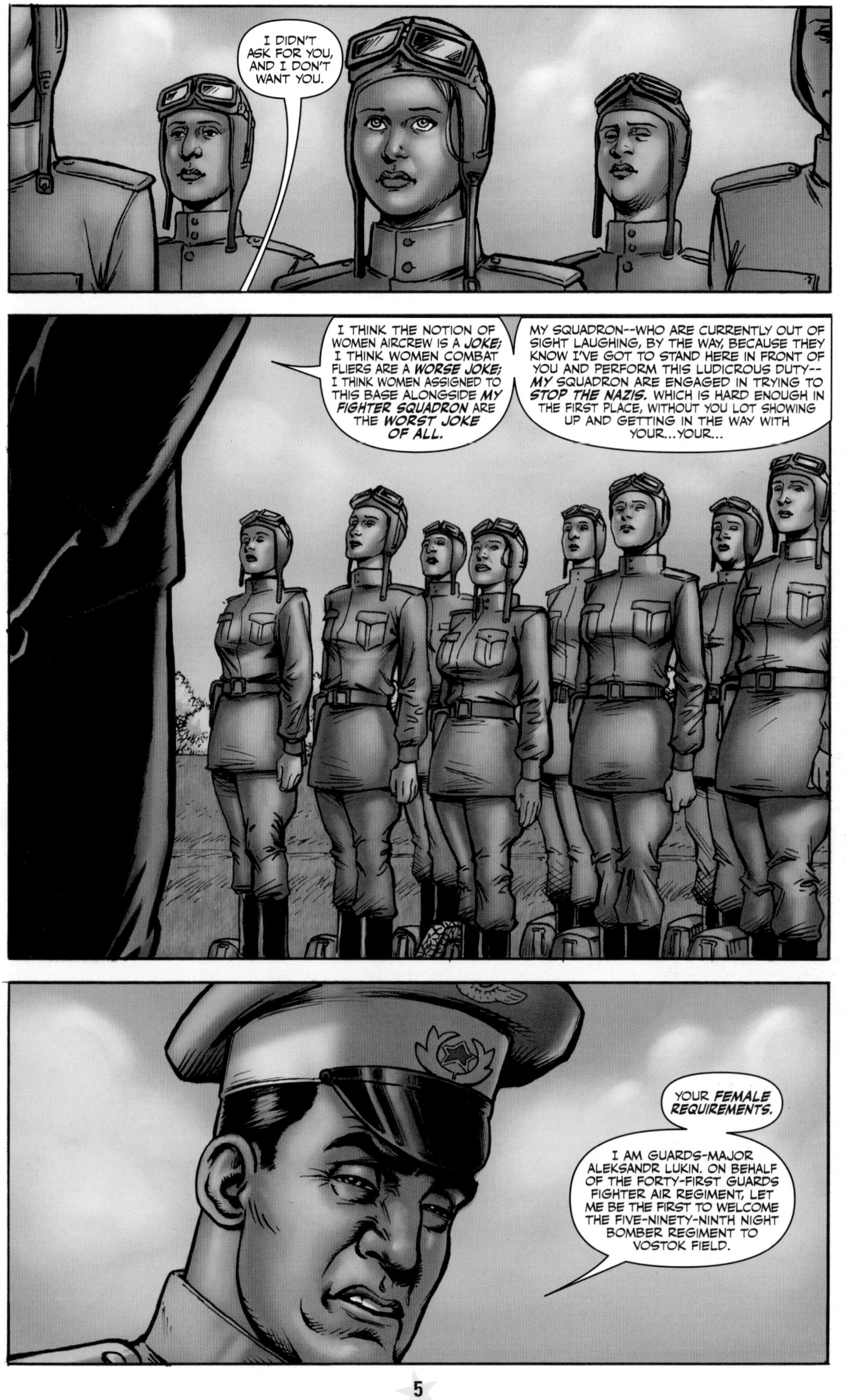
I DIDN'T ASK FOR YOU, AND I DON'T WANT YOU.
I THINK THE NOTION OF WOMEN AIRCREW IS A JOKE; I THINK WOMEN COMBAT FLIERS ARE A WORSE JOKE; I THINK WOMEN ASSIGNED TO THIS BASE ALONGSIDE MY FIGHTER SQUADRON ARE THE WORST JOKE OF ALL.
MY SQUADRON--WHO ARE CURRENTLY OUT OF SIGHT LAUGHING, BY THE WAY, BECAUSE THEY KNOW I'VE GOT TO STAND HERE IN FRONT OF YOU AND PERFORM THIS LUDICROUS DUTY--MY SQUADRON ARE ENGAGED IN TRYING TO STOP THE NAZIS. WHICH IS HARD ENOUGH IN THE FIRST PLACE, WITHOUT YOU LOT SHOWING UP AND GETTING IN THE WAY WITH YOUR...YOUR...
YOUR FEMALE REQUIREMENTS.
I AM GUARDS-MAJOR ALEKSANDR LUKIN. ON BEHALF OF THE FORTY-FIRST GUARDS FIGHTER AIR REGIMENT, LET ME BE THE FIRST TO WELCOME THE FIVE-NINETY-NINTH NIGHT BOMBER REGIMENT TO VOSTOK FIELD.

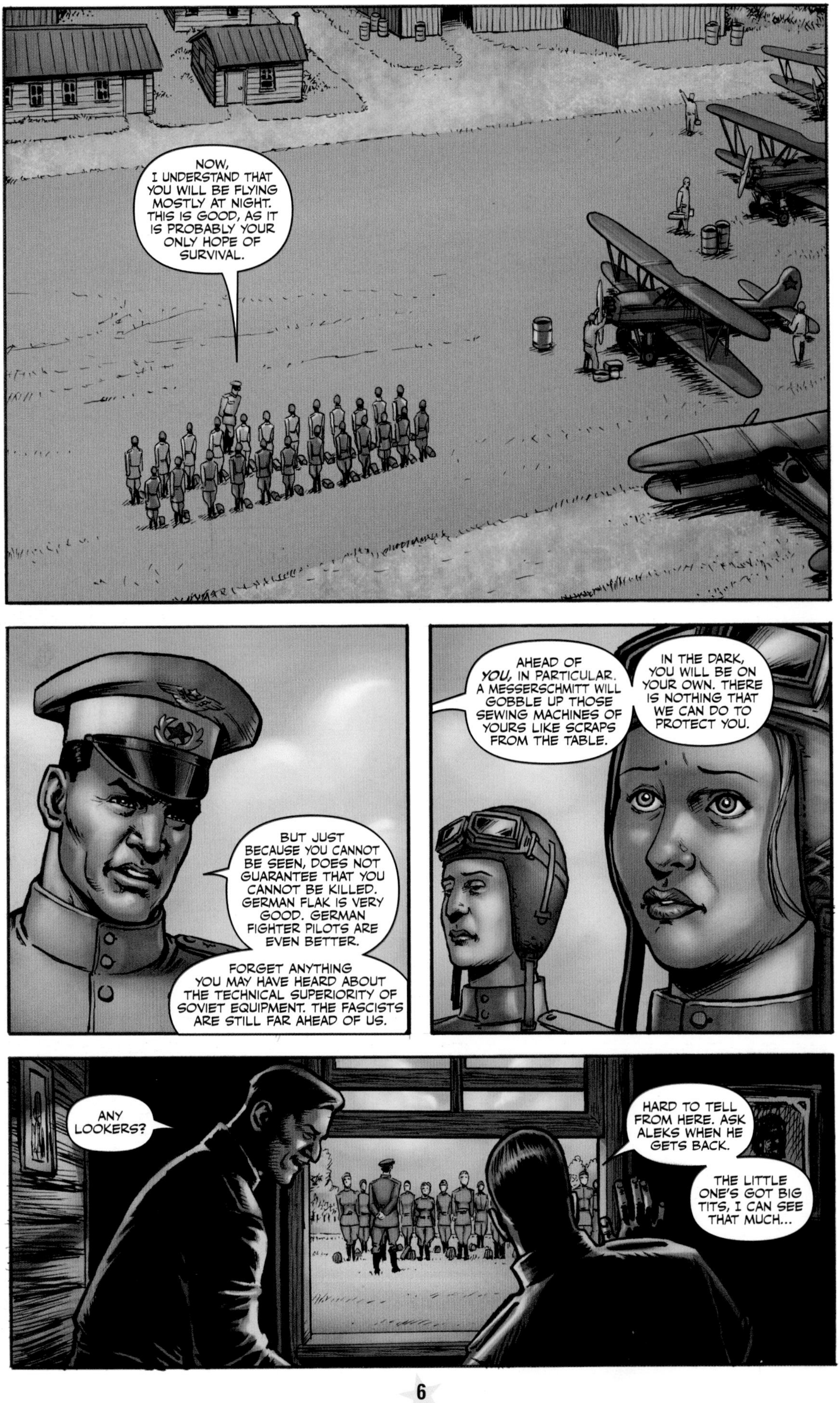
NOW, I UNDERSTAND THAT YOU WILL BE FLYING MOSTLY AT NIGHT. THIS IS GOOD, AS IT IS PROBABLY YOUR ONLY HOPE OF SURVIVAL.
BUT JUST BECAUSE YOU CANNOT BE SEEN, DOES NOT GUARANTEE THAT YOU CANNOT BE KILLED. GERMAN FLAK IS VERY GOOD. GERMAN FIGHTER PILOTS ARE EVEN BETTER.
FORGET ANYTHING YOU MAY HAVE HEARD ABOUT THE TECHNICAL SUPERIORITY OF SOVIET EQUIPMENT. THE FASCISTS ARE STILL FAR AHEAD OF US.
AHEAD OF *YOU,* IN PARTICULAR. A MESSERSCHMITT WILL GOBBLE UP THOSE SEWING MACHINES OF YOURS LIKE SCRAPS FROM THE TABLE.
IN THE DARK, YOU WILL BE ON YOUR OWN. THERE IS NOTHING THAT WE CAN DO TO PROTECT YOU.
ANY LOOKERS?
HARD TO TELL FROM HERE. ASK ALEKS WHEN HE GETS BACK.
THE LITTLE ONE'S GOT BIG TITS, I CAN SEE THAT MUCH...

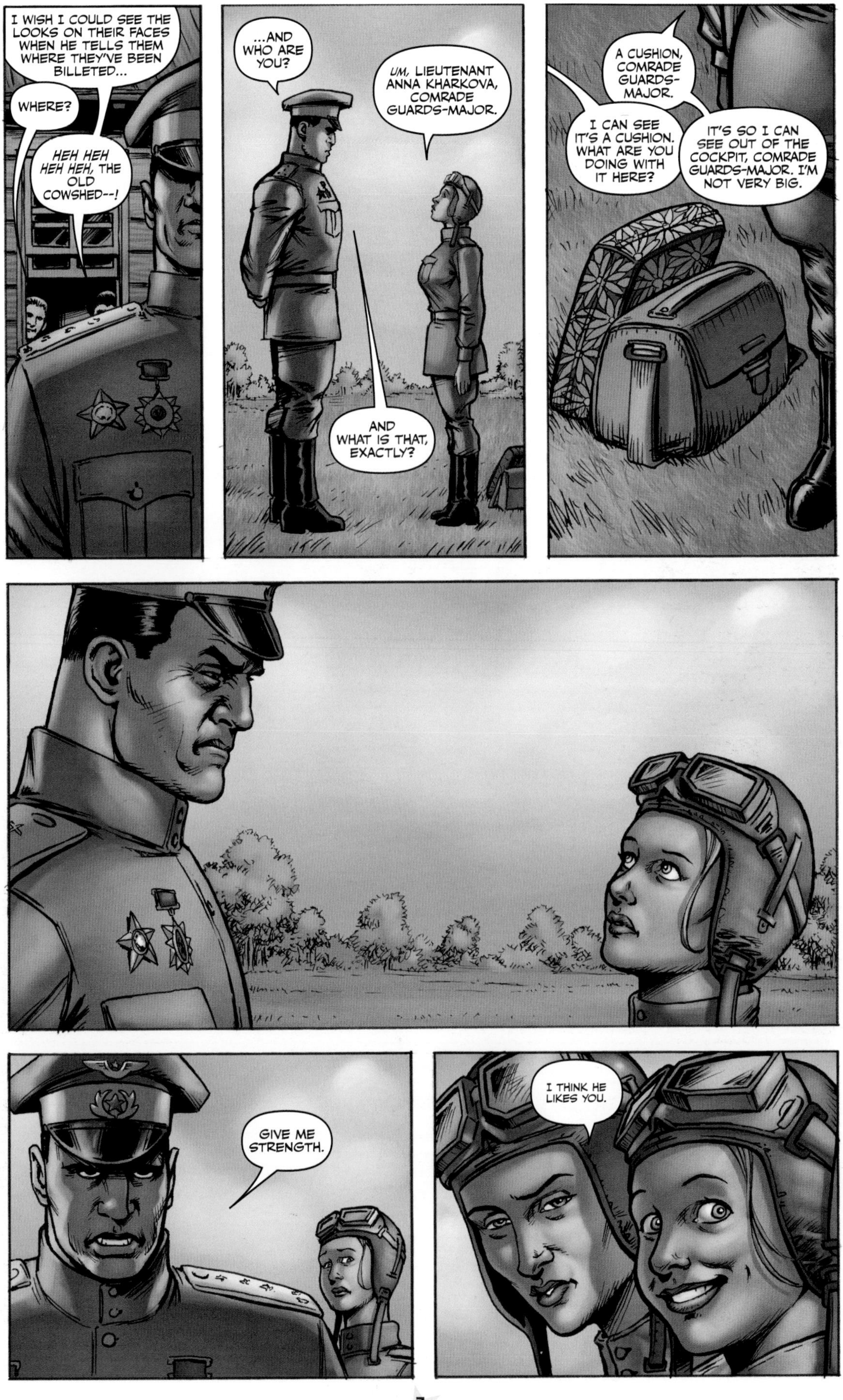

I WISH I COULD SEE THE LOOKS ON THEIR FACES WHEN HE TELLS THEM WHERE THEY'VE BEEN BILLETED...
WHERE?
HEH HEH HEH HEH, THE OLD COWSHED--!
...AND WHO ARE YOU?
UM, LIEUTENANT ANNA KHARKOVA, COMRADE GUARDS-MAJOR.
AND WHAT IS THAT, EXACTLY?
A CUSHION, COMRADE GUARDS-MAJOR.
I CAN SEE IT'S A CUSHION. WHAT ARE YOU DOING WITH IT HERE?
IT'S SO I CAN SEE OUT OF THE COCKPIT, COMRADE GUARDS-MAJOR. I'M NOT VERY BIG.
GIVE ME STRENGTH.
I THINK HE LIKES YOU.

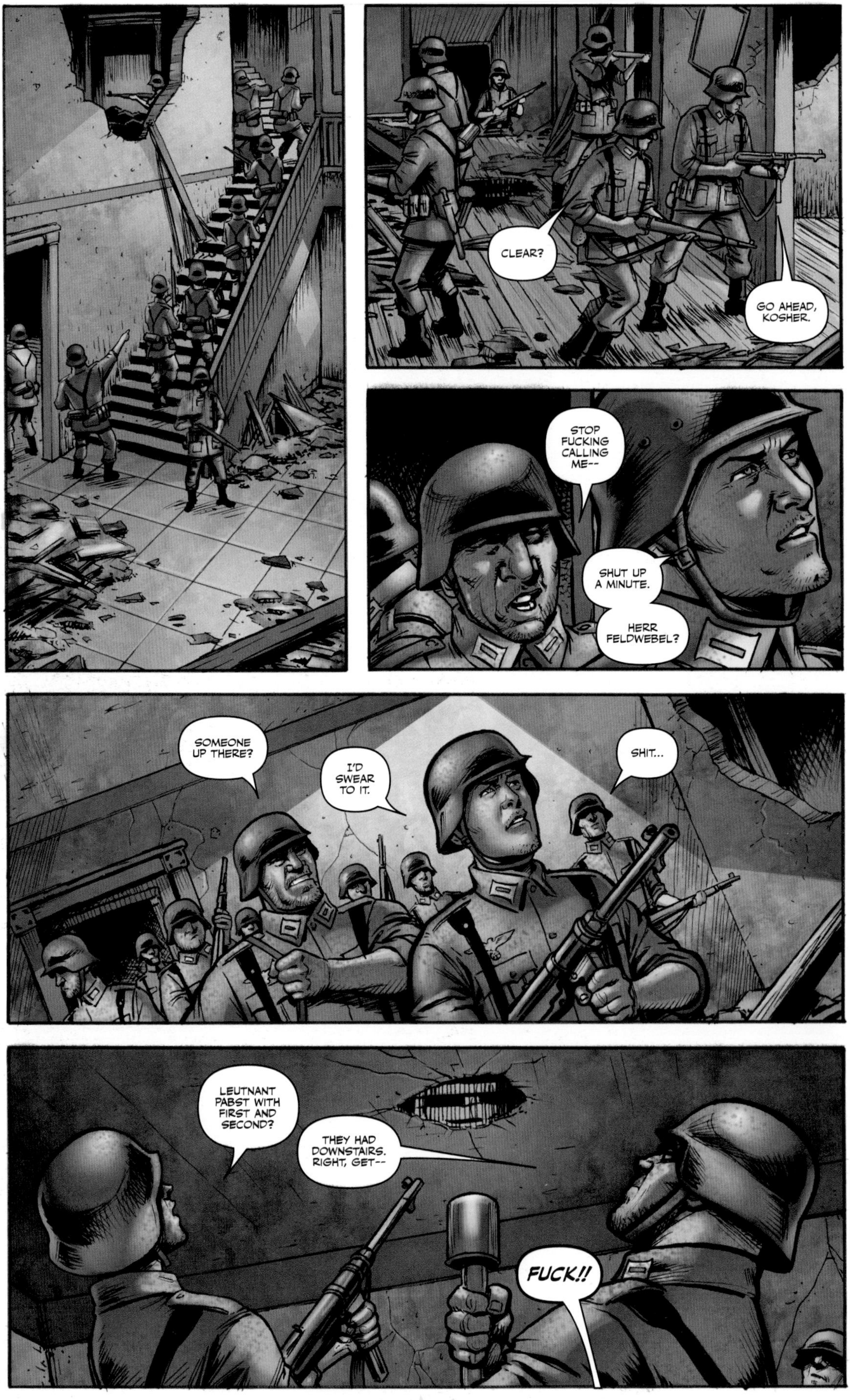
CLEAR?
GO AHEAD, KOSHER.
STOP FUCKING CALLING ME--
SHUT UP A MINUTE.
HERR FELDWEBEL?
SOMEONE UP THERE?
I'D SWEAR TO IT.
SHIT...
LEUTNANT PABST WITH FIRST AND SECOND?
THEY HAD DOWNSTAIRS. RIGHT, GET--
FUCK!!

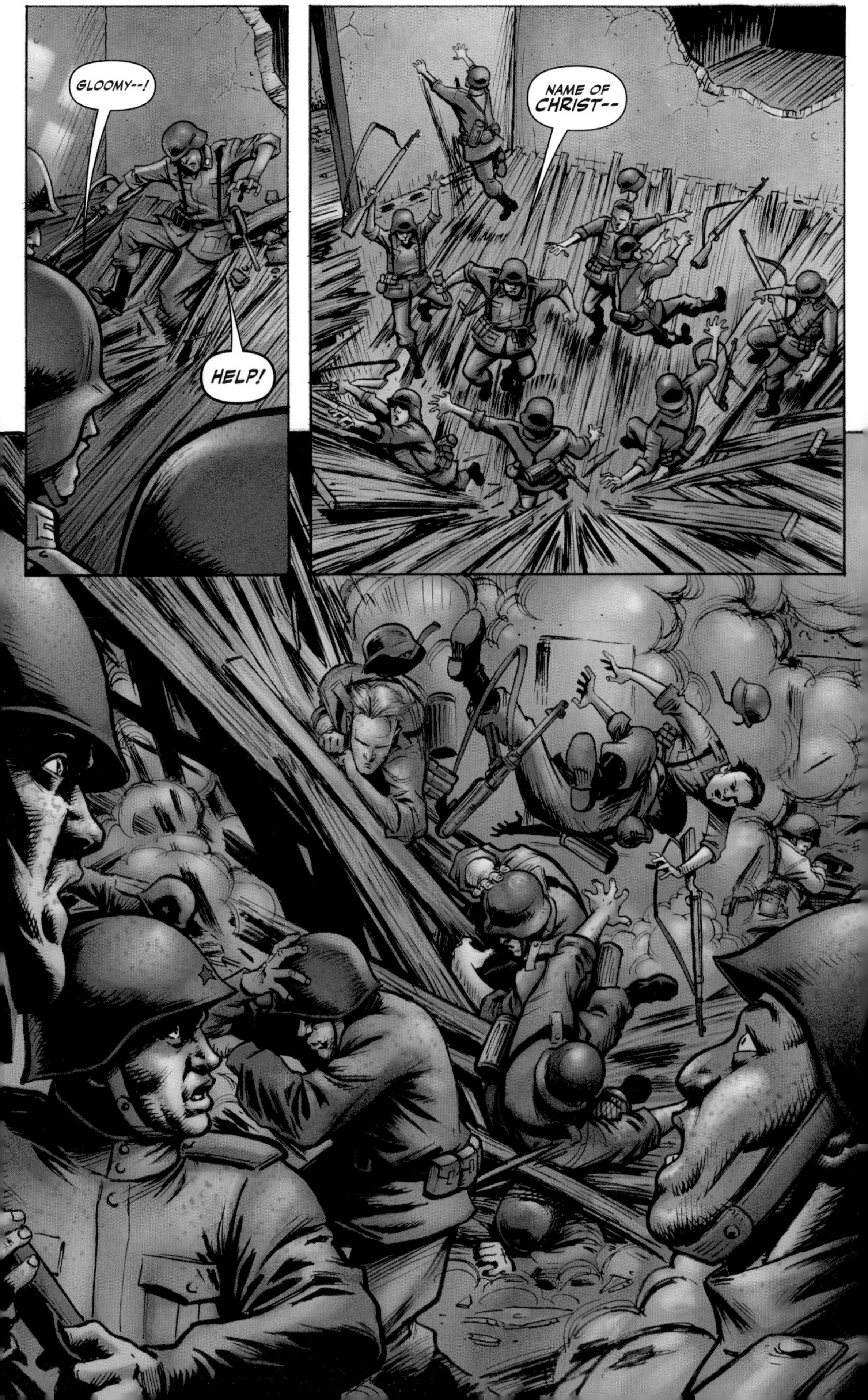
GLOOMY--!
HELP!
NAME OF CHRIST--

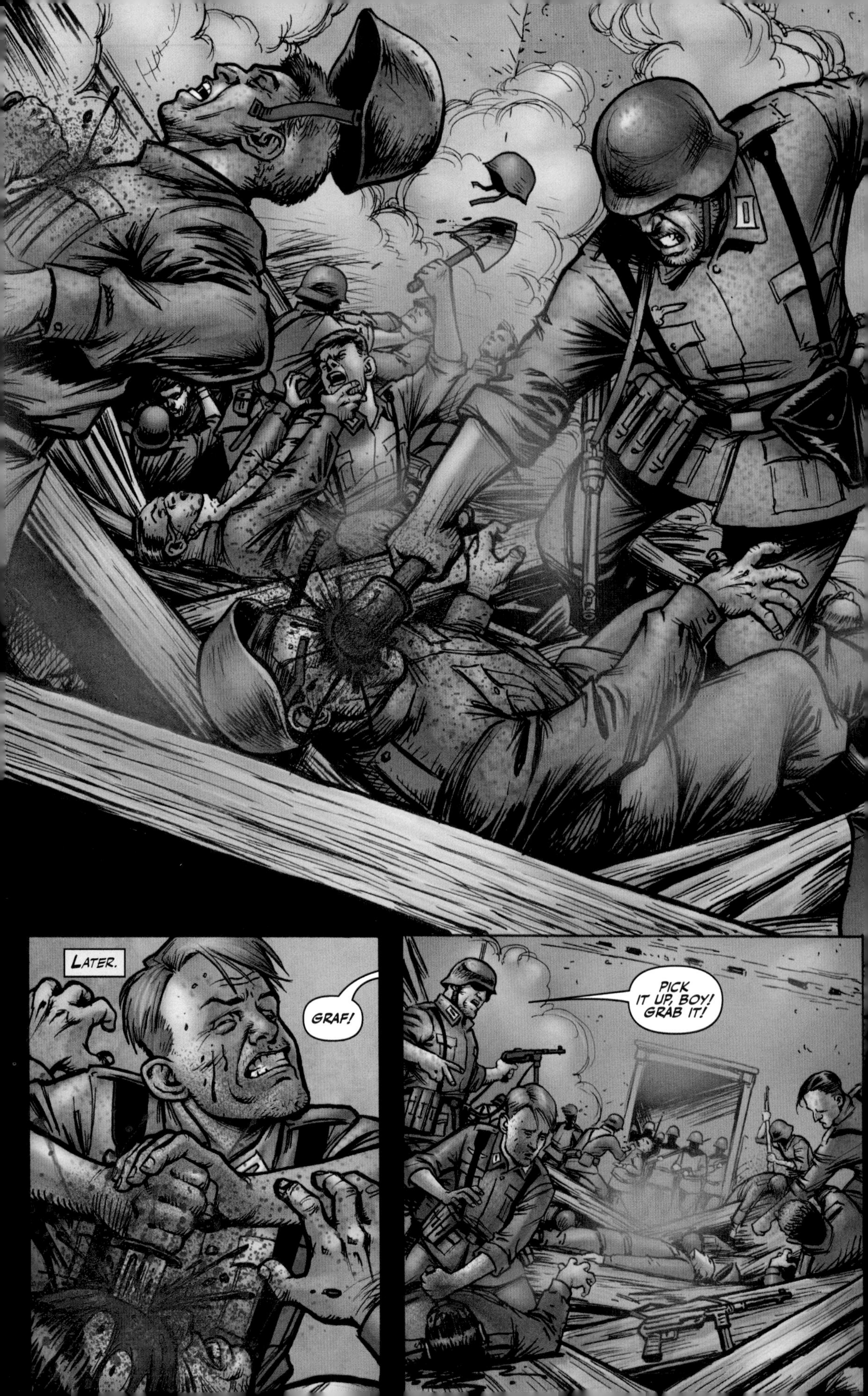
LATER.
GRAF!
PICK IT UP, BOY! GRAB IT!

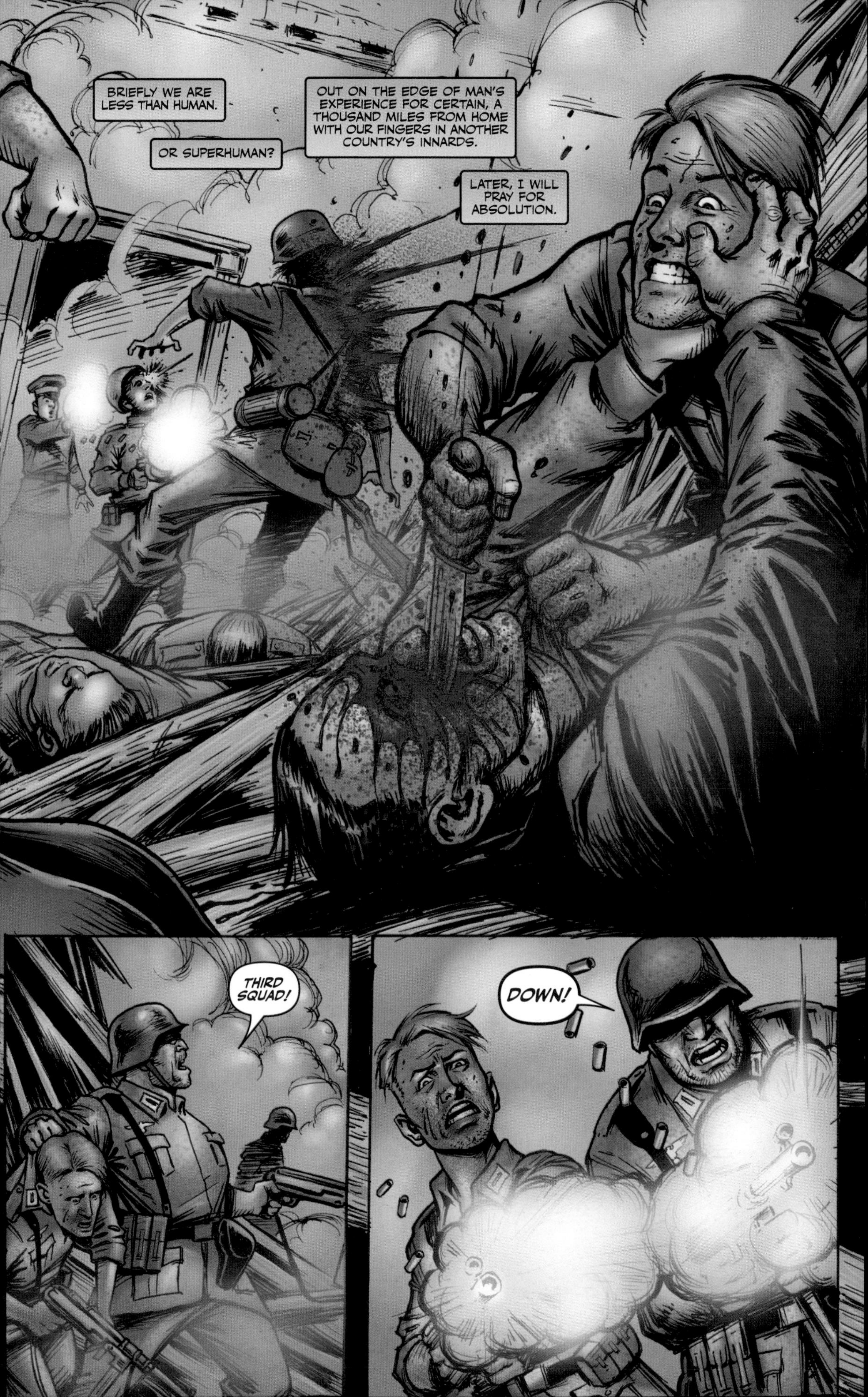
BRIEFLY WE ARE LESS THAN HUMAN.
OR SUPERHUMAN?
OUT ON THE EDGE OF MAN'S EXPERIENCE FOR CERTAIN, A THOUSAND MILES FROM HOME WITH OUR FINGERS IN ANOTHER COUNTRY'S INNARDS.
LATER, I WILL PRAY FOR ABSOLUTION.
THIRD SQUAD!
DOWN!

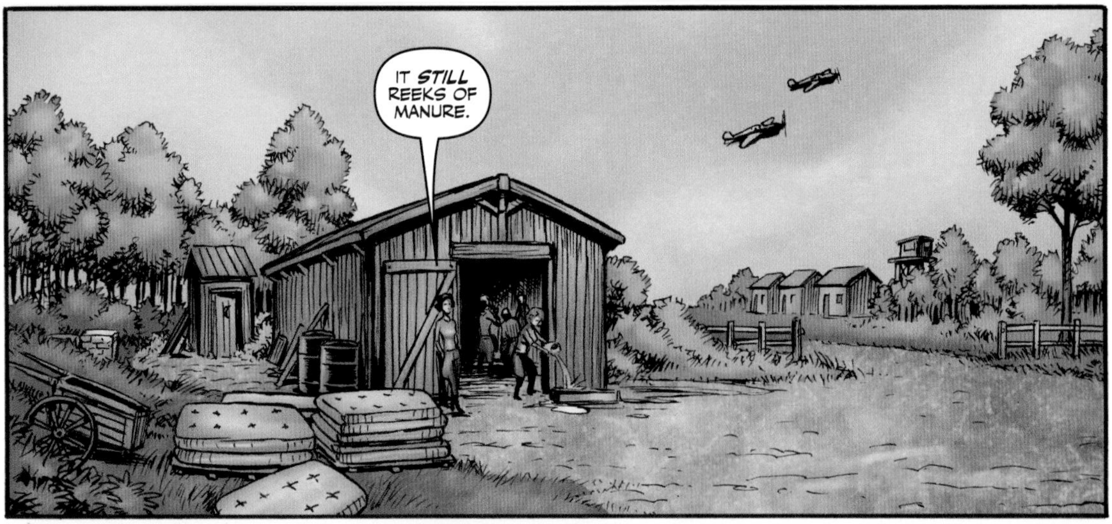
IT *STILL* REEKS OF MANURE.

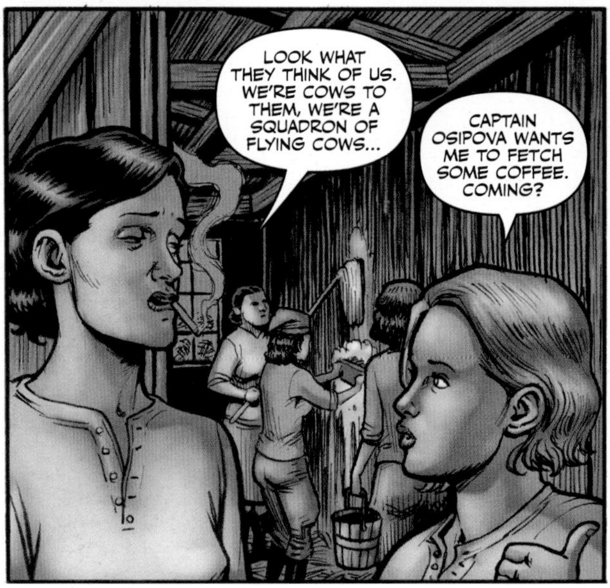
LOOK WHAT THEY THINK OF US. WE'RE COWS TO THEM, WE'RE A SQUADRON OF FLYING COWS...
CAPTAIN OSIPOVA WANTS ME TO FETCH SOME COFFEE. COMING?

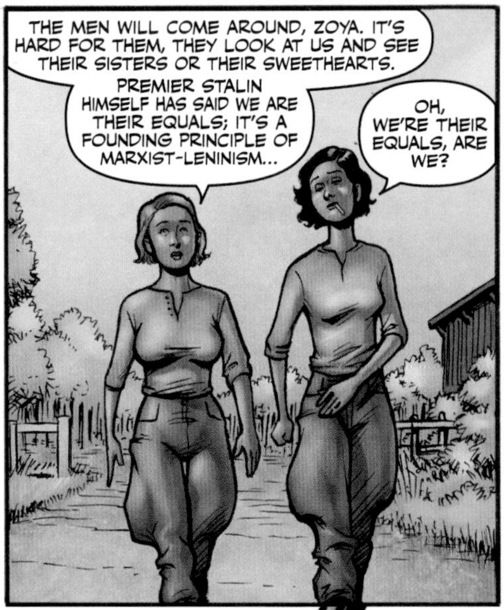
THE MEN WILL COME AROUND, ZOYA. IT'S HARD FOR THEM, THEY LOOK AT US AND SEE THEIR SISTERS OR THEIR SWEETHEARTS.
PREMIER STALIN HIMSELF HAS SAID WE ARE THEIR EQUALS; IT'S A FOUNDING PRINCIPLE OF MARXIST-LENINISM...
OH, WE'RE THEIR EQUALS, ARE WE?

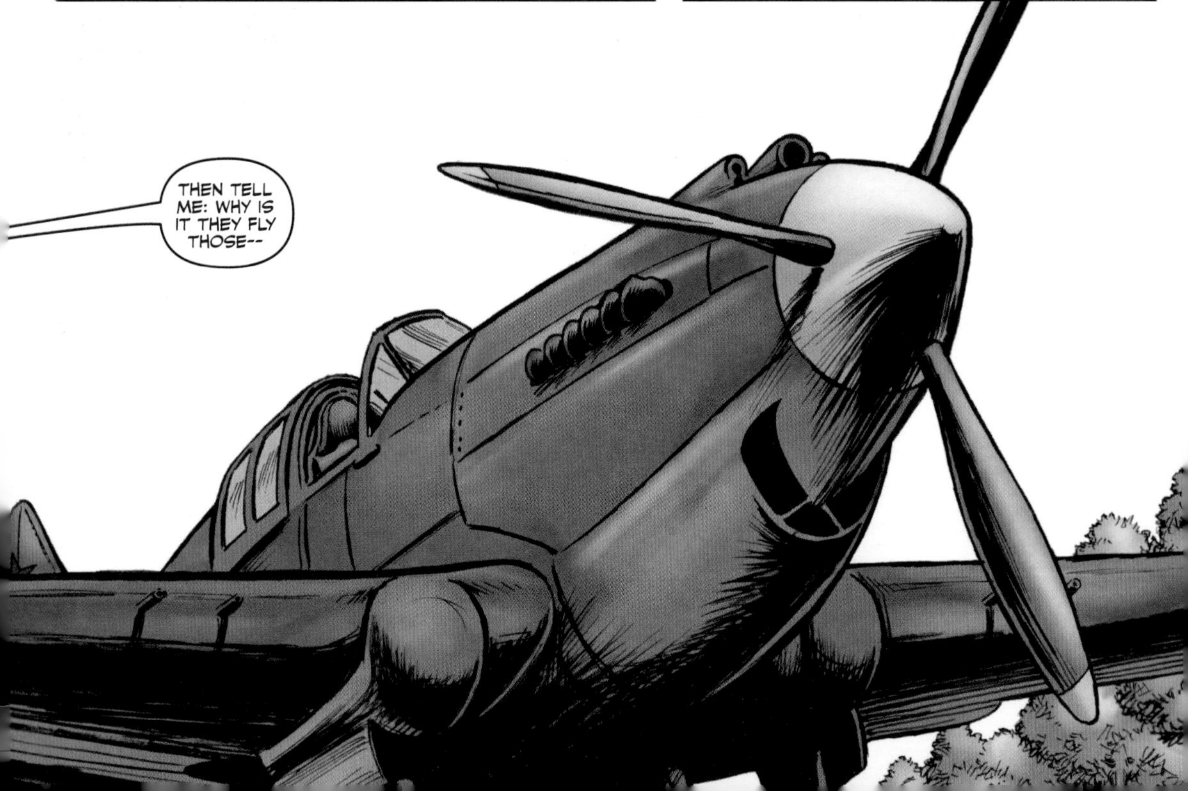
THEN TELL ME: WHY IS IT THEY FLY THOSE--

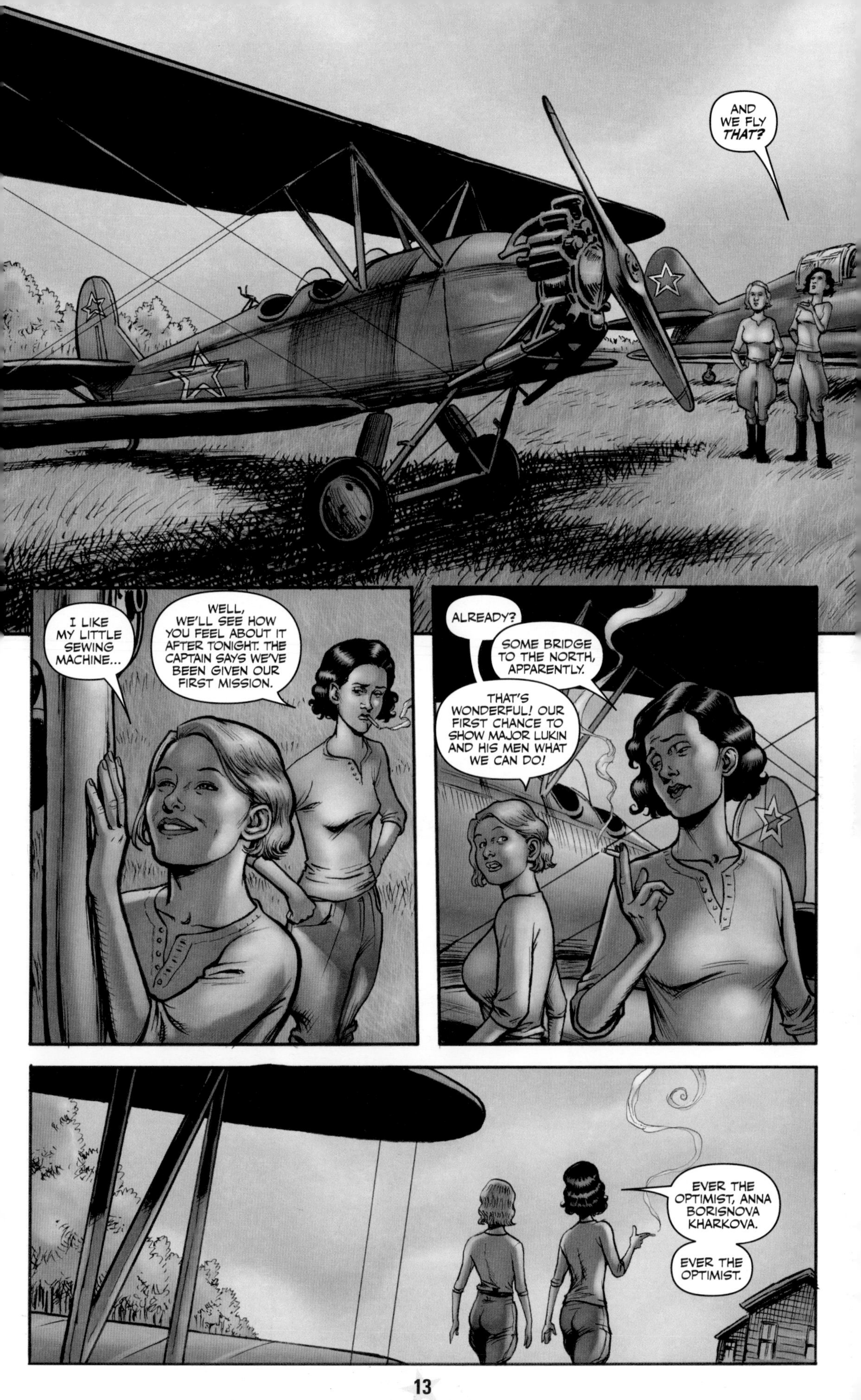
AND WE FLY *THAT?*
I LIKE MY LITTLE SEWING MACHINE...
WELL, WE'LL SEE HOW YOU FEEL ABOUT IT AFTER TONIGHT. THE CAPTAIN SAYS WE'VE BEEN GIVEN OUR FIRST MISSION.
ALREADY?
SOME BRIDGE TO THE NORTH, APPARENTLY.
THAT'S WONDERFUL! OUR FIRST CHANCE TO SHOW MAJOR LUKIN AND HIS MEN WHAT WE CAN DO!
EVER THE OPTIMIST, ANNA BORISNOVA KHARKOVA.
EVER THE OPTIMIST.

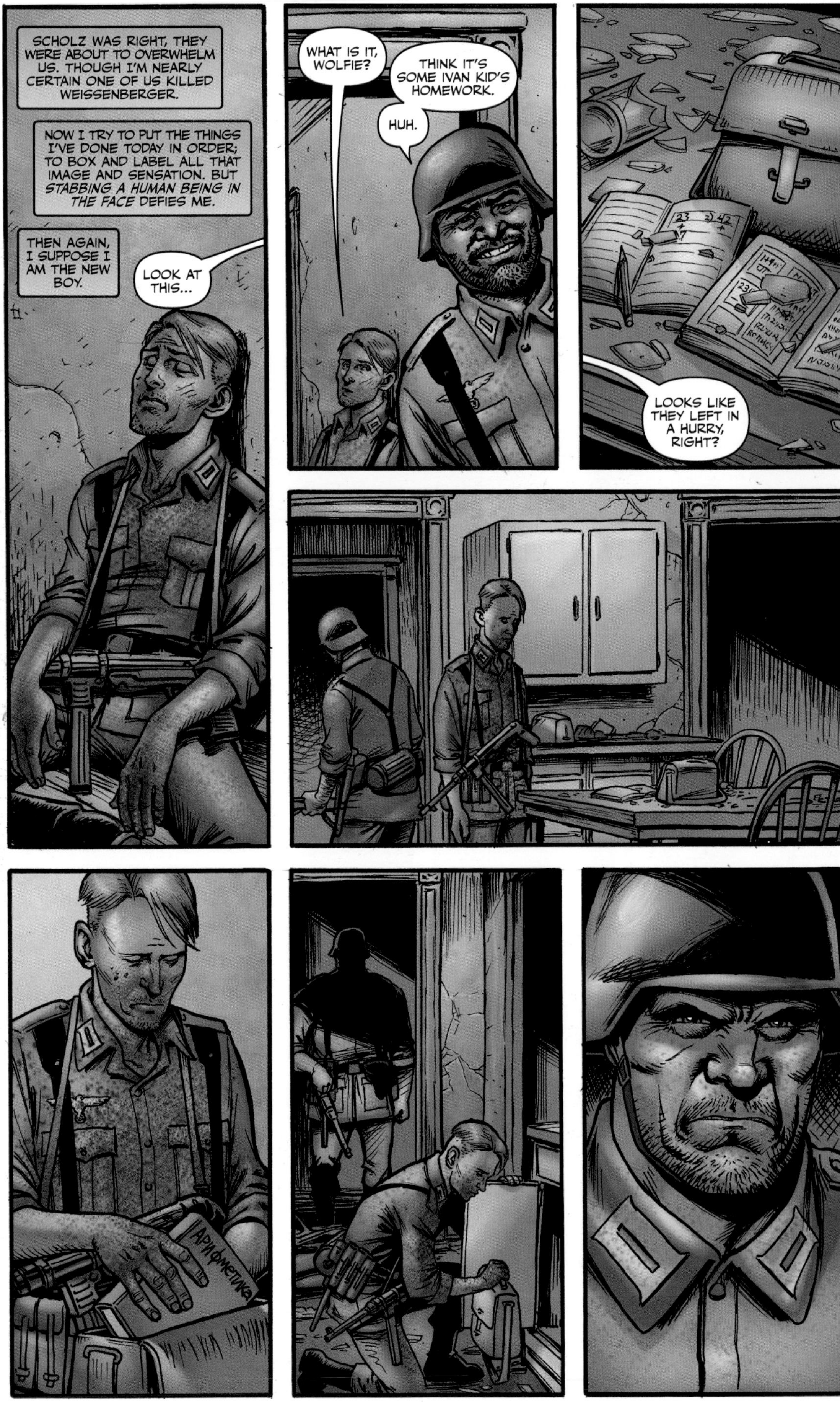
SCHOLZ WAS RIGHT, THEY WERE ABOUT TO OVERWHELM US. THOUGH I'M NEARLY CERTAIN ONE OF US KILLED WEISSENBERGER.
NOW I TRY TO PUT THE THINGS I'VE DONE TODAY IN ORDER; TO BOX AND LABEL ALL THAT IMAGE AND SENSATION. BUT *STABBING A HUMAN BEING IN THE FACE* DEFIES ME.
THEN AGAIN, I SUPPOSE I AM THE NEW BOY.
LOOK AT THIS...
WHAT IS IT, WOLFIE?
THINK IT'S SOME IVAN KID'S HOMEWORK.
HUH.
LOOKS LIKE THEY LEFT IN A HURRY, RIGHT?
АРИФМЕТИКА

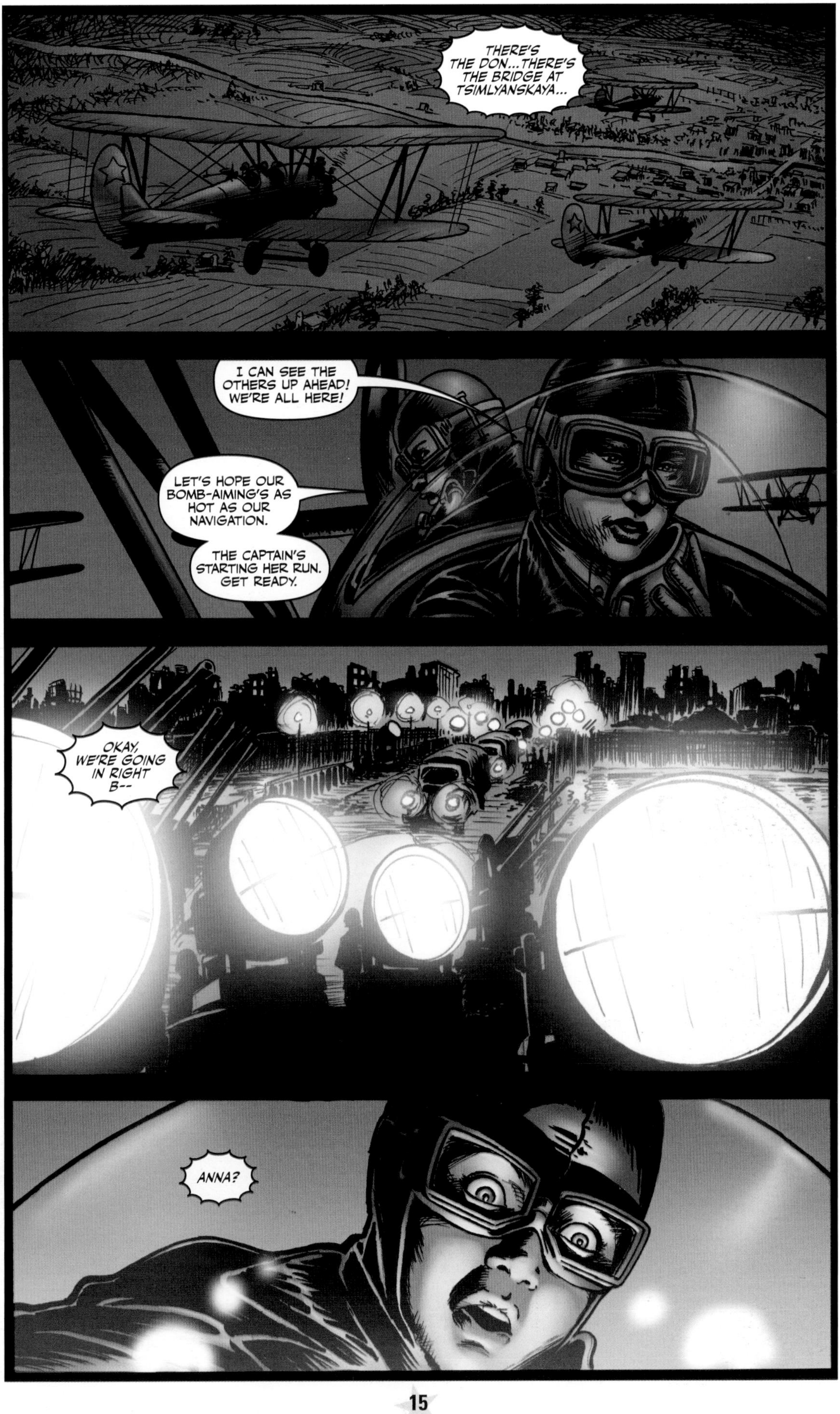
THERE'S THE DON...THERE'S THE BRIDGE AT TSIMLYANSKAYA...
I CAN SEE THE OTHERS UP AHEAD! WE'RE ALL HERE!
LET'S HOPE OUR BOMB-AIMING'S AS HOT AS OUR NAVIGATION.
THE CAPTAIN'S STARTING HER RUN. GET READY.
OKAY, WE'RE GOING IN RIGHT B--
ANNA?

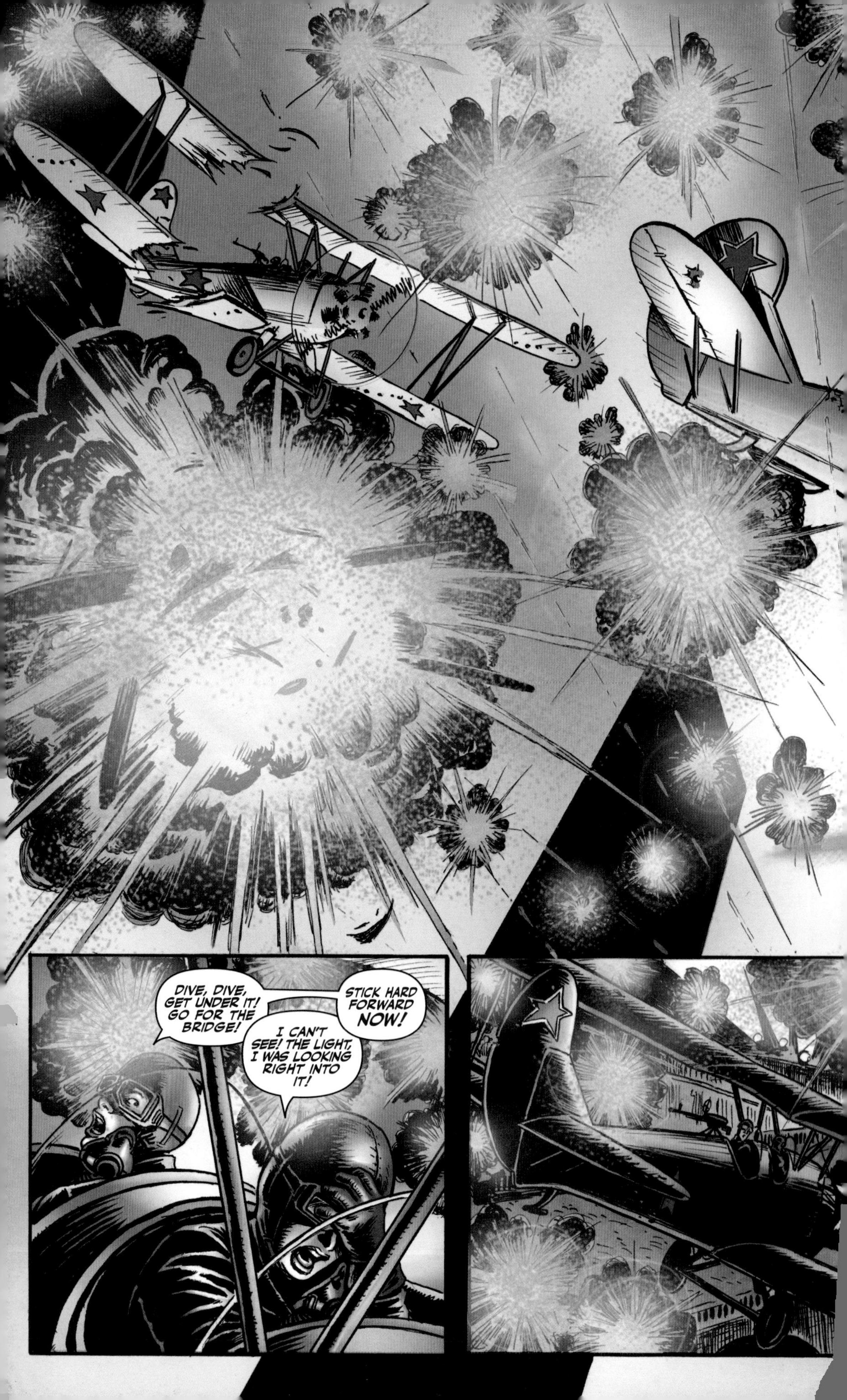
DIVE, DIVE, GET UNDER IT! GO FOR THE BRIDGE!
STICK HARD FORWARD NOW!
I CAN'T SEE! THE LIGHT, I WAS LOOKING RIGHT INTO IT!

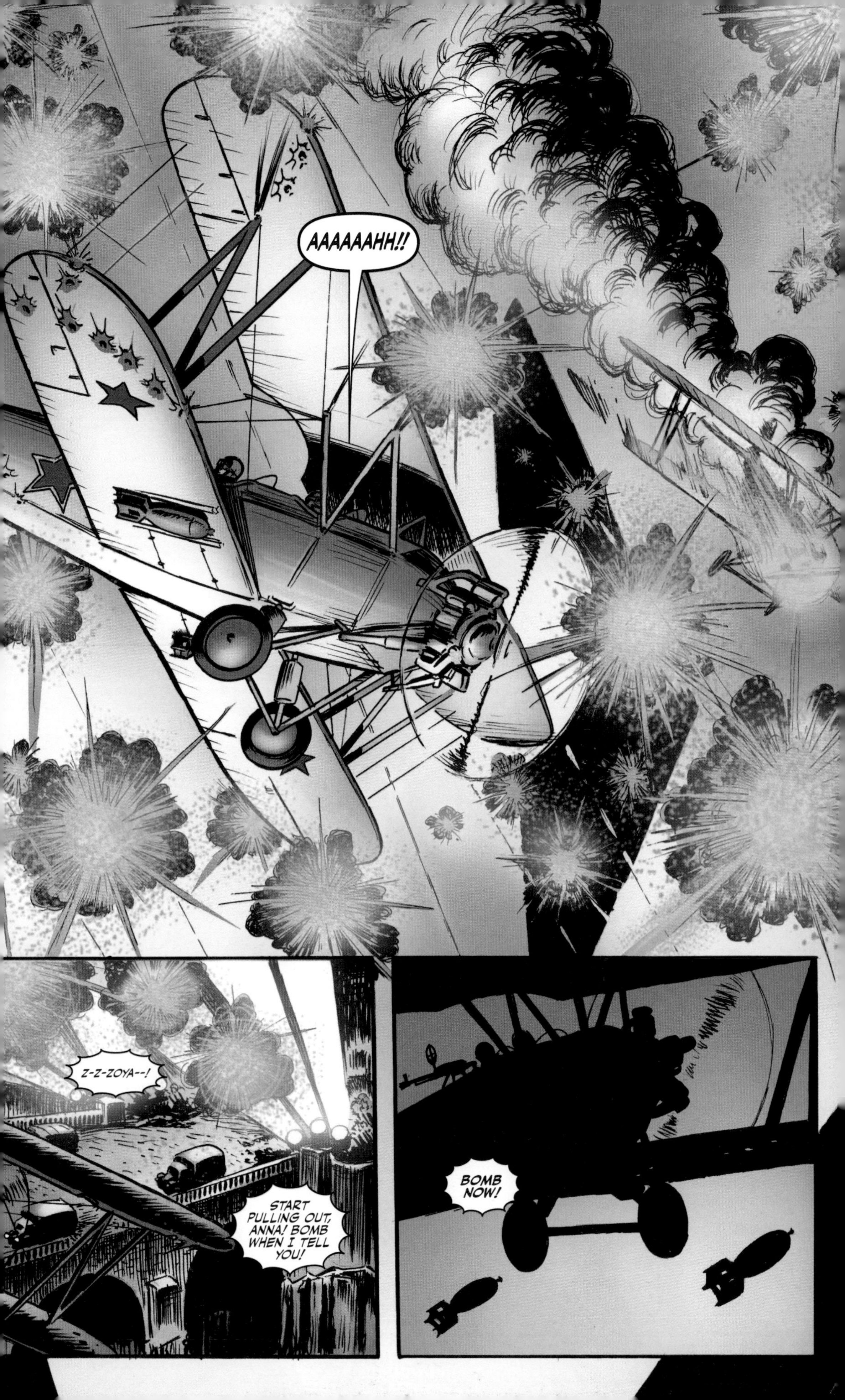
AAAAAAHH!!
Z-Z-ZOYA--!
START PULLING OUT, ANNA! BOMB WHEN I TELL YOU!
BOMB NOW!

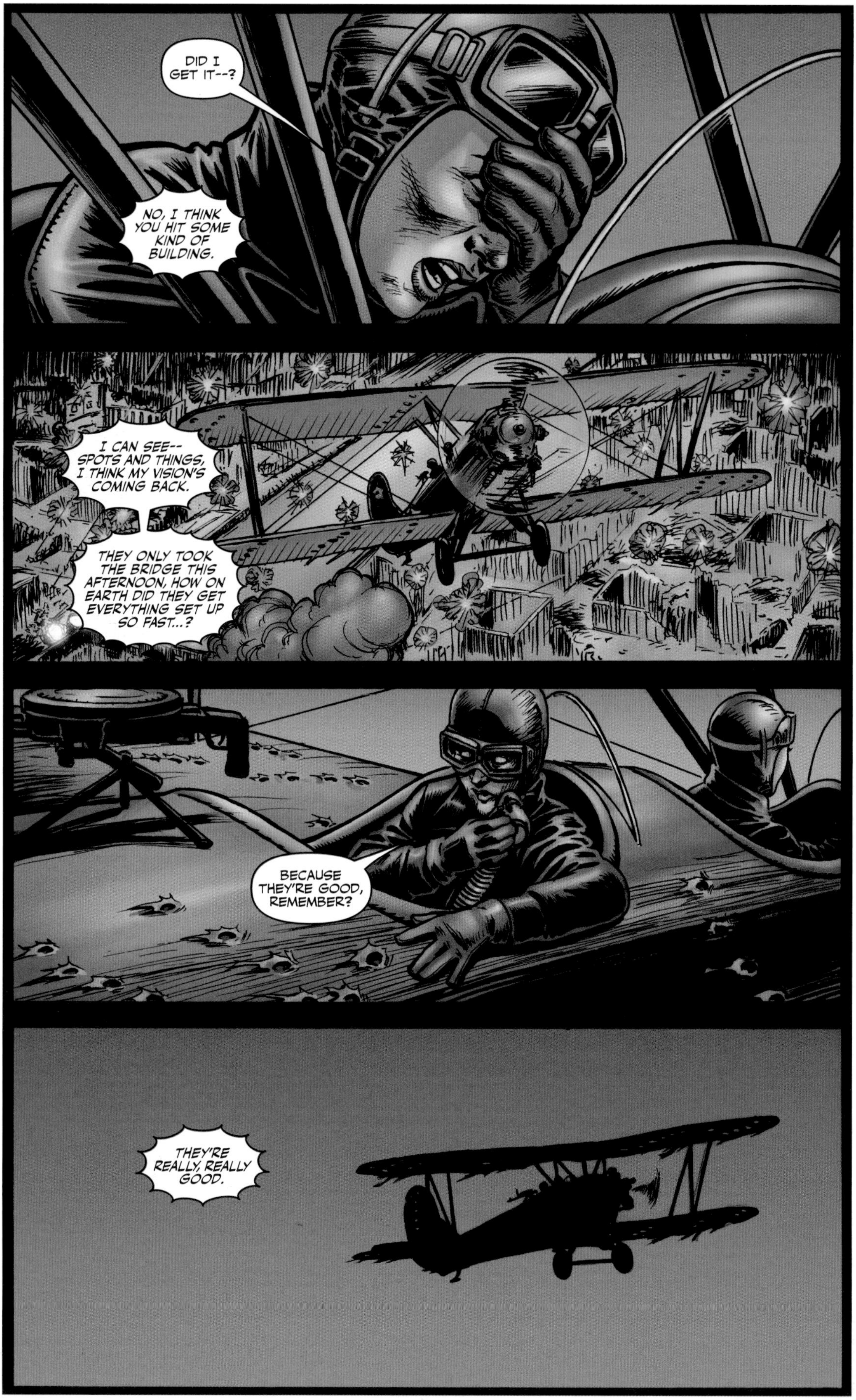
DID I GET IT--?
NO, I THINK YOU HIT SOME KIND OF BUILDING.
I CAN SEE-- SPOTS AND THINGS, I THINK MY VISION'S COMING BACK.
THEY ONLY TOOK THE BRIDGE THIS AFTERNOON, HOW ON EARTH DID THEY GET EVERYTHING SET UP SO FAST...?
BECAUSE THEY'RE GOOD, REMEMBER?
THEY'RE REALLY, REALLY GOOD.

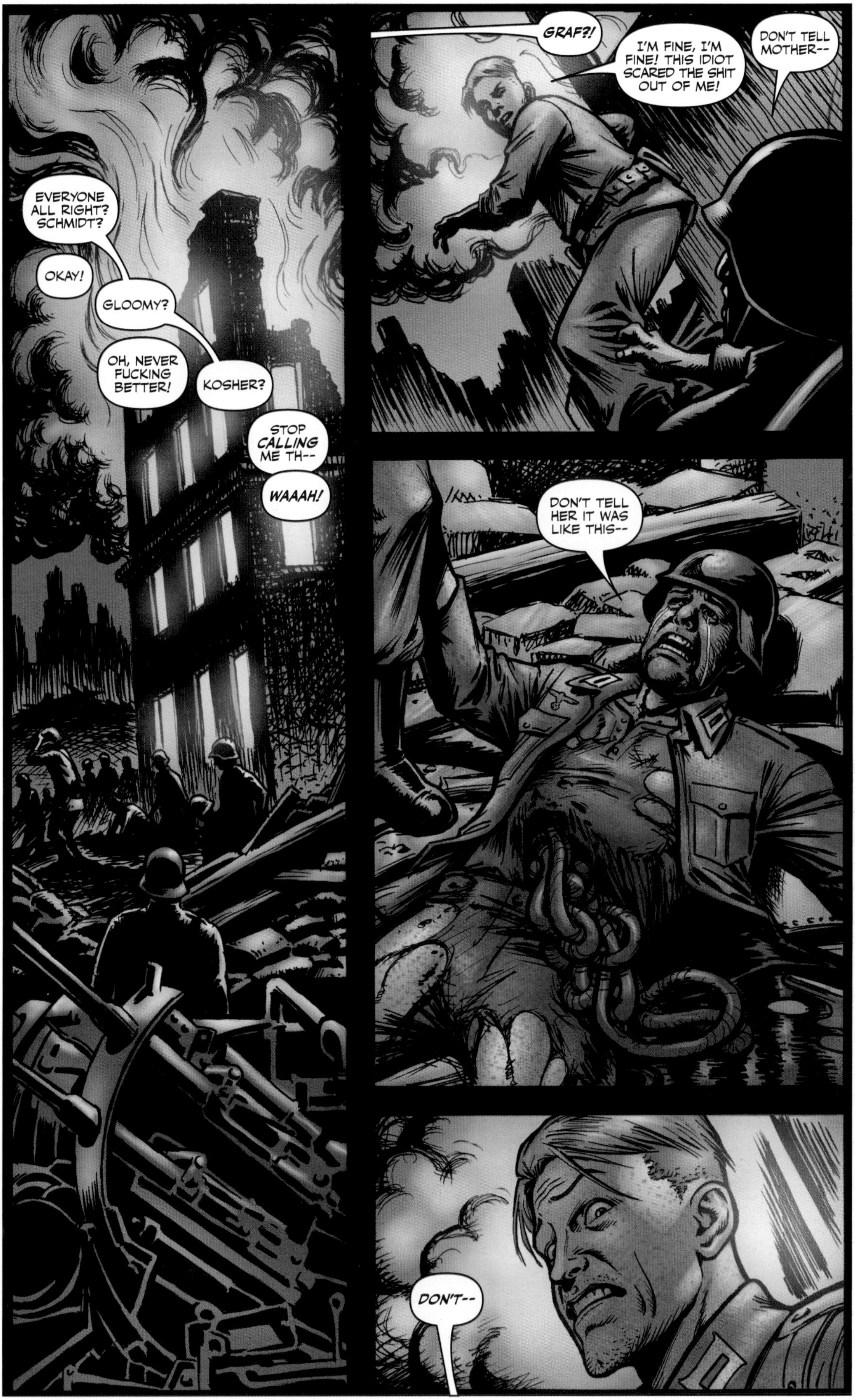

EVERYONE ALL RIGHT? SCHMIDT?
OKAY!
GLOOMY?
OH, NEVER FUCKING BETTER!
KOSHER?
STOP CALLING ME TH--
WAAAH!
GRAF?!
I'M FINE, I'M FINE! THIS IDIOT SCARED THE SHIT OUT OF ME!
DON'T TELL MOTHER--
DON'T TELL HER IT WAS LIKE THIS--
DON'T--

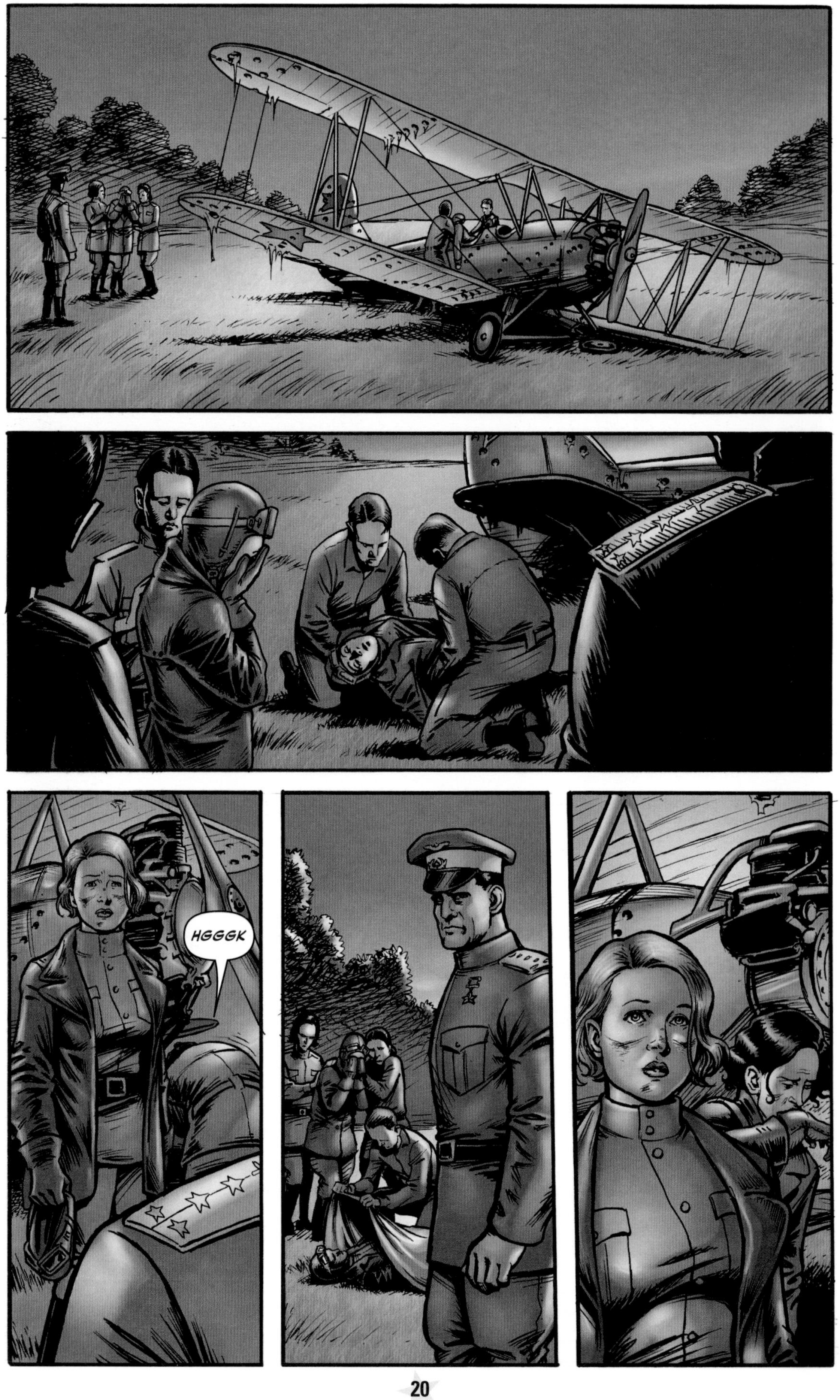
HGGGK

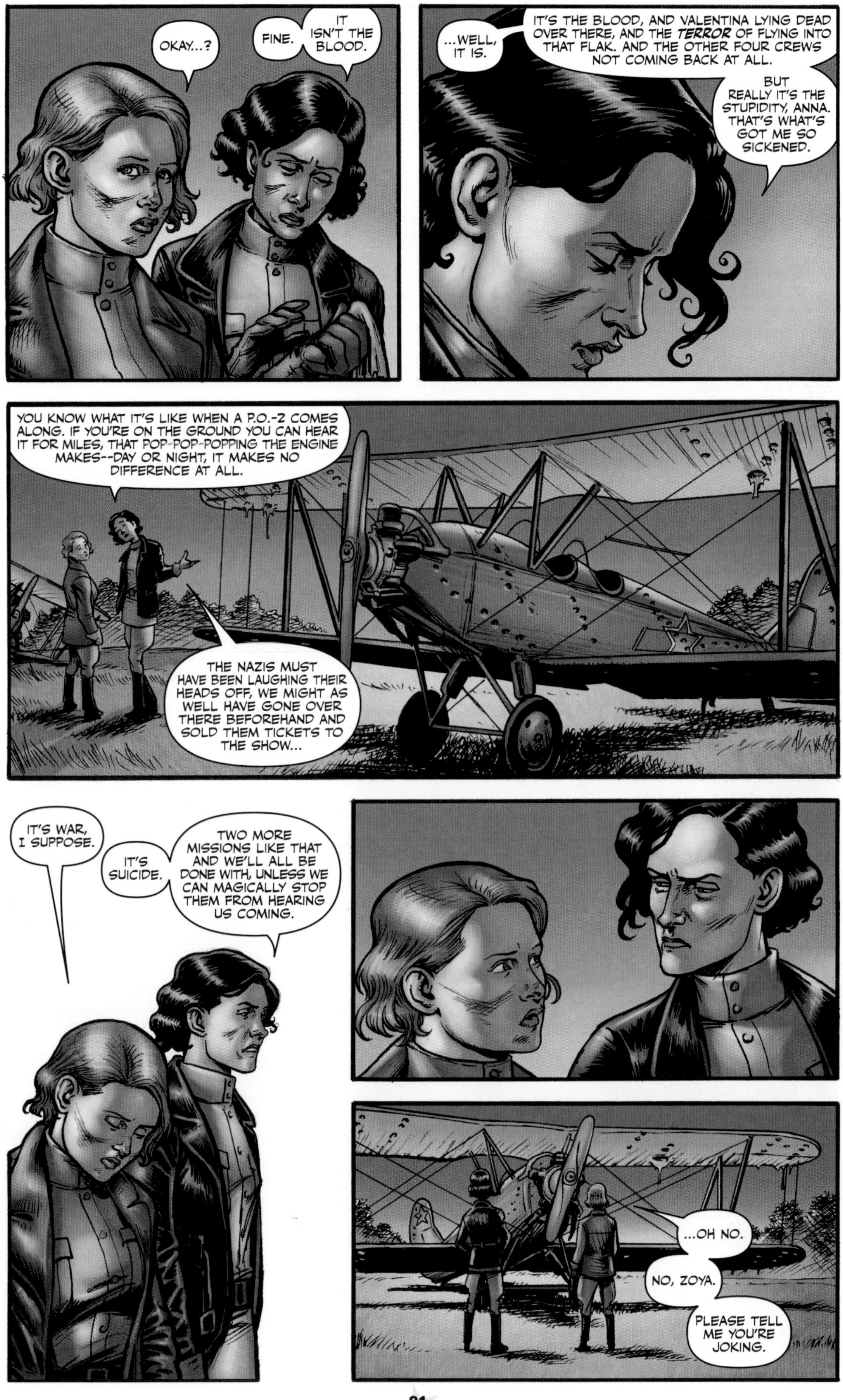
OKAY...?
FINE.
IT ISN'T THE BLOOD.
...WELL, IT IS.
IT'S THE BLOOD, AND VALENTINA LYING DEAD OVER THERE, AND THE *TERROR* OF FLYING INTO THAT FLAK. AND THE OTHER FOUR CREWS NOT COMING BACK AT ALL.
BUT REALLY IT'S THE STUPIDITY, ANNA. THAT'S WHAT'S GOT ME SO SICKENED.
YOU KNOW WHAT IT'S LIKE WHEN A P.O.-2 COMES ALONG. IF YOU'RE ON THE GROUND YOU CAN HEAR IT FOR MILES, THAT POP-POP-POPPING THE ENGINE MAKES--DAY OR NIGHT, IT MAKES NO DIFFERENCE AT ALL.
THE NAZIS MUST HAVE BEEN LAUGHING THEIR HEADS OFF, WE MIGHT AS WELL HAVE GONE OVER THERE BEFOREHAND AND SOLD THEM TICKETS TO THE SHOW...
IT'S WAR, I SUPPOSE.
IT'S SUICIDE.
TWO MORE MISSIONS LIKE THAT AND WE'LL ALL BE DONE WITH, UNLESS WE CAN MAGICALLY STOP THEM FROM HEARING US COMING.
...OH NO.
NO, ZOYA.
PLEASE TELL ME YOU'RE JOKING.

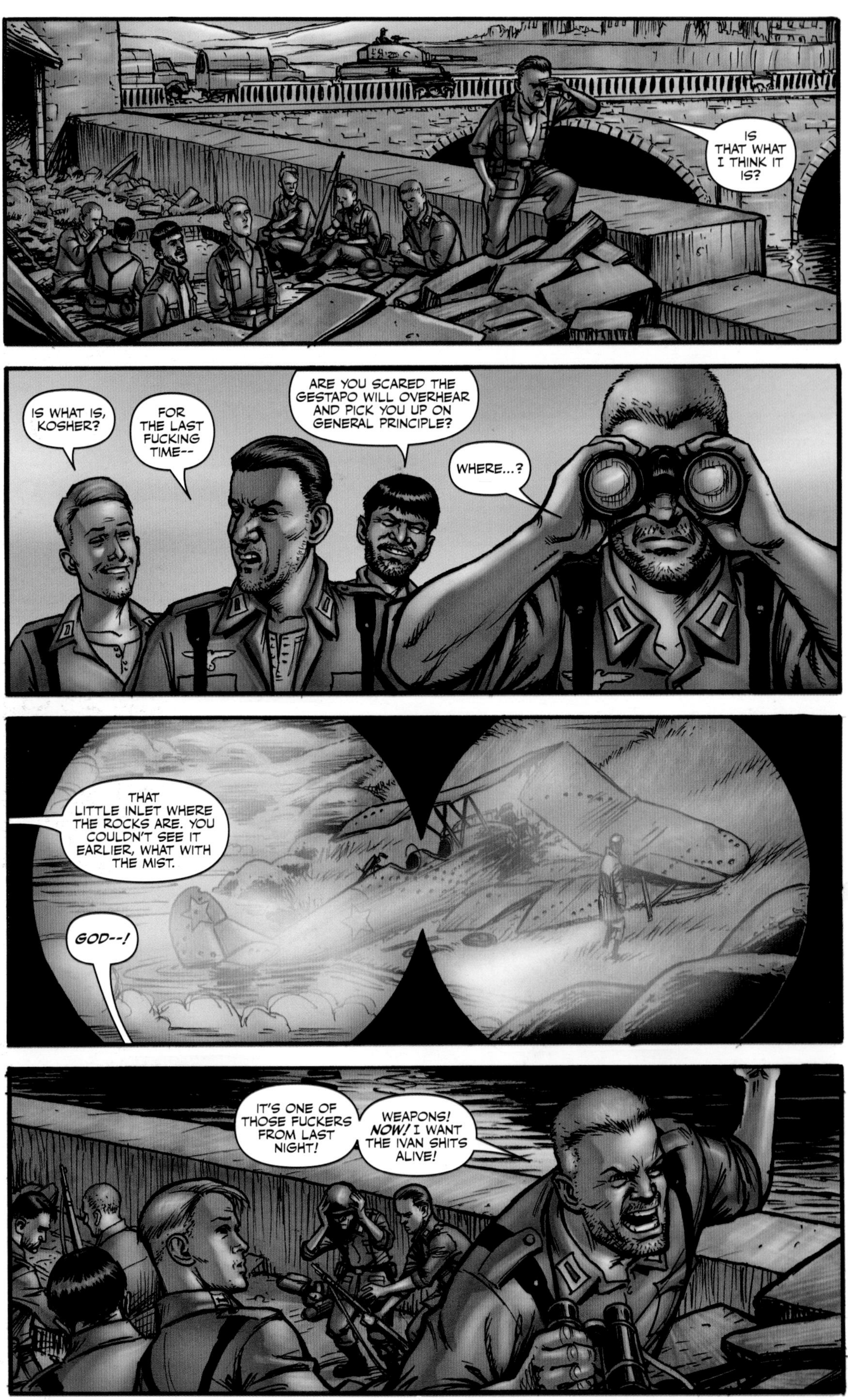
IS THAT WHAT I THINK IT IS?
IS WHAT IS, KOSHER?
FOR THE LAST FUCKING TIME--
ARE YOU SCARED THE GESTAPO WILL OVERHEAR AND PICK YOU UP ON GENERAL PRINCIPLE?
WHERE...?
THAT LITTLE INLET WHERE THE ROCKS ARE. YOU COULDN'T SEE IT EARLIER, WHAT WITH THE MIST.
GOD--!
IT'S ONE OF THOSE FUCKERS FROM LAST NIGHT!
WEAPONS! NOW! I WANT THE IVAN SHITS ALIVE!

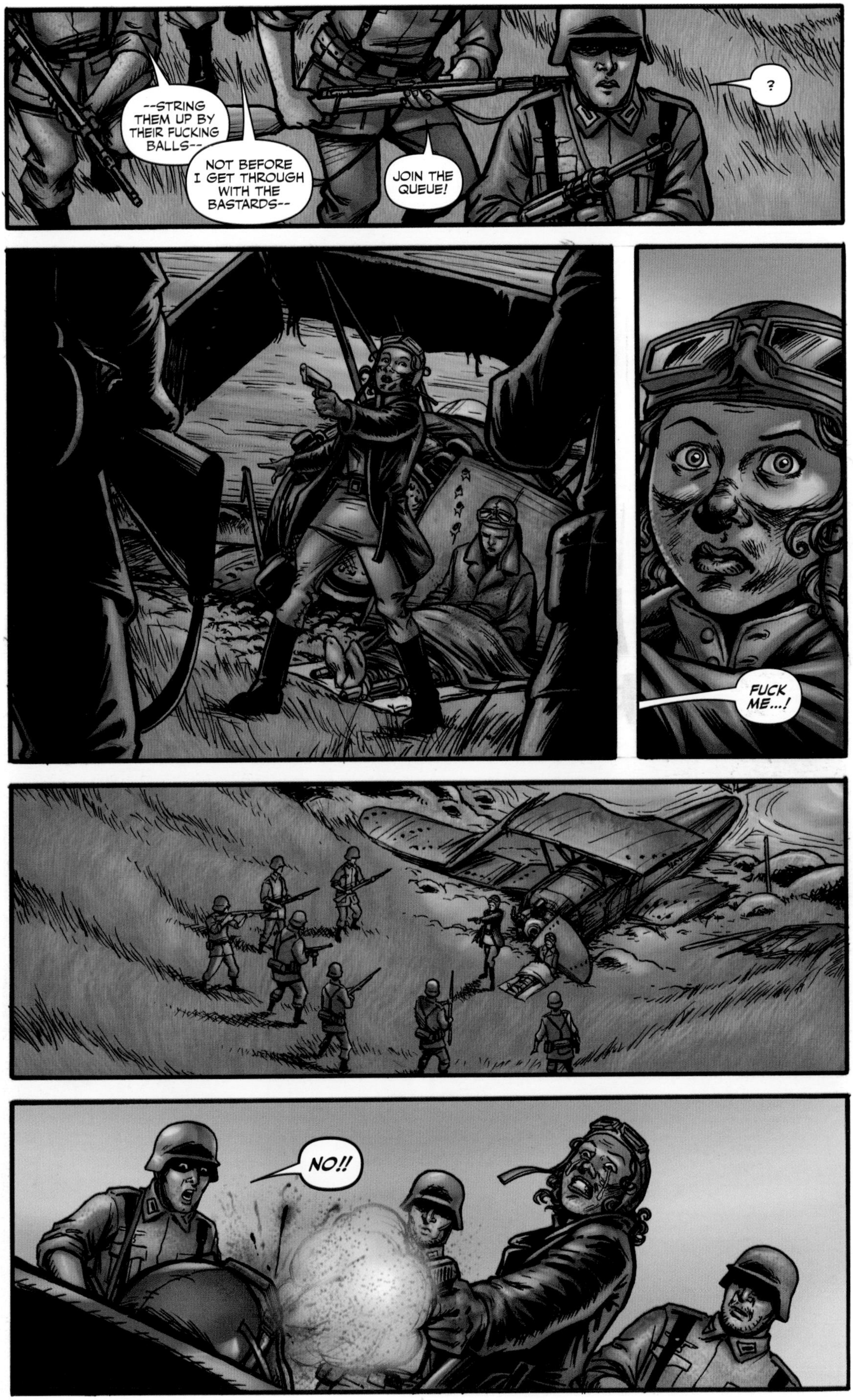
--STRING THEM UP BY THEIR FUCKING BALLS--
NOT BEFORE I GET THROUGH WITH THE BASTARDS--
JOIN THE QUEUE!
?
FUCK ME...!
NO!!

...FUCKING SAVAGES.

IT'S LIKE I'M ALWAYS SAYING. OLD ADOLF'S RIGHT: THEY'RE A LESSER RACE.

SENDING *WOMEN* OUT TO FIGHT, THEY'RE NOTHING BUT *SUB-HUMAN SCUM*...

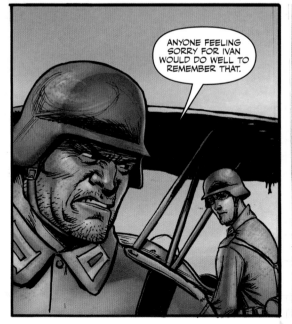

ANYONE FEELING SORRY FOR IVAN WOULD DO WELL TO REMEMBER THAT.

RIGHT, THROW THOSE PIECES OF SHIT IN THE RIVER.

BREAKFAST'S GETTING COLD.

Chapter 2

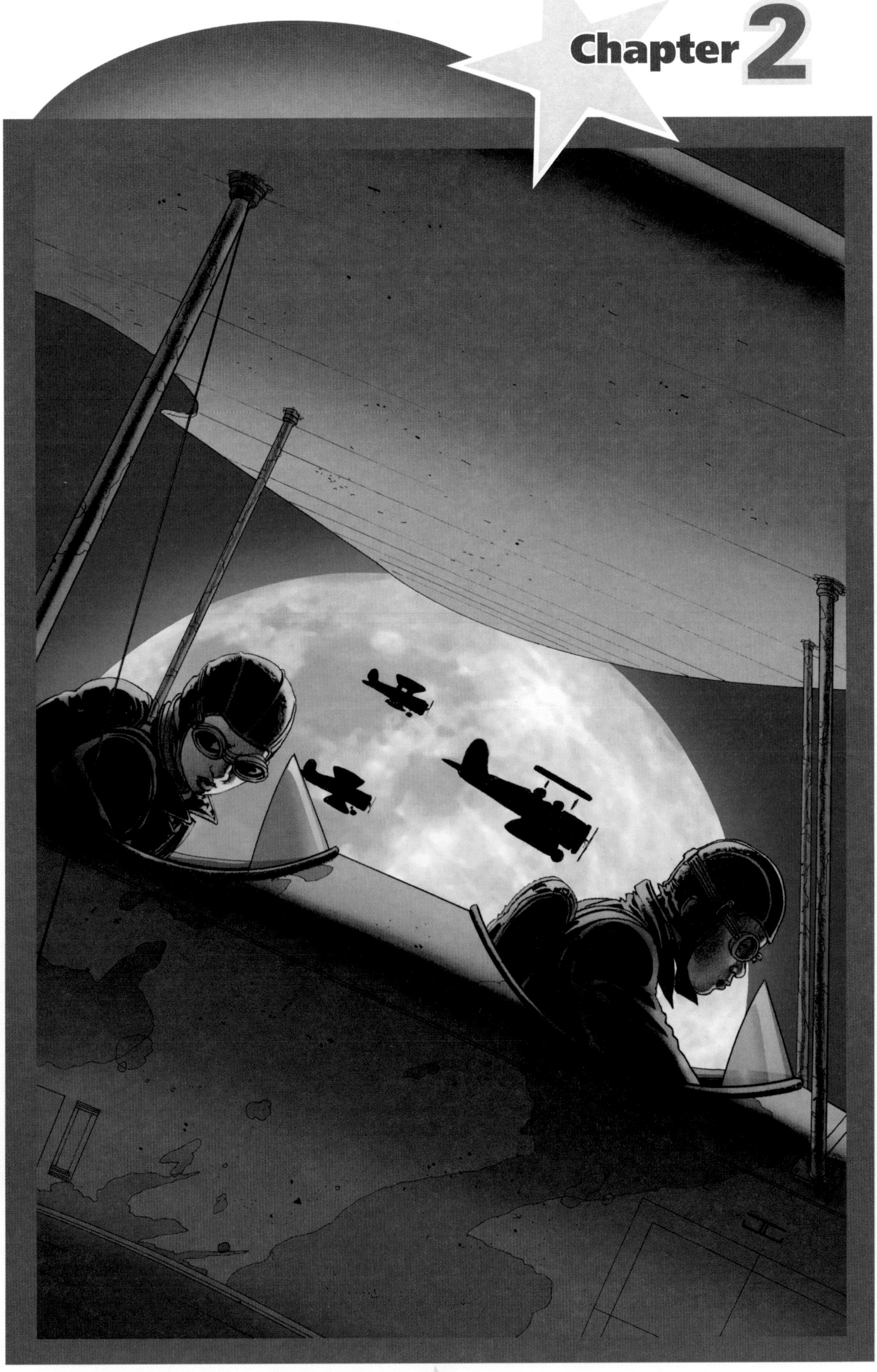

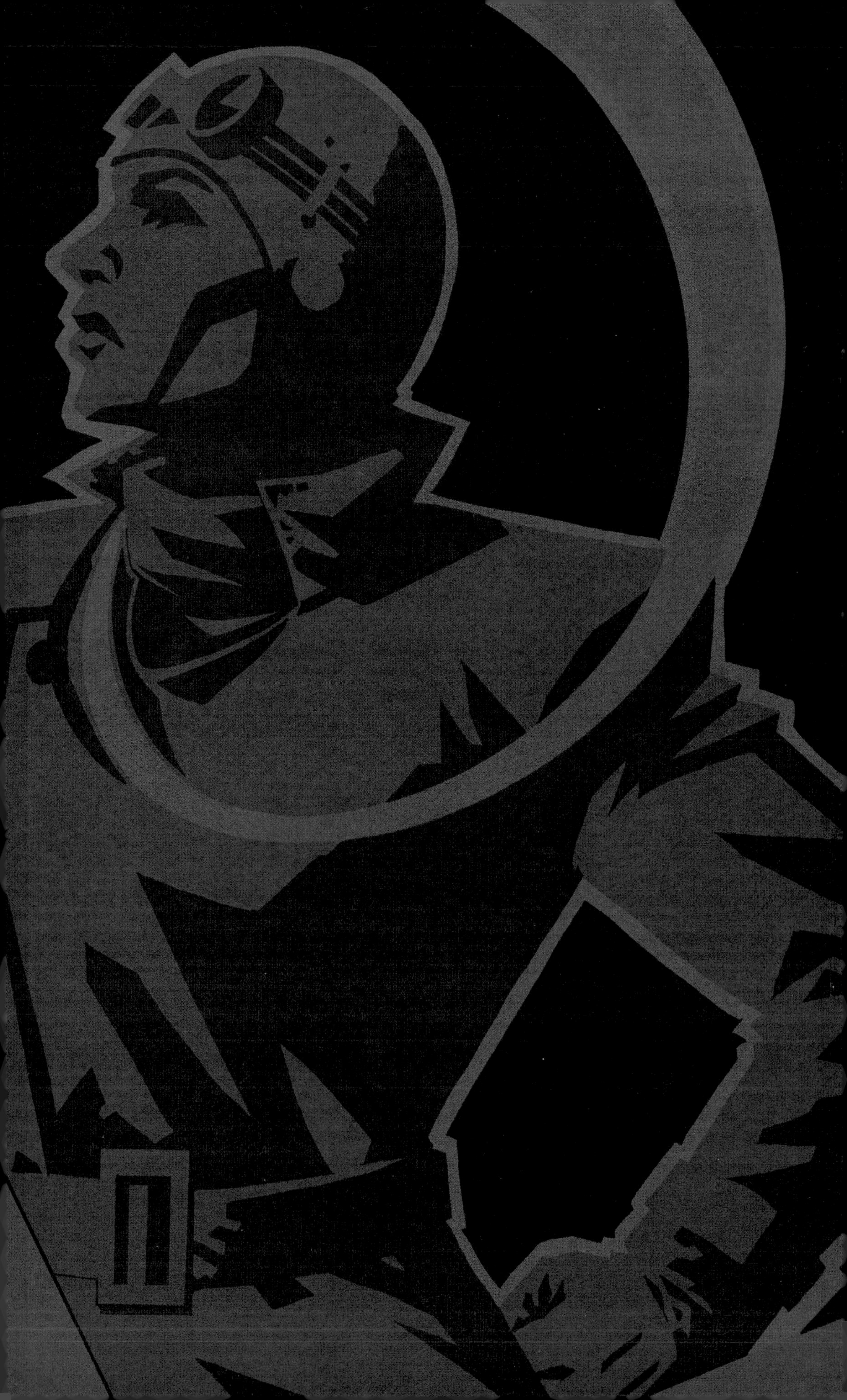

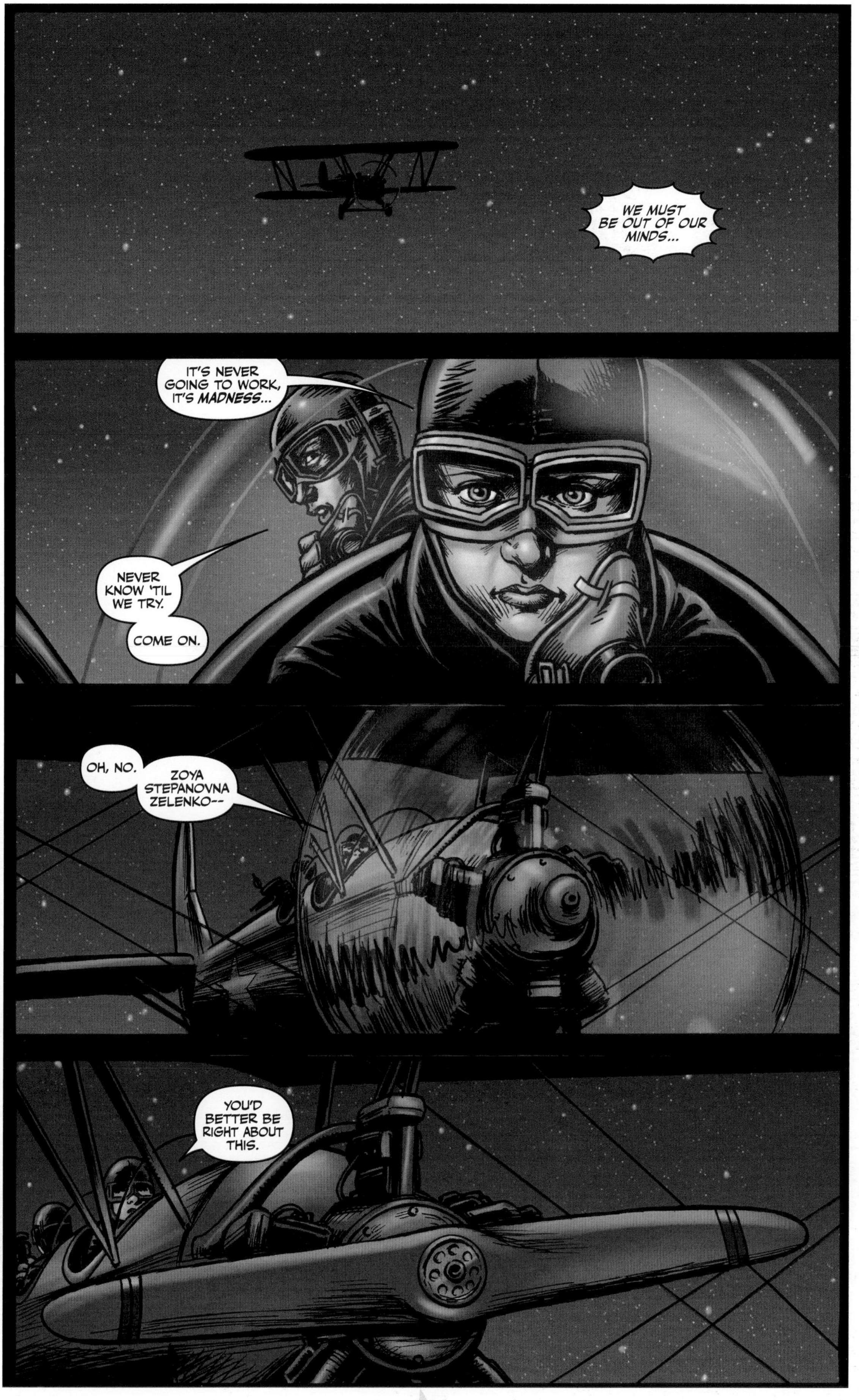
WE MUST BE OUT OF OUR MINDS...
IT'S NEVER GOING TO WORK, IT'S *MADNESS*...
NEVER KNOW 'TIL WE TRY.
COME ON.
OH, NO.
ZOYA STEPANOVNA ZELENKO--
YOU'D BETTER BE RIGHT ABOUT THIS.

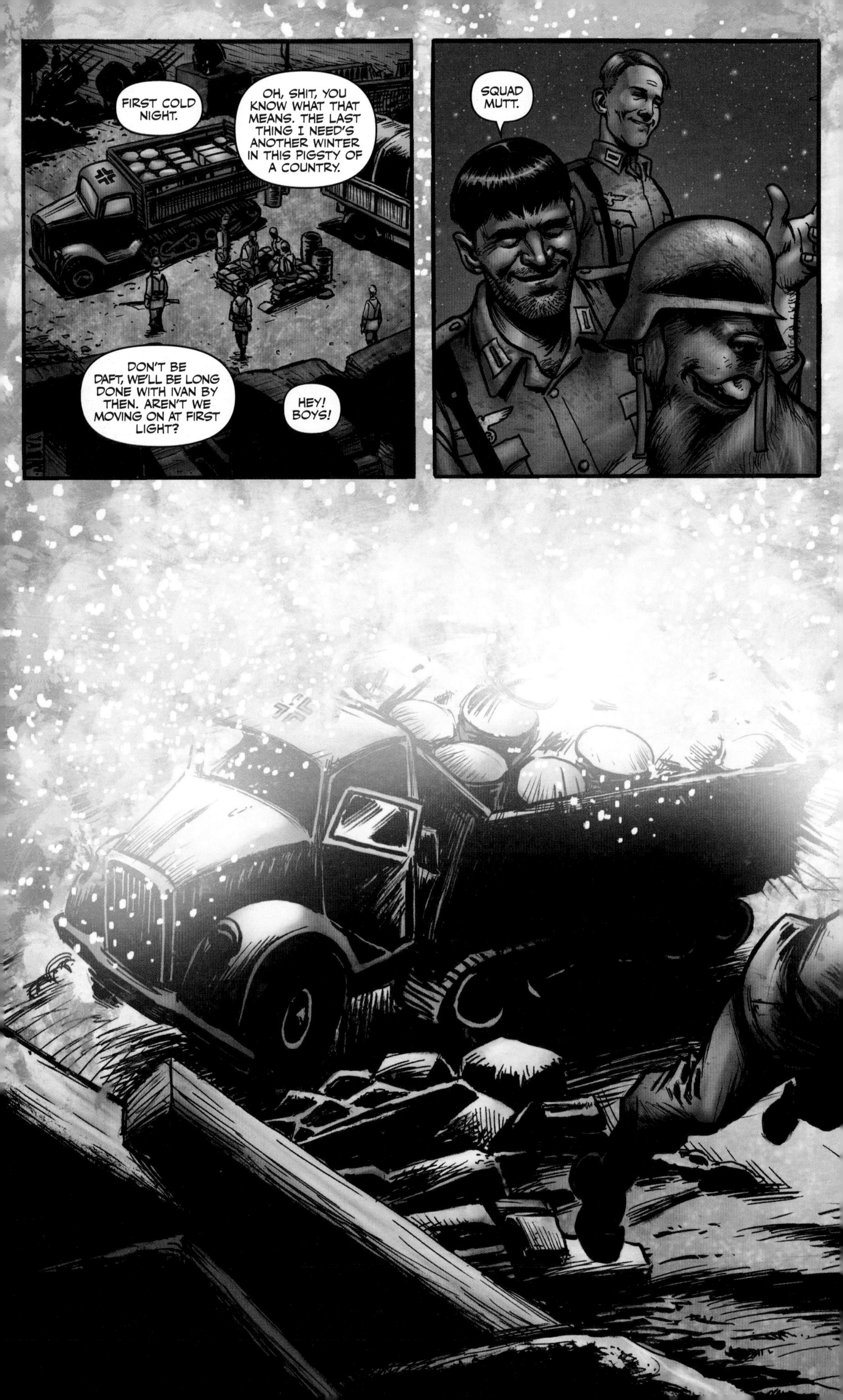
FIRST COLD NIGHT.
OH, SHIT, YOU KNOW WHAT THAT MEANS. THE LAST THING I NEED'S ANOTHER WINTER IN THIS PIGSTY OF A COUNTRY.
DON'T BE DAFT, WE'LL BE LONG DONE WITH IVAN BY THEN. AREN'T WE MOVING ON AT FIRST LIGHT?
HEY! BOYS!
SQUAD MUTT.

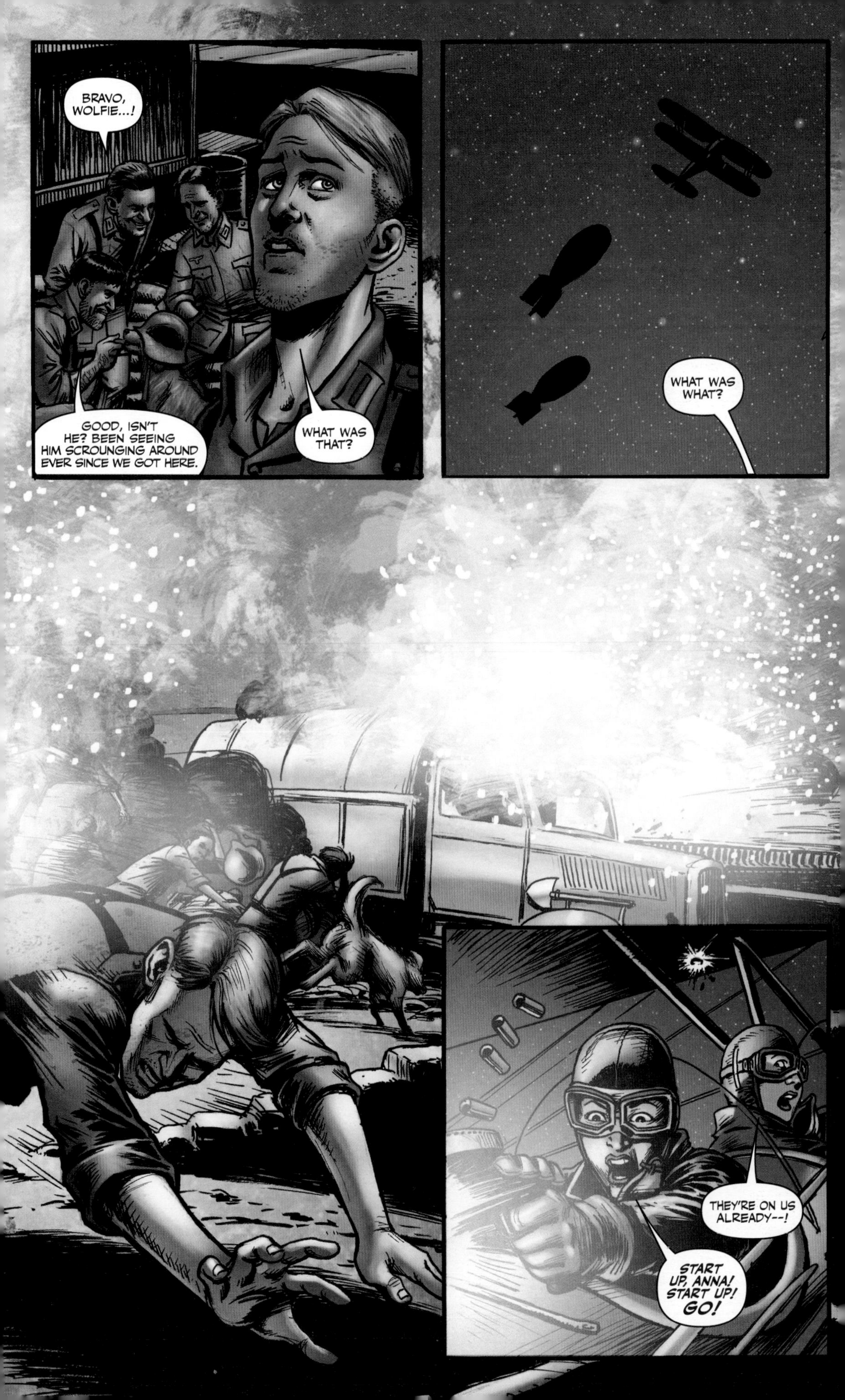
BRAVO, WOLFIE...!
GOOD, ISN'T HE? BEEN SEEING HIM SCROUNGING AROUND EVER SINCE WE GOT HERE.
WHAT WAS THAT?
WHAT WAS WHAT?
THEY'RE ON US ALREADY--!
START UP, ANNA! START UP! GO!

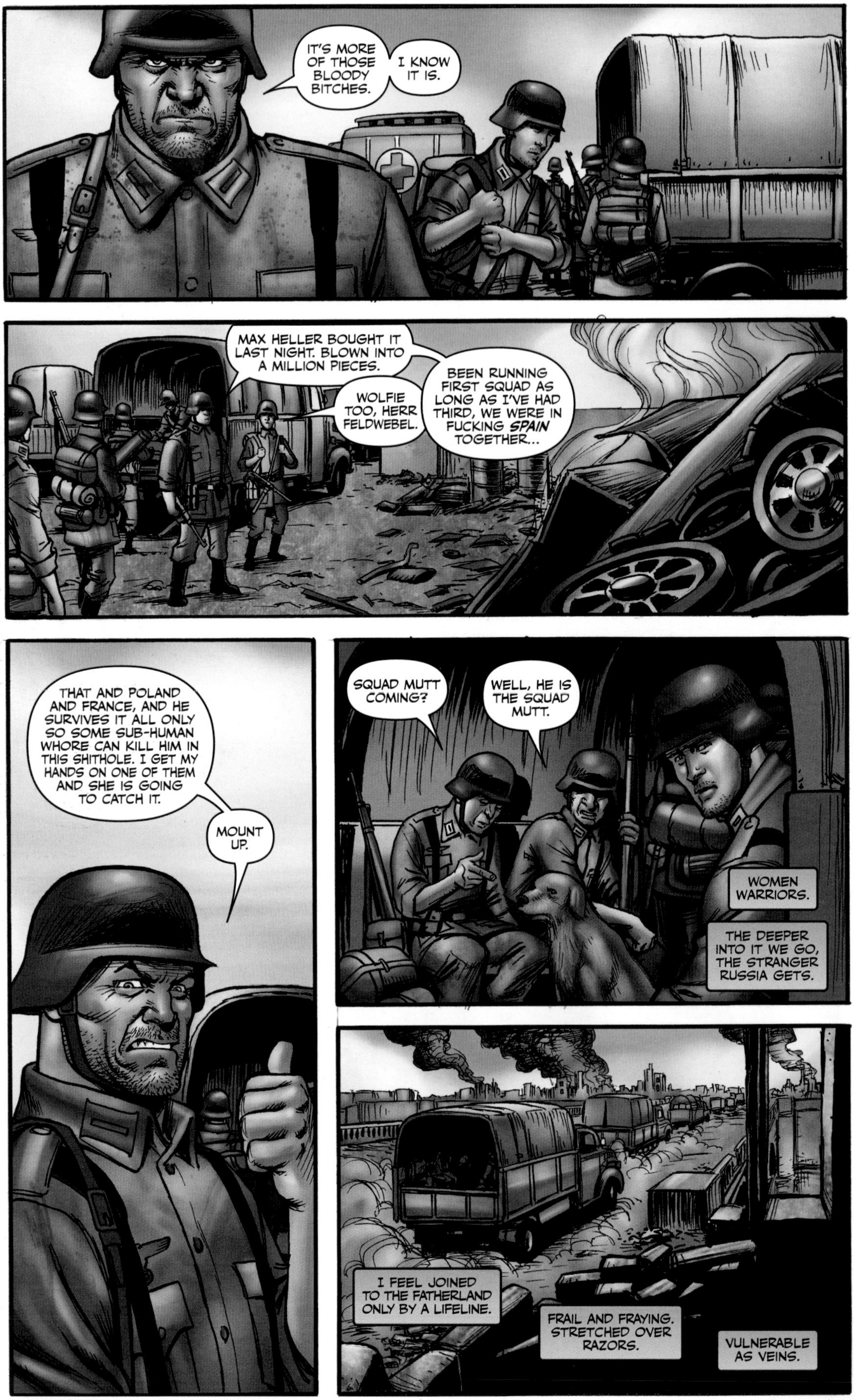

IT'S MORE OF THOSE BLOODY BITCHES.
I KNOW IT IS.
MAX HELLER BOUGHT IT LAST NIGHT. BLOWN INTO A MILLION PIECES.
WOLFIE TOO, HERR FELDWEBEL.
BEEN RUNNING FIRST SQUAD AS LONG AS I'VE HAD THIRD, WE WERE IN FUCKING SPAIN TOGETHER...
THAT AND POLAND AND FRANCE, AND HE SURVIVES IT ALL ONLY SO SOME SUB-HUMAN WHORE CAN KILL HIM IN THIS SHITHOLE. I GET MY HANDS ON ONE OF THEM AND SHE IS GOING TO CATCH IT.
MOUNT UP.
SQUAD MUTT COMING?
WELL, HE IS THE SQUAD MUTT.
WOMEN WARRIORS.
THE DEEPER INTO IT WE GO, THE STRANGER RUSSIA GETS.
I FEEL JOINED TO THE FATHERLAND ONLY BY A LIFELINE.
FRAIL AND FRAYING. STRETCHED OVER RAZORS.
VULNERABLE AS VEINS.

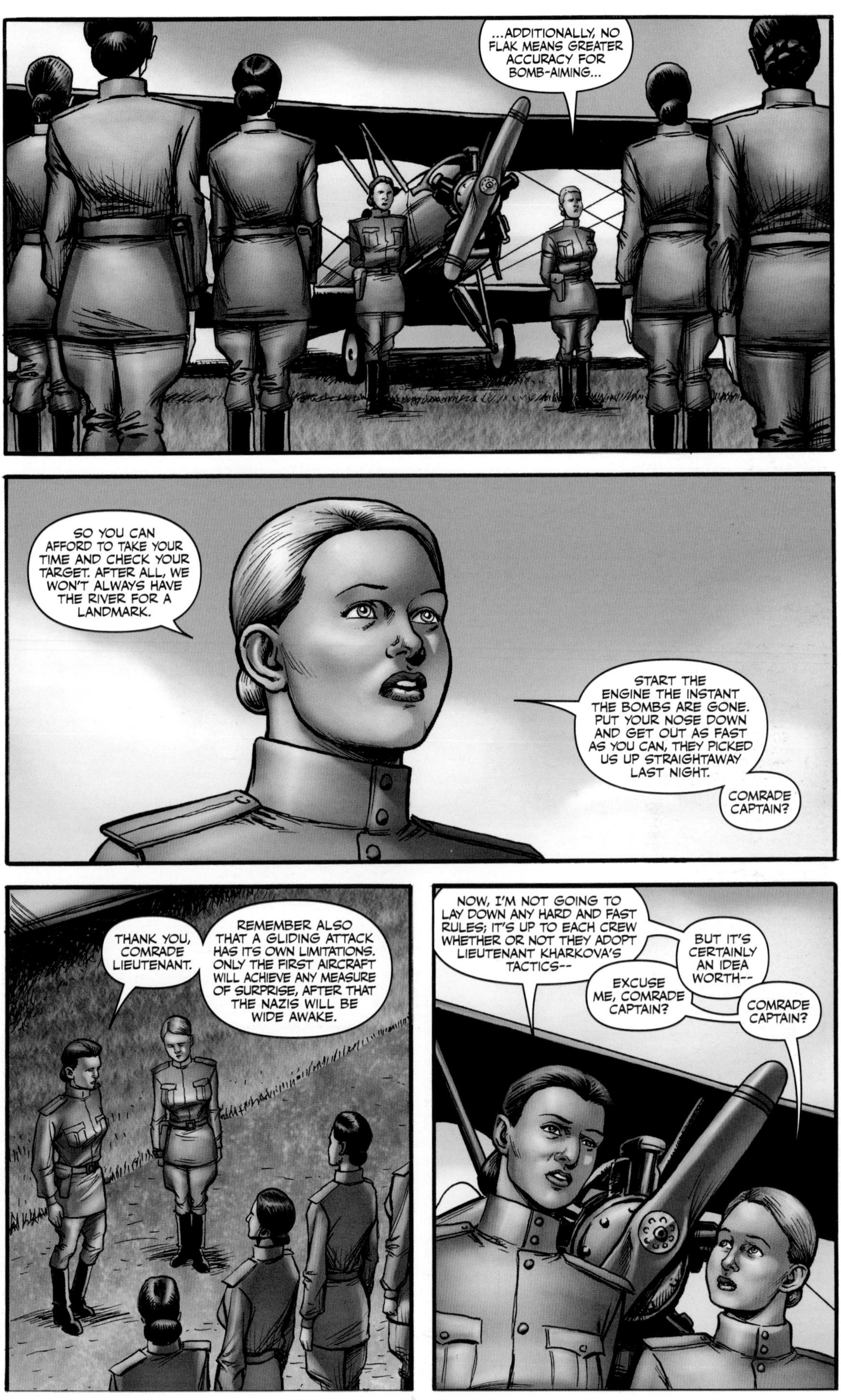
...ADDITIONALLY, NO FLAK MEANS GREATER ACCURACY FOR BOMB-AIMING...
SO YOU CAN AFFORD TO TAKE YOUR TIME AND CHECK YOUR TARGET. AFTER ALL, WE WON'T ALWAYS HAVE THE RIVER FOR A LANDMARK.
START THE ENGINE THE INSTANT THE BOMBS ARE GONE. PUT YOUR NOSE DOWN AND GET OUT AS FAST AS YOU CAN, THEY PICKED US UP STRAIGHTAWAY LAST NIGHT.
COMRADE CAPTAIN?
THANK YOU, COMRADE LIEUTENANT.
REMEMBER ALSO THAT A GLIDING ATTACK HAS ITS OWN LIMITATIONS. ONLY THE FIRST AIRCRAFT WILL ACHIEVE ANY MEASURE OF SURPRISE, AFTER THAT THE NAZIS WILL BE WIDE AWAKE.
NOW, I'M NOT GOING TO LAY DOWN ANY HARD AND FAST RULES; IT'S UP TO EACH CREW WHETHER OR NOT THEY ADOPT LIEUTENANT KHARKOVA'S TACTICS--
BUT IT'S CERTAINLY AN IDEA WORTH--
EXCUSE ME, COMRADE CAPTAIN?
COMRADE CAPTAIN?

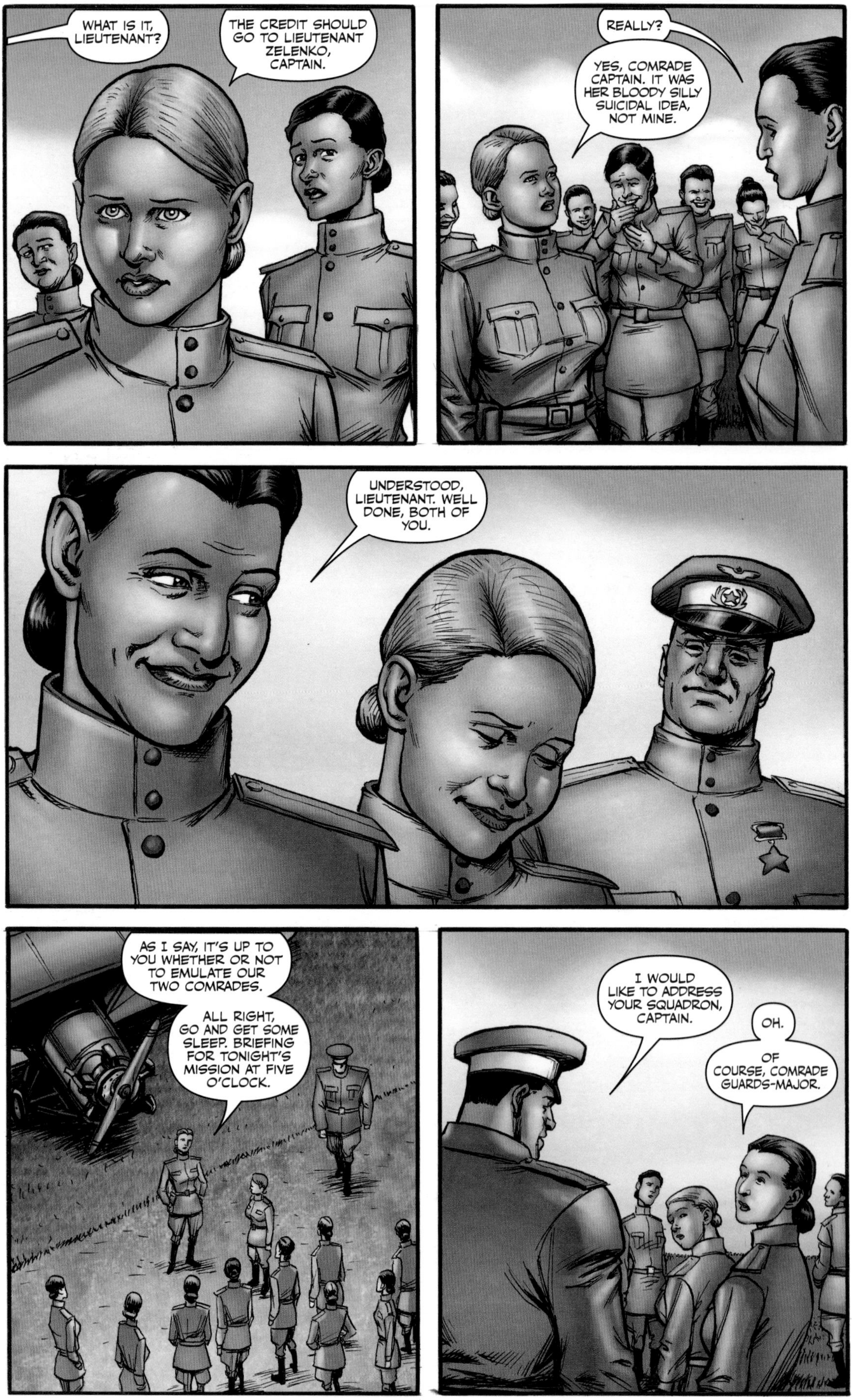
WHAT IS IT, LIEUTENANT?
THE CREDIT SHOULD GO TO LIEUTENANT ZELENKO, CAPTAIN.
REALLY?
YES, COMRADE CAPTAIN. IT WAS HER BLOODY SILLY SUICIDAL IDEA, NOT MINE.
UNDERSTOOD, LIEUTENANT. WELL DONE, BOTH OF YOU.
AS I SAY, IT'S UP TO YOU WHETHER OR NOT TO EMULATE OUR TWO COMRADES.
ALL RIGHT, GO AND GET SOME SLEEP. BRIEFING FOR TONIGHT'S MISSION AT FIVE O'CLOCK.
I WOULD LIKE TO ADDRESS YOUR SQUADRON, CAPTAIN.
OH.
OF COURSE, COMRADE GUARDS-MAJOR.

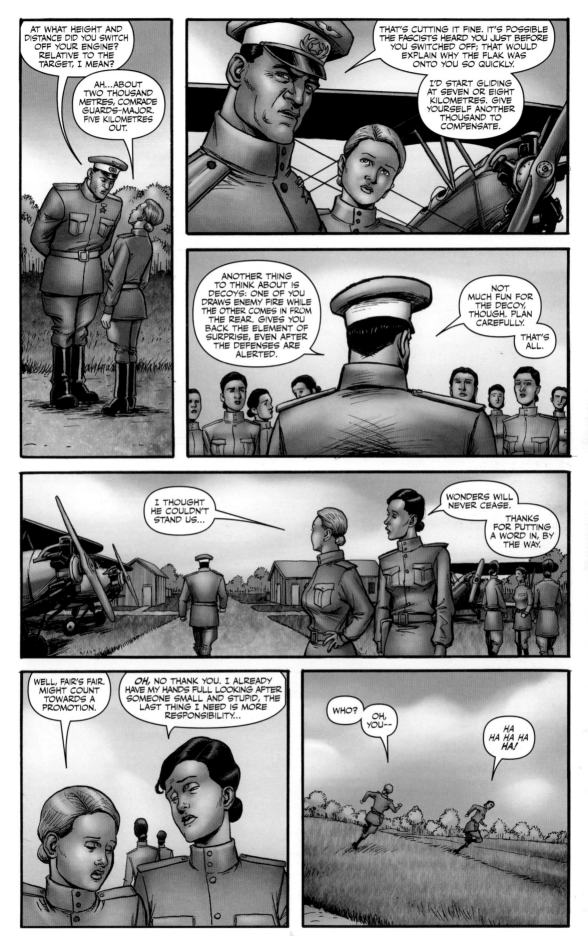

AT WHAT HEIGHT AND DISTANCE DID YOU SWITCH OFF YOUR ENGINE? RELATIVE TO THE TARGET, I MEAN?

AH...ABOUT TWO THOUSAND METRES, COMRADE GUARDS-MAJOR. FIVE KILOMETRES OUT.

THAT'S CUTTING IT FINE. IT'S POSSIBLE THE FASCISTS HEARD YOU JUST BEFORE YOU SWITCHED OFF; THAT WOULD EXPLAIN WHY THE FLAK WAS ONTO YOU SO QUICKLY.

I'D START GLIDING AT SEVEN OR EIGHT KILOMETRES. GIVE YOURSELF ANOTHER THOUSAND TO COMPENSATE.

ANOTHER THING TO THINK ABOUT IS DECOYS: ONE OF YOU DRAWS ENEMY FIRE WHILE THE OTHER COMES IN FROM THE REAR. GIVES YOU BACK THE ELEMENT OF SURPRISE, EVEN AFTER THE DEFENSES ARE ALERTED.

NOT MUCH FUN FOR THE DECOY, THOUGH. PLAN CAREFULLY.

THAT'S ALL.

I THOUGHT HE COULDN'T STAND US...

WONDERS WILL NEVER CEASE.

THANKS FOR PUTTING A WORD IN, BY THE WAY.

WELL, FAIR'S FAIR. MIGHT COUNT TOWARDS A PROMOTION.

OH, NO THANK YOU. I ALREADY HAVE MY HANDS FULL LOOKING AFTER SOMEONE SMALL AND STUPID, THE LAST THING I NEED IS MORE RESPONSIBILITY...

WHO?

OH, YOU--

HA HA HA HA HA!

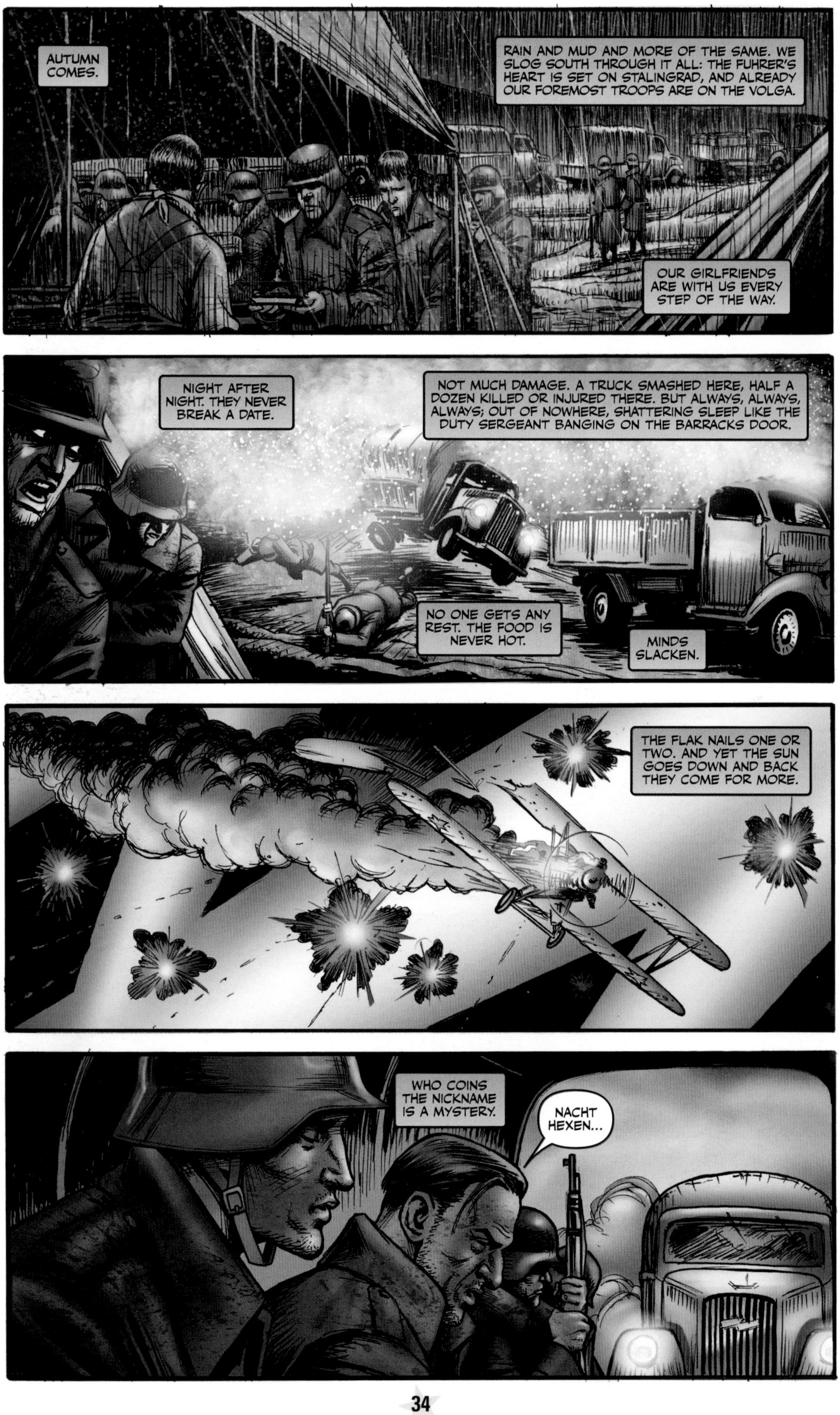
AUTUMN COMES.
RAIN AND MUD AND MORE OF THE SAME. WE SLOG SOUTH THROUGH IT ALL: THE FUHRER'S HEART IS SET ON STALINGRAD, AND ALREADY OUR FOREMOST TROOPS ARE ON THE VOLGA.
OUR GIRLFRIENDS ARE WITH US EVERY STEP OF THE WAY.
NIGHT AFTER NIGHT. THEY NEVER BREAK A DATE.
NOT MUCH DAMAGE. A TRUCK SMASHED HERE, HALF A DOZEN KILLED OR INJURED THERE. BUT ALWAYS, ALWAYS, ALWAYS; OUT OF NOWHERE, SHATTERING SLEEP LIKE THE DUTY SERGEANT BANGING ON THE BARRACKS DOOR.
NO ONE GETS ANY REST. THE FOOD IS NEVER HOT.
MINDS SLACKEN.
THE FLAK NAILS ONE OR TWO. AND YET THE SUN GOES DOWN AND BACK THEY COME FOR MORE.
WHO COINS THE NICKNAME IS A MYSTERY.
NACHT HEXEN...

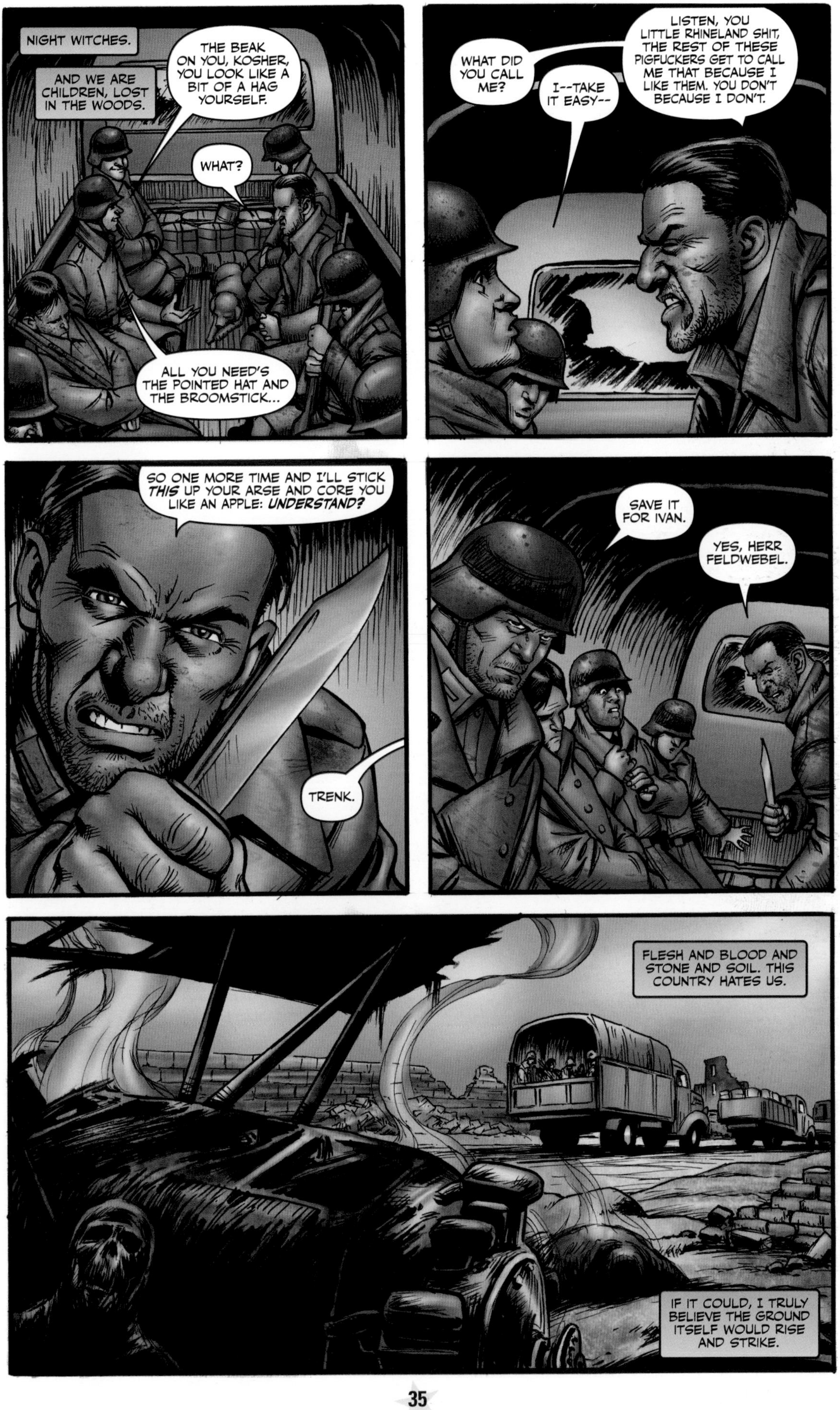
NIGHT WITCHES.
AND WE ARE CHILDREN, LOST IN THE WOODS.
THE BEAK ON YOU, KOSHER, YOU LOOK LIKE A BIT OF A HAG YOURSELF.
WHAT?
ALL YOU NEED'S THE POINTED HAT AND THE BROOMSTICK...
WHAT DID YOU CALL ME?
I--TAKE IT EASY--
LISTEN, YOU LITTLE RHINELAND SHIT, THE REST OF THESE PIGFUCKERS GET TO CALL ME THAT BECAUSE I LIKE THEM. YOU DON'T BECAUSE I DON'T.
SO ONE MORE TIME AND I'LL STICK *THIS* UP YOUR ARSE AND CORE YOU LIKE AN APPLE: ***UNDERSTAND?***
TRENK.
SAVE IT FOR IVAN.
YES, HERR FELDWEBEL.
FLESH AND BLOOD AND STONE AND SOIL. THIS COUNTRY HATES US.
IF IT COULD, I TRULY BELIEVE THE GROUND ITSELF WOULD RISE AND STRIKE.

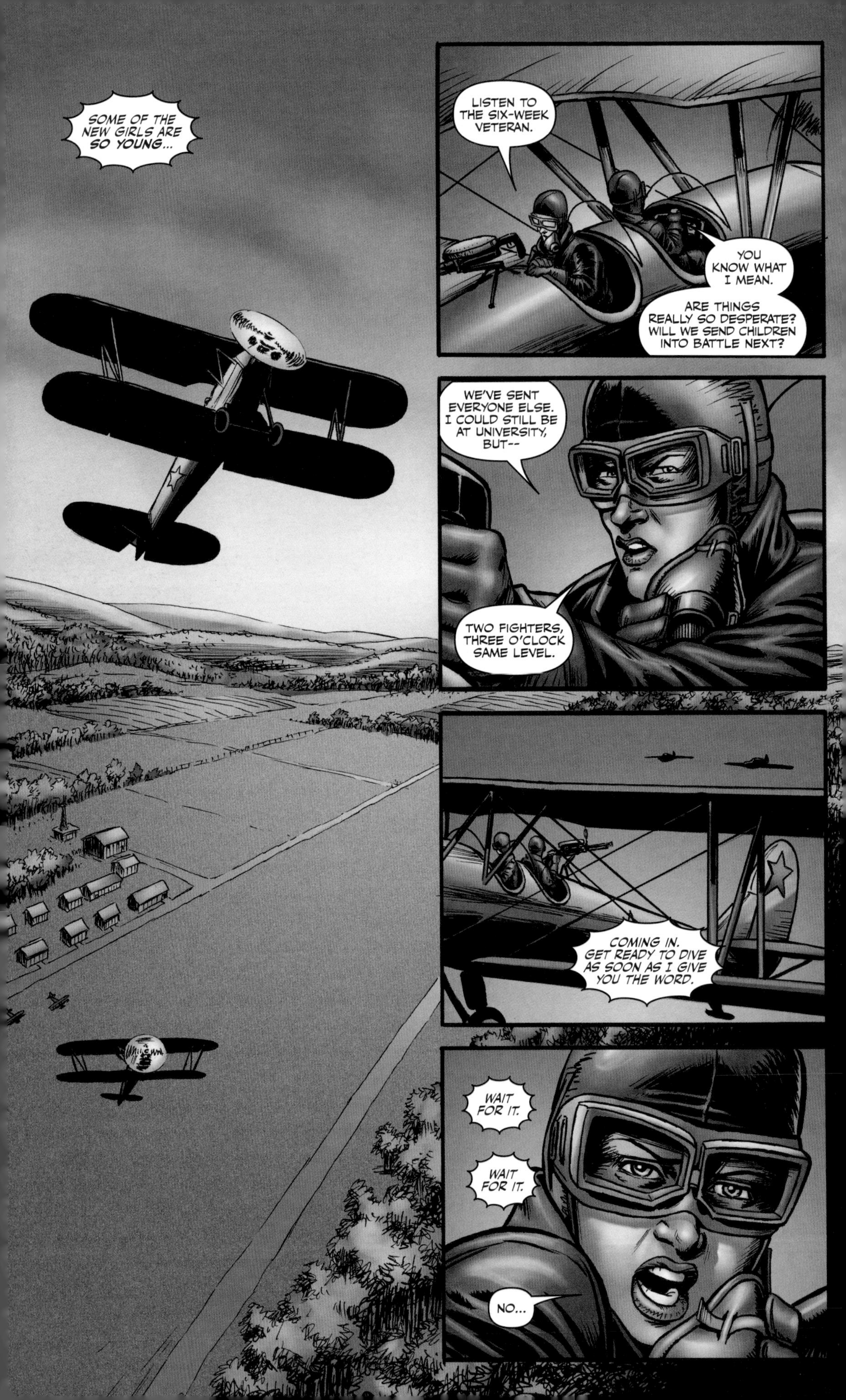
SOME OF THE NEW GIRLS ARE SO YOUNG...
LISTEN TO THE SIX-WEEK VETERAN.
YOU KNOW WHAT I MEAN.
ARE THINGS REALLY SO DESPERATE? WILL WE SEND CHILDREN INTO BATTLE NEXT?
WE'VE SENT EVERYONE ELSE. I COULD STILL BE AT UNIVERSITY, BUT--
TWO FIGHTERS, THREE O'CLOCK SAME LEVEL.
COMING IN. GET READY TO DIVE AS SOON AS I GIVE YOU THE WORD.
WAIT FOR IT.
WAIT FOR IT.
NO...

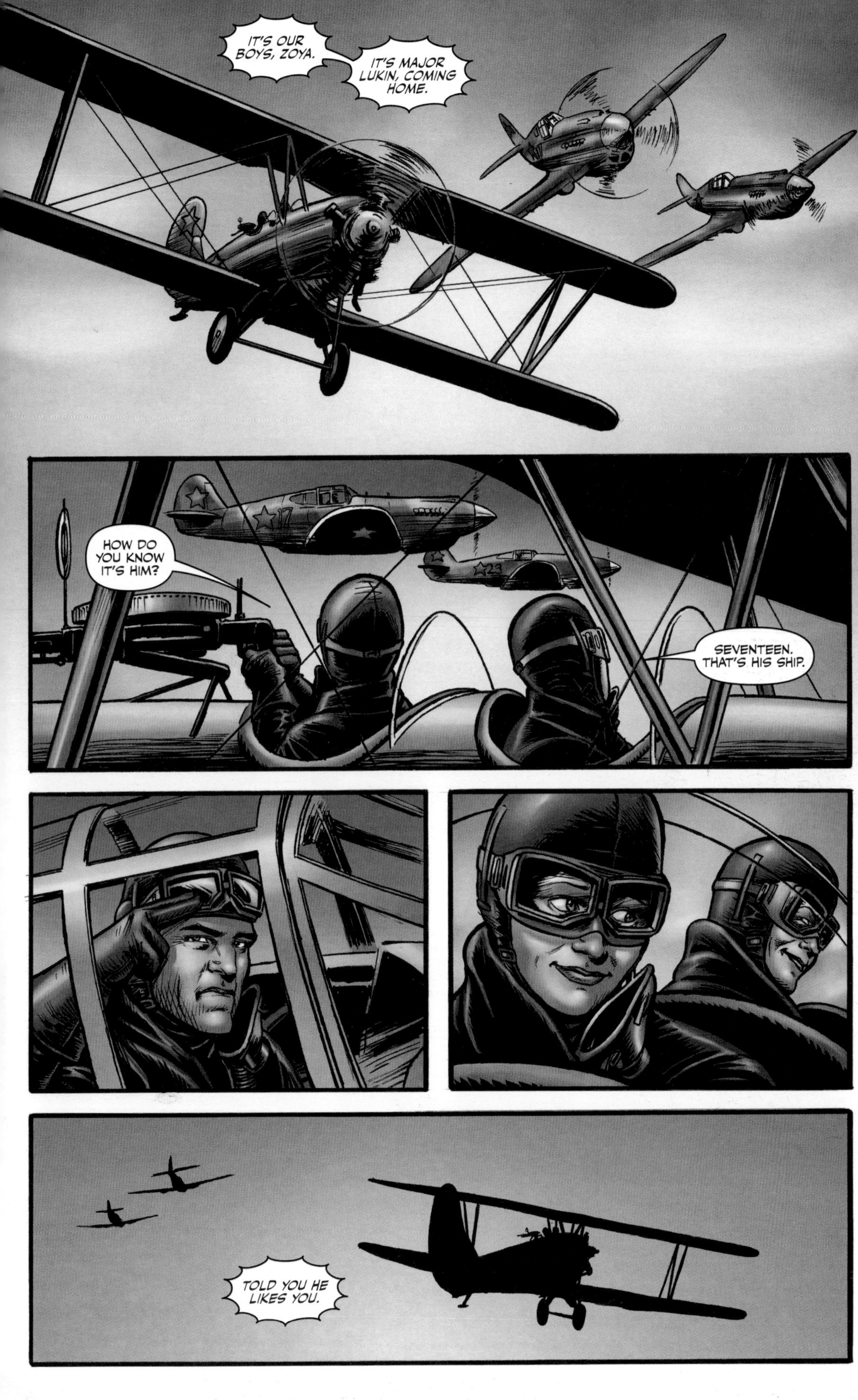
IT'S OUR BOYS, ZOYA.
IT'S MAJOR LUKIN, COMING HOME.
HOW DO YOU KNOW IT'S HIM?
SEVENTEEN. THAT'S HIS SHIP.
TOLD YOU HE LIKES YOU.

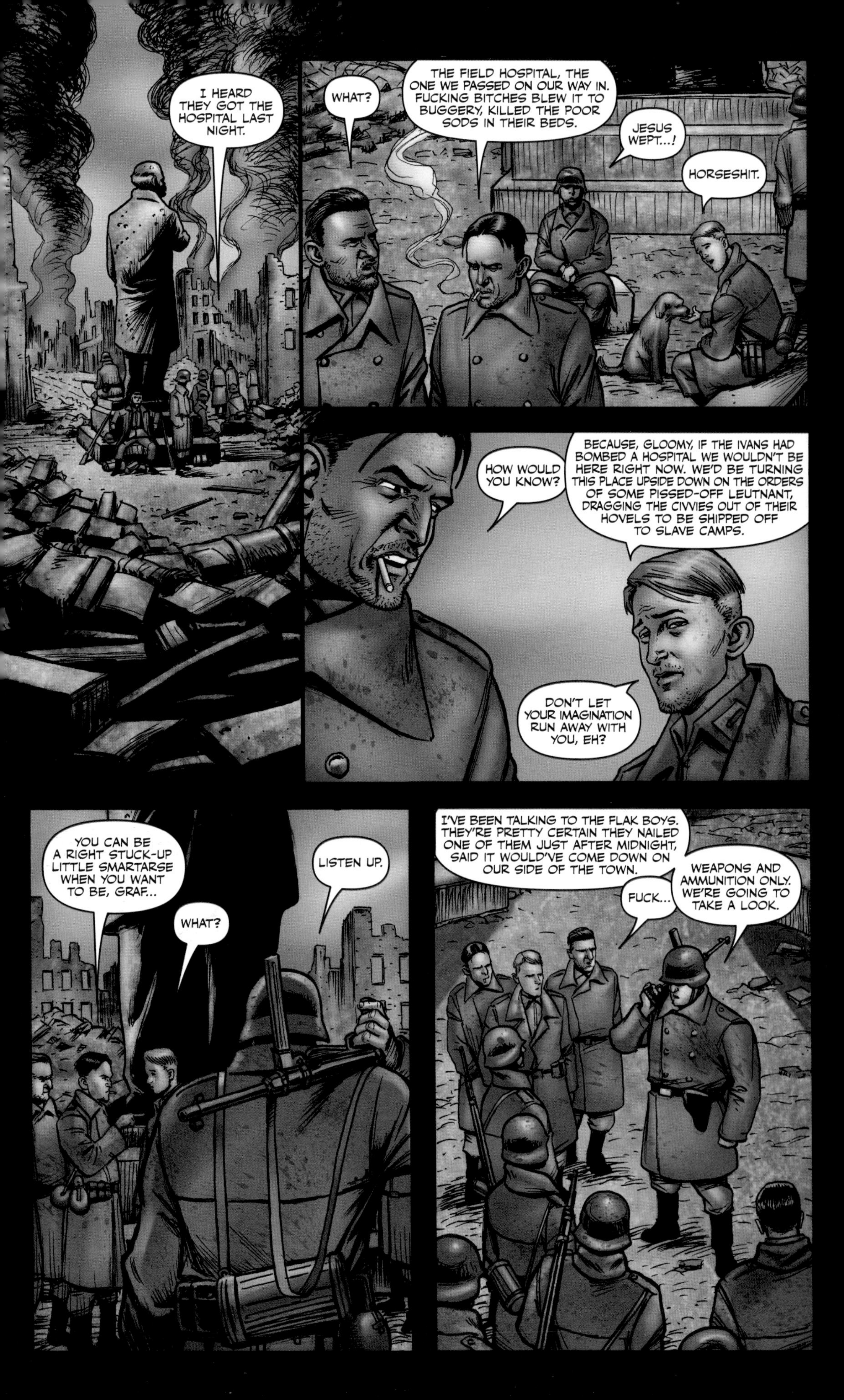
I HEARD THEY GOT THE HOSPITAL LAST NIGHT.
WHAT?
THE FIELD HOSPITAL, THE ONE WE PASSED ON OUR WAY IN. FUCKING BITCHES BLEW IT TO BUGGERY, KILLED THE POOR SODS IN THEIR BEDS.
JESUS WEPT...!
HORSESHIT.
HOW WOULD YOU KNOW?
BECAUSE, GLOOMY, IF THE IVANS HAD BOMBED A HOSPITAL WE WOULDN'T BE HERE RIGHT NOW. WE'D BE TURNING THIS PLACE UPSIDE DOWN ON THE ORDERS OF SOME PISSED-OFF LEUTNANT, DRAGGING THE CIVVIES OUT OF THEIR HOVELS TO BE SHIPPED OFF TO SLAVE CAMPS.
DON'T LET YOUR IMAGINATION RUN AWAY WITH YOU, EH?
YOU CAN BE A RIGHT STUCK-UP LITTLE SMARTARSE WHEN YOU WANT TO BE, GRAF...
WHAT?
LISTEN UP.
I'VE BEEN TALKING TO THE FLAK BOYS. THEY'RE PRETTY CERTAIN THEY NAILED ONE OF THEM JUST AFTER MIDNIGHT, SAID IT WOULD'VE COME DOWN ON OUR SIDE OF THE TOWN.
FUCK...
WEAPONS AND AMMUNITION ONLY. WE'RE GOING TO TAKE A LOOK.

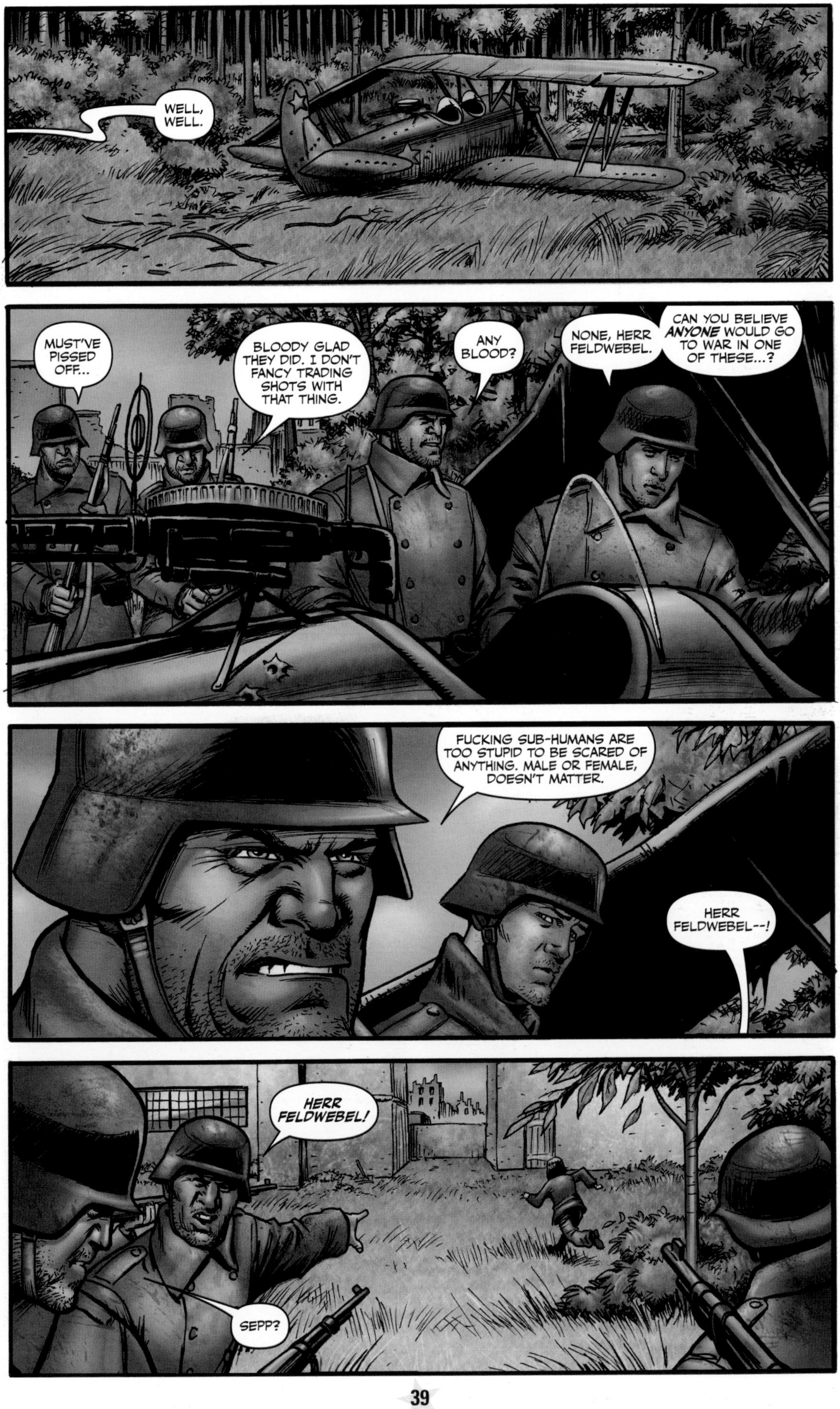
WELL, WELL.
MUST'VE PISSED OFF...
BLOODY GLAD THEY DID. I DON'T FANCY TRADING SHOTS WITH THAT THING.
ANY BLOOD?
NONE, HERR FELDWEBEL.
CAN YOU BELIEVE ANYONE WOULD GO TO WAR IN ONE OF THESE...?
FUCKING SUB-HUMANS ARE TOO STUPID TO BE SCARED OF ANYTHING. MALE OR FEMALE, DOESN'T MATTER.
HERR FELDWEBEL--!
HERR FELDWEBEL!
SEPP?

ALIVE.

SEPP THE SAVAGE.

BECAUSE HE NEVER, EVER GETS EXCITED.

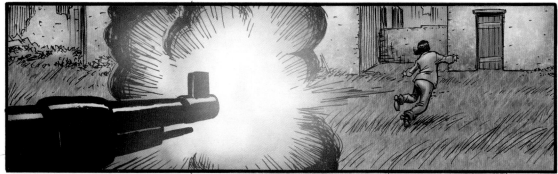

WHERE WAS--?

HIDING OUT 'TIL DARK, I BET YOU...

CAN'T BELIEVE WE *GOT ONE*--

SHE ISN'T A PILOT...!

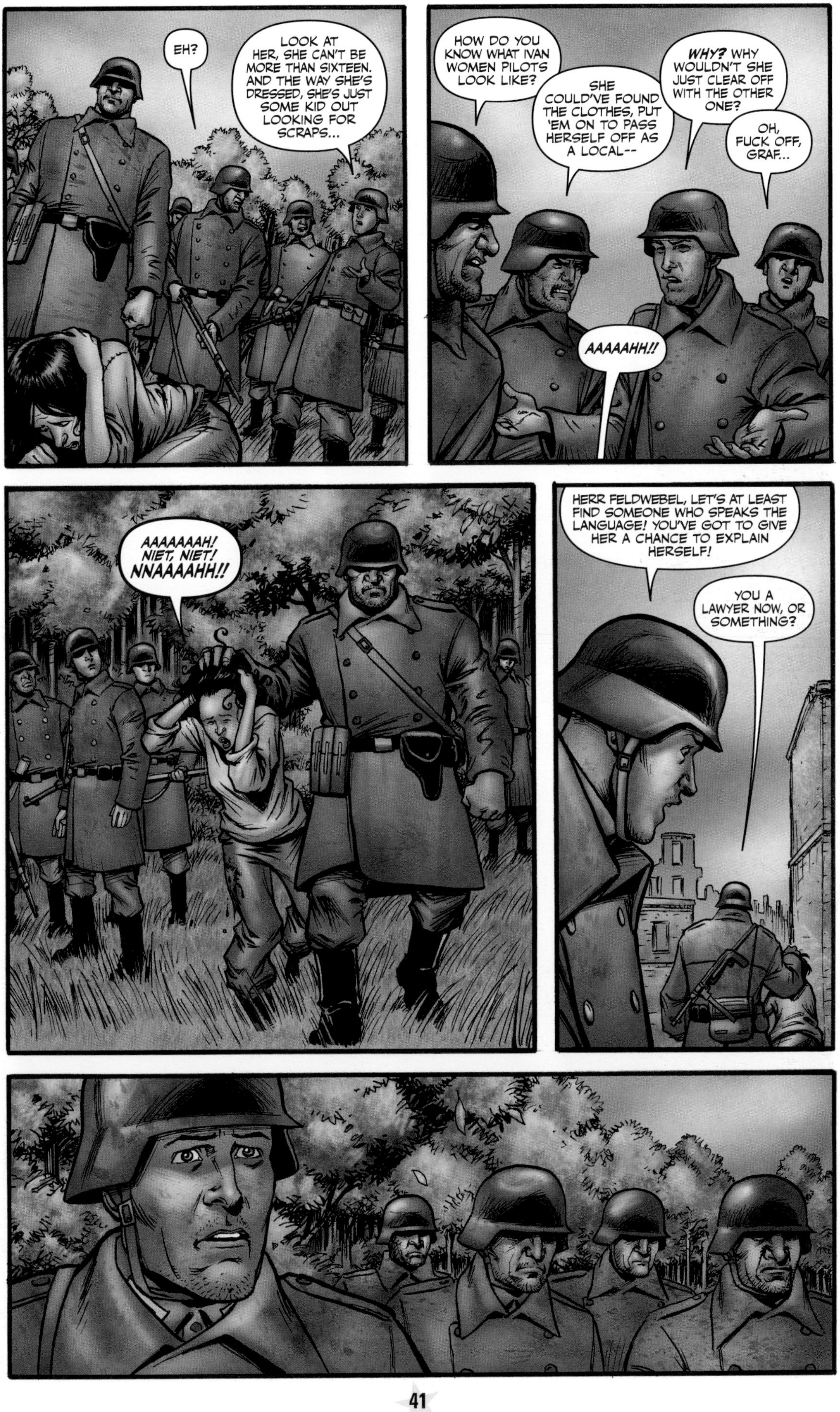
EH?
LOOK AT HER, SHE CAN'T BE MORE THAN SIXTEEN. AND THE WAY SHE'S DRESSED, SHE'S JUST SOME KID OUT LOOKING FOR SCRAPS...
HOW DO YOU KNOW WHAT IVAN WOMEN PILOTS LOOK LIKE?
SHE COULD'VE FOUND THE CLOTHES, PUT 'EM ON TO PASS HERSELF OFF AS A LOCAL--
WHY? WHY WOULDN'T SHE JUST CLEAR OFF WITH THE OTHER ONE?
OH, FUCK OFF, GRAF...
AAAAAHH!!
AAAAAAAH! NIET, NIET! NNAAAAHH!!
HERR FELDWEBEL, LET'S AT LEAST FIND SOMEONE WHO SPEAKS THE LANGUAGE! YOU'VE GOT TO GIVE HER A CHANCE TO EXPLAIN HERSELF!
YOU A LAWYER NOW, OR SOMETHING?

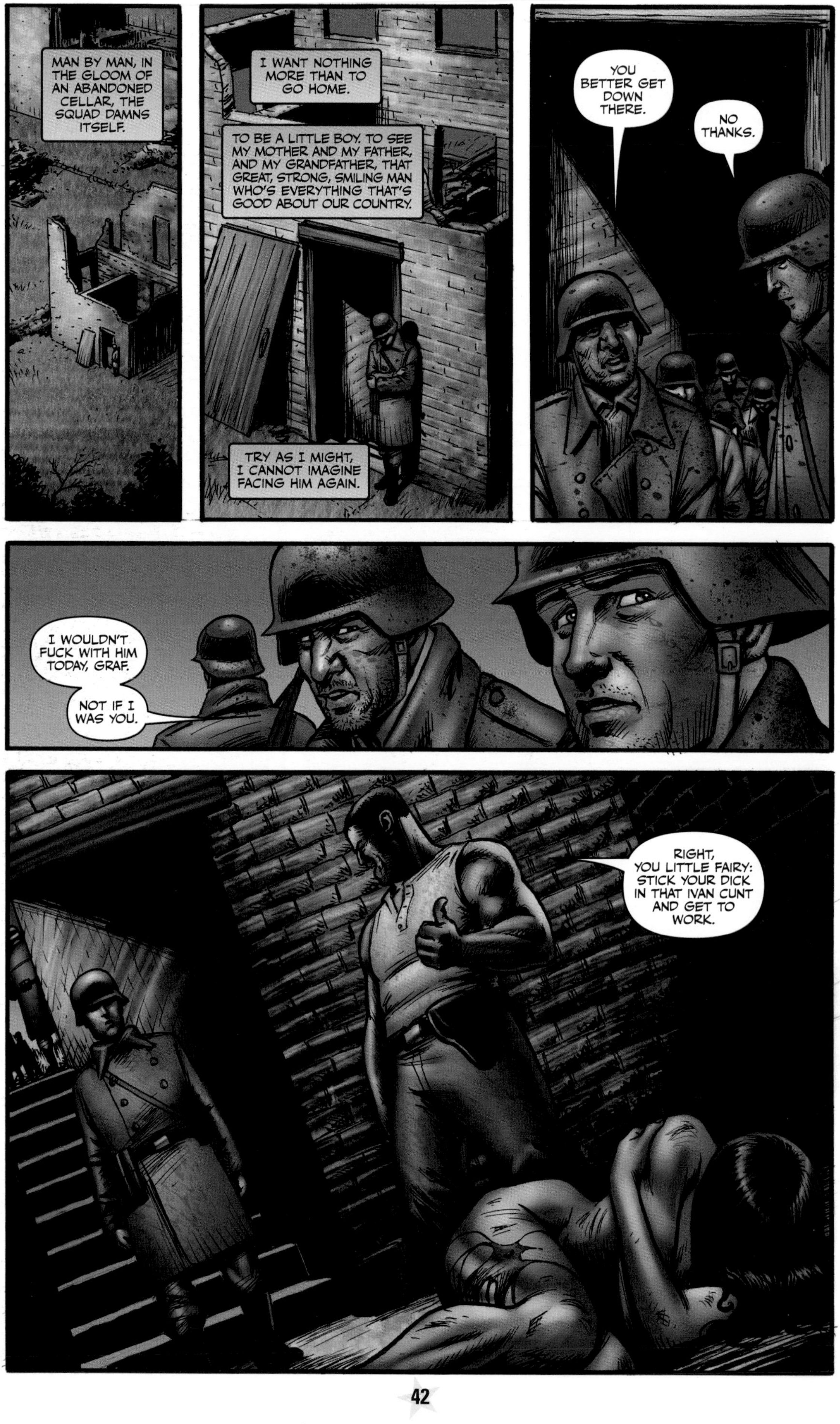
MAN BY MAN, IN THE GLOOM OF AN ABANDONED CELLAR, THE SQUAD DAMNS ITSELF.
I WANT NOTHING MORE THAN TO GO HOME.
TO BE A LITTLE BOY. TO SEE MY MOTHER AND MY FATHER, AND MY GRANDFATHER, THAT GREAT, STRONG, SMILING MAN WHO'S EVERYTHING THAT'S GOOD ABOUT OUR COUNTRY.
TRY AS I MIGHT, I CANNOT IMAGINE FACING HIM AGAIN.
YOU BETTER GET DOWN THERE.
NO THANKS.
I WOULDN'T FUCK WITH HIM TODAY, GRAF.
NOT IF I WAS YOU.
RIGHT, YOU LITTLE FAIRY: STICK YOUR DICK IN THAT IVAN CUNT AND GET TO WORK.

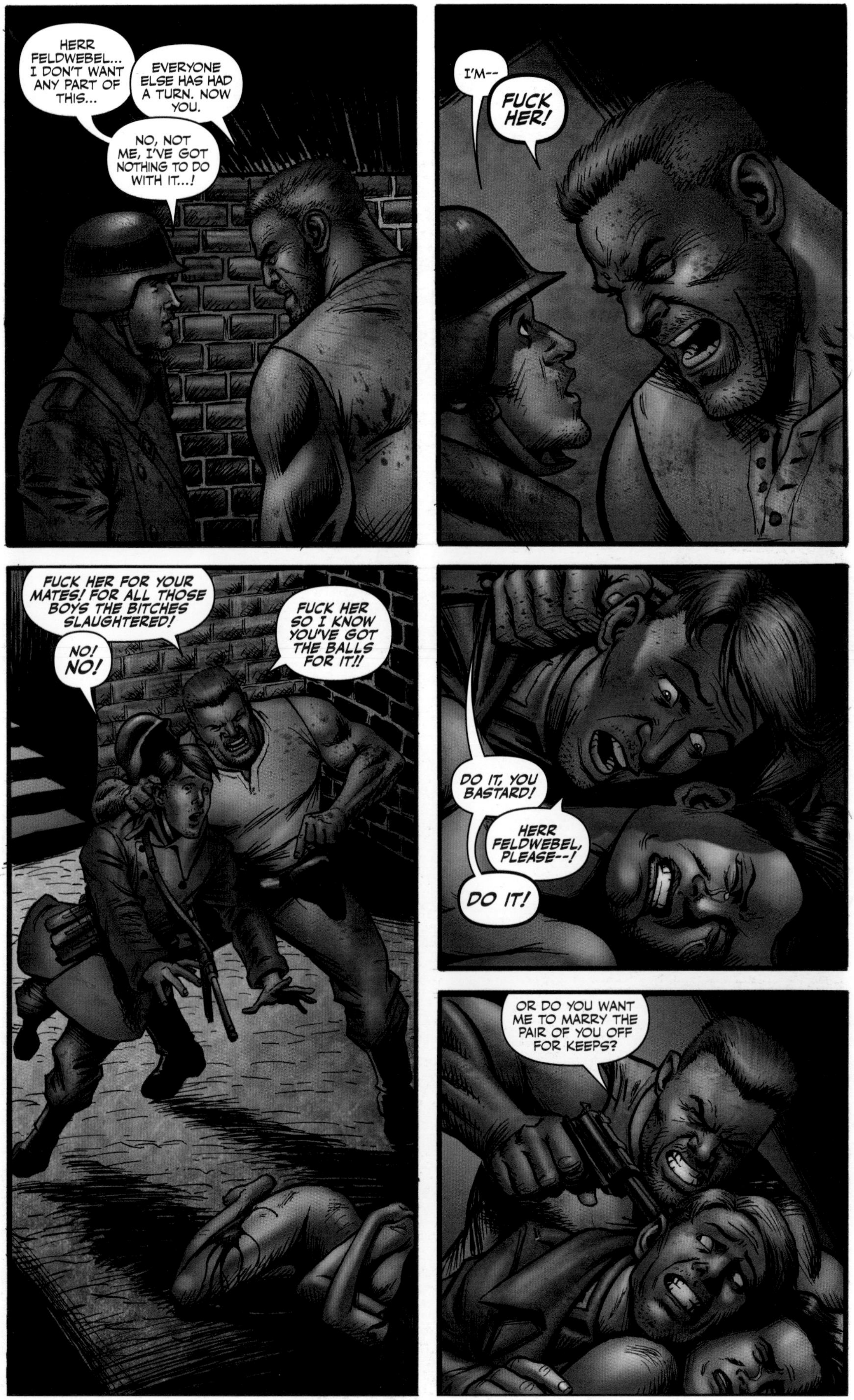
HERR FELDWEBEL... I DON'T WANT ANY PART OF THIS...
EVERYONE ELSE HAS HAD A TURN. NOW YOU.
NO, NOT ME, I'VE GOT NOTHING TO DO WITH IT...!
I'M--
FUCK HER!
FUCK HER FOR YOUR MATES! FOR ALL THOSE BOYS THE BITCHES SLAUGHTERED!
NO! NO!
FUCK HER SO I KNOW YOU'VE GOT THE BALLS FOR IT!!
DO IT, YOU BASTARD!
HERR FELDWEBEL, PLEASE--!
DO IT!
OR DO YOU WANT ME TO MARRY THE PAIR OF YOU OFF FOR KEEPS?

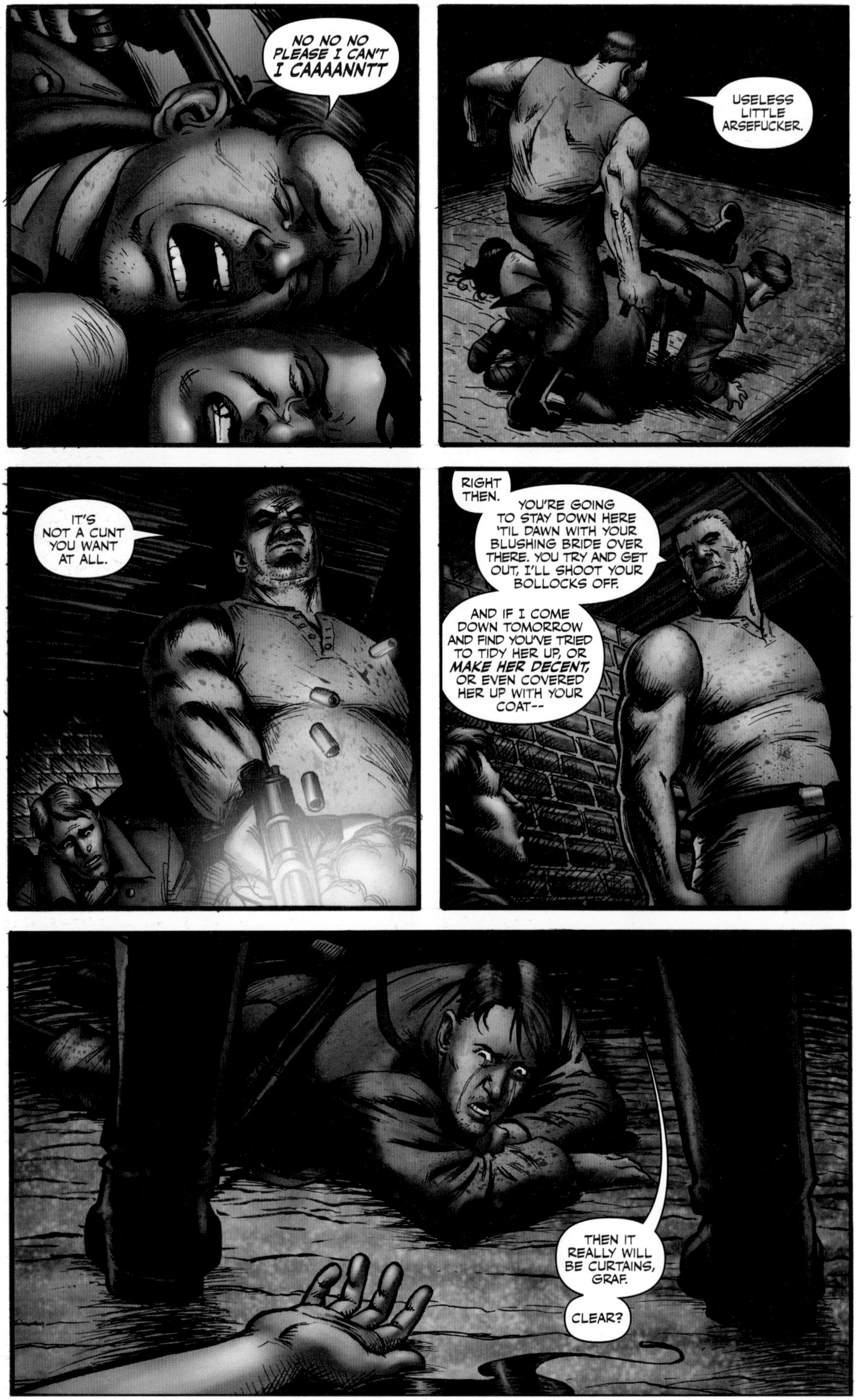
NO NO NO PLEASE I CAN'T I CAAAANNTT
USELESS LITTLE ARSEFUCKER.
IT'S NOT A CUNT YOU WANT AT ALL.
RIGHT THEN.
YOU'RE GOING TO STAY DOWN HERE 'TIL DAWN WITH YOUR BLUSHING BRIDE OVER THERE. YOU TRY AND GET OUT, I'LL SHOOT YOUR BOLLOCKS OFF.
AND IF I COME DOWN TOMORROW AND FIND YOU'VE TRIED TO TIDY HER UP, OR MAKE HER DECENT, OR EVEN COVERED HER UP WITH YOUR COAT--
THEN IT REALLY WILL BE CURTAINS, GRAF.
CLEAR?

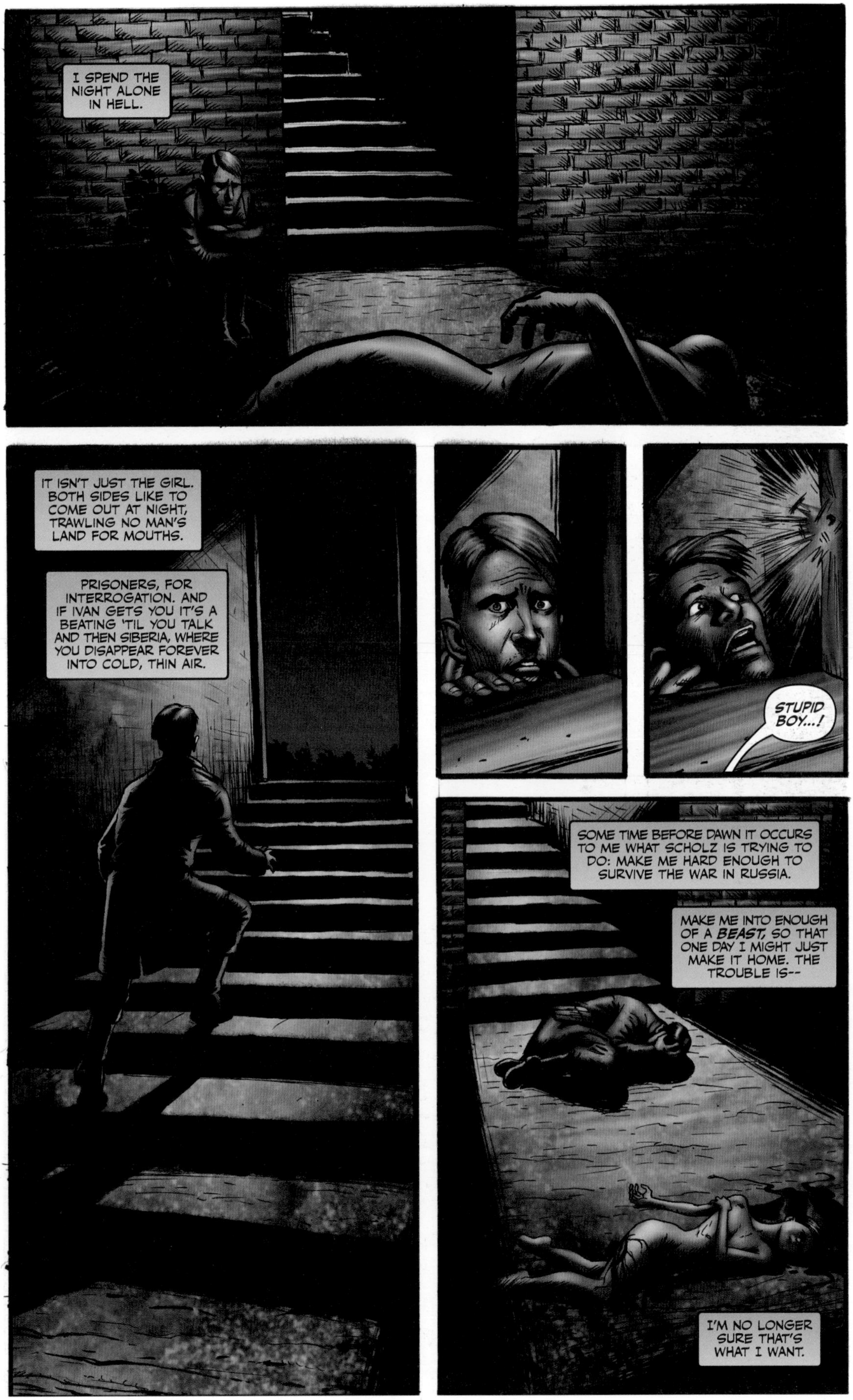
I SPEND THE NIGHT ALONE IN HELL.
IT ISN'T JUST THE GIRL. BOTH SIDES LIKE TO COME OUT AT NIGHT, TRAWLING NO MAN'S LAND FOR MOUTHS.
PRISONERS, FOR INTERROGATION. AND IF IVAN GETS YOU IT'S A BEATING 'TIL YOU TALK AND THEN SIBERIA, WHERE YOU DISAPPEAR FOREVER INTO COLD, THIN AIR.
STUPID BOY...!
SOME TIME BEFORE DAWN IT OCCURS TO ME WHAT SCHOLZ IS TRYING TO DO: MAKE ME HARD ENOUGH TO SURVIVE THE WAR IN RUSSIA.
MAKE ME INTO ENOUGH OF A *BEAST,* SO THAT ONE DAY I MIGHT JUST MAKE IT HOME. THE TROUBLE IS--
I'M NO LONGER SURE THAT'S WHAT I WANT.

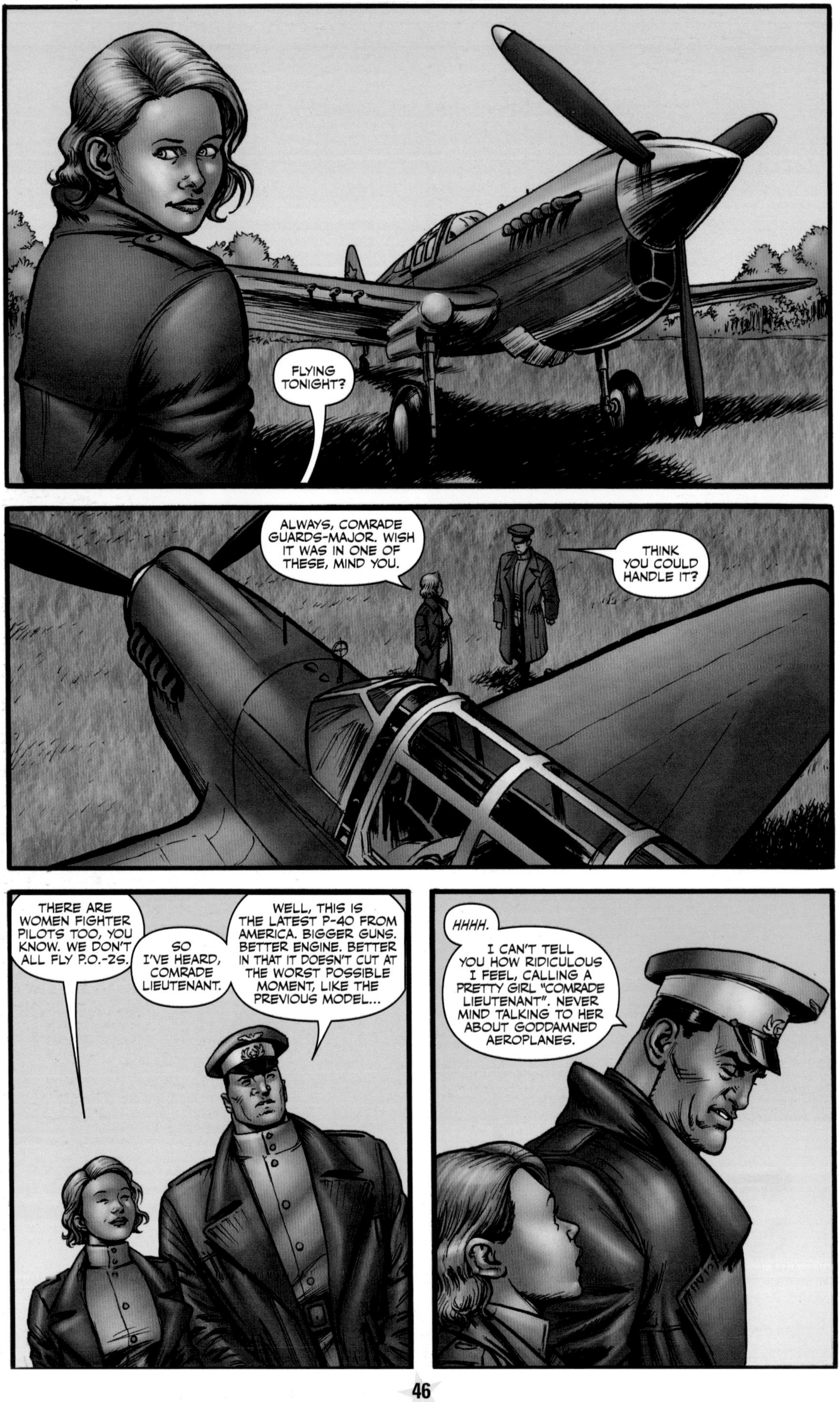
FLYING TONIGHT?
ALWAYS, COMRADE GUARDS-MAJOR. WISH IT WAS IN ONE OF THESE, MIND YOU.
THINK YOU COULD HANDLE IT?
THERE ARE WOMEN FIGHTER PILOTS TOO, YOU KNOW. WE DON'T ALL FLY P.O.-2S.
SO I'VE HEARD, COMRADE LIEUTENANT.
WELL, THIS IS THE LATEST P-40 FROM AMERICA. BIGGER GUNS. BETTER ENGINE. BETTER IN THAT IT DOESN'T CUT AT THE WORST POSSIBLE MOMENT, LIKE THE PREVIOUS MODEL...
HHHH.
I CAN'T TELL YOU HOW RIDICULOUS I FEEL, CALLING A PRETTY GIRL "COMRADE LIEUTENANT". NEVER MIND TALKING TO HER ABOUT GODDAMNED AEROPLANES.

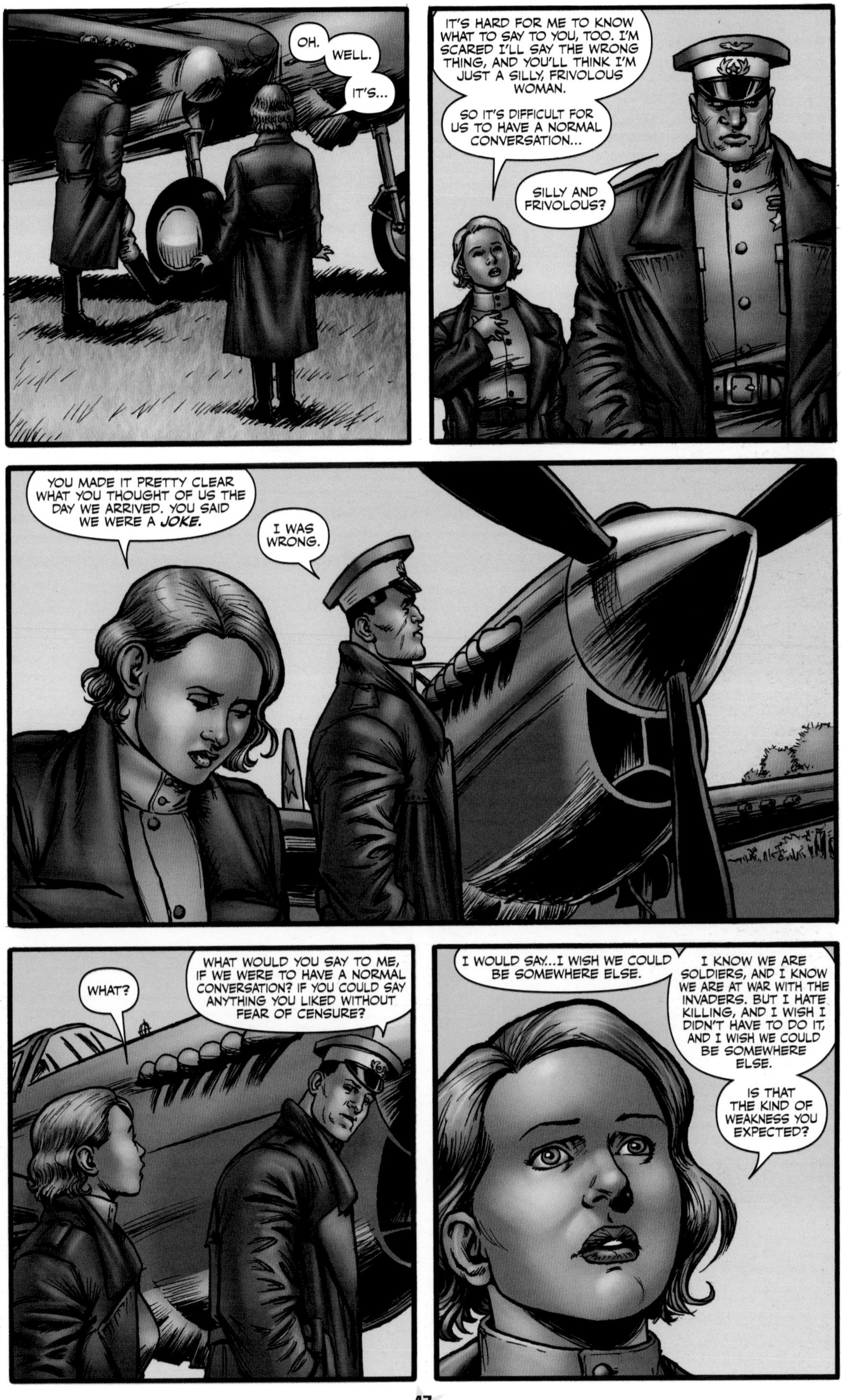

OH.
WELL.
IT'S...
IT'S HARD FOR ME TO KNOW WHAT TO SAY TO YOU, TOO. I'M SCARED I'LL SAY THE WRONG THING, AND YOU'LL THINK I'M JUST A SILLY, FRIVOLOUS WOMAN.
SO IT'S DIFFICULT FOR US TO HAVE A NORMAL CONVERSATION...
SILLY AND FRIVOLOUS?
YOU MADE IT PRETTY CLEAR WHAT YOU THOUGHT OF US THE DAY WE ARRIVED. YOU SAID WE WERE A ***JOKE.***
I WAS WRONG.
WHAT?
WHAT WOULD YOU SAY TO ME, IF WE WERE TO HAVE A NORMAL CONVERSATION? IF YOU COULD SAY ANYTHING YOU LIKED WITHOUT FEAR OF CENSURE?
I WOULD SAY...I WISH WE COULD BE SOMEWHERE ELSE.
I KNOW WE ARE SOLDIERS, AND I KNOW WE ARE AT WAR WITH THE INVADERS. BUT I HATE KILLING, AND I WISH I DIDN'T HAVE TO DO IT, AND I WISH WE COULD BE SOMEWHERE ELSE.
IS THAT THE KIND OF WEAKNESS YOU EXPECTED?

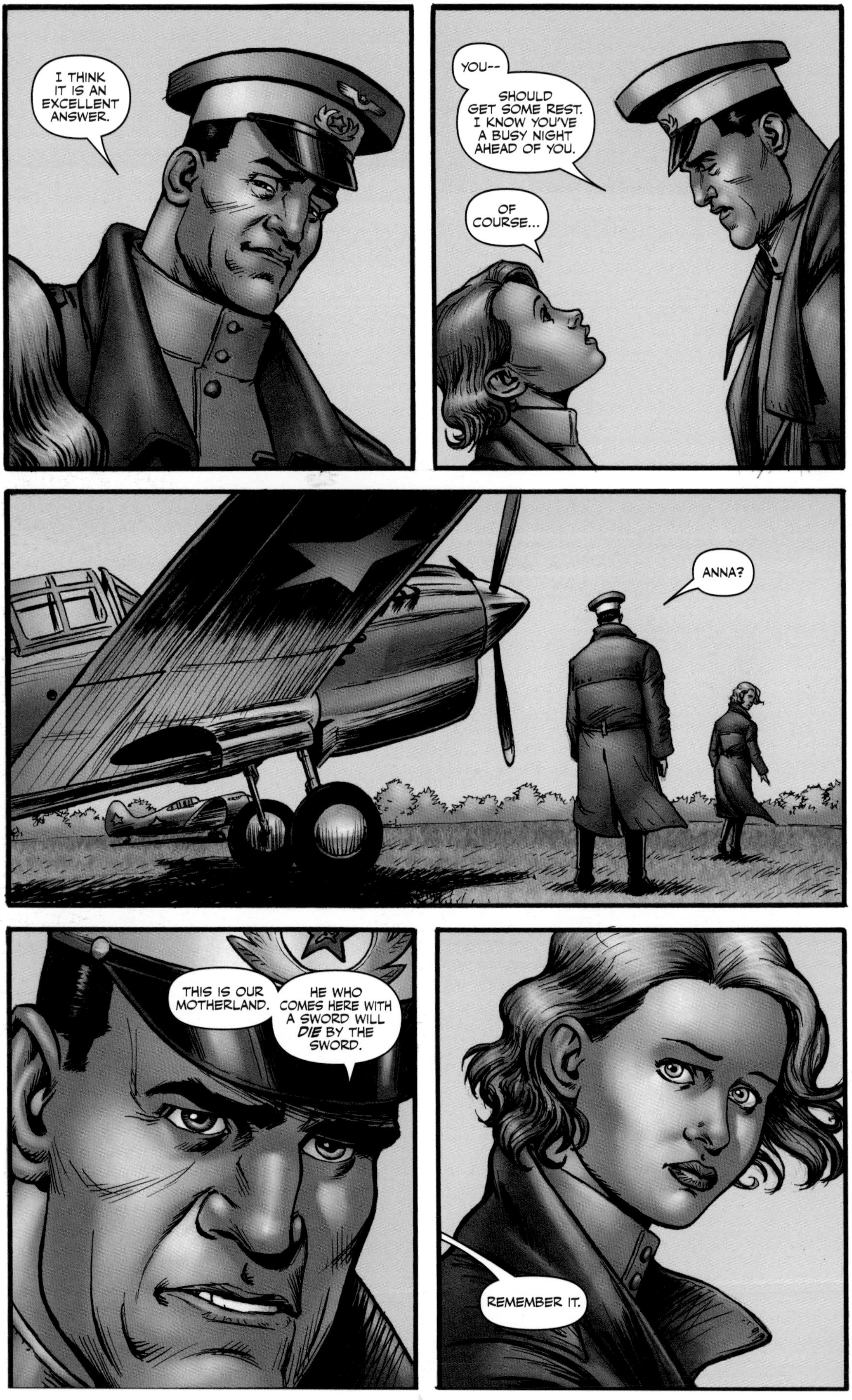
I THINK IT IS AN EXCELLENT ANSWER.
YOU--
SHOULD GET SOME REST. I KNOW YOU'VE A BUSY NIGHT AHEAD OF YOU.
OF COURSE...
ANNA?
THIS IS OUR MOTHERLAND.
HE WHO COMES HERE WITH A SWORD WILL DIE BY THE SWORD.
REMEMBER IT.

Chapter 3

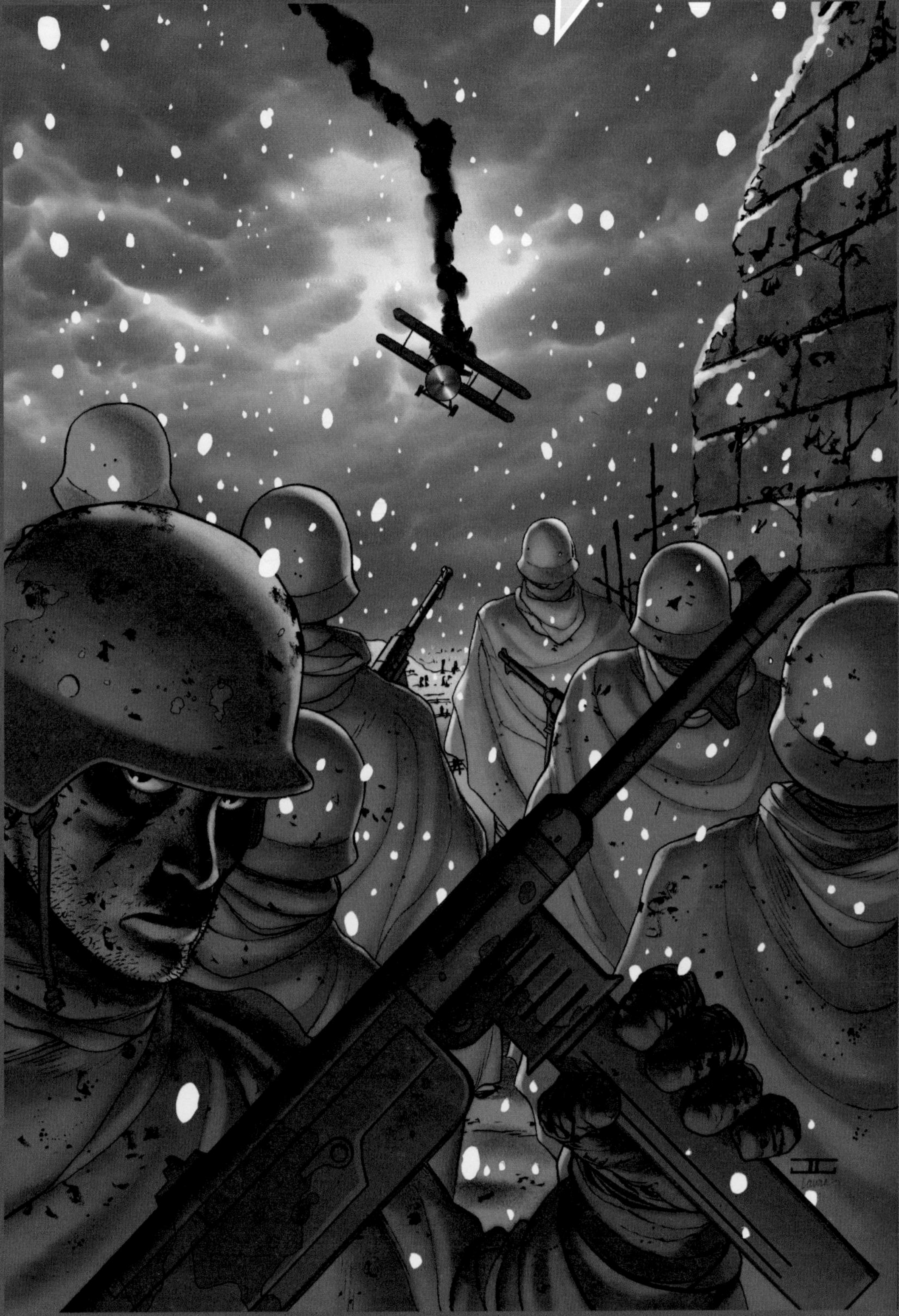

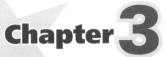

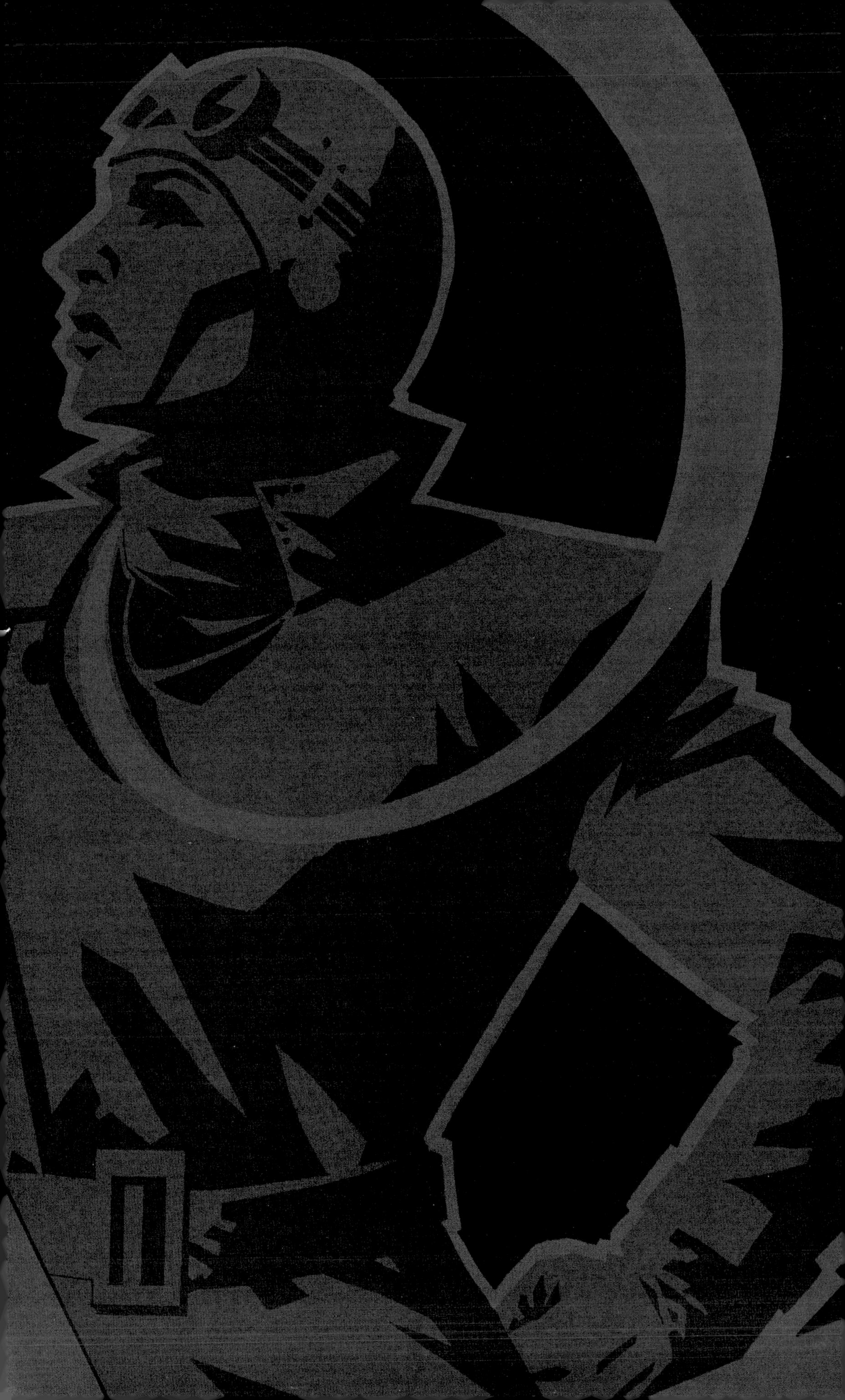

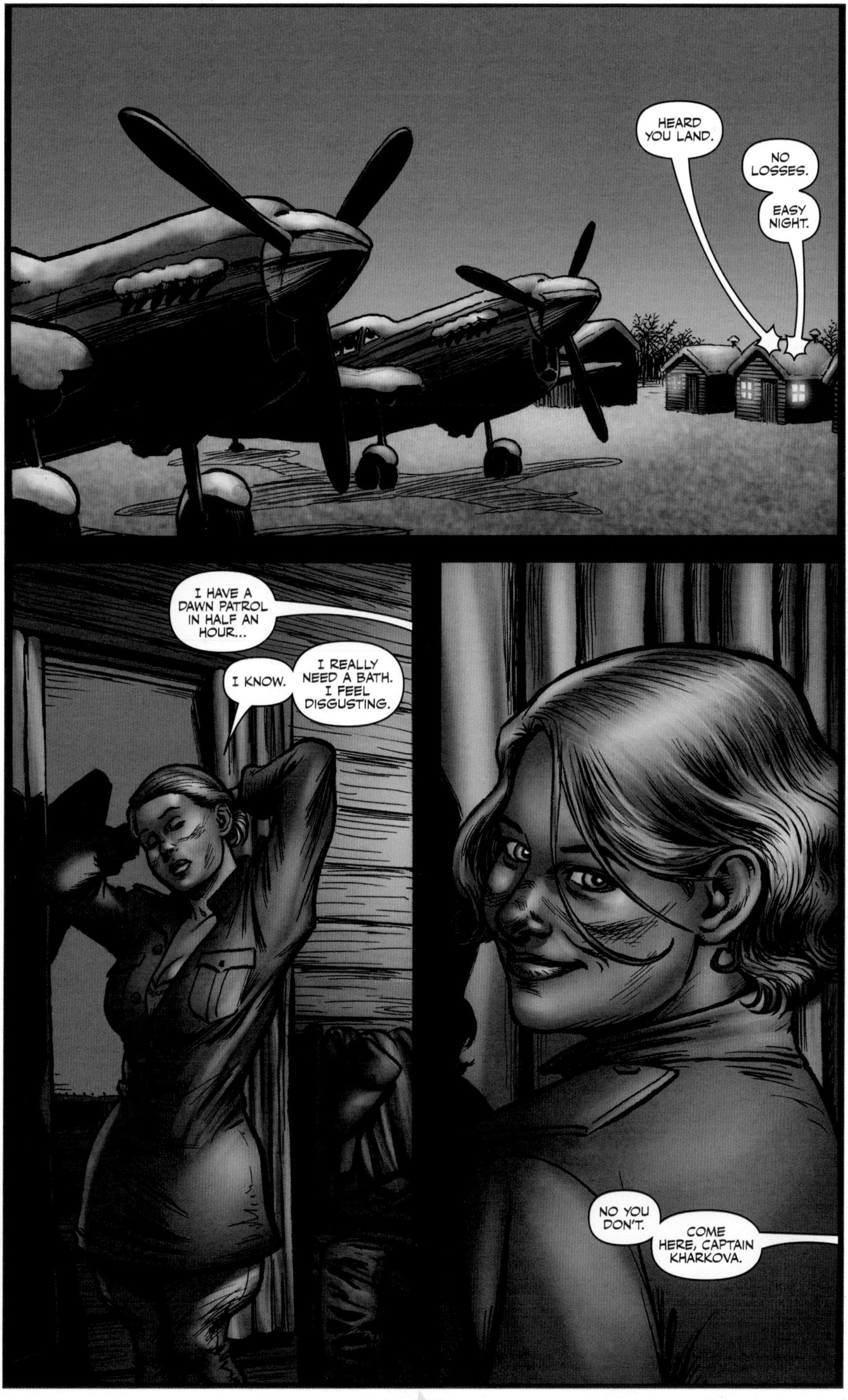
HEARD YOU LAND.
NO LOSSES.
EASY NIGHT.
I HAVE A DAWN PATROL IN HALF AN HOUR...
I KNOW.
I REALLY NEED A BATH. I FEEL DISGUSTING.
NO YOU DON'T.
COME HERE, CAPTAIN KHARKOVA.

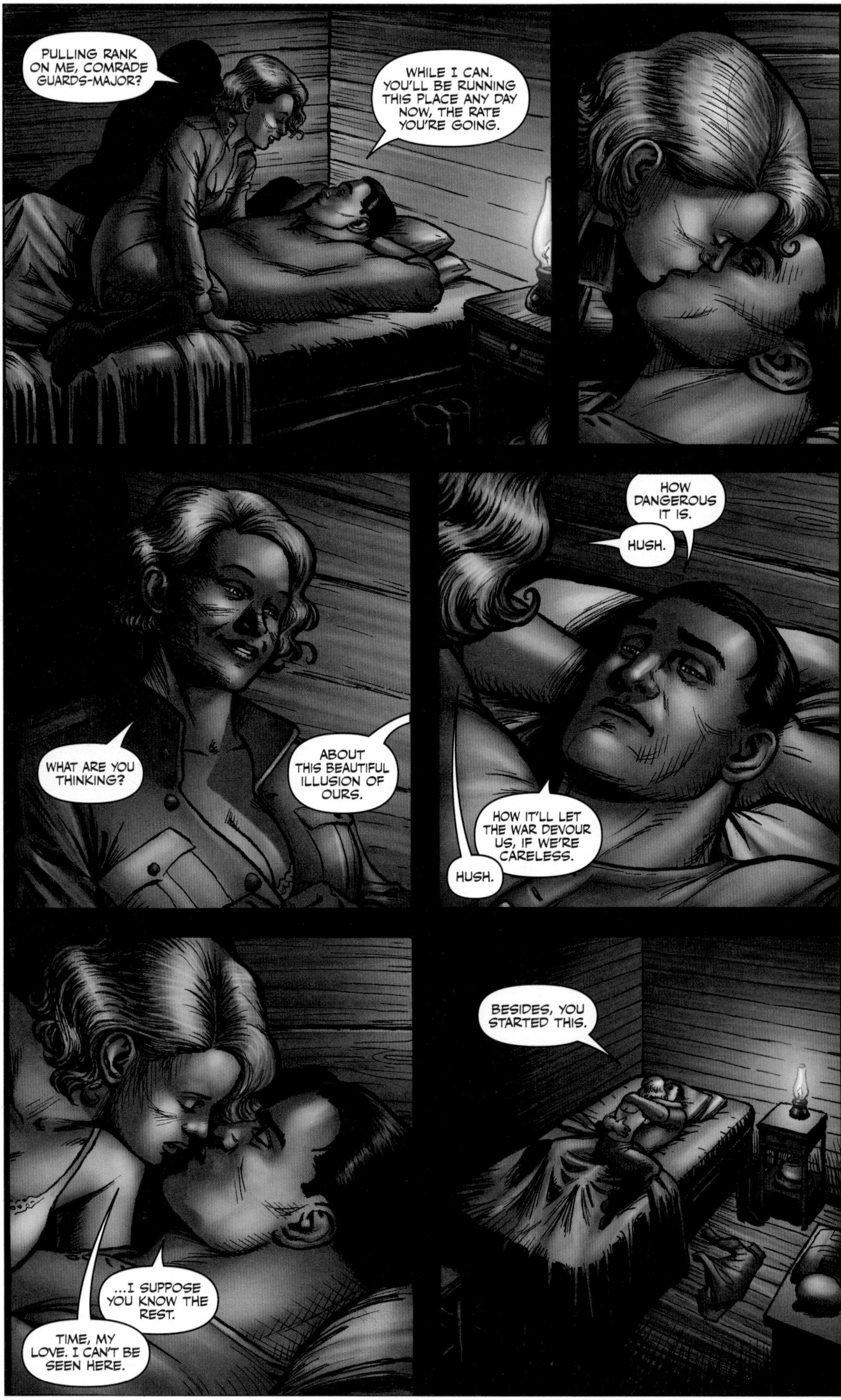
PULLING RANK ON ME, COMRADE GUARDS-MAJOR?
WHILE I CAN. YOU'LL BE RUNNING THIS PLACE ANY DAY NOW, THE RATE YOU'RE GOING.
WHAT ARE YOU THINKING?
ABOUT THIS BEAUTIFUL ILLUSION OF OURS.
HOW DANGEROUS IT IS.
HUSH.
HOW IT'LL LET THE WAR DEVOUR US, IF WE'RE CARELESS.
HUSH.
...I SUPPOSE YOU KNOW THE REST.
TIME, MY LOVE. I CAN'T BE SEEN HERE.
BESIDES, YOU STARTED THIS.

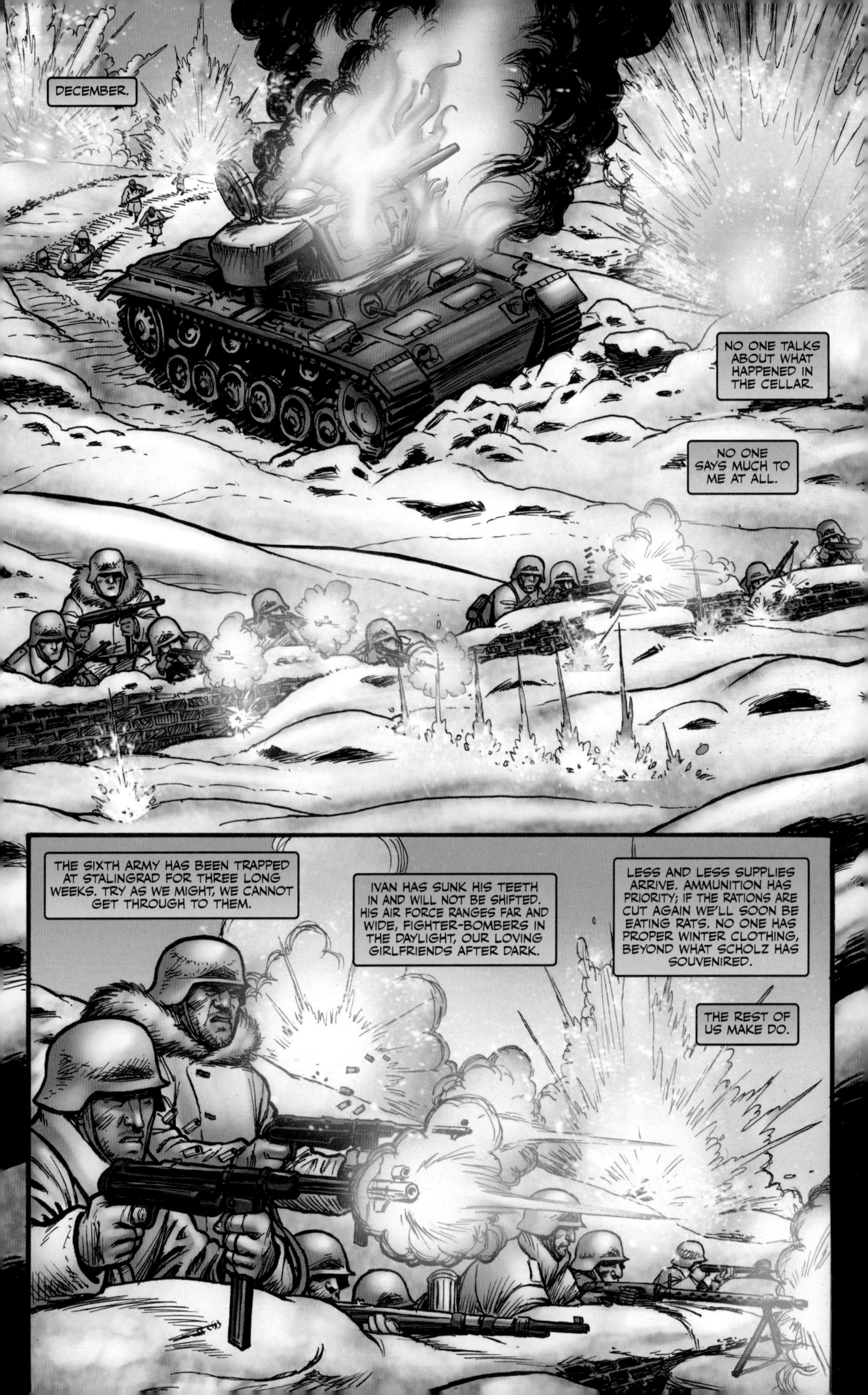
DECEMBER.
NO ONE TALKS ABOUT WHAT HAPPENED IN THE CELLAR.
NO ONE SAYS MUCH TO ME AT ALL.
THE SIXTH ARMY HAS BEEN TRAPPED AT STALINGRAD FOR THREE LONG WEEKS. TRY AS WE MIGHT, WE CANNOT GET THROUGH TO THEM.
IVAN HAS SUNK HIS TEETH IN AND WILL NOT BE SHIFTED. HIS AIR FORCE RANGES FAR AND WIDE, FIGHTER-BOMBERS IN THE DAYLIGHT, OUR LOVING GIRLFRIENDS AFTER DARK.
LESS AND LESS SUPPLIES ARRIVE. AMMUNITION HAS PRIORITY; IF THE RATIONS ARE CUT AGAIN WE'LL SOON BE EATING RATS. NO ONE HAS PROPER WINTER CLOTHING, BEYOND WHAT SCHOLZ HAS SOUVENIRED.
THE REST OF US MAKE DO.

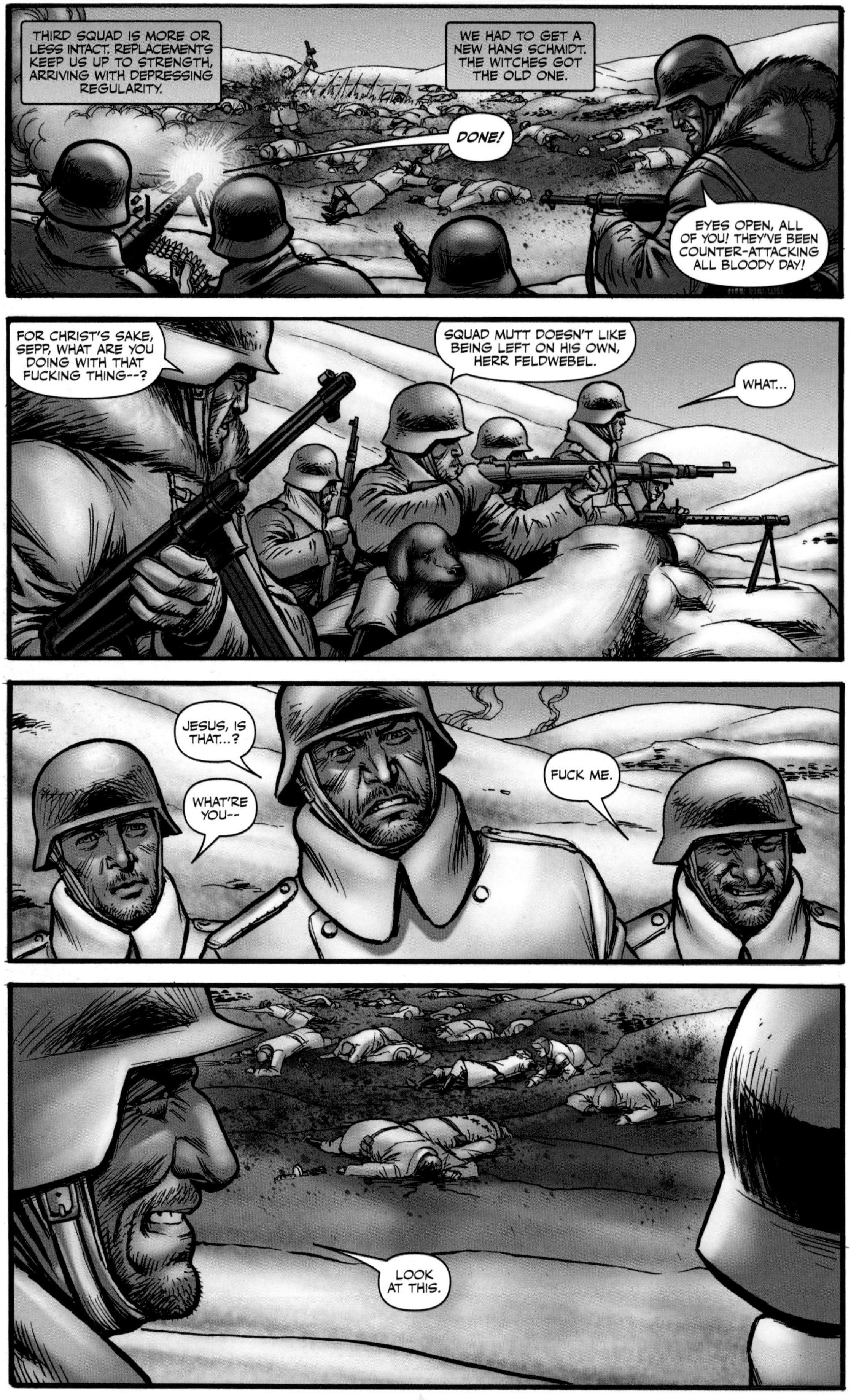
THIRD SQUAD IS MORE OR LESS INTACT. REPLACEMENTS KEEP US UP TO STRENGTH, ARRIVING WITH DEPRESSING REGULARITY.
WE HAD TO GET A NEW HANS SCHMIDT. THE WITCHES GOT THE OLD ONE.
DONE!
EYES OPEN, ALL OF YOU! THEY'VE BEEN COUNTER-ATTACKING ALL BLOODY DAY!
FOR CHRIST'S SAKE, SEPP, WHAT ARE YOU DOING WITH THAT FUCKING THING--?
SQUAD MUTT DOESN'T LIKE BEING LEFT ON HIS OWN, HERR FELDWEBEL.
WHAT...
JESUS, IS THAT...?
WHAT'RE YOU--
FUCK ME.
LOOK AT THIS.

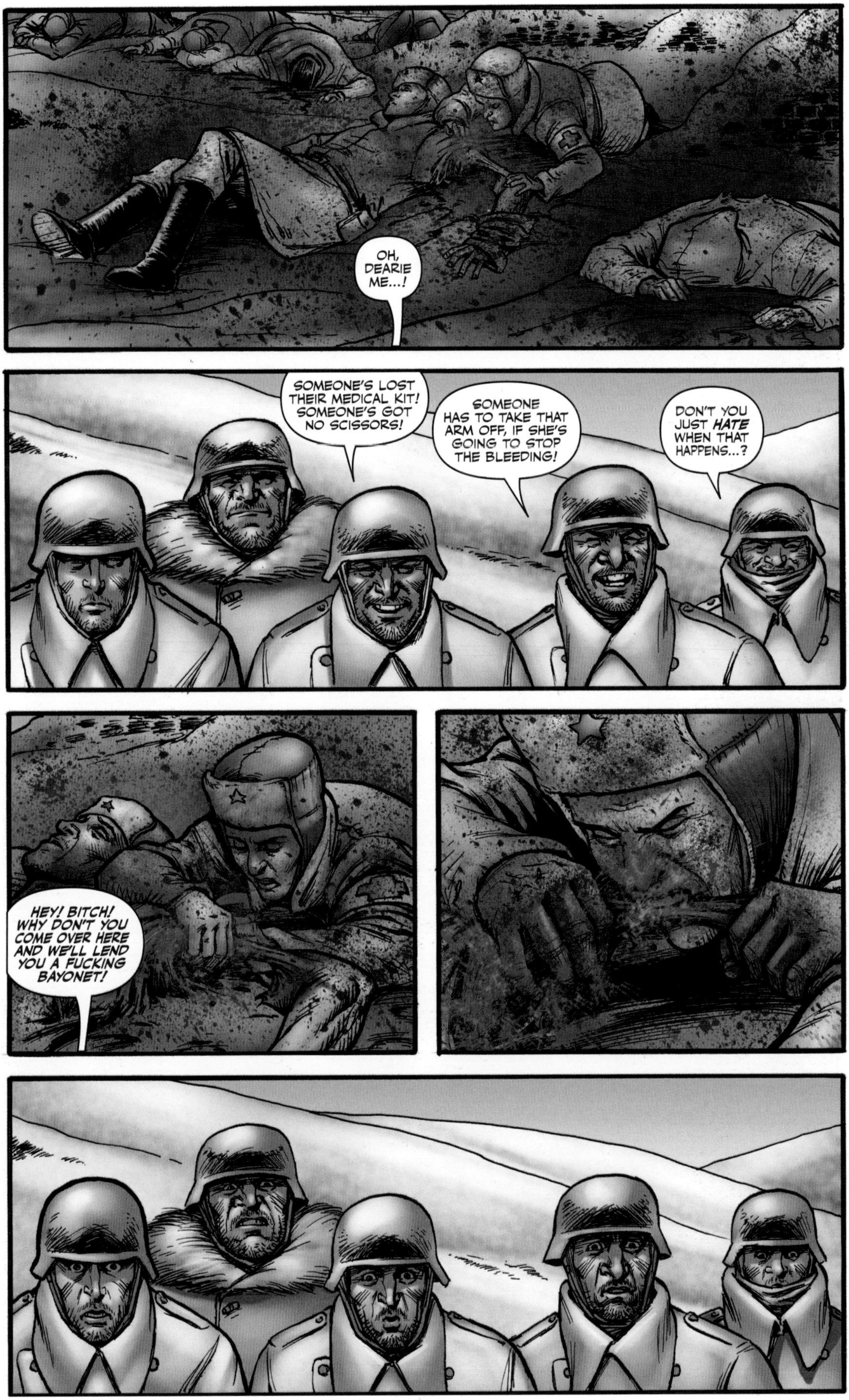
OH, DEARIE ME...!
SOMEONE'S LOST THEIR MEDICAL KIT! SOMEONE'S GOT NO SCISSORS!
SOMEONE HAS TO TAKE THAT ARM OFF, IF SHE'S GOING TO STOP THE BLEEDING!
DON'T YOU JUST HATE WHEN THAT HAPPENS...?
HEY! BITCH! WHY DON'T YOU COME OVER HERE AND WE'LL LEND YOU A FUCKING BAYONET!

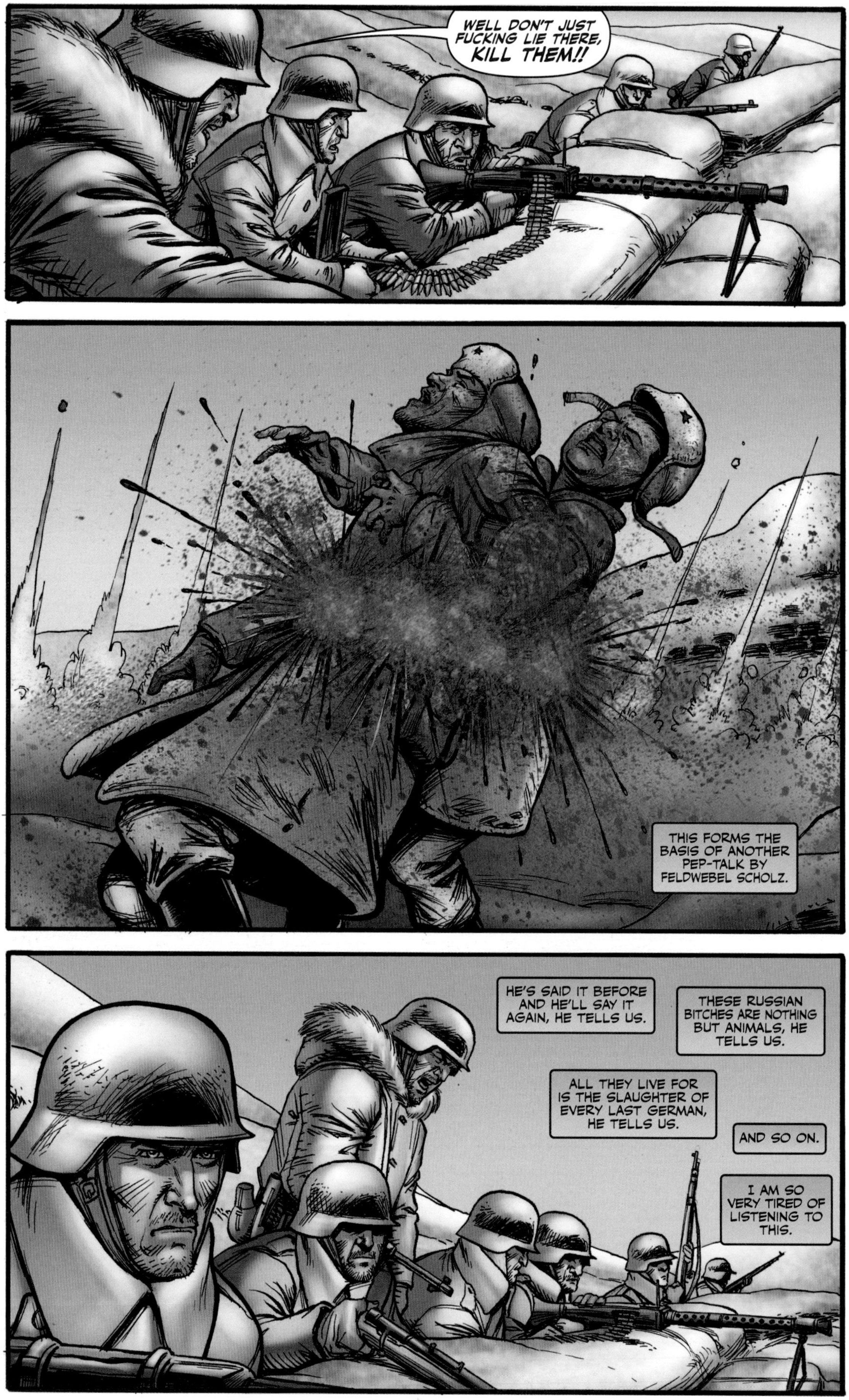
WELL DON'T JUST FUCKING LIE THERE, KILL THEM!!
THIS FORMS THE BASIS OF ANOTHER PEP-TALK BY FELDWEBEL SCHOLZ.
HE'S SAID IT BEFORE AND HE'LL SAY IT AGAIN, HE TELLS US.
THESE RUSSIAN BITCHES ARE NOTHING BUT ANIMALS, HE TELLS US.
ALL THEY LIVE FOR IS THE SLAUGHTER OF EVERY LAST GERMAN, HE TELLS US.
AND SO ON.
I AM SO VERY TIRED OF LISTENING TO THIS.

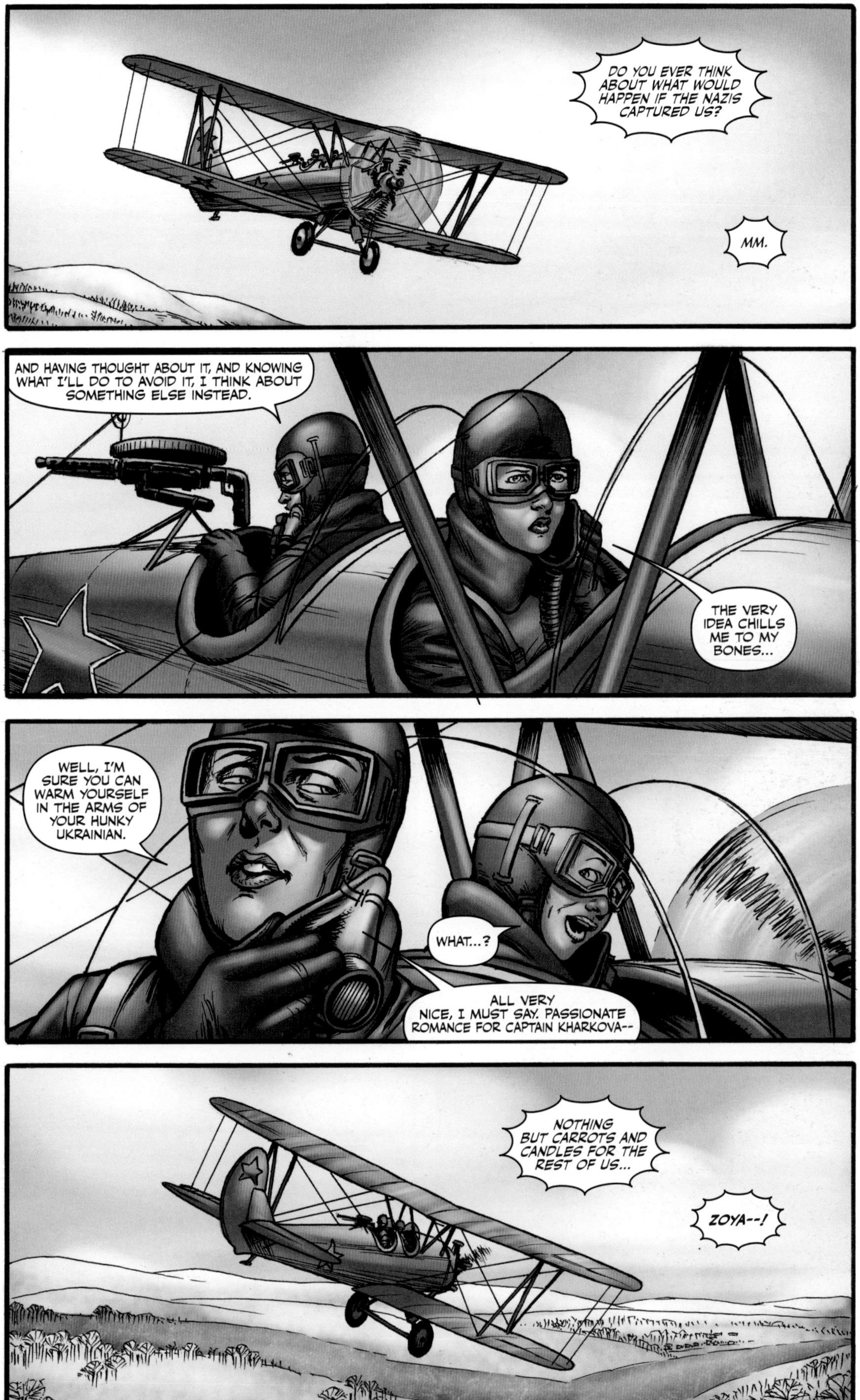
DO YOU EVER THINK ABOUT WHAT WOULD HAPPEN IF THE NAZIS CAPTURED US?
MM.
AND HAVING THOUGHT ABOUT IT, AND KNOWING WHAT I'LL DO TO AVOID IT, I THINK ABOUT SOMETHING ELSE INSTEAD.
THE VERY IDEA CHILLS ME TO MY BONES...
WELL, I'M SURE YOU CAN WARM YOURSELF IN THE ARMS OF YOUR HUNKY UKRAINIAN.
WHAT...?
ALL VERY NICE, I MUST SAY. PASSIONATE ROMANCE FOR CAPTAIN KHARKOVA--
NOTHING BUT CARROTS AND CANDLES FOR THE REST OF US...
ZOYA--!

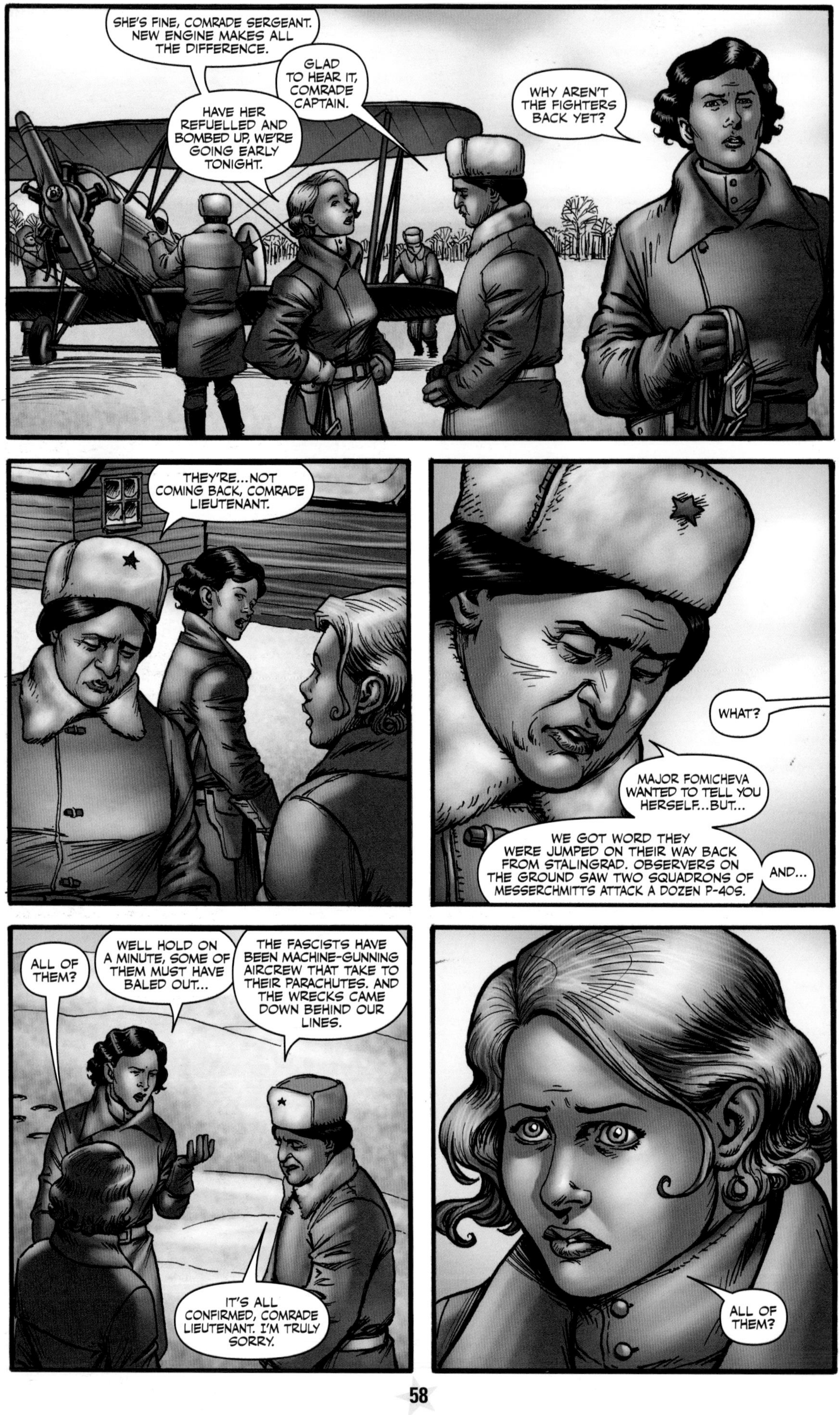
SHE'S FINE, COMRADE SERGEANT. NEW ENGINE MAKES ALL THE DIFFERENCE.
HAVE HER REFUELLED AND BOMBED UP, WE'RE GOING EARLY TONIGHT.
GLAD TO HEAR IT, COMRADE CAPTAIN.
WHY AREN'T THE FIGHTERS BACK YET?
THEY'RE...NOT COMING BACK, COMRADE LIEUTENANT.
WHAT?
MAJOR FOMICHEVA WANTED TO TELL YOU HERSELF...BUT...
WE GOT WORD THEY WERE JUMPED ON THEIR WAY BACK FROM STALINGRAD. OBSERVERS ON THE GROUND SAW TWO SQUADRONS OF MESSERSCHMITTS ATTACK A DOZEN P-40S.
AND...
ALL OF THEM?
WELL HOLD ON A MINUTE, SOME OF THEM MUST HAVE BALED OUT...
THE FASCISTS HAVE BEEN MACHINE-GUNNING AIRCREW THAT TAKE TO THEIR PARACHUTES. AND THE WRECKS CAME DOWN BEHIND OUR LINES.
IT'S ALL CONFIRMED, COMRADE LIEUTENANT. I'M TRULY SORRY.
ALL OF THEM?

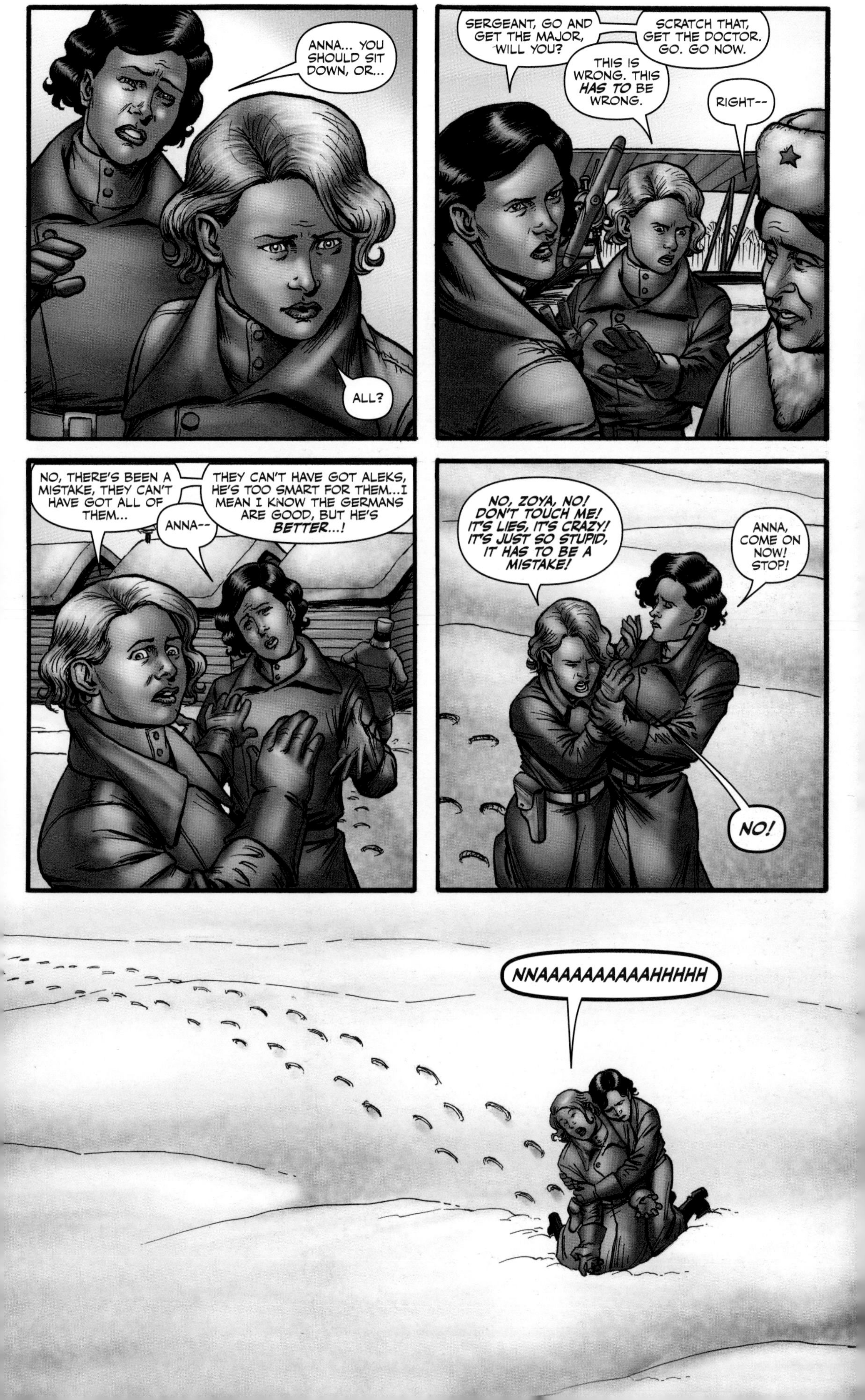
ANNA... YOU SHOULD SIT DOWN, OR...
ALL?
SERGEANT, GO AND GET THE MAJOR, WILL YOU?
SCRATCH THAT, GET THE DOCTOR. GO. GO NOW.
THIS IS WRONG. THIS *HAS TO* BE WRONG.
RIGHT--
NO, THERE'S BEEN A MISTAKE, THEY CAN'T HAVE GOT ALL OF THEM...
THEY CAN'T HAVE GOT ALEKS, HE'S TOO SMART FOR THEM...I MEAN I KNOW THE GERMANS ARE GOOD, BUT HE'S *BETTER*...!
ANNA--
NO, ZOYA, NO! DON'T TOUCH ME! IT'S LIES, IT'S CRAZY! IT'S JUST SO STUPID, IT HAS TO BE A MISTAKE!
ANNA, COME ON NOW! STOP!
NO!
NNAAAAAAAAAAHHHHH

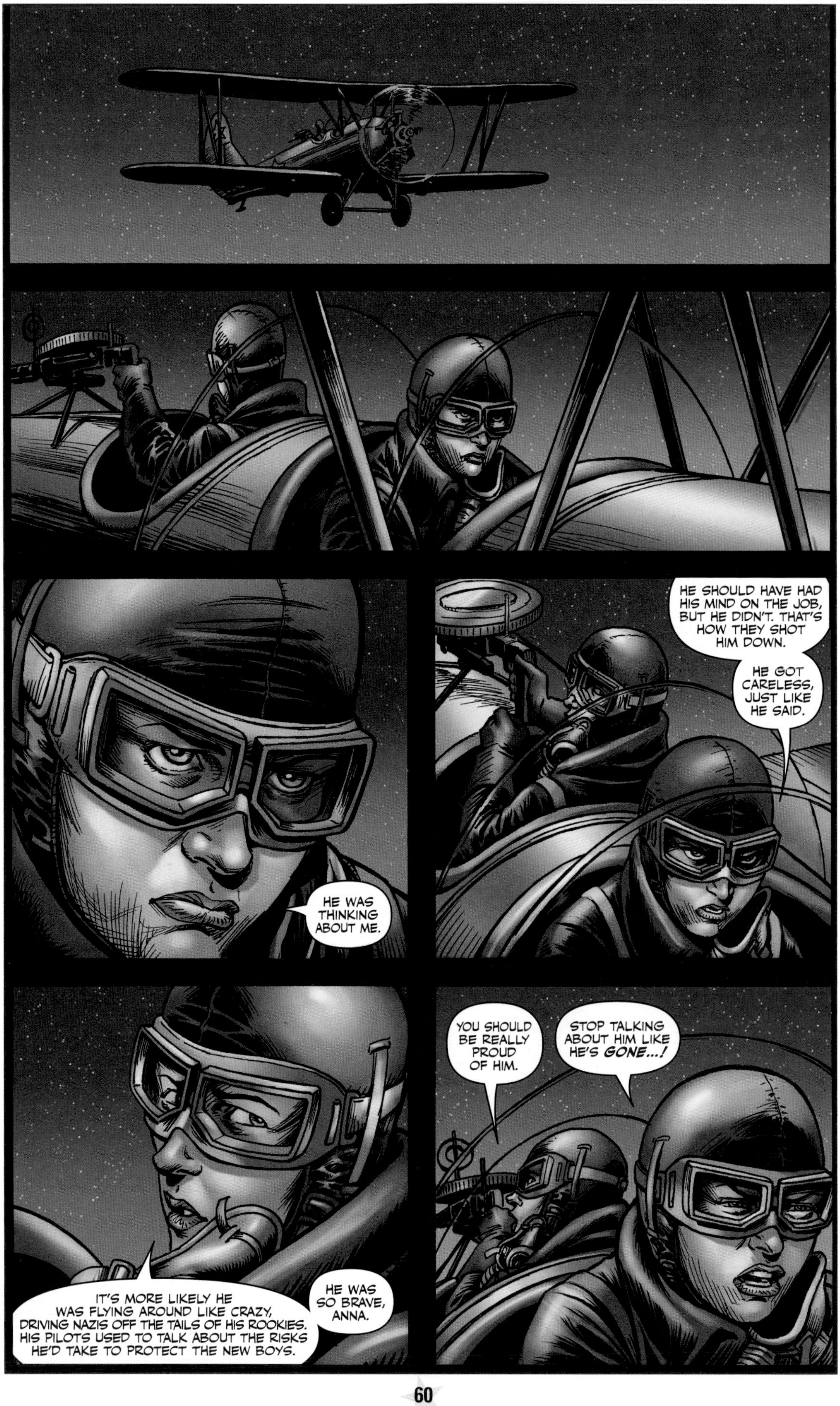
HE SHOULD HAVE HAD HIS MIND ON THE JOB, BUT HE DIDN'T. THAT'S HOW THEY SHOT HIM DOWN.
HE GOT CARELESS, JUST LIKE HE SAID.
HE WAS THINKING ABOUT ME.
IT'S MORE LIKELY HE WAS FLYING AROUND LIKE CRAZY, DRIVING NAZIS OFF THE TAILS OF HIS ROOKIES. HIS PILOTS USED TO TALK ABOUT THE RISKS HE'D TAKE TO PROTECT THE NEW BOYS.
HE WAS SO BRAVE, ANNA.
YOU SHOULD BE REALLY PROUD OF HIM.
STOP TALKING ABOUT HIM LIKE HE'S *GONE...!*

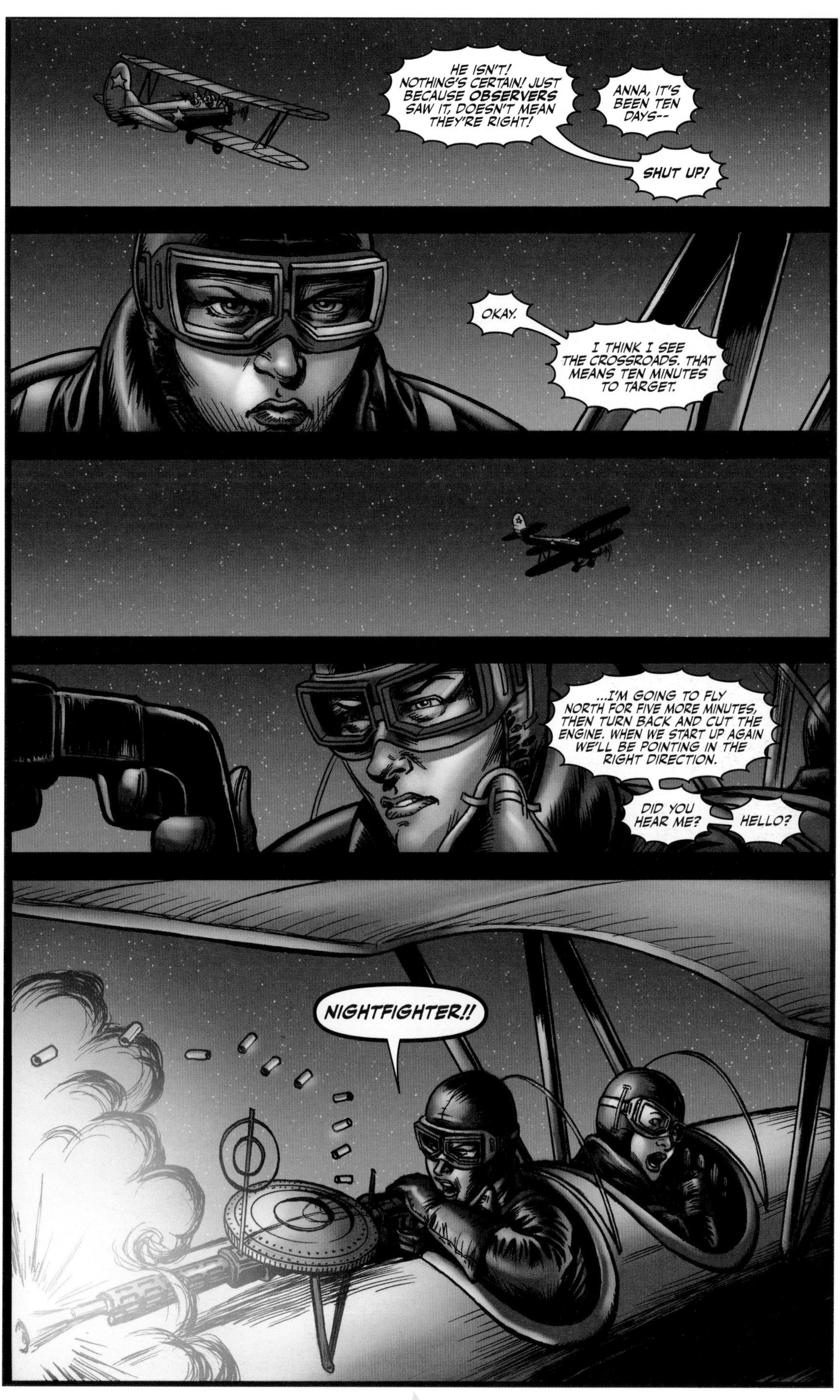
HE ISN'T! NOTHING'S CERTAIN! JUST BECAUSE OBSERVERS SAW IT, DOESN'T MEAN THEY'RE RIGHT!
ANNA, IT'S BEEN TEN DAYS--
SHUT UP!
OKAY.
I THINK I SEE THE CROSSROADS. THAT MEANS TEN MINUTES TO TARGET.
...I'M GOING TO FLY NORTH FOR FIVE MORE MINUTES, THEN TURN BACK AND CUT THE ENGINE. WHEN WE START UP AGAIN WE'LL BE POINTING IN THE RIGHT DIRECTION.
DID YOU HEAR ME?
HELLO?
NIGHTFIGHTER!!

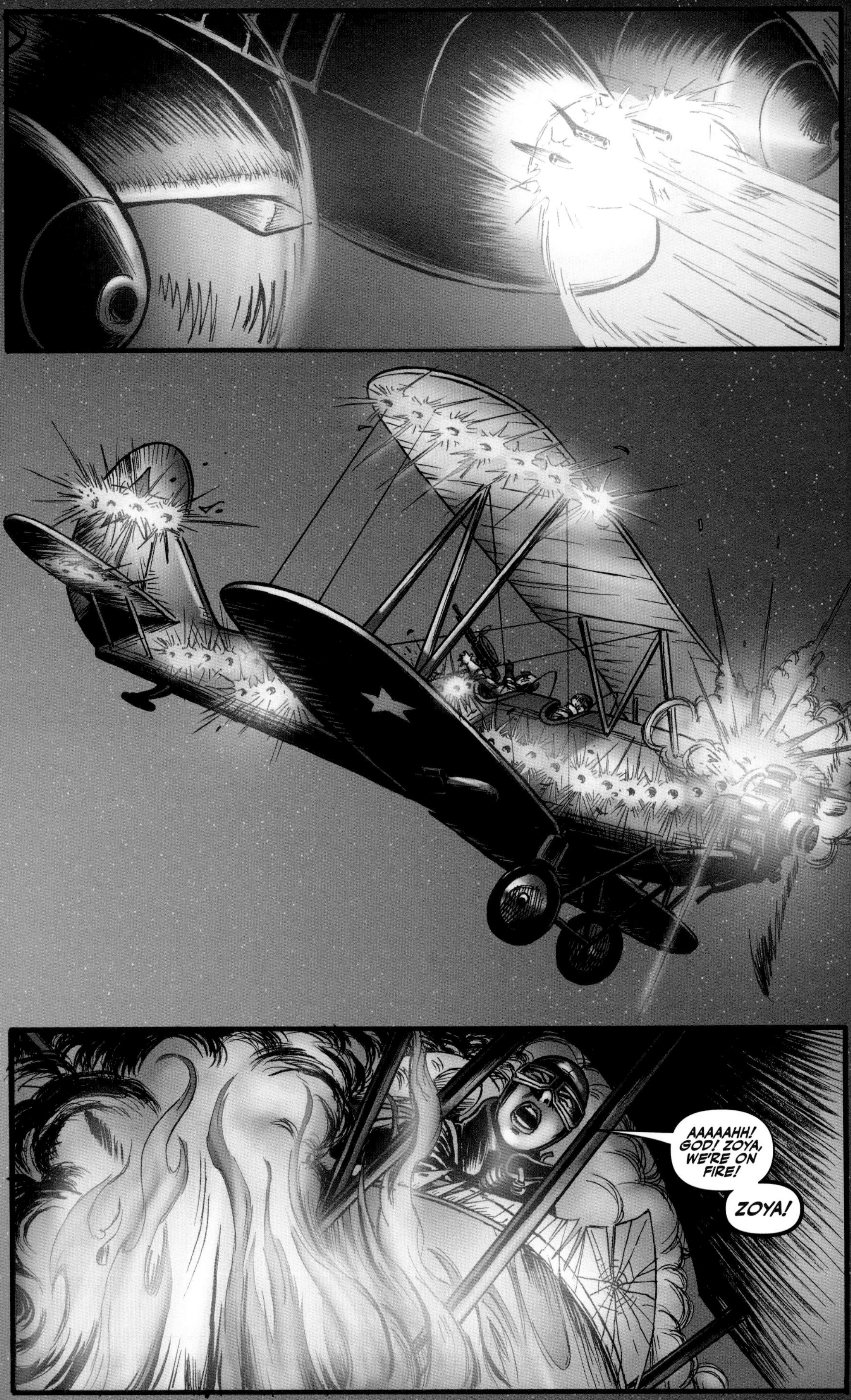
AAAAAHH! GOD! ZOYA, WE'RE ON FIRE!
ZOYA!

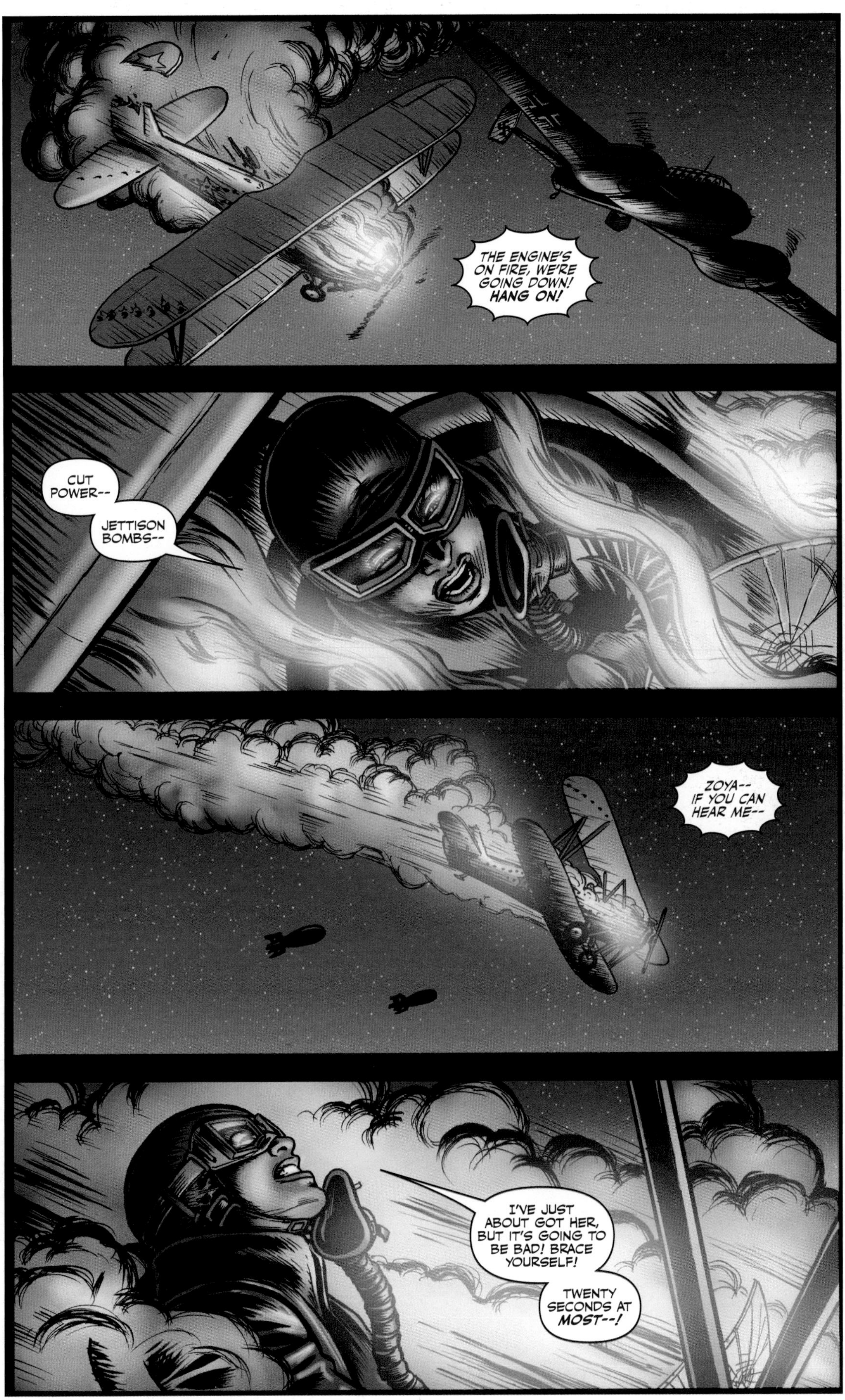
THE ENGINE'S ON FIRE, WE'RE GOING DOWN! HANG ON!
CUT POWER--
JETTISON BOMBS--
ZOYA-- IF YOU CAN HEAR ME--
I'VE JUST ABOUT GOT HER, BUT IT'S GOING TO BE BAD! BRACE YOURSELF!
TWENTY SECONDS AT MOST--!

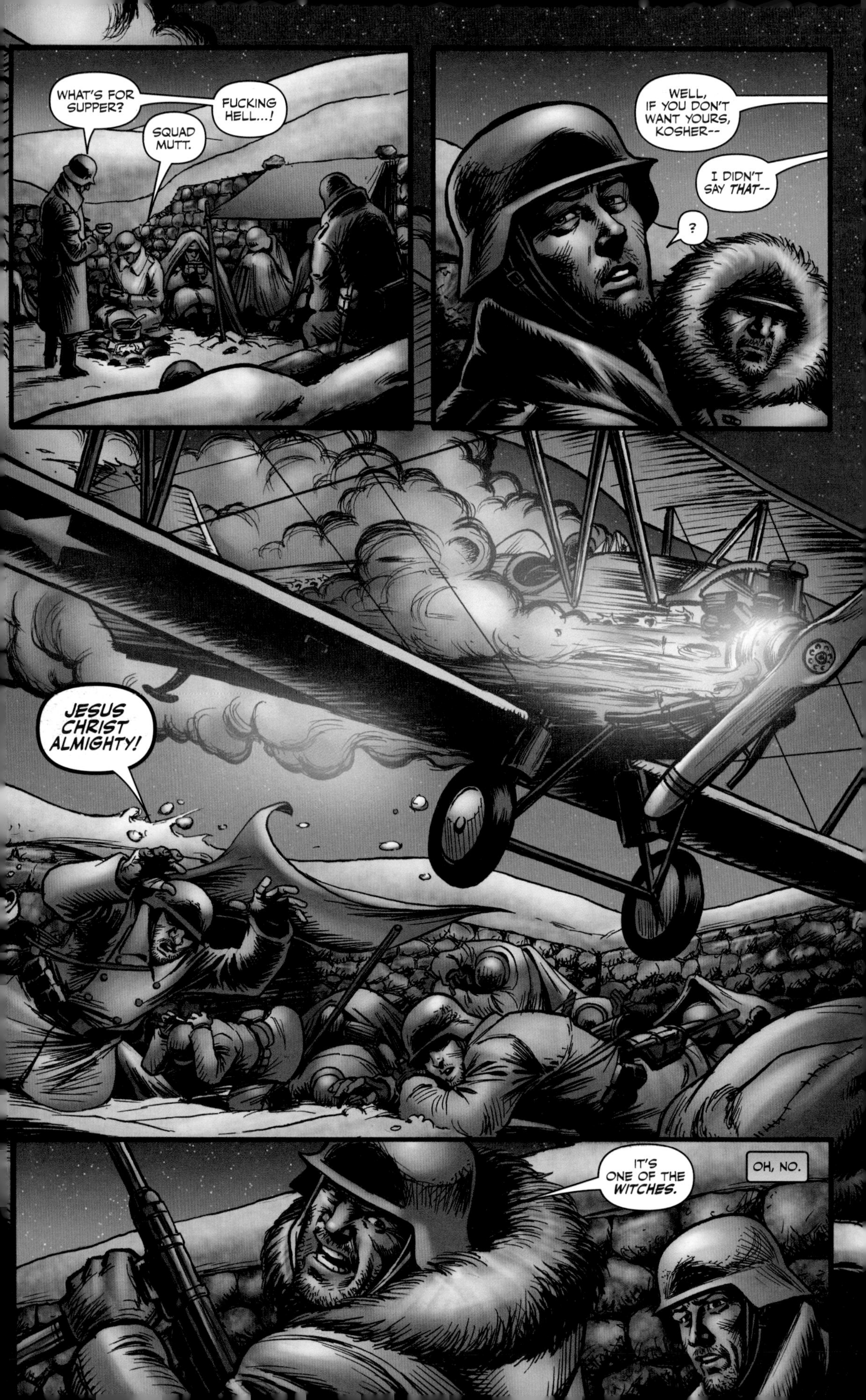
WHAT'S FOR SUPPER?
FUCKING HELL...!
SQUAD MUTT.
WELL, IF YOU DON'T WANT YOURS, KOSHER--
I DIDN'T SAY THAT--
?
JESUS CHRIST ALMIGHTY!
IT'S ONE OF THE WITCHES.
OH, NO.

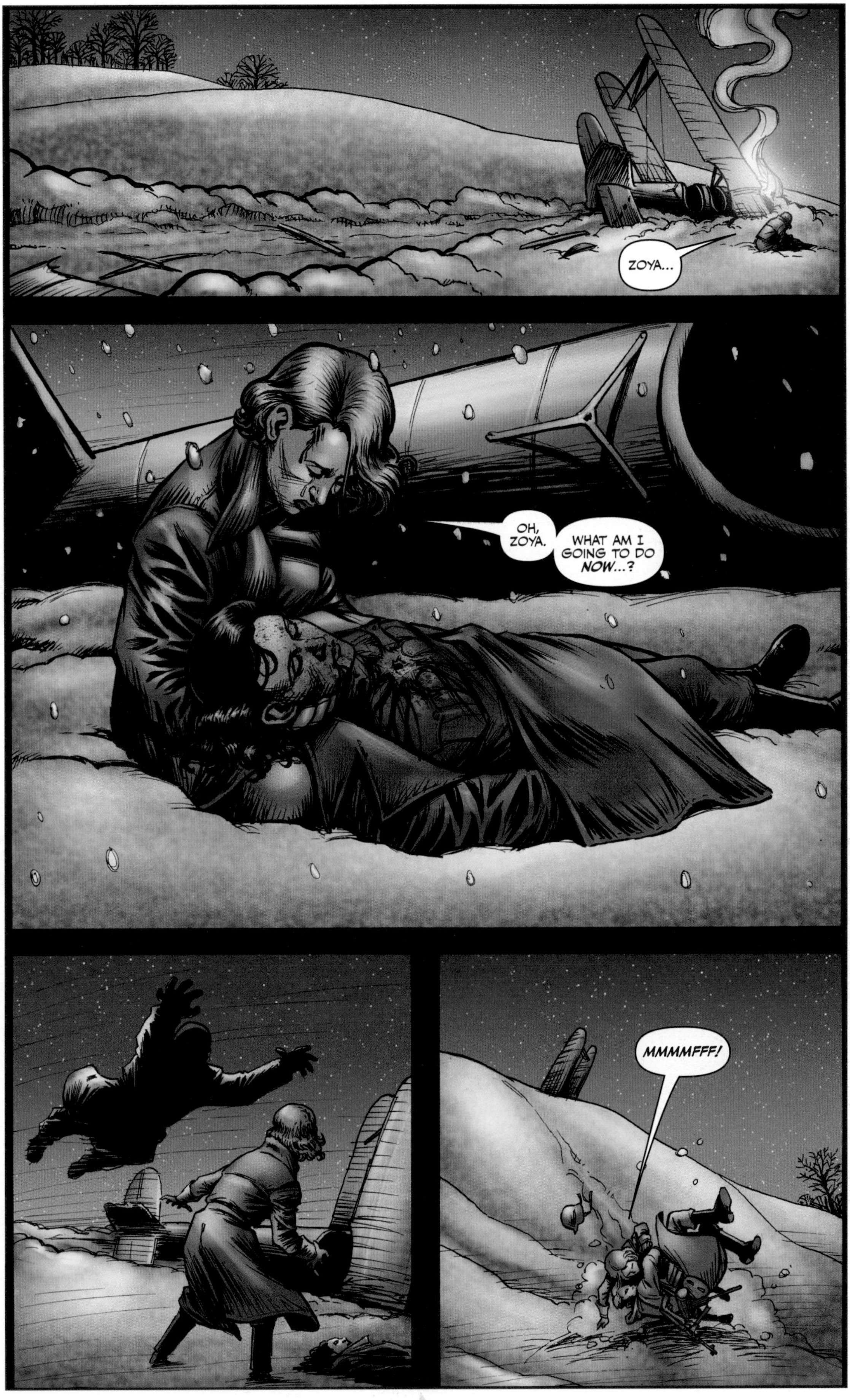
ZOYA...
OH, ZOYA.
WHAT AM I GOING TO DO NOW...?
MMMMFFF!

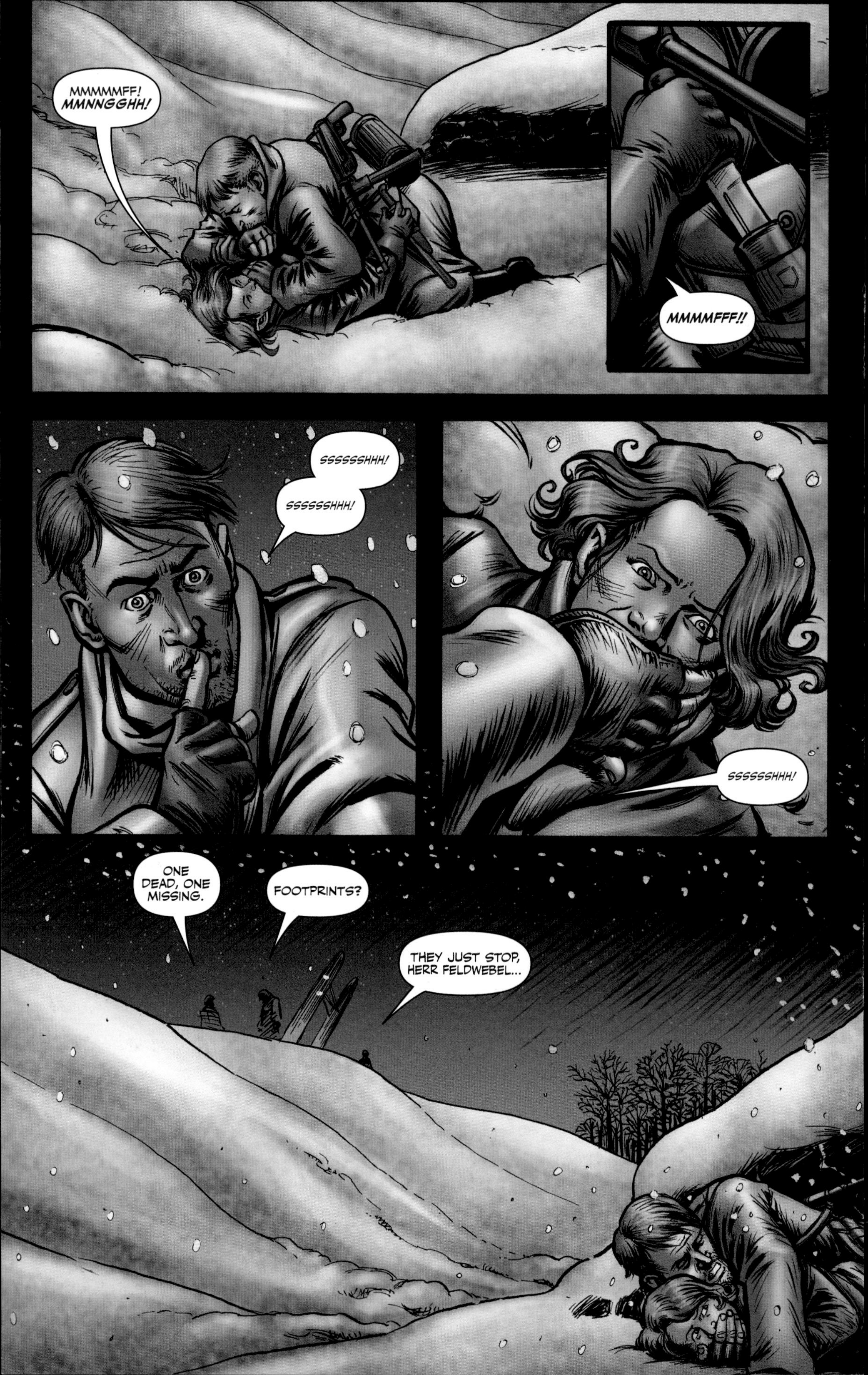
MMMMMFF! MMNNGGHH!
MMMMFFF!!
SSSSSSHHH!
SSSSSSHHH!
SSSSSSHHH!
ONE DEAD, ONE MISSING.
FOOTPRINTS?
THEY JUST STOP, HERR FELDWEBEL...

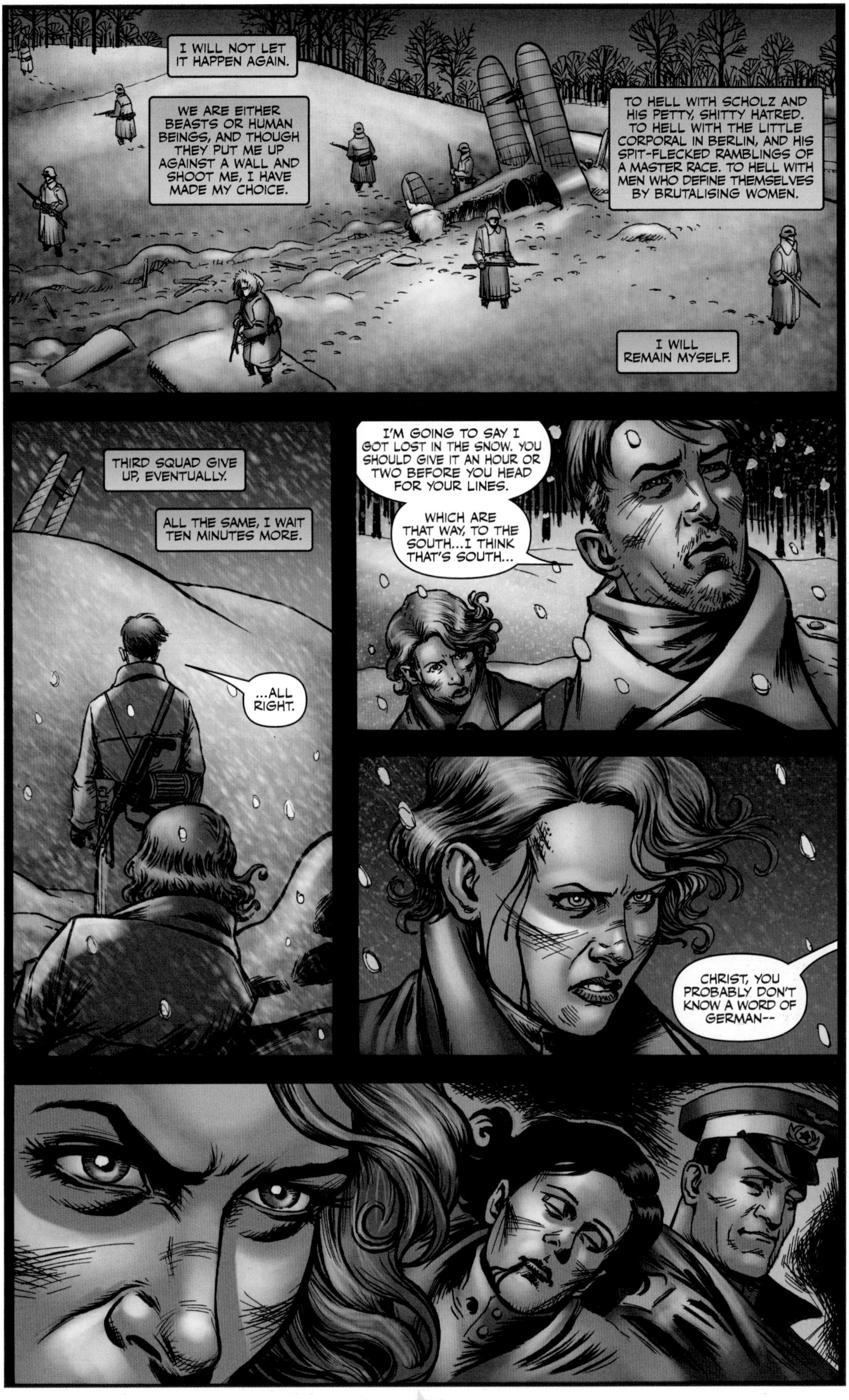
I WILL NOT LET IT HAPPEN AGAIN.
WE ARE EITHER BEASTS OR HUMAN BEINGS, AND THOUGH THEY PUT ME UP AGAINST A WALL AND SHOOT ME, I HAVE MADE MY CHOICE.
TO HELL WITH SCHOLZ AND HIS PETTY, SHITTY HATRED. TO HELL WITH THE LITTLE CORPORAL IN BERLIN, AND HIS SPIT-FLECKED RAMBLINGS OF A MASTER RACE. TO HELL WITH MEN WHO DEFINE THEMSELVES BY BRUTALISING WOMEN.
I WILL REMAIN MYSELF.
THIRD SQUAD GIVE UP, EVENTUALLY.
ALL THE SAME, I WAIT TEN MINUTES MORE.
...ALL RIGHT.
I'M GOING TO SAY I GOT LOST IN THE SNOW. YOU SHOULD GIVE IT AN HOUR OR TWO BEFORE YOU HEAD FOR YOUR LINES.
WHICH ARE THAT WAY, TO THE SOUTH...I THINK THAT'S SOUTH...
CHRIST, YOU PROBABLY DON'T KNOW A WORD OF GERMAN--

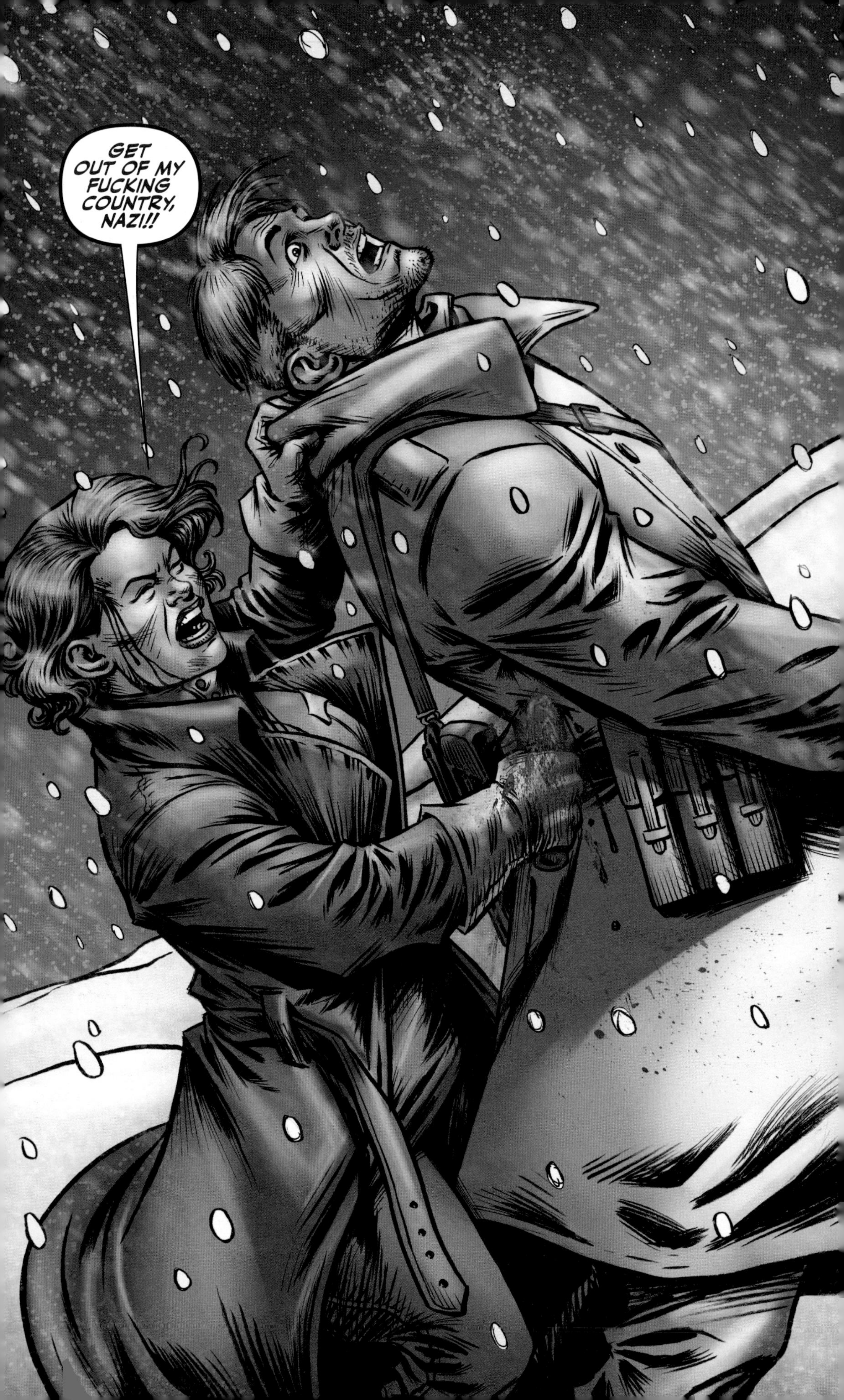
GET OUT OF MY FUCKING COUNTRY, NAZI!!

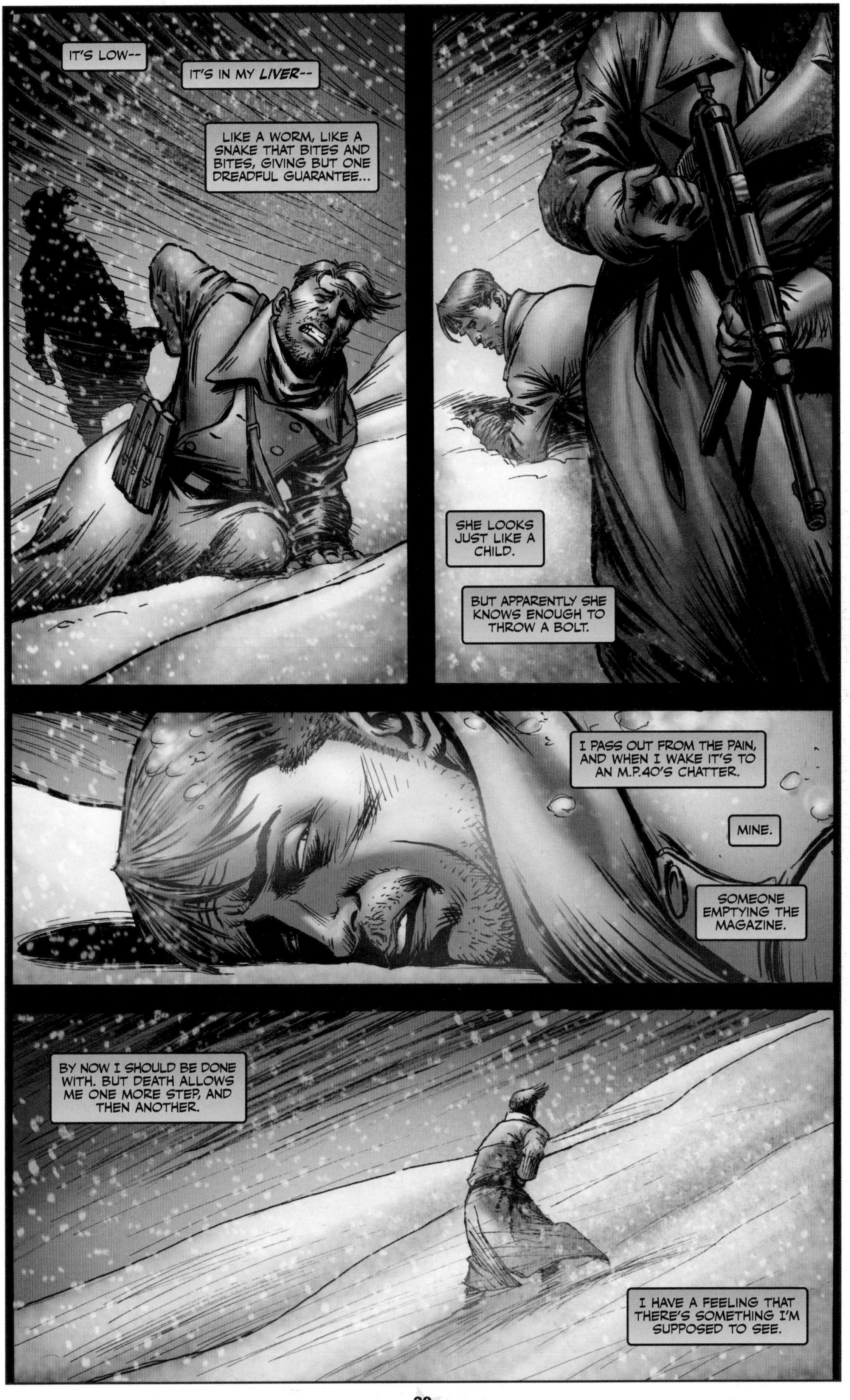
IT'S LOW--
IT'S IN MY LIVER--
LIKE A WORM, LIKE A SNAKE THAT BITES AND BITES, GIVING BUT ONE DREADFUL GUARANTEE...
SHE LOOKS JUST LIKE A CHILD.
BUT APPARENTLY SHE KNOWS ENOUGH TO THROW A BOLT.
I PASS OUT FROM THE PAIN, AND WHEN I WAKE IT'S TO AN M.P.40'S CHATTER.
MINE.
SOMEONE EMPTYING THE MAGAZINE.
BY NOW I SHOULD BE DONE WITH. BUT DEATH ALLOWS ME ONE MORE STEP, AND THEN ANOTHER.
I HAVE A FEELING THAT THERE'S SOMETHING I'M SUPPOSED TO SEE.

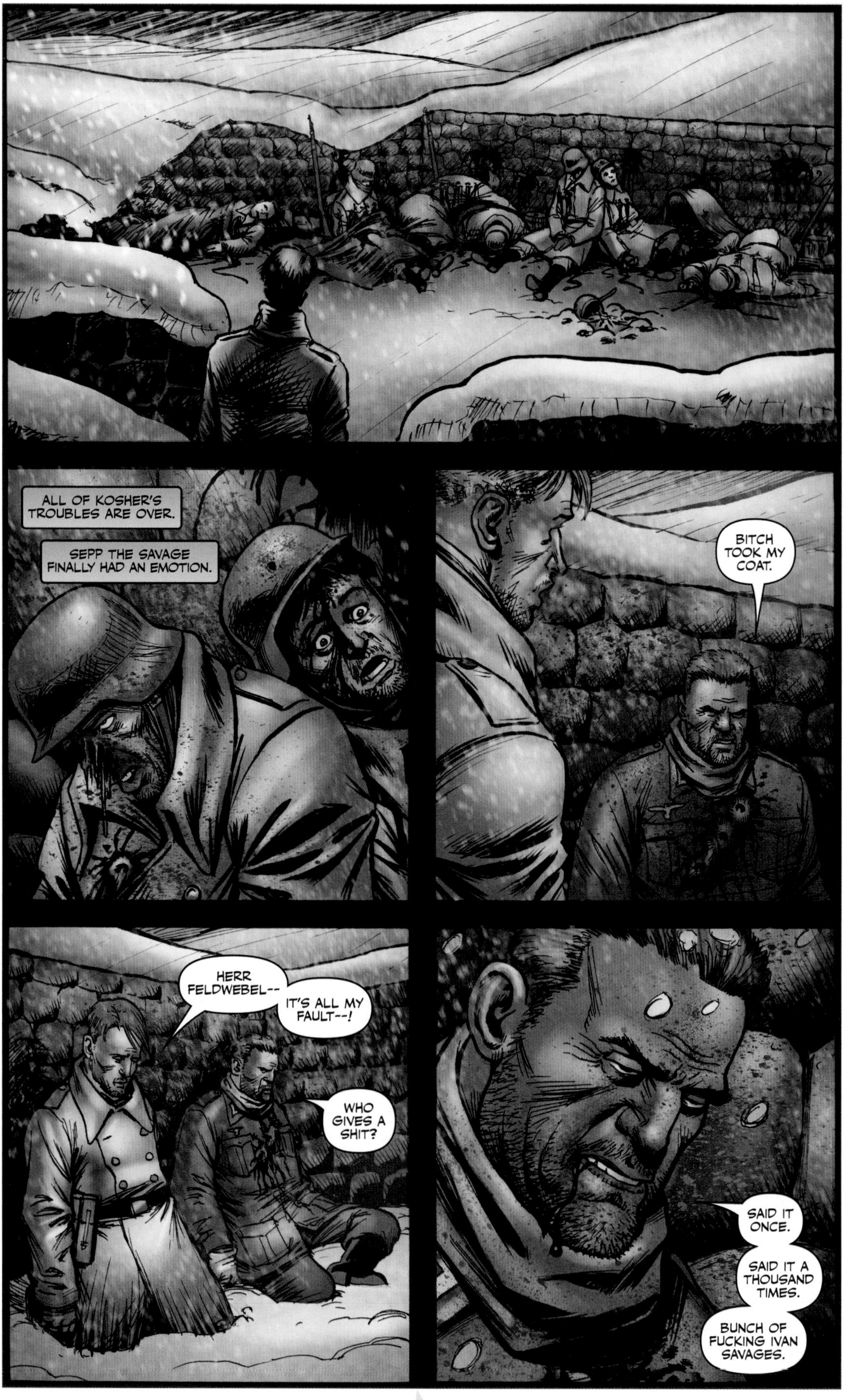
ALL OF KOSHER'S TROUBLES ARE OVER.
SEPP THE SAVAGE FINALLY HAD AN EMOTION.
BITCH TOOK MY COAT.
HERR FELDWEBEL--
IT'S ALL MY FAULT--!
WHO GIVES A SHIT?
SAID IT ONCE.
SAID IT A THOUSAND TIMES.
BUNCH OF FUCKING IVAN SAVAGES.

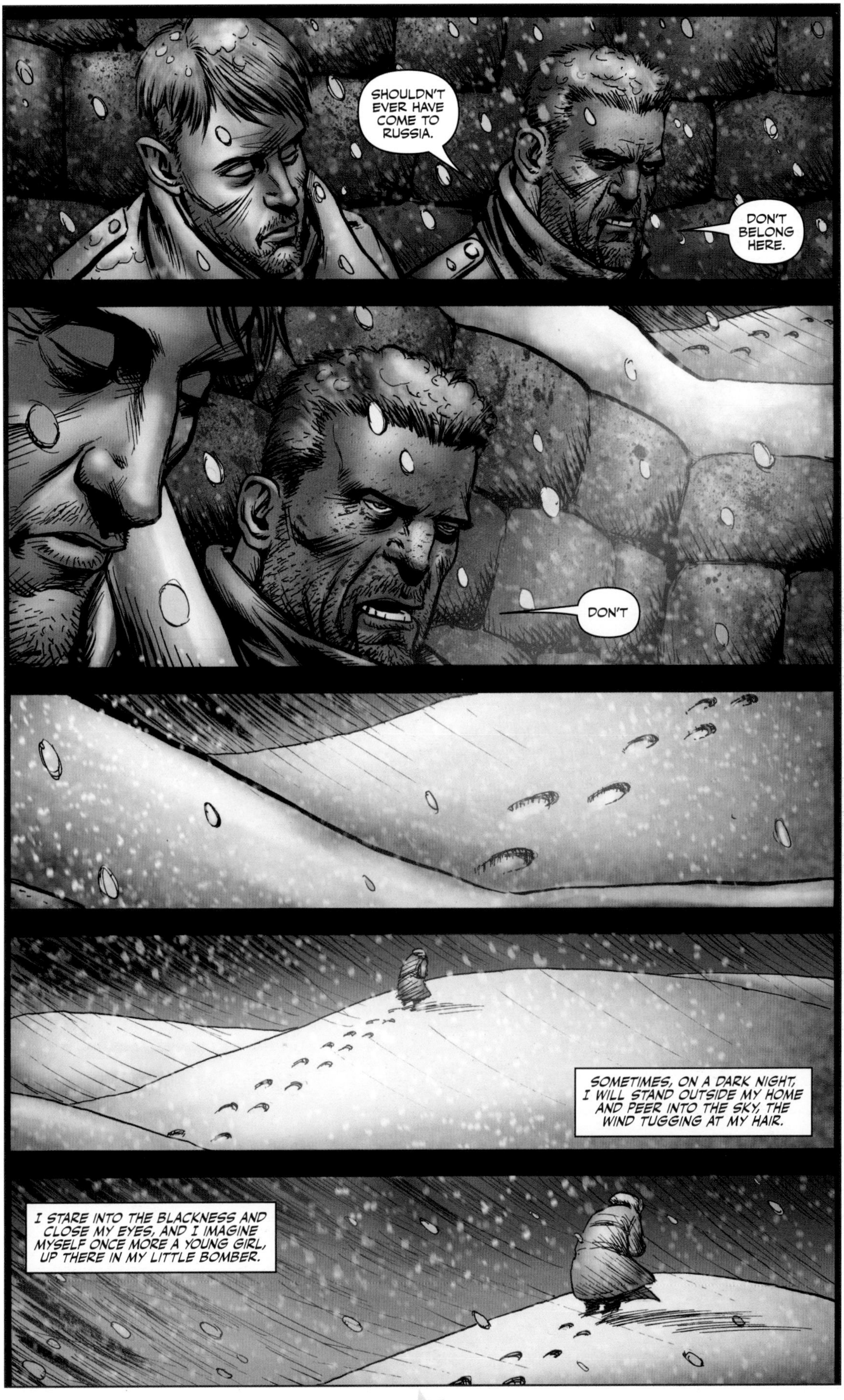
SHOULDN'T EVER HAVE COME TO RUSSIA.
DON'T BELONG HERE.
DON'T
SOMETIMES, ON A DARK NIGHT, I WILL STAND OUTSIDE MY HOME AND PEER INTO THE SKY, THE WIND TUGGING AT MY HAIR.
I STARE INTO THE BLACKNESS AND CLOSE MY EYES, AND I IMAGINE MYSELF ONCE MORE A YOUNG GIRL, UP THERE IN MY LITTLE BOMBER.

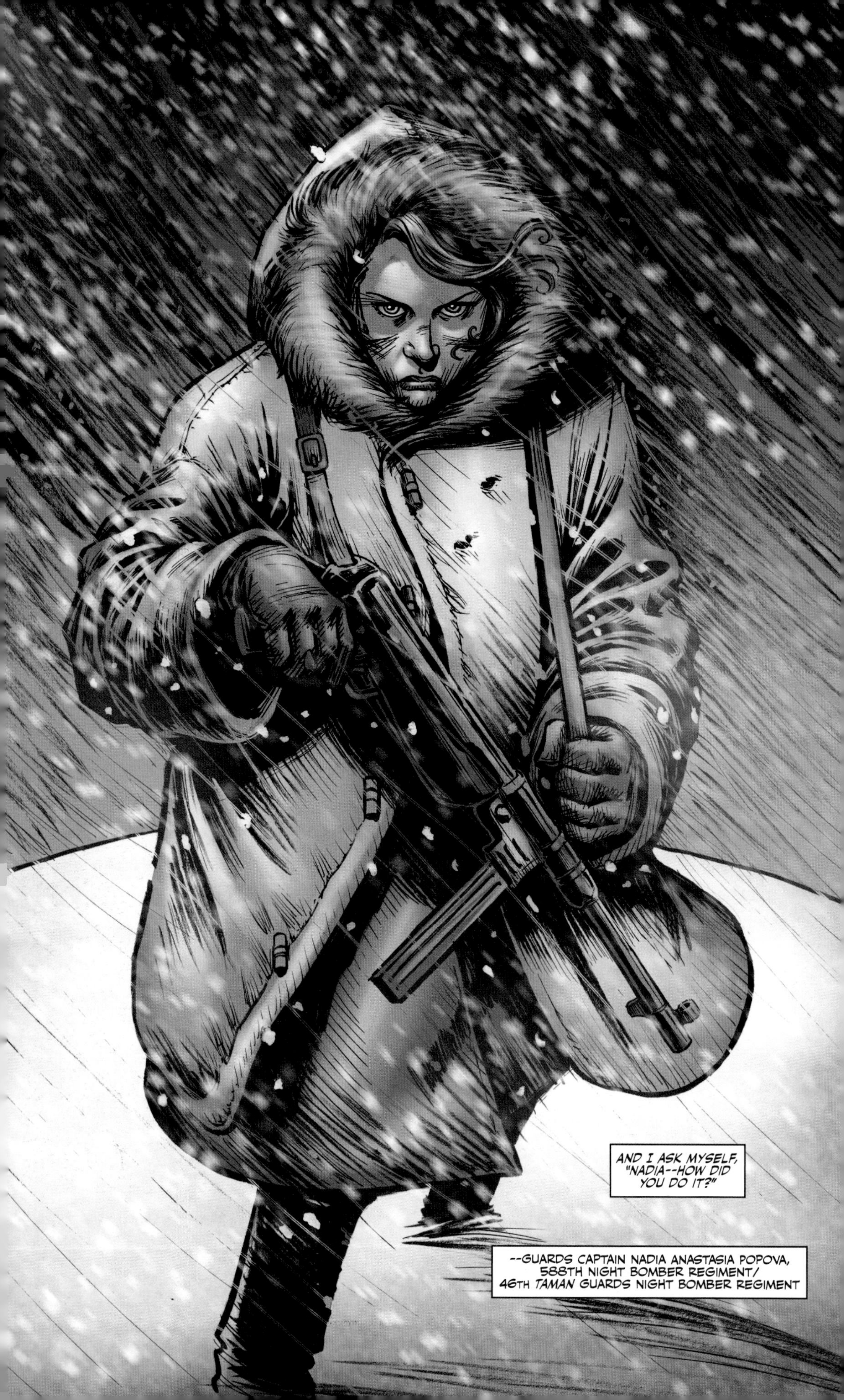
AND I ASK MYSELF, "NADIA--HOW DID YOU DO IT?"
--GUARDS CAPTAIN NADIA ANASTASIA POPOVA, 588TH NIGHT BOMBER REGIMENT/ 46TH *TAMAN* GUARDS NIGHT BOMBER REGIMENT

MOTHERLAND Chapter 1

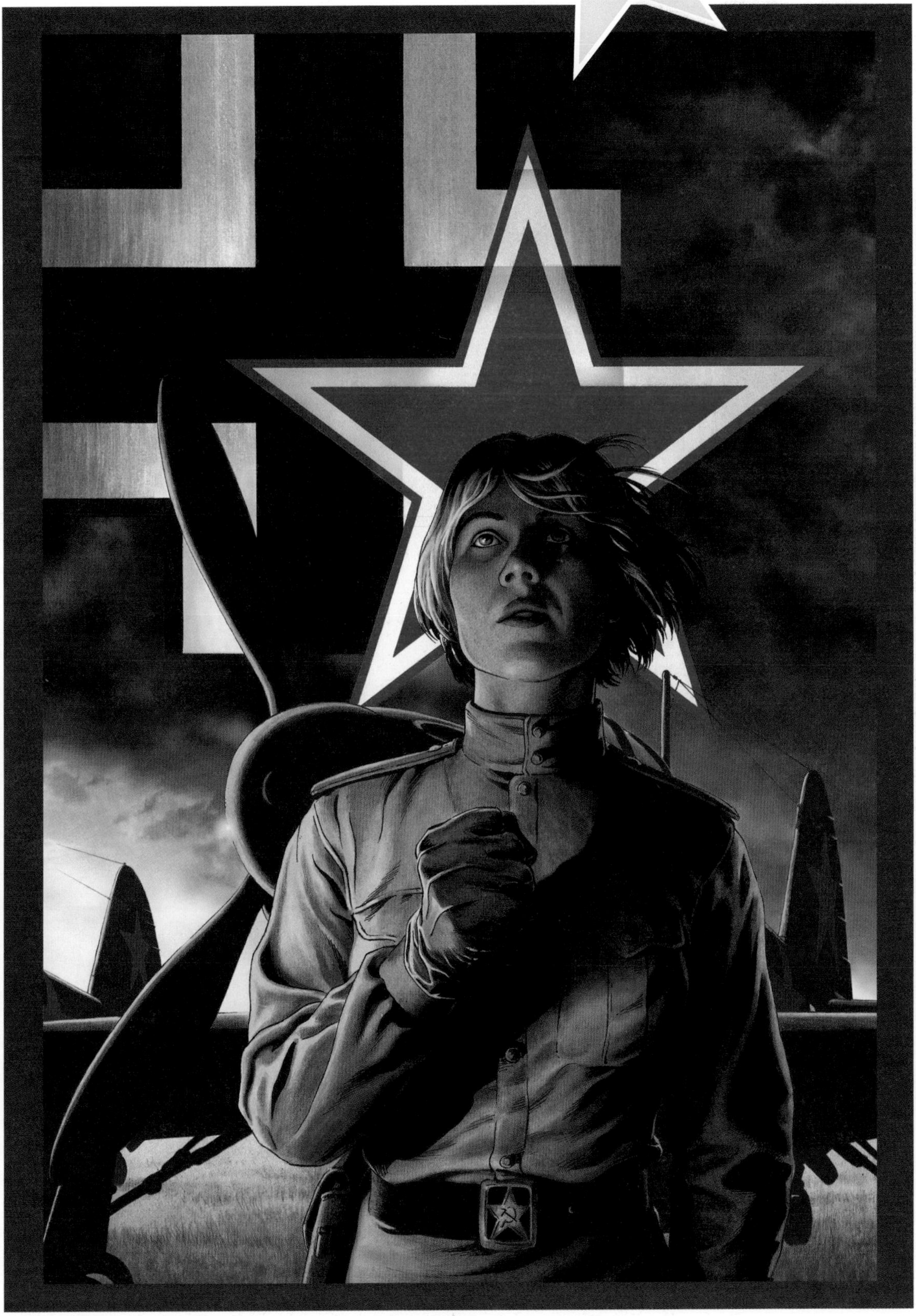

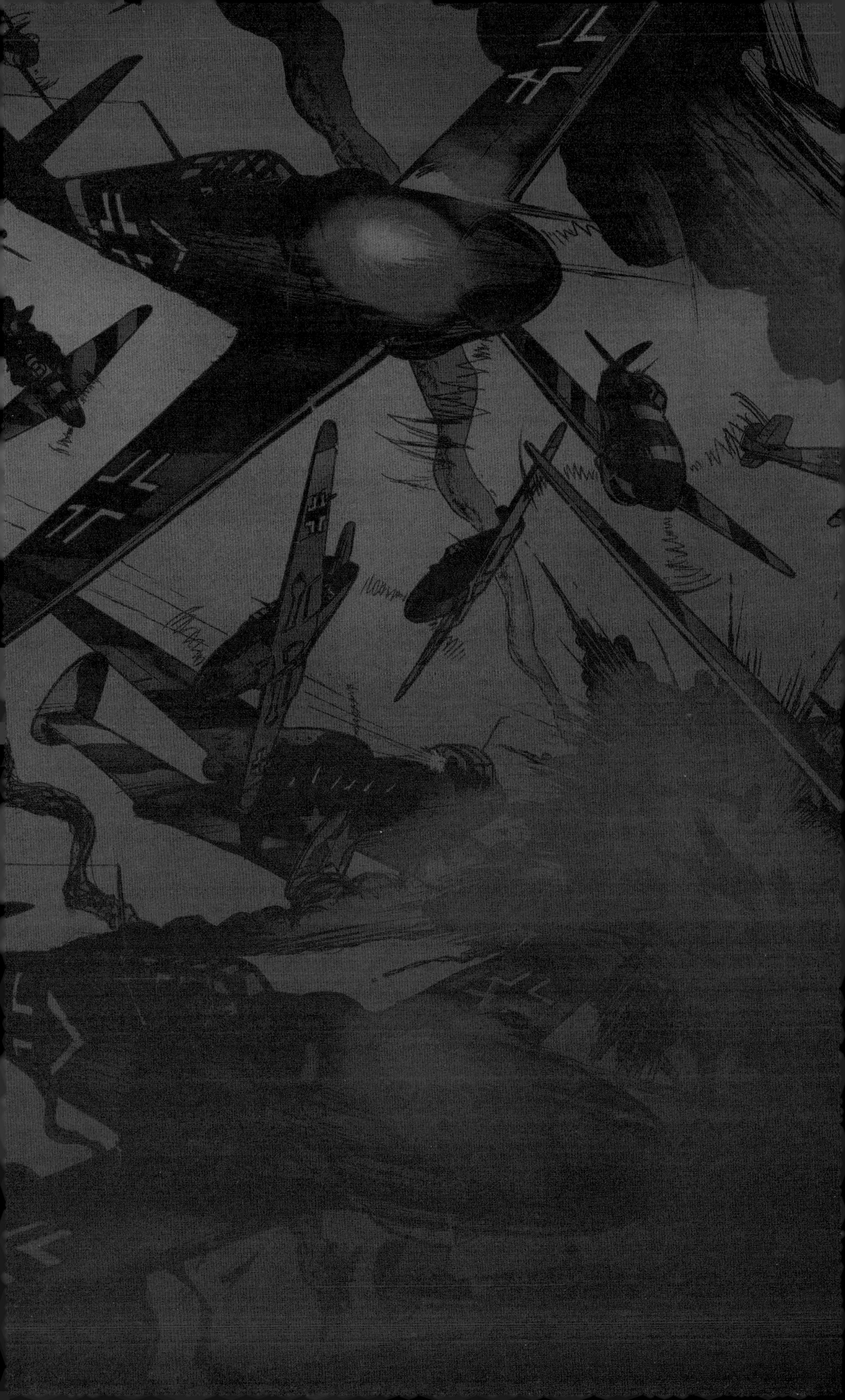

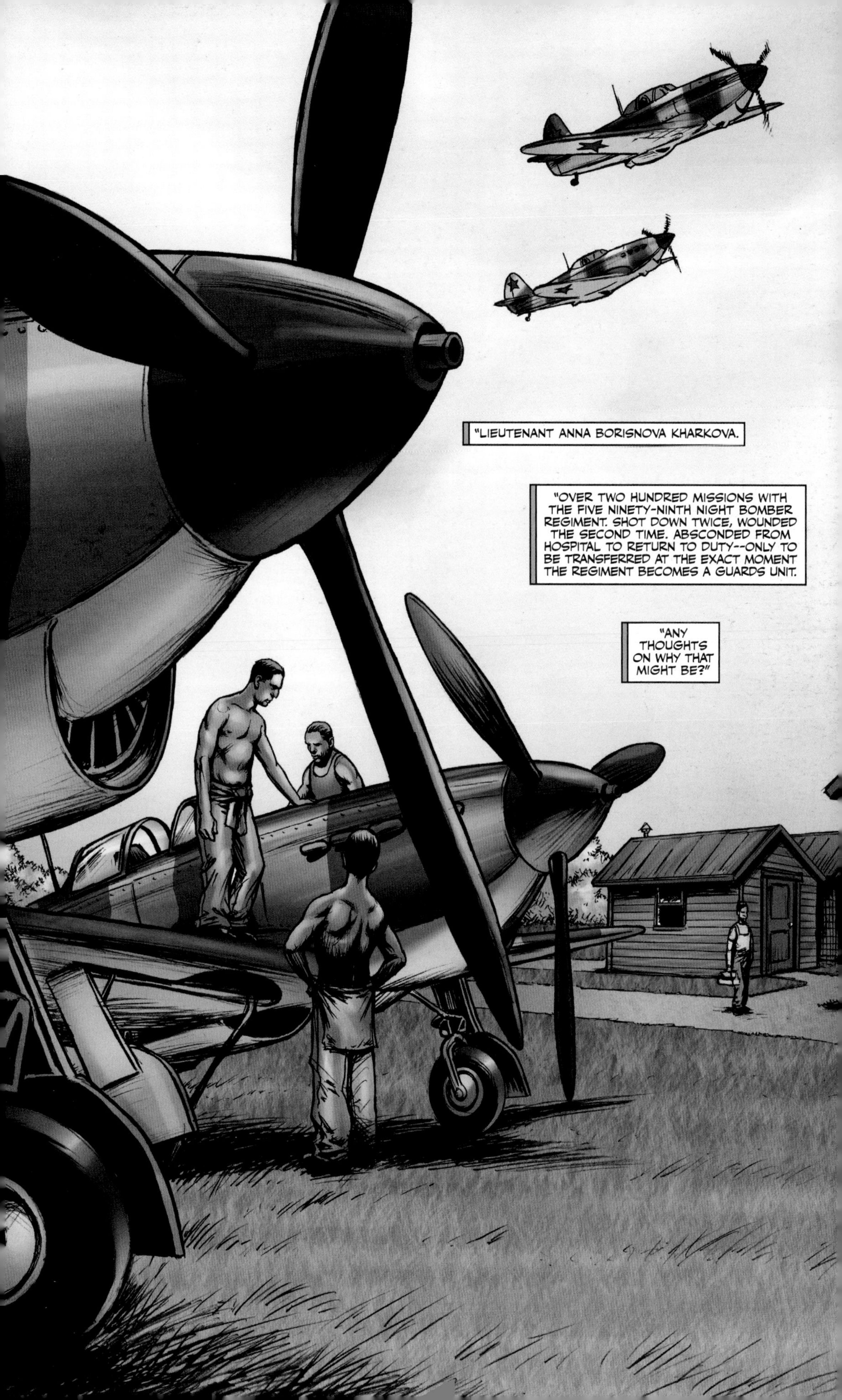
"LIEUTENANT ANNA BORISNOVA KHARKOVA.
"OVER TWO HUNDRED MISSIONS WITH THE FIVE NINETY-NINTH NIGHT BOMBER REGIMENT. SHOT DOWN TWICE, WOUNDED THE SECOND TIME. ABSCONDED FROM HOSPITAL TO RETURN TO DUTY--ONLY TO BE TRANSFERRED AT THE EXACT MOMENT THE REGIMENT BECOMES A GUARDS UNIT.
"ANY THOUGHTS ON WHY THAT MIGHT BE?"

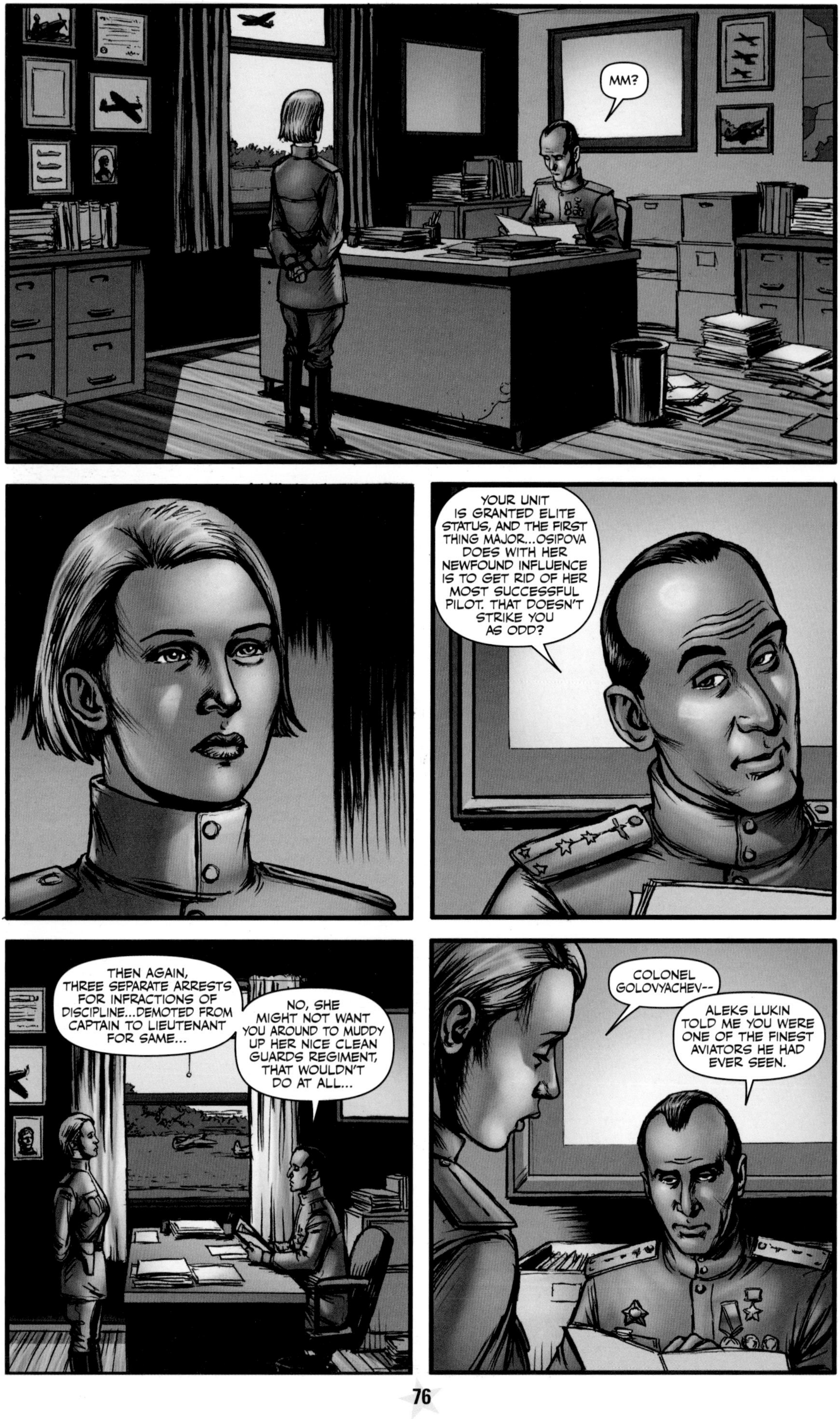
MM?
YOUR UNIT IS GRANTED ELITE STATUS, AND THE FIRST THING MAJOR...OSIPOVA DOES WITH HER NEWFOUND INFLUENCE IS TO GET RID OF HER MOST SUCCESSFUL PILOT. THAT DOESN'T STRIKE YOU AS ODD?
THEN AGAIN, THREE SEPARATE ARRESTS FOR INFRACTIONS OF DISCIPLINE...DEMOTED FROM CAPTAIN TO LIEUTENANT FOR SAME...
NO, SHE MIGHT NOT WANT YOU AROUND TO MUDDY UP HER NICE CLEAN GUARDS REGIMENT, THAT WOULDN'T DO AT ALL...
COLONEL GOLOVYACHEV--
ALEKS LUKIN TOLD ME YOU WERE ONE OF THE FINEST AVIATORS HE HAD EVER SEEN.

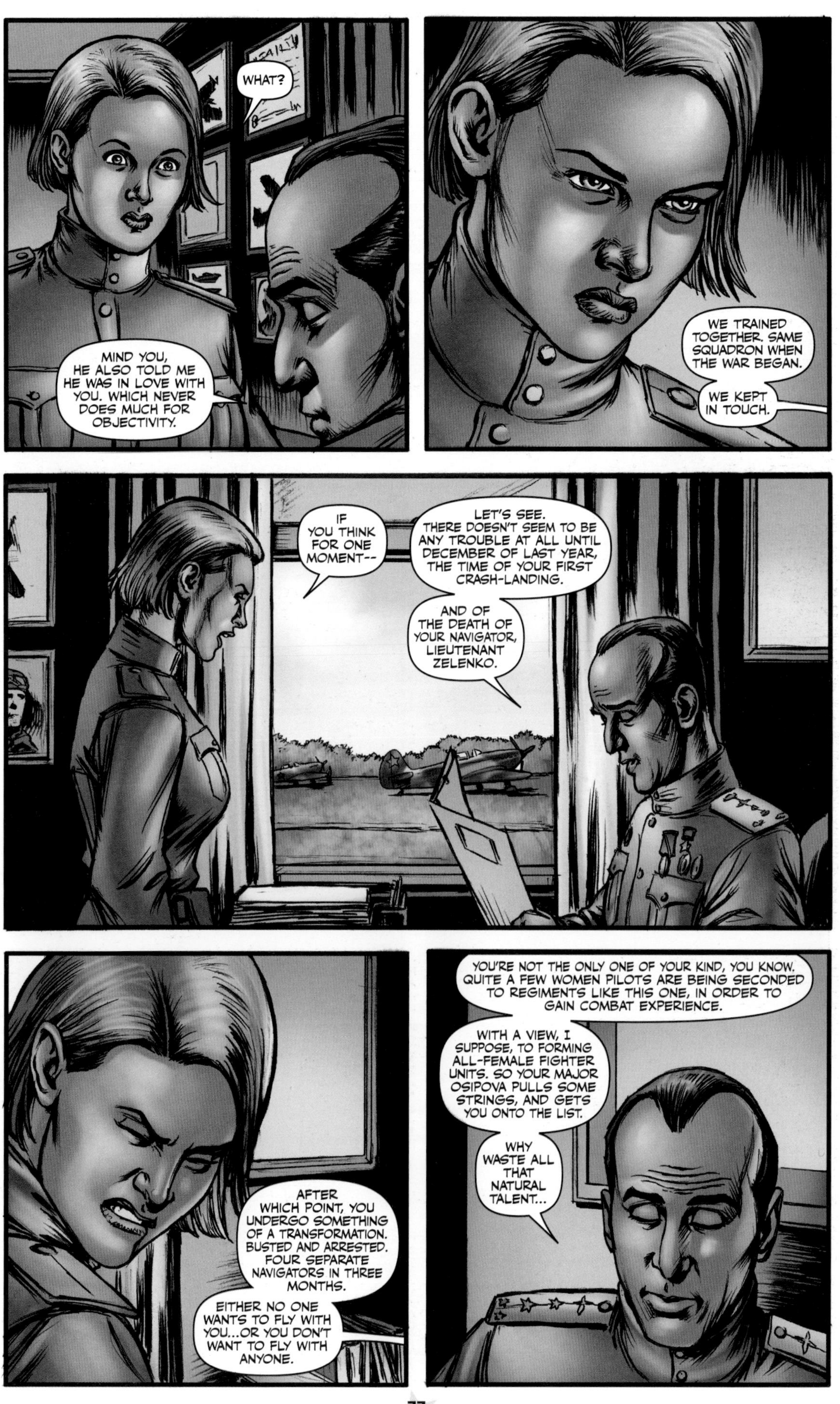
WHAT?
MIND YOU, HE ALSO TOLD ME HE WAS IN LOVE WITH YOU. WHICH NEVER DOES MUCH FOR OBJECTIVITY.
WE TRAINED TOGETHER. SAME SQUADRON WHEN THE WAR BEGAN.
WE KEPT IN TOUCH.
IF YOU THINK FOR ONE MOMENT--
LET'S SEE. THERE DOESN'T SEEM TO BE ANY TROUBLE AT ALL UNTIL DECEMBER OF LAST YEAR, THE TIME OF YOUR FIRST CRASH-LANDING.
AND OF THE DEATH OF YOUR NAVIGATOR, LIEUTENANT ZELENKO.
AFTER WHICH POINT, YOU UNDERGO SOMETHING OF A TRANSFORMATION. BUSTED AND ARRESTED. FOUR SEPARATE NAVIGATORS IN THREE MONTHS.
EITHER NO ONE WANTS TO FLY WITH YOU...OR YOU DON'T WANT TO FLY WITH ANYONE.
YOU'RE NOT THE ONLY ONE OF YOUR KIND, YOU KNOW. QUITE A FEW WOMEN PILOTS ARE BEING SECONDED TO REGIMENTS LIKE THIS ONE, IN ORDER TO GAIN COMBAT EXPERIENCE.
WITH A VIEW, I SUPPOSE, TO FORMING ALL-FEMALE FIGHTER UNITS. SO YOUR MAJOR OSIPOVA PULLS SOME STRINGS, AND GETS YOU ONTO THE LIST.
WHY WASTE ALL THAT NATURAL TALENT...

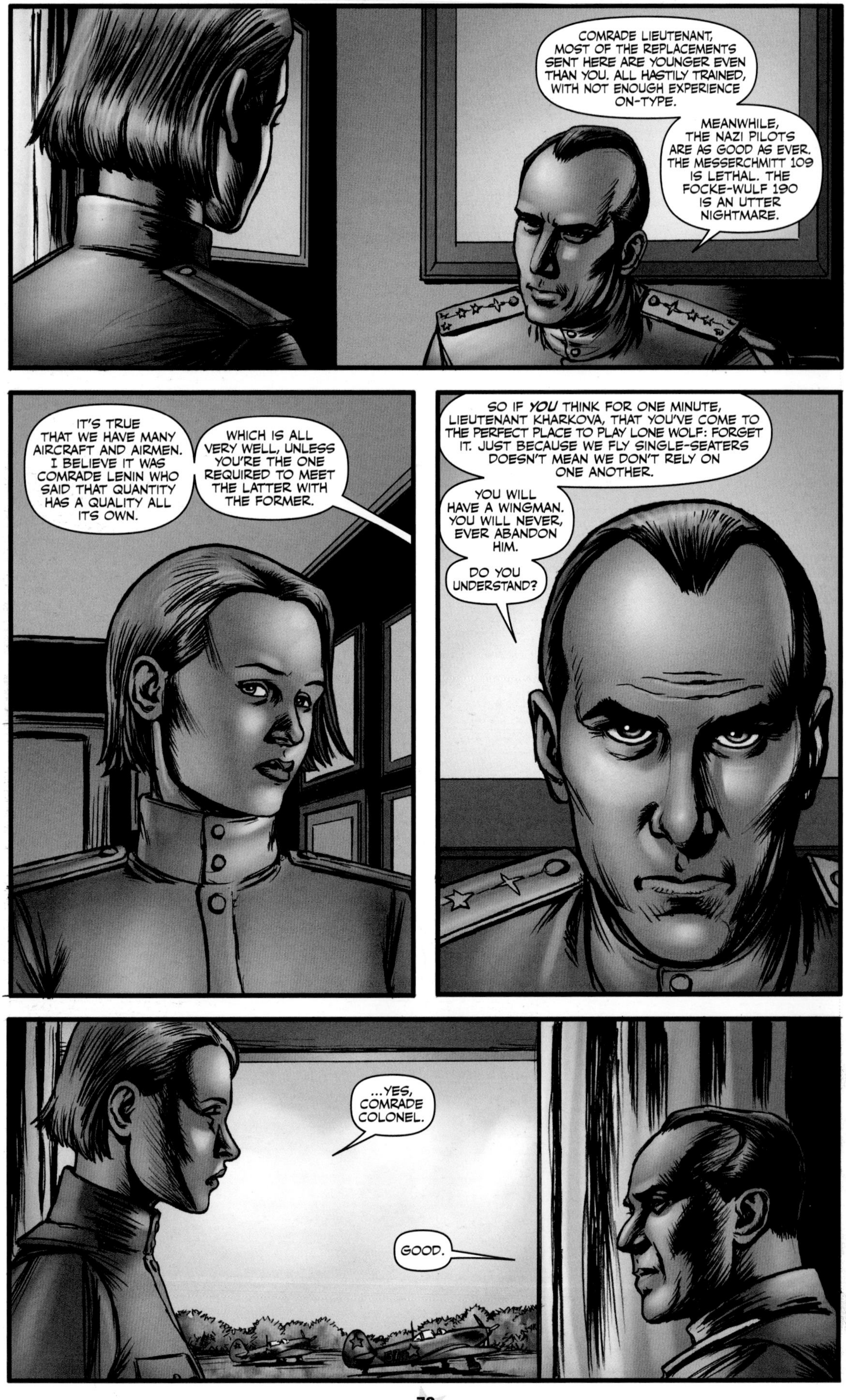
COMRADE LIEUTENANT, MOST OF THE REPLACEMENTS SENT HERE ARE YOUNGER EVEN THAN YOU. ALL HASTILY TRAINED, WITH NOT ENOUGH EXPERIENCE ON-TYPE.
MEANWHILE, THE NAZI PILOTS ARE AS GOOD AS EVER. THE MESSERSCHMITT 109 IS LETHAL. THE FOCKE-WULF 190 IS AN UTTER NIGHTMARE.
IT'S TRUE THAT WE HAVE MANY AIRCRAFT AND AIRMEN. I BELIEVE IT WAS COMRADE LENIN WHO SAID THAT QUANTITY HAS A QUALITY ALL ITS OWN.
WHICH IS ALL VERY WELL, UNLESS YOU'RE THE ONE REQUIRED TO MEET THE LATTER WITH THE FORMER.
SO IF *YOU* THINK FOR ONE MINUTE, LIEUTENANT KHARKOVA, THAT YOU'VE COME TO THE PERFECT PLACE TO PLAY LONE WOLF: FORGET IT. JUST BECAUSE WE FLY SINGLE-SEATERS DOESN'T MEAN WE DON'T RELY ON ONE ANOTHER.
YOU WILL HAVE A WINGMAN. YOU WILL NEVER, EVER ABANDON HIM.
DO YOU UNDERSTAND?
...YES, COMRADE COLONEL.
GOOD.

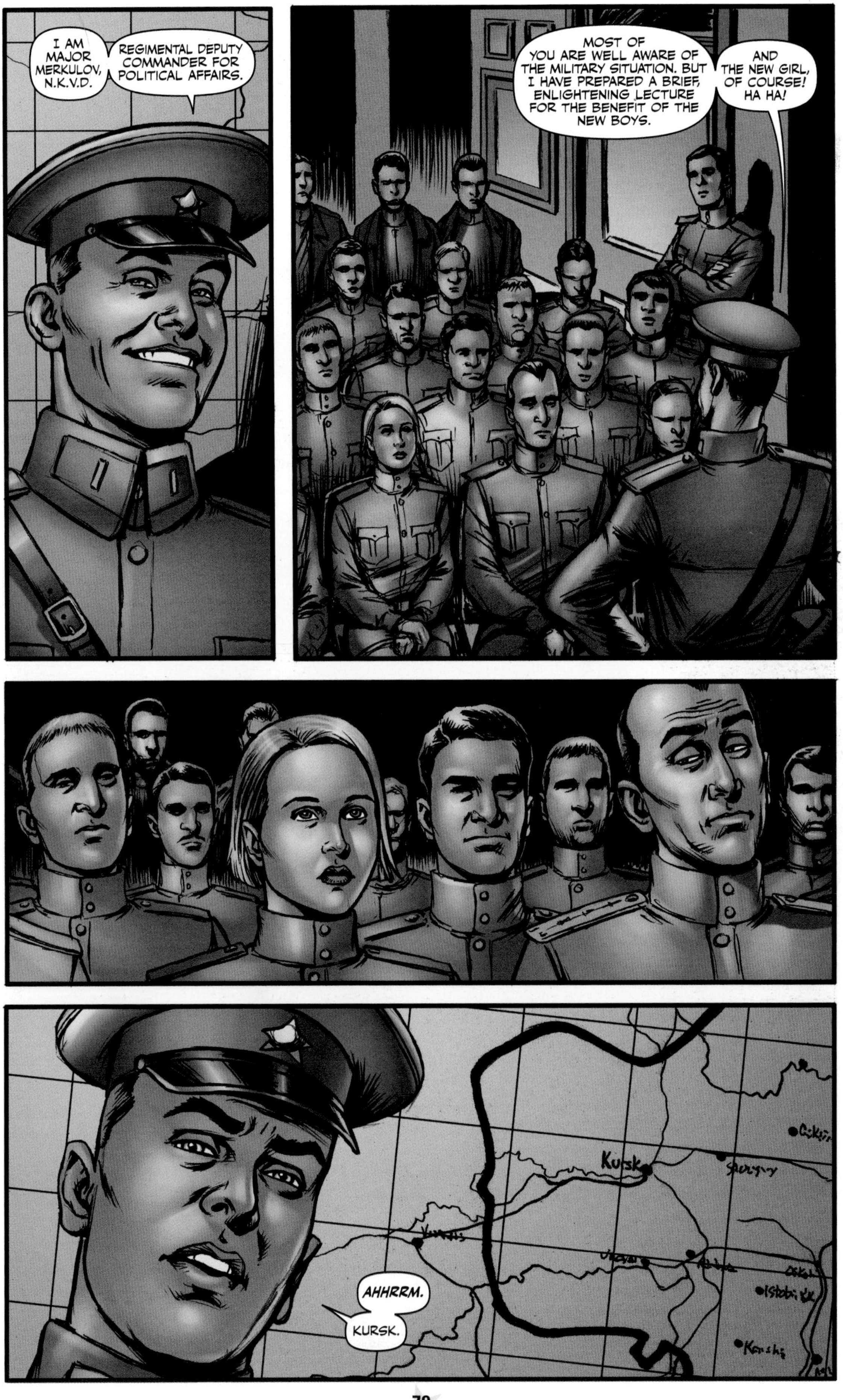
I AM MAJOR MERKULOV, N.K.V.D.
REGIMENTAL DEPUTY COMMANDER FOR POLITICAL AFFAIRS.
MOST OF YOU ARE WELL AWARE OF THE MILITARY SITUATION. BUT I HAVE PREPARED A BRIEF, ENLIGHTENING LECTURE FOR THE BENEFIT OF THE NEW BOYS.
AND THE NEW GIRL, OF COURSE! HA HA!
Kursk
AHHRRM.
KURSK.

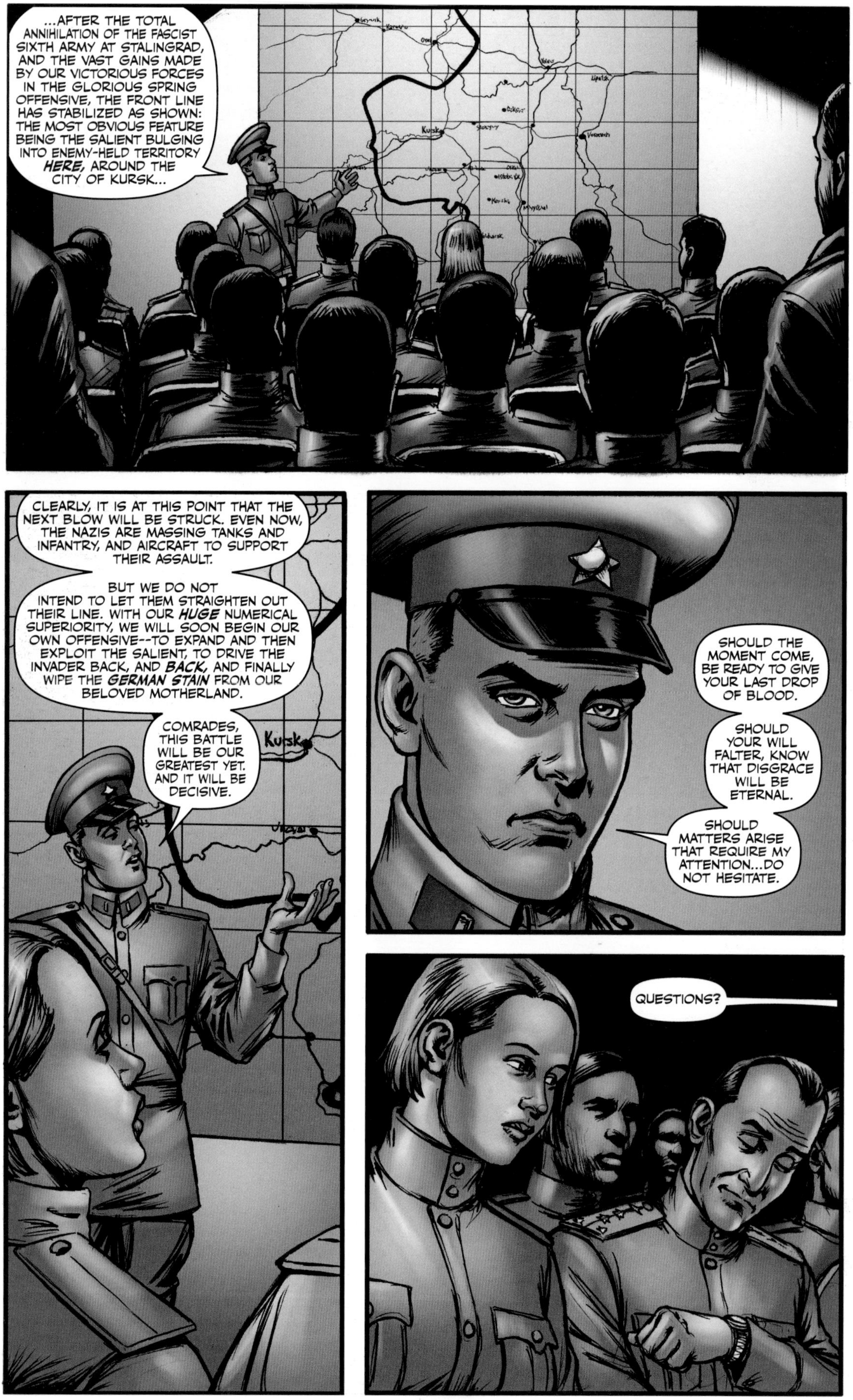
...AFTER THE TOTAL ANNIHILATION OF THE FASCIST SIXTH ARMY AT STALINGRAD, AND THE VAST GAINS MADE BY OUR VICTORIOUS FORCES IN THE GLORIOUS SPRING OFFENSIVE, THE FRONT LINE HAS STABILIZED AS SHOWN: THE MOST OBVIOUS FEATURE BEING THE SALIENT BULGING INTO ENEMY-HELD TERRITORY *HERE,* AROUND THE CITY OF KURSK...
Kursk
CLEARLY, IT IS AT THIS POINT THAT THE NEXT BLOW WILL BE STRUCK. EVEN NOW, THE NAZIS ARE MASSING TANKS AND INFANTRY, AND AIRCRAFT TO SUPPORT THEIR ASSAULT.
BUT WE DO NOT INTEND TO LET THEM STRAIGHTEN OUT THEIR LINE. WITH OUR *HUGE* NUMERICAL SUPERIORITY, WE WILL SOON BEGIN OUR OWN OFFENSIVE--TO EXPAND AND THEN EXPLOIT THE SALIENT, TO DRIVE THE INVADER BACK, AND *BACK,* AND FINALLY WIPE THE *GERMAN STAIN* FROM OUR BELOVED MOTHERLAND.
COMRADES, THIS BATTLE WILL BE OUR GREATEST YET. AND IT WILL BE DECISIVE.
Kursk
SHOULD THE MOMENT COME, BE READY TO GIVE YOUR LAST DROP OF BLOOD.
SHOULD YOUR WILL FALTER, KNOW THAT DISGRACE WILL BE ETERNAL.
SHOULD MATTERS ARISE THAT REQUIRE MY ATTENTION...DO NOT HESITATE.
QUESTIONS?

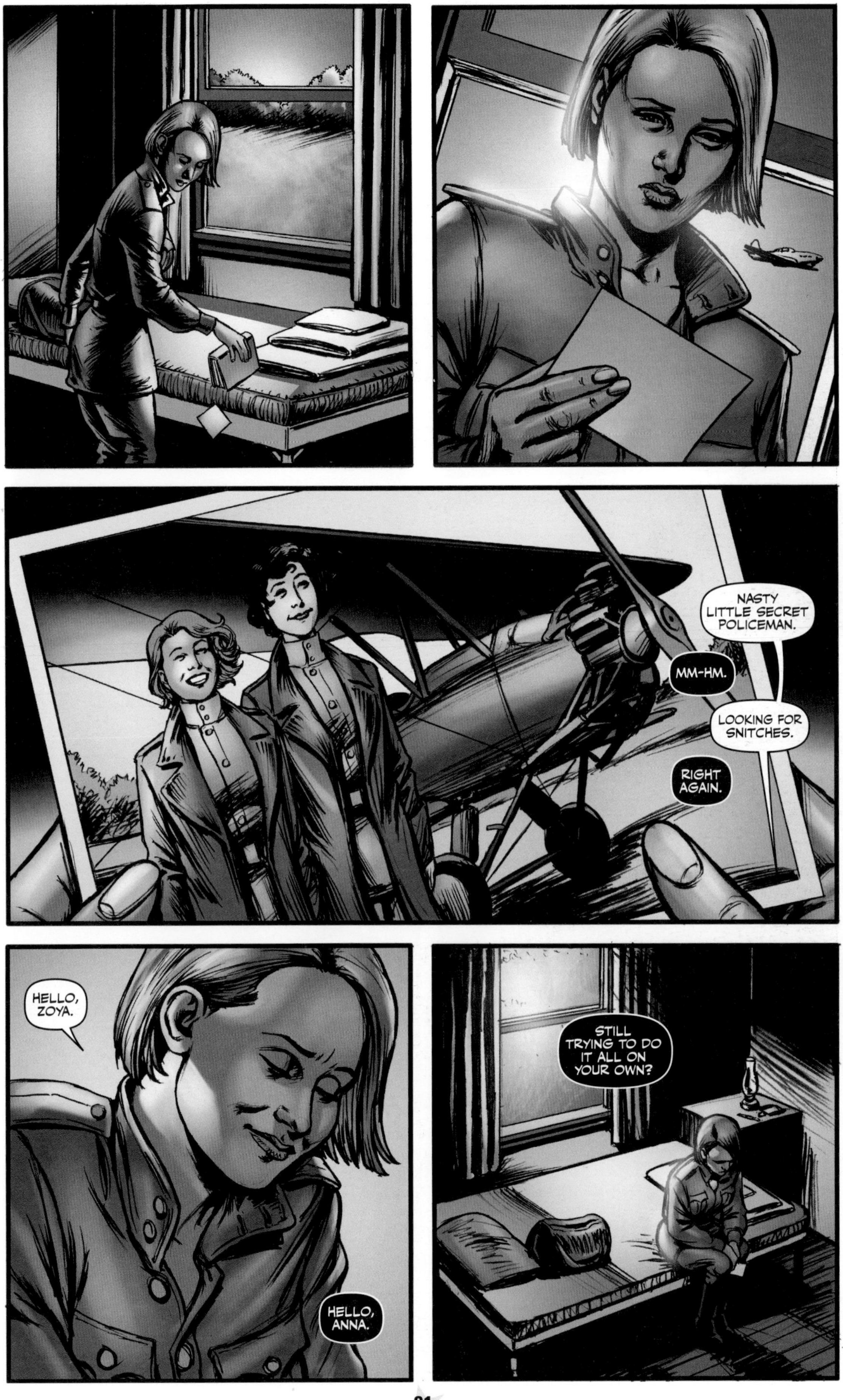
NASTY LITTLE SECRET POLICEMAN.
MM-HM.
LOOKING FOR SNITCHES.
RIGHT AGAIN.
HELLO, ZOYA.
HELLO, ANNA.
STILL TRYING TO DO IT ALL ON YOUR OWN?

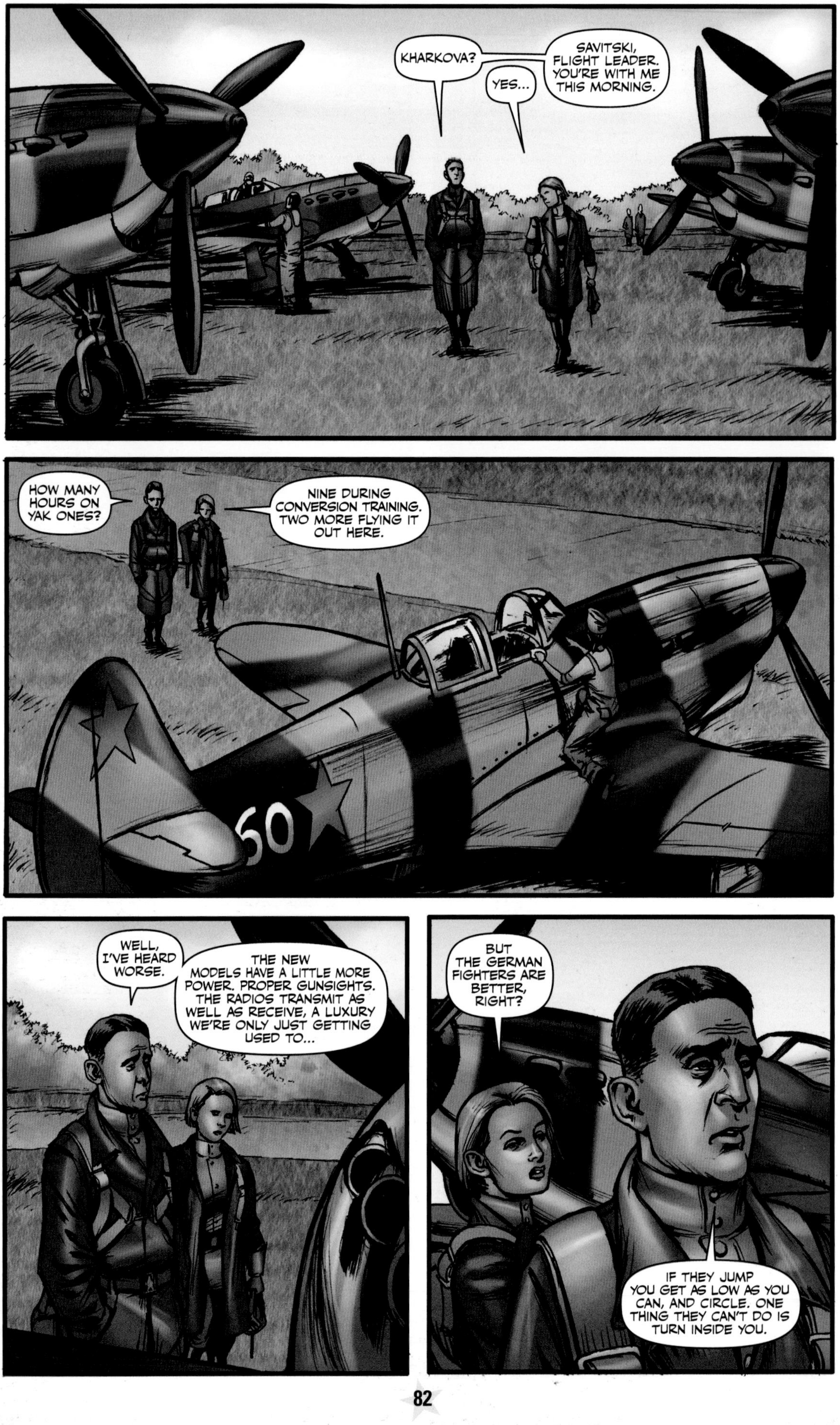
KHARKOVA?
YES...
SAVITSKI, FLIGHT LEADER. YOU'RE WITH ME THIS MORNING.
HOW MANY HOURS ON YAK ONES?
NINE DURING CONVERSION TRAINING. TWO MORE FLYING IT OUT HERE.
60
WELL, I'VE HEARD WORSE.
THE NEW MODELS HAVE A LITTLE MORE POWER. PROPER GUNSIGHTS. THE RADIOS TRANSMIT AS WELL AS RECEIVE, A LUXURY WE'RE ONLY JUST GETTING USED TO...
BUT THE GERMAN FIGHTERS ARE BETTER, RIGHT?
IF THEY JUMP YOU GET AS LOW AS YOU CAN, AND CIRCLE. ONE THING THEY CAN'T DO IS TURN INSIDE YOU.

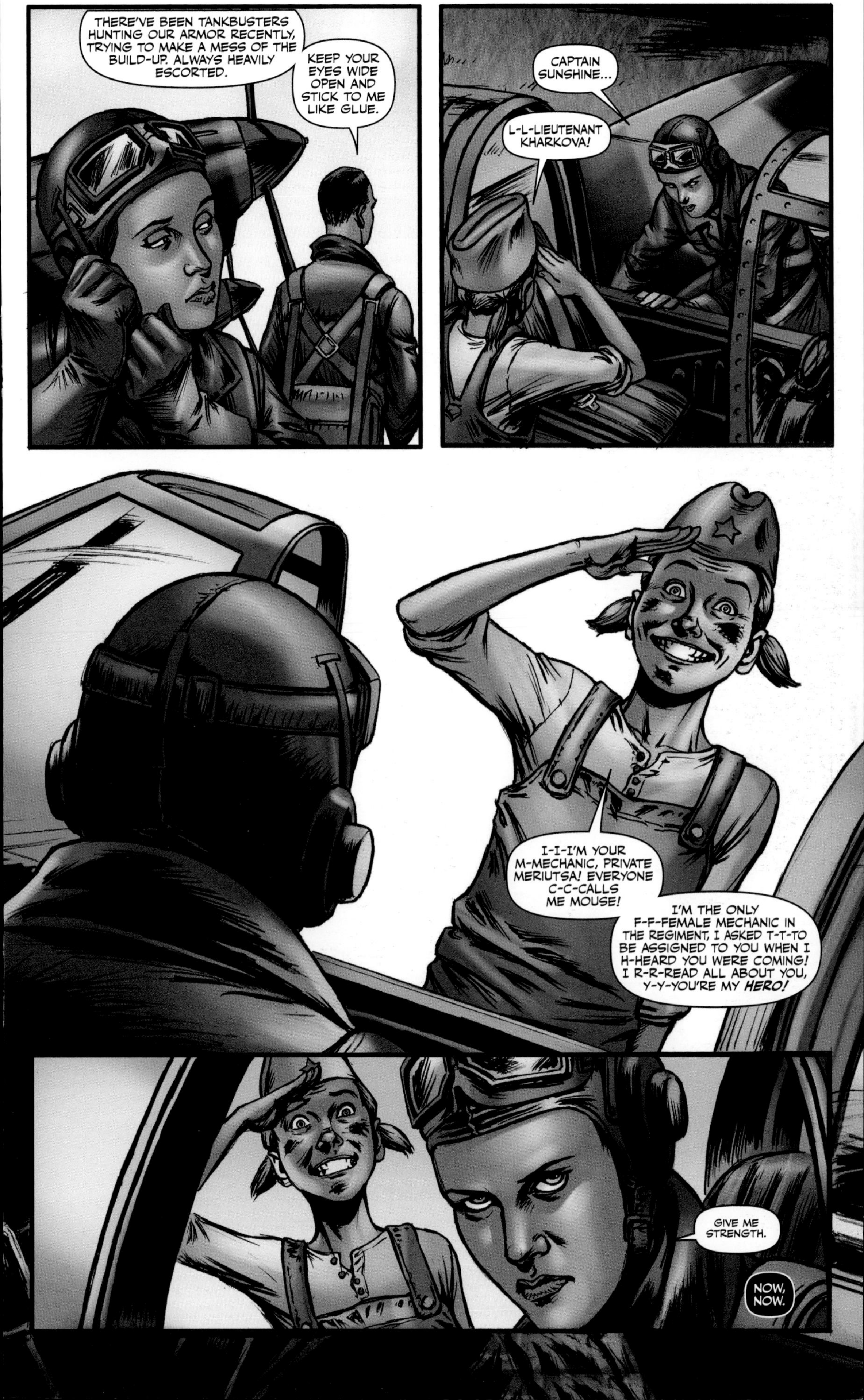
THERE'VE BEEN TANKBUSTERS HUNTING OUR ARMOR RECENTLY, TRYING TO MAKE A MESS OF THE BUILD-UP. ALWAYS HEAVILY ESCORTED.
KEEP YOUR EYES WIDE OPEN AND STICK TO ME LIKE GLUE.
CAPTAIN SUNSHINE...
L-L-LIEUTENANT KHARKOVA!
I-I-I'M YOUR M-MECHANIC, PRIVATE MERIUTSA! EVERYONE C-C-CALLS ME MOUSE!
I'M THE ONLY F-F-FEMALE MECHANIC IN THE REGIMENT, I ASKED T-T-TO BE ASSIGNED TO YOU WHEN I H-HEARD YOU WERE COMING! I R-R-READ ALL ABOUT YOU, Y-Y-YOU'RE MY ***HERO!***
GIVE ME STRENGTH.
NOW, NOW.

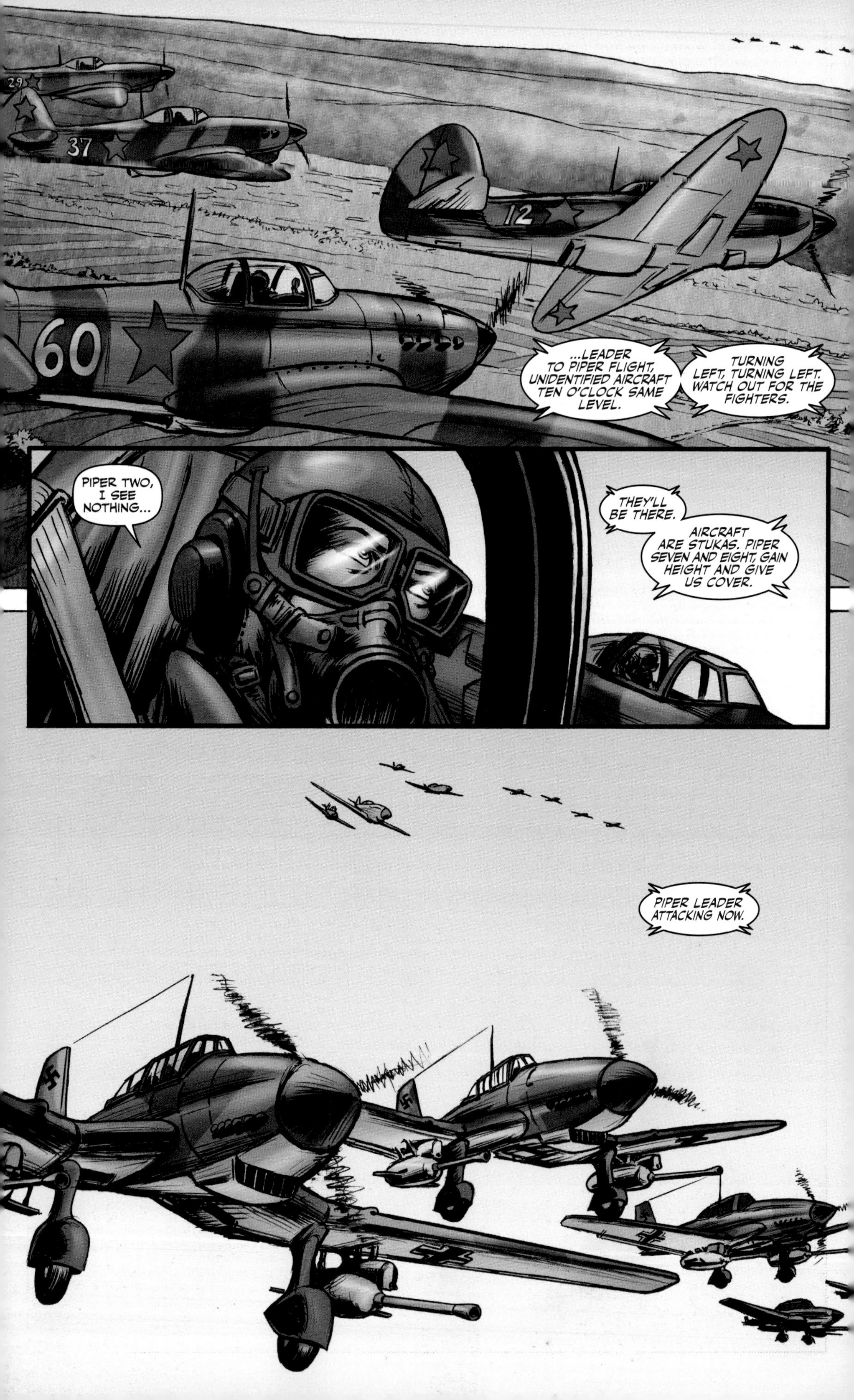
...LEADER TO PIPER FLIGHT, UNIDENTIFIED AIRCRAFT TEN O'CLOCK SAME LEVEL.
TURNING LEFT, TURNING LEFT. WATCH OUT FOR THE FIGHTERS.
PIPER TWO, I SEE NOTHING...
THEY'LL BE THERE.
AIRCRAFT ARE STUKAS. PIPER SEVEN AND EIGHT, GAIN HEIGHT AND GIVE US COVER.
PIPER LEADER ATTACKING NOW.

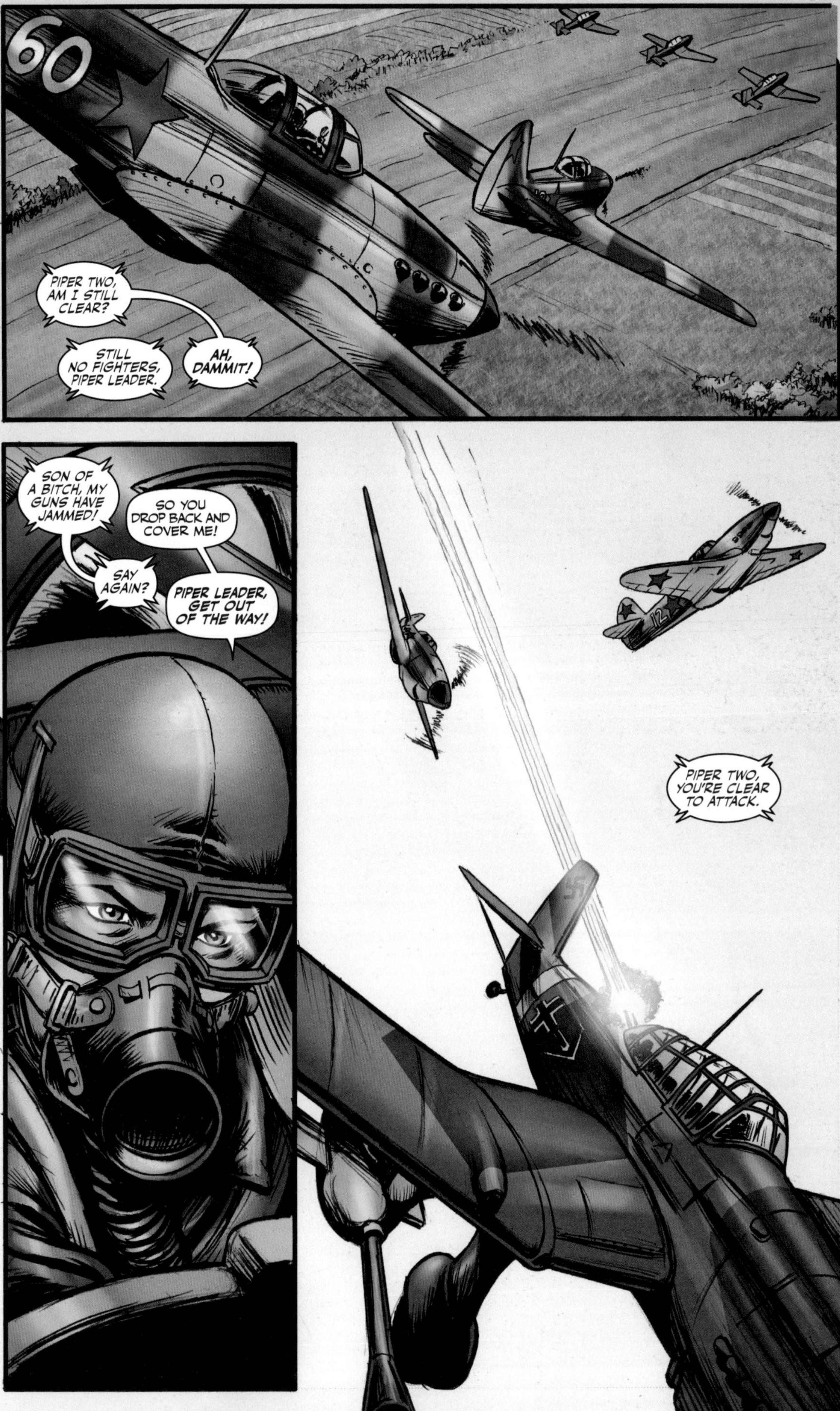
PIPER TWO, AM I STILL CLEAR?
STILL NO FIGHTERS, PIPER LEADER.
AH, DAMMIT!
SON OF A BITCH, MY GUNS HAVE JAMMED!
SO YOU DROP BACK AND COVER ME!
SAY AGAIN?
PIPER LEADER, GET OUT OF THE WAY!
PIPER TWO, YOU'RE CLEAR TO ATTACK.
12

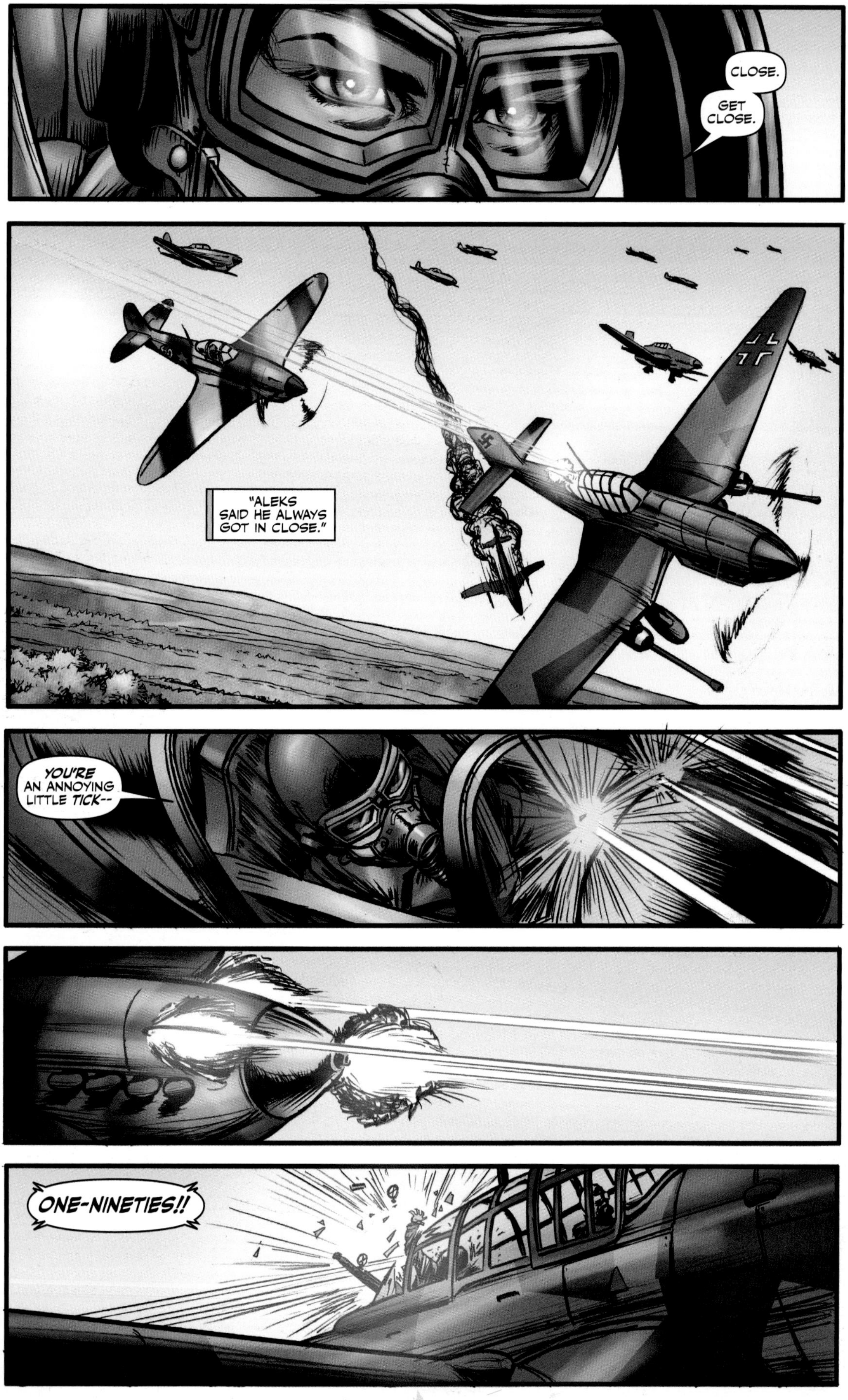
CLOSE.
GET CLOSE.
"ALEKS SAID HE ALWAYS GOT IN CLOSE."
YOU'RE AN ANNOYING LITTLE *TICK*--
ONE-NINETIES!!

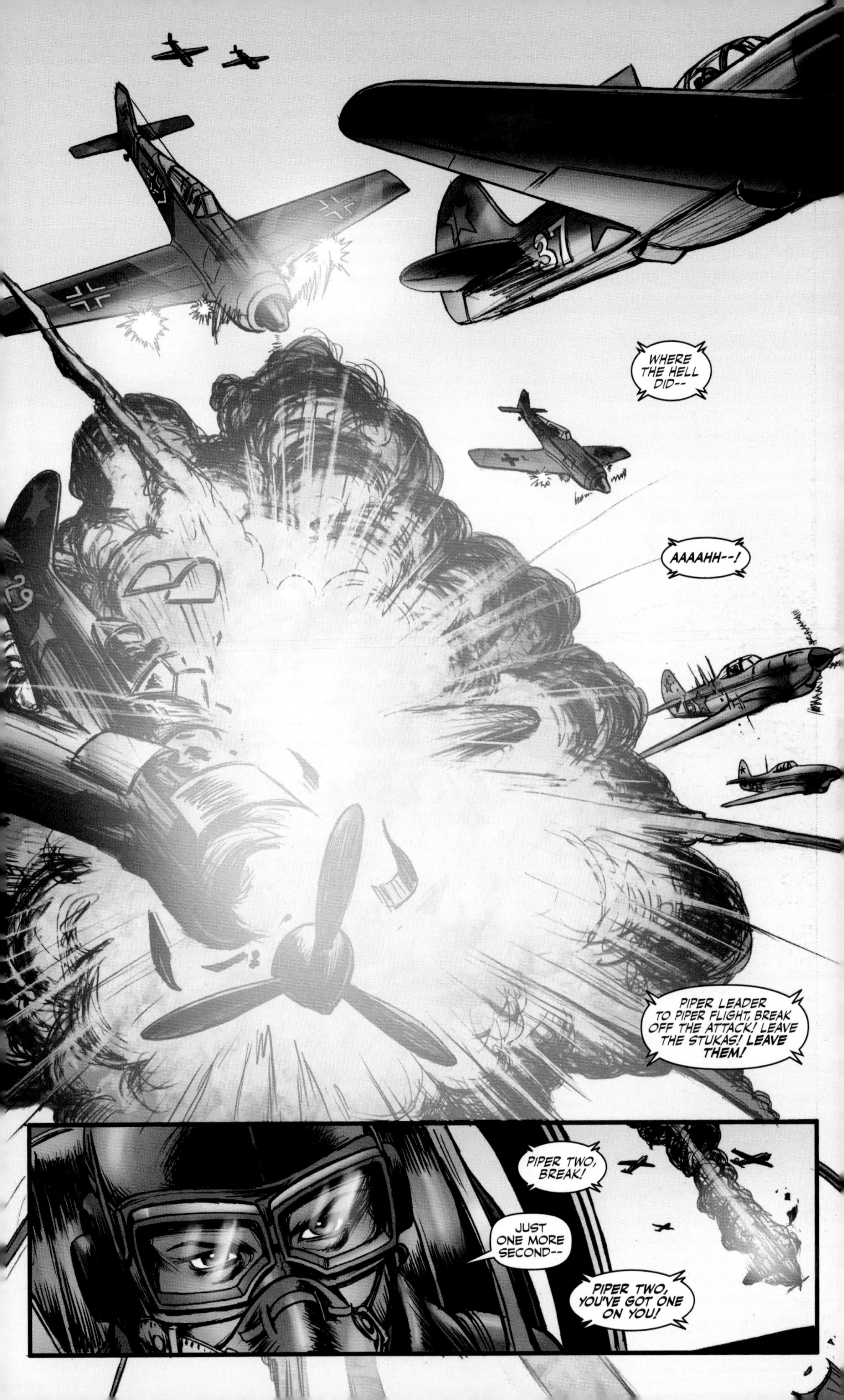
WHERE THE HELL DID--
AAAAHH--!
PIPER LEADER TO PIPER FLIGHT, BREAK OFF THE ATTACK! LEAVE THE STUKAS! LEAVE THEM!
PIPER TWO, BREAK!
JUST ONE MORE SECOND--
PIPER TWO, YOU'VE GOT ONE ON YOU!

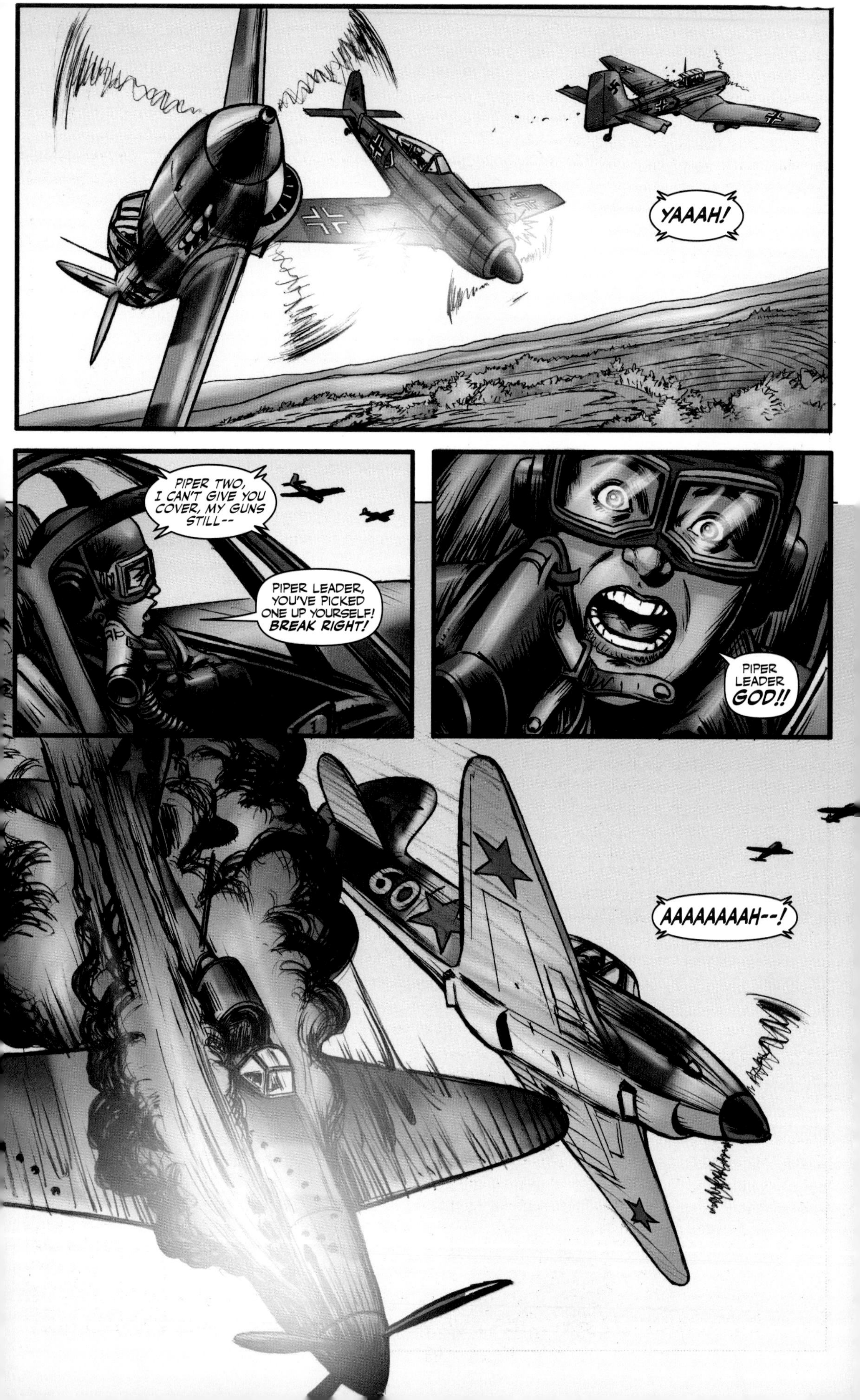
YAAAH!
PIPER TWO, I CAN'T GIVE YOU COVER, MY GUNS STILL--
PIPER LEADER, YOU'VE PICKED ONE UP YOURSELF! BREAK RIGHT!
PIPER LEADER GOD!!
AAAAAAAAH--!

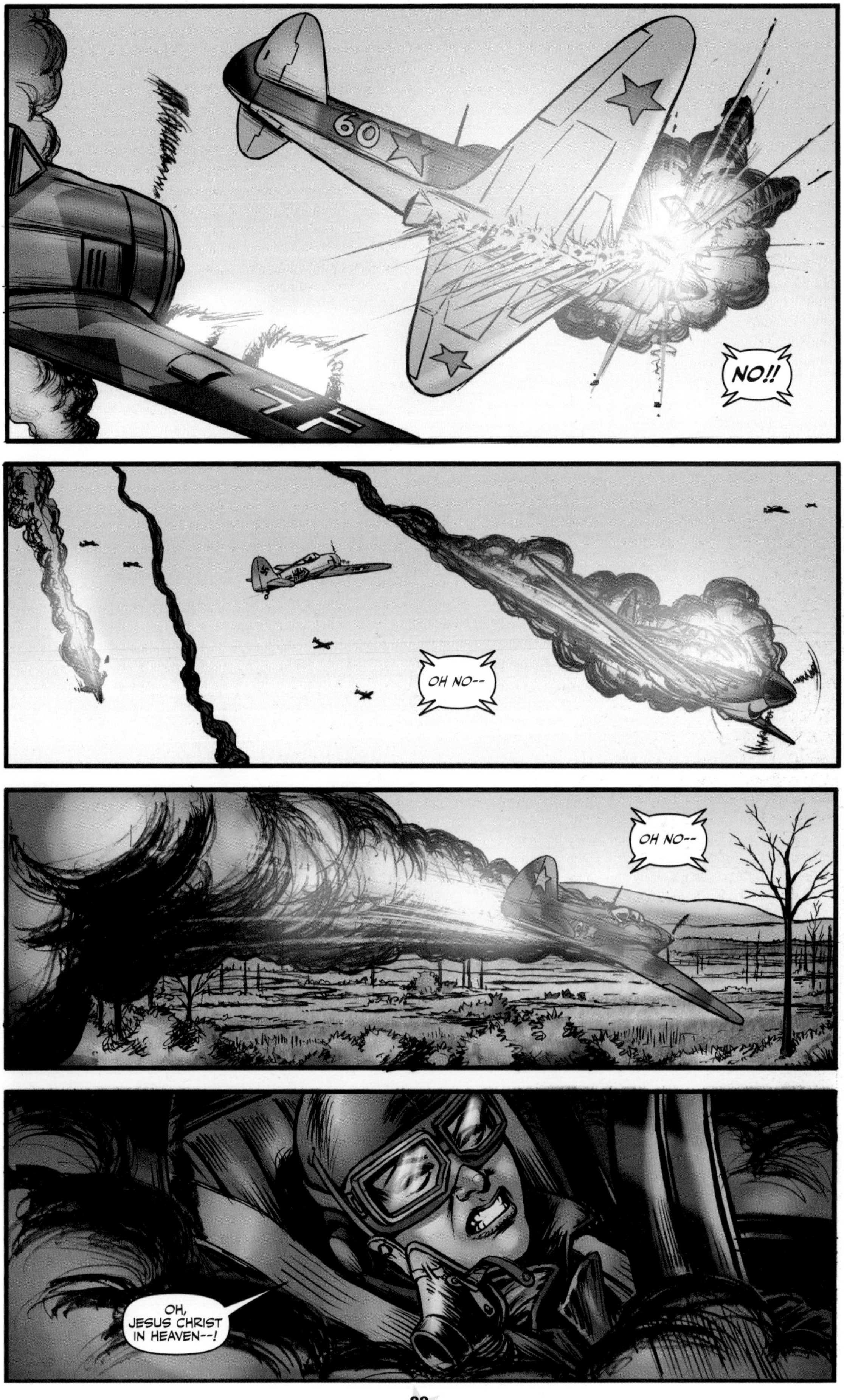
NO!!
OH NO--
OH NO--
OH,
JESUS CHRIST
IN HEAVEN--!

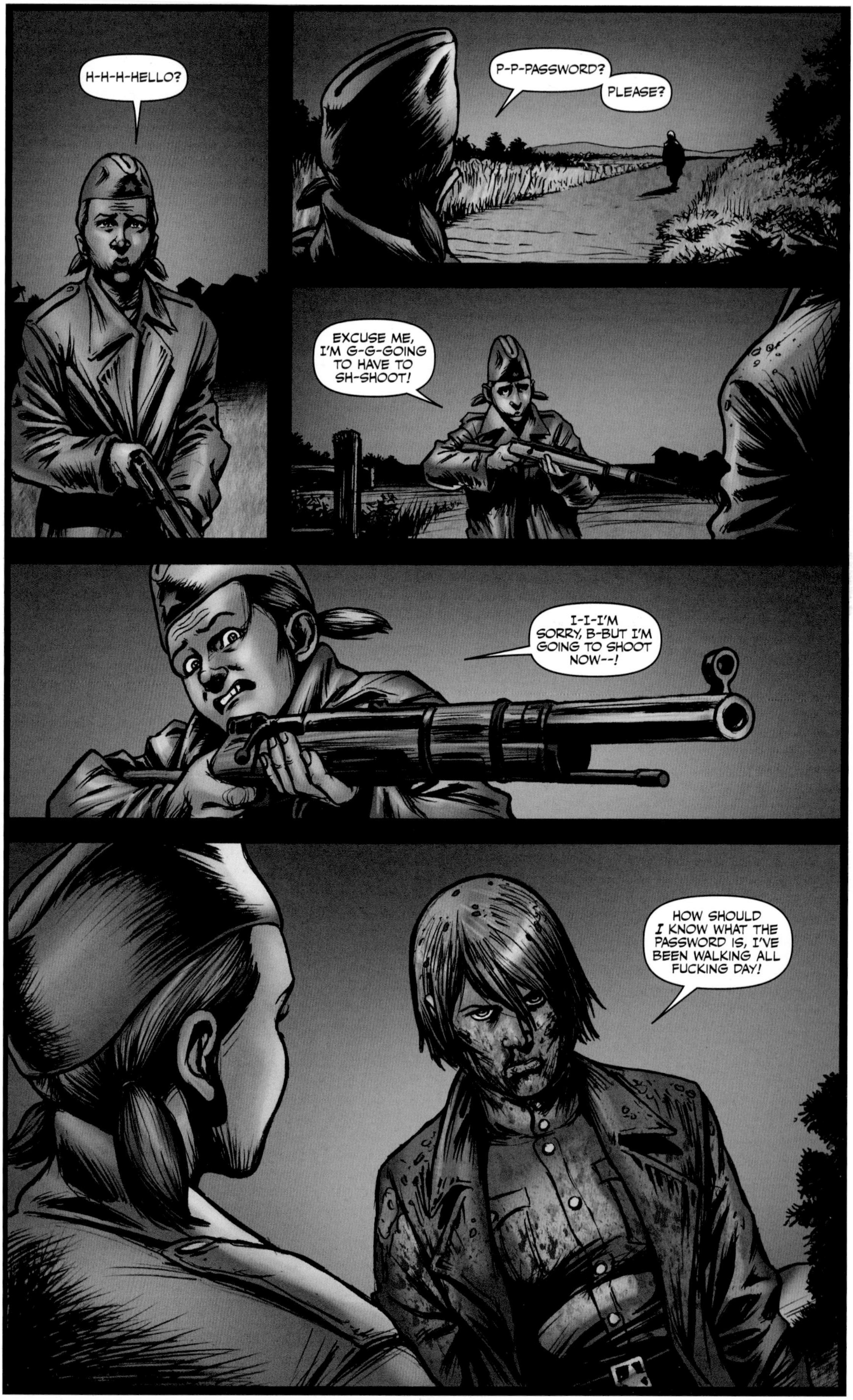
H-H-H-HELLO?
P-P-PASSWORD?
PLEASE?
EXCUSE ME, I'M G-G-GOING TO HAVE TO SH-SHOOT!
I-I-I'M SORRY, B-BUT I'M GOING TO SHOOT NOW--!
HOW SHOULD *I* KNOW WHAT THE PASSWORD IS, I'VE BEEN WALKING ALL FUCKING DAY!

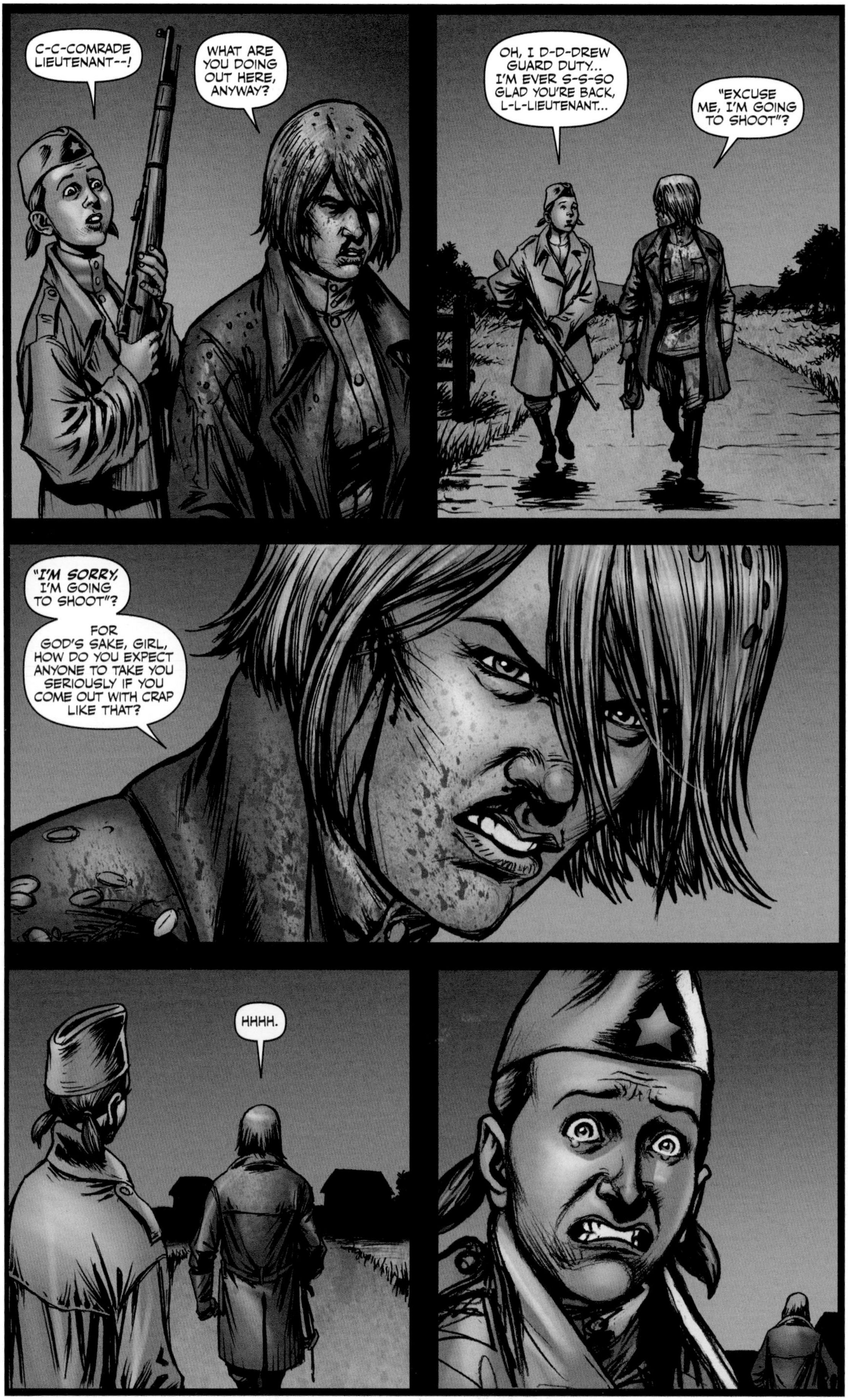
C-C-COMRADE LIEUTENANT--!
WHAT ARE YOU DOING OUT HERE, ANYWAY?
OH, I D-D-DREW GUARD DUTY... I'M EVER S-S-SO GLAD YOU'RE BACK, L-L-LIEUTENANT...
"EXCUSE ME, I'M GOING TO SHOOT"?
"*I'M SORRY,* I'M GOING TO SHOOT"?
FOR GOD'S SAKE, GIRL, HOW DO YOU EXPECT ANYONE TO TAKE YOU SERIOUSLY IF YOU COME OUT WITH CRAP LIKE THAT?
HHHH.

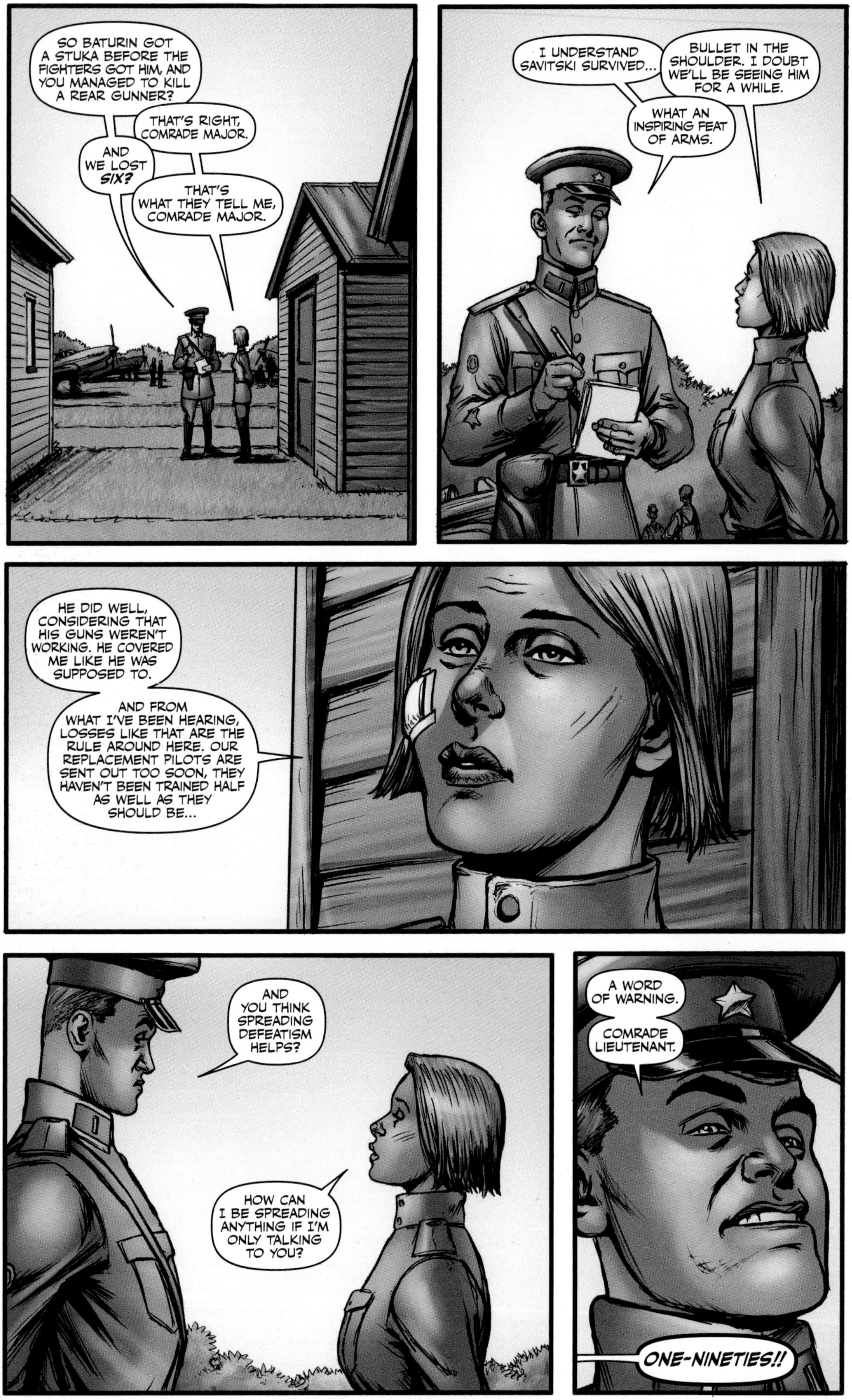
SO BATURIN GOT A STUKA BEFORE THE FIGHTERS GOT HIM, AND YOU MANAGED TO KILL A REAR GUNNER?
THAT'S RIGHT, COMRADE MAJOR.
AND WE LOST *SIX?*
THAT'S WHAT THEY TELL ME, COMRADE MAJOR.
I UNDERSTAND SAVITSKI SURVIVED...
BULLET IN THE SHOULDER. I DOUBT WE'LL BE SEEING HIM FOR A WHILE.
WHAT AN INSPIRING FEAT OF ARMS.
HE DID WELL, CONSIDERING THAT HIS GUNS WEREN'T WORKING. HE COVERED ME LIKE HE WAS SUPPOSED TO.
AND FROM WHAT I'VE BEEN HEARING, LOSSES LIKE THAT ARE THE RULE AROUND HERE. OUR REPLACEMENT PILOTS ARE SENT OUT TOO SOON, THEY HAVEN'T BEEN TRAINED HALF AS WELL AS THEY SHOULD BE...
AND YOU THINK SPREADING DEFEATISM HELPS?
HOW CAN I BE SPREADING ANYTHING IF I'M ONLY TALKING TO YOU?
A WORD OF WARNING.
COMRADE LIEUTENANT.
ONE-NINETIES!!

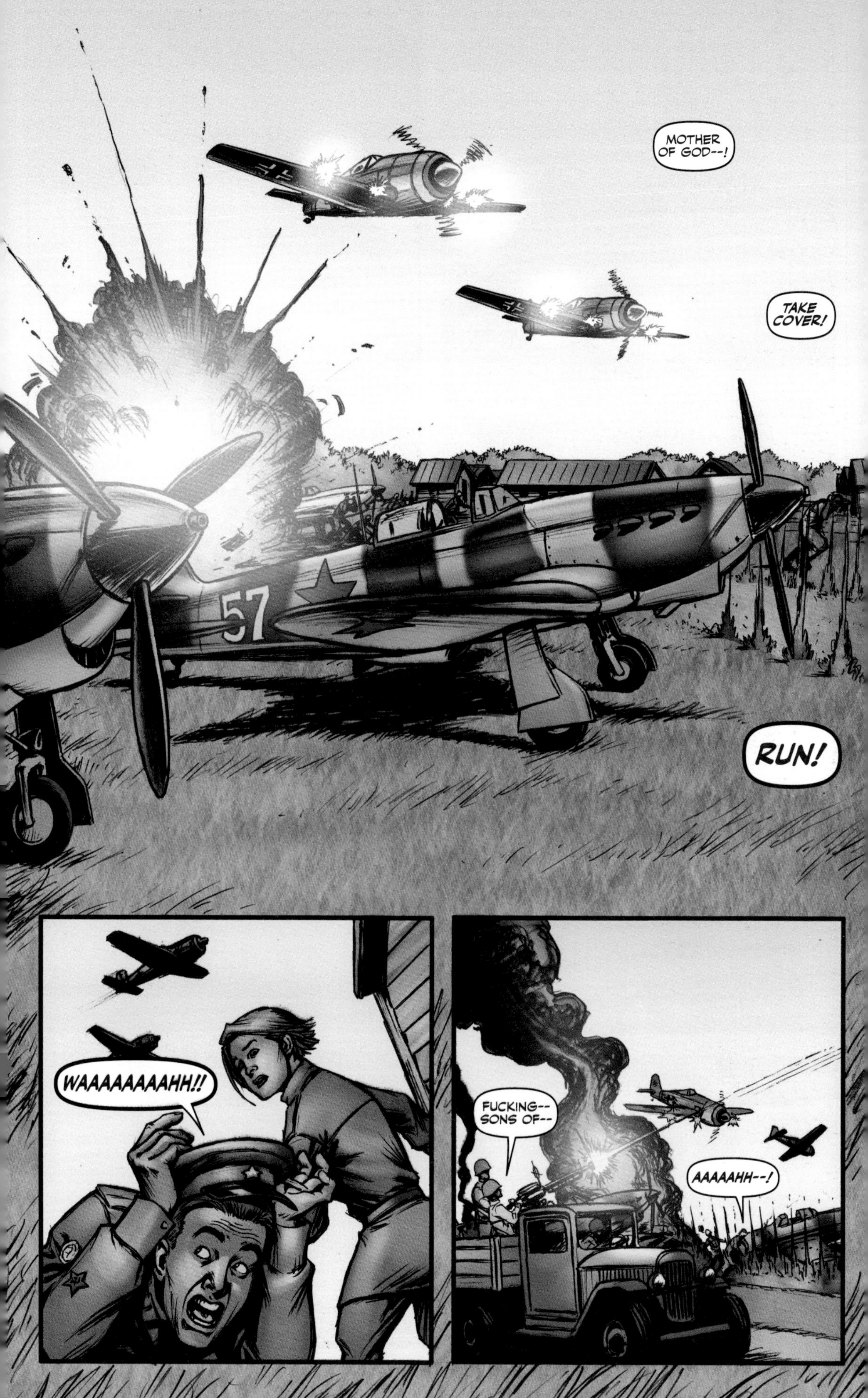
MOTHER OF GOD--!
TAKE COVER!
RUN!
WAAAAAAAAAHH!!
FUCKING-- SONS OF--
AAAAAHH--!

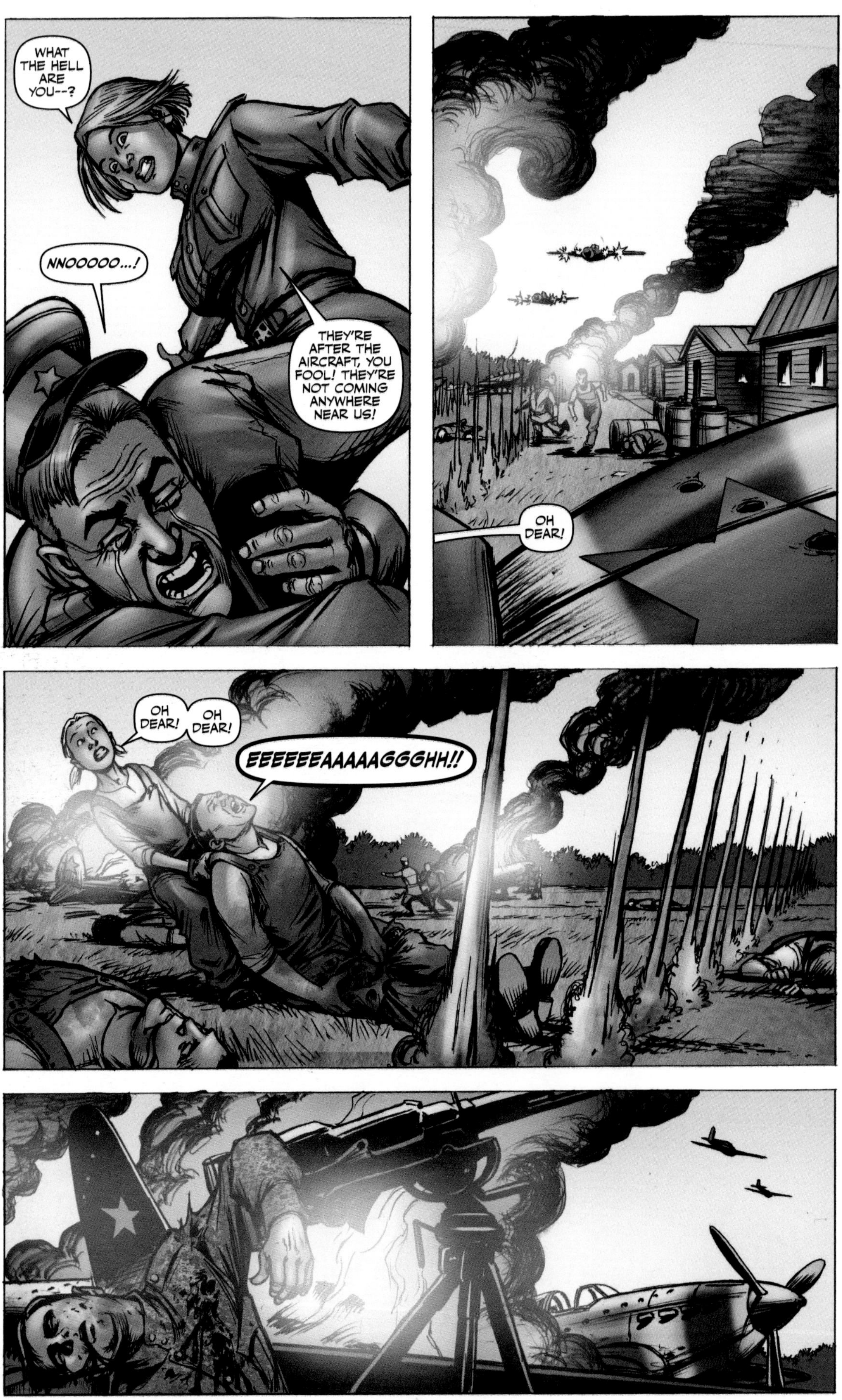
WHAT THE HELL ARE YOU--?
NNOOOOO...!
THEY'RE AFTER THE AIRCRAFT, YOU FOOL! THEY'RE NOT COMING ANYWHERE NEAR US!
OH DEAR!
OH DEAR!
OH DEAR!
EEEEEEAAAAAGGGHH!!

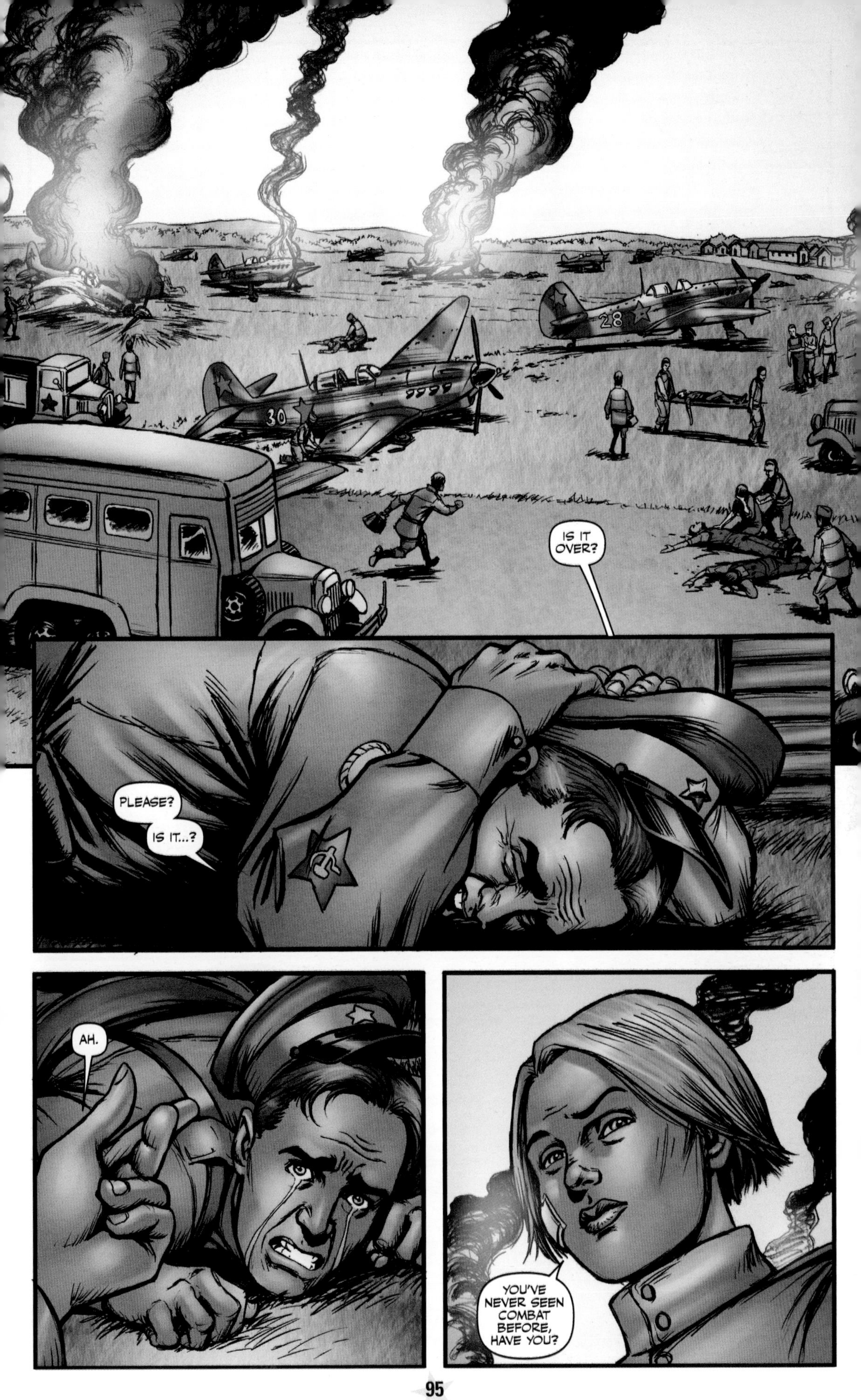
IS IT OVER?
PLEASE?
IS IT...?
AH.
YOU'VE NEVER SEEN COMBAT BEFORE, HAVE YOU?

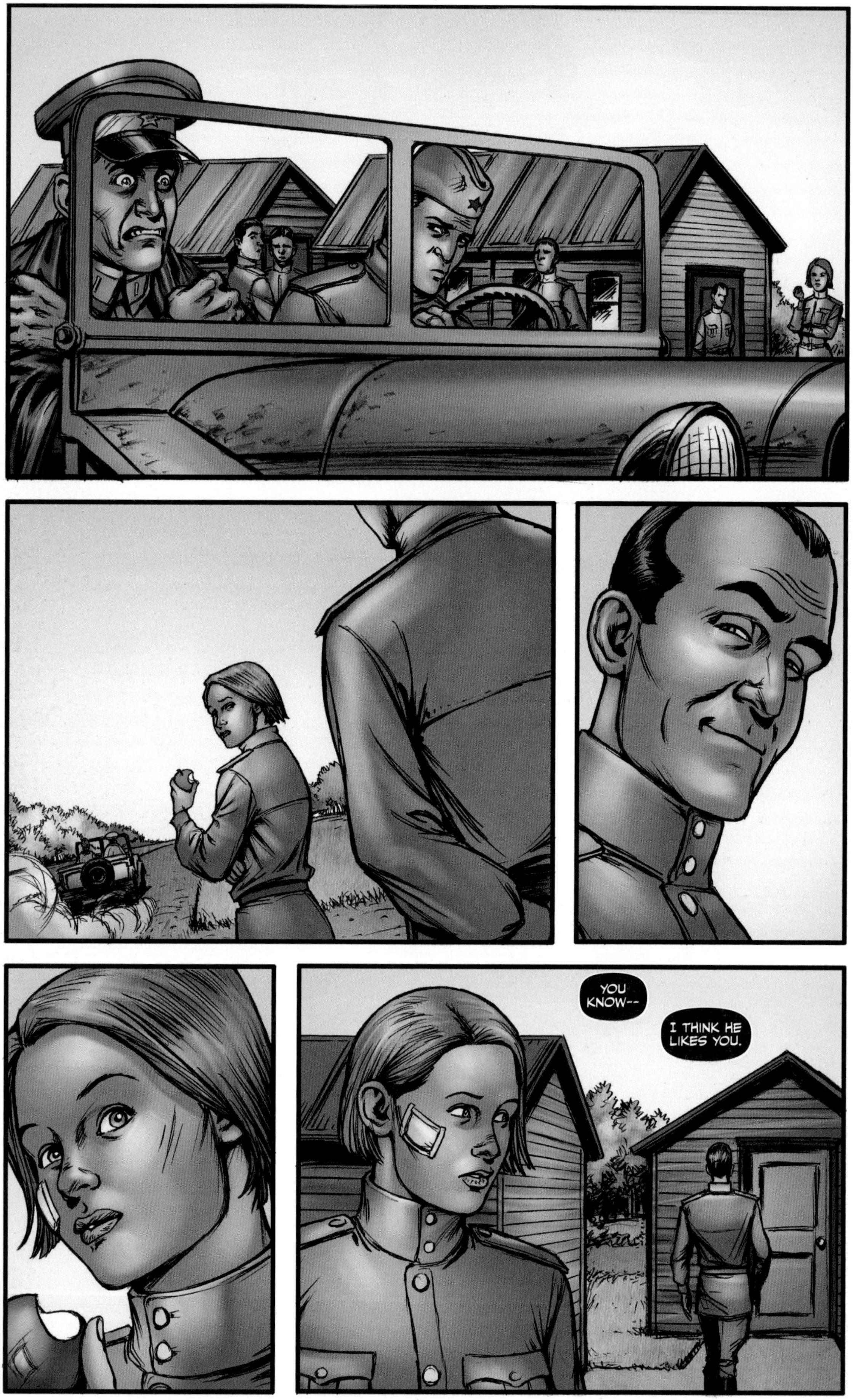
YOU KNOW--
I THINK HE LIKES YOU.

Chapter 2

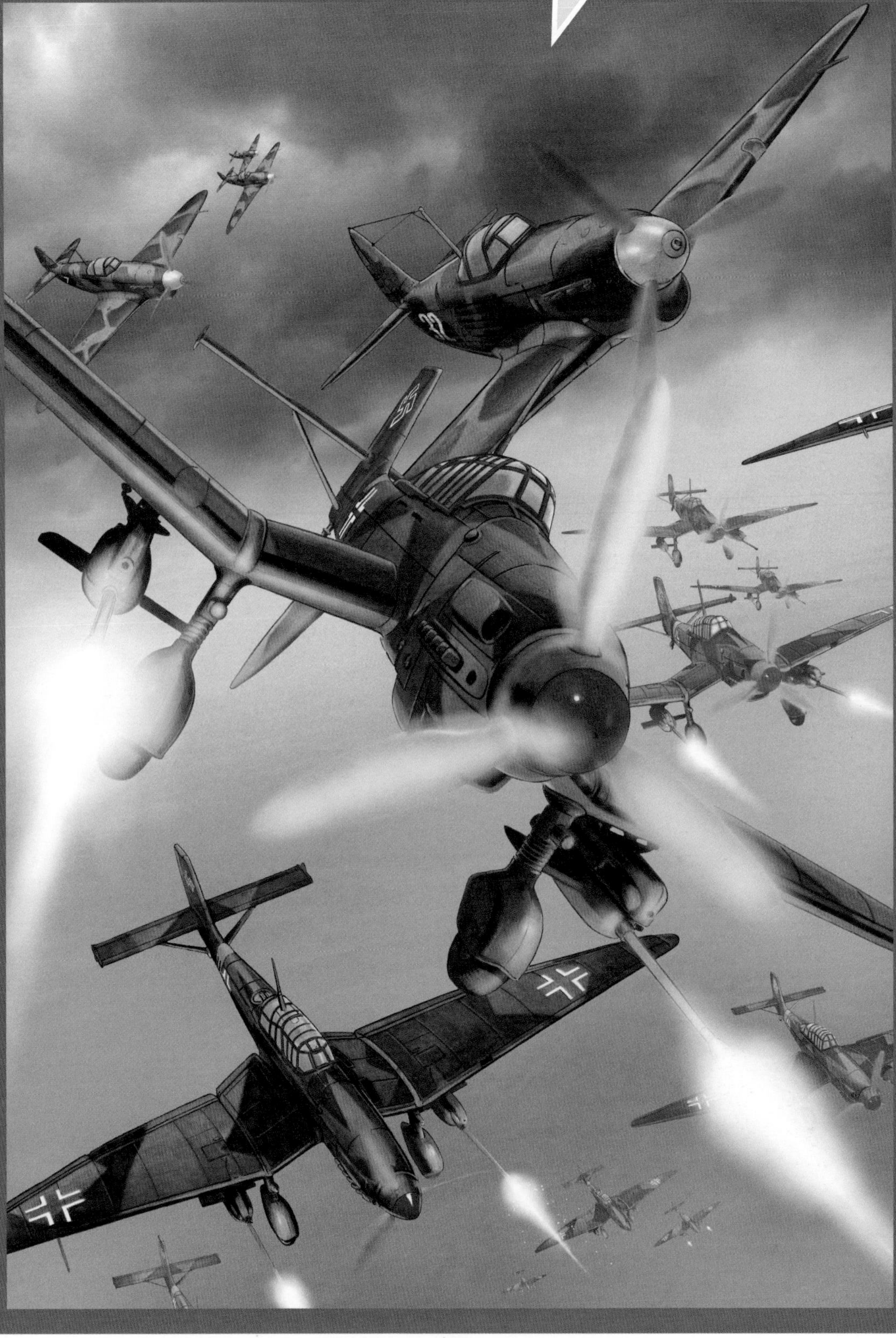
23

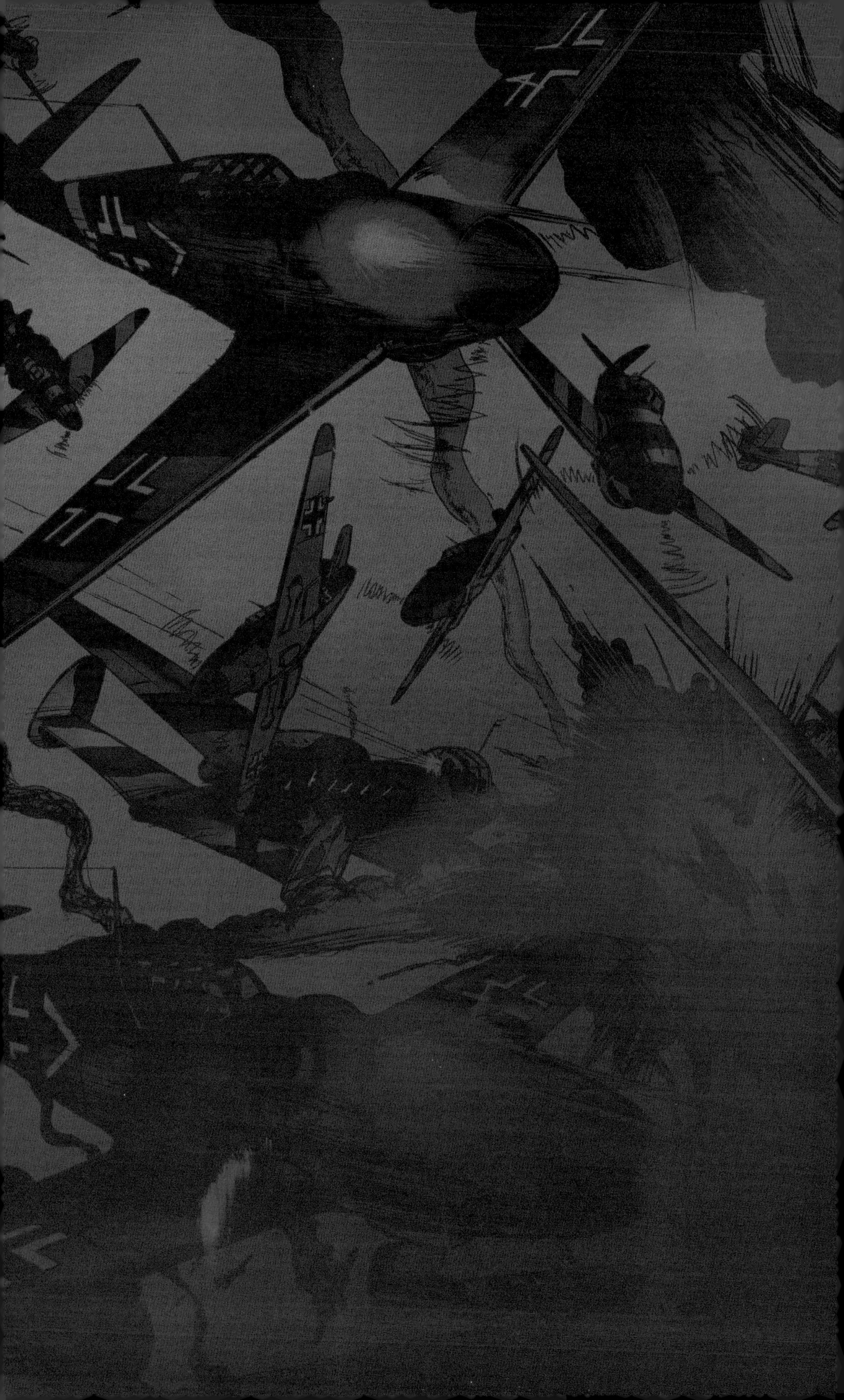

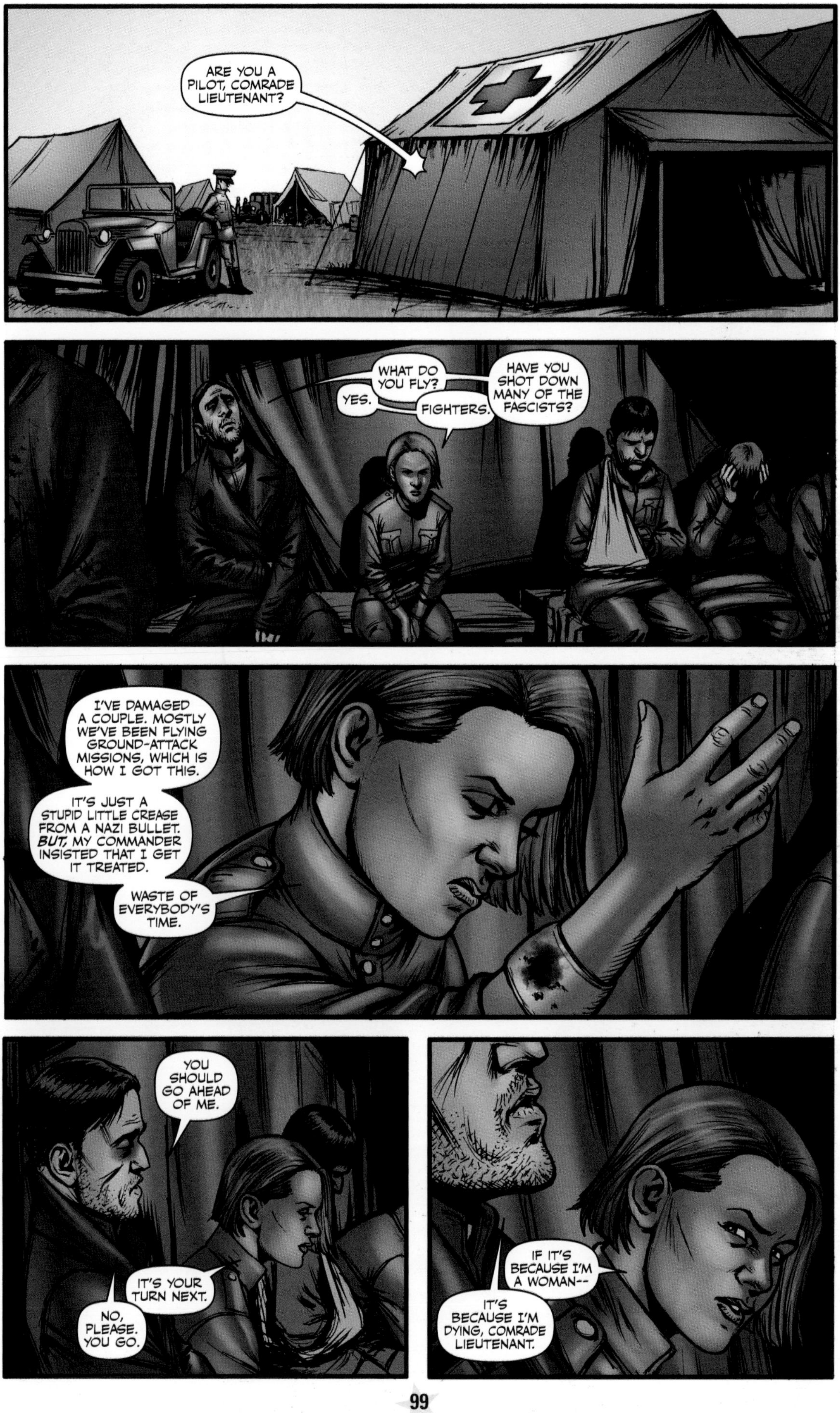
ARE YOU A PILOT, COMRADE LIEUTENANT?
YES.
WHAT DO YOU FLY?
FIGHTERS.
HAVE YOU SHOT DOWN MANY OF THE FASCISTS?
I'VE DAMAGED A COUPLE. MOSTLY WE'VE BEEN FLYING GROUND-ATTACK MISSIONS, WHICH IS HOW I GOT THIS.
IT'S JUST A STUPID LITTLE CREASE FROM A NAZI BULLET. BUT, MY COMMANDER INSISTED THAT I GET IT TREATED.
WASTE OF EVERYBODY'S TIME.
YOU SHOULD GO AHEAD OF ME.
IT'S YOUR TURN NEXT.
NO, PLEASE. YOU GO.
IF IT'S BECAUSE I'M A WOMAN--
IT'S BECAUSE I'M DYING, COMRADE LIEUTENANT.

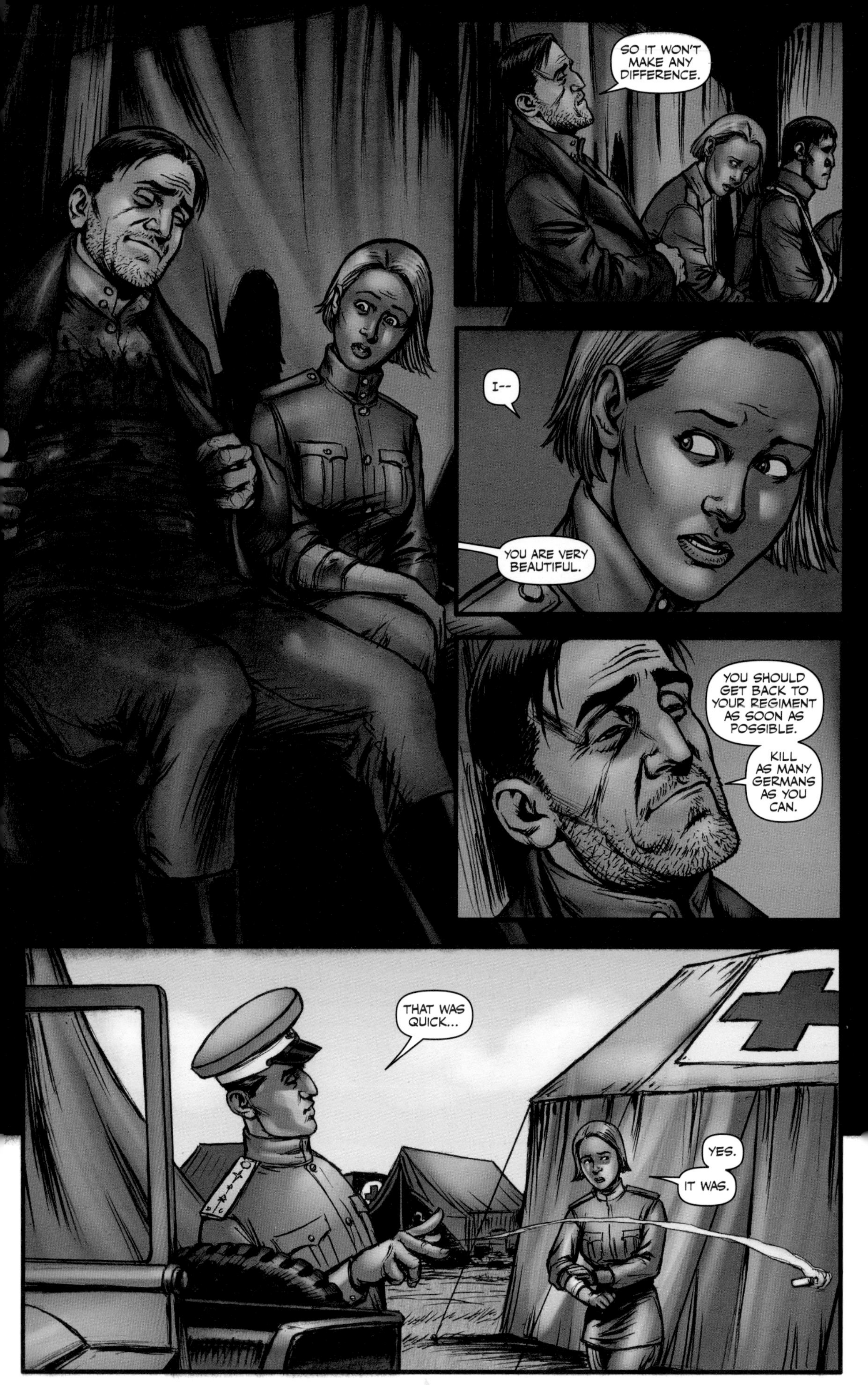
SO IT WON'T MAKE ANY DIFFERENCE.
I--
YOU ARE VERY BEAUTIFUL.
YOU SHOULD GET BACK TO YOUR REGIMENT AS SOON AS POSSIBLE.
KILL AS MANY GERMANS AS YOU CAN.
THAT WAS QUICK...
YES.
IT WAS.

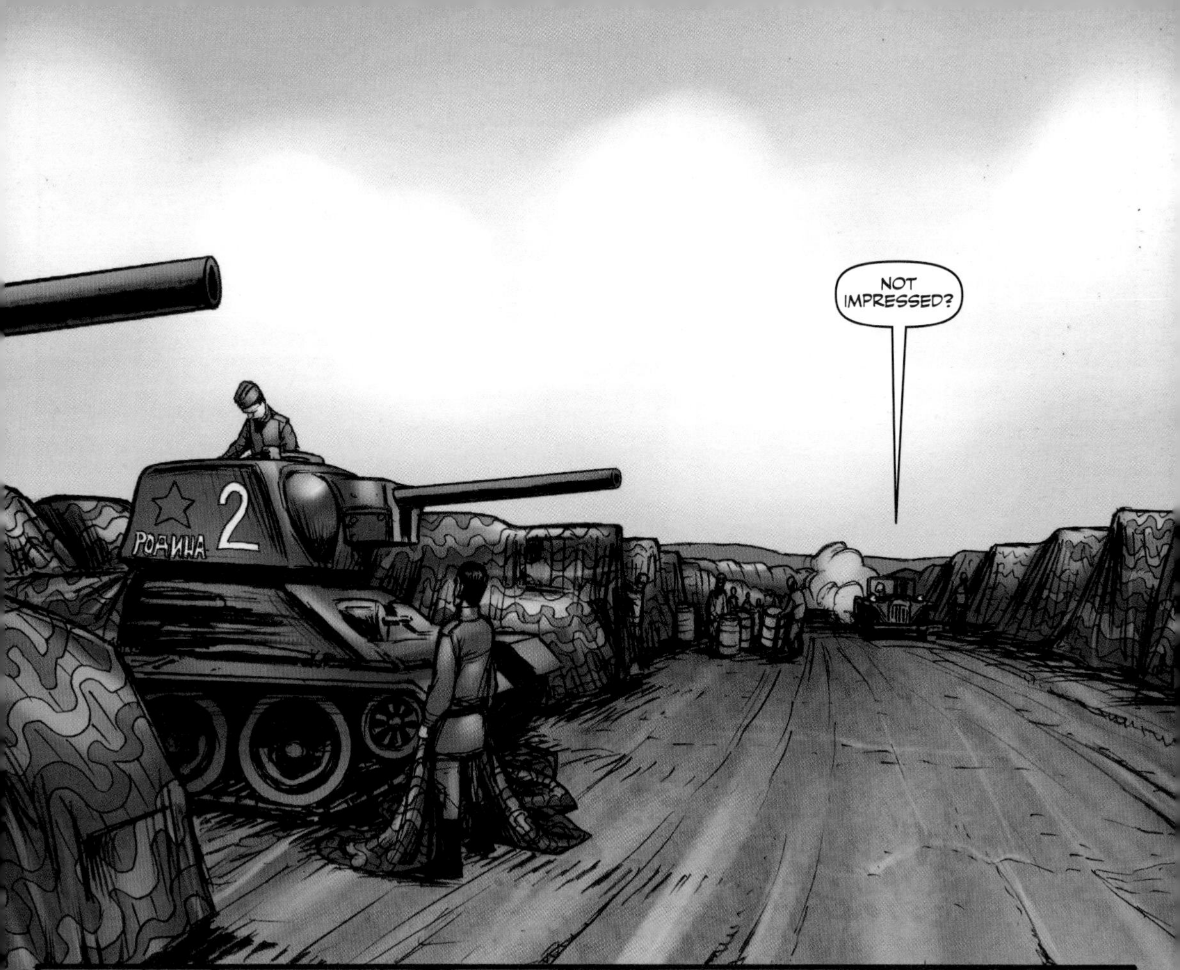

NOT IMPRESSED?
РОДИНА
2

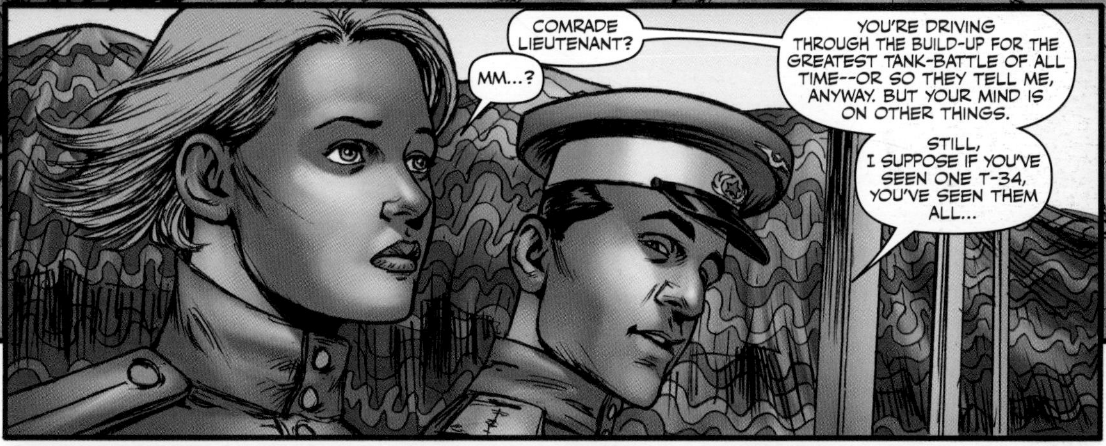

COMRADE LIEUTENANT?
MM...?
YOU'RE DRIVING THROUGH THE BUILD-UP FOR THE GREATEST TANK-BATTLE OF ALL TIME--OR SO THEY TELL ME, ANYWAY. BUT YOUR MIND IS ON OTHER THINGS.
STILL, I SUPPOSE IF YOU'VE SEEN ONE T-34, YOU'VE SEEN THEM ALL...

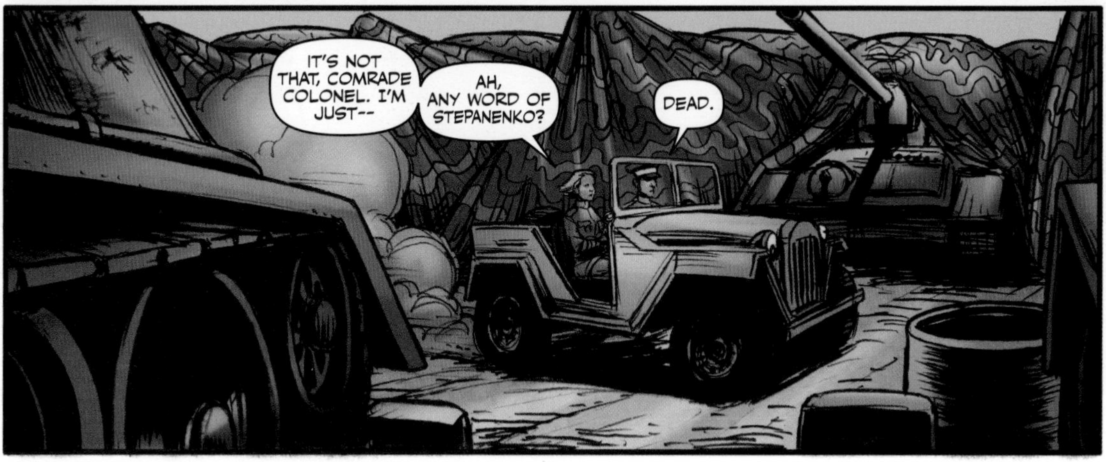

IT'S NOT THAT, COMRADE COLONEL. I'M JUST--
AH, ANY WORD OF STEPANENKO?
DEAD.

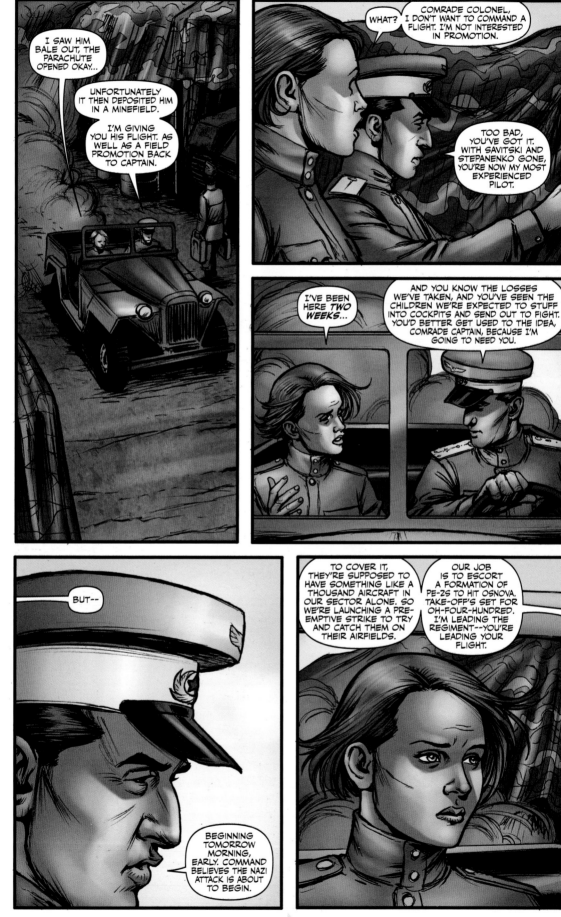

I SAW HIM BALE OUT, THE PARACHUTE OPENED OKAY...

UNFORTUNATELY IT THEN DEPOSITED HIM IN A MINEFIELD.

I'M GIVING YOU HIS FLIGHT. AS WELL AS A FIELD PROMOTION BACK TO CAPTAIN.

WHAT?

COMRADE COLONEL, I DON'T WANT TO COMMAND A FLIGHT. I'M NOT INTERESTED IN PROMOTION.

TOO BAD, YOU'VE GOT IT. WITH SAVITSKI AND STEPANENKO GONE, YOU'RE NOW MY MOST EXPERIENCED PILOT.

I'VE BEEN HERE TWO WEEKS...

AND YOU KNOW THE LOSSES WE'VE TAKEN, AND YOU'VE SEEN THE CHILDREN WE'RE EXPECTED TO STUFF INTO COCKPITS AND SEND OUT TO FIGHT. YOU'D BETTER GET USED TO THE IDEA, COMRADE CAPTAIN, BECAUSE I'M GOING TO NEED YOU.

BUT--

BEGINNING TOMORROW MORNING, EARLY. COMMAND BELIEVES THE NAZI ATTACK IS ABOUT TO BEGIN.

TO COVER IT, THEY'RE SUPPOSED TO HAVE SOMETHING LIKE A THOUSAND AIRCRAFT IN OUR SECTOR ALONE. SO WE'RE LAUNCHING A PRE-EMPTIVE STRIKE TO TRY AND CATCH THEM ON THEIR AIRFIELDS.

OUR JOB IS TO ESCORT A FORMATION OF PE-2S TO HIT OSNOVA. TAKE-OFF'S SET FOR OH-FOUR-HUNDRED. I'M LEADING THE REGIMENT--YOU'RE LEADING YOUR FLIGHT.

102

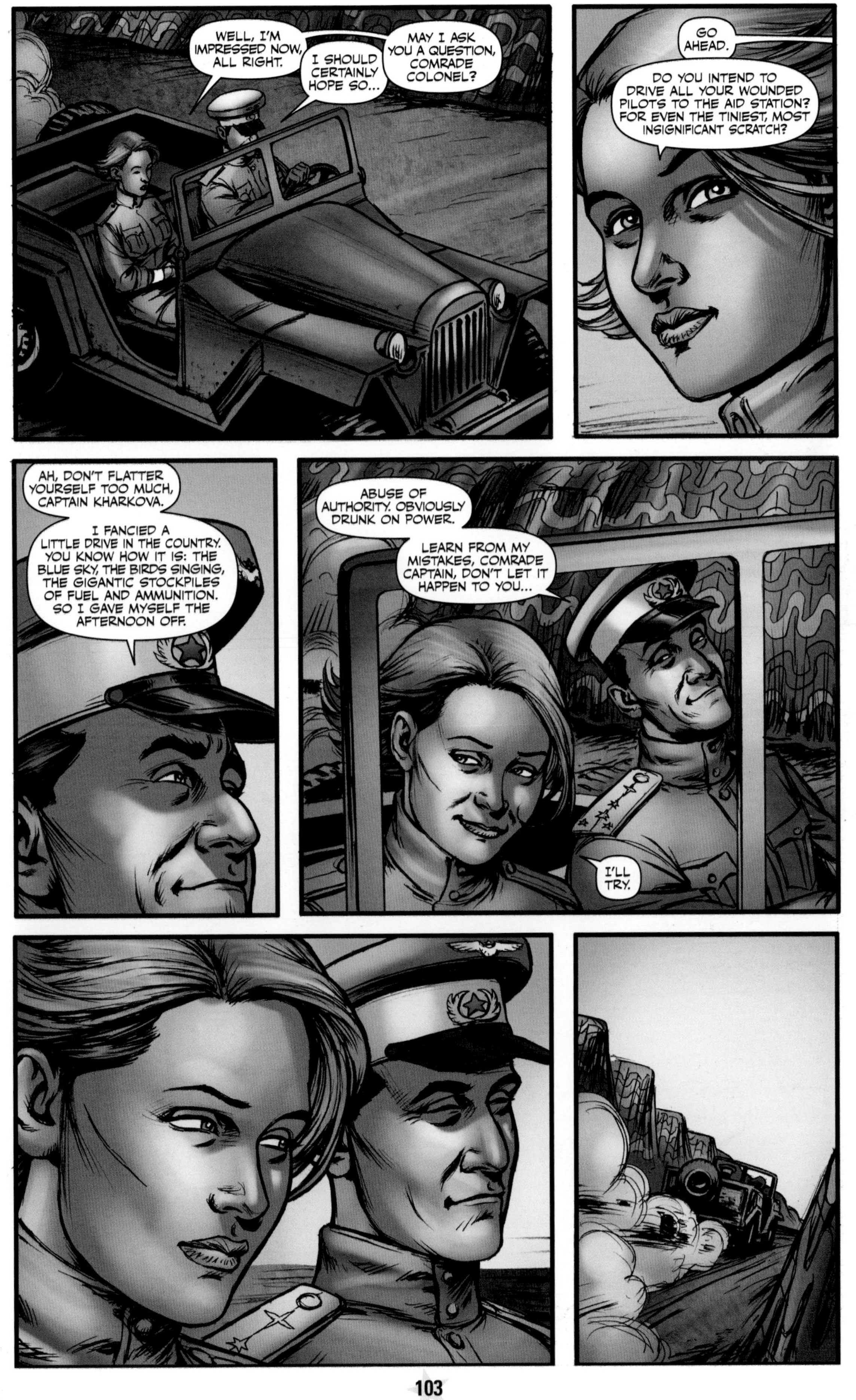
WELL, I'M IMPRESSED NOW, ALL RIGHT.
I SHOULD CERTAINLY HOPE SO...
MAY I ASK YOU A QUESTION, COMRADE COLONEL?
GO AHEAD.
DO YOU INTEND TO DRIVE ALL YOUR WOUNDED PILOTS TO THE AID STATION? FOR EVEN THE TINIEST, MOST INSIGNIFICANT SCRATCH?
AH, DON'T FLATTER YOURSELF TOO MUCH, CAPTAIN KHARKOVA.
I FANCIED A LITTLE DRIVE IN THE COUNTRY. YOU KNOW HOW IT IS: THE BLUE SKY, THE BIRDS SINGING, THE GIGANTIC STOCKPILES OF FUEL AND AMMUNITION. SO I GAVE MYSELF THE AFTERNOON OFF.
ABUSE OF AUTHORITY. OBVIOUSLY DRUNK ON POWER.
LEARN FROM MY MISTAKES, COMRADE CAPTAIN, DON'T LET IT HAPPEN TO YOU...
I'LL TRY.

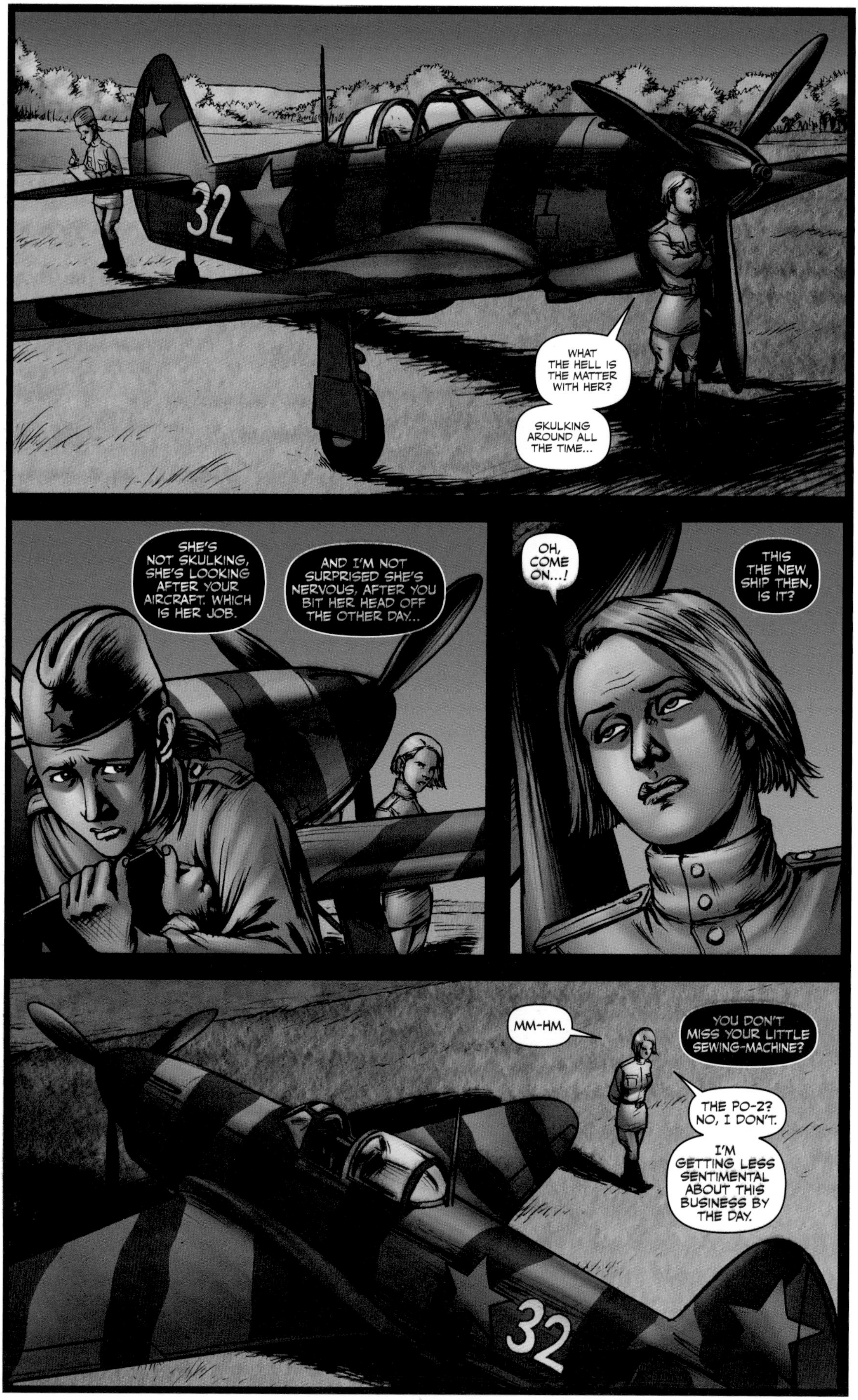
WHAT THE HELL IS THE MATTER WITH HER?
SKULKING AROUND ALL THE TIME...
SHE'S NOT SKULKING, SHE'S LOOKING AFTER YOUR AIRCRAFT. WHICH IS HER JOB.
AND I'M NOT SURPRISED SHE'S NERVOUS, AFTER YOU BIT HER HEAD OFF THE OTHER DAY...
OH, COME ON...!
THIS THE NEW SHIP THEN, IS IT?
MM-HM.
YOU DON'T MISS YOUR LITTLE SEWING-MACHINE?
THE PO-2? NO, I DON'T.
I'M GETTING LESS SENTIMENTAL ABOUT THIS BUSINESS BY THE DAY.

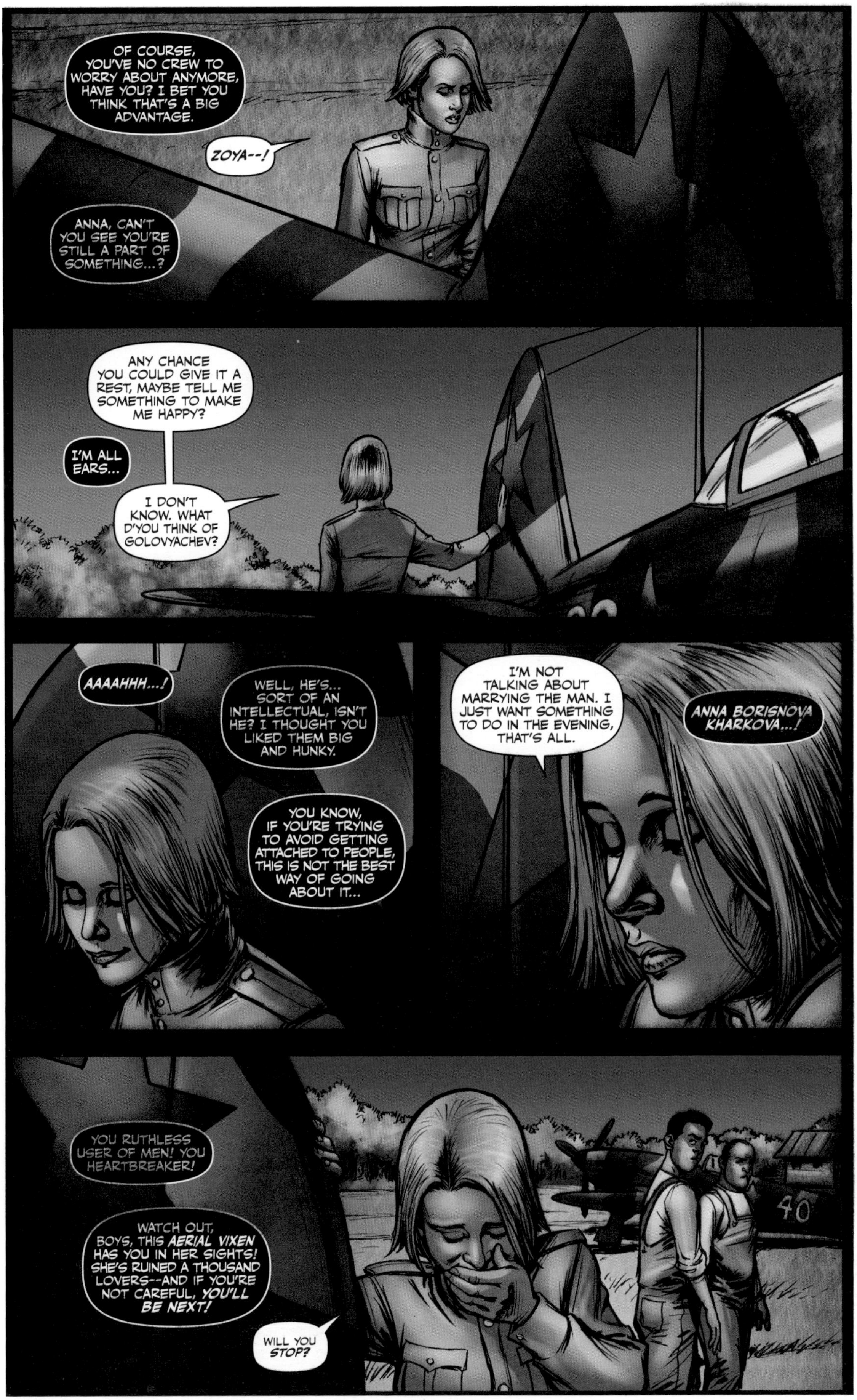
OF COURSE, YOU'VE NO CREW TO WORRY ABOUT ANYMORE, HAVE YOU? I BET YOU THINK THAT'S A BIG ADVANTAGE.
ZOYA--!
ANNA, CAN'T YOU SEE YOU'RE STILL A PART OF SOMETHING...?
ANY CHANCE YOU COULD GIVE IT A REST, MAYBE TELL ME SOMETHING TO MAKE ME HAPPY?
I'M ALL EARS...
I DON'T KNOW. WHAT D'YOU THINK OF GOLOVYACHEV?
AAAAHHH...!
WELL, HE'S... SORT OF AN INTELLECTUAL, ISN'T HE? I THOUGHT YOU LIKED THEM BIG AND HUNKY.
YOU KNOW, IF YOU'RE TRYING TO AVOID GETTING ATTACHED TO PEOPLE, THIS IS NOT THE BEST WAY OF GOING ABOUT IT...
I'M NOT TALKING ABOUT MARRYING THE MAN. I JUST WANT SOMETHING TO DO IN THE EVENING, THAT'S ALL.
ANNA BORISNOVA KHARKOVA...!
YOU RUTHLESS USER OF MEN! YOU HEARTBREAKER!
WATCH OUT, BOYS, THIS AERIAL VIXEN HAS YOU IN HER SIGHTS! SHE'S RUINED A THOUSAND LOVERS--AND IF YOU'RE NOT CAREFUL, YOU'LL BE NEXT!
WILL YOU STOP?
40

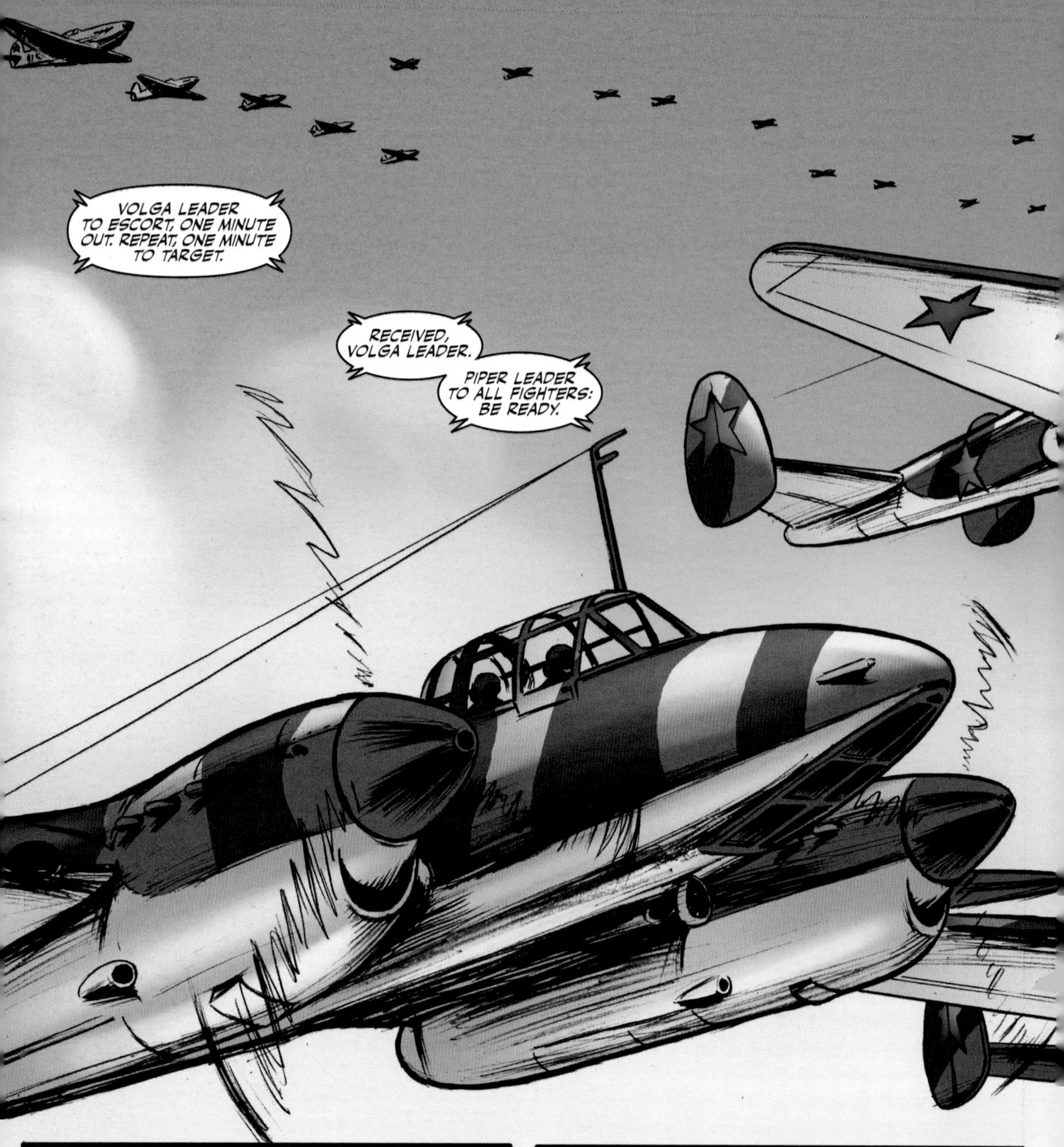
VOLGA LEADER TO ESCORT, ONE MINUTE OUT. REPEAT, ONE MINUTE TO TARGET.
RECEIVED, VOLGA LEADER.
PIPER LEADER TO ALL FIGHTERS: BE READY.

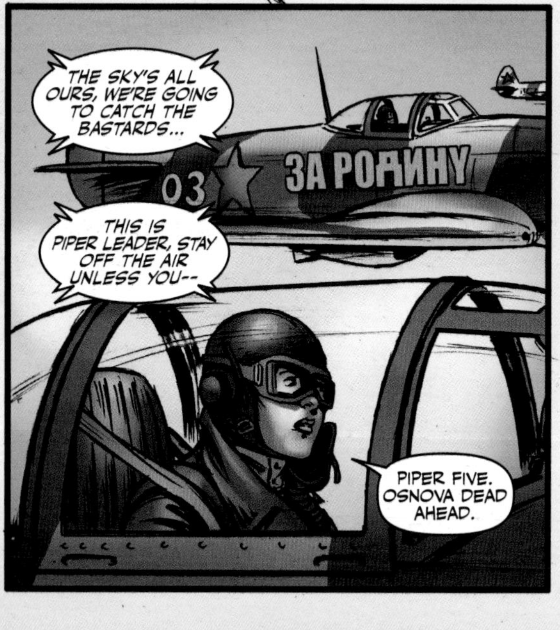
THE SKY'S ALL OURS, WE'RE GOING TO CATCH THE BASTARDS...
03
ЗА РОДИНУ
THIS IS PIPER LEADER, STAY OFF THE AIR UNLESS YOU--
PIPER FIVE. OSNOVA DEAD AHEAD.

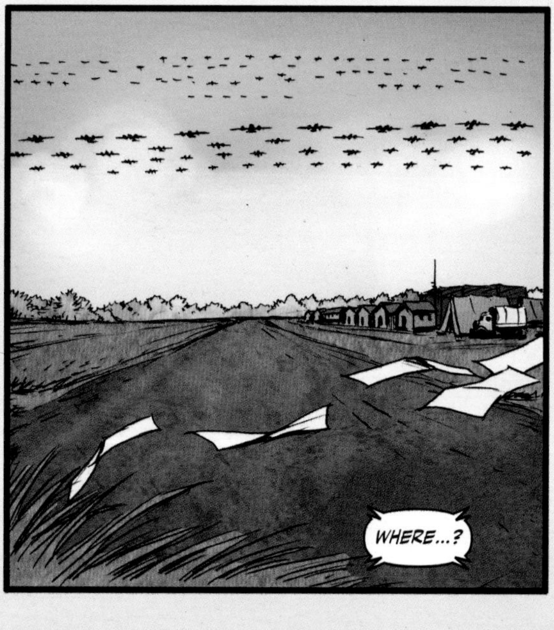
WHERE...?

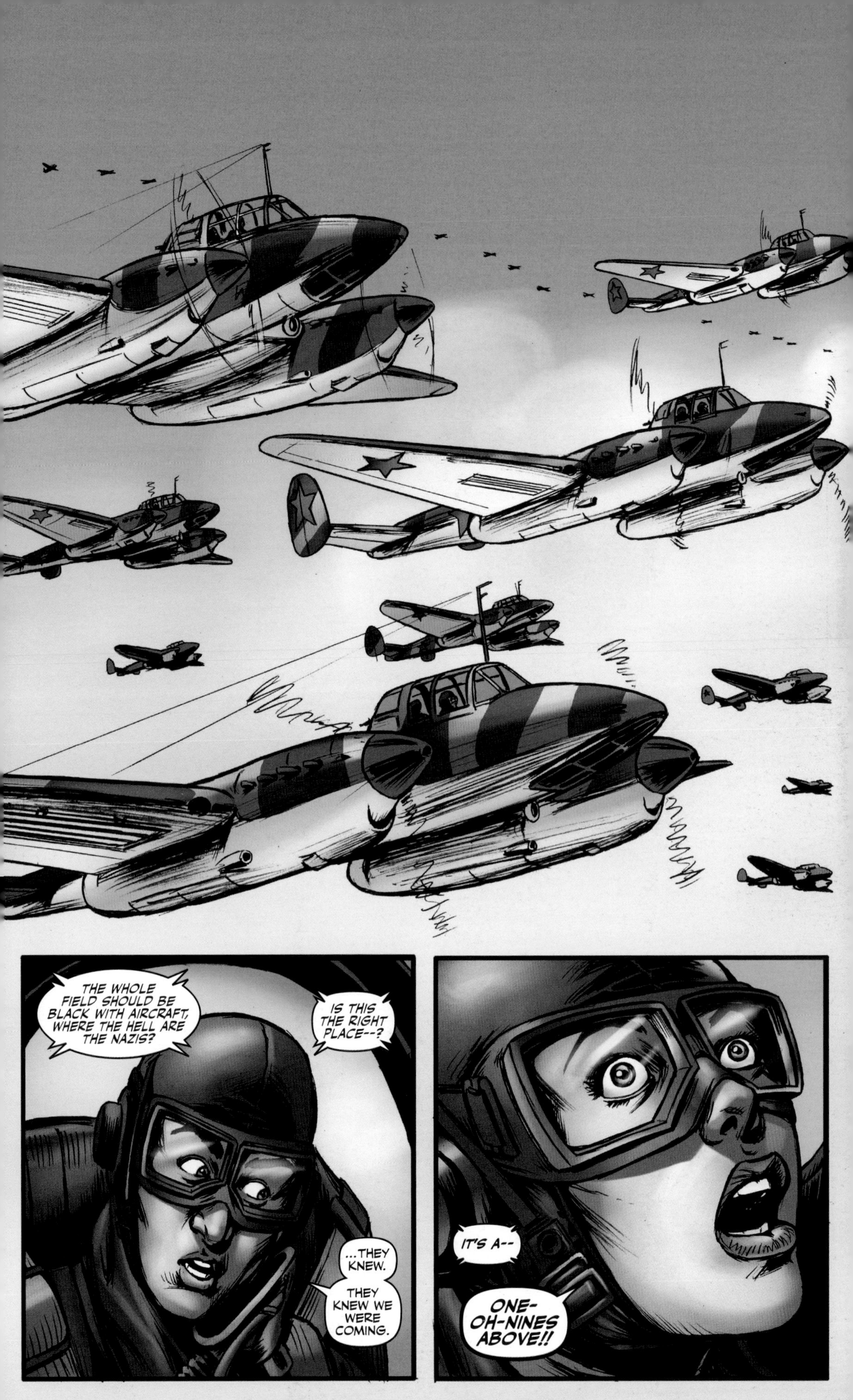

THE WHOLE FIELD SHOULD BE BLACK WITH AIRCRAFT, WHERE THE HELL ARE THE NAZIS?
IS THIS THE RIGHT PLACE--?
...THEY KNEW.
THEY KNEW WE WERE COMING.
IT'S A--
ONE-OH-NINES ABOVE!!

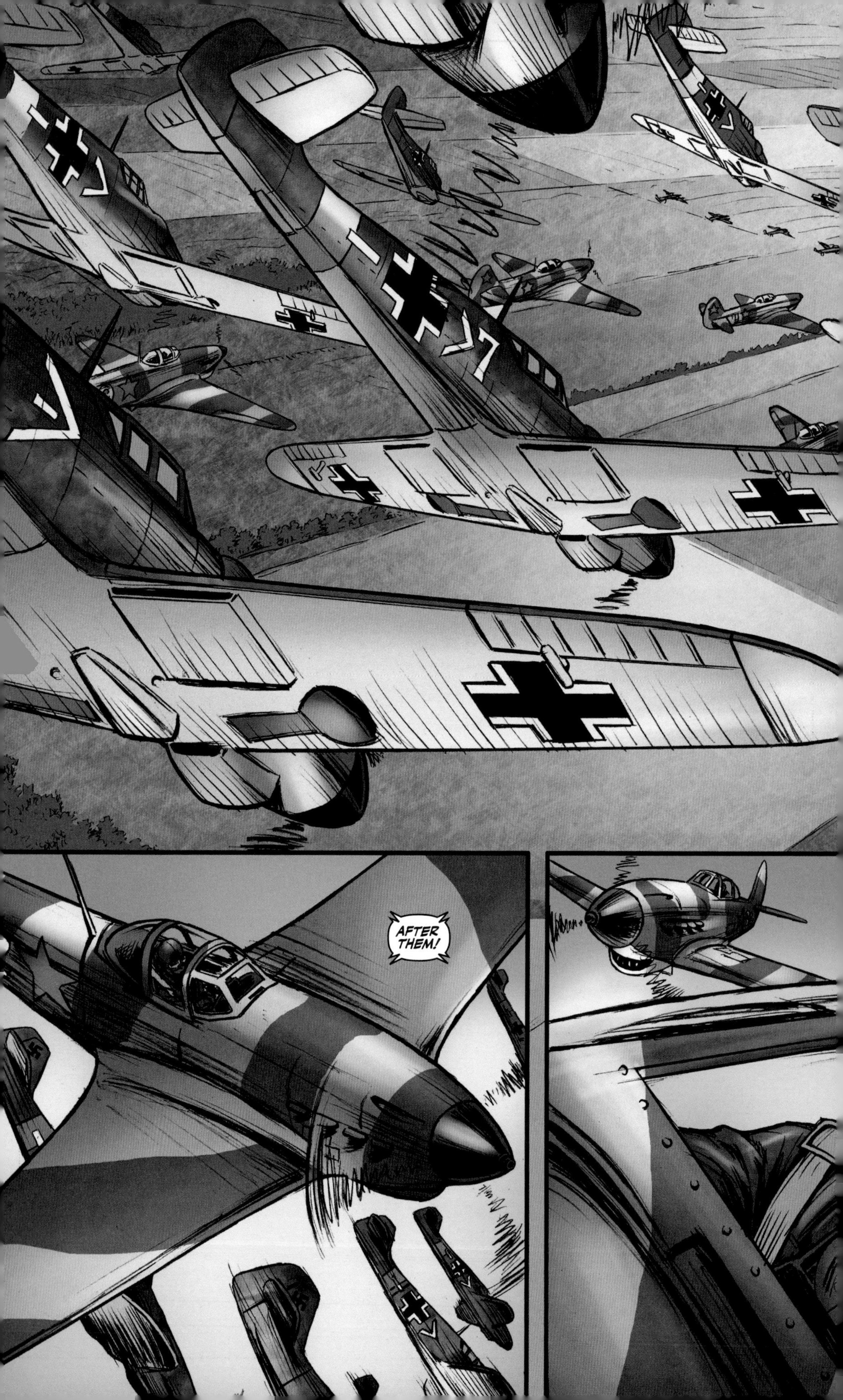
AFTER THEM!

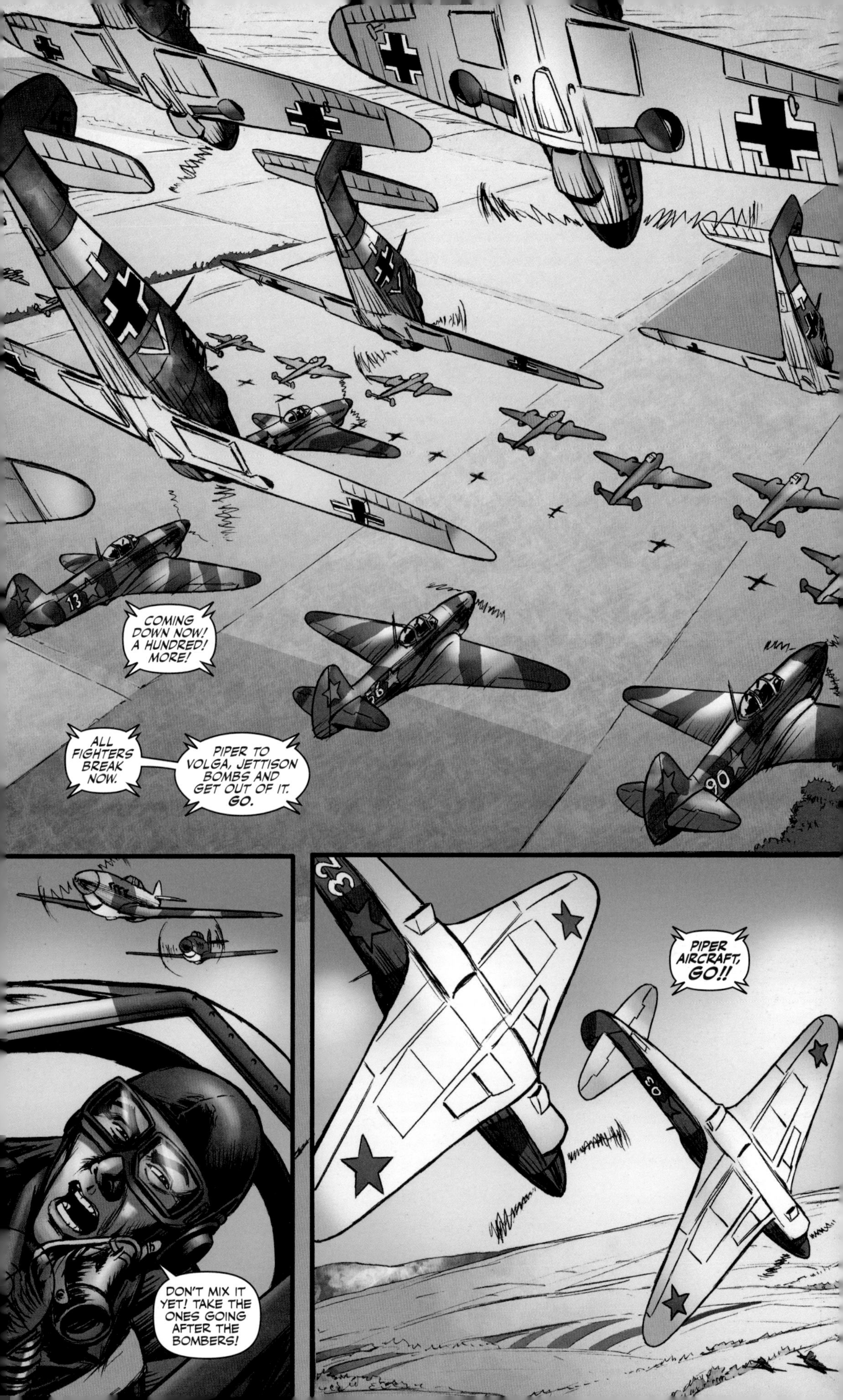
COMING DOWN NOW! A HUNDRED! MORE!
ALL FIGHTERS BREAK NOW.
PIPER TO VOLGA, JETTISON BOMBS AND GET OUT OF IT. GO.
DON'T MIX IT YET! TAKE THE ONES GOING AFTER THE BOMBERS!
PIPER AIRCRAFT, GO!!

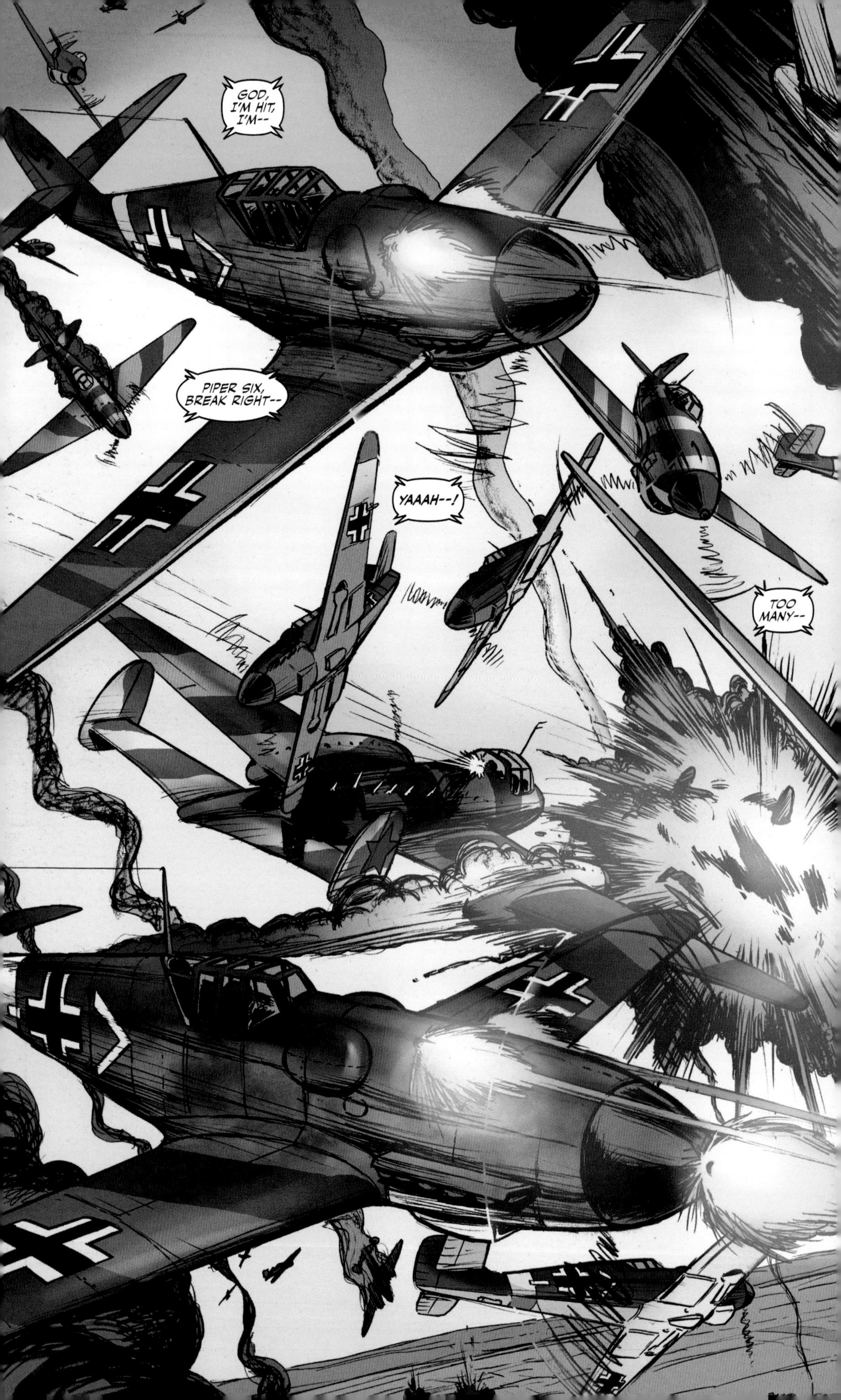
GOD, I'M HIT, I'M--
PIPER SIX, BREAK RIGHT--
YAAAH--!
TOO MANY--

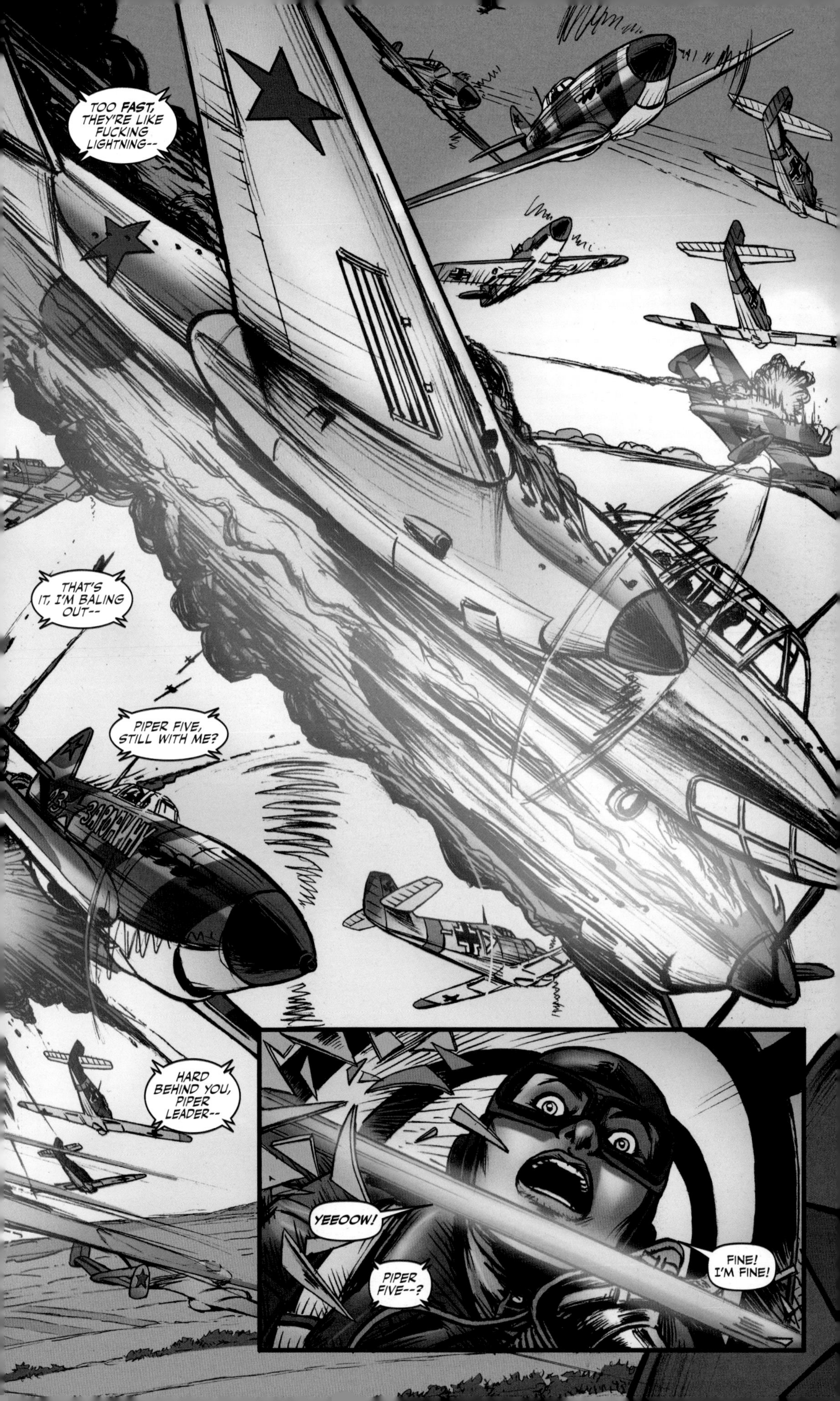
TOO FAST, THEY'RE LIKE FUCKING LIGHTNING--
THAT'S IT, I'M BALING OUT--
PIPER FIVE, STILL WITH ME?
HARD BEHIND YOU, PIPER LEADER--
YEEOOW!
PIPER FIVE--?
FINE! I'M FINE!

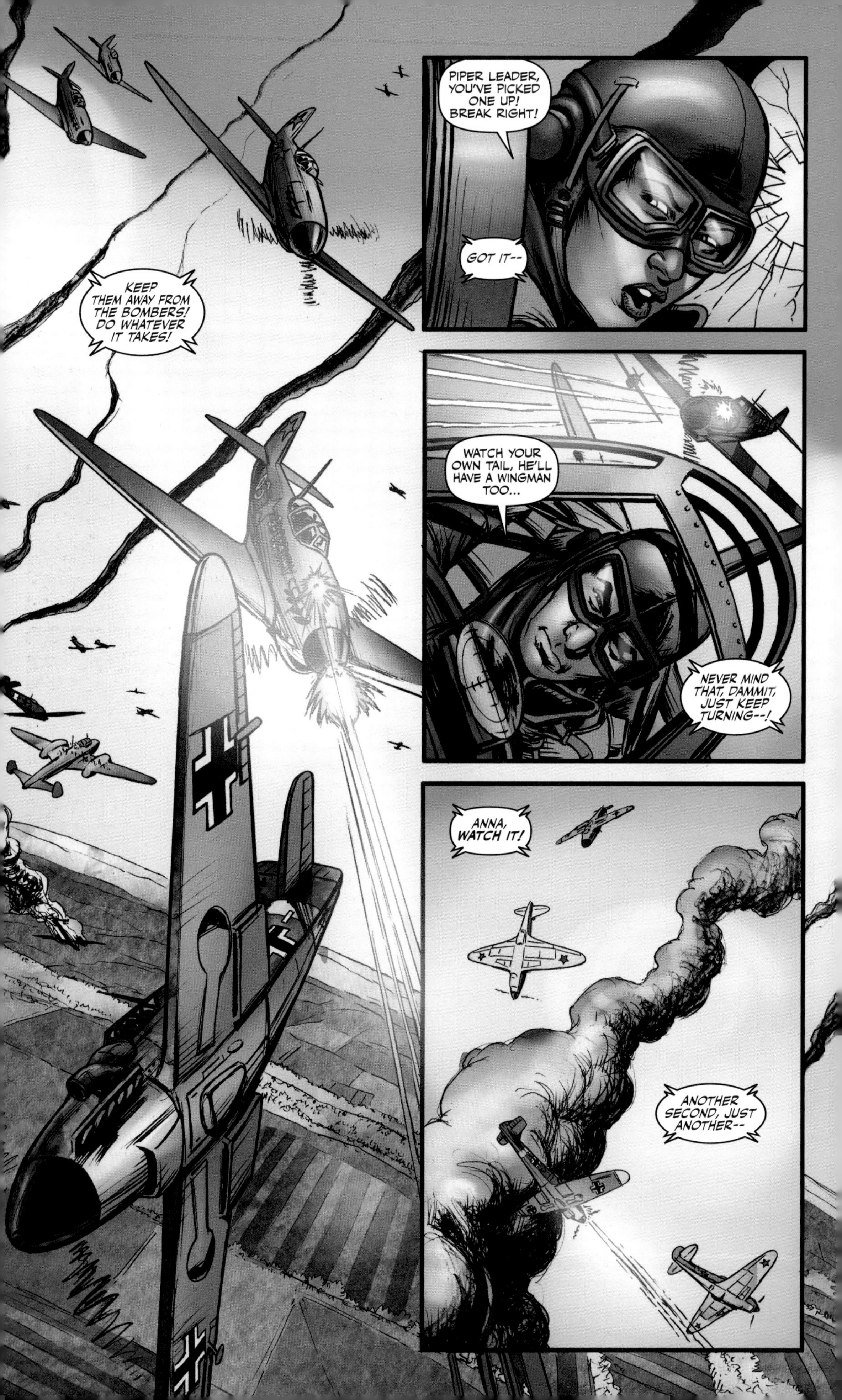
KEEP THEM AWAY FROM THE BOMBERS! DO WHATEVER IT TAKES!
PIPER LEADER, YOU'VE PICKED ONE UP! BREAK RIGHT!
GOT IT--
WATCH YOUR OWN TAIL, HE'LL HAVE A WINGMAN TOO...
NEVER MIND THAT, DAMMIT, JUST KEEP TURNING--!
ANNA, WATCH IT!
ANOTHER SECOND, JUST ANOTHER--

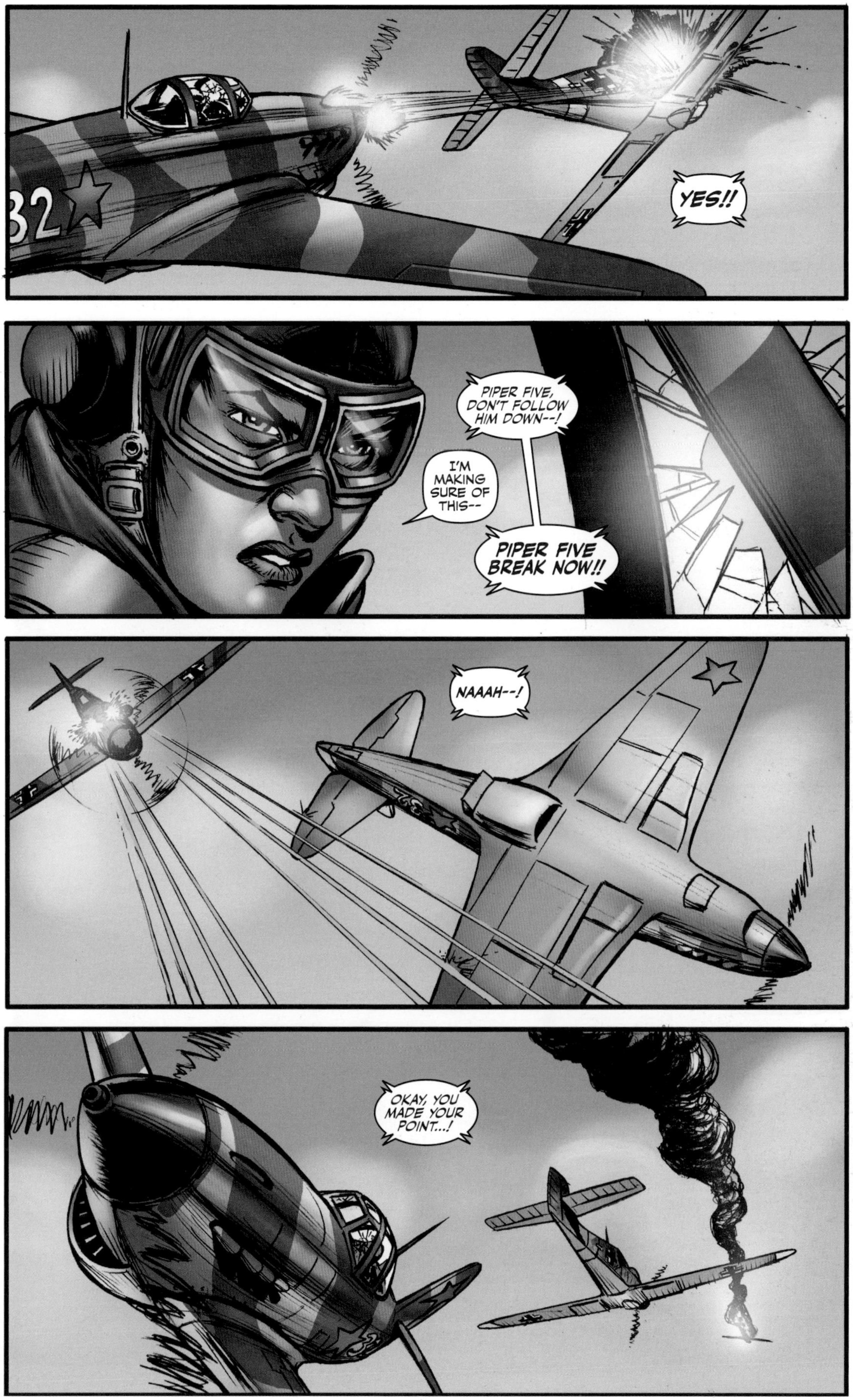
YES!!
PIPER FIVE, DON'T FOLLOW HIM DOWN--!
I'M MAKING SURE OF THIS--
PIPER FIVE BREAK NOW!!
NAAAH--!
OKAY, YOU MADE YOUR POINT...!

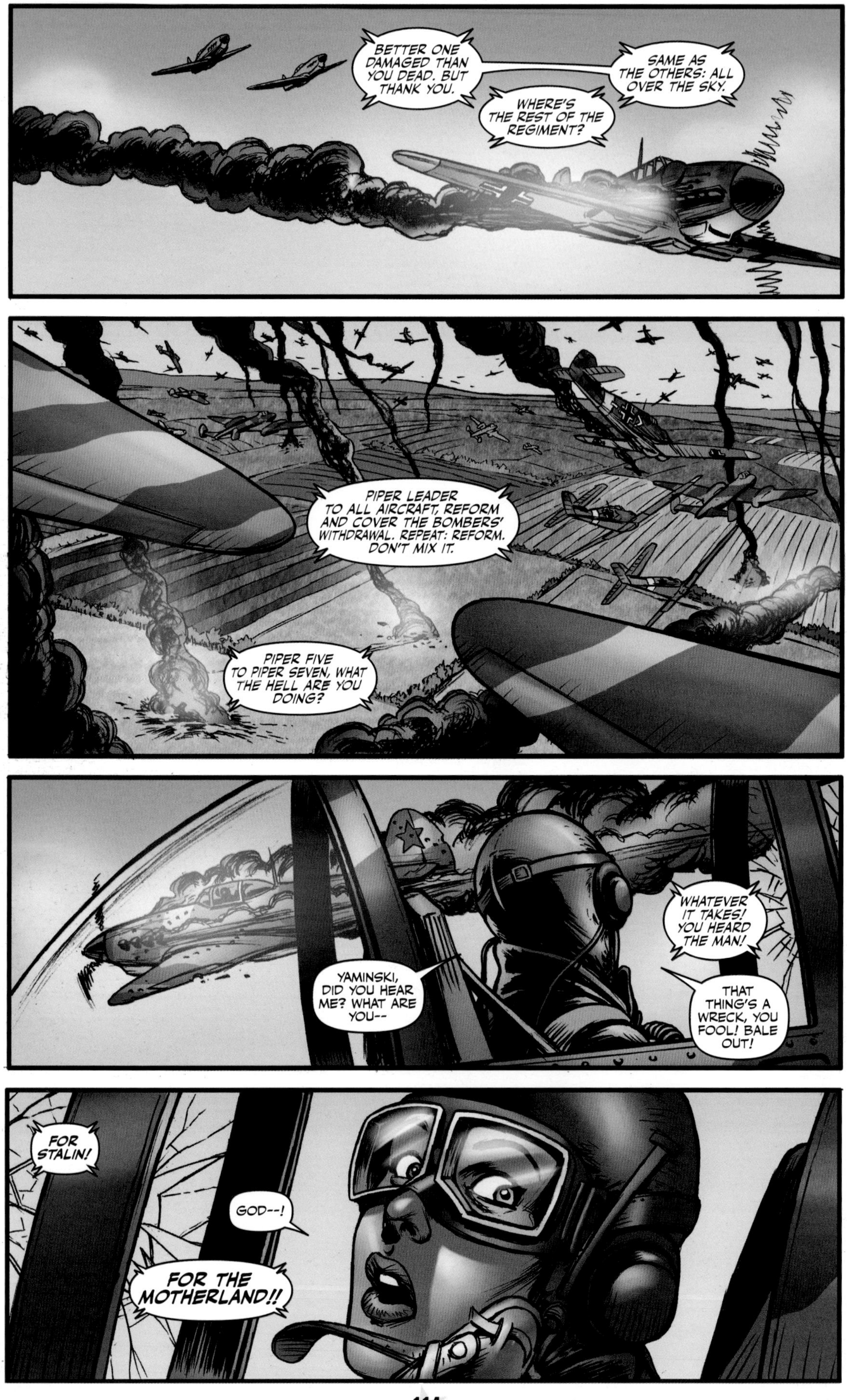

BETTER ONE DAMAGED THAN YOU DEAD. BUT THANK YOU.
WHERE'S THE REST OF THE REGIMENT?
SAME AS THE OTHERS: ALL OVER THE SKY.
PIPER LEADER TO ALL AIRCRAFT, REFORM AND COVER THE BOMBERS' WITHDRAWAL. REPEAT: REFORM. DON'T MIX IT.
PIPER FIVE TO PIPER SEVEN, WHAT THE HELL ARE YOU DOING?
YAMINSKI, DID YOU HEAR ME? WHAT ARE YOU--
WHATEVER IT TAKES! YOU HEARD THE MAN!
THAT THING'S A WRECK, YOU FOOL! BALE OUT!
FOR STALIN!
GOD--!
FOR THE MOTHERLAND!!

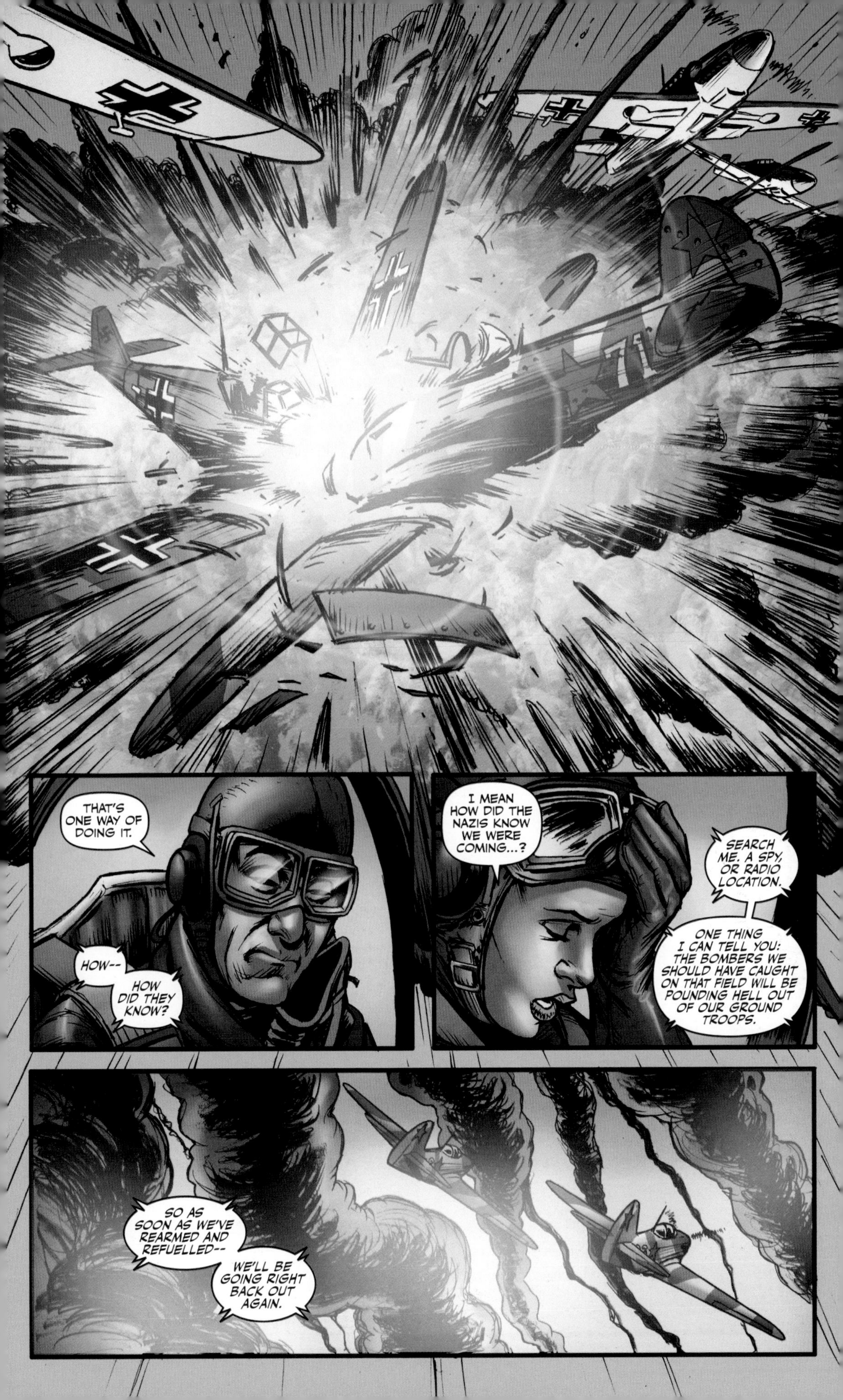
THAT'S ONE WAY OF DOING IT.
HOW--
HOW DID THEY KNOW?
I MEAN HOW DID THE NAZIS KNOW WE WERE COMING...?
SEARCH ME. A SPY, OR RADIO LOCATION.
ONE THING I CAN TELL YOU: THE BOMBERS WE SHOULD HAVE CAUGHT ON THAT FIELD WILL BE POUNDING HELL OUT OF OUR GROUND TROOPS.
SO AS SOON AS WE'VE REARMED AND REFUELLED--
WE'LL BE GOING RIGHT BACK OUT AGAIN.

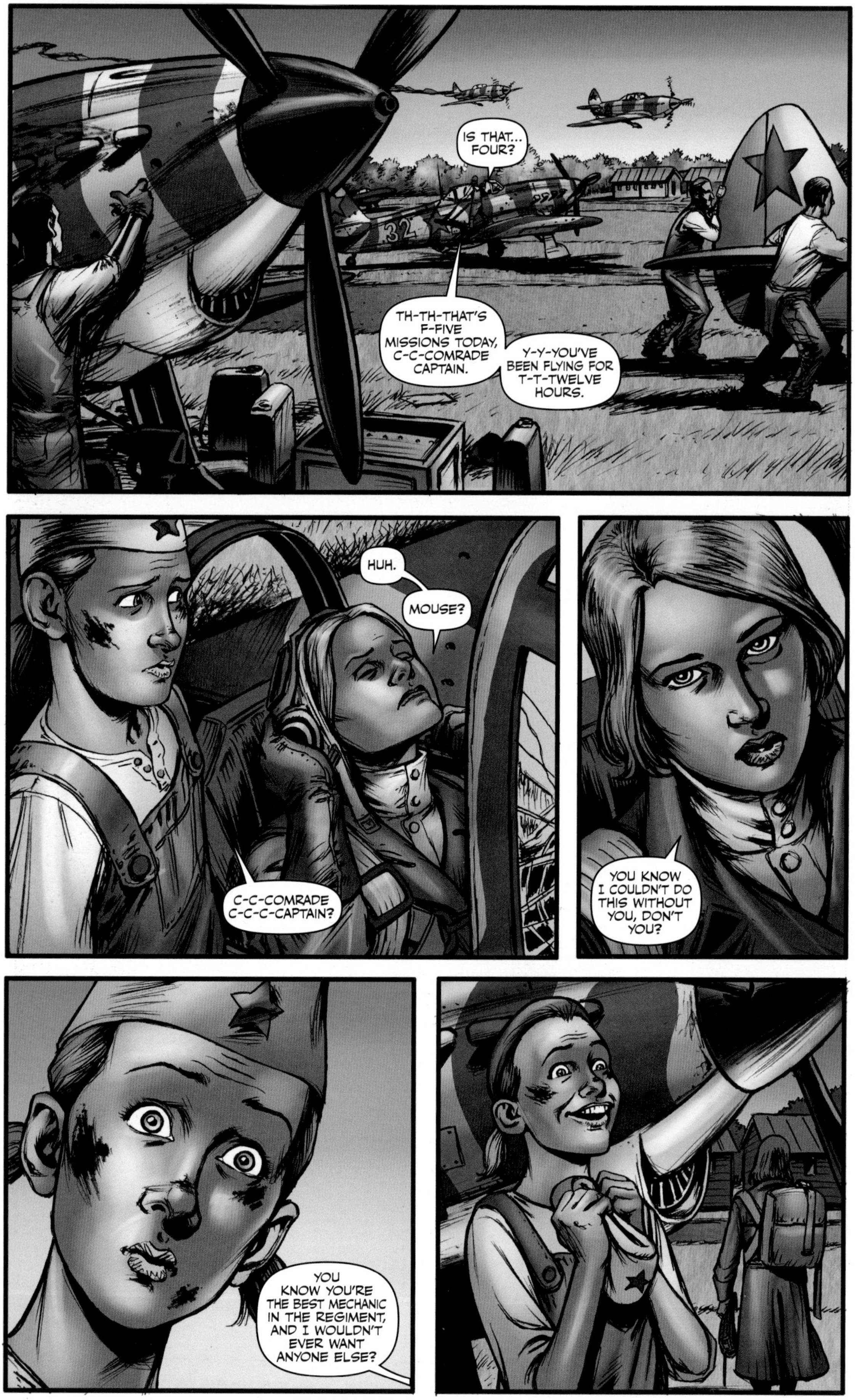
IS THAT... FOUR?
TH-TH-THAT'S F-FIVE MISSIONS TODAY, C-C-COMRADE CAPTAIN.
Y-Y-YOU'VE BEEN FLYING FOR T-T-TWELVE HOURS.
32
HUH.
MOUSE?
C-C-COMRADE C-C-C-CAPTAIN?
YOU KNOW I COULDN'T DO THIS WITHOUT YOU, DON'T YOU?
YOU KNOW YOU'RE THE BEST MECHANIC IN THE REGIMENT, AND I WOULDN'T EVER WANT ANYONE ELSE?

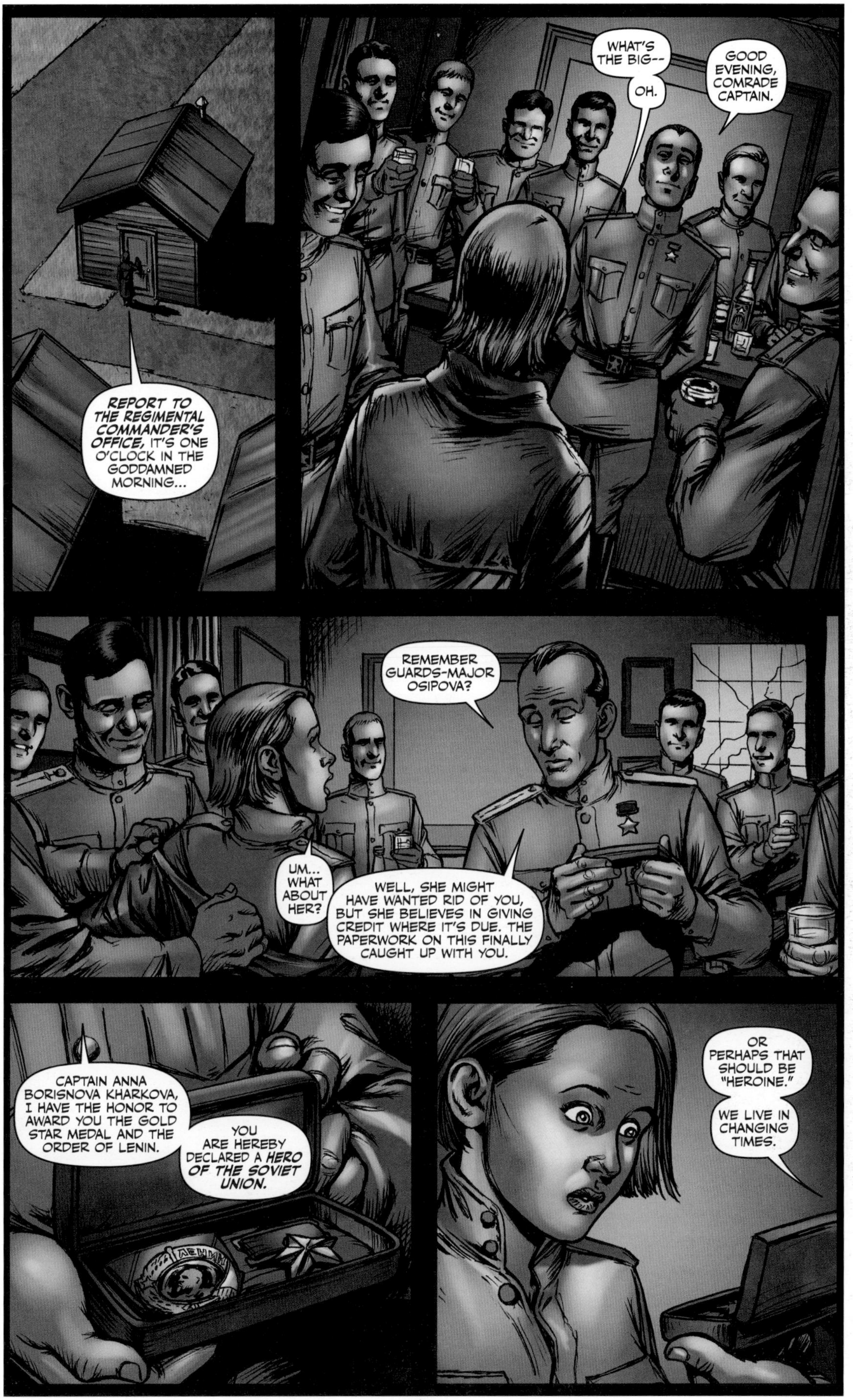
REPORT TO THE REGIMENTAL COMMANDER'S OFFICE, IT'S ONE O'CLOCK IN THE GODDAMNED MORNING...
WHAT'S THE BIG--
OH.
GOOD EVENING, COMRADE CAPTAIN.
REMEMBER GUARDS-MAJOR OSIPOVA?
UM... WHAT ABOUT HER?
WELL, SHE MIGHT HAVE WANTED RID OF YOU, BUT SHE BELIEVES IN GIVING CREDIT WHERE IT'S DUE. THE PAPERWORK ON THIS FINALLY CAUGHT UP WITH YOU.
CAPTAIN ANNA BORISNOVA KHARKOVA, I HAVE THE HONOR TO AWARD YOU THE GOLD STAR MEDAL AND THE ORDER OF LENIN.
YOU ARE HEREBY DECLARED A HERO OF THE SOVIET UNION.
OR PERHAPS THAT SHOULD BE "HEROINE."
WE LIVE IN CHANGING TIMES.

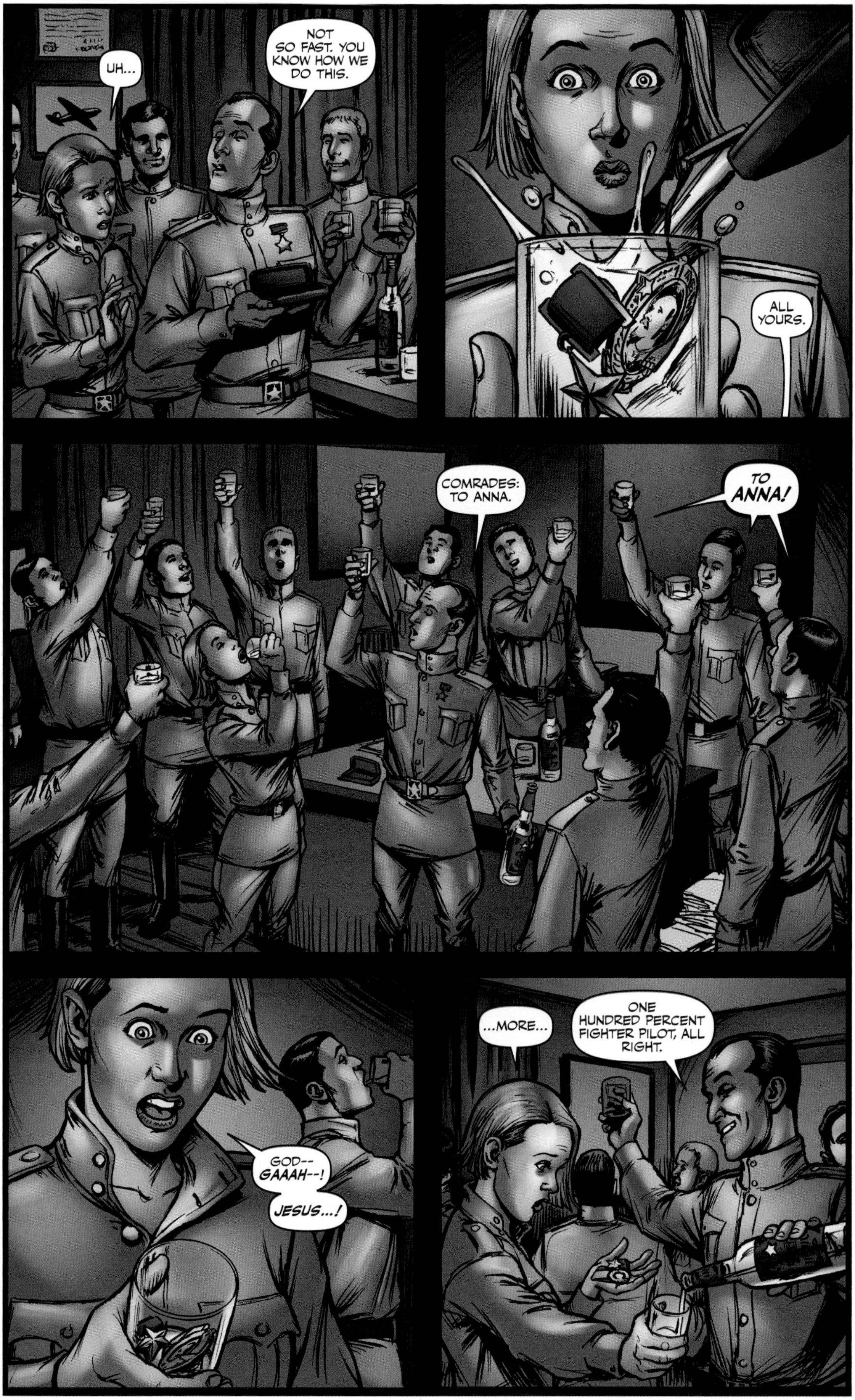
UH...
NOT SO FAST. YOU KNOW HOW WE DO THIS.
ALL YOURS.
COMRADES: TO ANNA.
TO ANNA!
GOD-- GAAAH--!
JESUS...!
...MORE...
ONE HUNDRED PERCENT FIGHTER PILOT, ALL RIGHT.

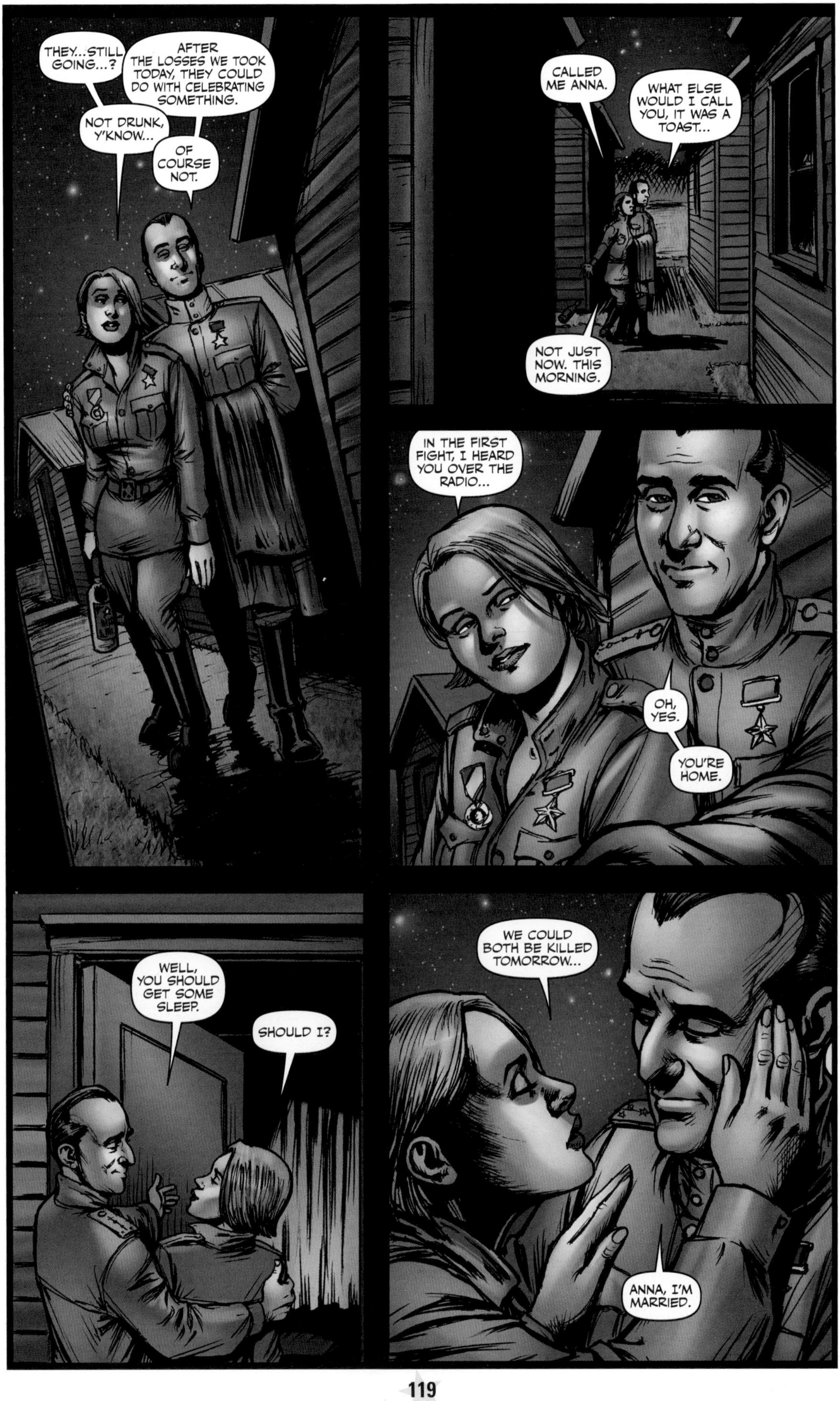
THEY...STILL GOING...?
AFTER THE LOSSES WE TOOK TODAY, THEY COULD DO WITH CELEBRATING SOMETHING.
NOT DRUNK, Y'KNOW...
OF COURSE NOT.
CALLED ME ANNA.
WHAT ELSE WOULD I CALL YOU, IT WAS A TOAST...
NOT JUST NOW. THIS MORNING.
IN THE FIRST FIGHT, I HEARD YOU OVER THE RADIO...
OH, YES.
YOU'RE HOME.
WELL, YOU SHOULD GET SOME SLEEP.
SHOULD I?
WE COULD BOTH BE KILLED TOMORROW...
ANNA, I'M MARRIED.

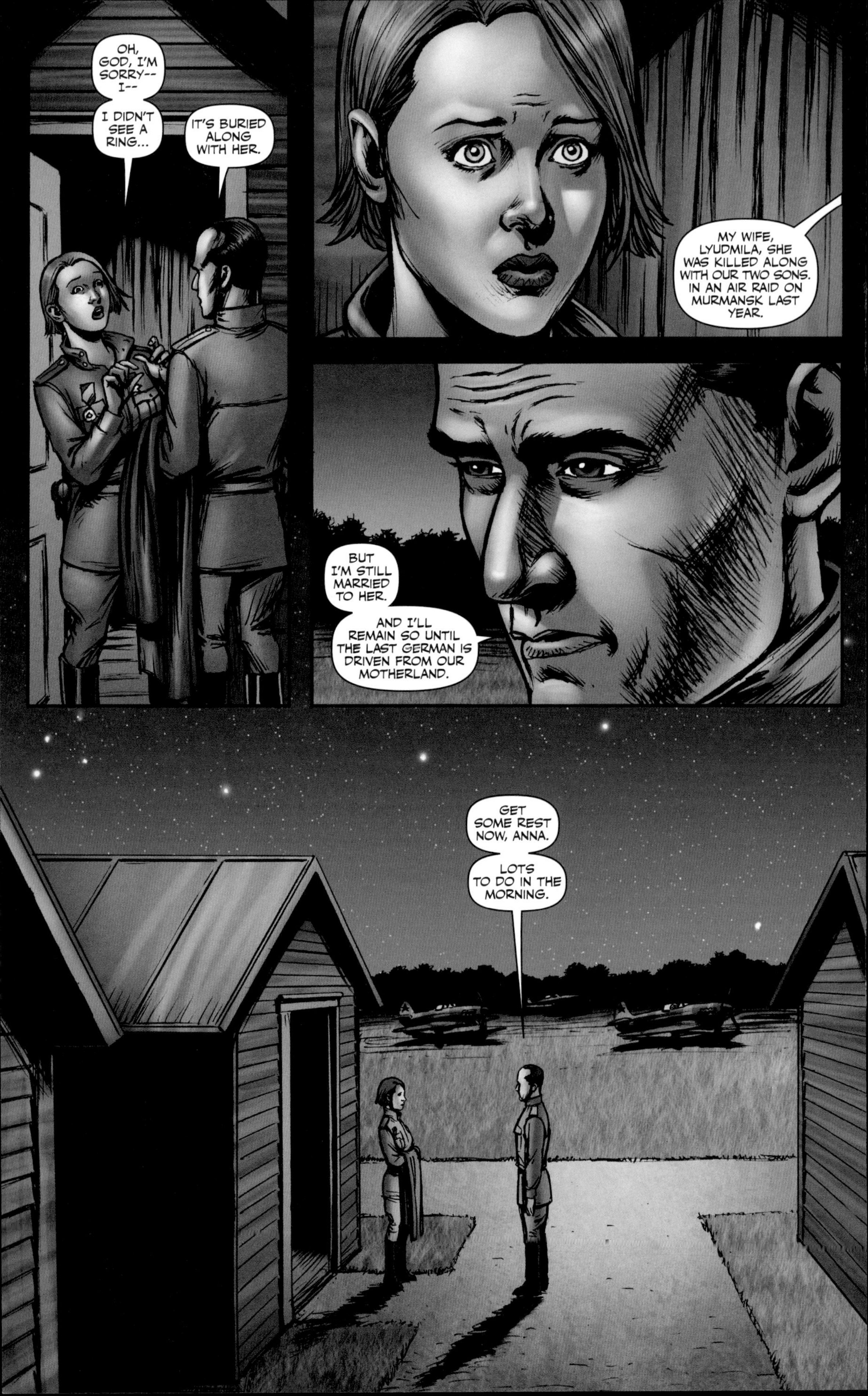
OH, GOD, I'M SORRY-- I--
I DIDN'T SEE A RING...
IT'S BURIED ALONG WITH HER.
MY WIFE, LYUDMILA, SHE WAS KILLED ALONG WITH OUR TWO SONS. IN AN AIR RAID ON MURMANSK LAST YEAR.
BUT I'M STILL MARRIED TO HER.
AND I'LL REMAIN SO UNTIL THE LAST GERMAN IS DRIVEN FROM OUR MOTHERLAND.
GET SOME REST NOW, ANNA.
LOTS TO DO IN THE MORNING.

Chapter 3

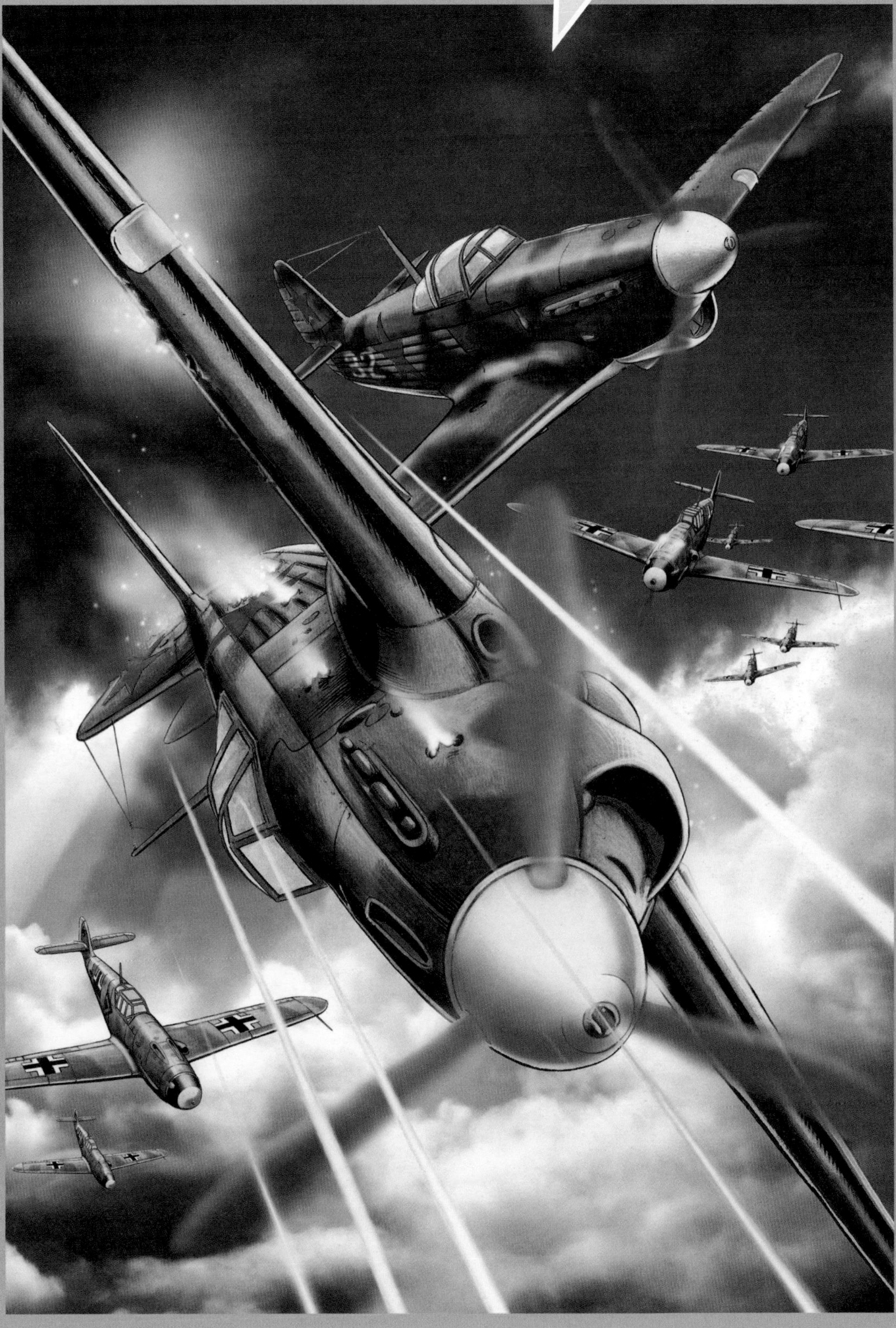

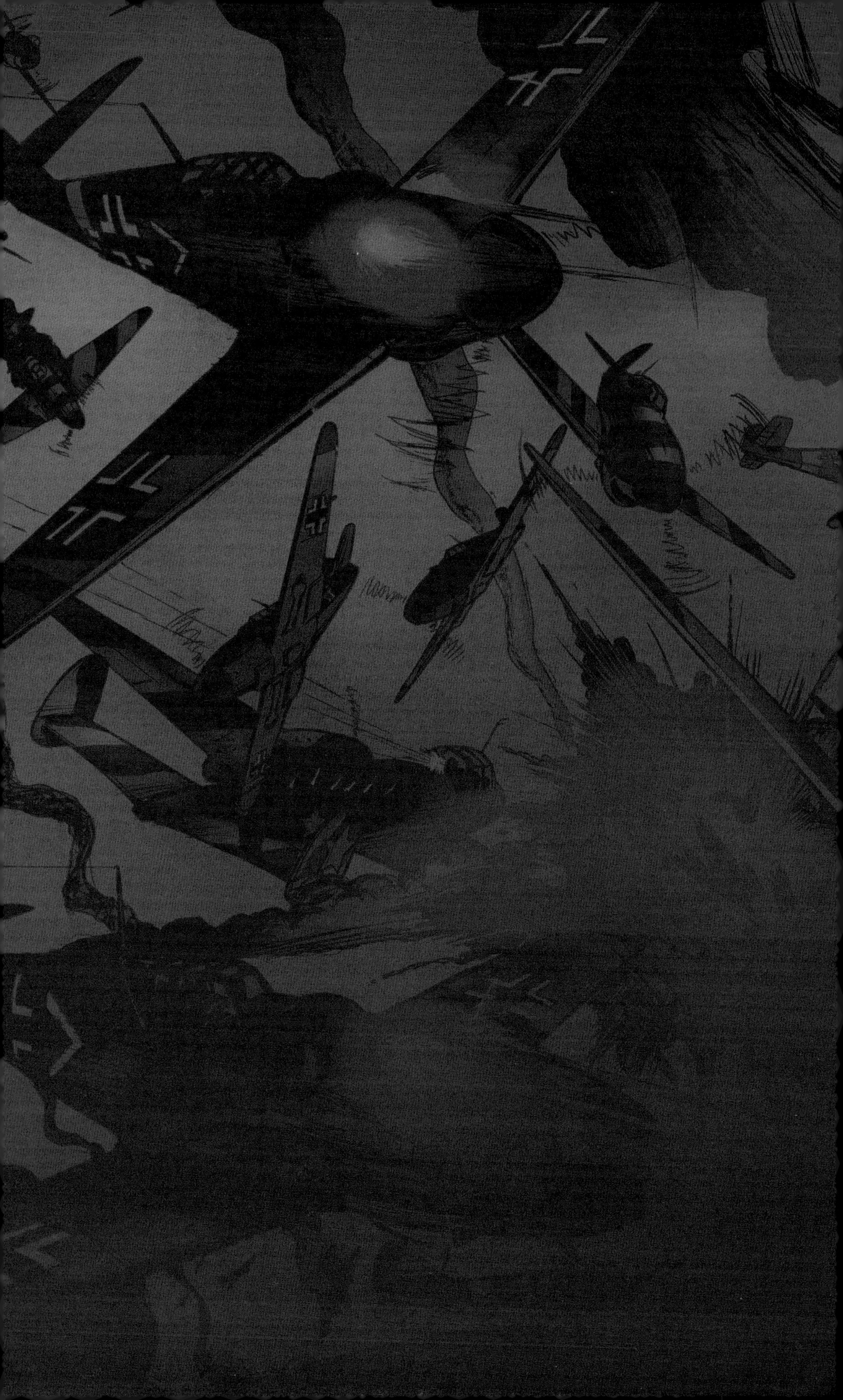

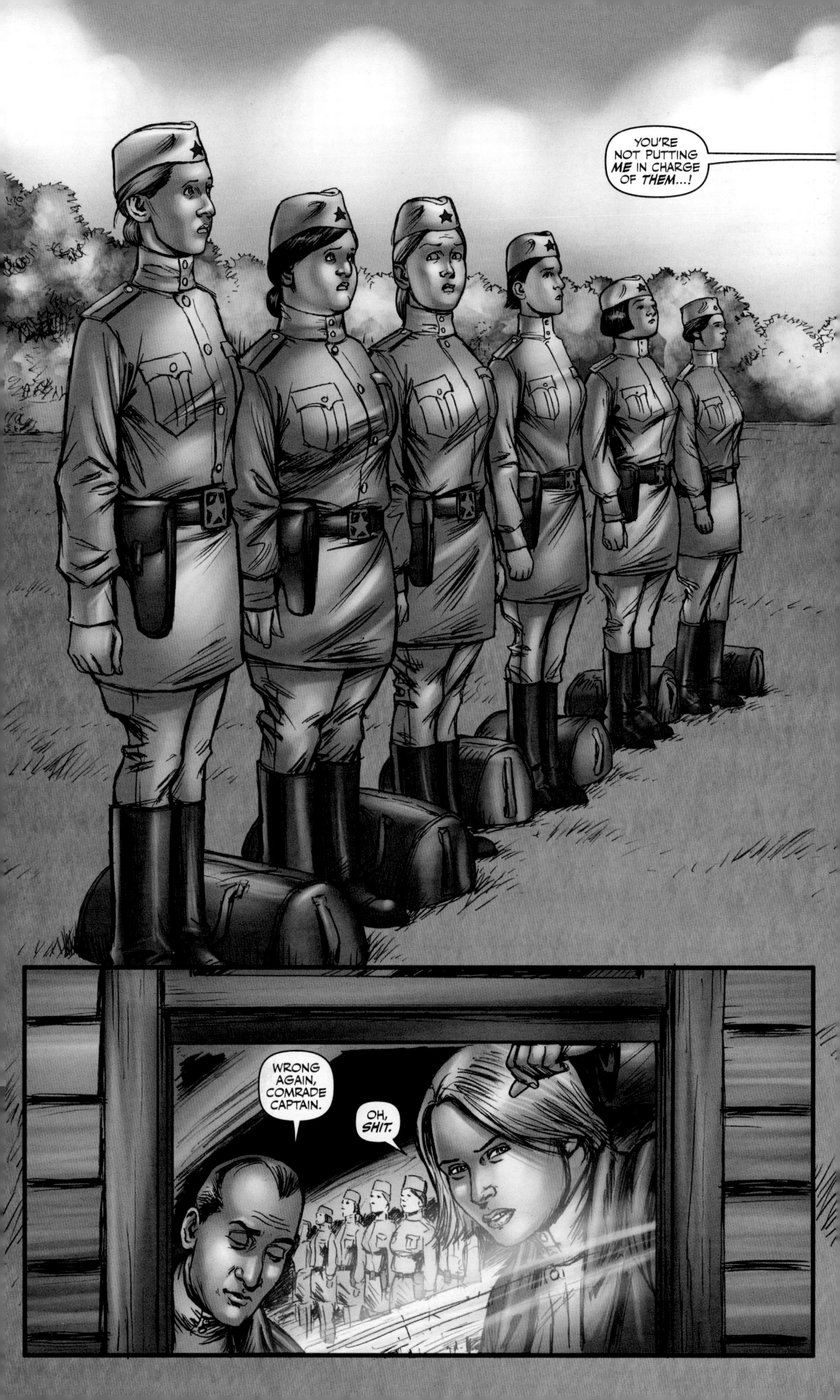
YOU'RE NOT PUTTING ME IN CHARGE OF THEM...!
WRONG AGAIN, COMRADE CAPTAIN.
OH, SHIT.

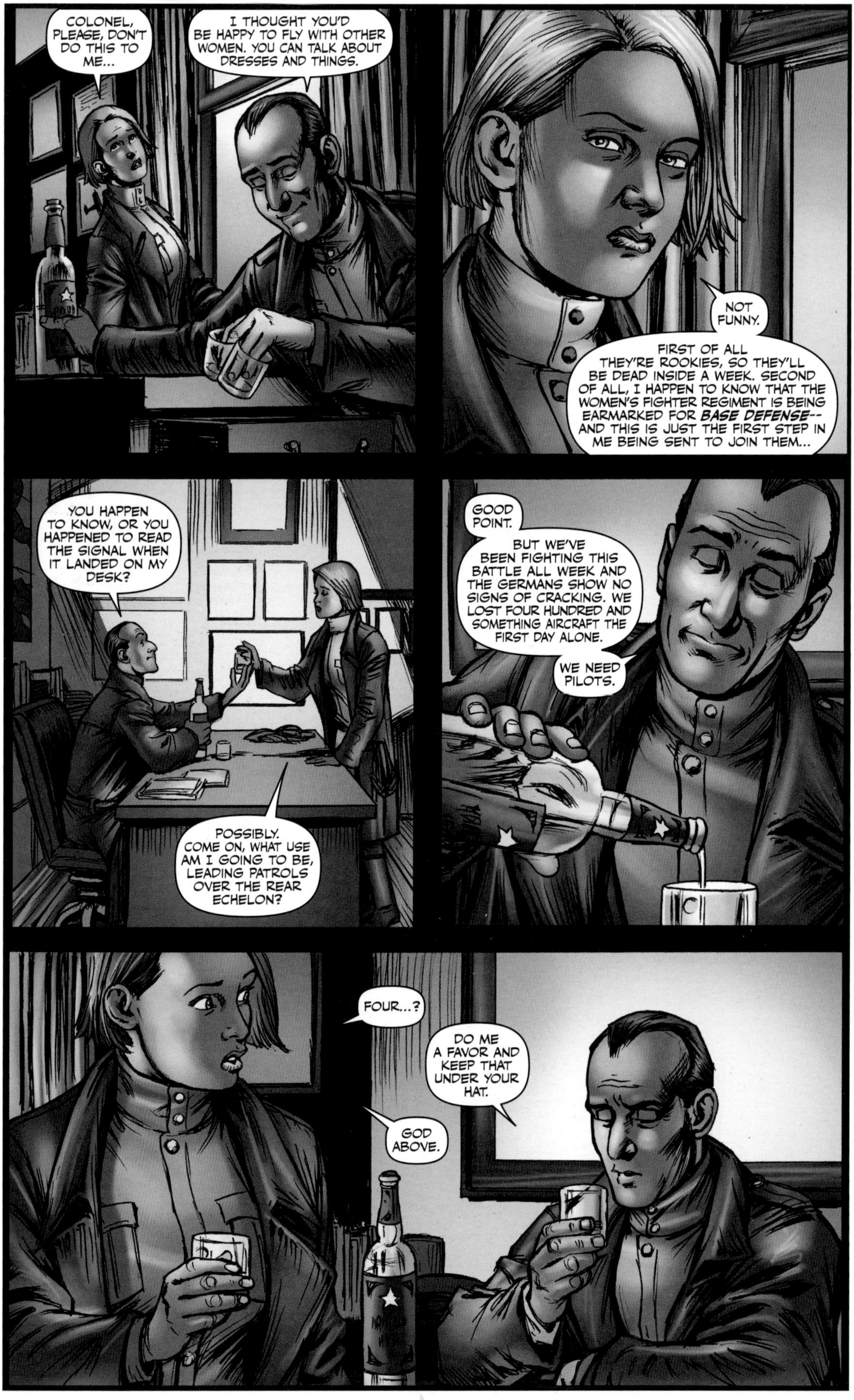
COLONEL, PLEASE, DON'T DO THIS TO ME...
I THOUGHT YOU'D BE HAPPY TO FLY WITH OTHER WOMEN. YOU CAN TALK ABOUT DRESSES AND THINGS.
NOT FUNNY.
FIRST OF ALL THEY'RE ROOKIES, SO THEY'LL BE DEAD INSIDE A WEEK. SECOND OF ALL, I HAPPEN TO KNOW THAT THE WOMEN'S FIGHTER REGIMENT IS BEING EARMARKED FOR BASE DEFENSE-- AND THIS IS JUST THE FIRST STEP IN ME BEING SENT TO JOIN THEM...
YOU HAPPEN TO KNOW, OR YOU HAPPENED TO READ THE SIGNAL WHEN IT LANDED ON MY DESK?
POSSIBLY. COME ON, WHAT USE AM I GOING TO BE, LEADING PATROLS OVER THE REAR ECHELON?
GOOD POINT.
BUT WE'VE BEEN FIGHTING THIS BATTLE ALL WEEK AND THE GERMANS SHOW NO SIGNS OF CRACKING. WE LOST FOUR HUNDRED AND SOMETHING AIRCRAFT THE FIRST DAY ALONE.
WE NEED PILOTS.
FOUR...?
DO ME A FAVOR AND KEEP THAT UNDER YOUR HAT.
GOD ABOVE.

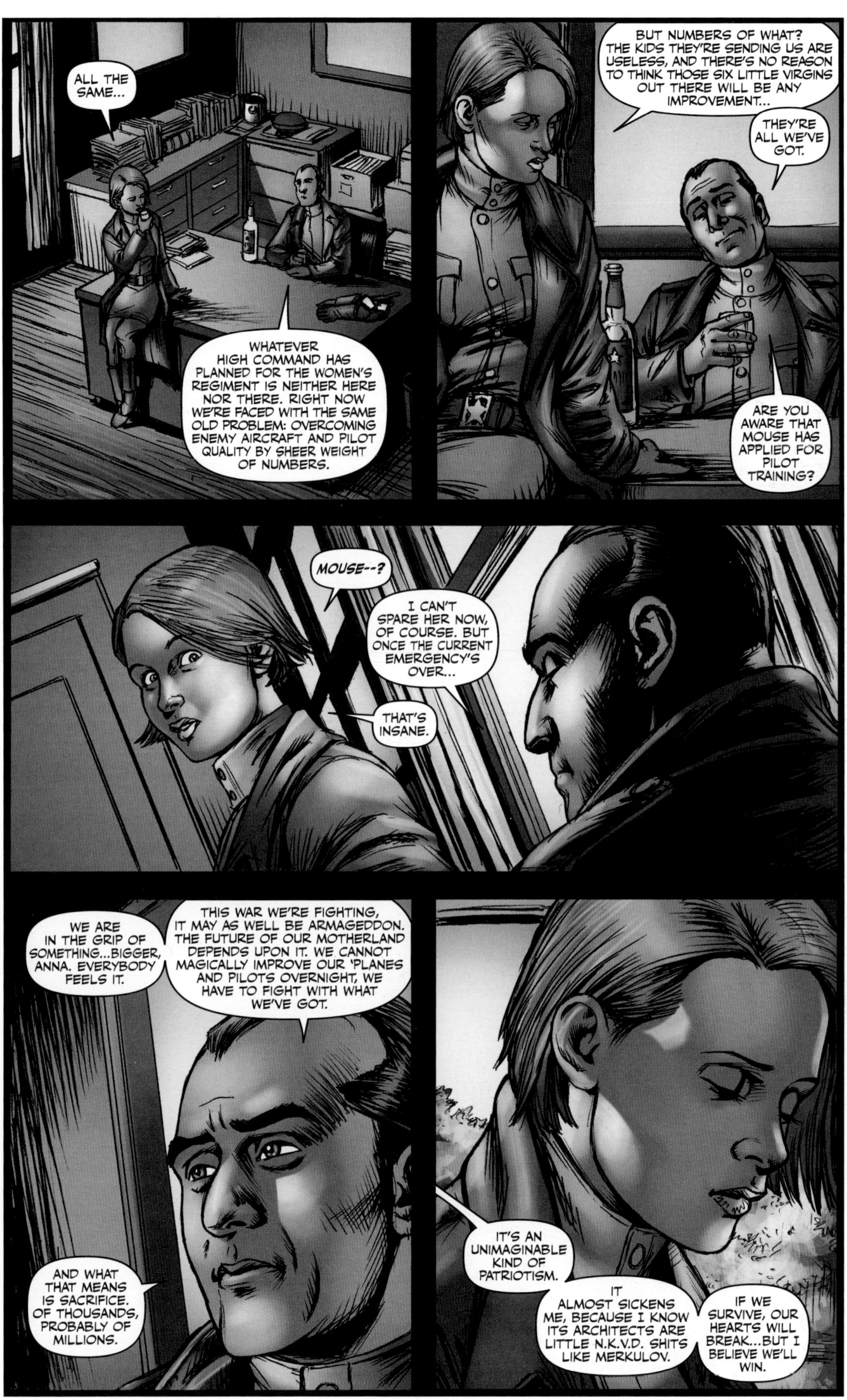

ALL THE SAME...
WHATEVER HIGH COMMAND HAS PLANNED FOR THE WOMEN'S REGIMENT IS NEITHER HERE NOR THERE. RIGHT NOW WE'RE FACED WITH THE SAME OLD PROBLEM: OVERCOMING ENEMY AIRCRAFT AND PILOT QUALITY BY SHEER WEIGHT OF NUMBERS.
BUT NUMBERS OF WHAT? THE KIDS THEY'RE SENDING US ARE USELESS, AND THERE'S NO REASON TO THINK THOSE SIX LITTLE VIRGINS OUT THERE WILL BE ANY IMPROVEMENT...
THEY'RE ALL WE'VE GOT.
ARE YOU AWARE THAT MOUSE HAS APPLIED FOR PILOT TRAINING?
MOUSE--?
I CAN'T SPARE HER NOW, OF COURSE. BUT ONCE THE CURRENT EMERGENCY'S OVER...
THAT'S INSANE.
WE ARE IN THE GRIP OF SOMETHING...BIGGER, ANNA. EVERYBODY FEELS IT.
THIS WAR WE'RE FIGHTING, IT MAY AS WELL BE ARMAGEDDON. THE FUTURE OF OUR MOTHERLAND DEPENDS UPON IT. WE CANNOT MAGICALLY IMPROVE OUR 'PLANES AND PILOTS OVERNIGHT, WE HAVE TO FIGHT WITH WHAT WE'VE GOT.
AND WHAT THAT MEANS IS SACRIFICE. OF THOUSANDS, PROBABLY OF MILLIONS.
IT'S AN UNIMAGINABLE KIND OF PATRIOTISM.
IT ALMOST SICKENS ME, BECAUSE I KNOW ITS ARCHITECTS ARE LITTLE N.K.V.D. SHITS LIKE MERKULOV.
IF WE SURVIVE, OUR HEARTS WILL BREAK...BUT I BELIEVE WE'LL WIN.

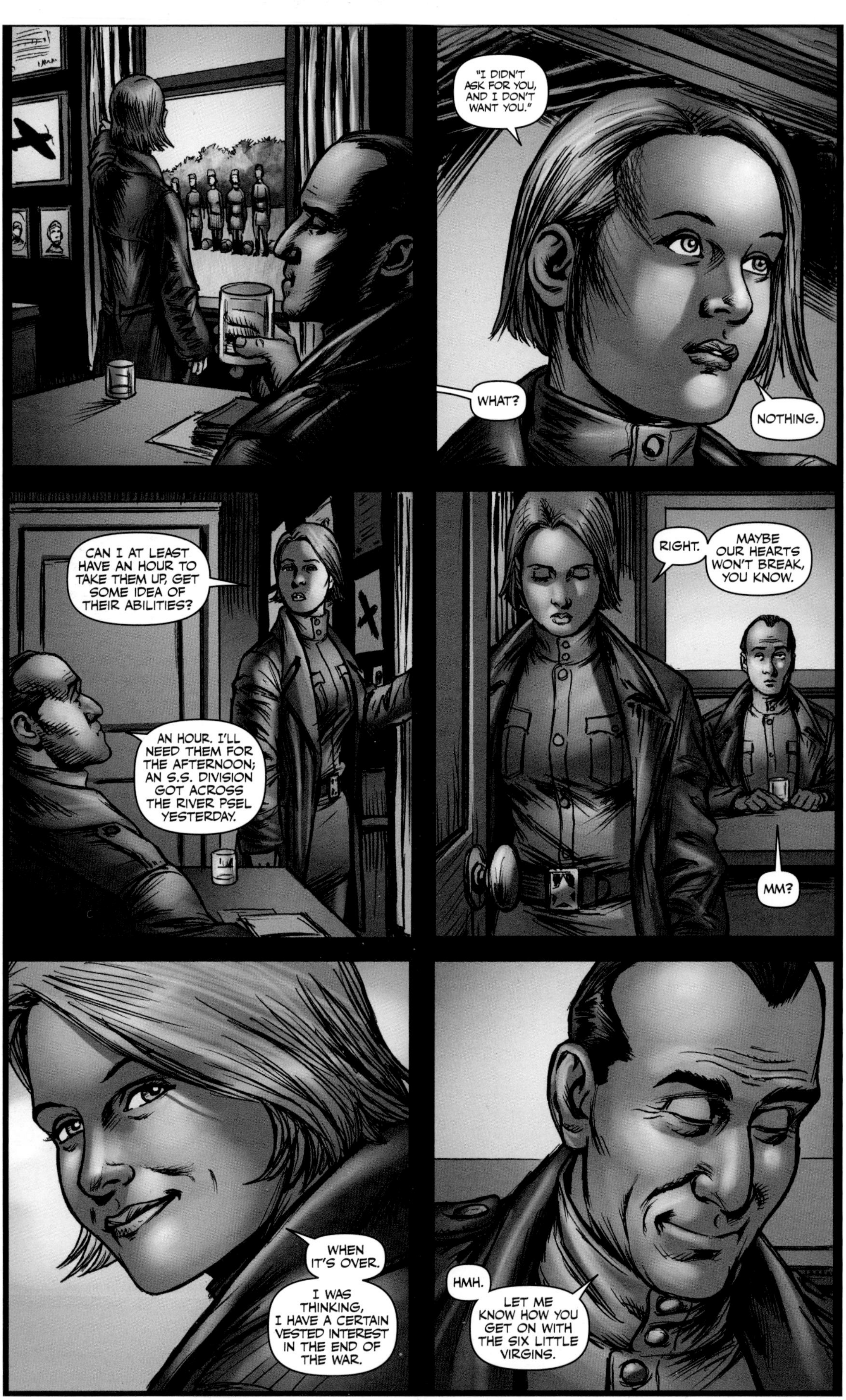
"I DIDN'T ASK FOR YOU, AND I DON'T WANT YOU."
WHAT?
NOTHING.
CAN I AT LEAST HAVE AN HOUR TO TAKE THEM UP, GET SOME IDEA OF THEIR ABILITIES?
AN HOUR. I'LL NEED THEM FOR THE AFTERNOON; AN S.S. DIVISION GOT ACROSS THE RIVER PSEL YESTERDAY.
RIGHT.
MAYBE OUR HEARTS WON'T BREAK, YOU KNOW.
MM?
WHEN IT'S OVER.
I WAS THINKING, I HAVE A CERTAIN VESTED INTEREST IN THE END OF THE WAR.
HMH.
LET ME KNOW HOW YOU GET ON WITH THE SIX LITTLE VIRGINS.

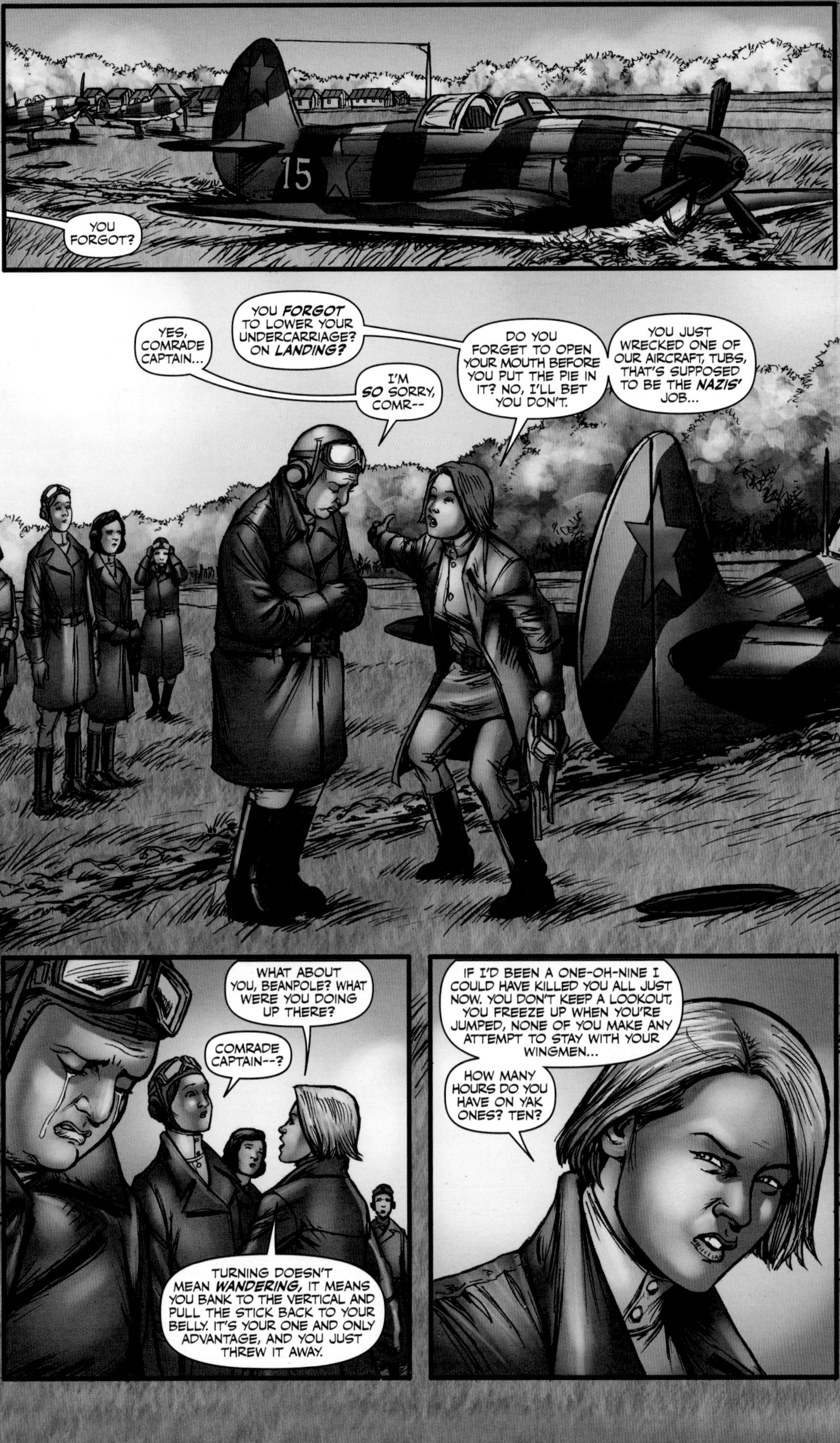
YOU FORGOT?
YOU FORGOT TO LOWER YOUR UNDERCARRIAGE? ON LANDING?
YES, COMRADE CAPTAIN...
I'M SO SORRY, COMR--
DO YOU FORGET TO OPEN YOUR MOUTH BEFORE YOU PUT THE PIE IN IT? NO, I'LL BET YOU DON'T.
YOU JUST WRECKED ONE OF OUR AIRCRAFT, TUBS, THAT'S SUPPOSED TO BE THE NAZIS' JOB...
WHAT ABOUT YOU, BEANPOLE? WHAT WERE YOU DOING UP THERE?
COMRADE CAPTAIN--?
TURNING DOESN'T MEAN WANDERING, IT MEANS YOU BANK TO THE VERTICAL AND PULL THE STICK BACK TO YOUR BELLY. IT'S YOUR ONE AND ONLY ADVANTAGE, AND YOU JUST THREW IT AWAY.
IF I'D BEEN A ONE-OH-NINE I COULD HAVE KILLED YOU ALL JUST NOW. YOU DON'T KEEP A LOOKOUT, YOU FREEZE UP WHEN YOU'RE JUMPED, NONE OF YOU MAKE ANY ATTEMPT TO STAY WITH YOUR WINGMEN...
HOW MANY HOURS DO YOU HAVE ON YAK ONES? TEN?

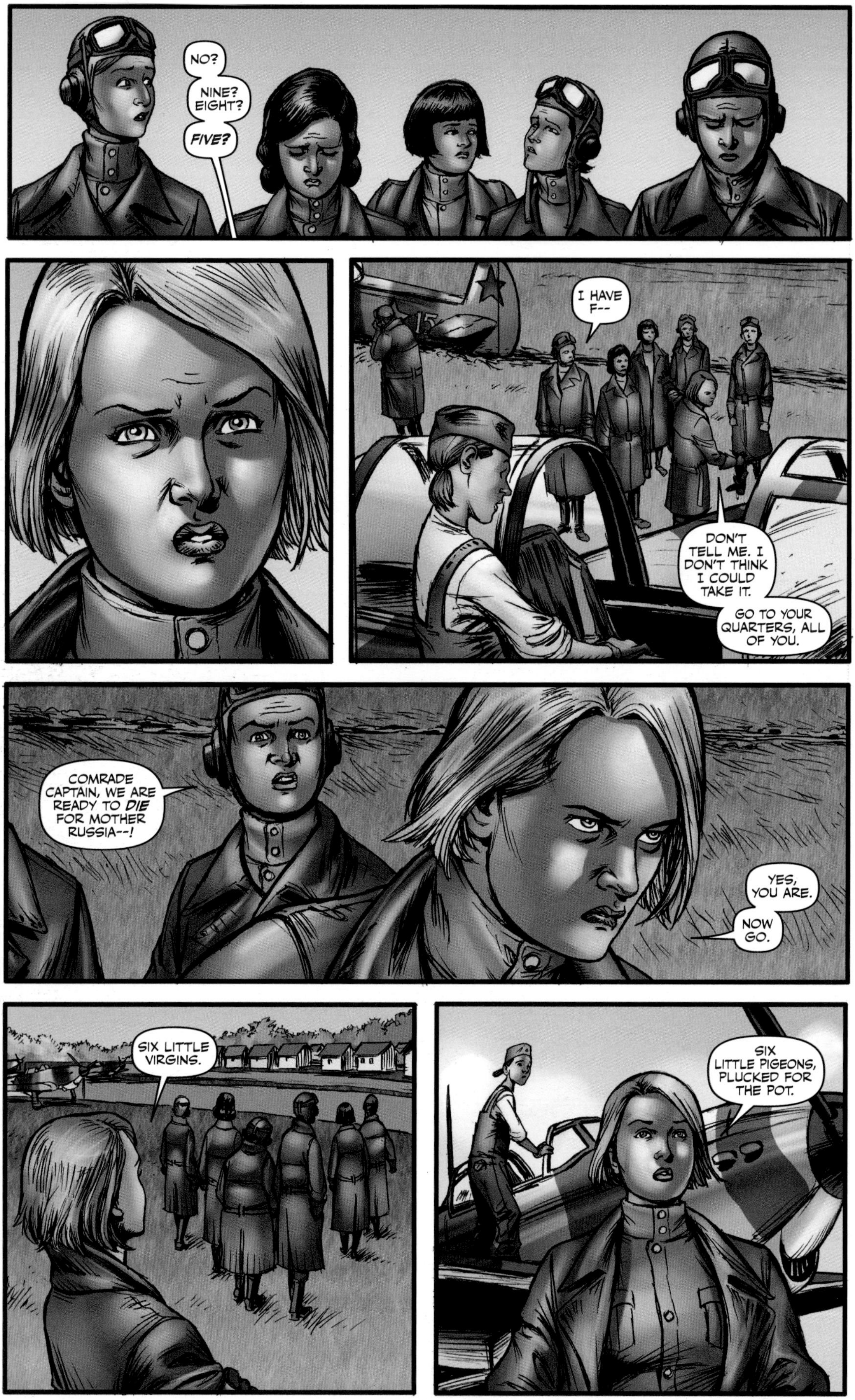
NO?
NINE? EIGHT?
FIVE?
I HAVE F--
DON'T TELL ME. I DON'T THINK I COULD TAKE IT.
GO TO YOUR QUARTERS, ALL OF YOU.
COMRADE CAPTAIN, WE ARE READY TO DIE FOR MOTHER RUSSIA--!
YES, YOU ARE.
NOW GO.
SIX LITTLE VIRGINS.
SIX LITTLE PIGEONS, PLUCKED FOR THE POT.

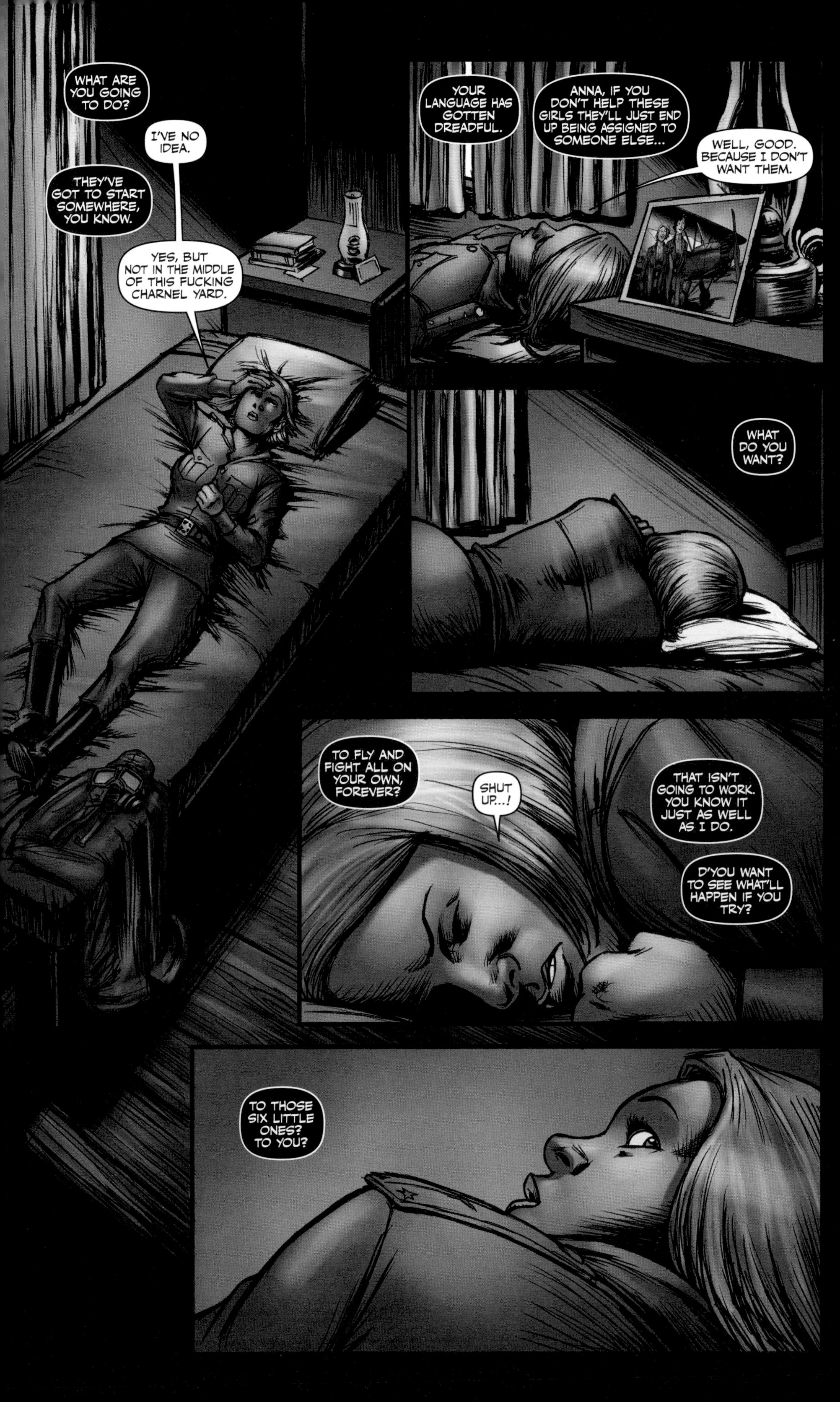
WHAT ARE YOU GOING TO DO?
I'VE NO IDEA.
THEY'VE GOT TO START SOMEWHERE, YOU KNOW.
YES, BUT NOT IN THE MIDDLE OF THIS FUCKING CHARNEL YARD.
YOUR LANGUAGE HAS GOTTEN DREADFUL.
ANNA, IF YOU DON'T HELP THESE GIRLS THEY'LL JUST END UP BEING ASSIGNED TO SOMEONE ELSE...
WELL, GOOD. BECAUSE I DON'T WANT THEM.
WHAT DO YOU WANT?
TO FLY AND FIGHT ALL ON YOUR OWN, FOREVER?
SHUT UP...!
THAT ISN'T GOING TO WORK. YOU KNOW IT JUST AS WELL AS I DO.
D'YOU WANT TO SEE WHAT'LL HAPPEN IF YOU TRY?
TO THOSE SIX LITTLE ONES? TO YOU?

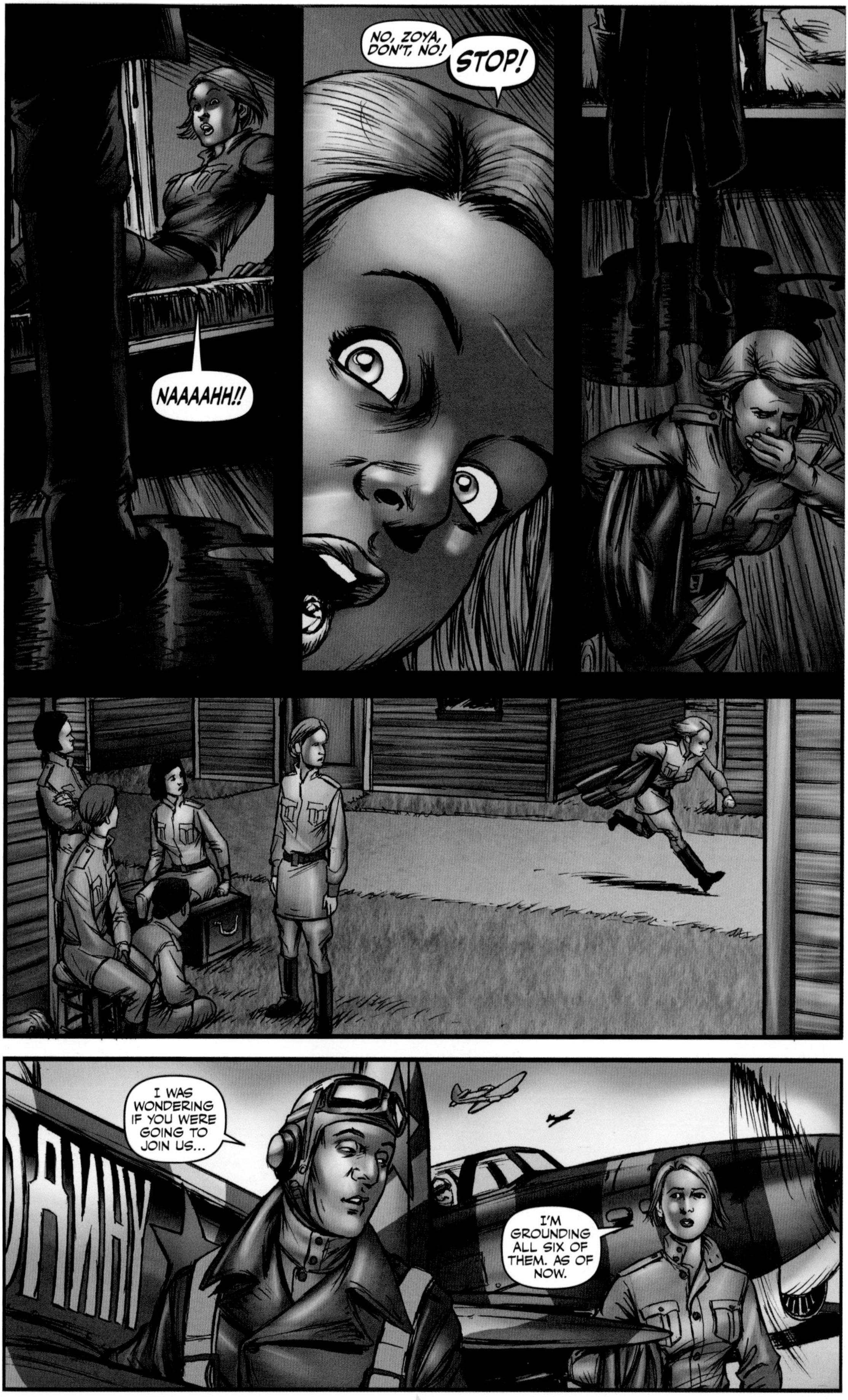
NAAAAHH!!
NO, ZOYA, DON'T, NO!
STOP!
I WAS WONDERING IF YOU WERE GOING TO JOIN US...
I'M GROUNDING ALL SIX OF THEM. AS OF NOW.

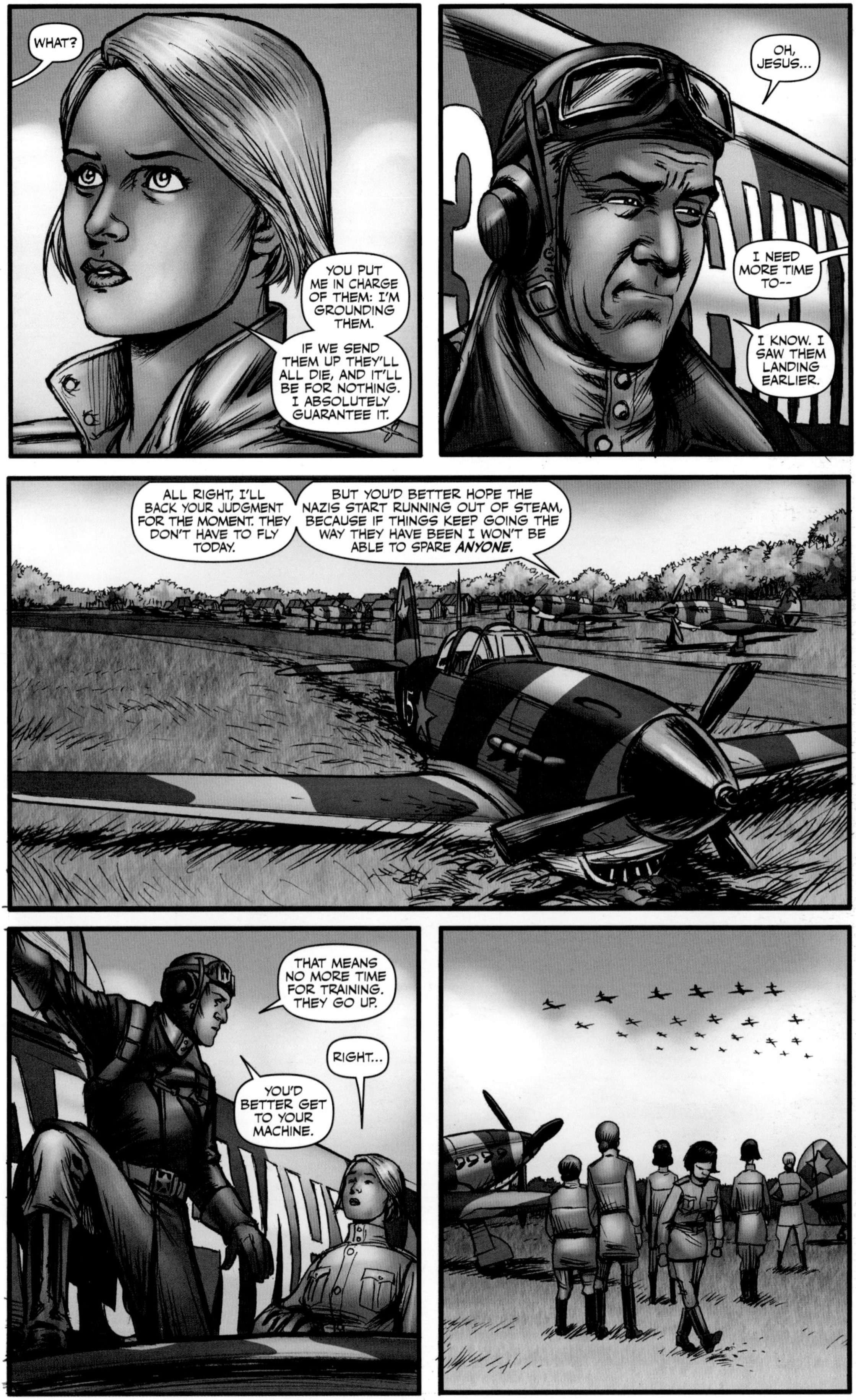
WHAT?
YOU PUT ME IN CHARGE OF THEM: I'M GROUNDING THEM.
IF WE SEND THEM UP THEY'LL ALL DIE, AND IT'LL BE FOR NOTHING. I ABSOLUTELY GUARANTEE IT.
OH, JESUS...
I NEED MORE TIME TO--
I KNOW. I SAW THEM LANDING EARLIER.
ALL RIGHT, I'LL BACK YOUR JUDGMENT FOR THE MOMENT. THEY DON'T HAVE TO FLY TODAY.
BUT YOU'D BETTER HOPE THE NAZIS START RUNNING OUT OF STEAM, BECAUSE IF THINGS KEEP GOING THE WAY THEY HAVE BEEN I WON'T BE ABLE TO SPARE *ANYONE.*
THAT MEANS NO MORE TIME FOR TRAINING. THEY GO UP.
RIGHT...
YOU'D BETTER GET TO YOUR MACHINE.

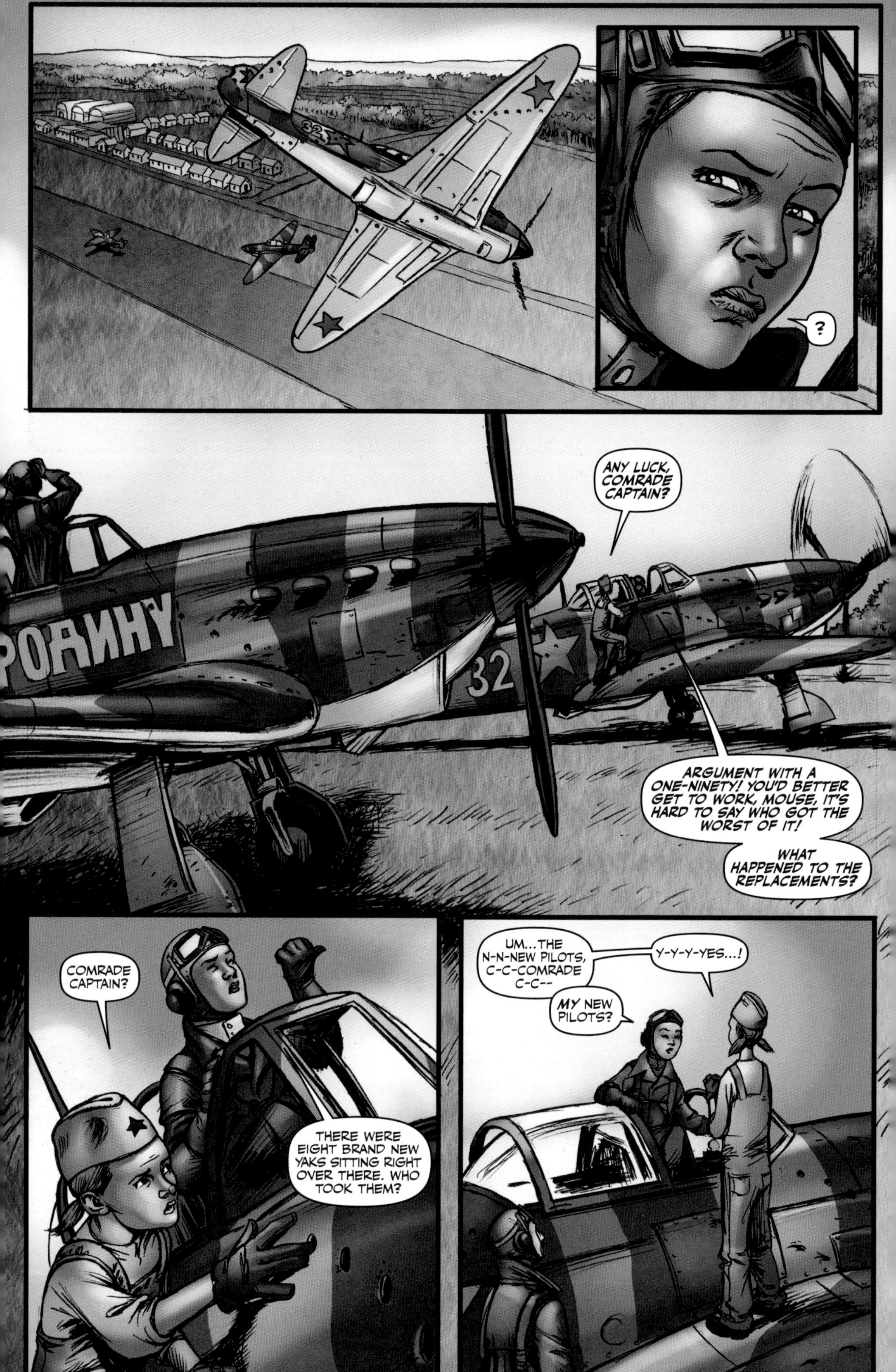
?
ANY LUCK, COMRADE CAPTAIN?
ARGUMENT WITH A ONE-NINETY! YOU'D BETTER GET TO WORK, MOUSE, IT'S HARD TO SAY WHO GOT THE WORST OF IT!
WHAT HAPPENED TO THE REPLACEMENTS?
COMRADE CAPTAIN?
THERE WERE EIGHT BRAND NEW YAKS SITTING RIGHT OVER THERE. WHO TOOK THEM?
UM...THE N-N-NEW PILOTS, C-C-COMRADE C-C--
MY NEW PILOTS?
Y-Y-Y-YES...!

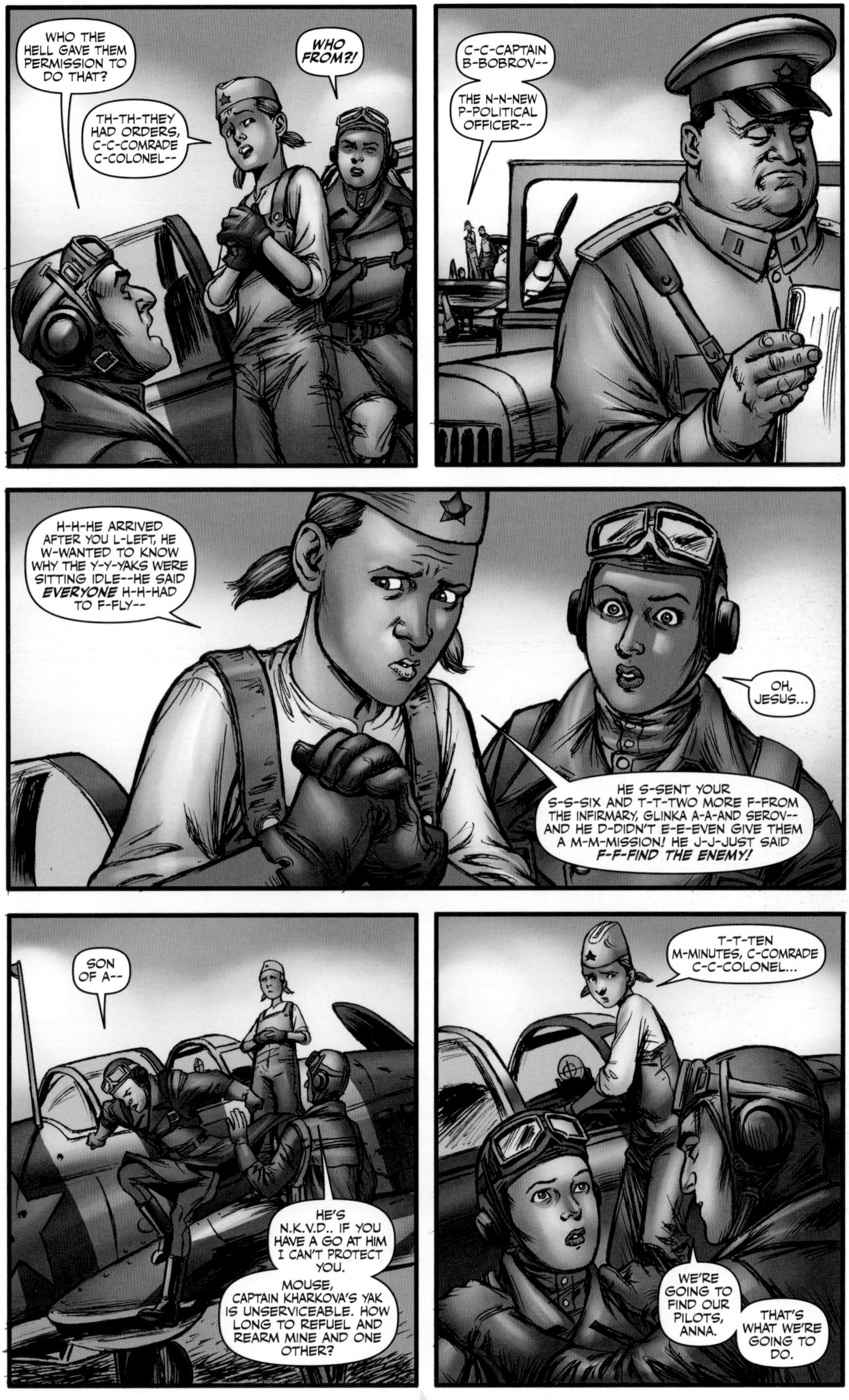
WHO THE HELL GAVE THEM PERMISSION TO DO THAT?
WHO FROM?!
TH-TH-THEY HAD ORDERS, C-C-COMRADE C-COLONEL--
C-C-CAPTAIN B-BOBROV--
THE N-N-NEW P-POLITICAL OFFICER--
H-H-HE ARRIVED AFTER YOU L-LEFT, HE W-WANTED TO KNOW WHY THE Y-Y-YAKS WERE SITTING IDLE--HE SAID EVERYONE H-H-HAD TO F-FLY--
OH, JESUS...
HE S-SENT YOUR S-S-SIX AND T-T-TWO MORE F-FROM THE INFIRMARY, GLINKA A-A-AND SEROV-- AND HE D-DIDN'T E-E-EVEN GIVE THEM A M-M-MISSION! HE J-J-JUST SAID F-F-FIND THE ENEMY!
SON OF A--
HE'S N.K.V.D.. IF YOU HAVE A GO AT HIM I CAN'T PROTECT YOU.
MOUSE, CAPTAIN KHARKOVA'S YAK IS UNSERVICEABLE. HOW LONG TO REFUEL AND REARM MINE AND ONE OTHER?
T-T-TEN M-MINUTES, C-COMRADE C-C-COLONEL...
WE'RE GOING TO FIND OUR PILOTS, ANNA.
THAT'S WHAT WE'RE GOING TO DO.

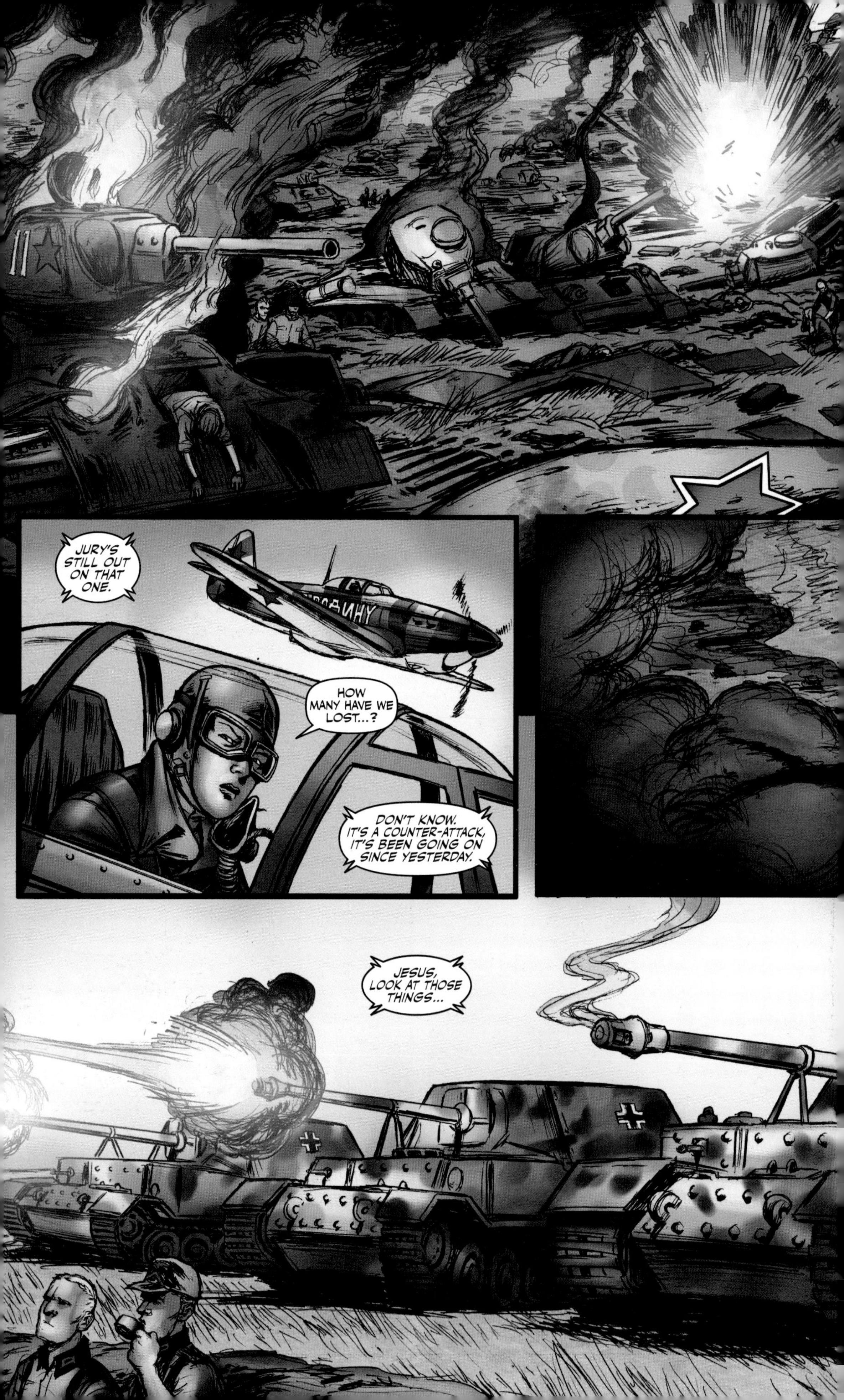
JURY'S STILL OUT ON THAT ONE.
HOW MANY HAVE WE LOST...?
DON'T KNOW. IT'S A COUNTER-ATTACK, IT'S BEEN GOING ON SINCE YESTERDAY.
JESUS, LOOK AT THOSE THINGS...

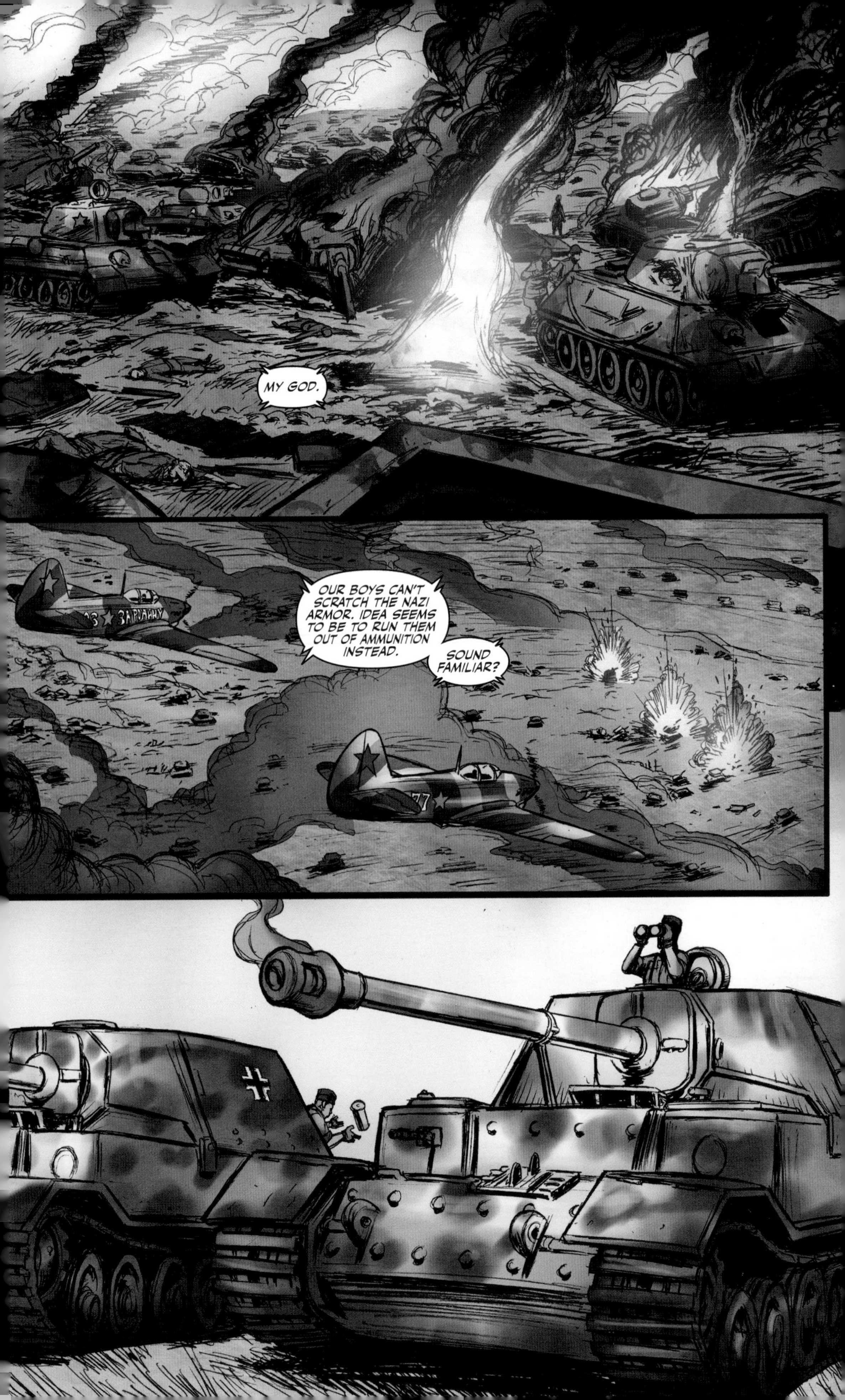
MY GOD.
OUR BOYS CAN'T SCRATCH THE NAZI ARMOR. IDEA SEEMS TO BE TO RUN THEM OUT OF AMMUNITION INSTEAD.
SOUND FAMILIAR?

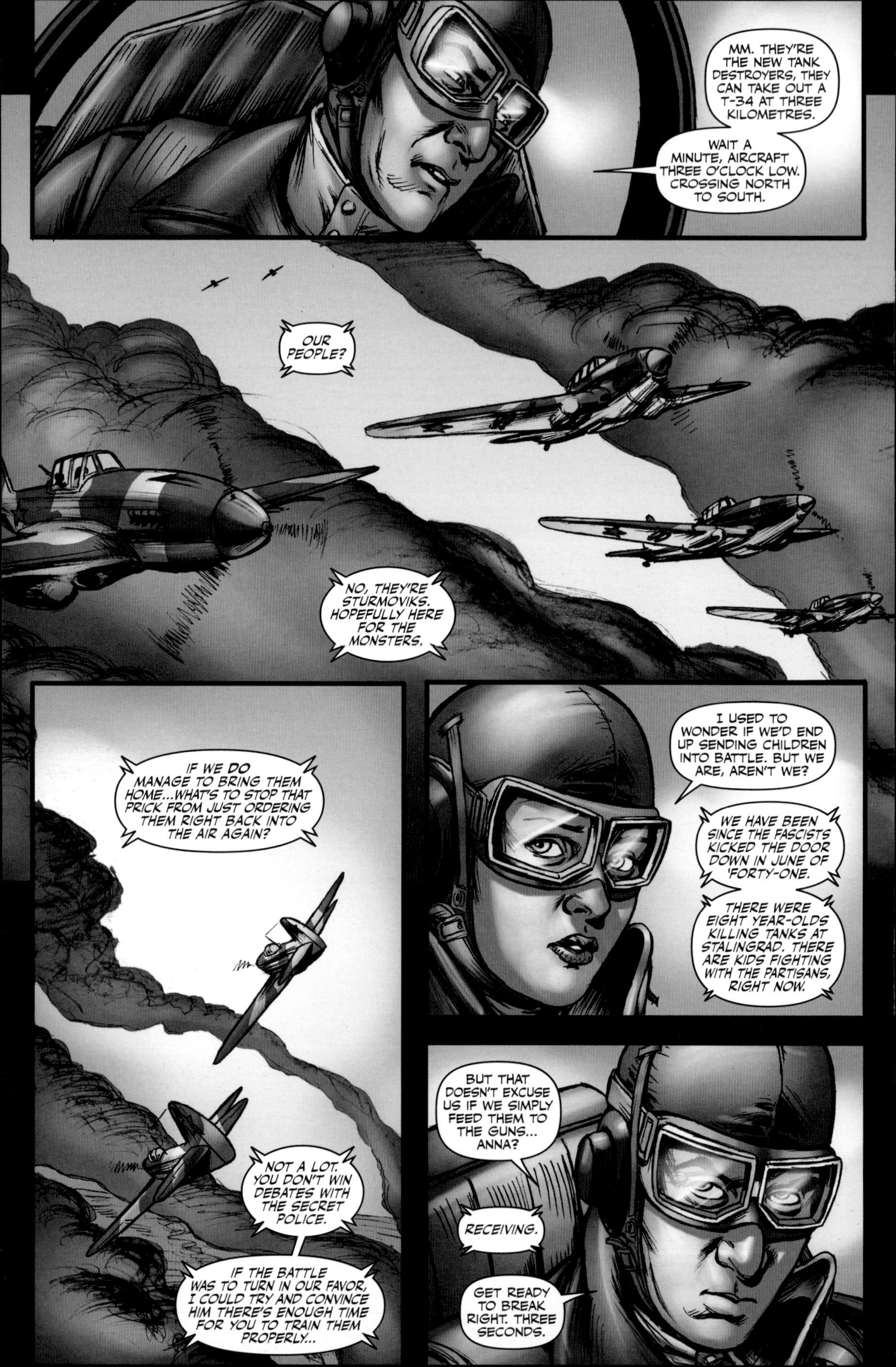
MM. THEY'RE THE NEW TANK DESTROYERS, THEY CAN TAKE OUT A T-34 AT THREE KILOMETRES.
WAIT A MINUTE, AIRCRAFT THREE O'CLOCK LOW. CROSSING NORTH TO SOUTH.
OUR PEOPLE?
NO, THEY'RE STURMOVIKS. HOPEFULLY HERE FOR THE MONSTERS.
IF WE DO MANAGE TO BRING THEM HOME...WHAT'S TO STOP THAT PRICK FROM JUST ORDERING THEM RIGHT BACK INTO THE AIR AGAIN?
NOT A LOT. YOU DON'T WIN DEBATES WITH THE SECRET POLICE.
IF THE BATTLE WAS TO TURN IN OUR FAVOR, I COULD TRY AND CONVINCE HIM THERE'S ENOUGH TIME FOR YOU TO TRAIN THEM PROPERLY...
I USED TO WONDER IF WE'D END UP SENDING CHILDREN INTO BATTLE. BUT WE ARE, AREN'T WE?
WE HAVE BEEN SINCE THE FASCISTS KICKED THE DOOR DOWN IN JUNE OF 'FORTY-ONE.
THERE WERE EIGHT YEAR-OLDS KILLING TANKS AT STALINGRAD. THERE ARE KIDS FIGHTING WITH THE PARTISANS, RIGHT NOW.
BUT THAT DOESN'T EXCUSE US IF WE SIMPLY FEED THEM TO THE GUNS... ANNA?
RECEIVING.
GET READY TO BREAK RIGHT. THREE SECONDS.

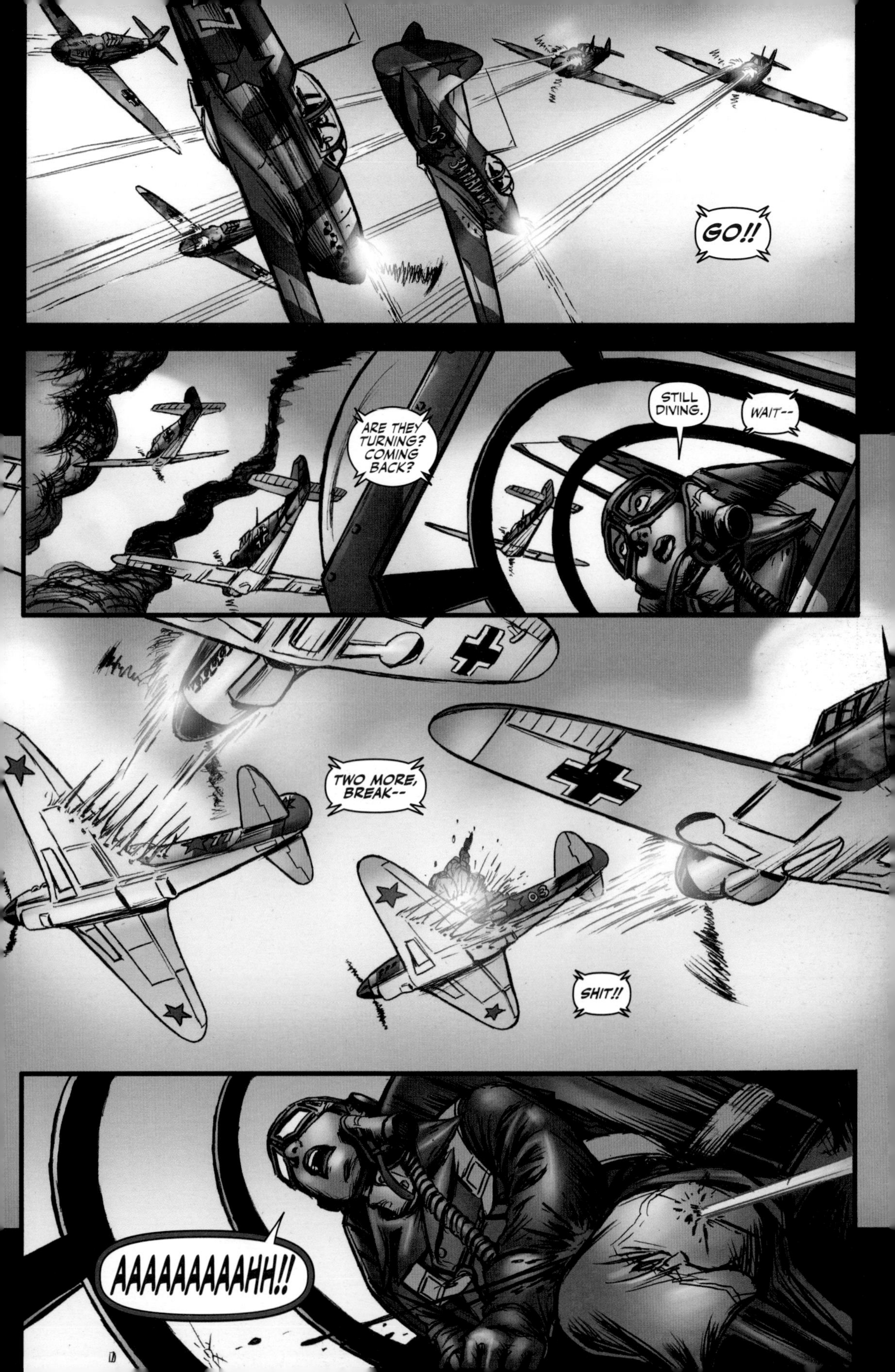
GO!!
ARE THEY TURNING? COMING BACK?
STILL DIVING.
WAIT--
TWO MORE, BREAK--
SHIT!!
AAAAAAAAAHH!!

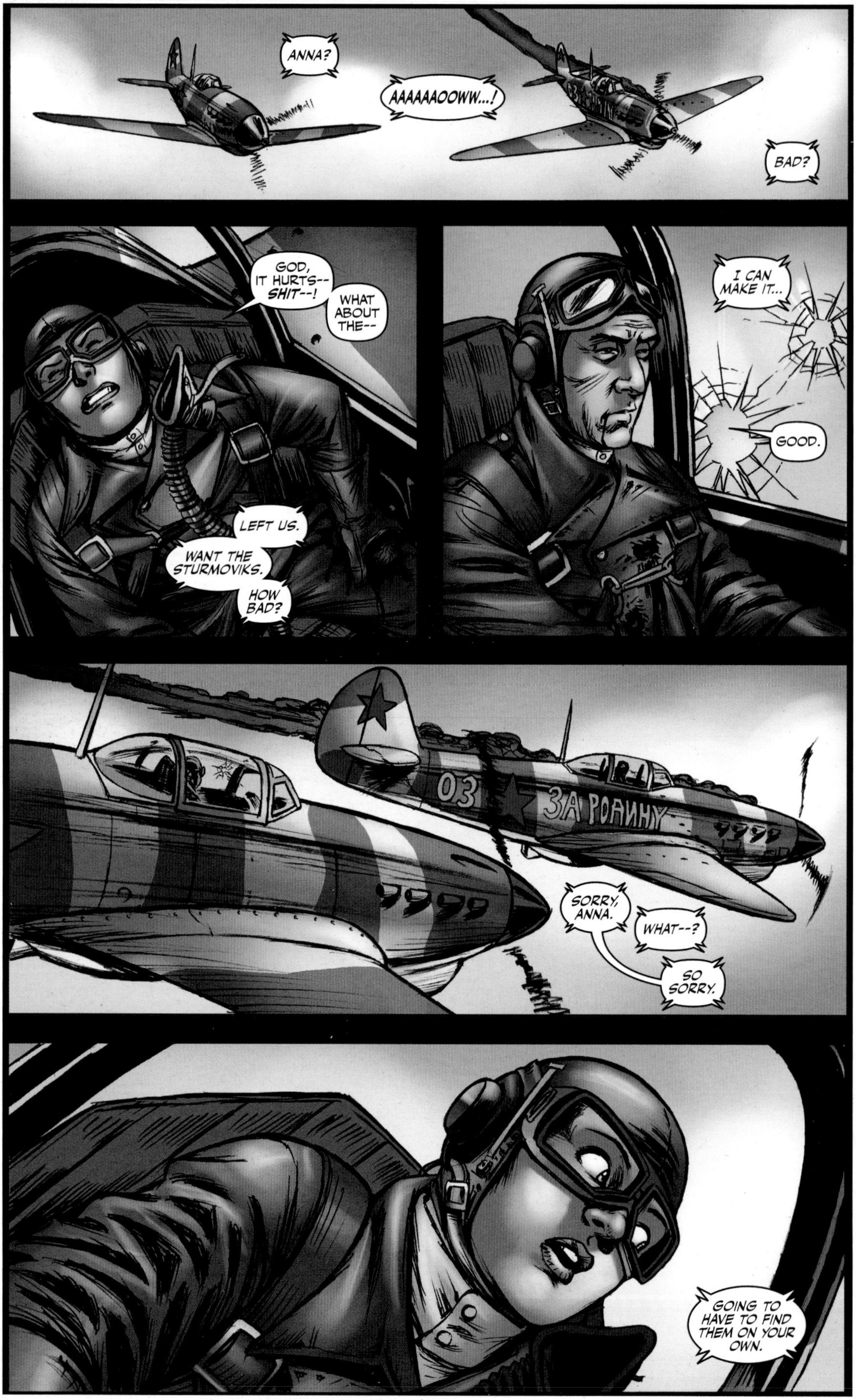
ANNA?
AAAAAAOOWW...!
BAD?
GOD, IT HURTS-- SHIT--!
WHAT ABOUT THE--
LEFT US.
WANT THE STURMOVIKS.
HOW BAD?
I CAN MAKE IT...
GOOD.
03
ЗА РОДИНУ
SORRY, ANNA.
WHAT--?
SO SORRY.
GOING TO HAVE TO FIND THEM ON YOUR OWN.

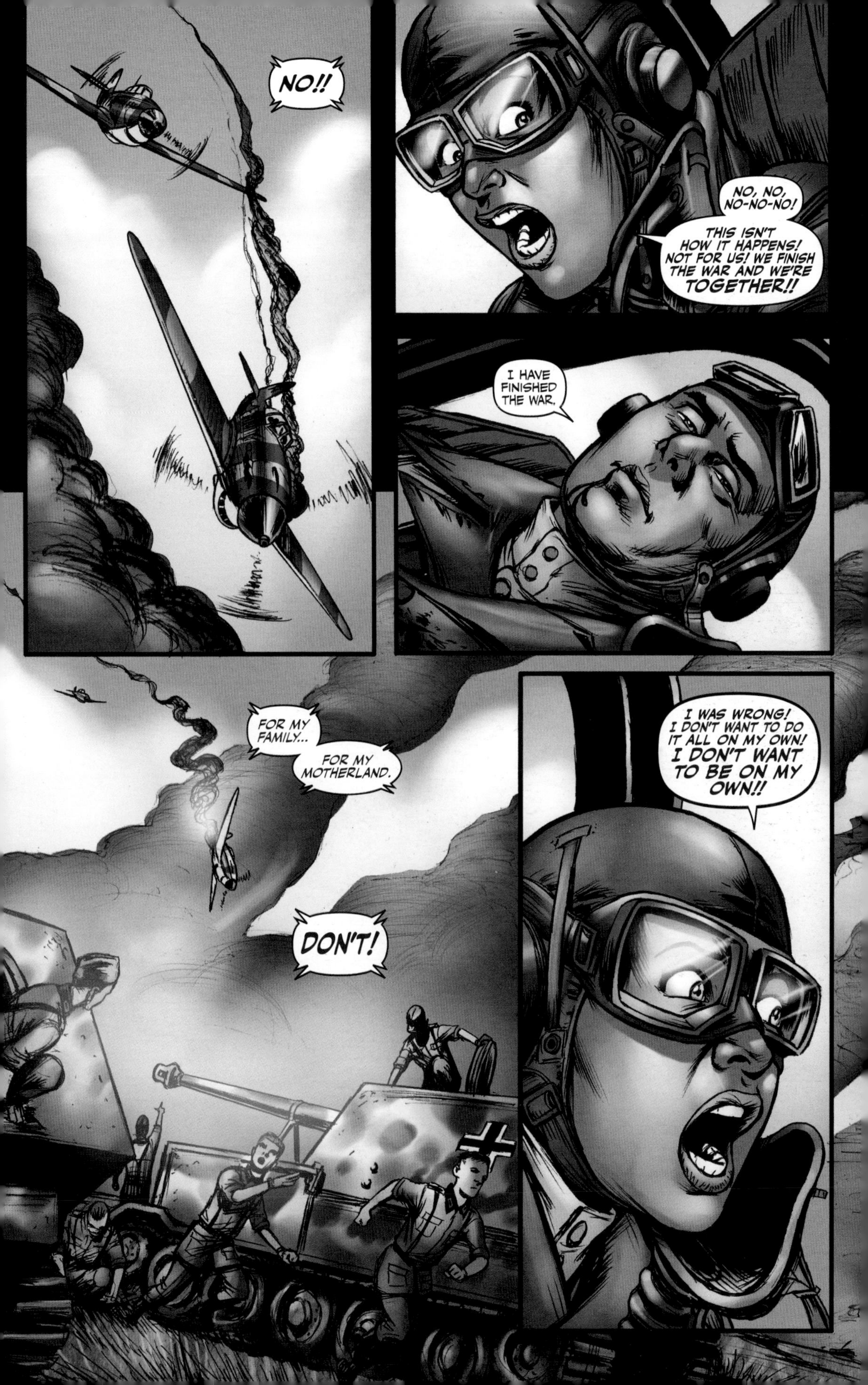
NO!!
NO, NO, NO-NO-NO!
THIS ISN'T HOW IT HAPPENS! NOT FOR US! WE FINISH THE WAR AND WE'RE TOGETHER!!
I HAVE FINISHED THE WAR.
FOR MY FAMILY...
FOR MY MOTHERLAND.
DON'T!
I WAS WRONG! I DON'T WANT TO DO IT ALL ON MY OWN! I DON'T WANT TO BE ON MY OWN!!

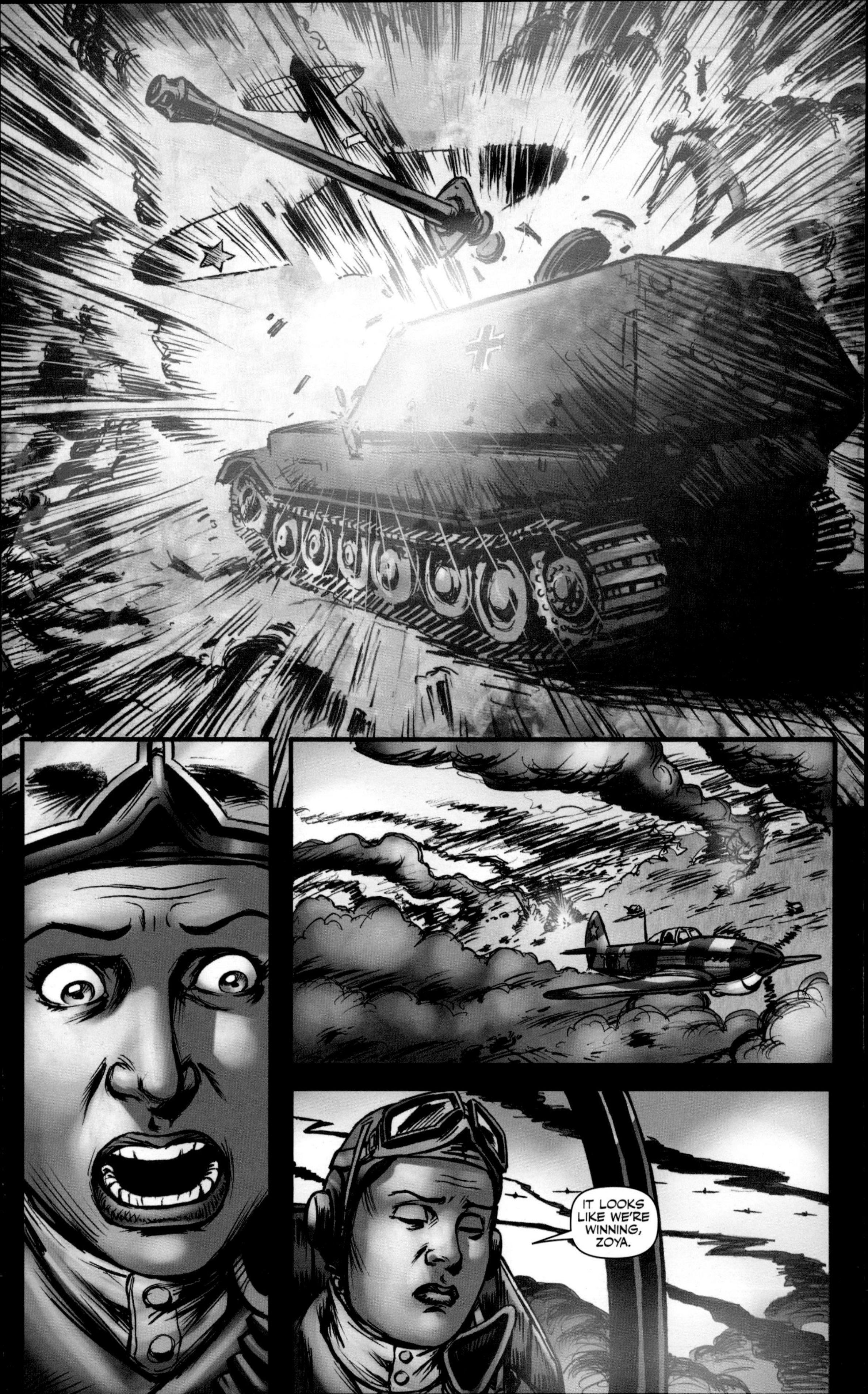
IT LOOKS LIKE WE'RE WINNING, ZOYA.

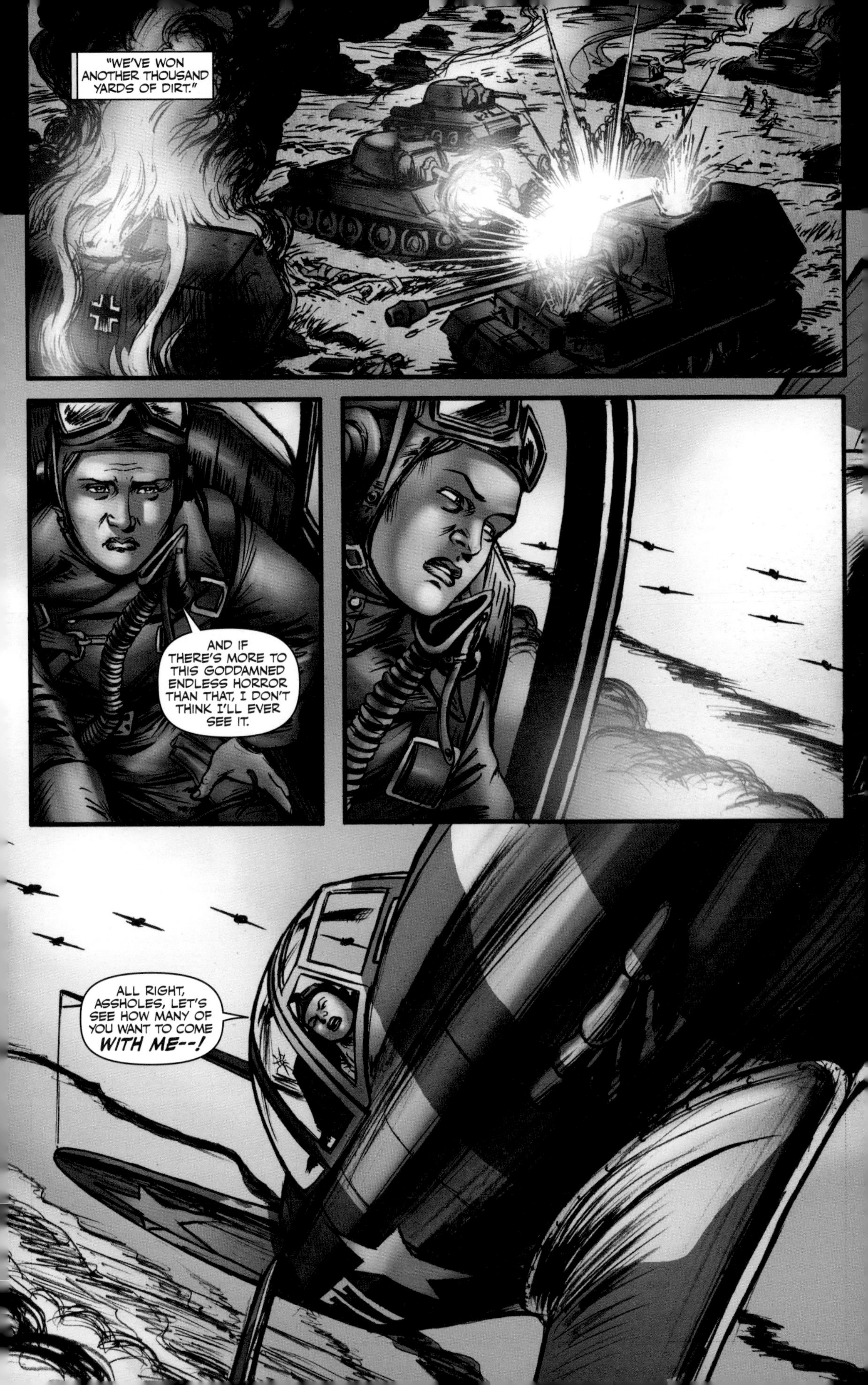
"WE'VE WON ANOTHER THOUSAND YARDS OF DIRT."
AND IF THERE'S MORE TO THIS GODDAMNED ENDLESS HORROR THAN THAT, I DON'T THINK I'LL EVER SEE IT.
ALL RIGHT, ASSHOLES, LET'S SEE HOW MANY OF YOU WANT TO COME WITH ME--!

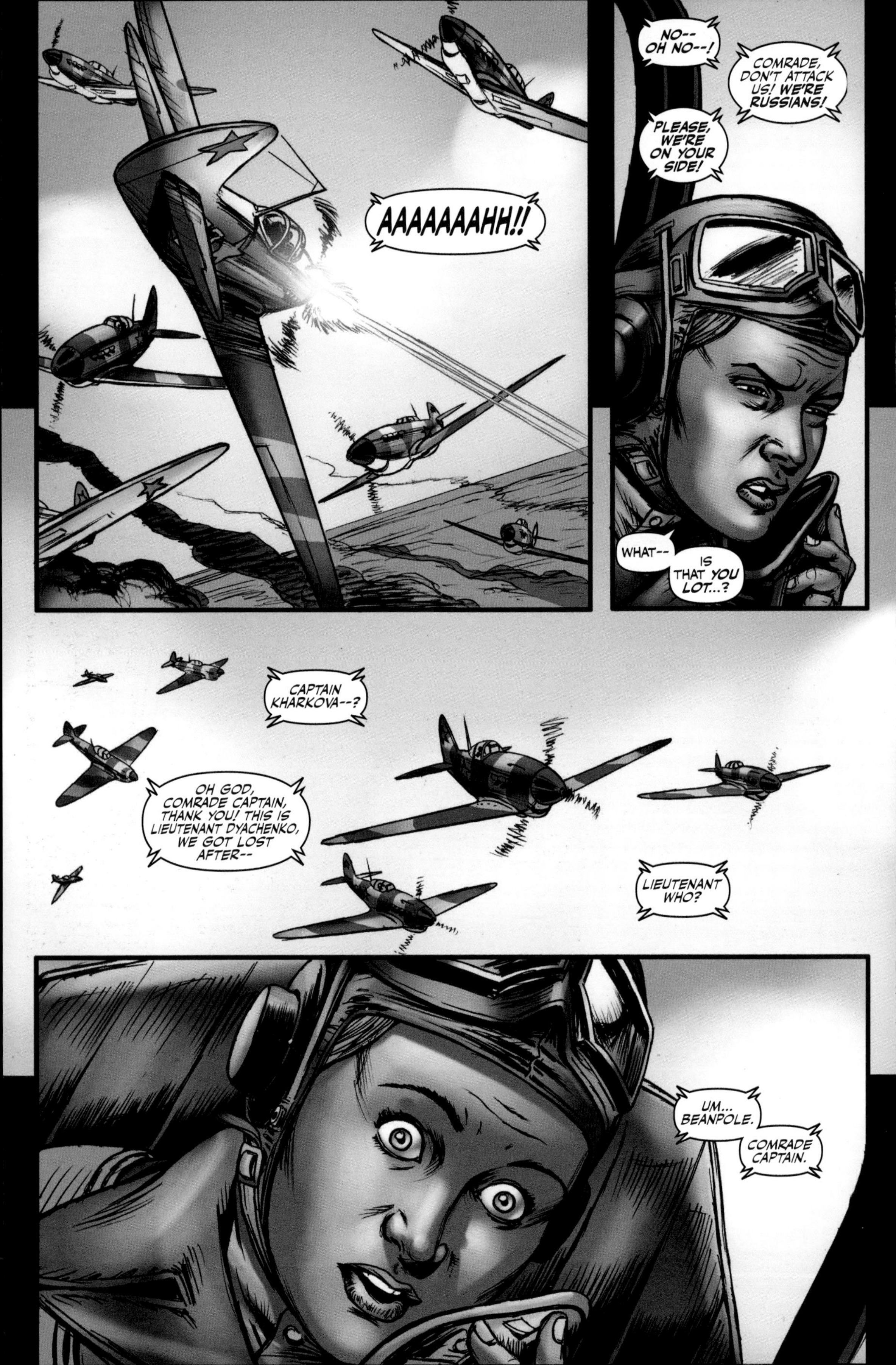
AAAAAAAHH!!
NO-- OH NO--!
COMRADE, DON'T ATTACK US! WE'RE RUSSIANS!
PLEASE, WE'RE ON YOUR SIDE!
WHAT--
IS THAT YOU LOT...?
CAPTAIN KHARKOVA--?
OH GOD, COMRADE CAPTAIN, THANK YOU! THIS IS LIEUTENANT DYACHENKO, WE GOT LOST AFTER--
LIEUTENANT WHO?
UM... BEANPOLE.
COMRADE CAPTAIN.

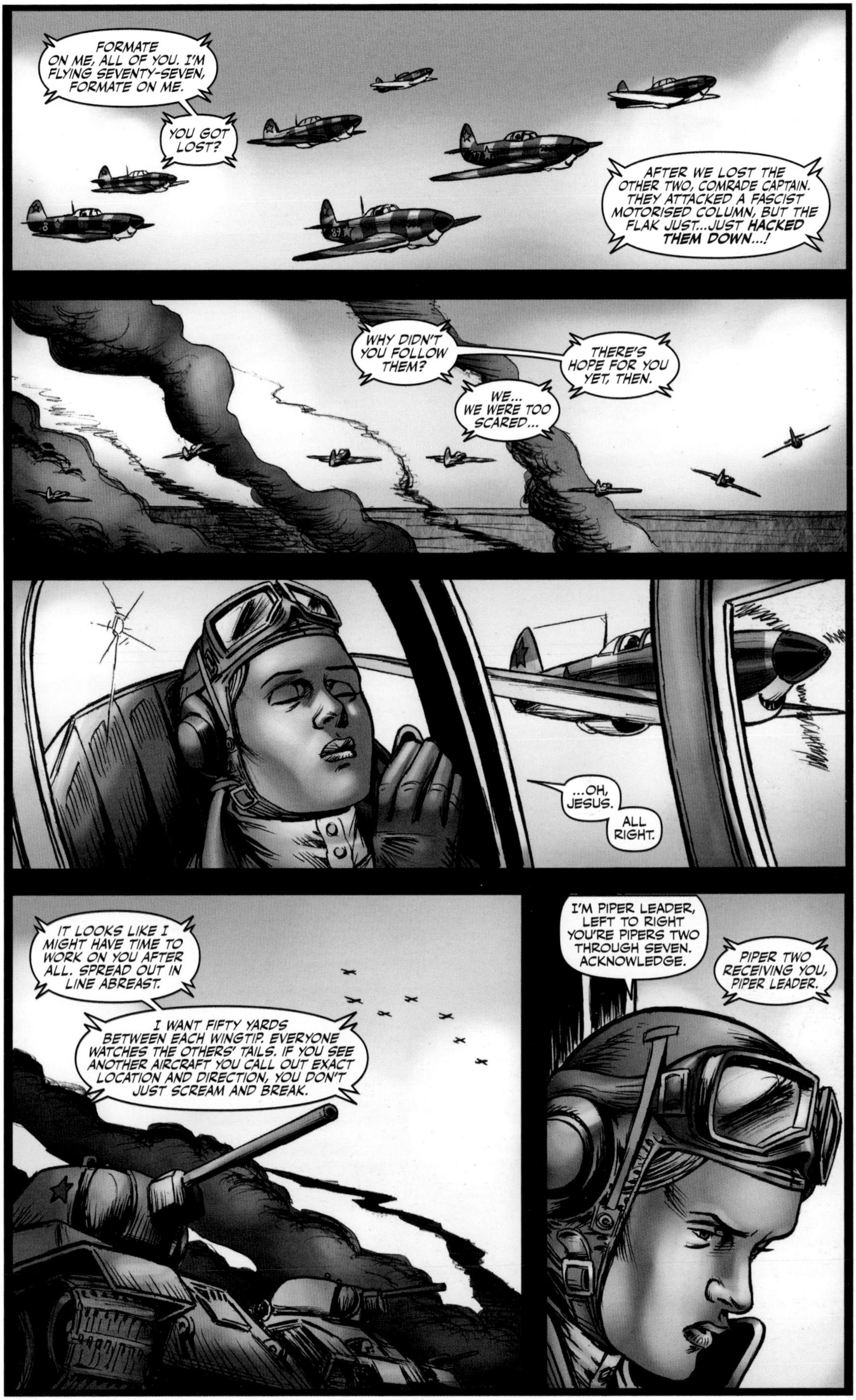
FORMATE ON ME, ALL OF YOU. I'M FLYING SEVENTY-SEVEN, FORMATE ON ME.
YOU GOT LOST?
AFTER WE LOST THE OTHER TWO, COMRADE CAPTAIN. THEY ATTACKED A FASCIST MOTORISED COLUMN, BUT THE FLAK JUST...JUST HACKED THEM DOWN...!
WHY DIDN'T YOU FOLLOW THEM?
WE... WE WERE TOO SCARED...
THERE'S HOPE FOR YOU YET, THEN.
...OH, JESUS.
ALL RIGHT.
IT LOOKS LIKE I MIGHT HAVE TIME TO WORK ON YOU AFTER ALL. SPREAD OUT IN LINE ABREAST.
I WANT FIFTY YARDS BETWEEN EACH WINGTIP. EVERYONE WATCHES THE OTHERS' TAILS. IF YOU SEE ANOTHER AIRCRAFT YOU CALL OUT EXACT LOCATION AND DIRECTION, YOU DON'T JUST SCREAM AND BREAK.
I'M PIPER LEADER, LEFT TO RIGHT YOU'RE PIPERS TWO THROUGH SEVEN. ACKNOWLEDGE.
PIPER TWO RECEIVING YOU, PIPER LEADER.

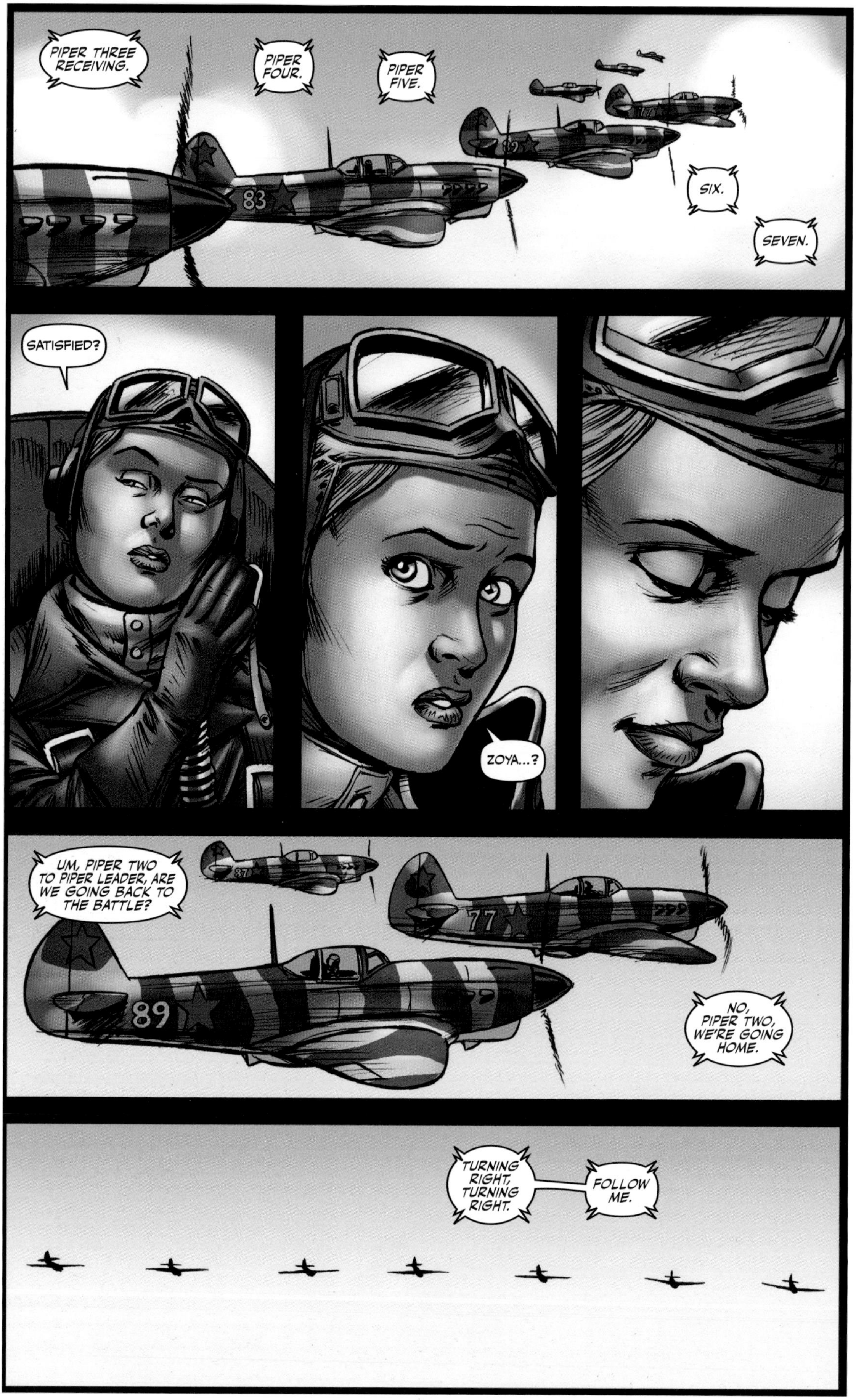
PIPER THREE RECEIVING.
PIPER FOUR.
PIPER FIVE.
SIX.
SEVEN.
SATISFIED?
ZOYA...?
UM, PIPER TWO TO PIPER LEADER, ARE WE GOING BACK TO THE BATTLE?
NO, PIPER TWO, WE'RE GOING HOME.
TURNING RIGHT, TURNING RIGHT.
FOLLOW ME.

THE FALL AND RISE OF ANNA KHARKOVA

Chapter 1

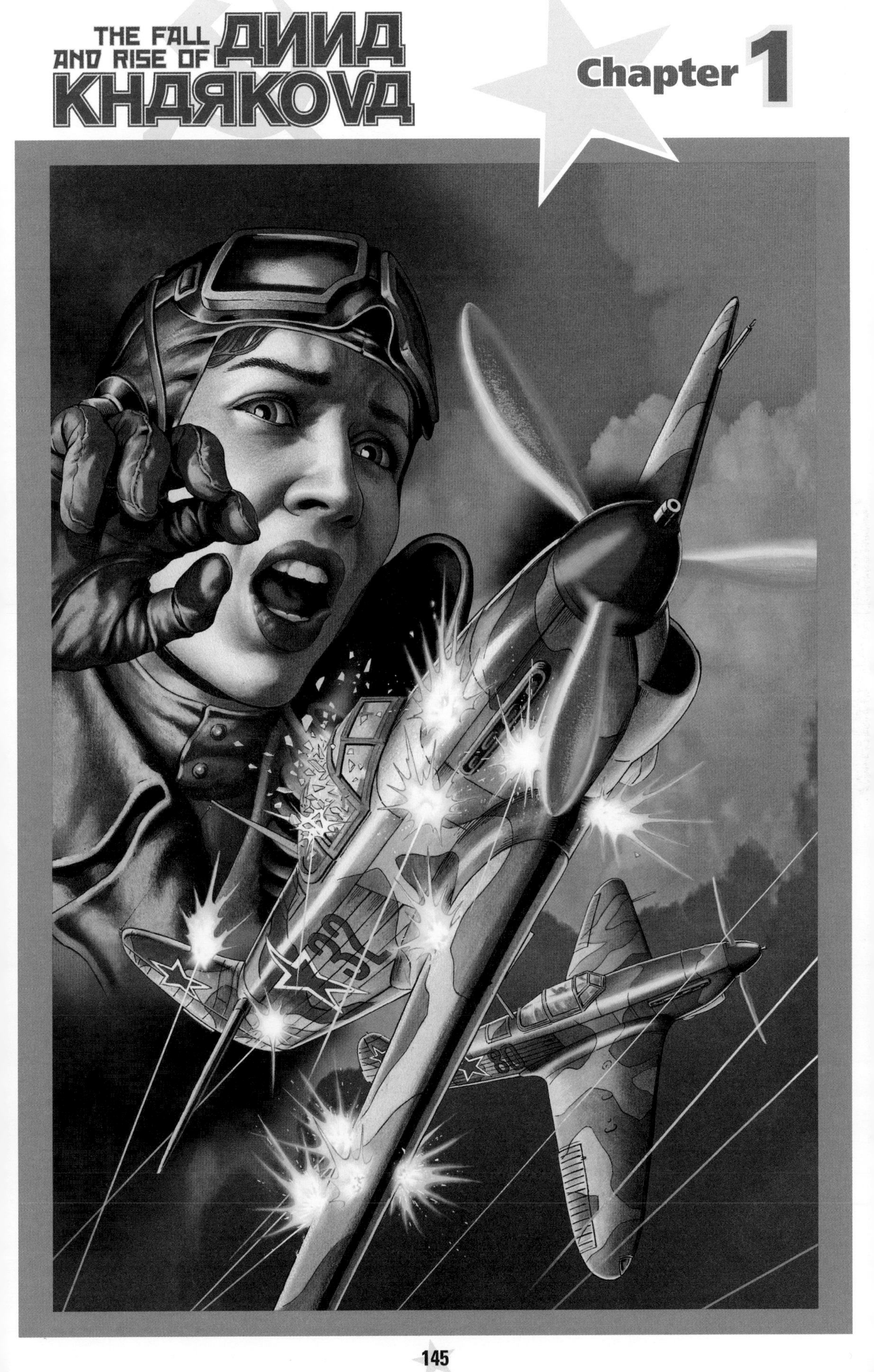

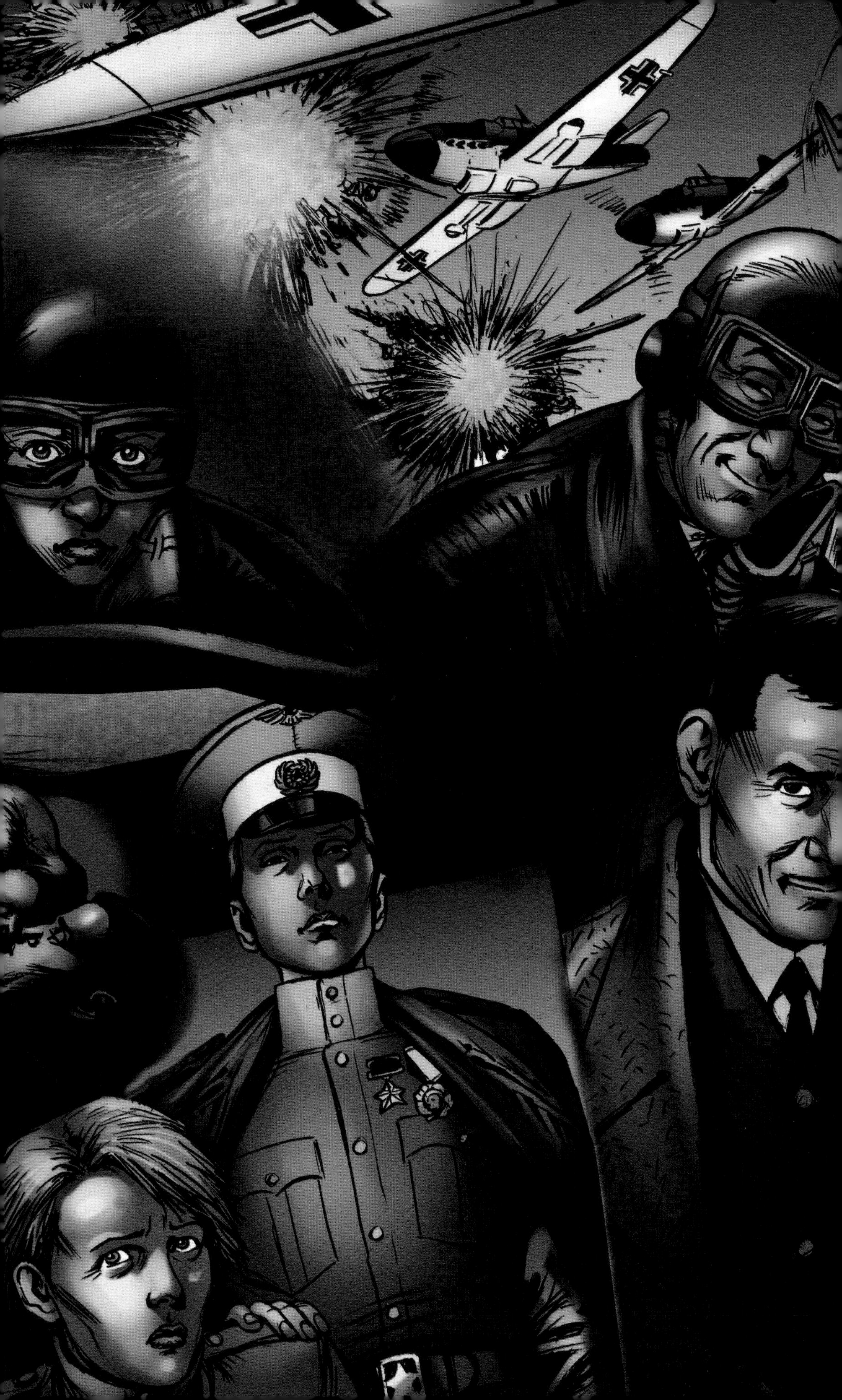

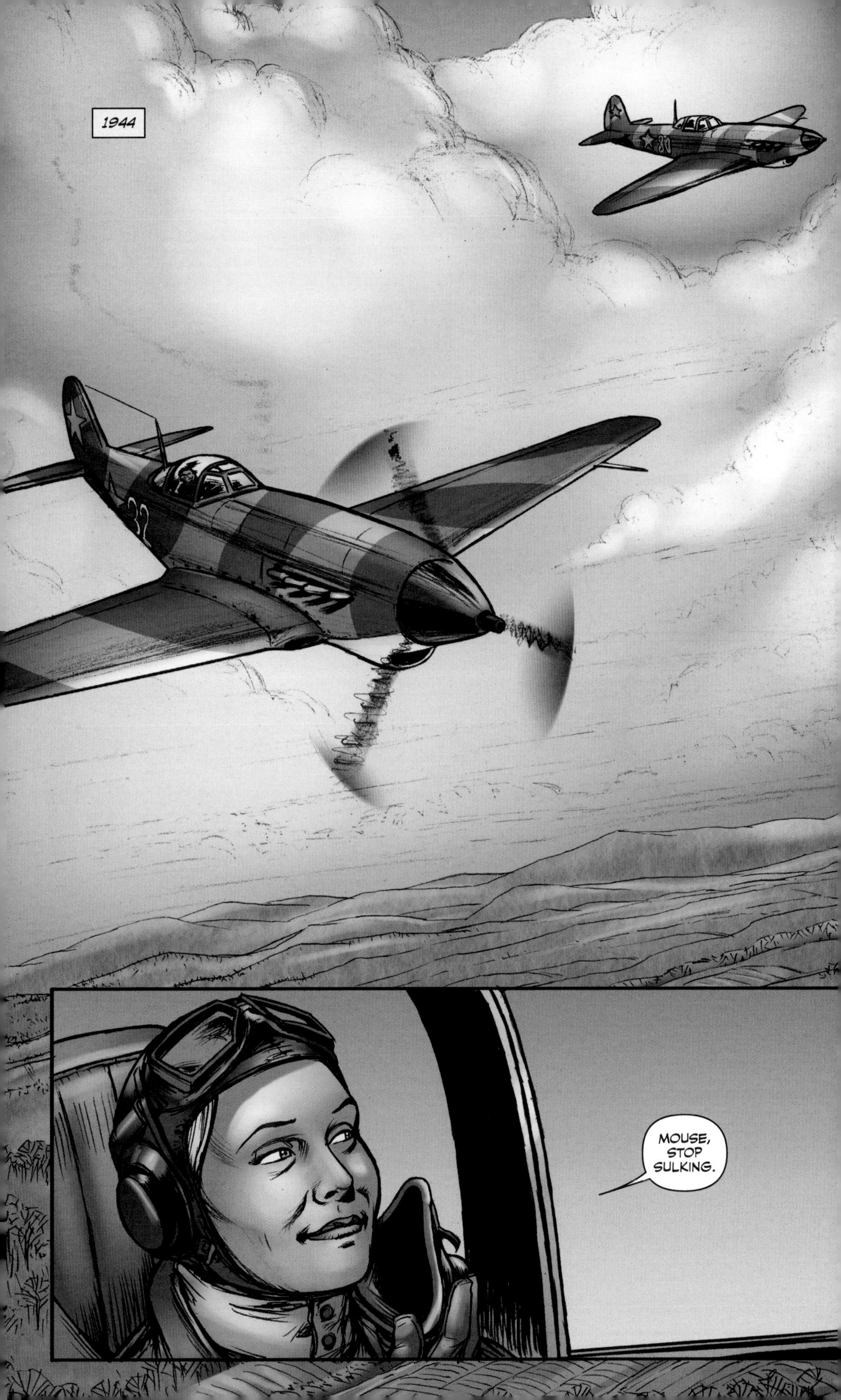
1944
MOUSE, STOP SULKING.

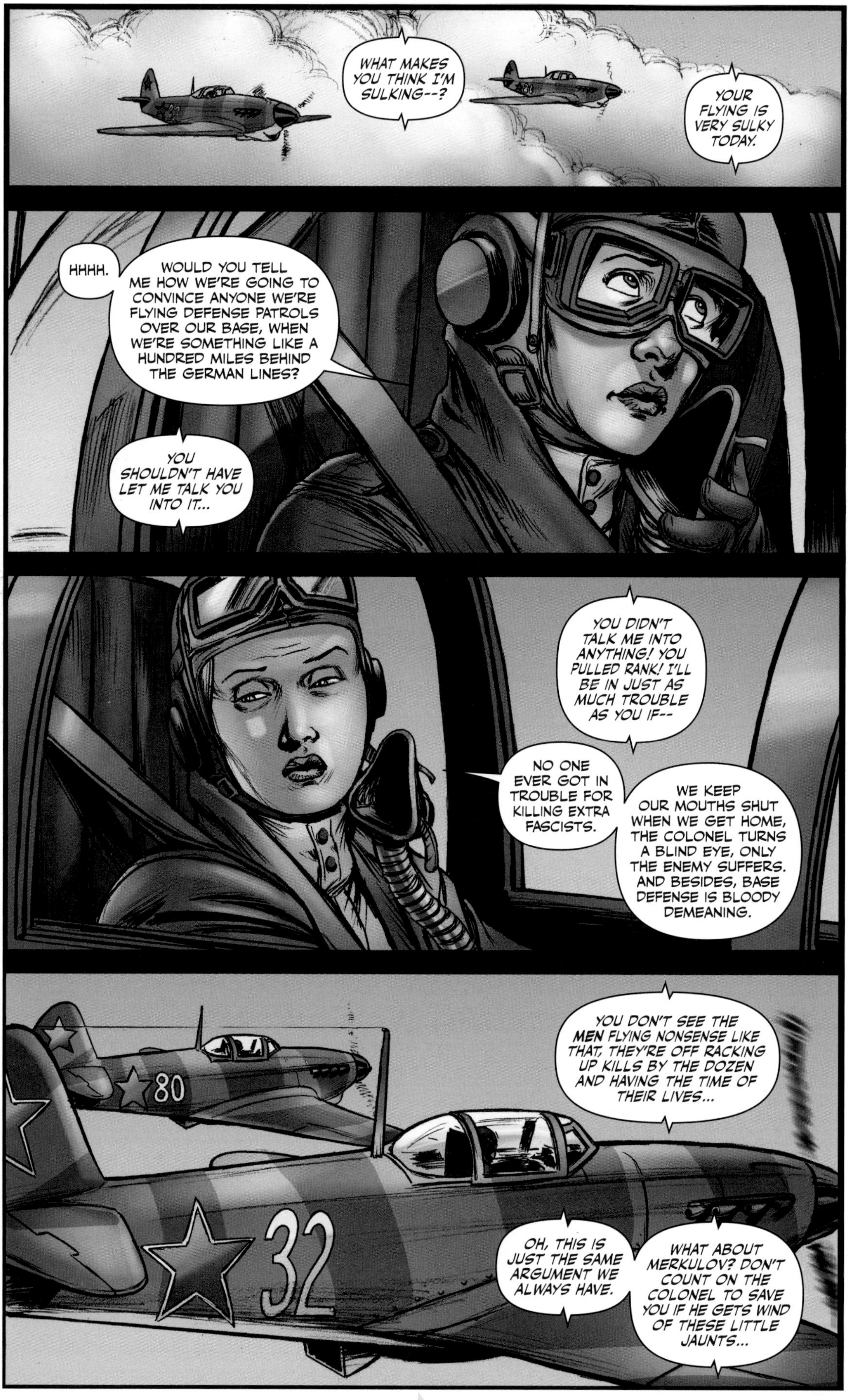
WHAT MAKES YOU THINK I'M SULKING--?
YOUR FLYING IS VERY SULKY TODAY.
HHHH.
WOULD YOU TELL ME HOW WE'RE GOING TO CONVINCE ANYONE WE'RE FLYING DEFENSE PATROLS OVER OUR BASE, WHEN WE'RE SOMETHING LIKE A HUNDRED MILES BEHIND THE GERMAN LINES?
YOU SHOULDN'T HAVE LET ME TALK YOU INTO IT...
YOU DIDN'T TALK ME INTO ANYTHING! YOU PULLED RANK! I'LL BE IN JUST AS MUCH TROUBLE AS YOU IF--
NO ONE EVER GOT IN TROUBLE FOR KILLING EXTRA FASCISTS.
WE KEEP OUR MOUTHS SHUT WHEN WE GET HOME, THE COLONEL TURNS A BLIND EYE, ONLY THE ENEMY SUFFERS. AND BESIDES, BASE DEFENSE IS BLOODY DEMEANING.
80
YOU DON'T SEE THE MEN FLYING NONSENSE LIKE THAT, THEY'RE OFF RACKING UP KILLS BY THE DOZEN AND HAVING THE TIME OF THEIR LIVES...
32
OH, THIS IS JUST THE SAME ARGUMENT WE ALWAYS HAVE.
WHAT ABOUT MERKULOV? DON'T COUNT ON THE COLONEL TO SAVE YOU IF HE GETS WIND OF THESE LITTLE JAUNTS...

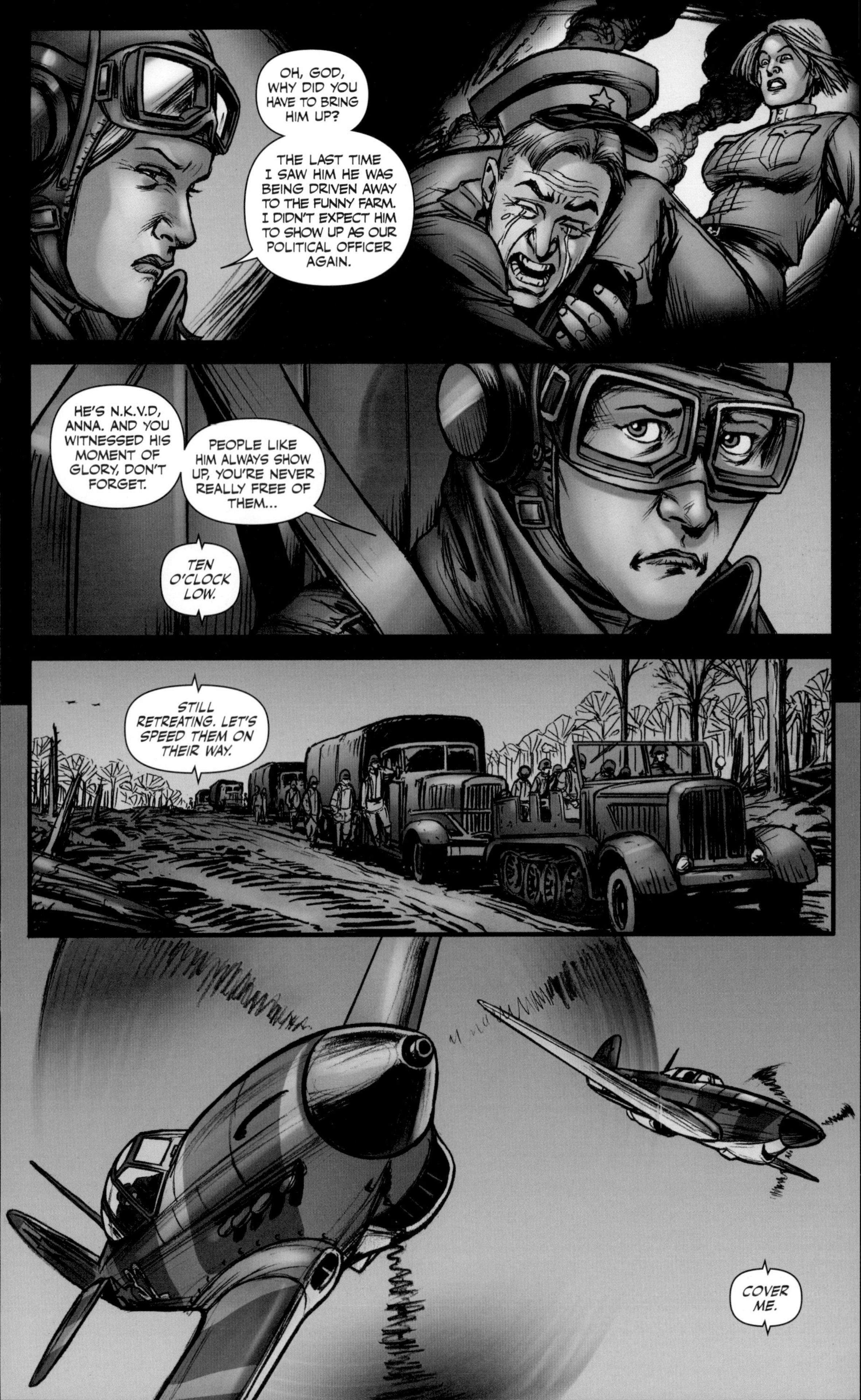
OH, GOD, WHY DID YOU HAVE TO BRING HIM UP?
THE LAST TIME I SAW HIM HE WAS BEING DRIVEN AWAY TO THE FUNNY FARM. I DIDN'T EXPECT HIM TO SHOW UP AS OUR POLITICAL OFFICER AGAIN.
HE'S N.K.V.D, ANNA. AND YOU WITNESSED HIS MOMENT OF GLORY, DON'T FORGET.
PEOPLE LIKE HIM ALWAYS SHOW UP, YOU'RE NEVER REALLY FREE OF THEM...
TEN O'CLOCK LOW.
STILL RETREATING. LET'S SPEED THEM ON THEIR WAY.
COVER ME.

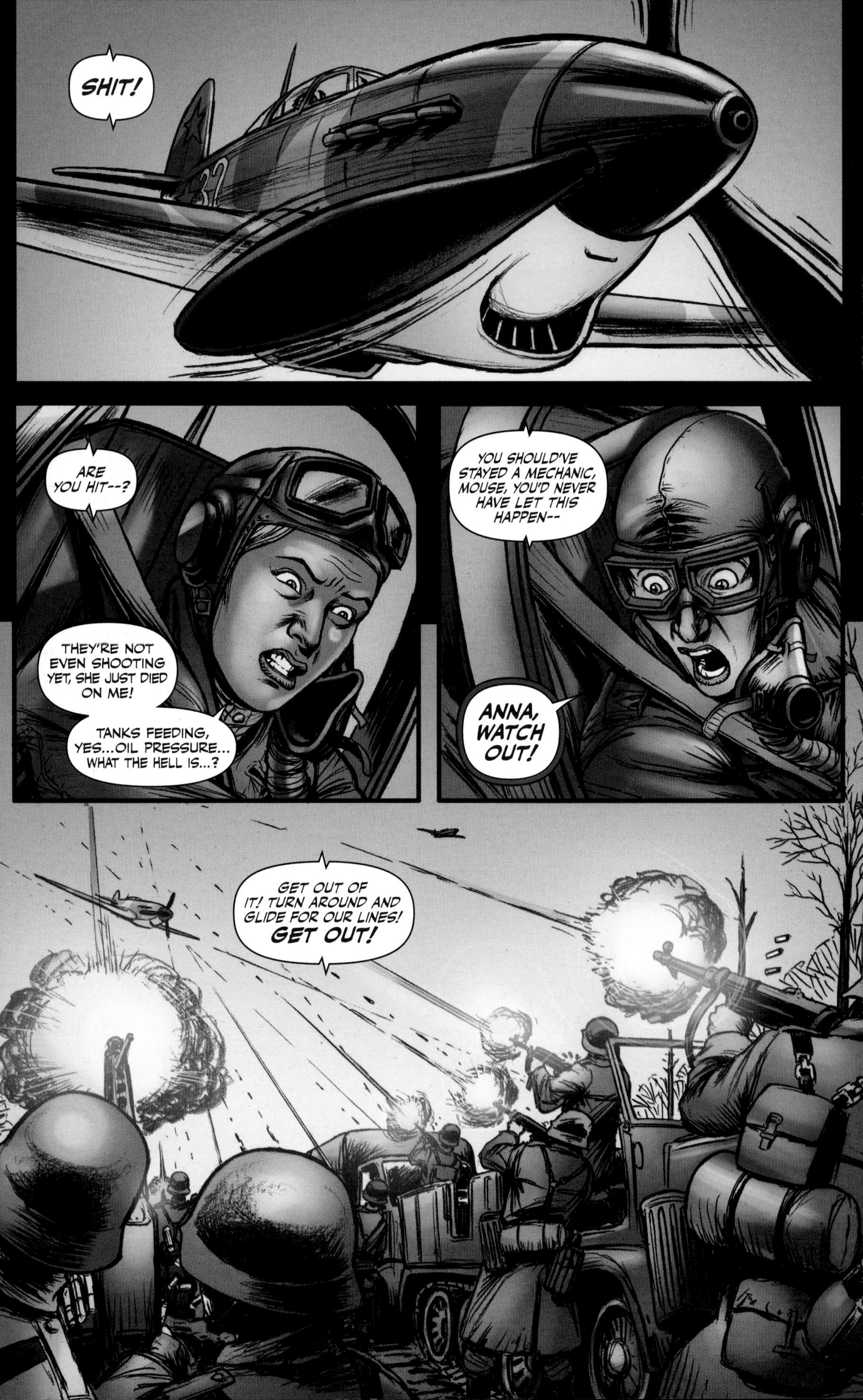
SHIT!
ARE YOU HIT--?
THEY'RE NOT EVEN SHOOTING YET, SHE JUST DIED ON ME!
TANKS FEEDING, YES...OIL PRESSURE... WHAT THE HELL IS...?
YOU SHOULD'VE STAYED A MECHANIC, MOUSE, YOU'D NEVER HAVE LET THIS HAPPEN--
ANNA, WATCH OUT!
GET OUT OF IT! TURN AROUND AND GLIDE FOR OUR LINES! GET OUT!

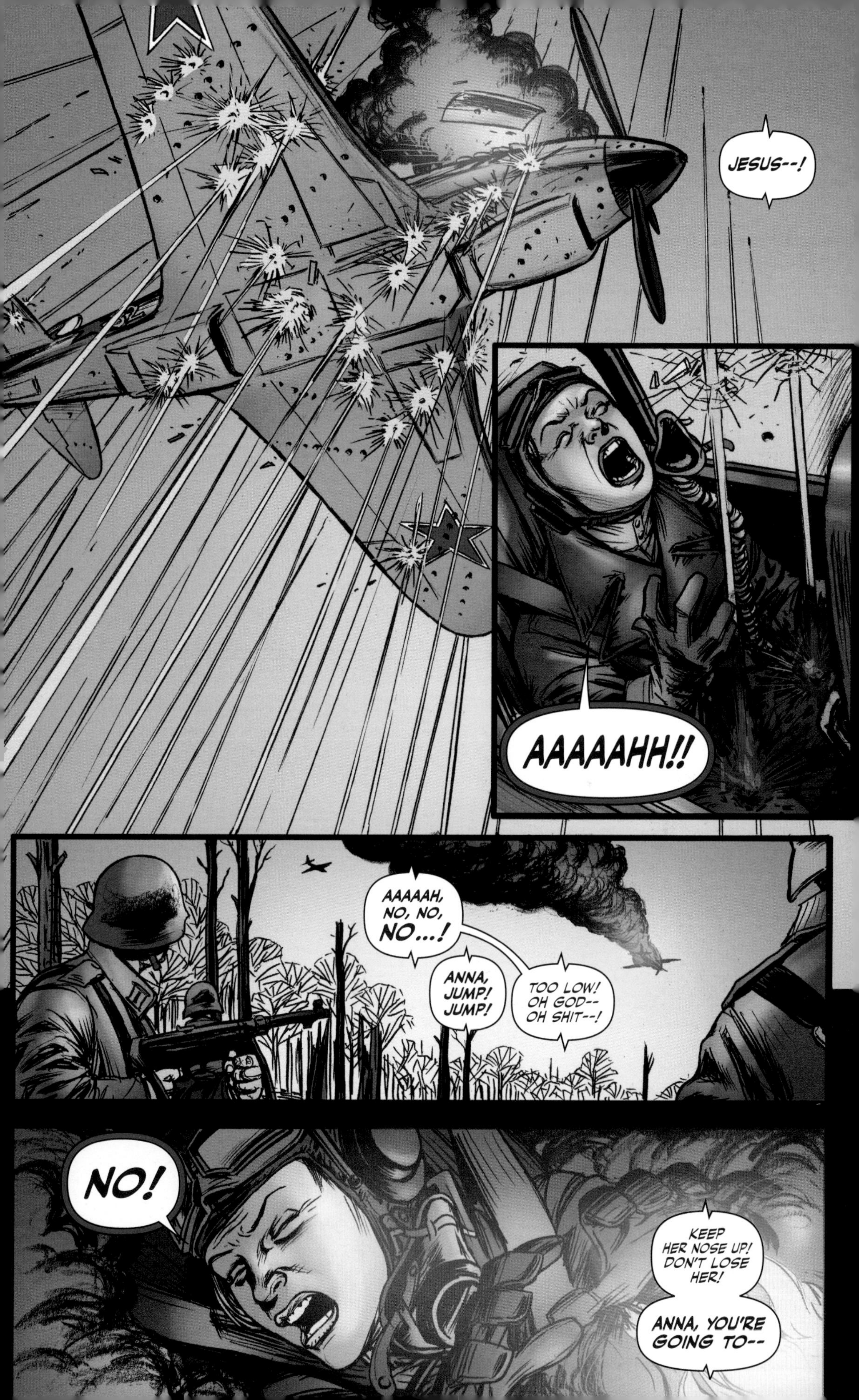
JESUS--!
AAAAAHH!!
AAAAAH, NO, NO, NO...!
ANNA, JUMP! JUMP!
TOO LOW! OH GOD-- OH SHIT--!
NO!
KEEP HER NOSE UP! DON'T LOSE HER!
ANNA, YOU'RE GOING TO--

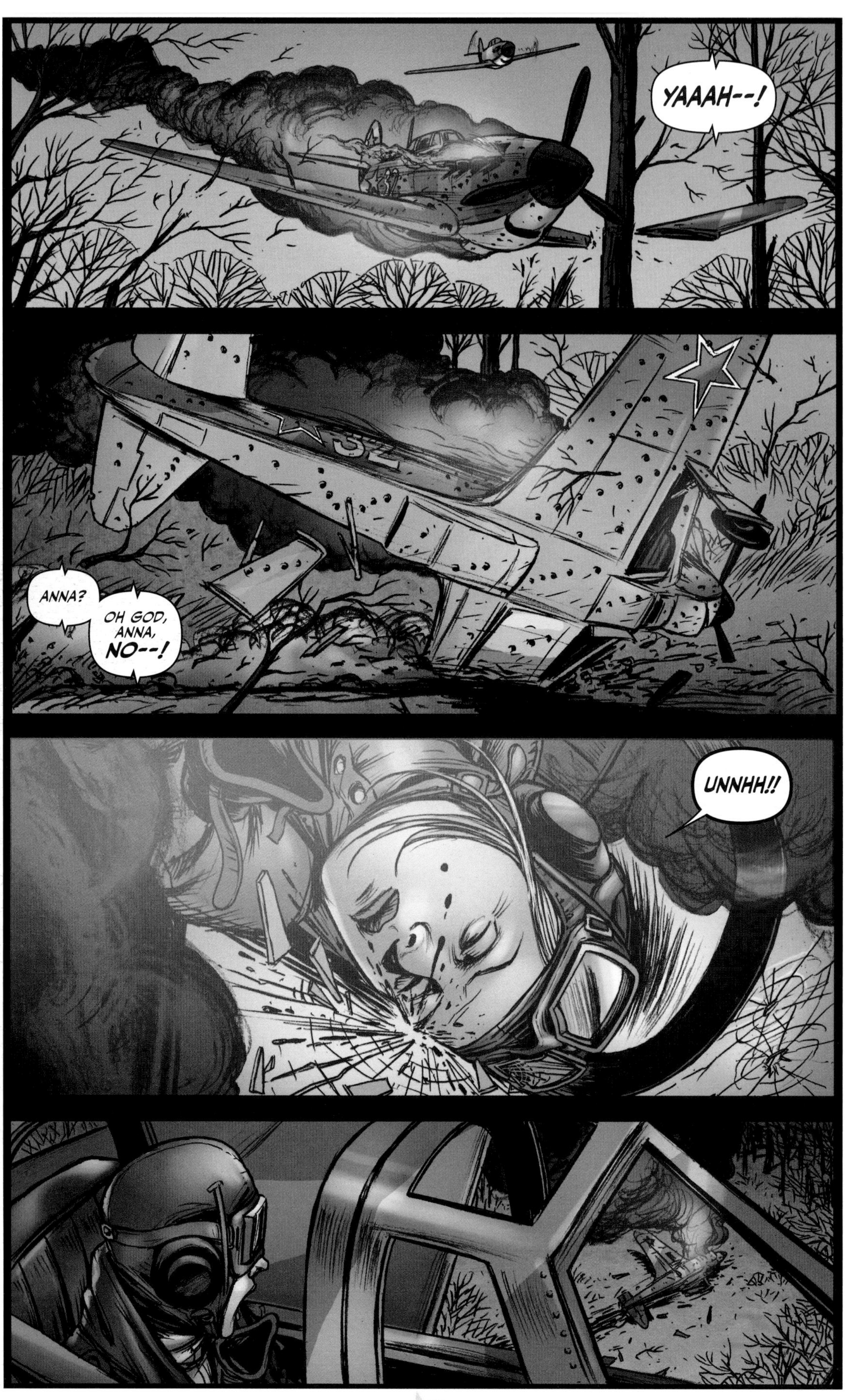
YAAAH--!
ANNA?
OH GOD, ANNA, NO--!
UNNHH!!

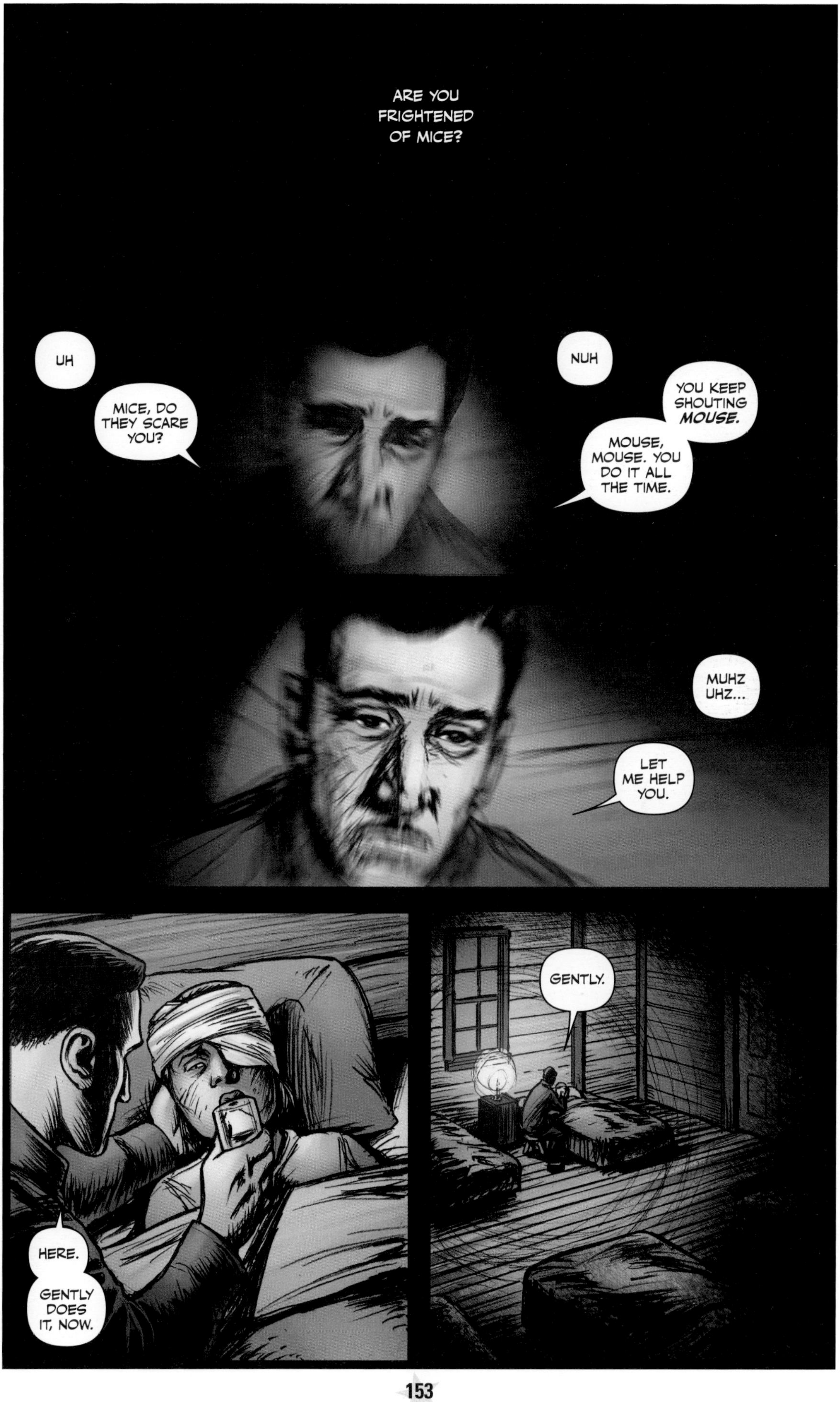
ARE YOU FRIGHTENED OF MICE?
UH
MICE, DO THEY SCARE YOU?
NUH
YOU KEEP SHOUTING *MOUSE.*
MOUSE, MOUSE. YOU DO IT ALL THE TIME.
MUHZ UHZ...
LET ME HELP YOU.
HERE.
GENTLY DOES IT, NOW.
GENTLY.

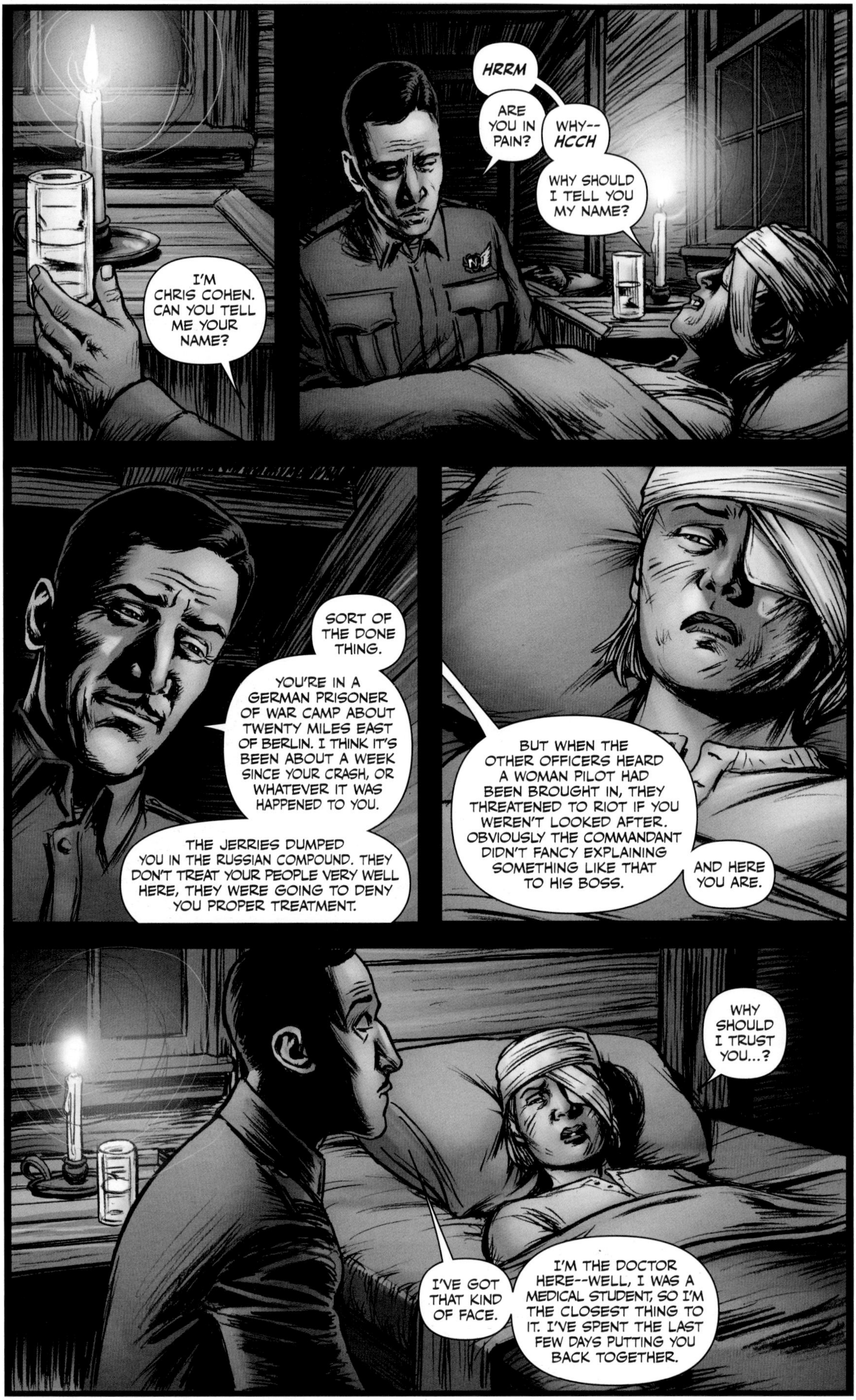
I'M CHRIS COHEN. CAN YOU TELL ME YOUR NAME?
HRRM
ARE YOU IN PAIN?
WHY-- HCCH
WHY SHOULD I TELL YOU MY NAME?
SORT OF THE DONE THING.
YOU'RE IN A GERMAN PRISONER OF WAR CAMP ABOUT TWENTY MILES EAST OF BERLIN. I THINK IT'S BEEN ABOUT A WEEK SINCE YOUR CRASH, OR WHATEVER IT WAS HAPPENED TO YOU.
THE JERRIES DUMPED YOU IN THE RUSSIAN COMPOUND. THEY DON'T TREAT YOUR PEOPLE VERY WELL HERE, THEY WERE GOING TO DENY YOU PROPER TREATMENT.
BUT WHEN THE OTHER OFFICERS HEARD A WOMAN PILOT HAD BEEN BROUGHT IN, THEY THREATENED TO RIOT IF YOU WEREN'T LOOKED AFTER. OBVIOUSLY THE COMMANDANT DIDN'T FANCY EXPLAINING SOMETHING LIKE THAT TO HIS BOSS.
AND HERE YOU ARE.
WHY SHOULD I TRUST YOU...?
I'VE GOT THAT KIND OF FACE.
I'M THE DOCTOR HERE--WELL, I WAS A MEDICAL STUDENT, SO I'M THE CLOSEST THING TO IT. I'VE SPENT THE LAST FEW DAYS PUTTING YOU BACK TOGETHER.

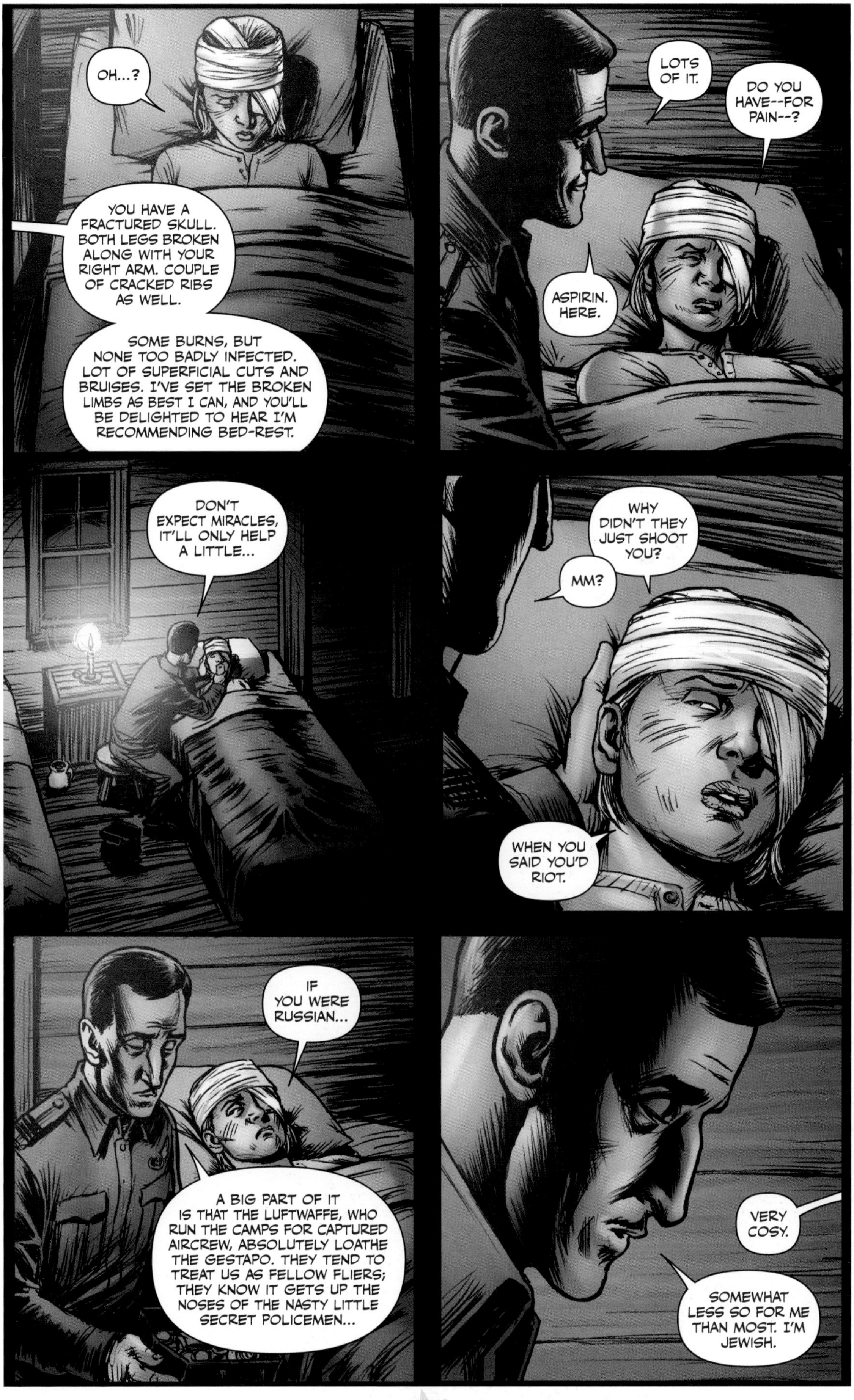
OH...?
YOU HAVE A FRACTURED SKULL. BOTH LEGS BROKEN ALONG WITH YOUR RIGHT ARM. COUPLE OF CRACKED RIBS AS WELL.
SOME BURNS, BUT NONE TOO BADLY INFECTED. LOT OF SUPERFICIAL CUTS AND BRUISES. I'VE SET THE BROKEN LIMBS AS BEST I CAN, AND YOU'LL BE DELIGHTED TO HEAR I'M RECOMMENDING BED-REST.
LOTS OF IT.
DO YOU HAVE--FOR PAIN--?
ASPIRIN. HERE.
DON'T EXPECT MIRACLES, IT'LL ONLY HELP A LITTLE...
WHY DIDN'T THEY JUST SHOOT YOU?
MM?
WHEN YOU SAID YOU'D RIOT.
IF YOU WERE RUSSIAN...
A BIG PART OF IT IS THAT THE LUFTWAFFE, WHO RUN THE CAMPS FOR CAPTURED AIRCREW, ABSOLUTELY LOATHE THE GESTAPO. THEY TEND TO TREAT US AS FELLOW FLIERS; THEY KNOW IT GETS UP THE NOSES OF THE NASTY LITTLE SECRET POLICEMEN...
VERY COSY.
SOMEWHAT LESS SO FOR ME THAN MOST. I'M JEWISH.

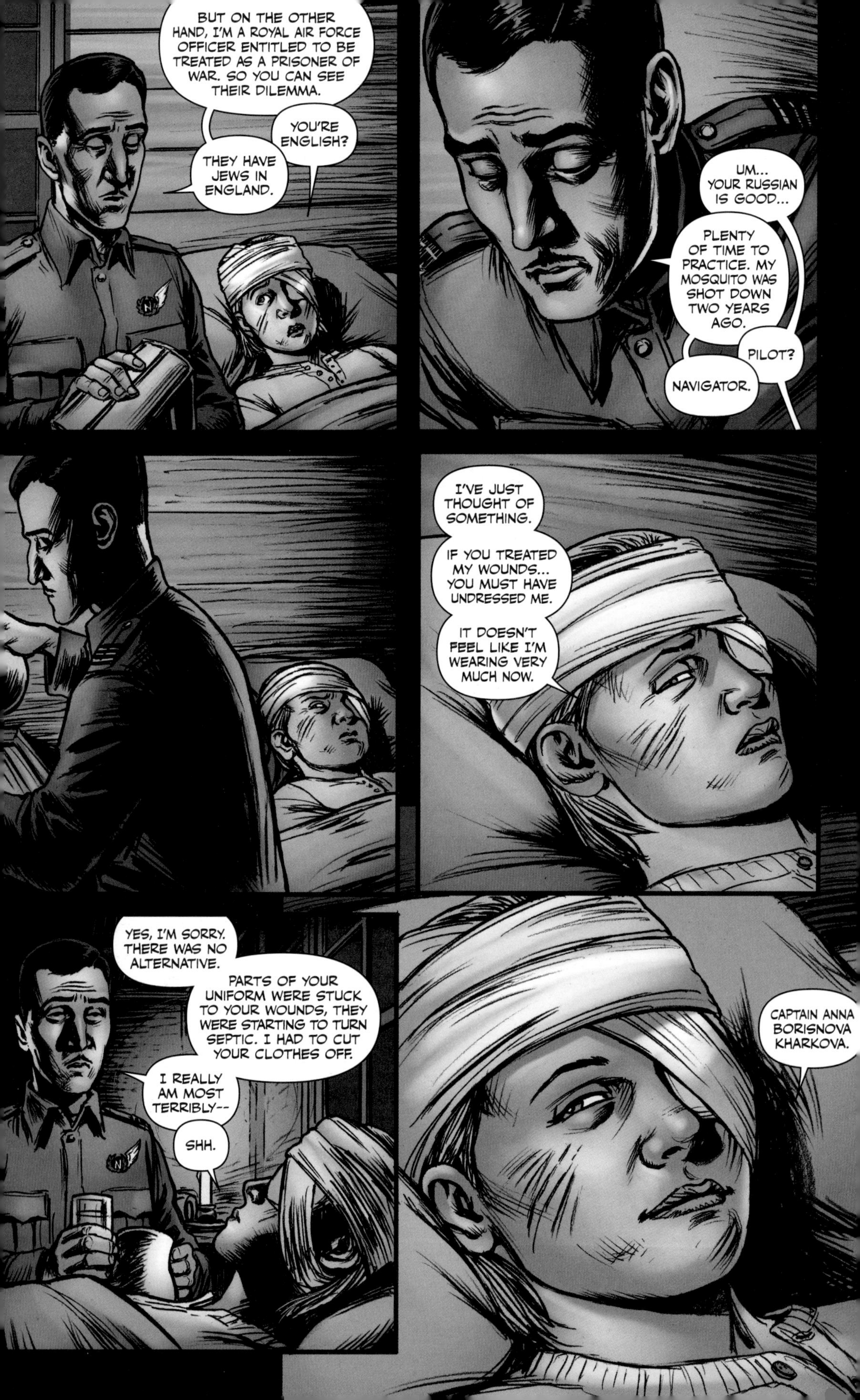
BUT ON THE OTHER HAND, I'M A ROYAL AIR FORCE OFFICER ENTITLED TO BE TREATED AS A PRISONER OF WAR. SO YOU CAN SEE THEIR DILEMMA.
YOU'RE ENGLISH?
THEY HAVE JEWS IN ENGLAND.
UM... YOUR RUSSIAN IS GOOD...
PLENTY OF TIME TO PRACTICE. MY MOSQUITO WAS SHOT DOWN TWO YEARS AGO.
PILOT?
NAVIGATOR.
I'VE JUST THOUGHT OF SOMETHING.
IF YOU TREATED MY WOUNDS... YOU MUST HAVE UNDRESSED ME.
IT DOESN'T FEEL LIKE I'M WEARING VERY MUCH NOW.
YES, I'M SORRY. THERE WAS NO ALTERNATIVE.
PARTS OF YOUR UNIFORM WERE STUCK TO YOUR WOUNDS, THEY WERE STARTING TO TURN SEPTIC. I HAD TO CUT YOUR CLOTHES OFF.
I REALLY AM MOST TERRIBLY--
SHH.
CAPTAIN ANNA BORISNOVA KHARKOVA.

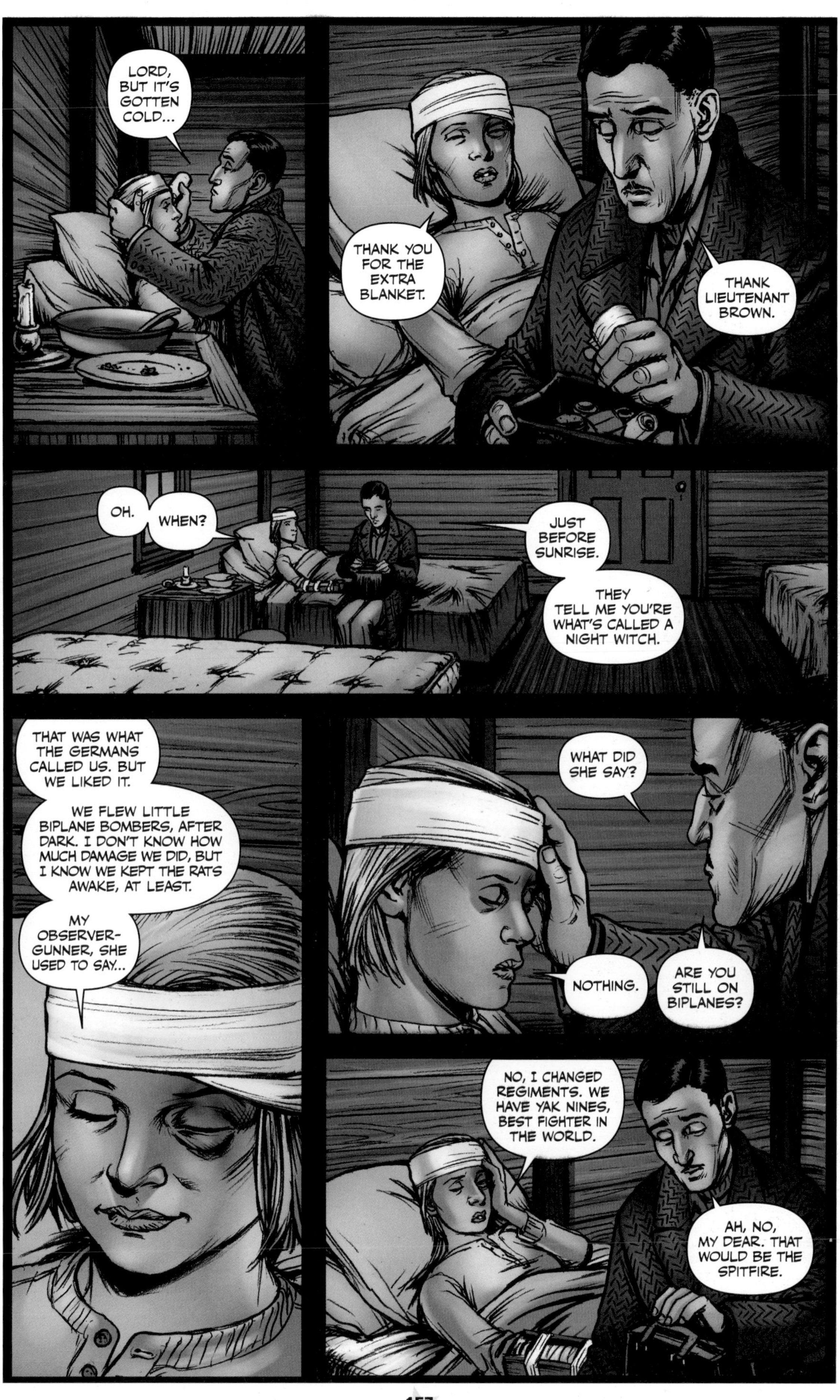
LORD, BUT IT'S GOTTEN COLD...
THANK YOU FOR THE EXTRA BLANKET.
THANK LIEUTENANT BROWN.
OH.
WHEN?
JUST BEFORE SUNRISE.
THEY TELL ME YOU'RE WHAT'S CALLED A NIGHT WITCH.
THAT WAS WHAT THE GERMANS CALLED US. BUT WE LIKED IT.
WE FLEW LITTLE BIPLANE BOMBERS, AFTER DARK. I DON'T KNOW HOW MUCH DAMAGE WE DID, BUT I KNOW WE KEPT THE RATS AWAKE, AT LEAST.
MY OBSERVER-GUNNER, SHE USED TO SAY...
WHAT DID SHE SAY?
NOTHING.
ARE YOU STILL ON BIPLANES?
NO, I CHANGED REGIMENTS. WE HAVE YAK NINES, BEST FIGHTER IN THE WORLD.
AH, NO, MY DEAR. THAT WOULD BE THE SPITFIRE.

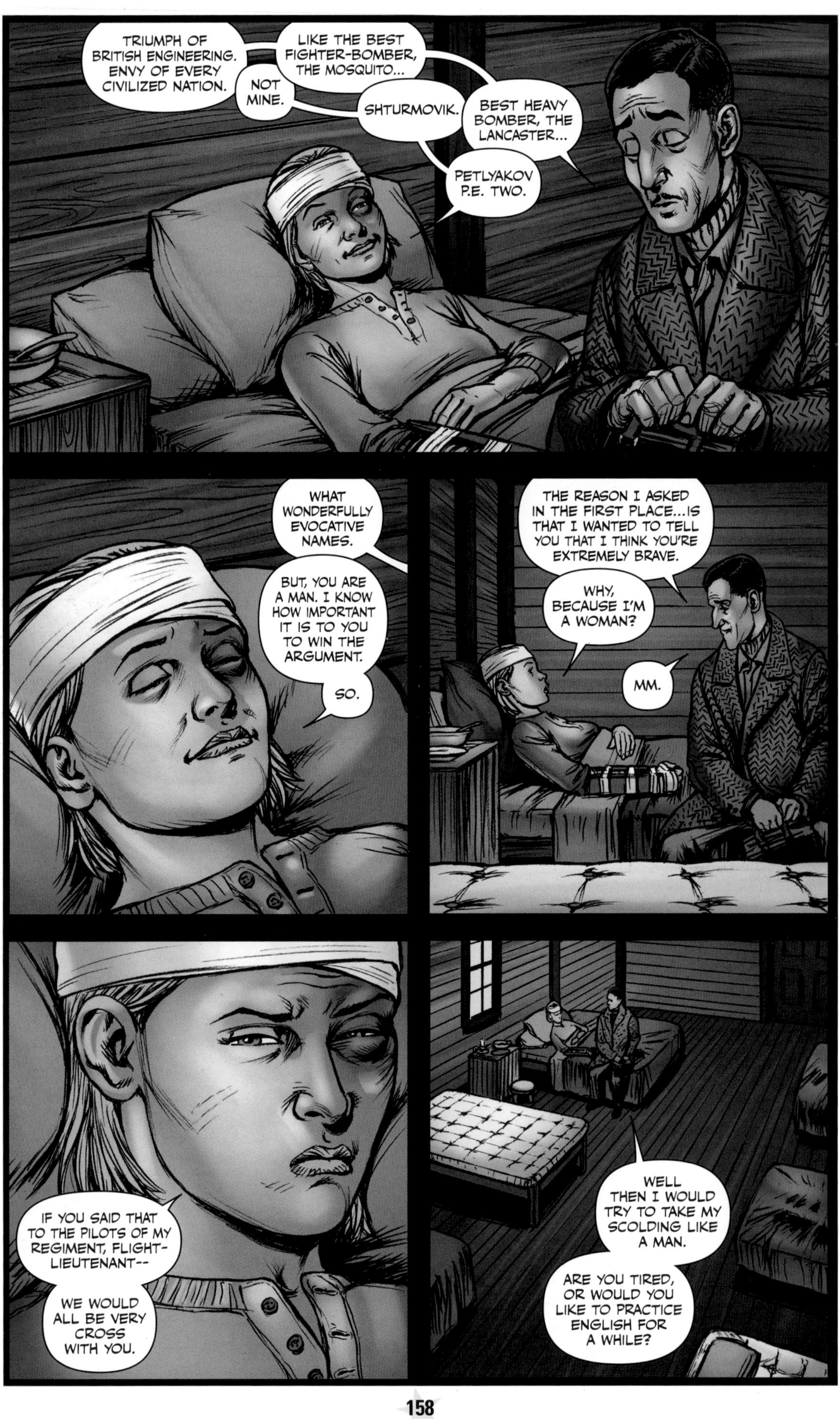
TRIUMPH OF BRITISH ENGINEERING. ENVY OF EVERY CIVILIZED NATION.
LIKE THE BEST FIGHTER-BOMBER, THE MOSQUITO...
NOT MINE.
SHTURMOVIK.
BEST HEAVY BOMBER, THE LANCASTER...
PETLYAKOV P.E. TWO.
WHAT WONDERFULLY EVOCATIVE NAMES.
BUT, YOU ARE A MAN. I KNOW HOW IMPORTANT IT IS TO YOU TO WIN THE ARGUMENT.
SO.
THE REASON I ASKED IN THE FIRST PLACE...IS THAT I WANTED TO TELL YOU THAT I THINK YOU'RE EXTREMELY BRAVE.
WHY, BECAUSE I'M A WOMAN?
MM.
IF YOU SAID THAT TO THE PILOTS OF MY REGIMENT, FLIGHT-LIEUTENANT--
WE WOULD ALL BE VERY CROSS WITH YOU.
WELL THEN I WOULD TRY TO TAKE MY SCOLDING LIKE A MAN.
ARE YOU TIRED, OR WOULD YOU LIKE TO PRACTICE ENGLISH FOR A WHILE?

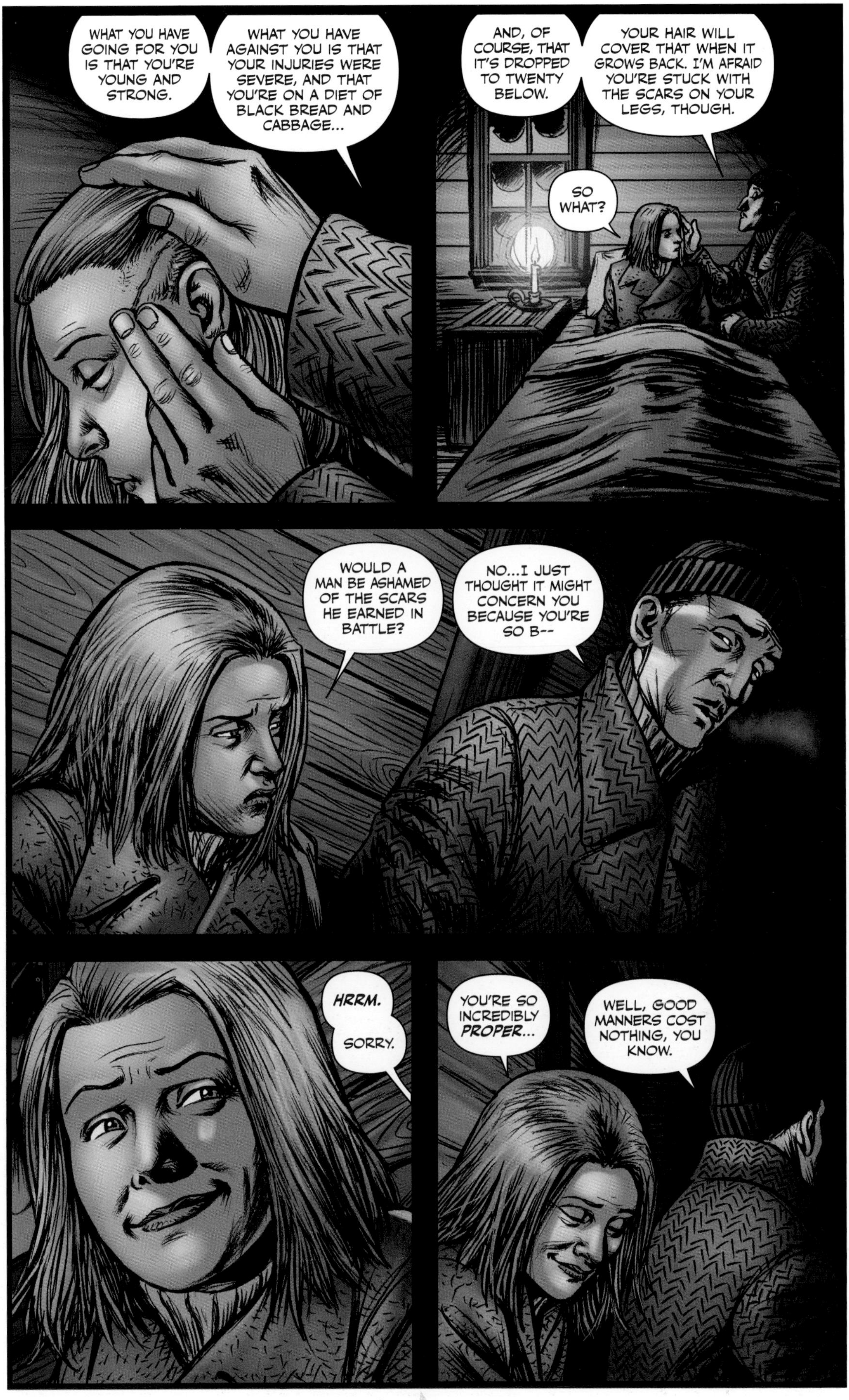

WHAT YOU HAVE GOING FOR YOU IS THAT YOU'RE YOUNG AND STRONG.
WHAT YOU HAVE AGAINST YOU IS THAT YOUR INJURIES WERE SEVERE, AND THAT YOU'RE ON A DIET OF BLACK BREAD AND CABBAGE...
AND, OF COURSE, THAT IT'S DROPPED TO TWENTY BELOW.
YOUR HAIR WILL COVER THAT WHEN IT GROWS BACK. I'M AFRAID YOU'RE STUCK WITH THE SCARS ON YOUR LEGS, THOUGH.
SO WHAT?
WOULD A MAN BE ASHAMED OF THE SCARS HE EARNED IN BATTLE?
NO...I JUST THOUGHT IT MIGHT CONCERN YOU BECAUSE YOU'RE SO B--
HRRM.
SORRY.
YOU'RE SO INCREDIBLY *PROPER*...
WELL, GOOD MANNERS COST NOTHING, YOU KNOW.

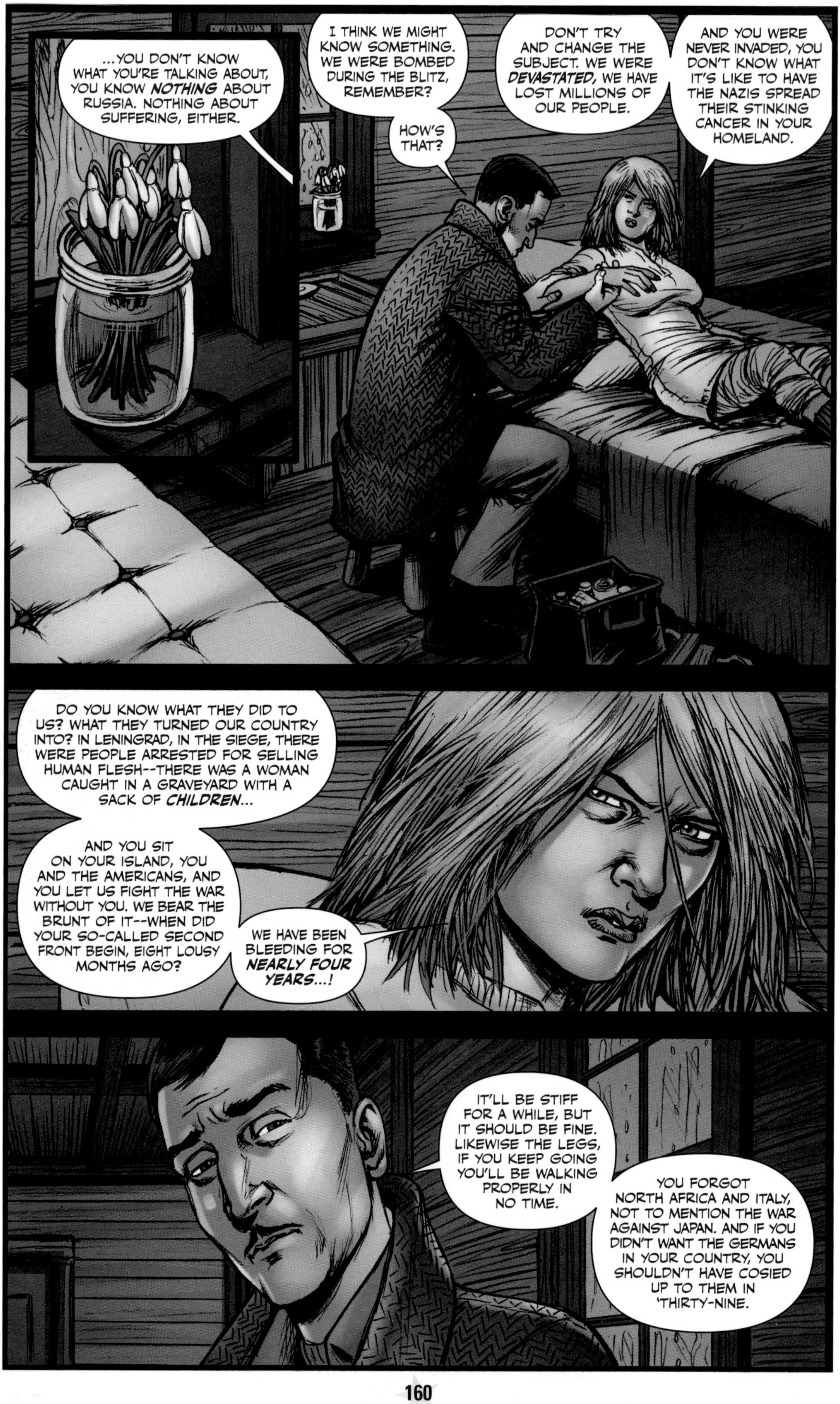
...YOU DON'T KNOW WHAT YOU'RE TALKING ABOUT, YOU KNOW NOTHING ABOUT RUSSIA. NOTHING ABOUT SUFFERING, EITHER.
I THINK WE MIGHT KNOW SOMETHING. WE WERE BOMBED DURING THE BLITZ, REMEMBER?
HOW'S THAT?
DON'T TRY AND CHANGE THE SUBJECT. WE WERE DEVASTATED, WE HAVE LOST MILLIONS OF OUR PEOPLE.
AND YOU WERE NEVER INVADED, YOU DON'T KNOW WHAT IT'S LIKE TO HAVE THE NAZIS SPREAD THEIR STINKING CANCER IN YOUR HOMELAND.
DO YOU KNOW WHAT THEY DID TO US? WHAT THEY TURNED OUR COUNTRY INTO? IN LENINGRAD, IN THE SIEGE, THERE WERE PEOPLE ARRESTED FOR SELLING HUMAN FLESH--THERE WAS A WOMAN CAUGHT IN A GRAVEYARD WITH A SACK OF CHILDREN...
AND YOU SIT ON YOUR ISLAND, YOU AND THE AMERICANS, AND YOU LET US FIGHT THE WAR WITHOUT YOU. WE BEAR THE BRUNT OF IT--WHEN DID YOUR SO-CALLED SECOND FRONT BEGIN, EIGHT LOUSY MONTHS AGO?
WE HAVE BEEN BLEEDING FOR NEARLY FOUR YEARS...!
IT'LL BE STIFF FOR A WHILE, BUT IT SHOULD BE FINE. LIKEWISE THE LEGS, IF YOU KEEP GOING YOU'LL BE WALKING PROPERLY IN NO TIME.
YOU FORGOT NORTH AFRICA AND ITALY, NOT TO MENTION THE WAR AGAINST JAPAN. AND IF YOU DIDN'T WANT THE GERMANS IN YOUR COUNTRY, YOU SHOULDN'T HAVE COSIED UP TO THEM IN 'THIRTY-NINE.

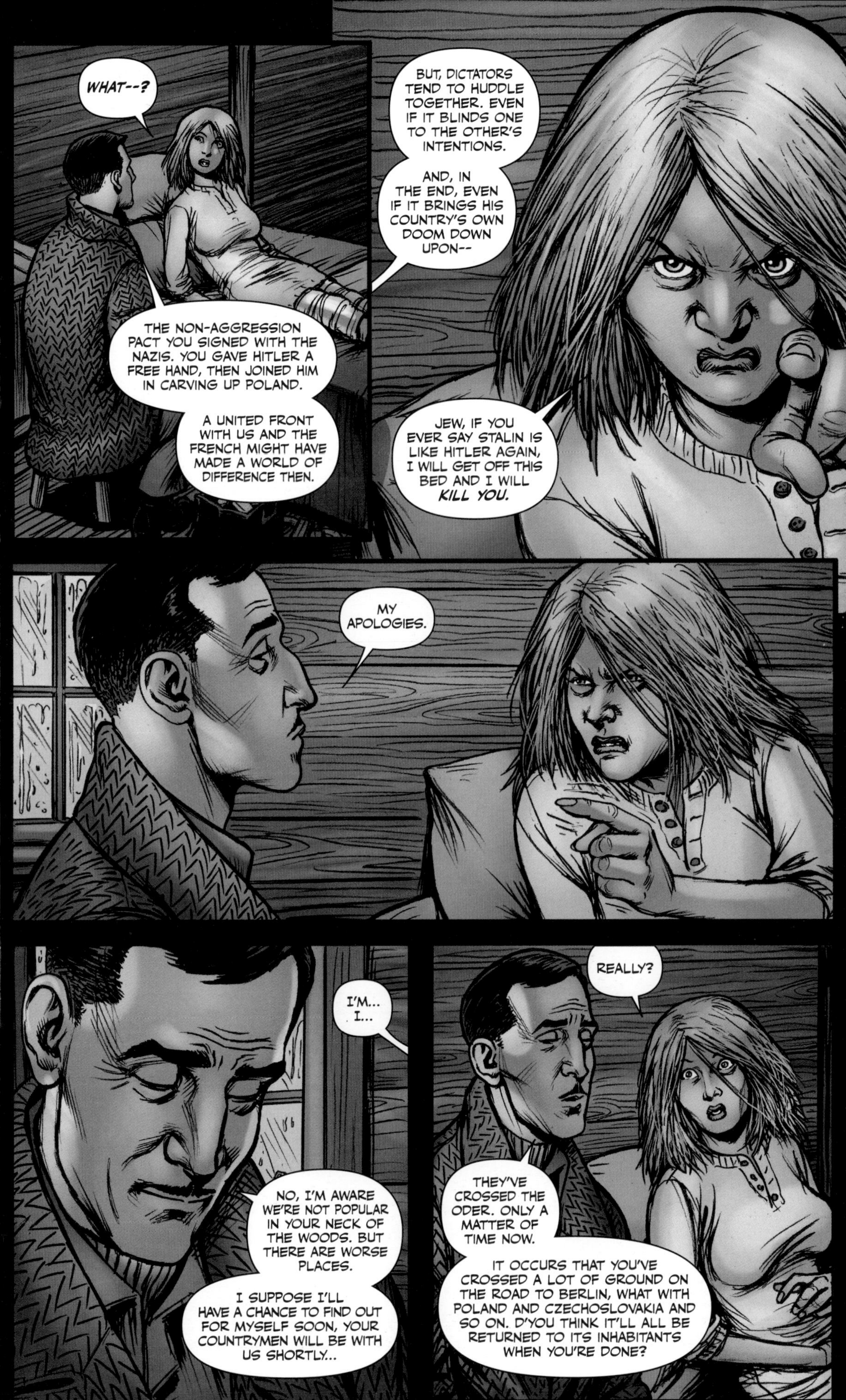
WHAT--?
THE NON-AGGRESSION PACT YOU SIGNED WITH THE NAZIS. YOU GAVE HITLER A FREE HAND, THEN JOINED HIM IN CARVING UP POLAND.
A UNITED FRONT WITH US AND THE FRENCH MIGHT HAVE MADE A WORLD OF DIFFERENCE THEN.
BUT, DICTATORS TEND TO HUDDLE TOGETHER. EVEN IF IT BLINDS ONE TO THE OTHER'S INTENTIONS.
AND, IN THE END, EVEN IF IT BRINGS HIS COUNTRY'S OWN DOOM DOWN UPON--
JEW, IF YOU EVER SAY STALIN IS LIKE HITLER AGAIN, I WILL GET OFF THIS BED AND I WILL KILL YOU.
MY APOLOGIES.
I'M... I...
NO, I'M AWARE WE'RE NOT POPULAR IN YOUR NECK OF THE WOODS. BUT THERE ARE WORSE PLACES.
I SUPPOSE I'LL HAVE A CHANCE TO FIND OUT FOR MYSELF SOON, YOUR COUNTRYMEN WILL BE WITH US SHORTLY...
REALLY?
THEY'VE CROSSED THE ODER. ONLY A MATTER OF TIME NOW.
IT OCCURS THAT YOU'VE CROSSED A LOT OF GROUND ON THE ROAD TO BERLIN, WHAT WITH POLAND AND CZECHOSLOVAKIA AND SO ON. D'YOU THINK IT'LL ALL BE RETURNED TO ITS INHABITANTS WHEN YOU'RE DONE?

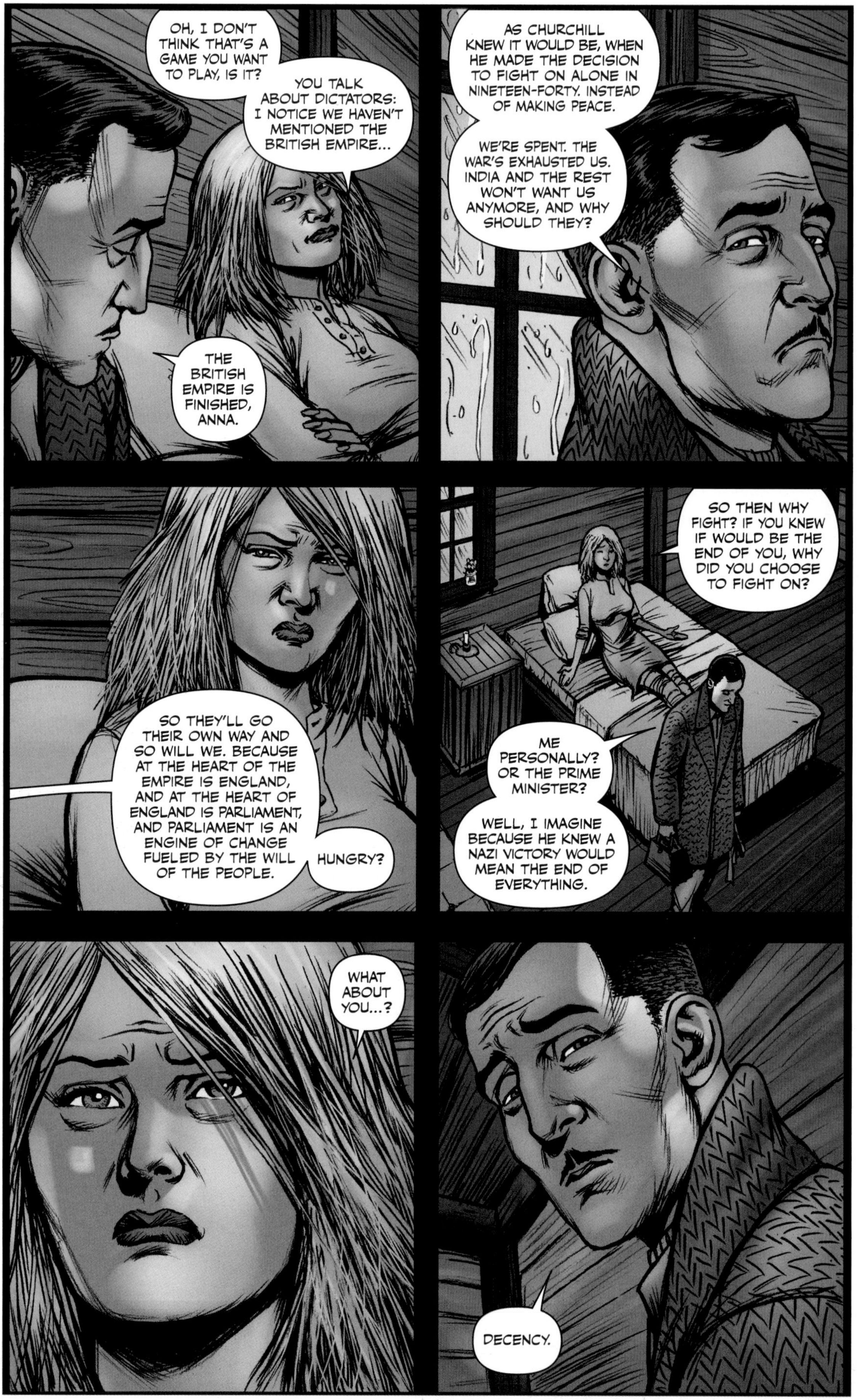
OH, I DON'T THINK THAT'S A GAME YOU WANT TO PLAY, IS IT?
YOU TALK ABOUT DICTATORS: I NOTICE WE HAVEN'T MENTIONED THE BRITISH EMPIRE...
THE BRITISH EMPIRE IS FINISHED, ANNA.
AS CHURCHILL KNEW IT WOULD BE, WHEN HE MADE THE DECISION TO FIGHT ON ALONE IN NINETEEN-FORTY. INSTEAD OF MAKING PEACE.
WE'RE SPENT. THE WAR'S EXHAUSTED US. INDIA AND THE REST WON'T WANT US ANYMORE, AND WHY SHOULD THEY?
SO THEY'LL GO THEIR OWN WAY AND SO WILL WE. BECAUSE AT THE HEART OF THE EMPIRE IS ENGLAND, AND AT THE HEART OF ENGLAND IS PARLIAMENT, AND PARLIAMENT IS AN ENGINE OF CHANGE FUELED BY THE WILL OF THE PEOPLE.
HUNGRY?
SO THEN WHY FIGHT? IF YOU KNEW IF WOULD BE THE END OF YOU, WHY DID YOU CHOOSE TO FIGHT ON?
ME PERSONALLY? OR THE PRIME MINISTER?
WELL, I IMAGINE BECAUSE HE KNEW A NAZI VICTORY WOULD MEAN THE END OF EVERYTHING.
WHAT ABOUT YOU...?
DECENCY.

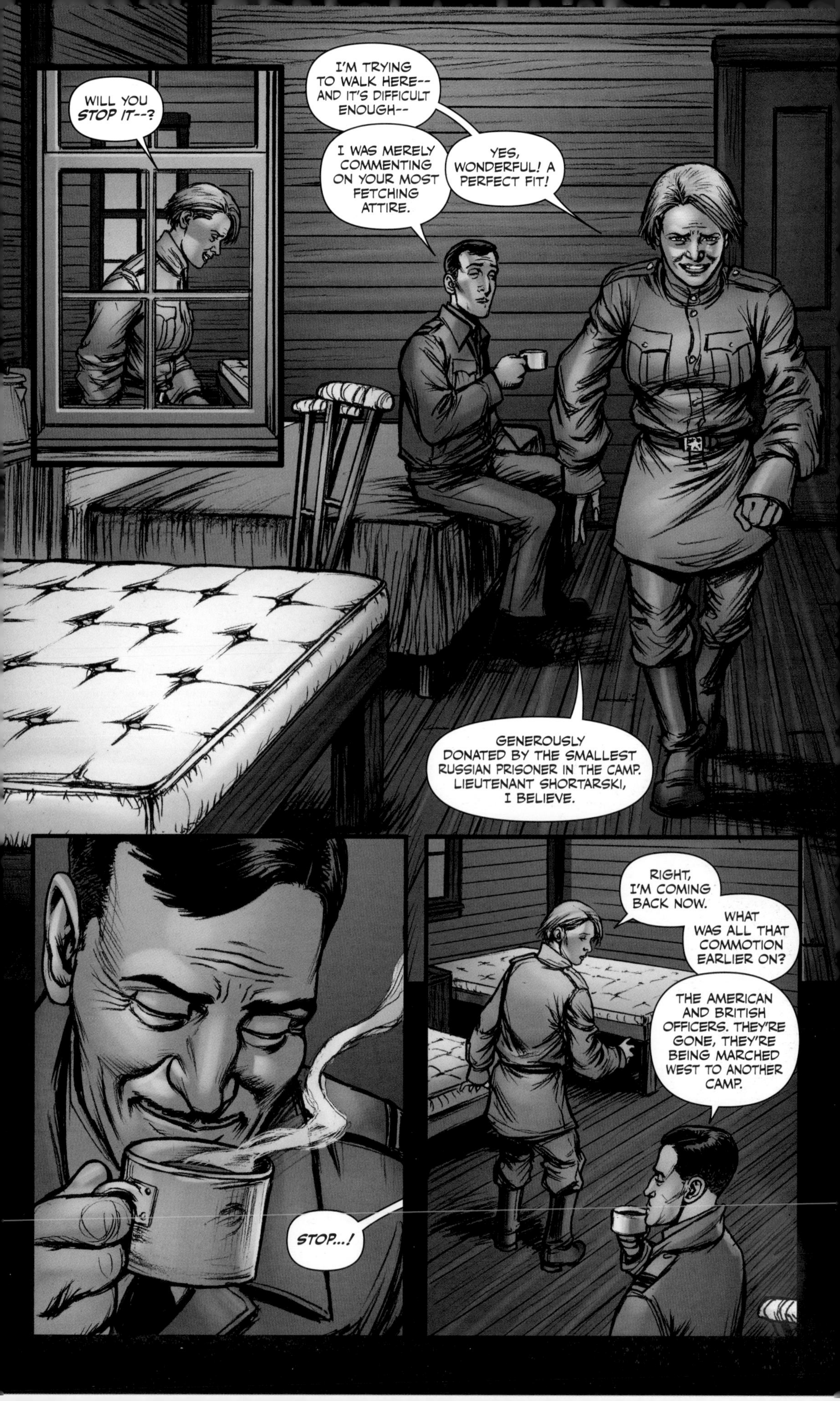
WILL YOU *STOP IT--?*
I'M TRYING TO WALK HERE-- AND IT'S DIFFICULT ENOUGH--
YES, WONDERFUL! A PERFECT FIT!
I WAS MERELY COMMENTING ON YOUR MOST FETCHING ATTIRE.
GENEROUSLY DONATED BY THE SMALLEST RUSSIAN PRISONER IN THE CAMP. LIEUTENANT SHORTARSKI, I BELIEVE.
STOP...!
RIGHT, I'M COMING BACK NOW.
WHAT WAS ALL THAT COMMOTION EARLIER ON?
THE AMERICAN AND BRITISH OFFICERS. THEY'RE GONE, THEY'RE BEING MARCHED WEST TO ANOTHER CAMP.

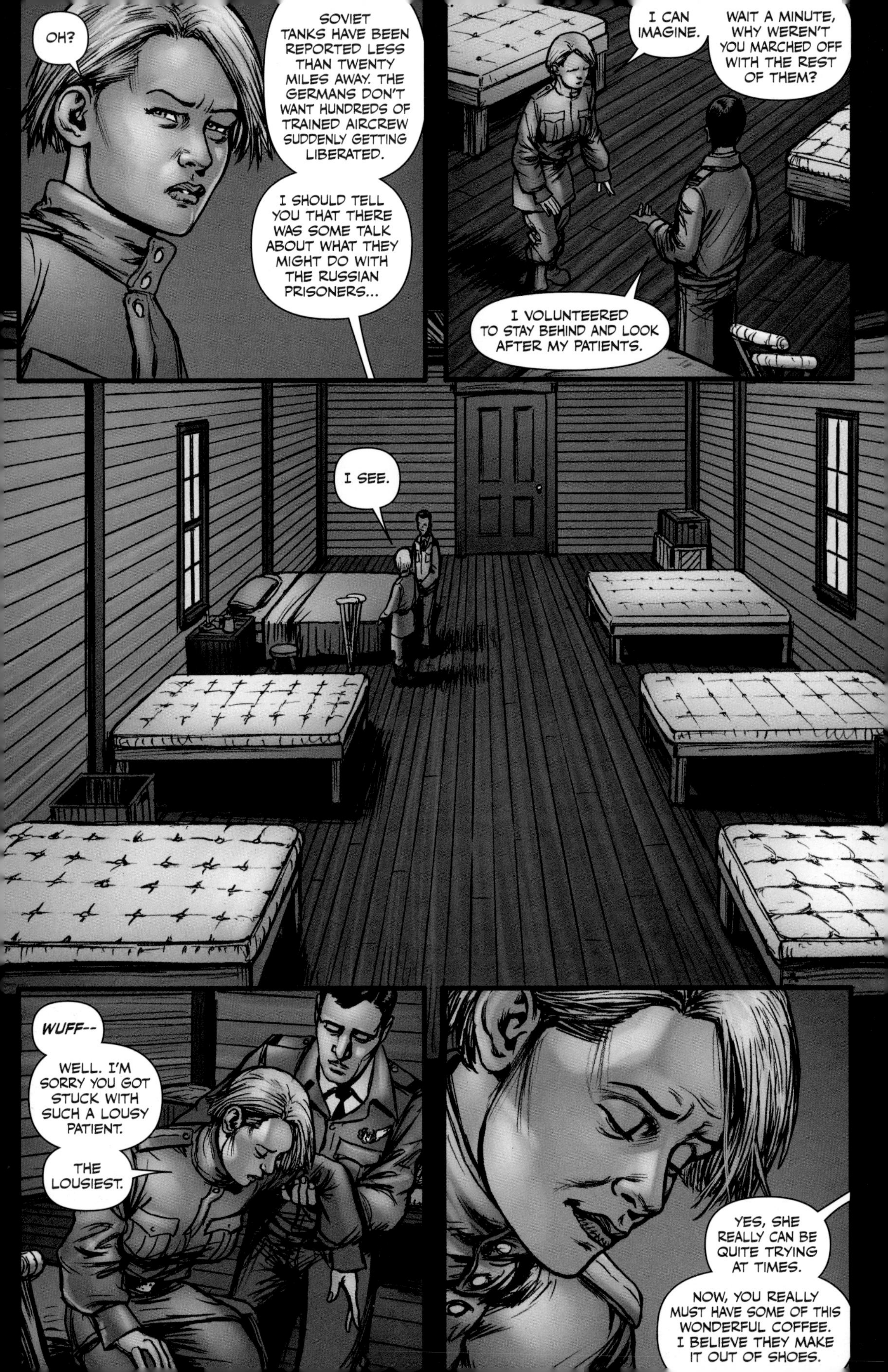
OH?
SOVIET TANKS HAVE BEEN REPORTED LESS THAN TWENTY MILES AWAY. THE GERMANS DON'T WANT HUNDREDS OF TRAINED AIRCREW SUDDENLY GETTING LIBERATED.
I SHOULD TELL YOU THAT THERE WAS SOME TALK ABOUT WHAT THEY MIGHT DO WITH THE RUSSIAN PRISONERS...
I CAN IMAGINE.
WAIT A MINUTE, WHY WEREN'T YOU MARCHED OFF WITH THE REST OF THEM?
I VOLUNTEERED TO STAY BEHIND AND LOOK AFTER MY PATIENTS.
I SEE.
WUFF--
WELL. I'M SORRY YOU GOT STUCK WITH SUCH A LOUSY PATIENT.
THE LOUSIEST.
YES, SHE REALLY CAN BE QUITE TRYING AT TIMES.
NOW, YOU REALLY MUST HAVE SOME OF THIS WONDERFUL COFFEE. I BELIEVE THEY MAKE IT OUT OF SHOES.

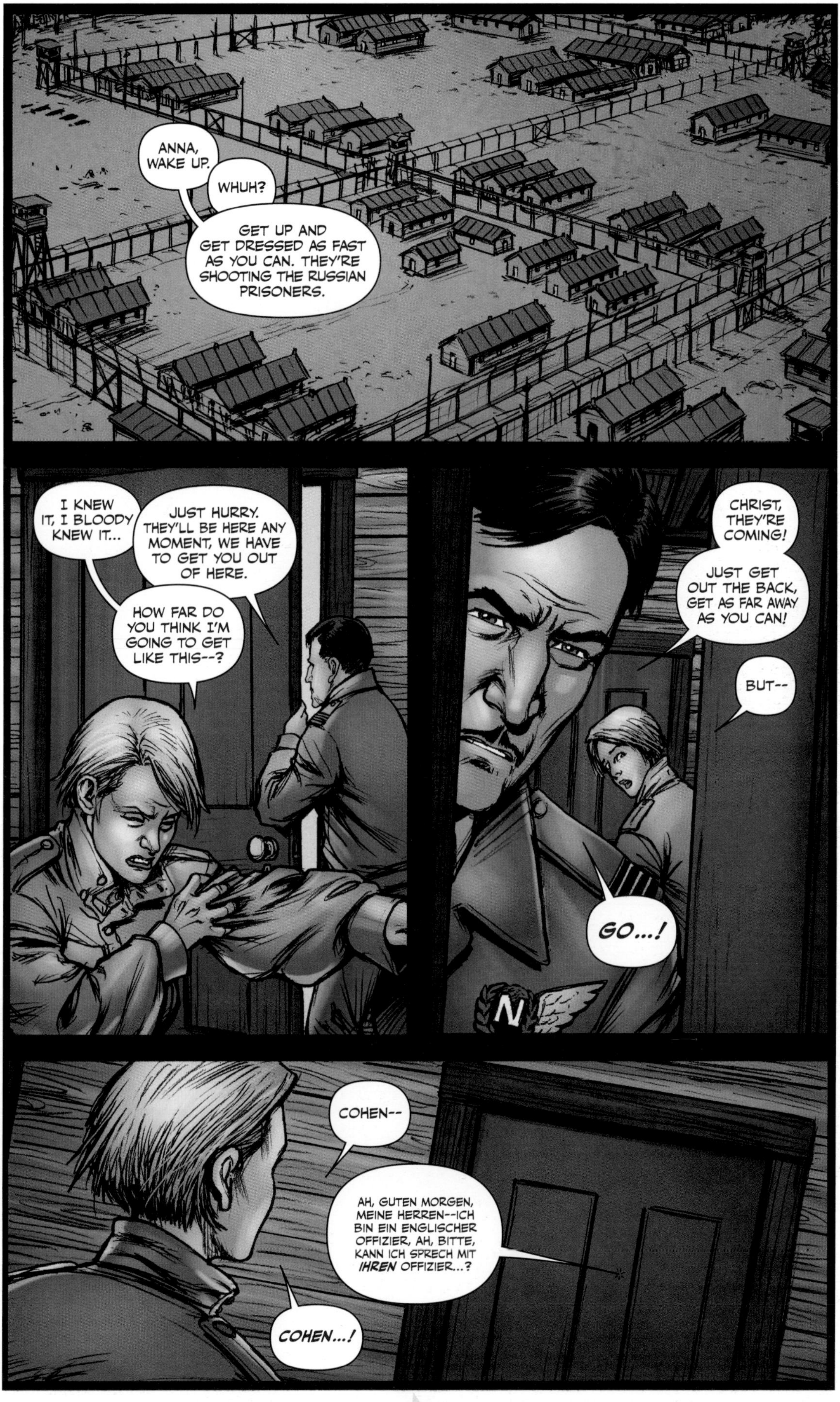
ANNA, WAKE UP.
WHUH?
GET UP AND GET DRESSED AS FAST AS YOU CAN. THEY'RE SHOOTING THE RUSSIAN PRISONERS.
I KNEW IT, I BLOODY KNEW IT...
JUST HURRY. THEY'LL BE HERE ANY MOMENT, WE HAVE TO GET YOU OUT OF HERE.
HOW FAR DO YOU THINK I'M GOING TO GET LIKE THIS--?
CHRIST, THEY'RE COMING!
JUST GET OUT THE BACK, GET AS FAR AWAY AS YOU CAN!
BUT--
GO...!
COHEN--
AH, GUTEN MORGEN, MEINE HERREN--ICH BIN EIN ENGLISCHER OFFIZIER, AH, BITTE, KANN ICH SPRECH MIT *IHREN* OFFIZIER...?
COHEN...!

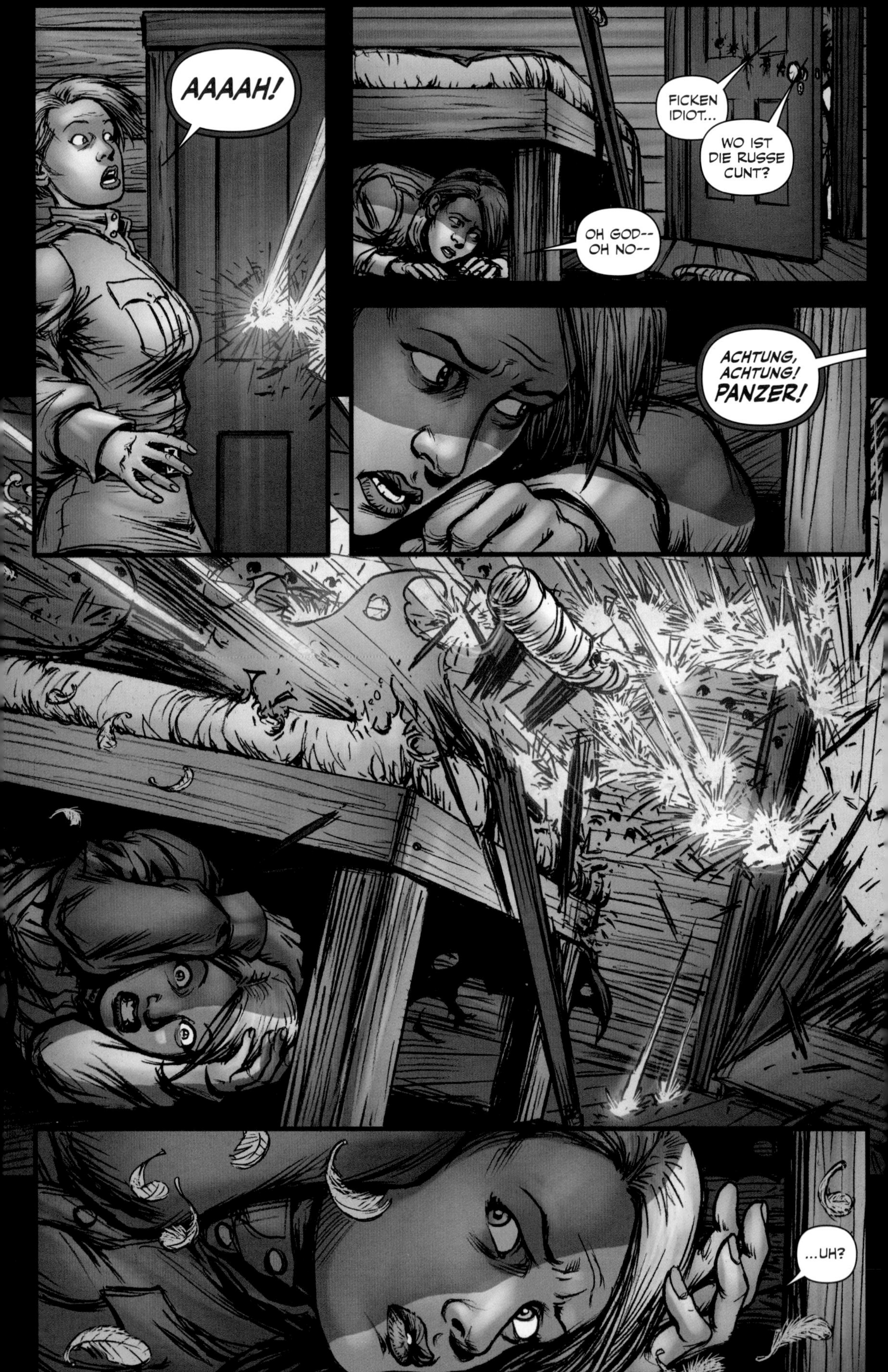
AAAAH!
FICKEN IDIOT...
WO IST DIE RUSSE CUNT?
OH GOD-- OH NO--
ACHTUNG, ACHTUNG! PANZER!
...UH?

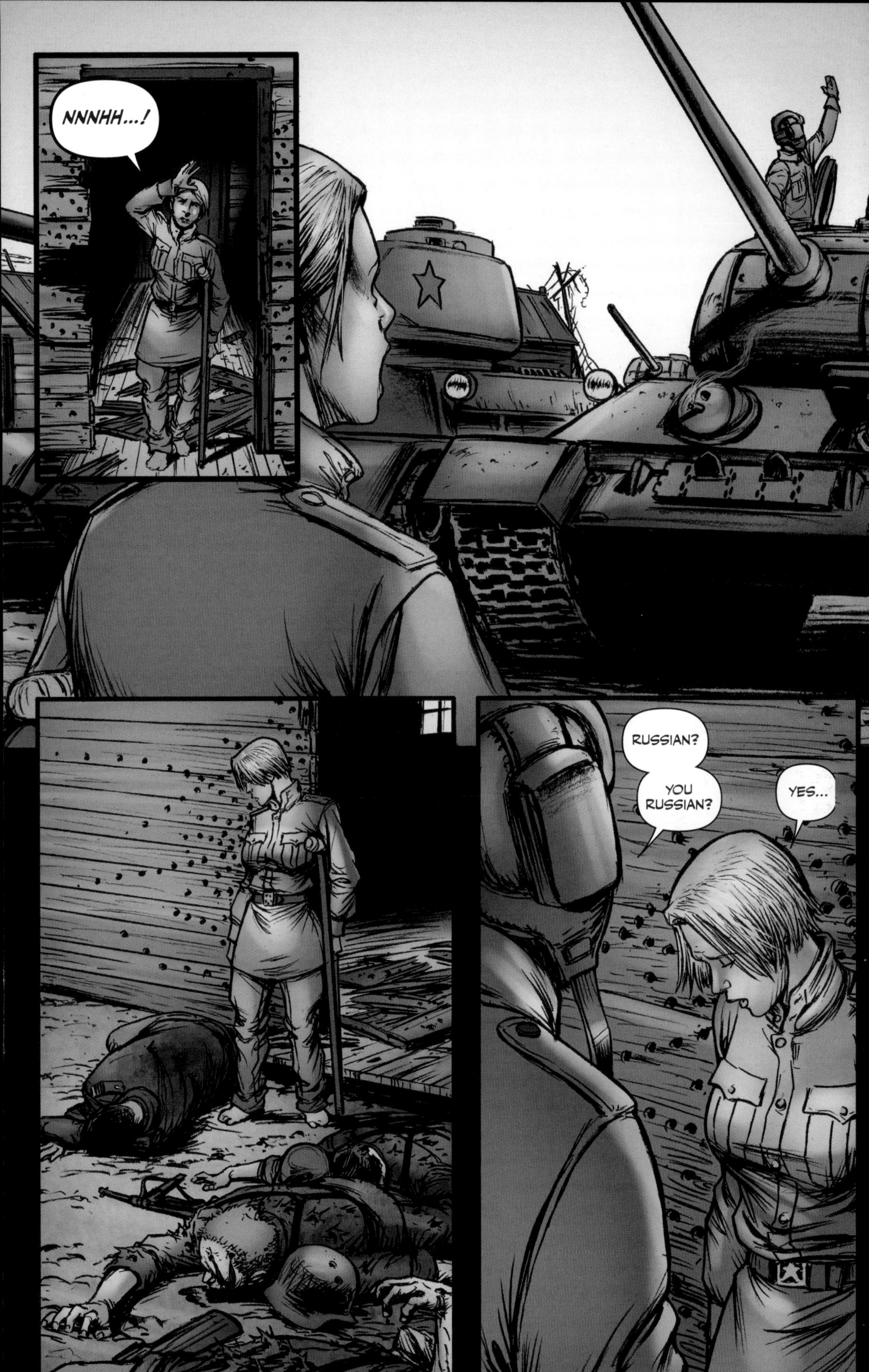
NNNHH...!
RUSSIAN?
YOU RUSSIAN?
YES...

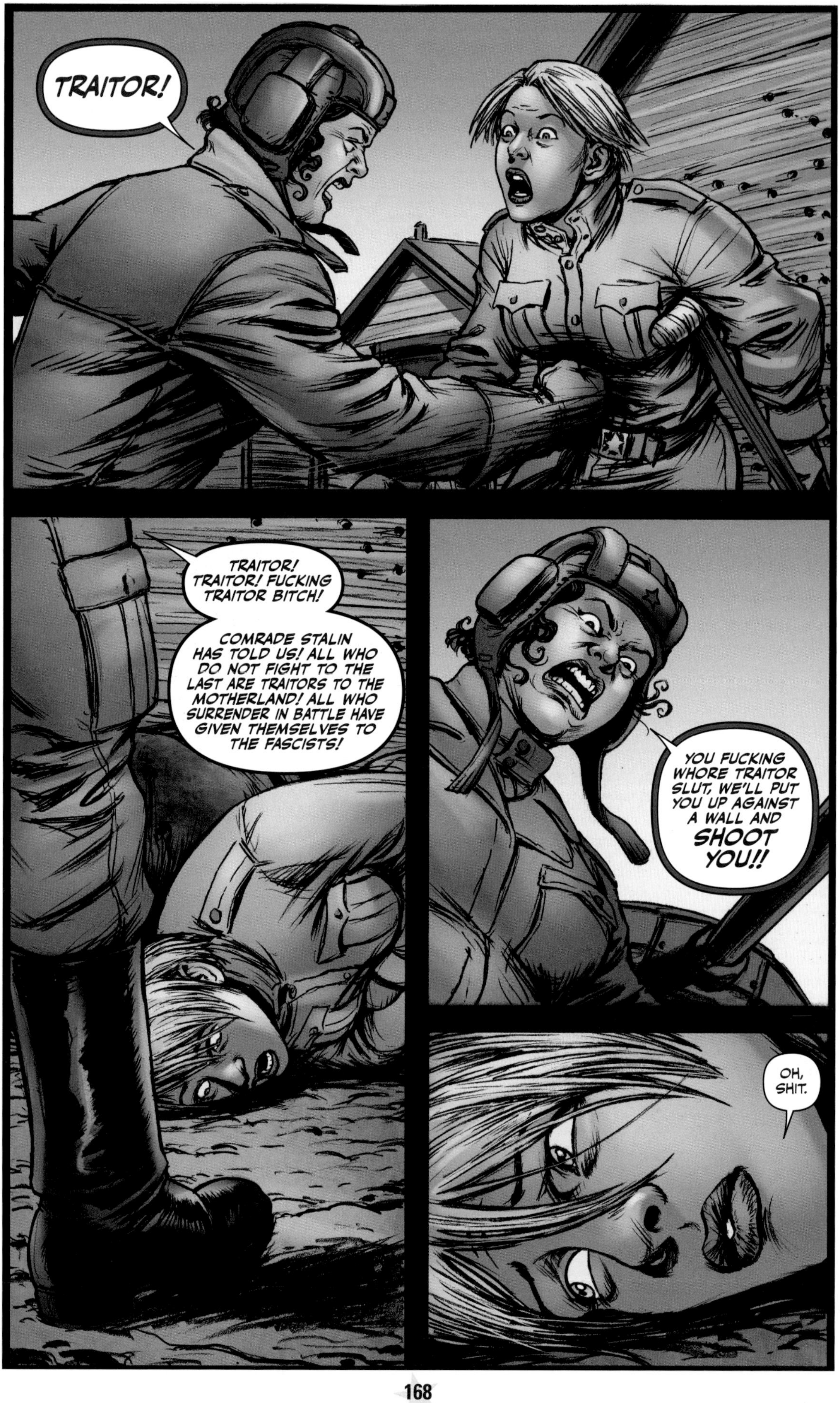
TRAITOR!
TRAITOR! TRAITOR! FUCKING TRAITOR BITCH!
COMRADE STALIN HAS TOLD US! ALL WHO DO NOT FIGHT TO THE LAST ARE TRAITORS TO THE MOTHERLAND! ALL WHO SURRENDER IN BATTLE HAVE GIVEN THEMSELVES TO THE FASCISTS!
YOU FUCKING WHORE TRAITOR SLUT, WE'LL PUT YOU UP AGAINST A WALL AND SHOOT YOU!!
OH, SHIT.

Chapter 2

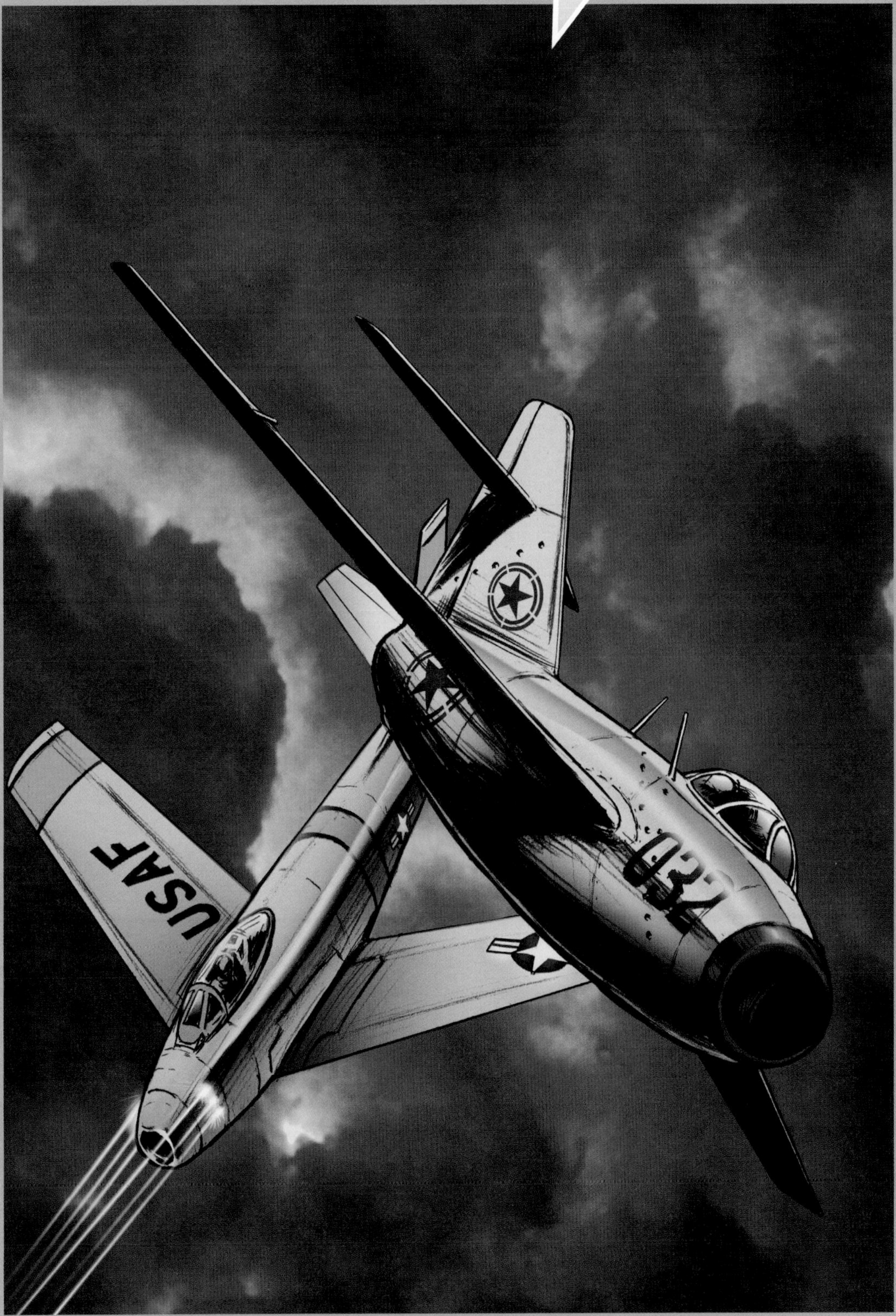
USAF

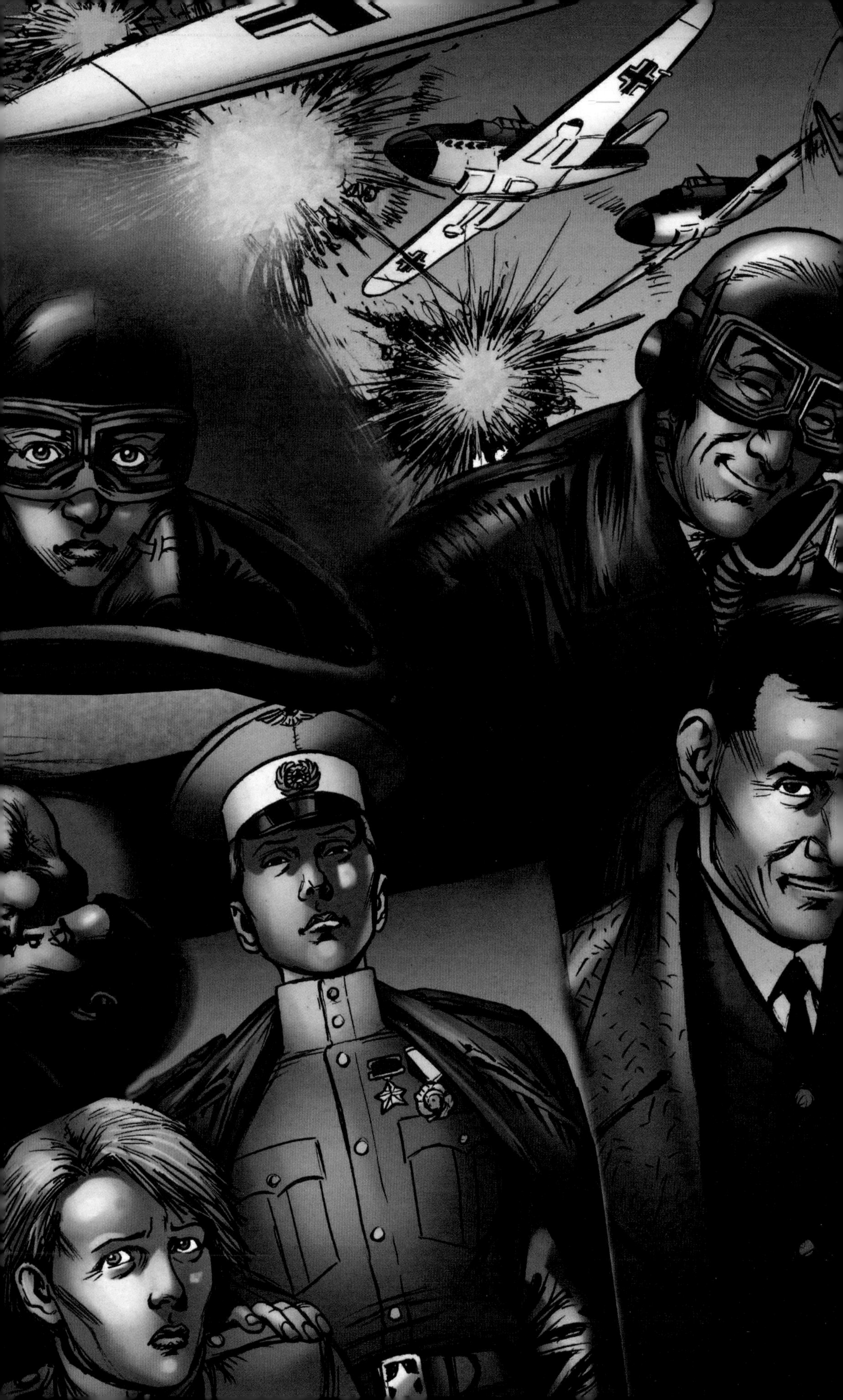

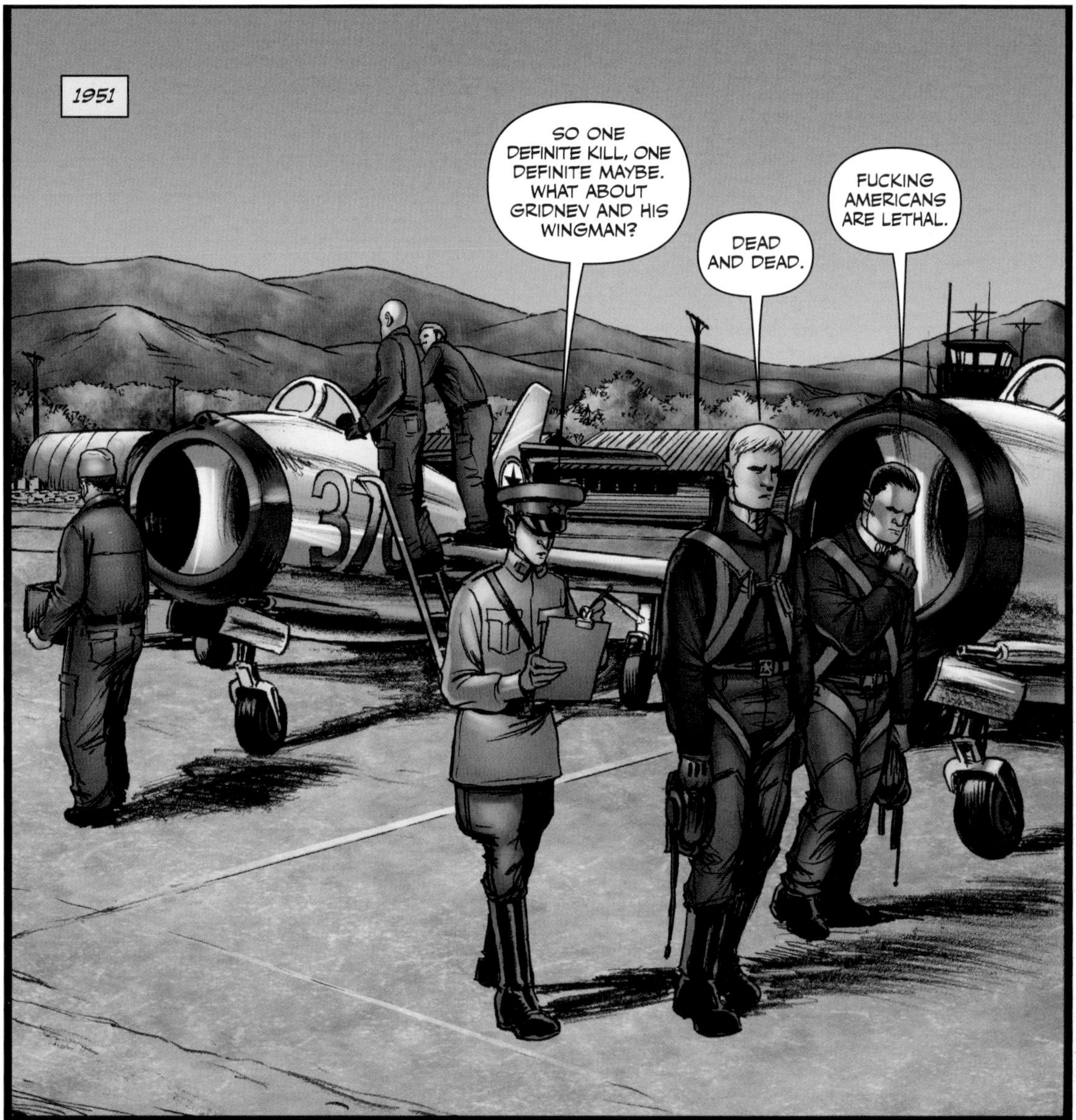
1951
SO ONE DEFINITE KILL, ONE DEFINITE MAYBE. WHAT ABOUT GRIDNEV AND HIS WINGMAN?
DEAD AND DEAD.
FUCKING AMERICANS ARE LETHAL.

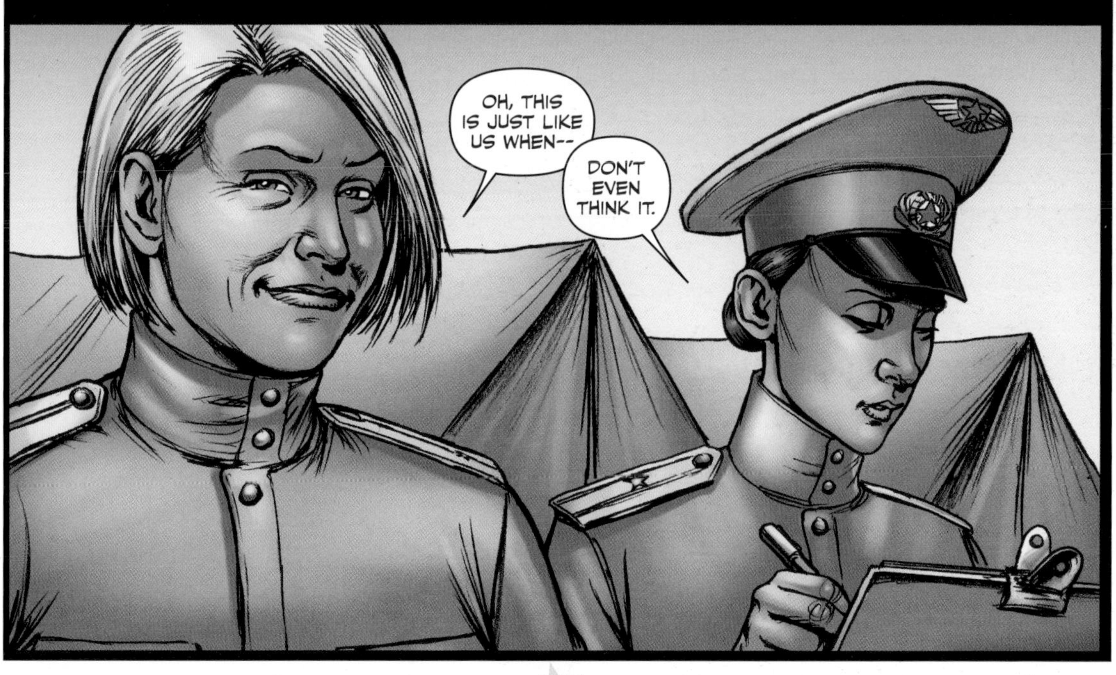
OH, THIS IS JUST LIKE US WHEN--
DON'T EVEN THINK IT.

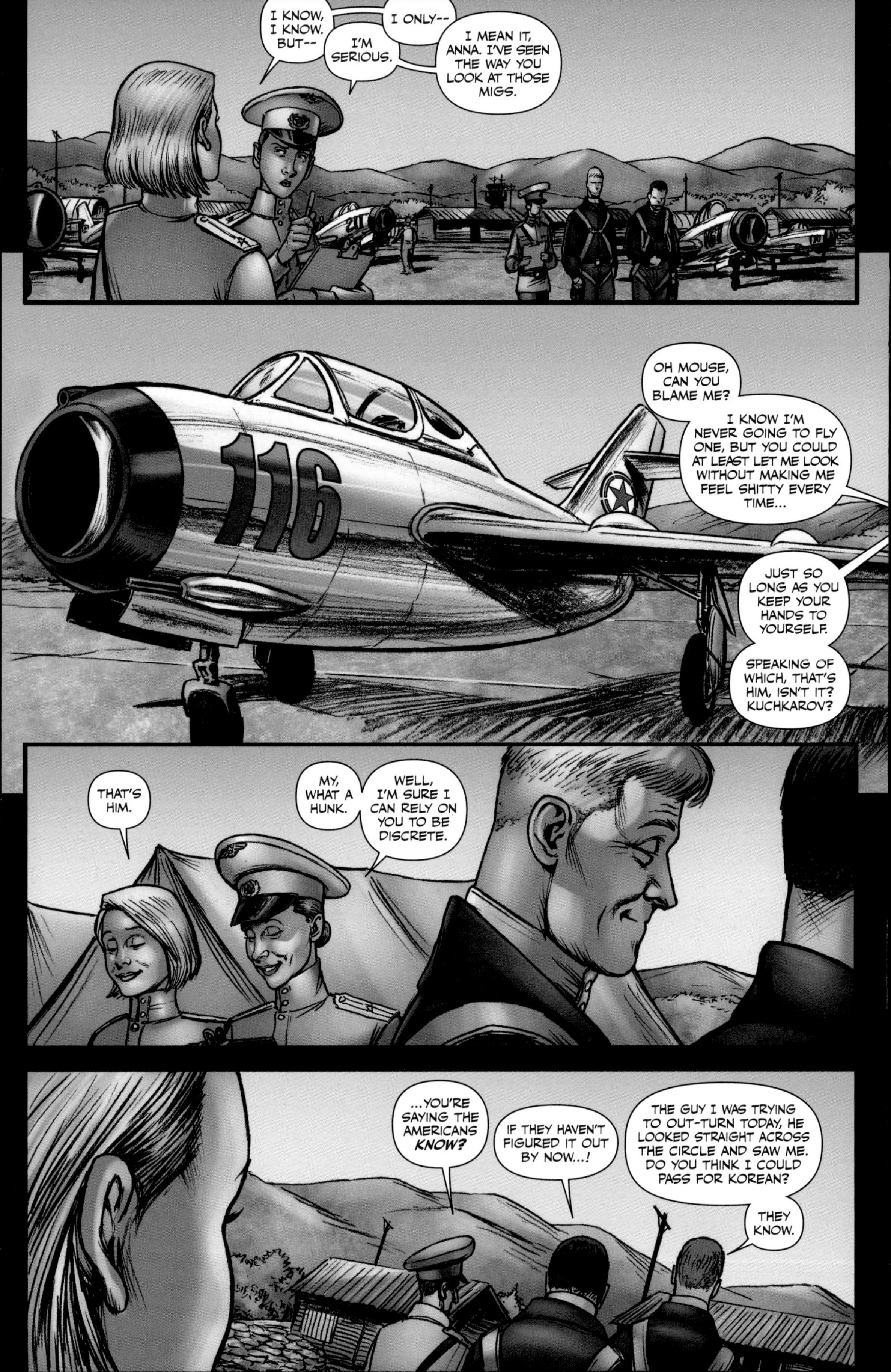
I KNOW, I KNOW. BUT--
I'M SERIOUS.
I ONLY--
I MEAN IT, ANNA. I'VE SEEN THE WAY YOU LOOK AT THOSE MIGS.
211
116
OH MOUSE, CAN YOU BLAME ME?
I KNOW I'M NEVER GOING TO FLY ONE, BUT YOU COULD AT LEAST LET ME LOOK WITHOUT MAKING ME FEEL SHITTY EVERY TIME...
JUST SO LONG AS YOU KEEP YOUR HANDS TO YOURSELF.
SPEAKING OF WHICH, THAT'S HIM, ISN'T IT? KUCHKAROV?
THAT'S HIM.
MY, WHAT A HUNK.
WELL, I'M SURE I CAN RELY ON YOU TO BE DISCRETE.
...YOU'RE SAYING THE AMERICANS *KNOW?*
IF THEY HAVEN'T FIGURED IT OUT BY NOW...!
THE GUY I WAS TRYING TO OUT-TURN TODAY, HE LOOKED STRAIGHT ACROSS THE CIRCLE AND SAW ME. DO YOU THINK I COULD PASS FOR KOREAN?
THEY KNOW.

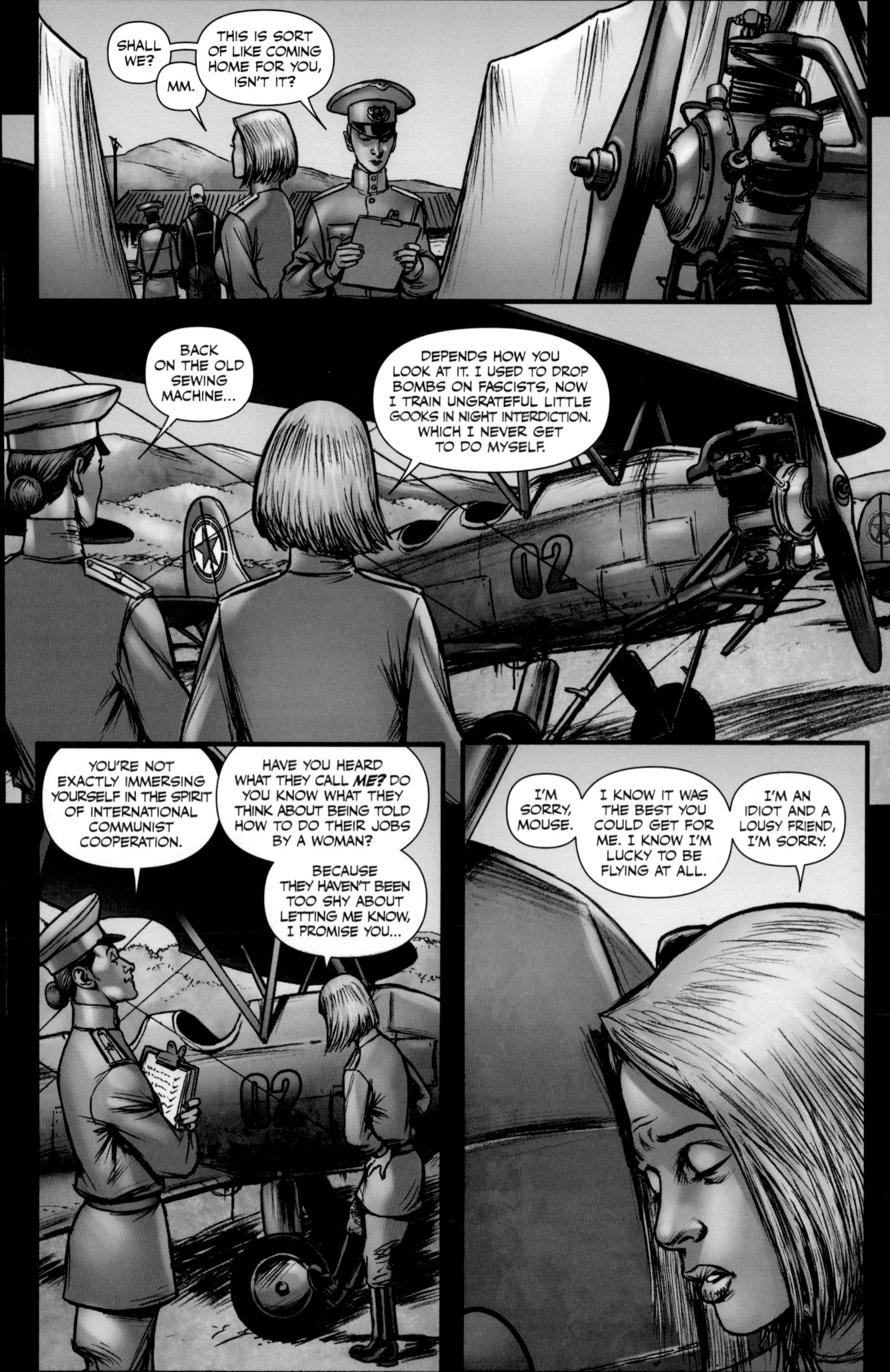
SHALL WE?
THIS IS SORT OF LIKE COMING HOME FOR YOU, ISN'T IT?
MM.
BACK ON THE OLD SEWING MACHINE...
DEPENDS HOW YOU LOOK AT IT. I USED TO DROP BOMBS ON FASCISTS, NOW I TRAIN UNGRATEFUL LITTLE GOOKS IN NIGHT INTERDICTION. WHICH I NEVER GET TO DO MYSELF.
02
YOU'RE NOT EXACTLY IMMERSING YOURSELF IN THE SPIRIT OF INTERNATIONAL COMMUNIST COOPERATION.
HAVE YOU HEARD WHAT THEY CALL ***ME?*** DO YOU KNOW WHAT THEY THINK ABOUT BEING TOLD HOW TO DO THEIR JOBS BY A WOMAN?
BECAUSE THEY HAVEN'T BEEN TOO SHY ABOUT LETTING ME KNOW, I PROMISE YOU...
02
I'M SORRY, MOUSE.
I KNOW IT WAS THE BEST YOU COULD GET FOR ME. I KNOW I'M LUCKY TO BE FLYING AT ALL.
I'M AN IDIOT AND A LOUSY FRIEND, I'M SORRY.

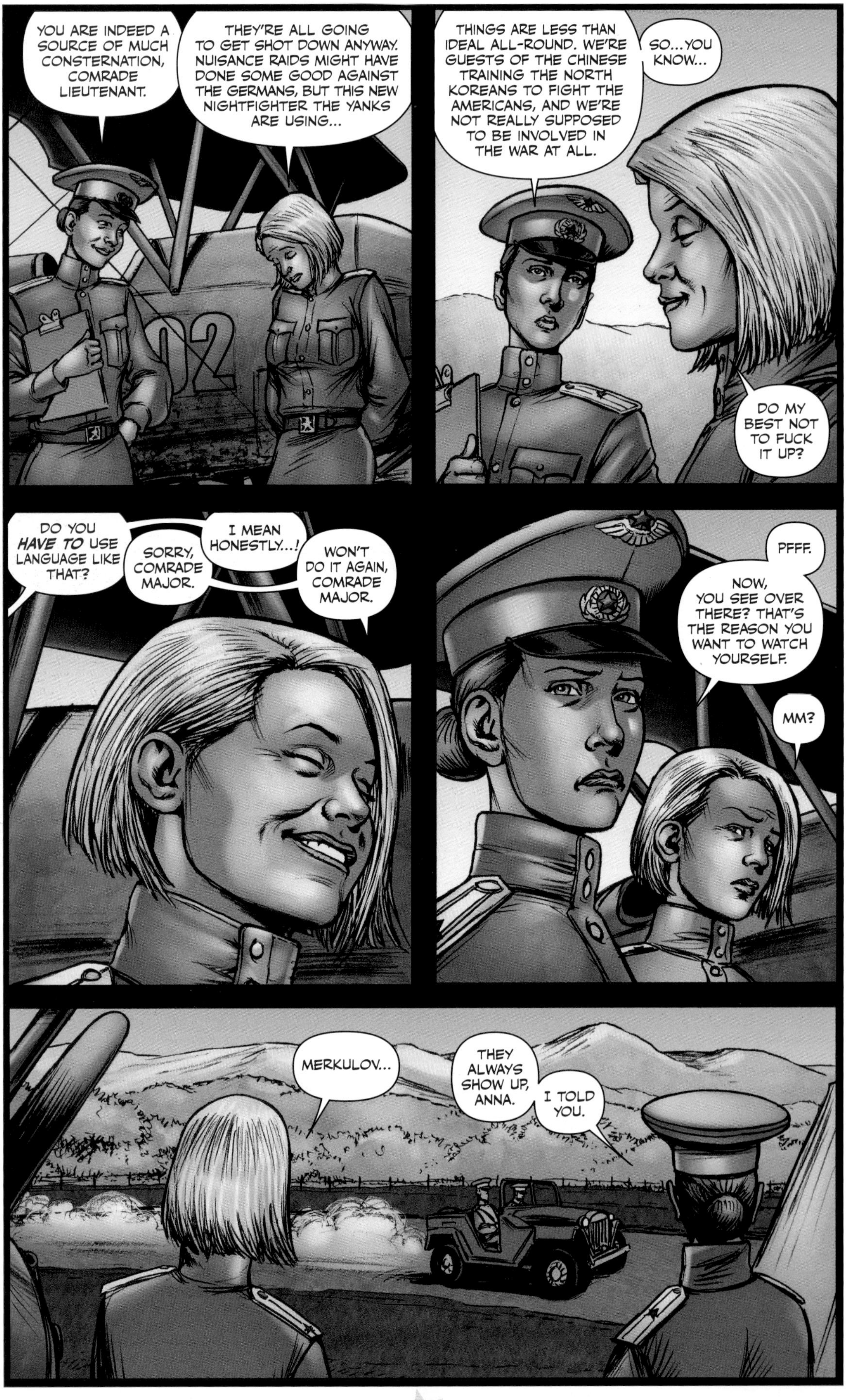
YOU ARE INDEED A SOURCE OF MUCH CONSTERNATION, COMRADE LIEUTENANT.
THEY'RE ALL GOING TO GET SHOT DOWN ANYWAY. NUISANCE RAIDS MIGHT HAVE DONE SOME GOOD AGAINST THE GERMANS, BUT THIS NEW NIGHTFIGHTER THE YANKS ARE USING...
THINGS ARE LESS THAN IDEAL ALL-ROUND. WE'RE GUESTS OF THE CHINESE TRAINING THE NORTH KOREANS TO FIGHT THE AMERICANS, AND WE'RE NOT REALLY SUPPOSED TO BE INVOLVED IN THE WAR AT ALL.
SO...YOU KNOW...
DO MY BEST NOT TO FUCK IT UP?
DO YOU *HAVE TO* USE LANGUAGE LIKE THAT?
SORRY, COMRADE MAJOR.
I MEAN HONESTLY...!
WON'T DO IT AGAIN, COMRADE MAJOR.
PFFF.
NOW, YOU SEE OVER THERE? THAT'S THE REASON YOU WANT TO WATCH YOURSELF.
MM?
MERKULOV...
THEY ALWAYS SHOW UP, ANNA.
I TOLD YOU.

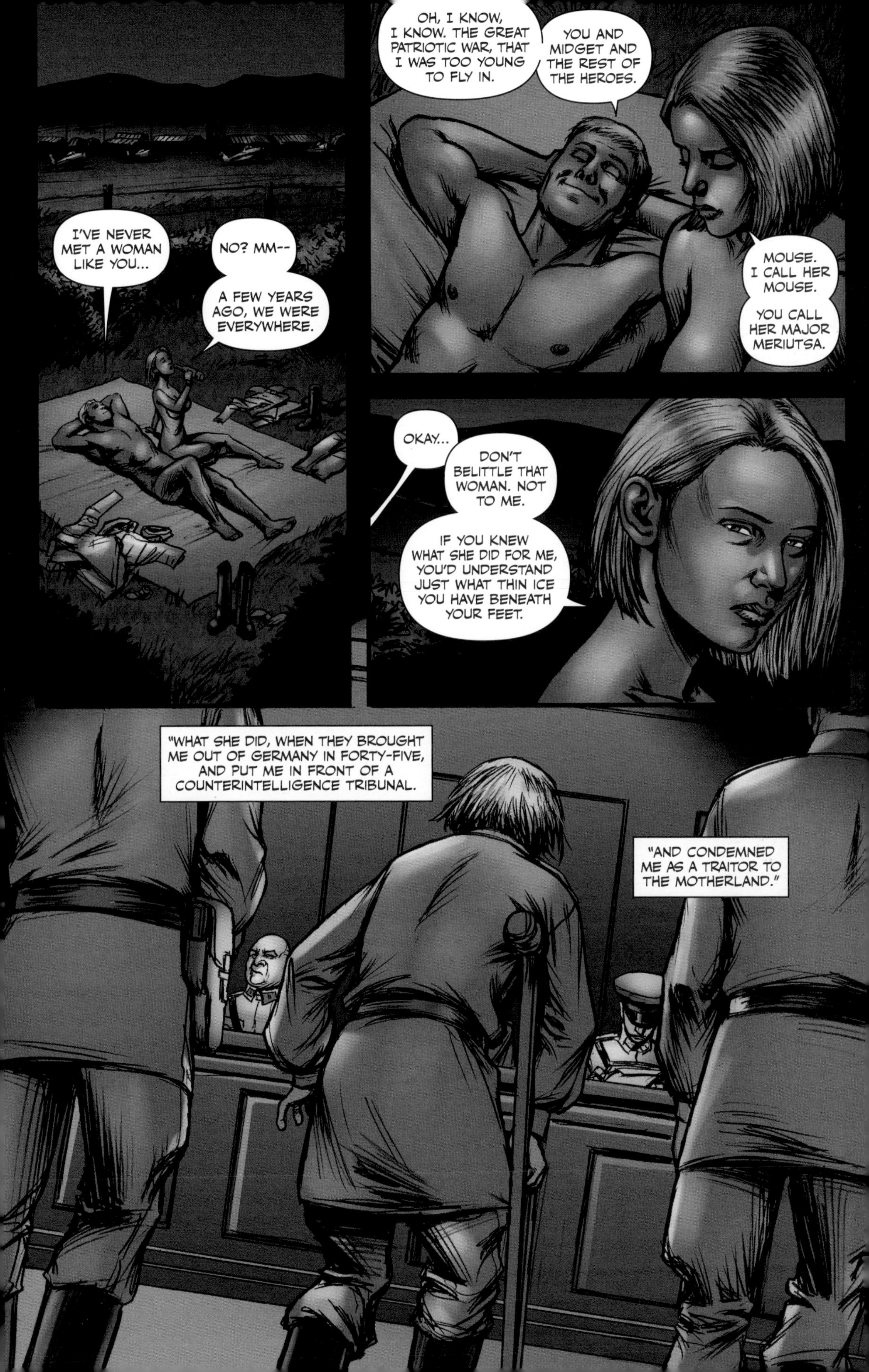
I'VE NEVER MET A WOMAN LIKE YOU...
NO? MM--
A FEW YEARS AGO, WE WERE EVERYWHERE.
OH, I KNOW, I KNOW. THE GREAT PATRIOTIC WAR, THAT I WAS TOO YOUNG TO FLY IN.
YOU AND MIDGET AND THE REST OF THE HEROES.
MOUSE. I CALL HER MOUSE.
YOU CALL HER MAJOR MERIUTSA.
OKAY...
DON'T BELITTLE THAT WOMAN. NOT TO ME.
IF YOU KNEW WHAT SHE DID FOR ME, YOU'D UNDERSTAND JUST WHAT THIN ICE YOU HAVE BENEATH YOUR FEET.
"WHAT SHE DID, WHEN THEY BROUGHT ME OUT OF GERMANY IN FORTY-FIVE, AND PUT ME IN FRONT OF A COUNTERINTELLIGENCE TRIBUNAL.
"AND CONDEMNED ME AS A TRAITOR TO THE MOTHERLAND."

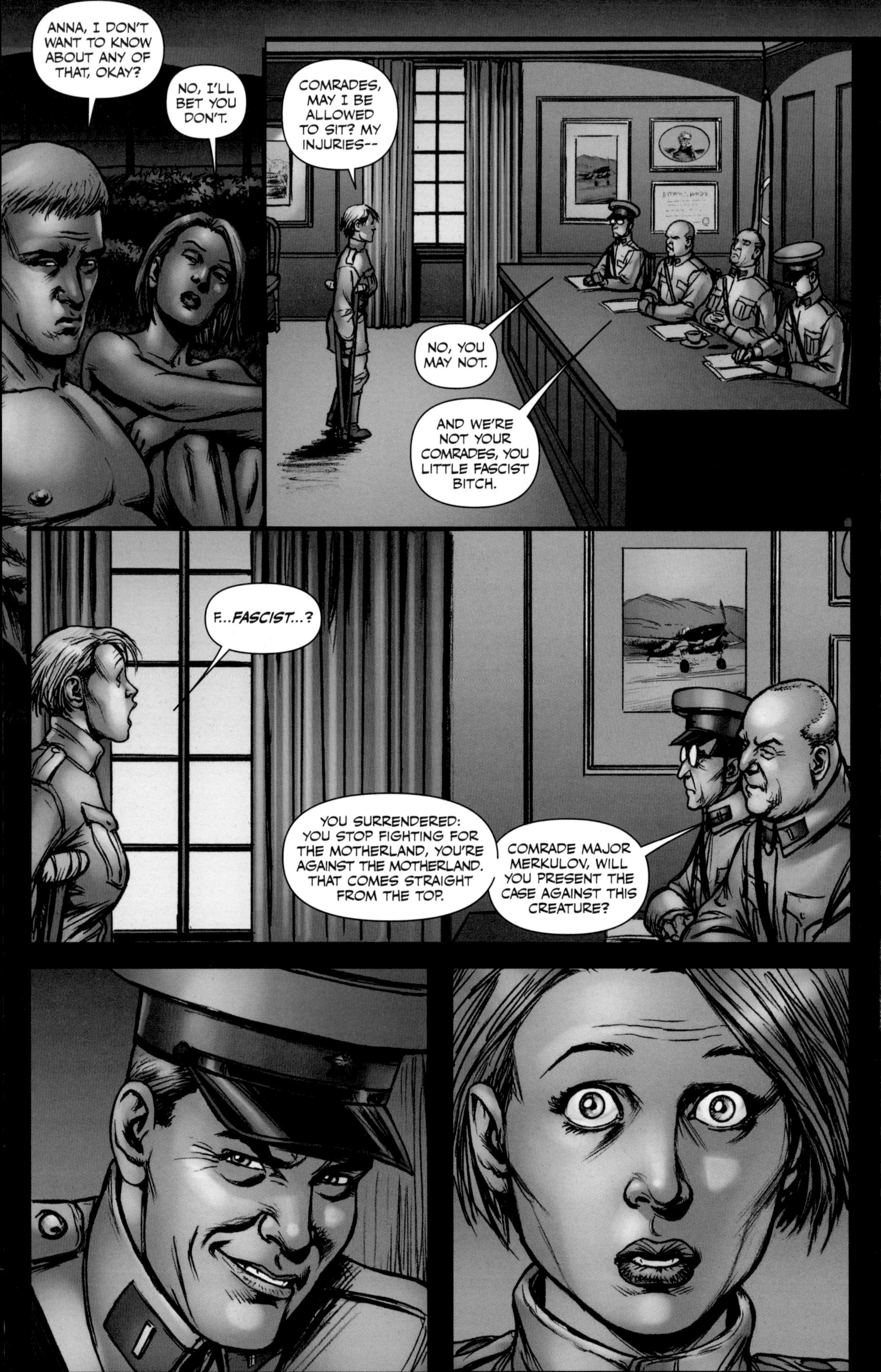
ANNA, I DON'T WANT TO KNOW ABOUT ANY OF THAT, OKAY?
NO, I'LL BET YOU DON'T.
COMRADES, MAY I BE ALLOWED TO SIT? MY INJURIES--
NO, YOU MAY NOT.
AND WE'RE NOT YOUR COMRADES, YOU LITTLE FASCIST BITCH.
F...*FASCIST*...?
YOU SURRENDERED: YOU STOP FIGHTING FOR THE MOTHERLAND, YOU'RE AGAINST THE MOTHERLAND. THAT COMES STRAIGHT FROM THE TOP.
COMRADE MAJOR MERKULOV, WILL YOU PRESENT THE CASE AGAINST THIS CREATURE?

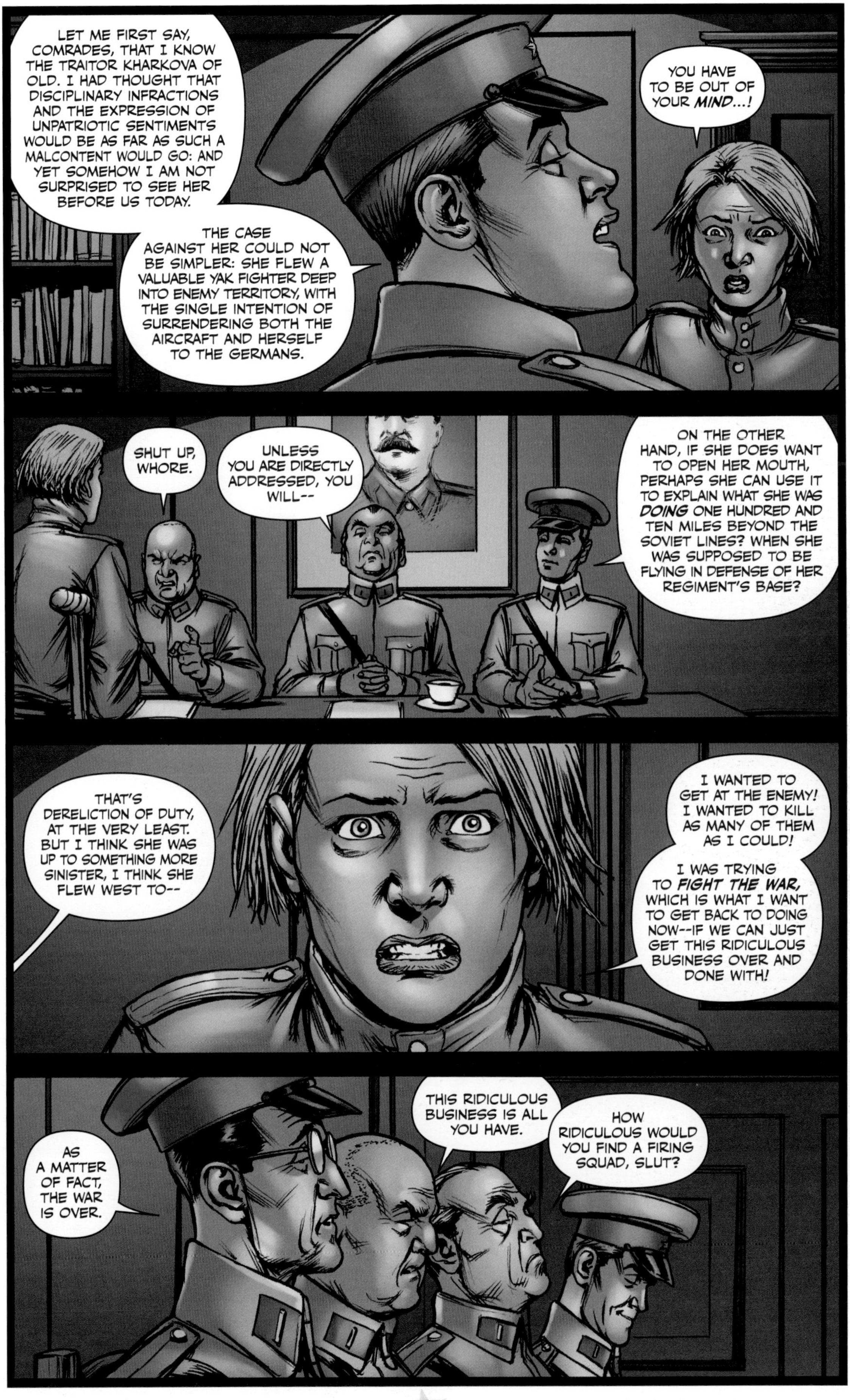
LET ME FIRST SAY, COMRADES, THAT I KNOW THE TRAITOR KHARKOVA OF OLD. I HAD THOUGHT THAT DISCIPLINARY INFRACTIONS AND THE EXPRESSION OF UNPATRIOTIC SENTIMENTS WOULD BE AS FAR AS SUCH A MALCONTENT WOULD GO: AND YET SOMEHOW I AM NOT SURPRISED TO SEE HER BEFORE US TODAY.
YOU HAVE TO BE OUT OF YOUR *MIND*...!
THE CASE AGAINST HER COULD NOT BE SIMPLER: SHE FLEW A VALUABLE YAK FIGHTER DEEP INTO ENEMY TERRITORY, WITH THE SINGLE INTENTION OF SURRENDERING BOTH THE AIRCRAFT AND HERSELF TO THE GERMANS.
SHUT UP, WHORE.
UNLESS YOU ARE DIRECTLY ADDRESSED, YOU WILL--
ON THE OTHER HAND, IF SHE DOES WANT TO OPEN HER MOUTH, PERHAPS SHE CAN USE IT TO EXPLAIN WHAT SHE WAS *DOING* ONE HUNDRED AND TEN MILES BEYOND THE SOVIET LINES? WHEN SHE WAS SUPPOSED TO BE FLYING IN DEFENSE OF HER REGIMENT'S BASE?
THAT'S DERELICTION OF DUTY, AT THE VERY LEAST. BUT I THINK SHE WAS UP TO SOMETHING MORE SINISTER, I THINK SHE FLEW WEST TO--
I WANTED TO GET AT THE ENEMY! I WANTED TO KILL AS MANY OF THEM AS I COULD!
I WAS TRYING TO *FIGHT THE WAR,* WHICH IS WHAT I WANT TO GET BACK TO DOING NOW--IF WE CAN JUST GET THIS RIDICULOUS BUSINESS OVER AND DONE WITH!
AS A MATTER OF FACT, THE WAR IS OVER.
THIS RIDICULOUS BUSINESS IS ALL YOU HAVE.
HOW RIDICULOUS WOULD YOU FIND A FIRING SQUAD, SLUT?

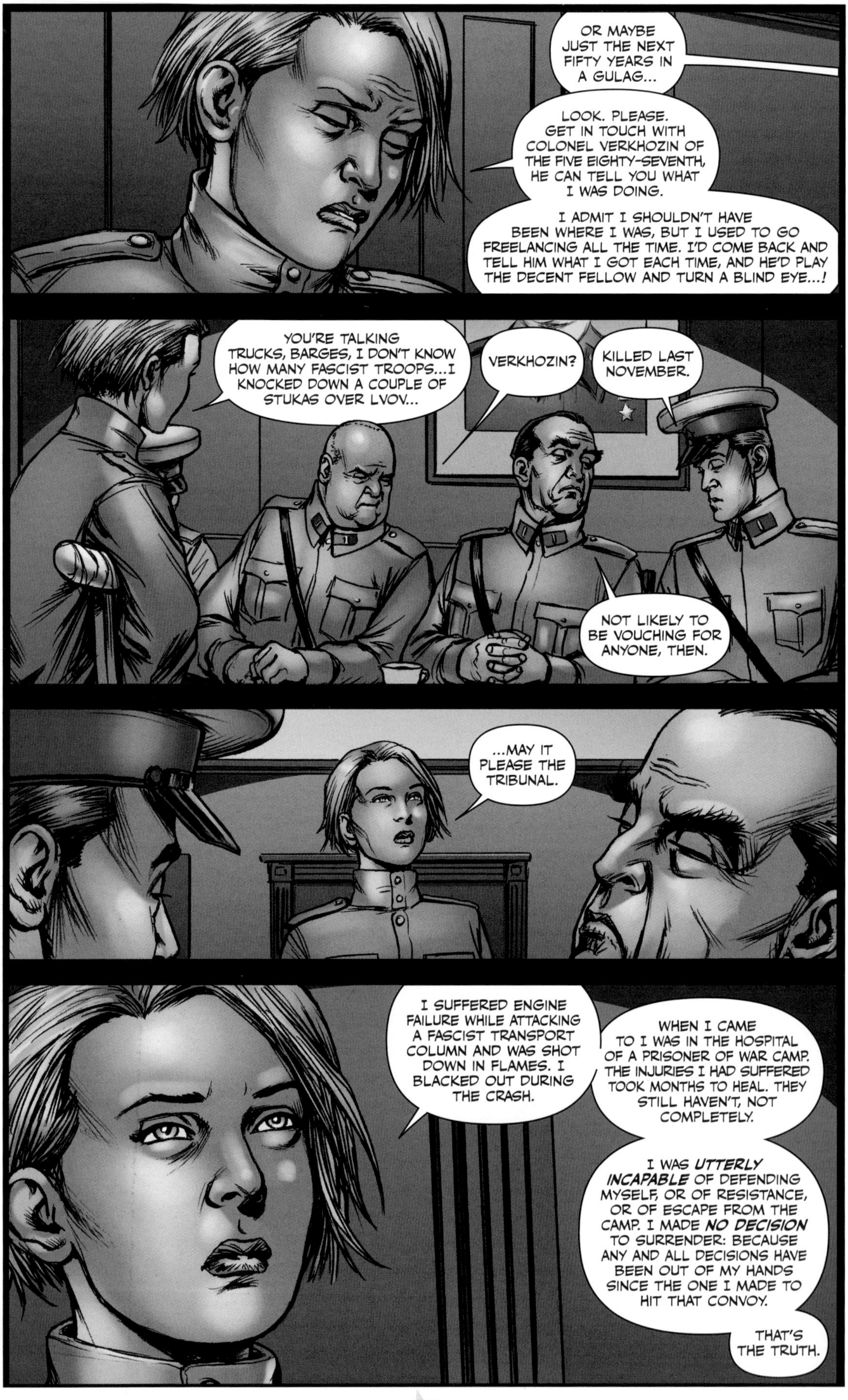
OR MAYBE JUST THE NEXT FIFTY YEARS IN A GULAG...
LOOK. PLEASE. GET IN TOUCH WITH COLONEL VERKHOZIN OF THE FIVE EIGHTY-SEVENTH, HE CAN TELL YOU WHAT I WAS DOING.
I ADMIT I SHOULDN'T HAVE BEEN WHERE I WAS, BUT I USED TO GO FREELANCING ALL THE TIME. I'D COME BACK AND TELL HIM WHAT I GOT EACH TIME, AND HE'D PLAY THE DECENT FELLOW AND TURN A BLIND EYE...!
YOU'RE TALKING TRUCKS, BARGES, I DON'T KNOW HOW MANY FASCIST TROOPS...I KNOCKED DOWN A COUPLE OF STUKAS OVER LVOV...
VERKHOZIN?
KILLED LAST NOVEMBER.
NOT LIKELY TO BE VOUCHING FOR ANYONE, THEN.
...MAY IT PLEASE THE TRIBUNAL.
I SUFFERED ENGINE FAILURE WHILE ATTACKING A FASCIST TRANSPORT COLUMN AND WAS SHOT DOWN IN FLAMES. I BLACKED OUT DURING THE CRASH.
WHEN I CAME TO I WAS IN THE HOSPITAL OF A PRISONER OF WAR CAMP. THE INJURIES I HAD SUFFERED TOOK MONTHS TO HEAL. THEY STILL HAVEN'T, NOT COMPLETELY.
I WAS *UTTERLY INCAPABLE* OF DEFENDING MYSELF, OR OF RESISTANCE, OR OF ESCAPE FROM THE CAMP. I MADE *NO DECISION* TO SURRENDER: BECAUSE ANY AND ALL DECISIONS HAVE BEEN OUT OF MY HANDS SINCE THE ONE I MADE TO HIT THAT CONVOY.
THAT'S THE TRUTH.

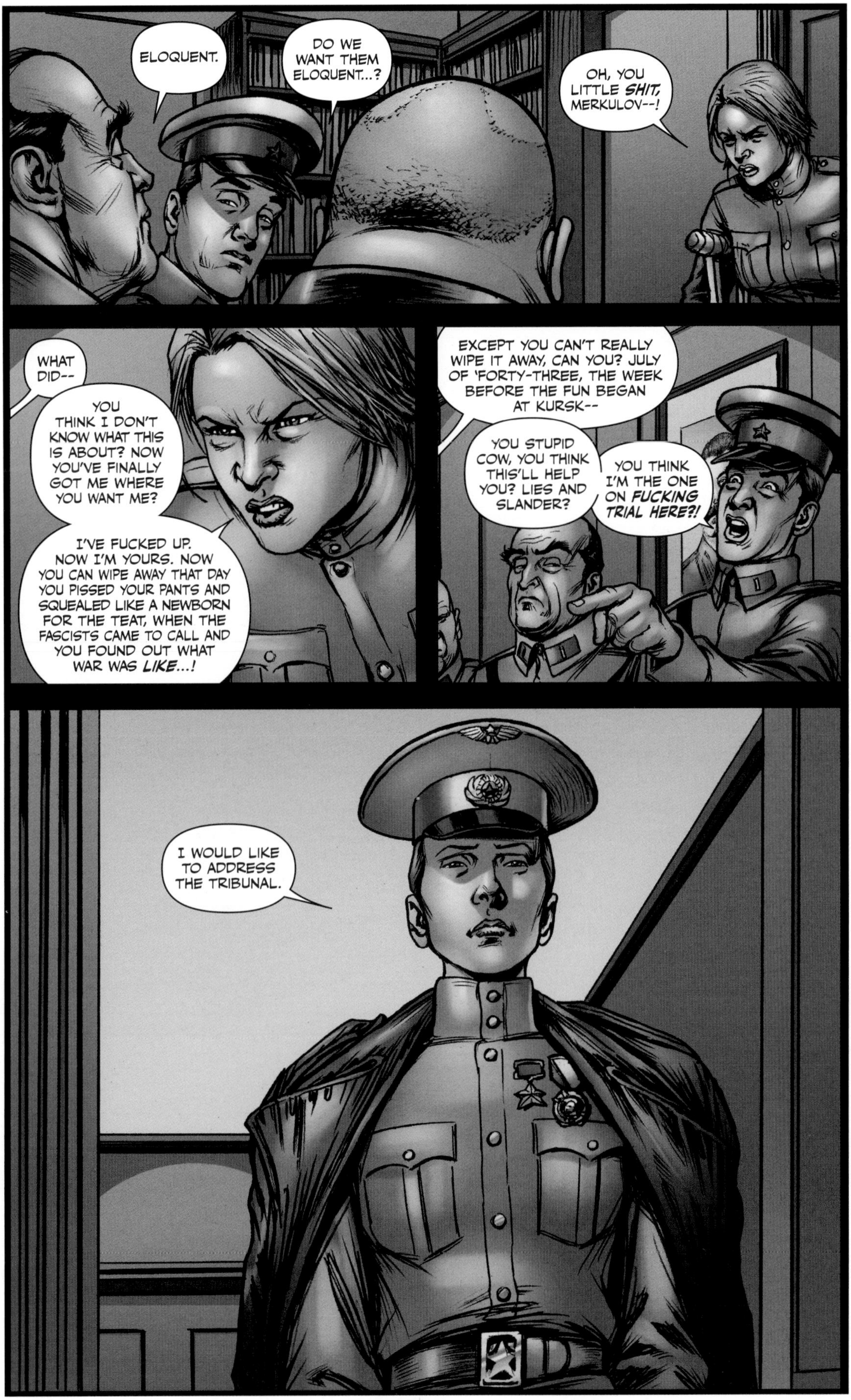
ELOQUENT.
DO WE WANT THEM ELOQUENT...?
OH, YOU LITTLE SHIT, MERKULOV--!
WHAT DID--
YOU THINK I DON'T KNOW WHAT THIS IS ABOUT? NOW YOU'VE FINALLY GOT ME WHERE YOU WANT ME?
I'VE FUCKED UP. NOW I'M YOURS. NOW YOU CAN WIPE AWAY THAT DAY YOU PISSED YOUR PANTS AND SQUEALED LIKE A NEWBORN FOR THE TEAT, WHEN THE FASCISTS CAME TO CALL AND YOU FOUND OUT WHAT WAR WAS LIKE...!
EXCEPT YOU CAN'T REALLY WIPE IT AWAY, CAN YOU? JULY OF 'FORTY-THREE, THE WEEK BEFORE THE FUN BEGAN AT KURSK--
YOU STUPID COW, YOU THINK THIS'LL HELP YOU? LIES AND SLANDER?
YOU THINK I'M THE ONE ON FUCKING TRIAL HERE?!
I WOULD LIKE TO ADDRESS THE TRIBUNAL.

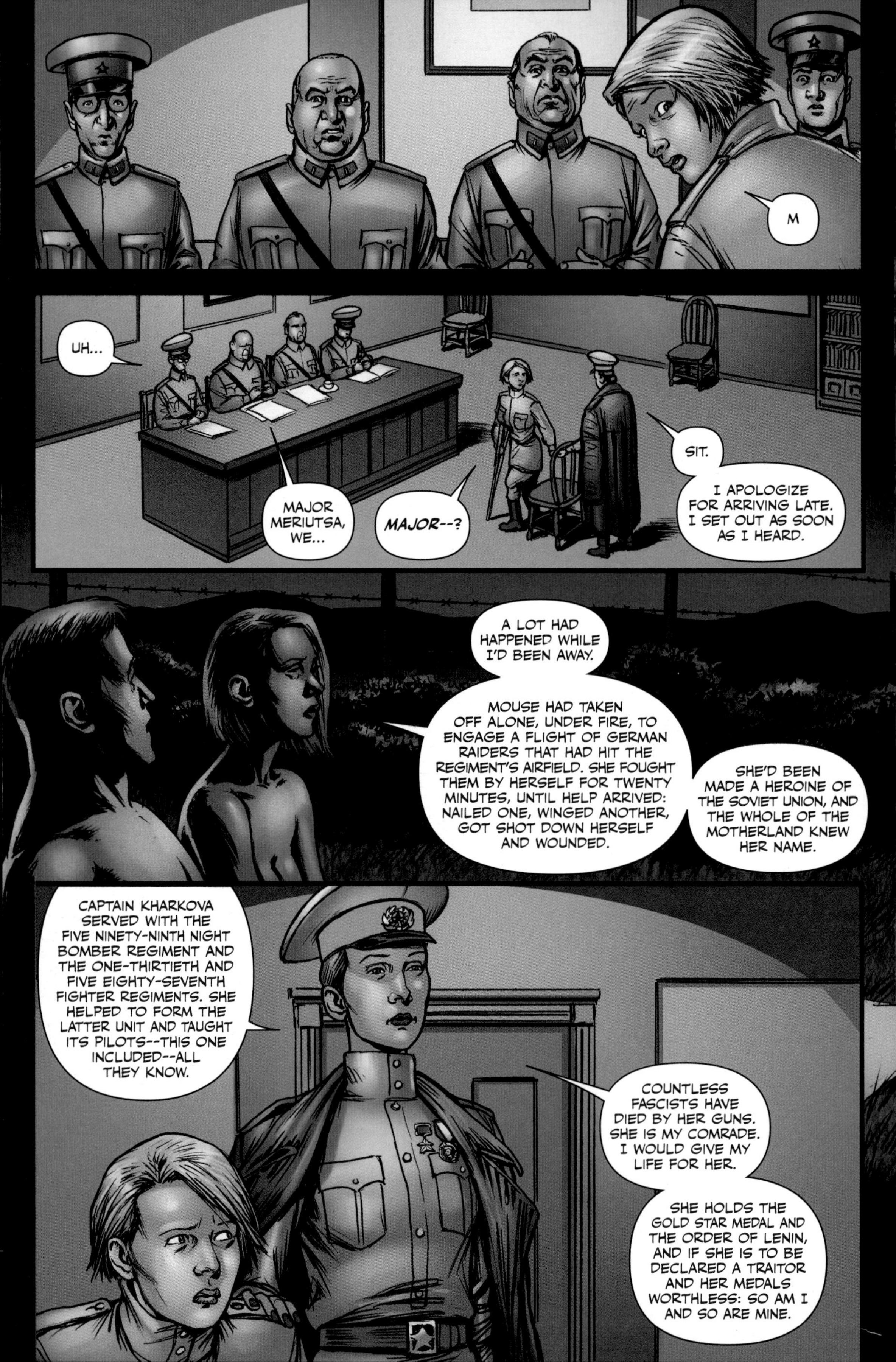
M
UH...
MAJOR MERIUTSA, WE...
MAJOR--?
SIT.
I APOLOGIZE FOR ARRIVING LATE. I SET OUT AS SOON AS I HEARD.
A LOT HAD HAPPENED WHILE I'D BEEN AWAY.
MOUSE HAD TAKEN OFF ALONE, UNDER FIRE, TO ENGAGE A FLIGHT OF GERMAN RAIDERS THAT HAD HIT THE REGIMENT'S AIRFIELD. SHE FOUGHT THEM BY HERSELF FOR TWENTY MINUTES, UNTIL HELP ARRIVED: NAILED ONE, WINGED ANOTHER, GOT SHOT DOWN HERSELF AND WOUNDED.
SHE'D BEEN MADE A HEROINE OF THE SOVIET UNION, AND THE WHOLE OF THE MOTHERLAND KNEW HER NAME.
CAPTAIN KHARKOVA SERVED WITH THE FIVE NINETY-NINTH NIGHT BOMBER REGIMENT AND THE ONE-THIRTIETH AND FIVE EIGHTY-SEVENTH FIGHTER REGIMENTS. SHE HELPED TO FORM THE LATTER UNIT AND TAUGHT ITS PILOTS--THIS ONE INCLUDED--ALL THEY KNOW.
COUNTLESS FASCISTS HAVE DIED BY HER GUNS. SHE IS MY COMRADE. I WOULD GIVE MY LIFE FOR HER.
SHE HOLDS THE GOLD STAR MEDAL AND THE ORDER OF LENIN, AND IF SHE IS TO BE DECLARED A TRAITOR AND HER MEDALS WORTHLESS: SO AM I AND SO ARE MINE.

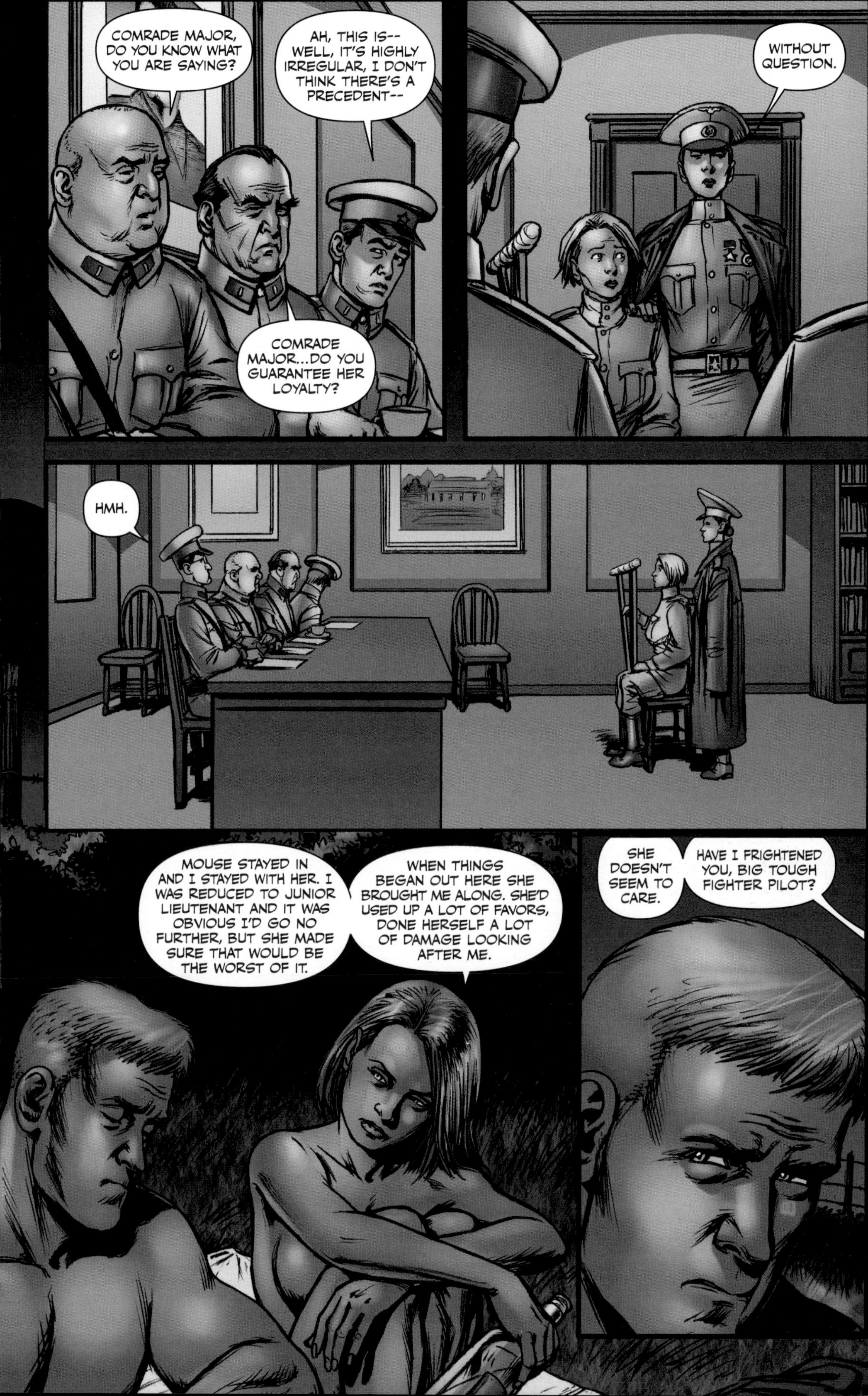
COMRADE MAJOR, DO YOU KNOW WHAT YOU ARE SAYING?
AH, THIS IS-- WELL, IT'S HIGHLY IRREGULAR, I DON'T THINK THERE'S A PRECEDENT--
COMRADE MAJOR...DO YOU GUARANTEE HER LOYALTY?
WITHOUT QUESTION.
HMH.
MOUSE STAYED IN AND I STAYED WITH HER. I WAS REDUCED TO JUNIOR LIEUTENANT AND IT WAS OBVIOUS I'D GO NO FURTHER, BUT SHE MADE SURE THAT WOULD BE THE WORST OF IT.
WHEN THINGS BEGAN OUT HERE SHE BROUGHT ME ALONG. SHE'D USED UP A LOT OF FAVORS, DONE HERSELF A LOT OF DAMAGE LOOKING AFTER ME.
SHE DOESN'T SEEM TO CARE.
HAVE I FRIGHTENED YOU, BIG TOUGH FIGHTER PILOT?

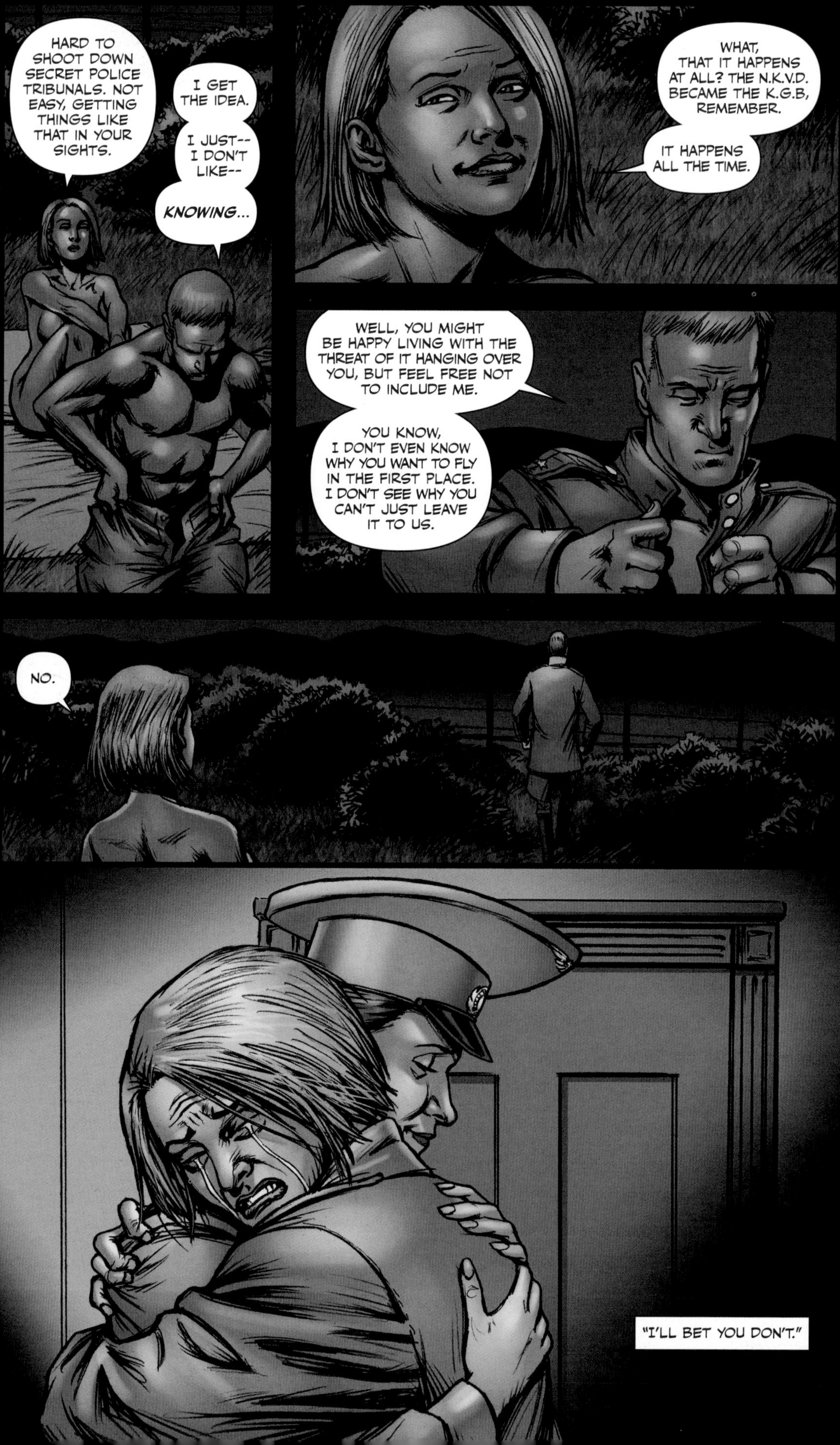
HARD TO SHOOT DOWN SECRET POLICE TRIBUNALS. NOT EASY, GETTING THINGS LIKE THAT IN YOUR SIGHTS.
I GET THE IDEA.
I JUST-- I DON'T LIKE--
KNOWING...
WHAT, THAT IT HAPPENS AT ALL? THE N.K.V.D. BECAME THE K.G.B, REMEMBER.
IT HAPPENS ALL THE TIME.
WELL, YOU MIGHT BE HAPPY LIVING WITH THE THREAT OF IT HANGING OVER YOU, BUT FEEL FREE NOT TO INCLUDE ME.
YOU KNOW, I DON'T EVEN KNOW WHY YOU WANT TO FLY IN THE FIRST PLACE. I DON'T SEE WHY YOU CAN'T JUST LEAVE IT TO US.
NO.
"I'LL BET YOU DON'T."

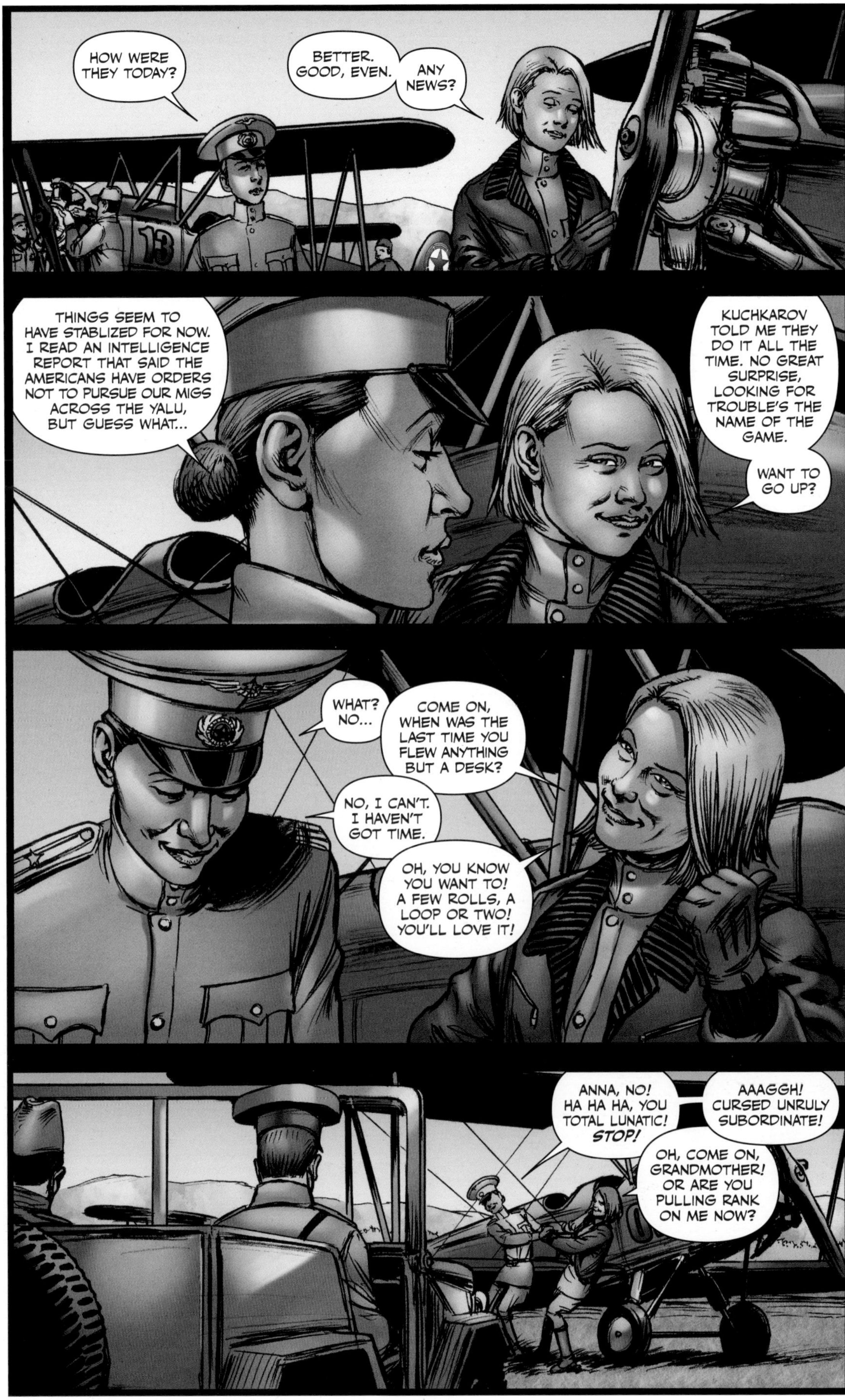
HOW WERE THEY TODAY?
BETTER. GOOD, EVEN.
ANY NEWS?
13
THINGS SEEM TO HAVE STABLIZED FOR NOW. I READ AN INTELLIGENCE REPORT THAT SAID THE AMERICANS HAVE ORDERS NOT TO PURSUE OUR MIGS ACROSS THE YALU, BUT GUESS WHAT...
KUCHKAROV TOLD ME THEY DO IT ALL THE TIME. NO GREAT SURPRISE, LOOKING FOR TROUBLE'S THE NAME OF THE GAME.
WANT TO GO UP?
WHAT? NO...
COME ON, WHEN WAS THE LAST TIME YOU FLEW ANYTHING BUT A DESK?
NO, I CAN'T. I HAVEN'T GOT TIME.
OH, YOU KNOW YOU WANT TO! A FEW ROLLS, A LOOP OR TWO! YOU'LL LOVE IT!
ANNA, NO! HA HA HA, YOU TOTAL LUNATIC! STOP!
AAAGGH! CURSED UNRULY SUBORDINATE!
OH, COME ON, GRANDMOTHER! OR ARE YOU PULLING RANK ON ME NOW?

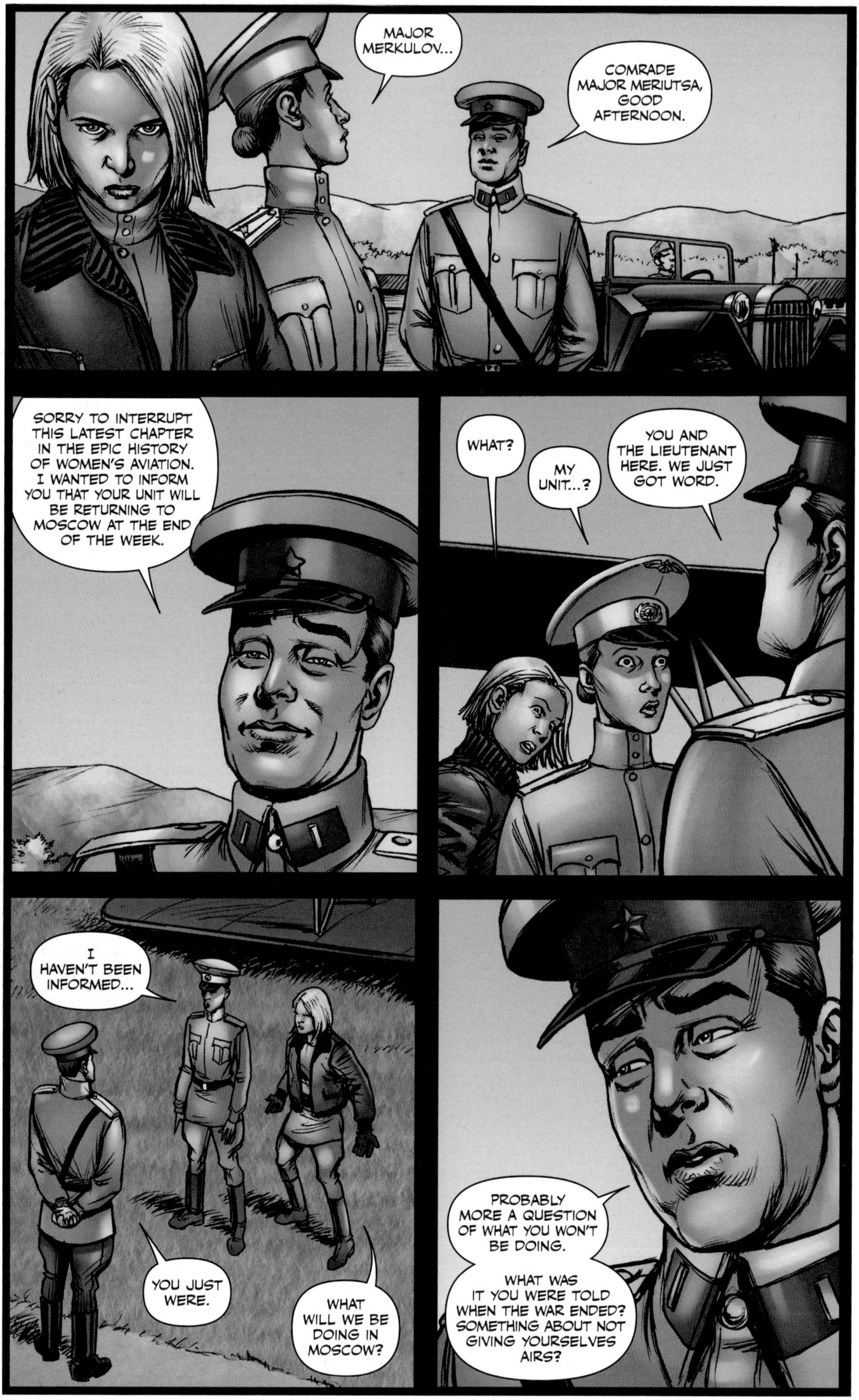

MAJOR MERKULOV...
COMRADE MAJOR MERIUTSA, GOOD AFTERNOON.
SORRY TO INTERRUPT THIS LATEST CHAPTER IN THE EPIC HISTORY OF WOMEN'S AVIATION. I WANTED TO INFORM YOU THAT YOUR UNIT WILL BE RETURNING TO MOSCOW AT THE END OF THE WEEK.
WHAT?
MY UNIT...?
YOU AND THE LIEUTENANT HERE. WE JUST GOT WORD.
I HAVEN'T BEEN INFORMED...
YOU JUST WERE.
WHAT WILL WE BE DOING IN MOSCOW?
PROBABLY MORE A QUESTION OF WHAT YOU WON'T BE DOING.
WHAT WAS IT YOU WERE TOLD WHEN THE WAR ENDED? SOMETHING ABOUT NOT GIVING YOURSELVES AIRS?

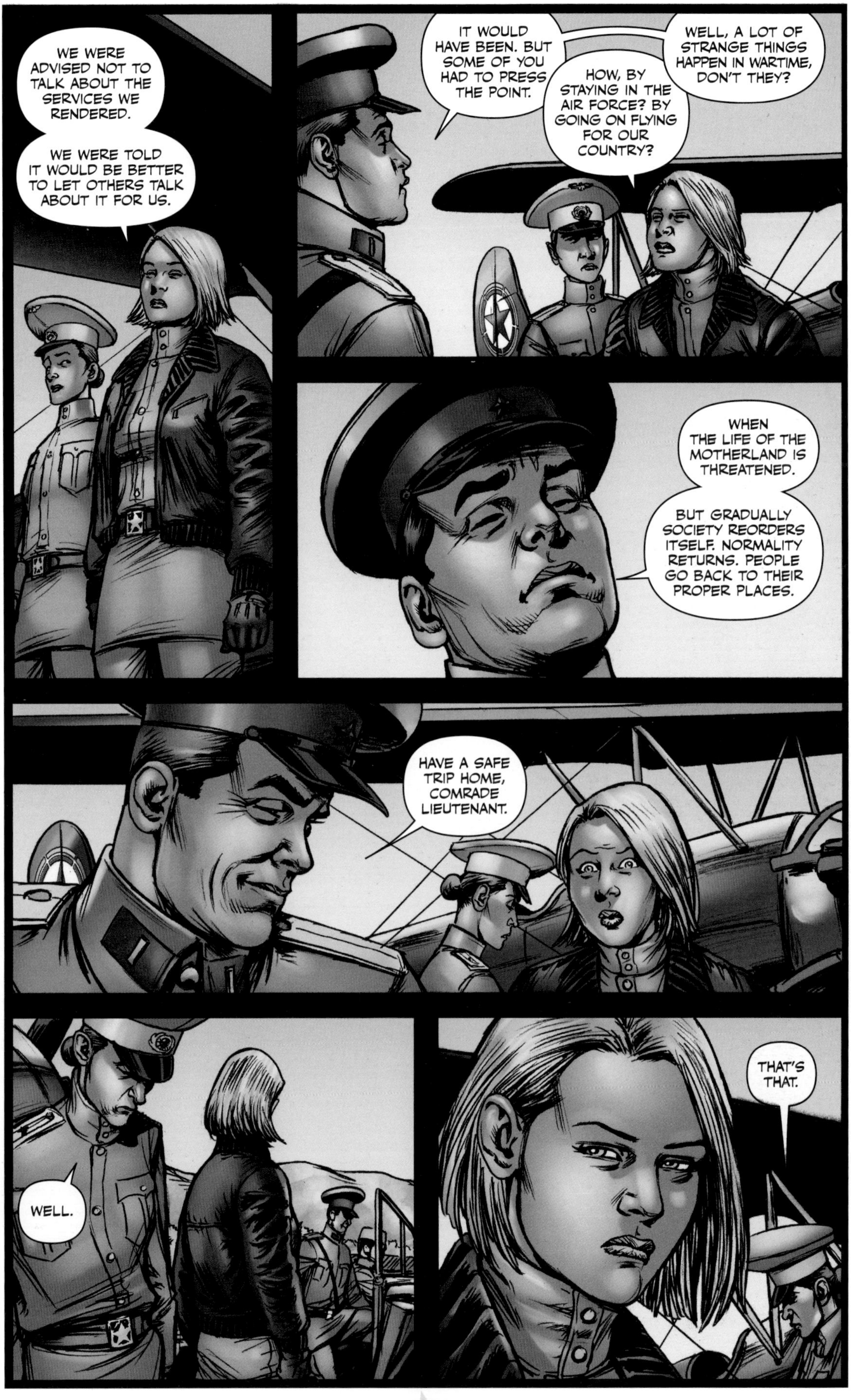
WE WERE ADVISED NOT TO TALK ABOUT THE SERVICES WE RENDERED.
WE WERE TOLD IT WOULD BE BETTER TO LET OTHERS TALK ABOUT IT FOR US.
IT WOULD HAVE BEEN. BUT SOME OF YOU HAD TO PRESS THE POINT.
HOW, BY STAYING IN THE AIR FORCE? BY GOING ON FLYING FOR OUR COUNTRY?
WELL, A LOT OF STRANGE THINGS HAPPEN IN WARTIME, DON'T THEY?
WHEN THE LIFE OF THE MOTHERLAND IS THREATENED.
BUT GRADUALLY SOCIETY REORDERS ITSELF. NORMALITY RETURNS. PEOPLE GO BACK TO THEIR PROPER PLACES.
HAVE A SAFE TRIP HOME, COMRADE LIEUTENANT.
WELL.
THAT'S THAT.

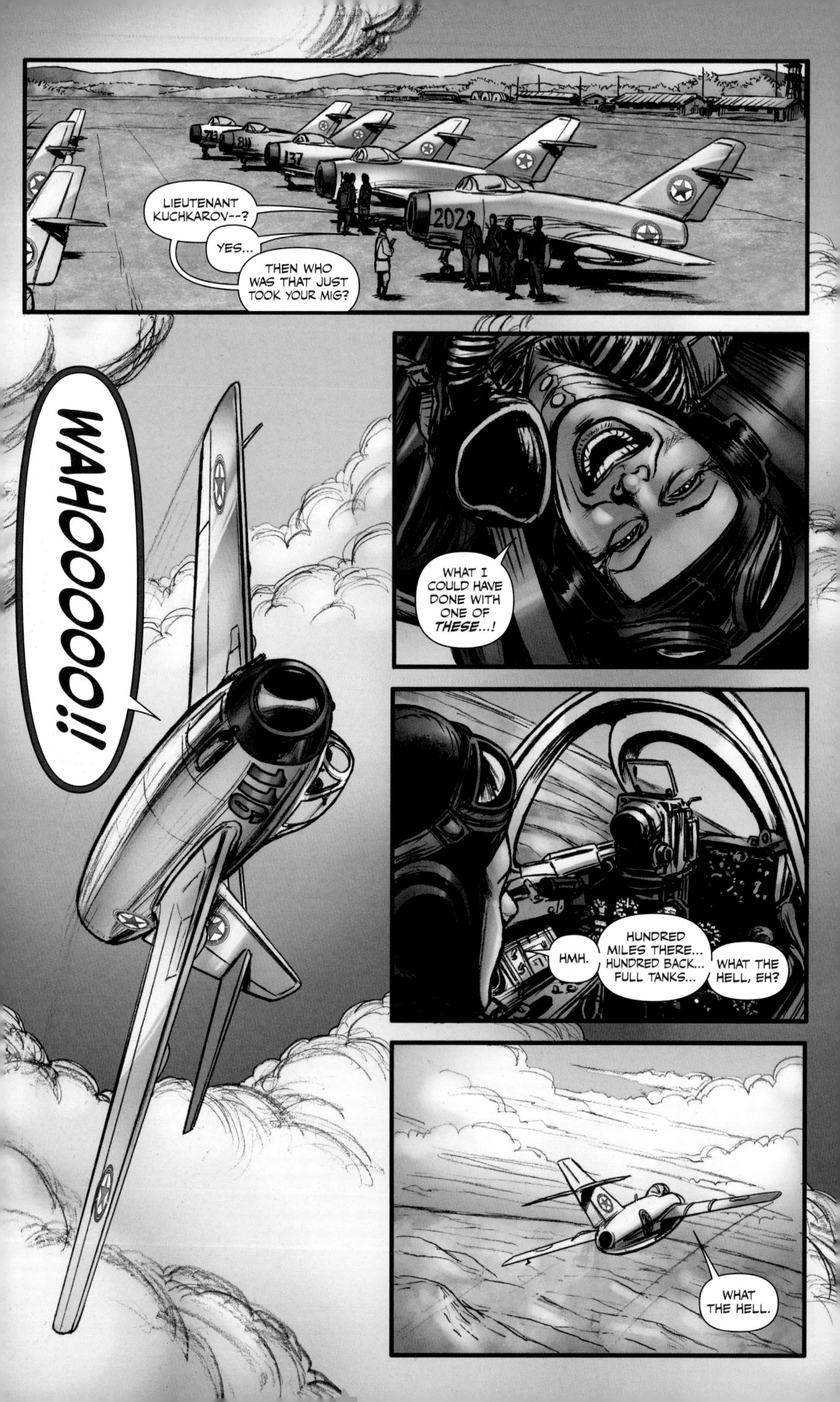

LIEUTENANT KUCHKAROV--?
YES...
THEN WHO WAS THAT JUST TOOK YOUR MIG?
WAHOOOOO!!
WHAT I COULD HAVE DONE WITH ONE OF *THESE*...!
HMH.
HUNDRED MILES THERE... HUNDRED BACK... FULL TANKS...
WHAT THE HELL, EH?
WHAT THE HELL.

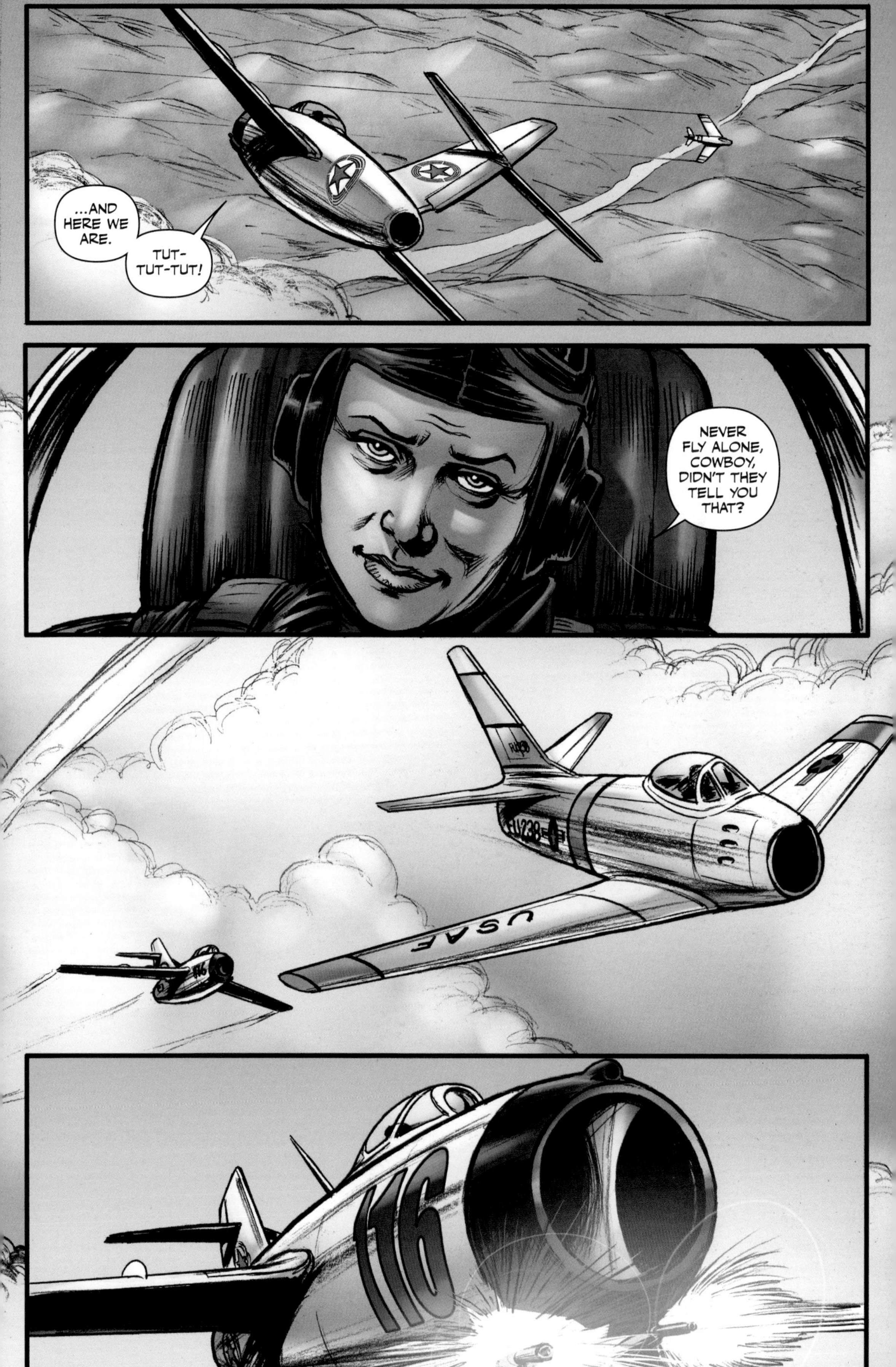

...AND HERE WE ARE.
TUT-TUT-TUT!
NEVER FLY ALONE, COWBOY, DIDN'T THEY TELL YOU THAT?
FU-238
USAF
116

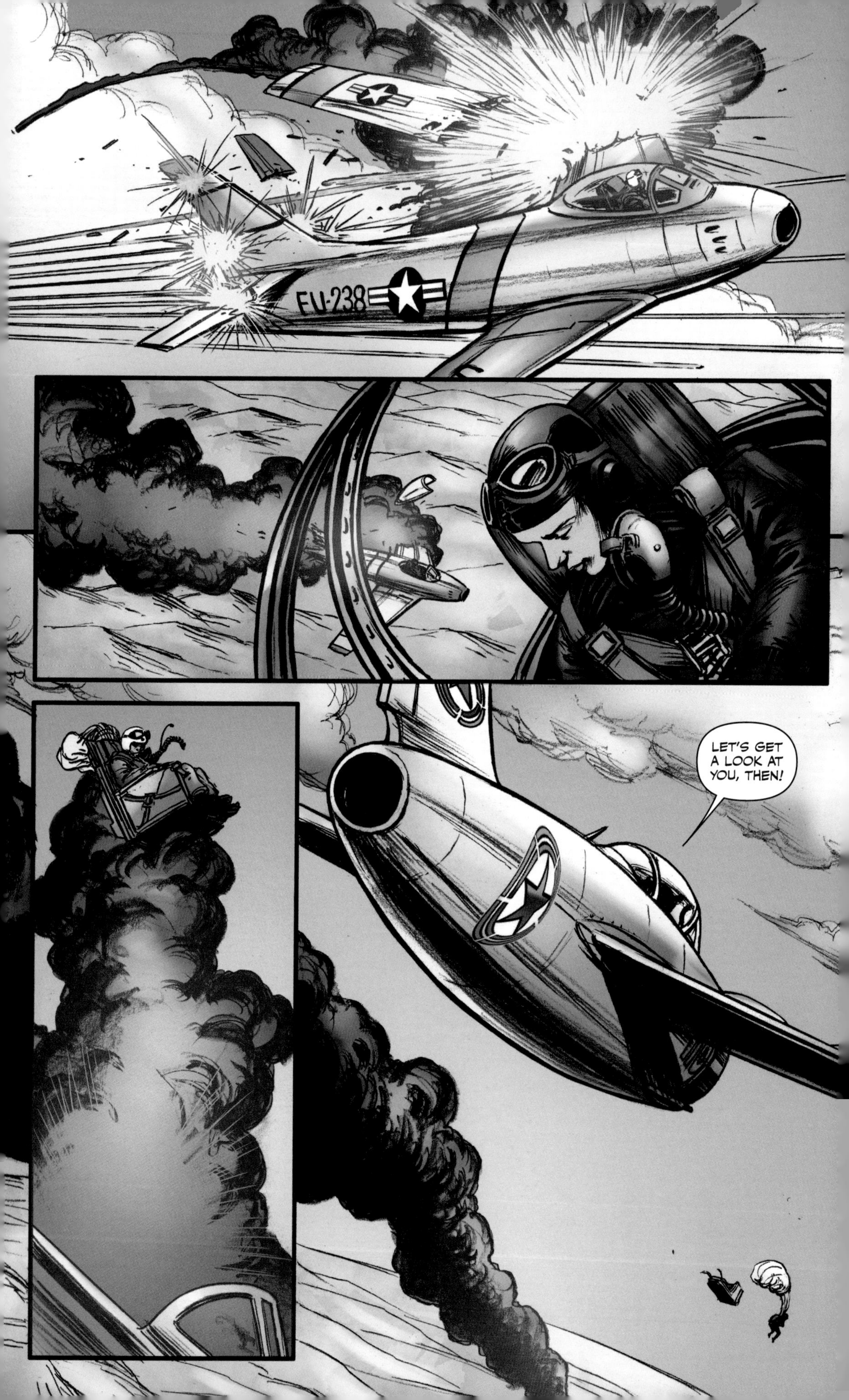
FU-238
LET'S GET A LOOK AT YOU, THEN!

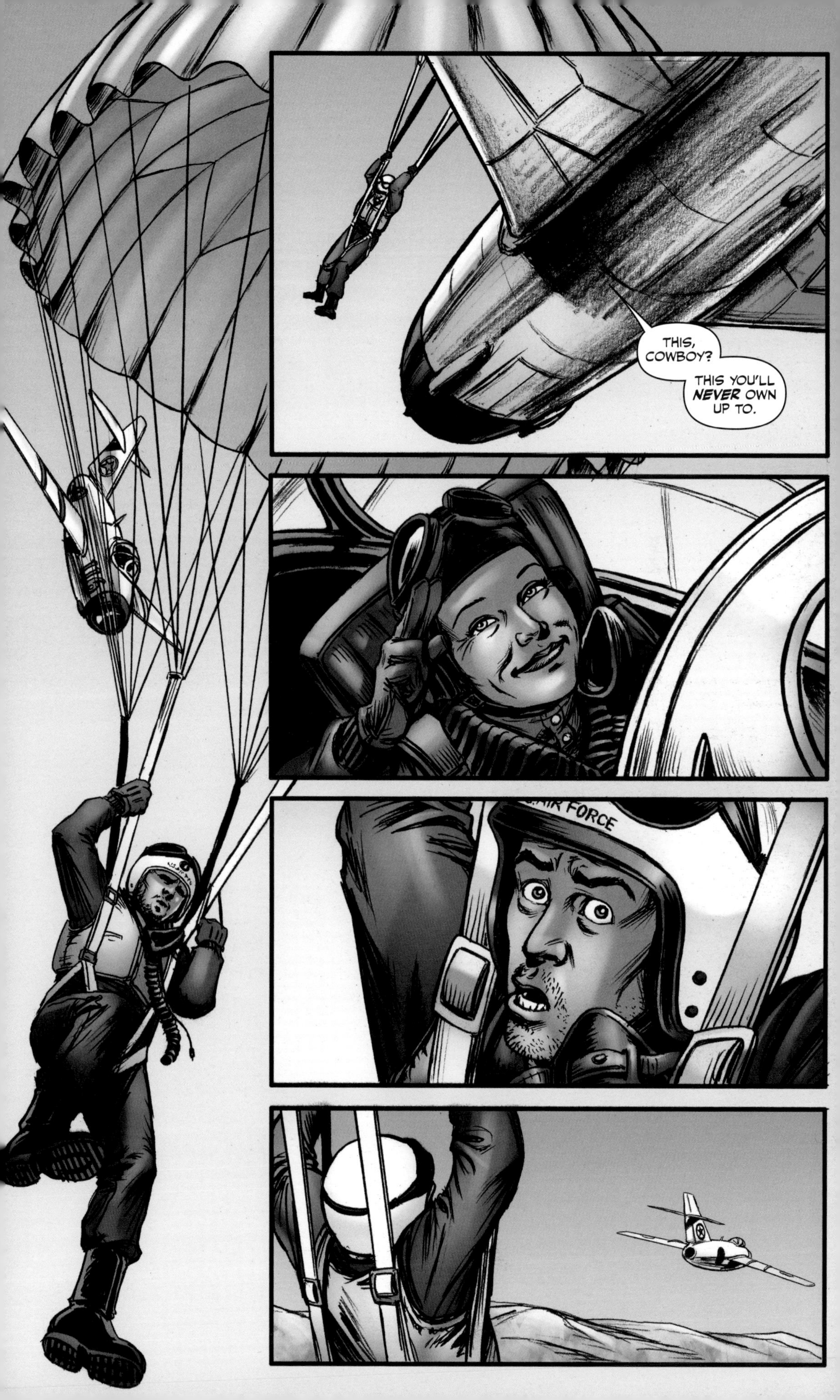
THIS, COWBOY?
THIS YOU'LL NEVER OWN UP TO.
IR FORCE

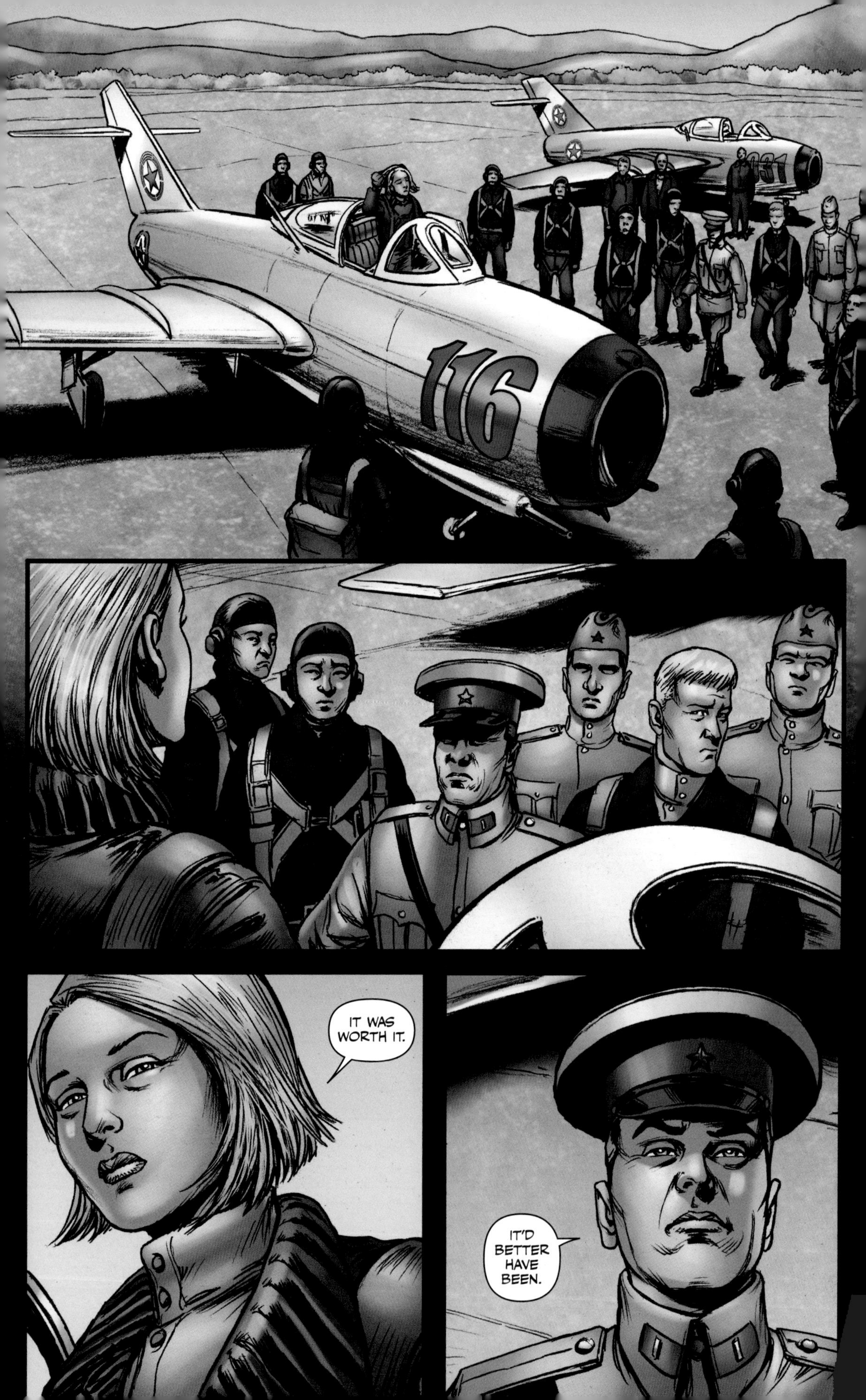
116
031
IT WAS WORTH IT.
IT'D BETTER HAVE BEEN.

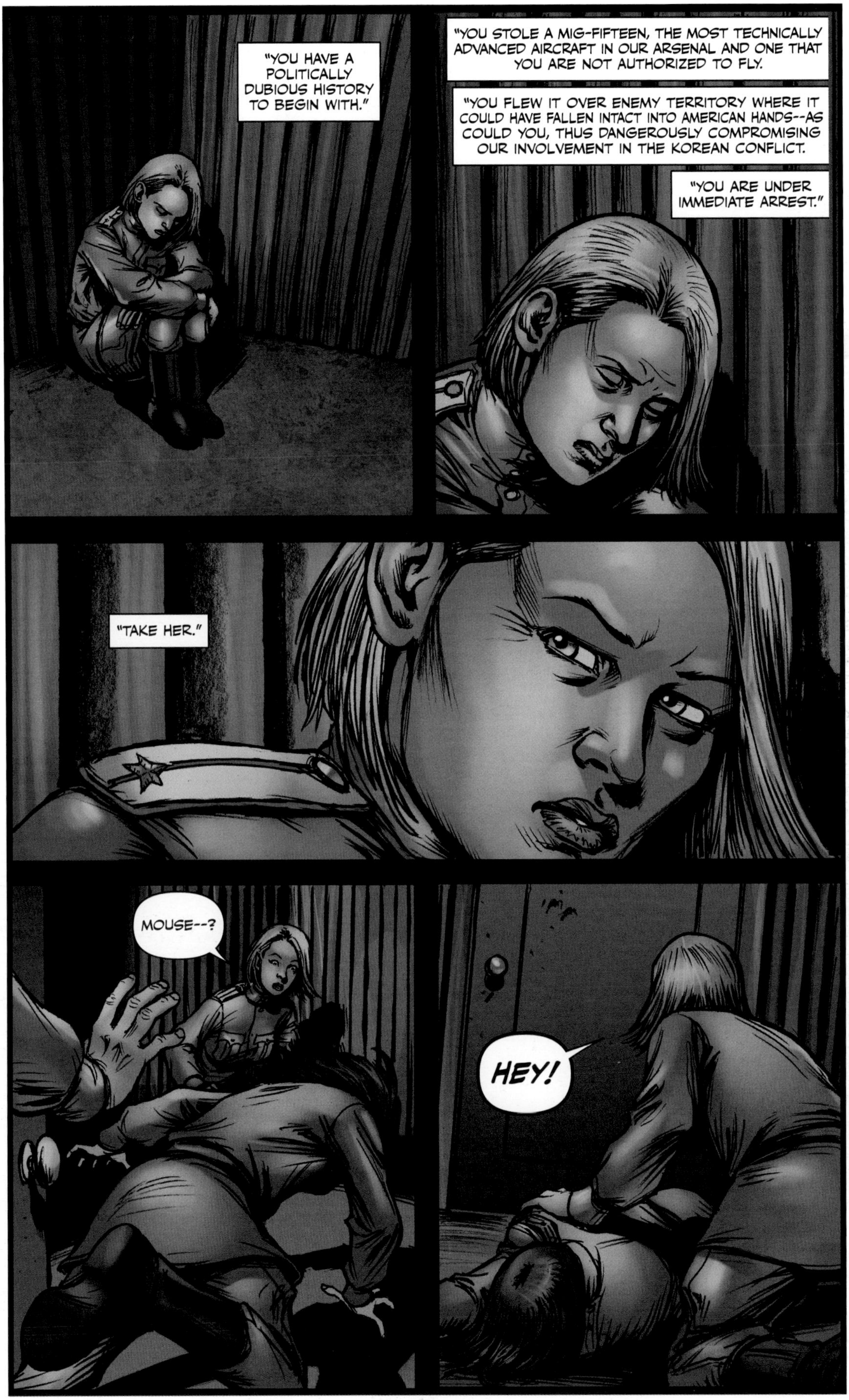
"YOU HAVE A POLITICALLY DUBIOUS HISTORY TO BEGIN WITH."
"YOU STOLE A MIG-FIFTEEN, THE MOST TECHNICALLY ADVANCED AIRCRAFT IN OUR ARSENAL AND ONE THAT YOU ARE NOT AUTHORIZED TO FLY.
"YOU FLEW IT OVER ENEMY TERRITORY WHERE IT COULD HAVE FALLEN INTACT INTO AMERICAN HANDS--AS COULD YOU, THUS DANGEROUSLY COMPROMISING OUR INVOLVEMENT IN THE KOREAN CONFLICT.
"YOU ARE UNDER IMMEDIATE ARREST."
"TAKE HER."
MOUSE--?
HEY!

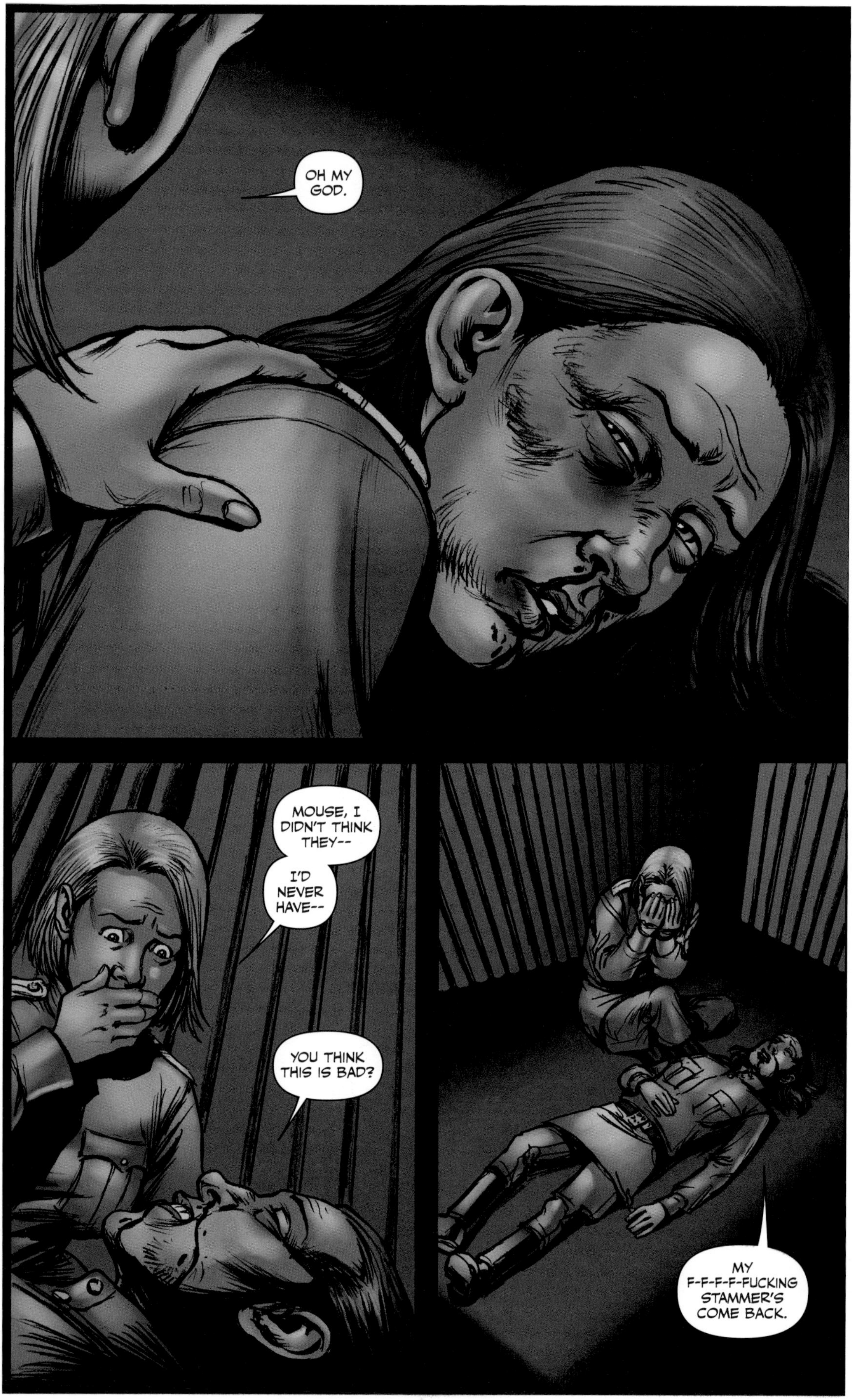

OH MY GOD.
MOUSE, I DIDN'T THINK THEY--
I'D NEVER HAVE--
YOU THINK THIS IS BAD?
MY F-F-F-F-FUCKING STAMMER'S COME BACK.

Chapter 3

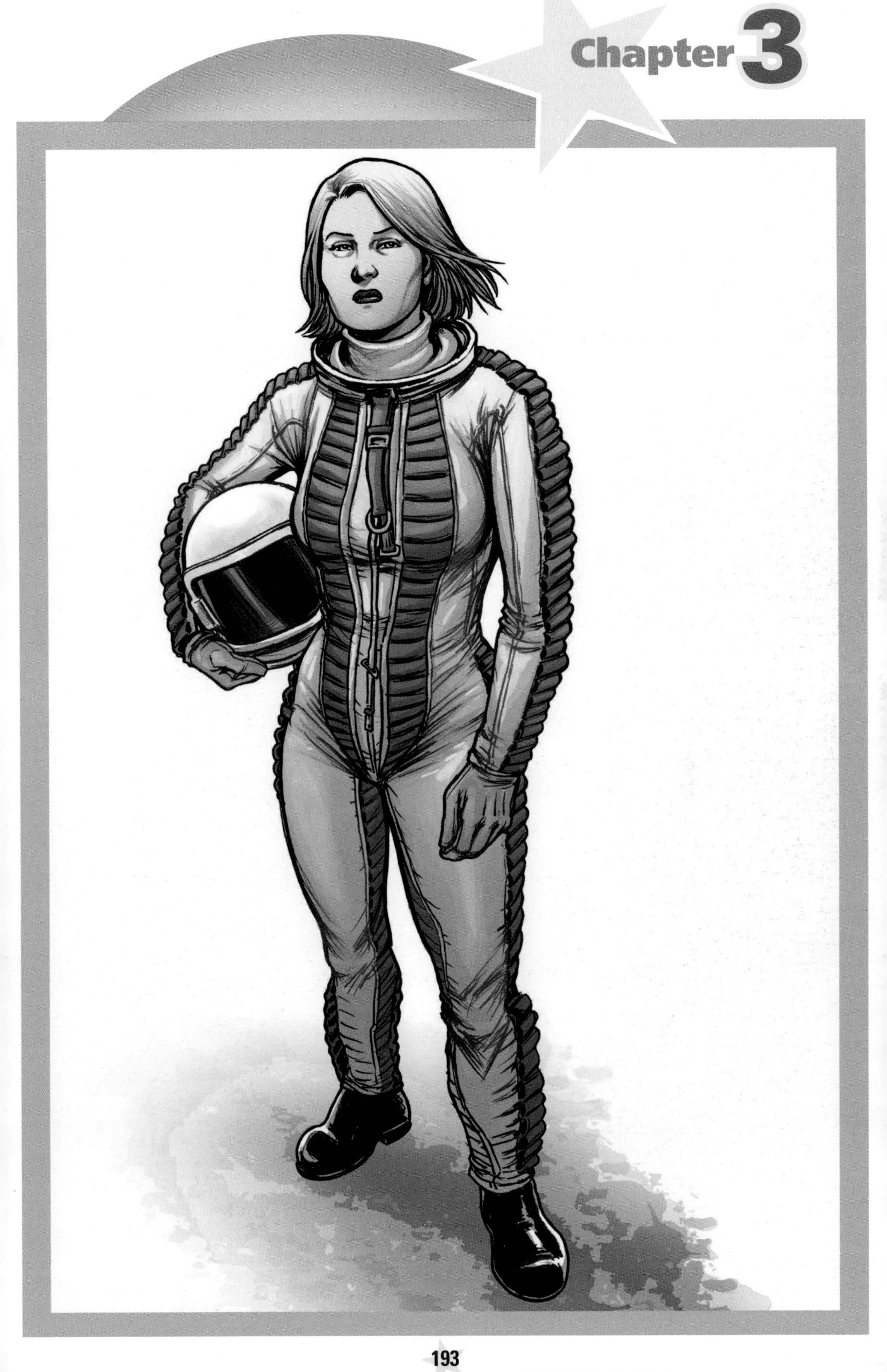

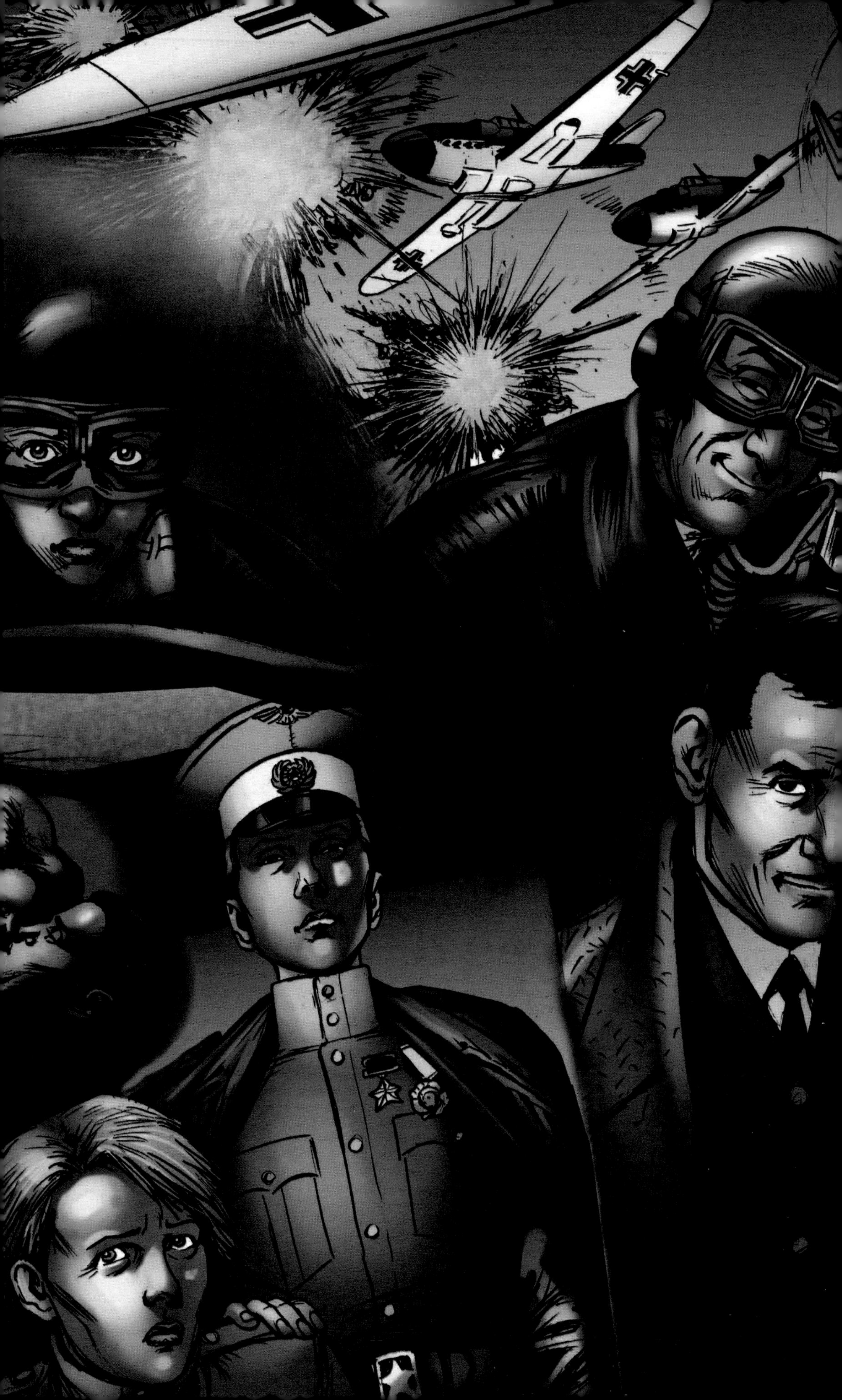

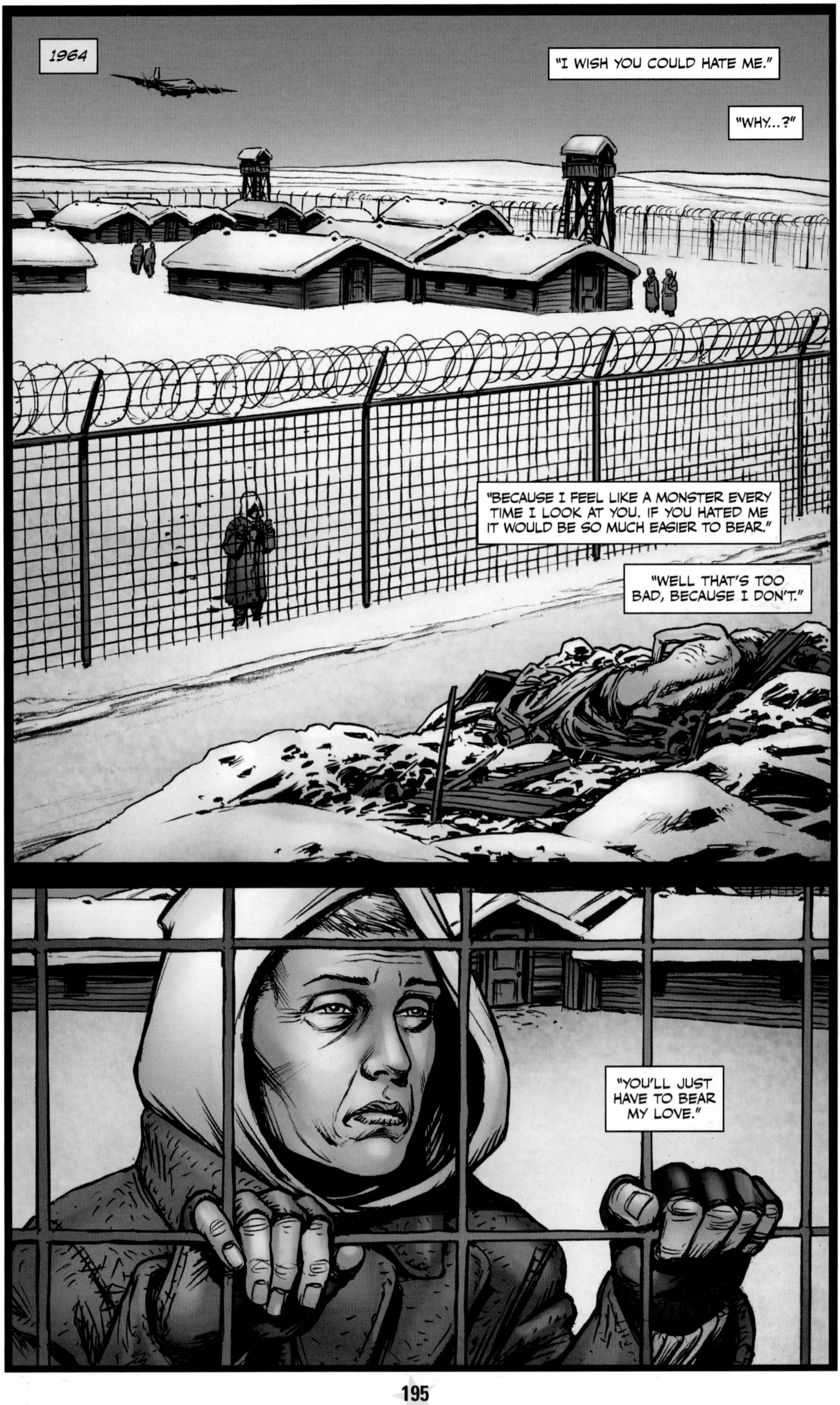
1964
"I WISH YOU COULD HATE ME."
"WHY...?"
"BECAUSE I FEEL LIKE A MONSTER EVERY TIME I LOOK AT YOU. IF YOU HATED ME IT WOULD BE SO MUCH EASIER TO BEAR."
"WELL THAT'S TOO BAD, BECAUSE I DON'T."
"YOU'LL JUST HAVE TO BEAR MY LOVE."

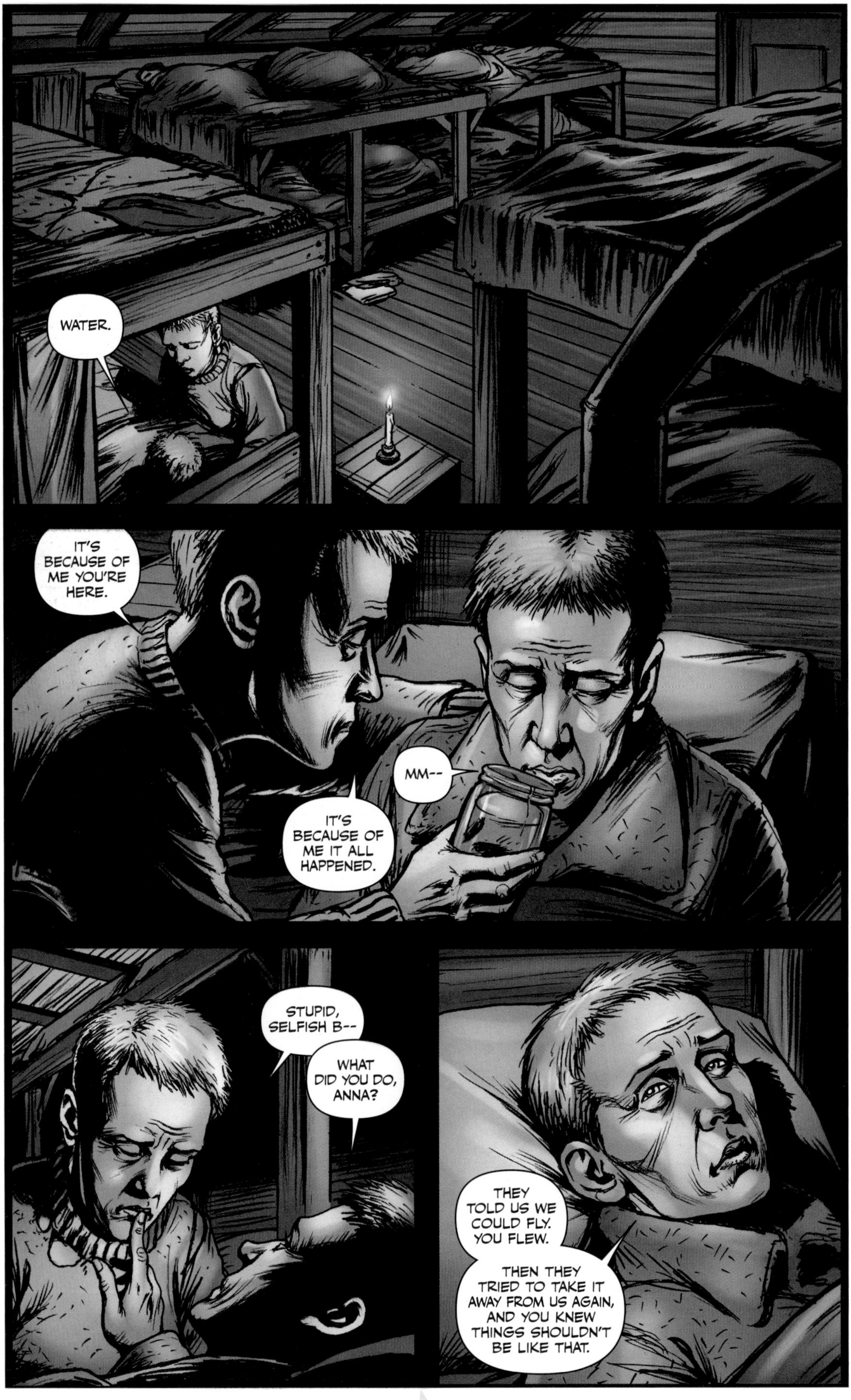
WATER.
IT'S BECAUSE OF ME YOU'RE HERE.
MM--
IT'S BECAUSE OF ME IT ALL HAPPENED.
STUPID, SELFISH B--
WHAT DID YOU DO, ANNA?
THEY TOLD US WE COULD FLY. YOU FLEW.
THEN THEY TRIED TO TAKE IT AWAY FROM US AGAIN, AND YOU KNEW THINGS SHOULDN'T BE LIKE THAT.

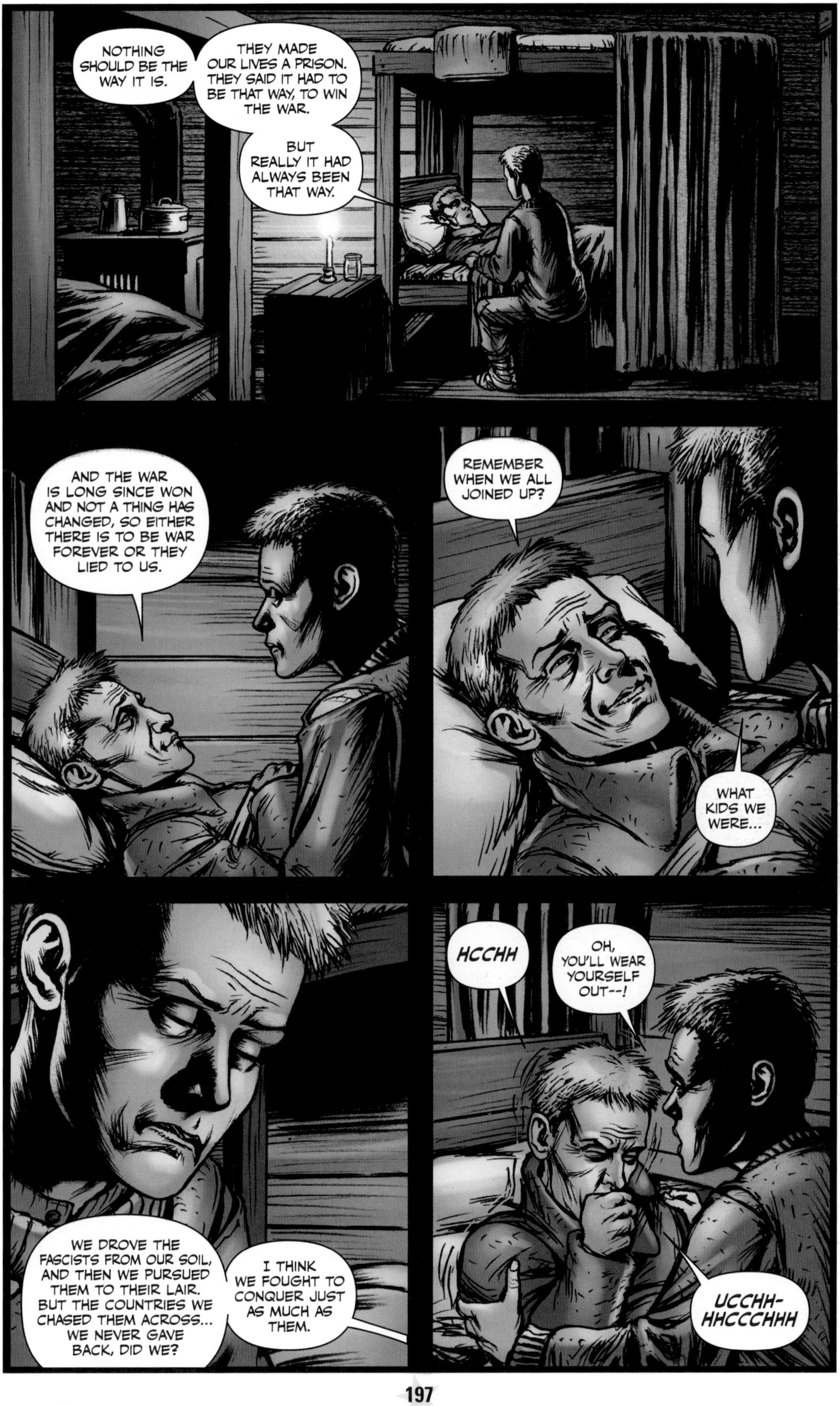
NOTHING SHOULD BE THE WAY IT IS.
THEY MADE OUR LIVES A PRISON. THEY SAID IT HAD TO BE THAT WAY, TO WIN THE WAR.
BUT REALLY IT HAD ALWAYS BEEN THAT WAY.
AND THE WAR IS LONG SINCE WON AND NOT A THING HAS CHANGED, SO EITHER THERE IS TO BE WAR FOREVER OR THEY LIED TO US.
REMEMBER WHEN WE ALL JOINED UP?
WHAT KIDS WE WERE...
WE DROVE THE FASCISTS FROM OUR SOIL, AND THEN WE PURSUED THEM TO THEIR LAIR. BUT THE COUNTRIES WE CHASED THEM ACROSS... WE NEVER GAVE BACK, DID WE?
I THINK WE FOUGHT TO CONQUER JUST AS MUCH AS THEM.
HCCHH
OH, YOU'LL WEAR YOURSELF OUT--!
UCCHH-HHCCCHHH

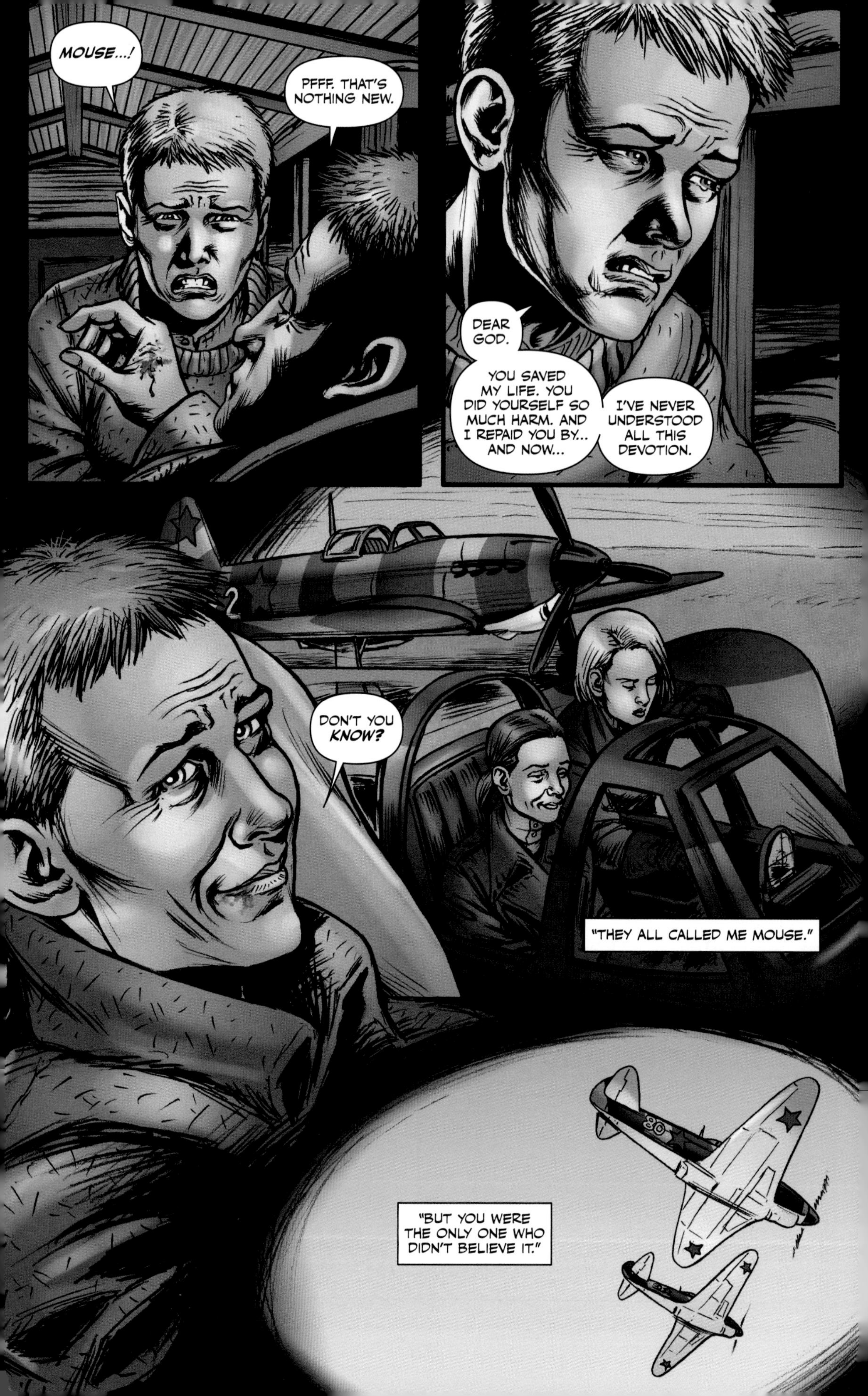
MOUSE...!
PFFF. THAT'S NOTHING NEW.
DEAR GOD.
YOU SAVED MY LIFE. YOU DID YOURSELF SO MUCH HARM. AND I REPAID YOU BY... AND NOW...
I'VE NEVER UNDERSTOOD ALL THIS DEVOTION.
DON'T YOU *KNOW?*
"THEY ALL CALLED ME MOUSE."
"BUT YOU WERE THE ONLY ONE WHO DIDN'T BELIEVE IT."

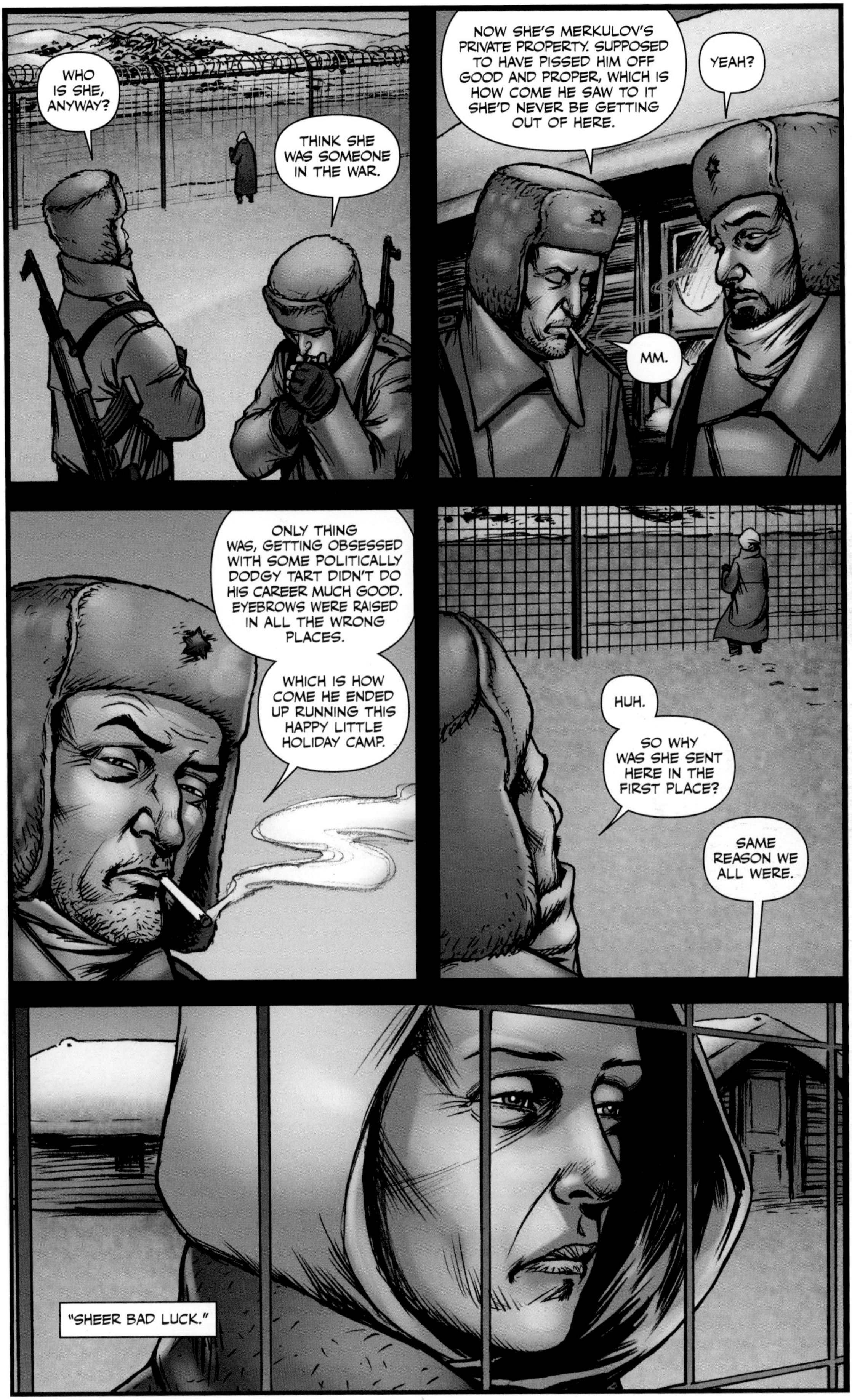
WHO IS SHE, ANYWAY?
THINK SHE WAS SOMEONE IN THE WAR.
NOW SHE'S MERKULOV'S PRIVATE PROPERTY. SUPPOSED TO HAVE PISSED HIM OFF GOOD AND PROPER, WHICH IS HOW COME HE SAW TO IT SHE'D NEVER BE GETTING OUT OF HERE.
YEAH?
MM.
ONLY THING WAS, GETTING OBSESSED WITH SOME POLITICALLY DODGY TART DIDN'T DO HIS CAREER MUCH GOOD. EYEBROWS WERE RAISED IN ALL THE WRONG PLACES.
WHICH IS HOW COME HE ENDED UP RUNNING THIS HAPPY LITTLE HOLIDAY CAMP.
HUH.
SO WHY WAS SHE SENT HERE IN THE FIRST PLACE?
SAME REASON WE ALL WERE.
"SHEER BAD LUCK."

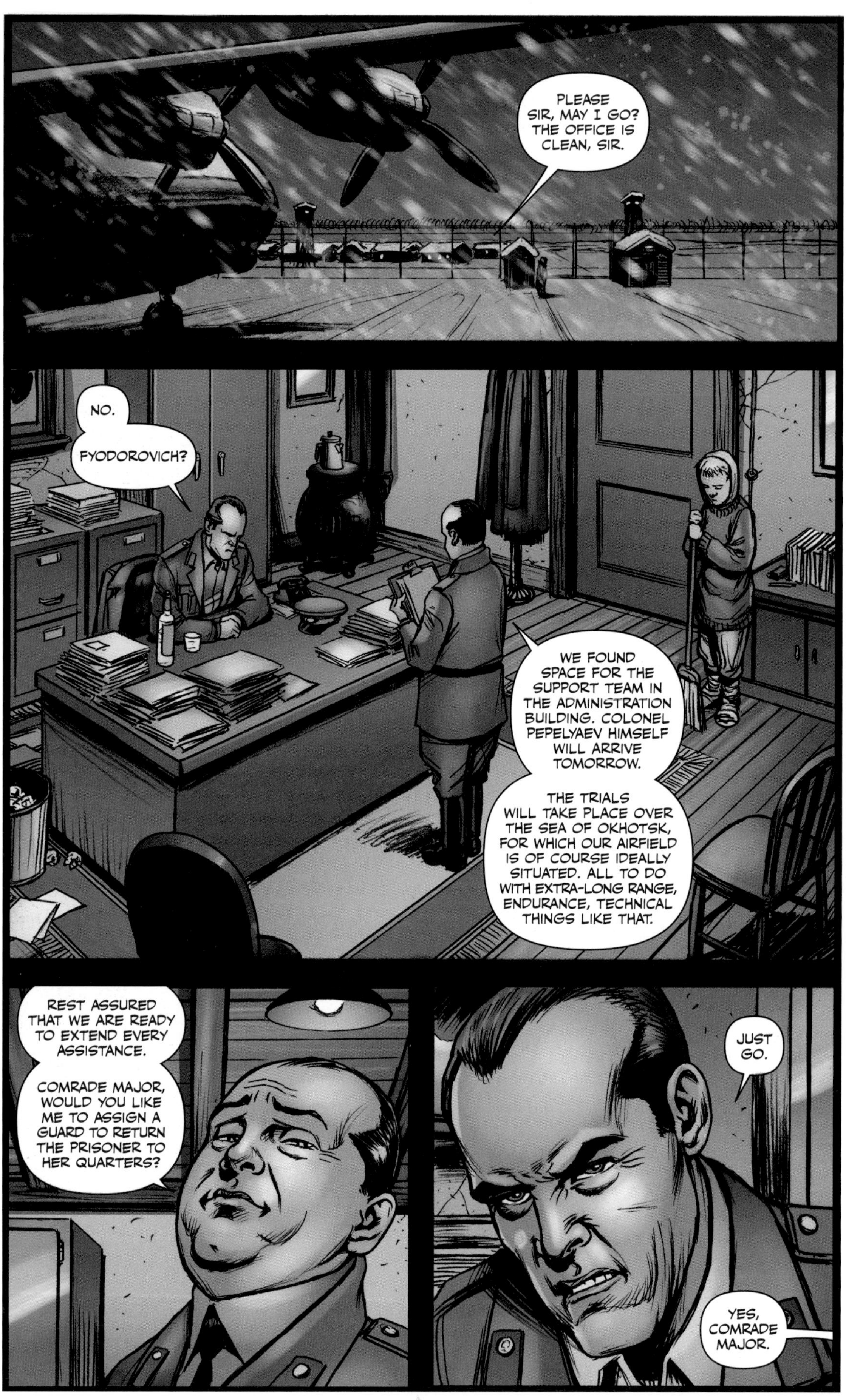
PLEASE SIR, MAY I GO? THE OFFICE IS CLEAN, SIR.
NO.
FYODOROVICH?
WE FOUND SPACE FOR THE SUPPORT TEAM IN THE ADMINISTRATION BUILDING. COLONEL PEPELYAEV HIMSELF WILL ARRIVE TOMORROW.
THE TRIALS WILL TAKE PLACE OVER THE SEA OF OKHOTSK, FOR WHICH OUR AIRFIELD IS OF COURSE IDEALLY SITUATED. ALL TO DO WITH EXTRA-LONG RANGE, ENDURANCE, TECHNICAL THINGS LIKE THAT.
REST ASSURED THAT WE ARE READY TO EXTEND EVERY ASSISTANCE.
COMRADE MAJOR, WOULD YOU LIKE ME TO ASSIGN A GUARD TO RETURN THE PRISONER TO HER QUARTERS?
JUST GO.
YES, COMRADE MAJOR.

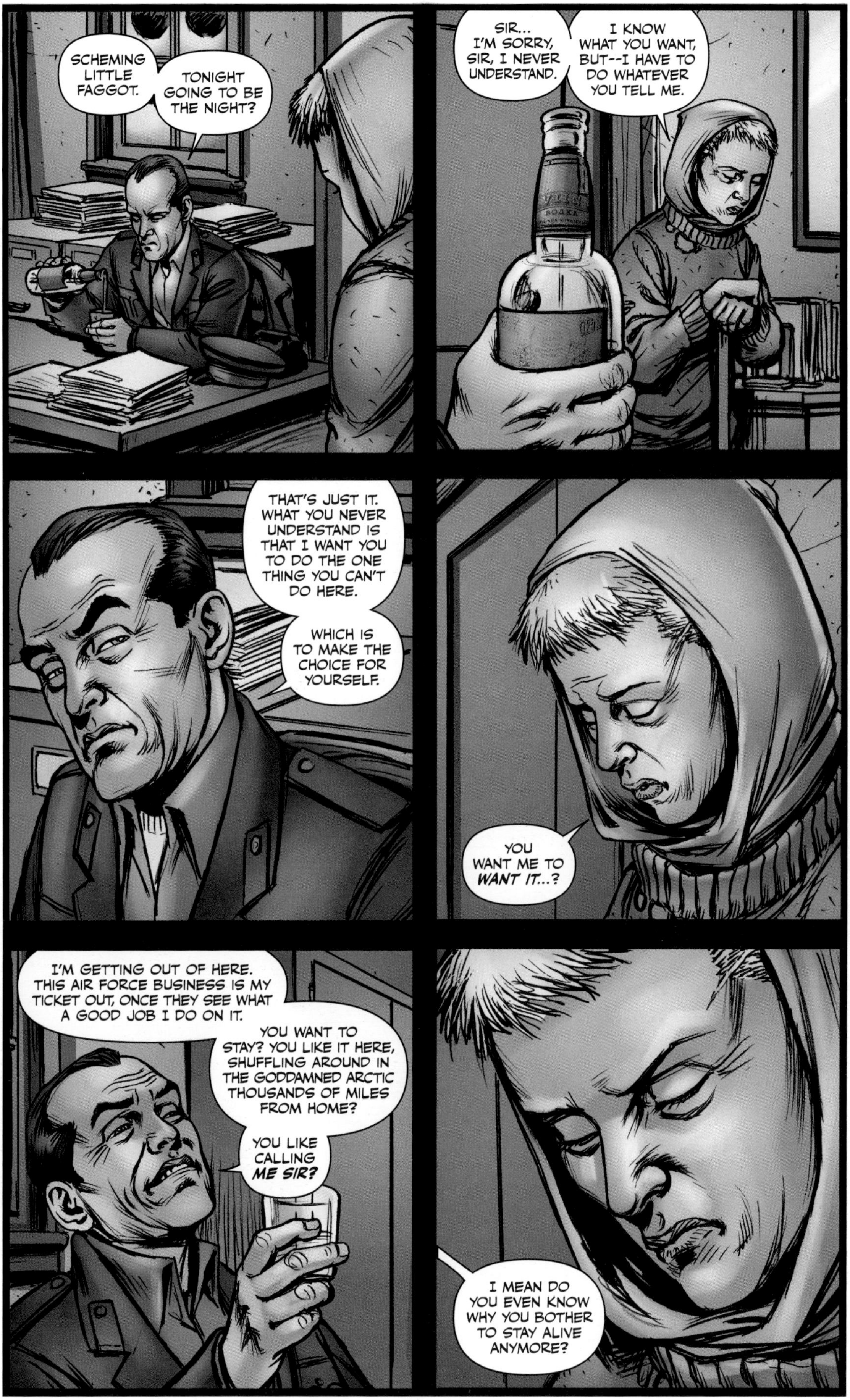
SCHEMING LITTLE FAGGOT.
TONIGHT GOING TO BE THE NIGHT?
SIR... I'M SORRY, SIR, I NEVER UNDERSTAND.
I KNOW WHAT YOU WANT, BUT--I HAVE TO DO WHATEVER YOU TELL ME.
THAT'S JUST IT. WHAT YOU NEVER UNDERSTAND IS THAT I WANT YOU TO DO THE ONE THING YOU CAN'T DO HERE.
WHICH IS TO MAKE THE CHOICE FOR YOURSELF.
YOU WANT ME TO *WANT IT*...?
I'M GETTING OUT OF HERE. THIS AIR FORCE BUSINESS IS MY TICKET OUT, ONCE THEY SEE WHAT A GOOD JOB I DO ON IT.
YOU WANT TO STAY? YOU LIKE IT HERE, SHUFFLING AROUND IN THE GODDAMNED ARCTIC THOUSANDS OF MILES FROM HOME?
YOU LIKE CALLING *ME SIR?*
I MEAN DO YOU EVEN KNOW WHY YOU BOTHER TO STAY ALIVE ANYMORE?

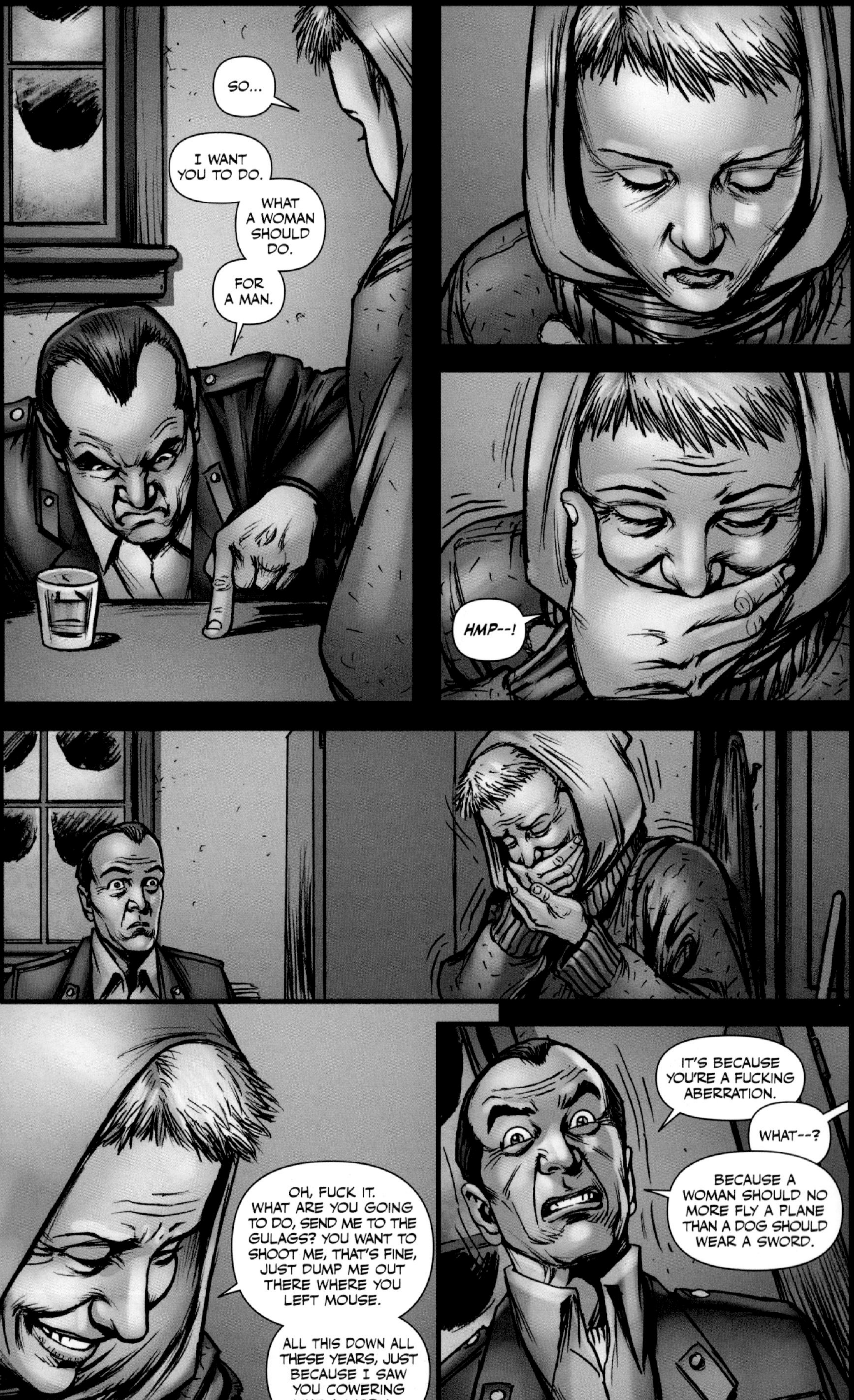
SO...
I WANT YOU TO DO.
WHAT A WOMAN SHOULD DO.
FOR A MAN.
HMP--!
OH, FUCK IT. WHAT ARE YOU GOING TO DO, SEND ME TO THE GULAGS? YOU WANT TO SHOOT ME, THAT'S FINE, JUST DUMP ME OUT THERE WHERE YOU LEFT MOUSE.
ALL THIS DOWN ALL THESE YEARS, JUST BECAUSE I SAW YOU COWERING LIKE A WORM...
IT'S BECAUSE YOU'RE A FUCKING ABERRATION.
WHAT--?
BECAUSE A WOMAN SHOULD NO MORE FLY A PLANE THAN A DOG SHOULD WEAR A SWORD.

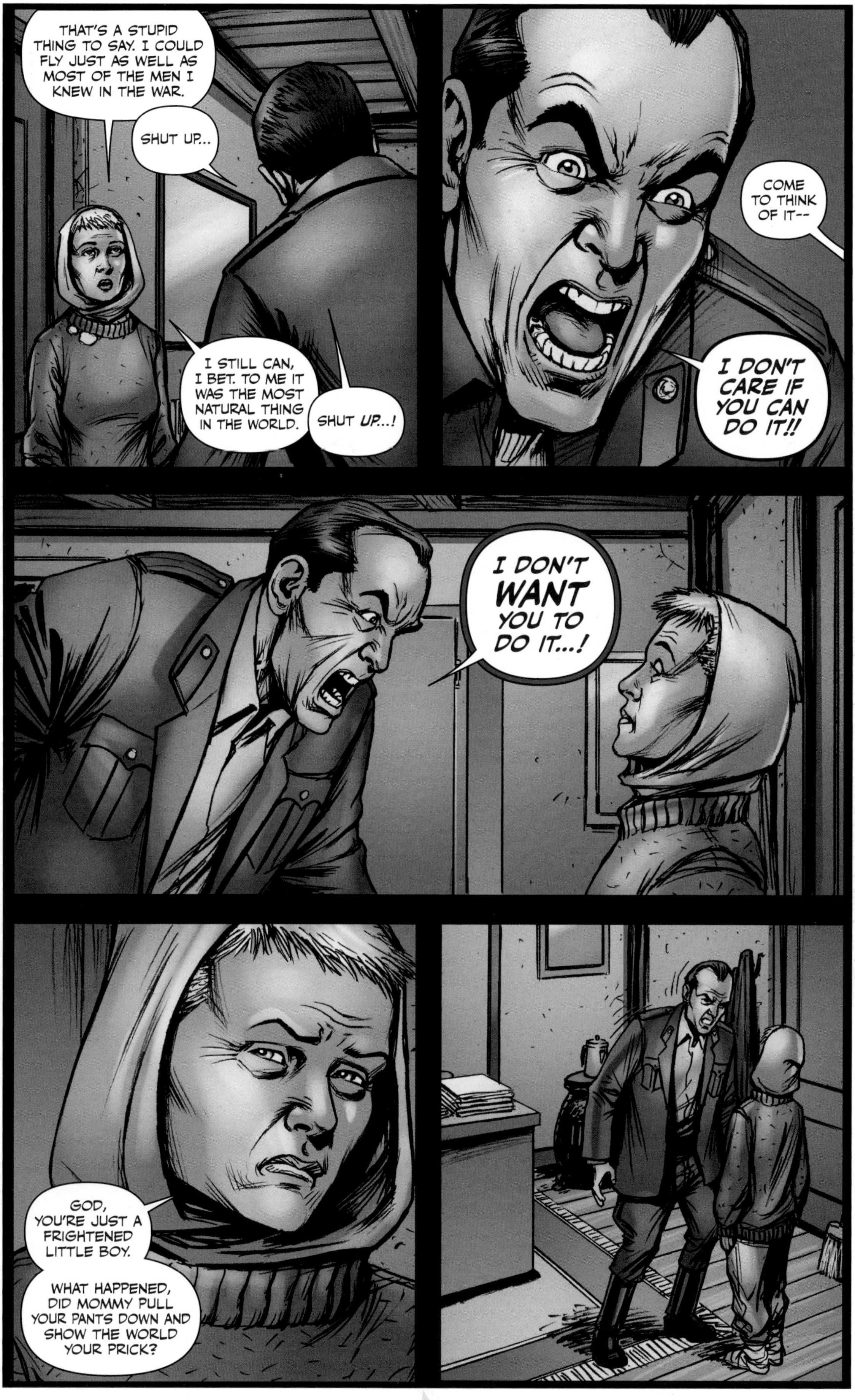
THAT'S A STUPID THING TO SAY. I COULD FLY JUST AS WELL AS MOST OF THE MEN I KNEW IN THE WAR.
SHUT UP...
I STILL CAN, I BET. TO ME IT WAS THE MOST NATURAL THING IN THE WORLD.
SHUT UP...!
COME TO THINK OF IT--
I DON'T CARE IF YOU CAN DO IT!!
I DON'T WANT YOU TO DO IT...!
GOD, YOU'RE JUST A FRIGHTENED LITTLE BOY.
WHAT HAPPENED, DID MOMMY PULL YOUR PANTS DOWN AND SHOW THE WORLD YOUR PRICK?

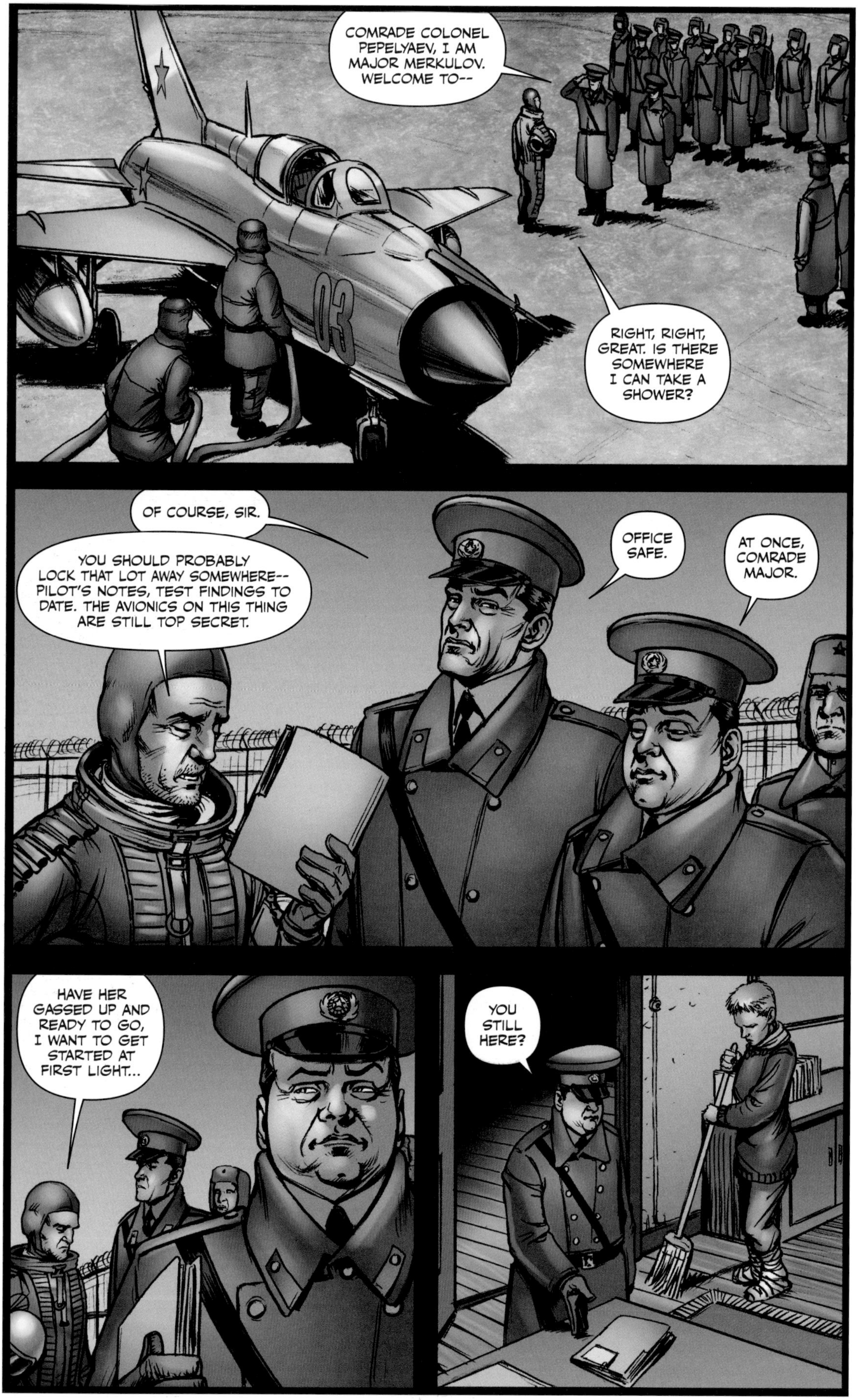
COMRADE COLONEL PEPELYAEV, I AM MAJOR MERKULOV. WELCOME TO--
RIGHT, RIGHT, GREAT. IS THERE SOMEWHERE I CAN TAKE A SHOWER?
OF COURSE, SIR.
YOU SHOULD PROBABLY LOCK THAT LOT AWAY SOMEWHERE-- PILOT'S NOTES, TEST FINDINGS TO DATE. THE AVIONICS ON THIS THING ARE STILL TOP SECRET.
OFFICE SAFE.
AT ONCE, COMRADE MAJOR.
HAVE HER GASSED UP AND READY TO GO, I WANT TO GET STARTED AT FIRST LIGHT...
YOU STILL HERE?

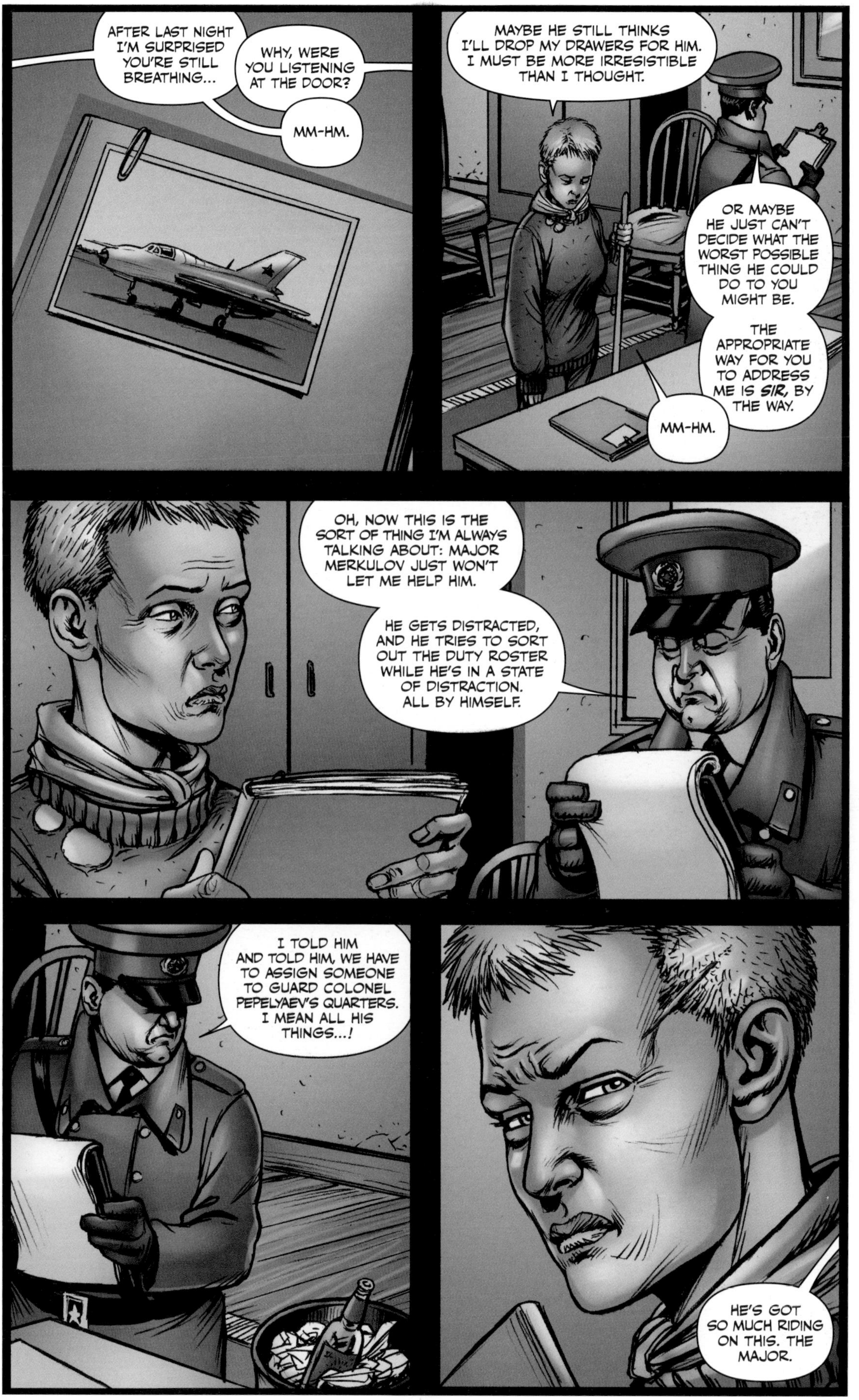
AFTER LAST NIGHT I'M SURPRISED YOU'RE STILL BREATHING...
WHY, WERE YOU LISTENING AT THE DOOR?
MM-HM.
MAYBE HE STILL THINKS I'LL DROP MY DRAWERS FOR HIM. I MUST BE MORE IRRESISTIBLE THAN I THOUGHT.
OR MAYBE HE JUST CAN'T DECIDE WHAT THE WORST POSSIBLE THING HE COULD DO TO YOU MIGHT BE.
THE APPROPRIATE WAY FOR YOU TO ADDRESS ME IS *SIR,* BY THE WAY.
MM-HM.
OH, NOW THIS IS THE SORT OF THING I'M ALWAYS TALKING ABOUT: MAJOR MERKULOV JUST WON'T LET ME HELP HIM.
HE GETS DISTRACTED, AND HE TRIES TO SORT OUT THE DUTY ROSTER WHILE HE'S IN A STATE OF DISTRACTION. ALL BY HIMSELF.
I TOLD HIM AND TOLD HIM, WE HAVE TO ASSIGN SOMEONE TO GUARD COLONEL PEPELYAEV'S QUARTERS. I MEAN ALL HIS THINGS...!
HE'S GOT SO MUCH RIDING ON THIS. THE MAJOR.

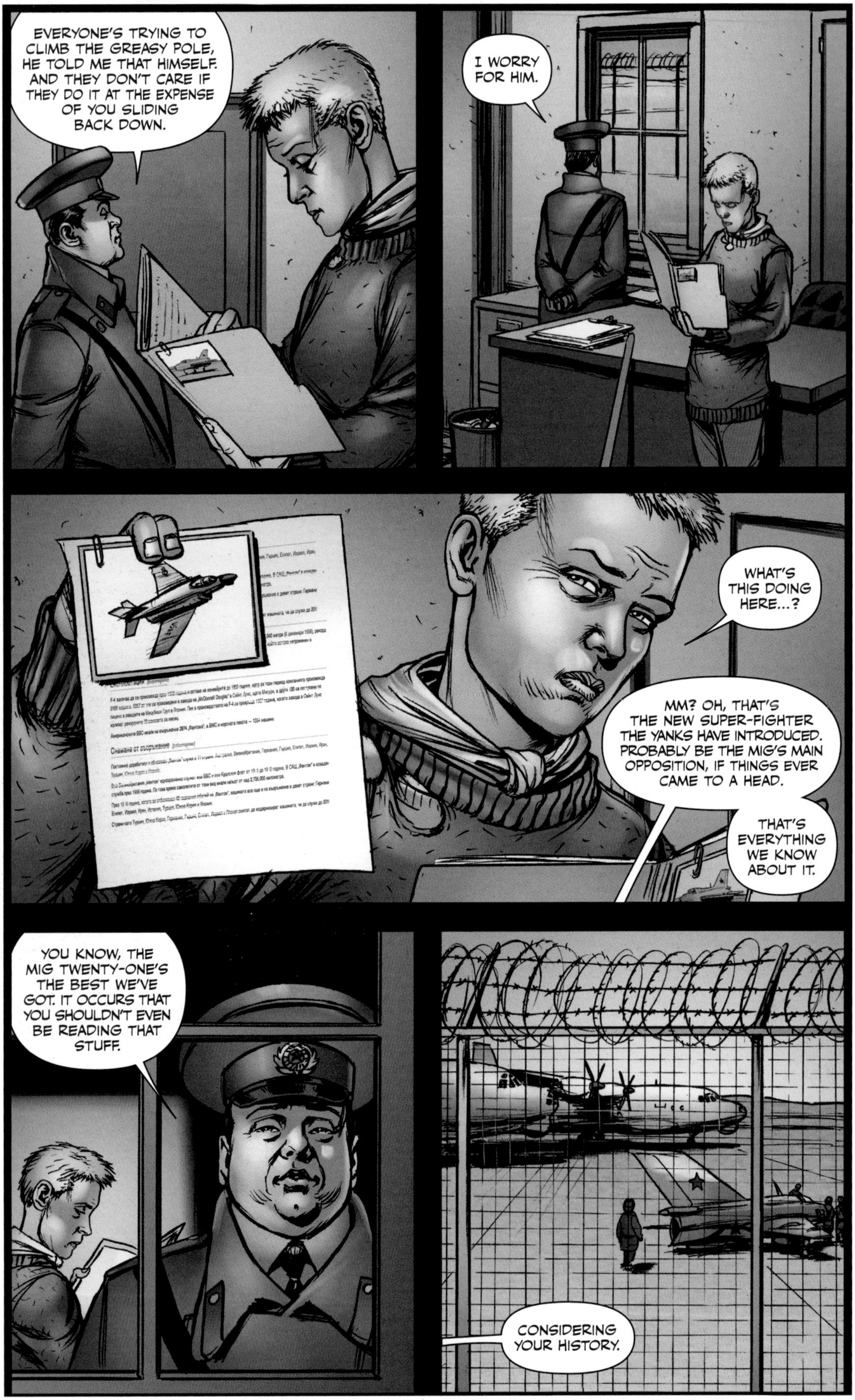
EVERYONE'S TRYING TO CLIMB THE GREASY POLE, HE TOLD ME THAT HIMSELF. AND THEY DON'T CARE IF THEY DO IT AT THE EXPENSE OF YOU SLIDING BACK DOWN.
I WORRY FOR HIM.
WHAT'S THIS DOING HERE...?
MM? OH, THAT'S THE NEW SUPER-FIGHTER THE YANKS HAVE INTRODUCED. PROBABLY BE THE MIG'S MAIN OPPOSITION, IF THINGS EVER CAME TO A HEAD.
THAT'S EVERYTHING WE KNOW ABOUT IT.
YOU KNOW, THE MIG TWENTY-ONE'S THE BEST WE'VE GOT. IT OCCURS THAT YOU SHOULDN'T EVEN BE READING THAT STUFF.
CONSIDERING YOUR HISTORY.

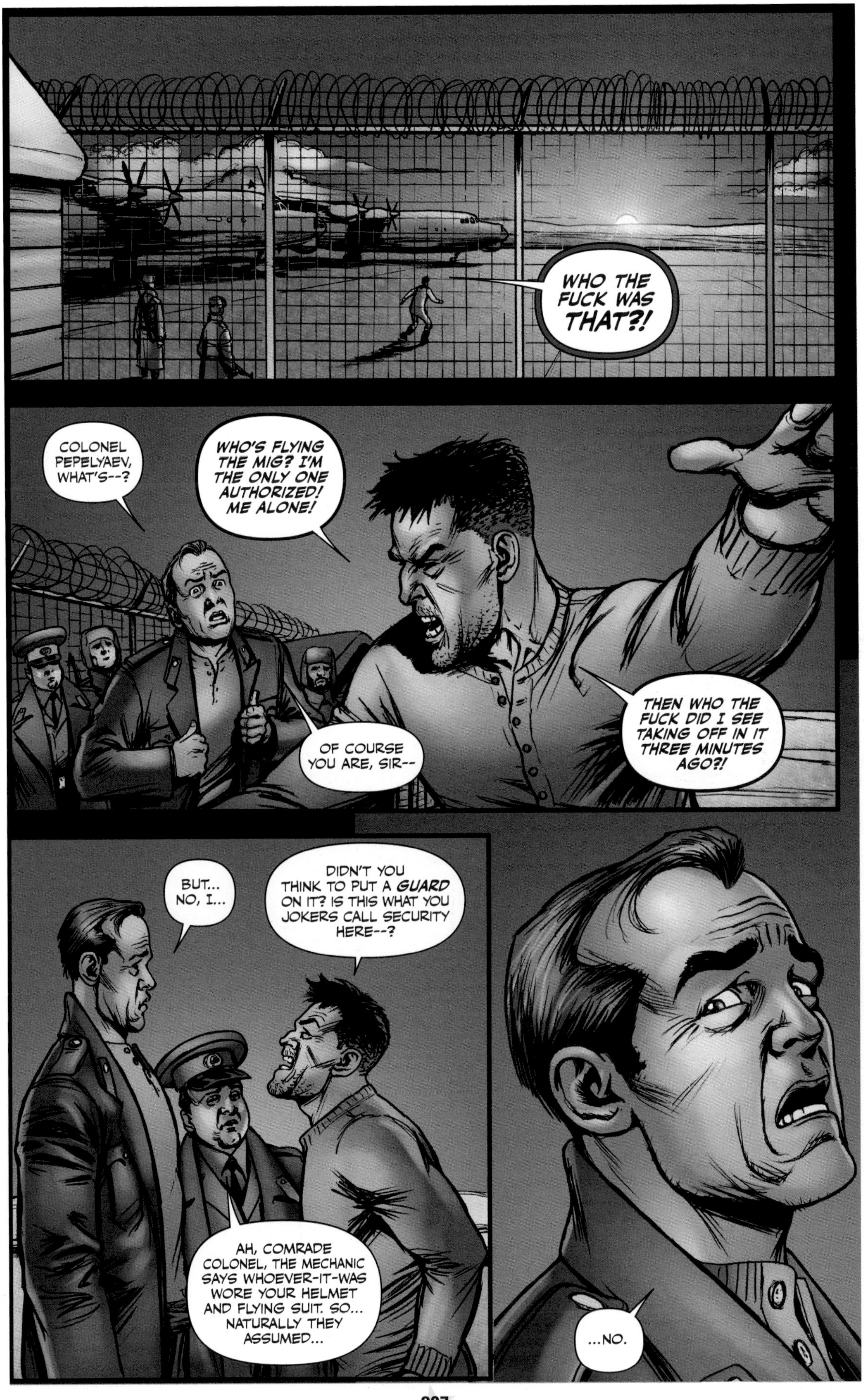
WHO THE FUCK WAS THAT?!
COLONEL PEPELYAEV, WHAT'S--?
WHO'S FLYING THE MIG? I'M THE ONLY ONE AUTHORIZED! ME ALONE!
OF COURSE YOU ARE, SIR--
THEN WHO THE FUCK DID I SEE TAKING OFF IN IT THREE MINUTES AGO?!
BUT... NO, I...
DIDN'T YOU THINK TO PUT A GUARD ON IT? IS THIS WHAT YOU JOKERS CALL SECURITY HERE--?
AH, COMRADE COLONEL, THE MECHANIC SAYS WHOEVER-IT-WAS WORE YOUR HELMET AND FLYING SUIT. SO... NATURALLY THEY ASSUMED...
...NO.

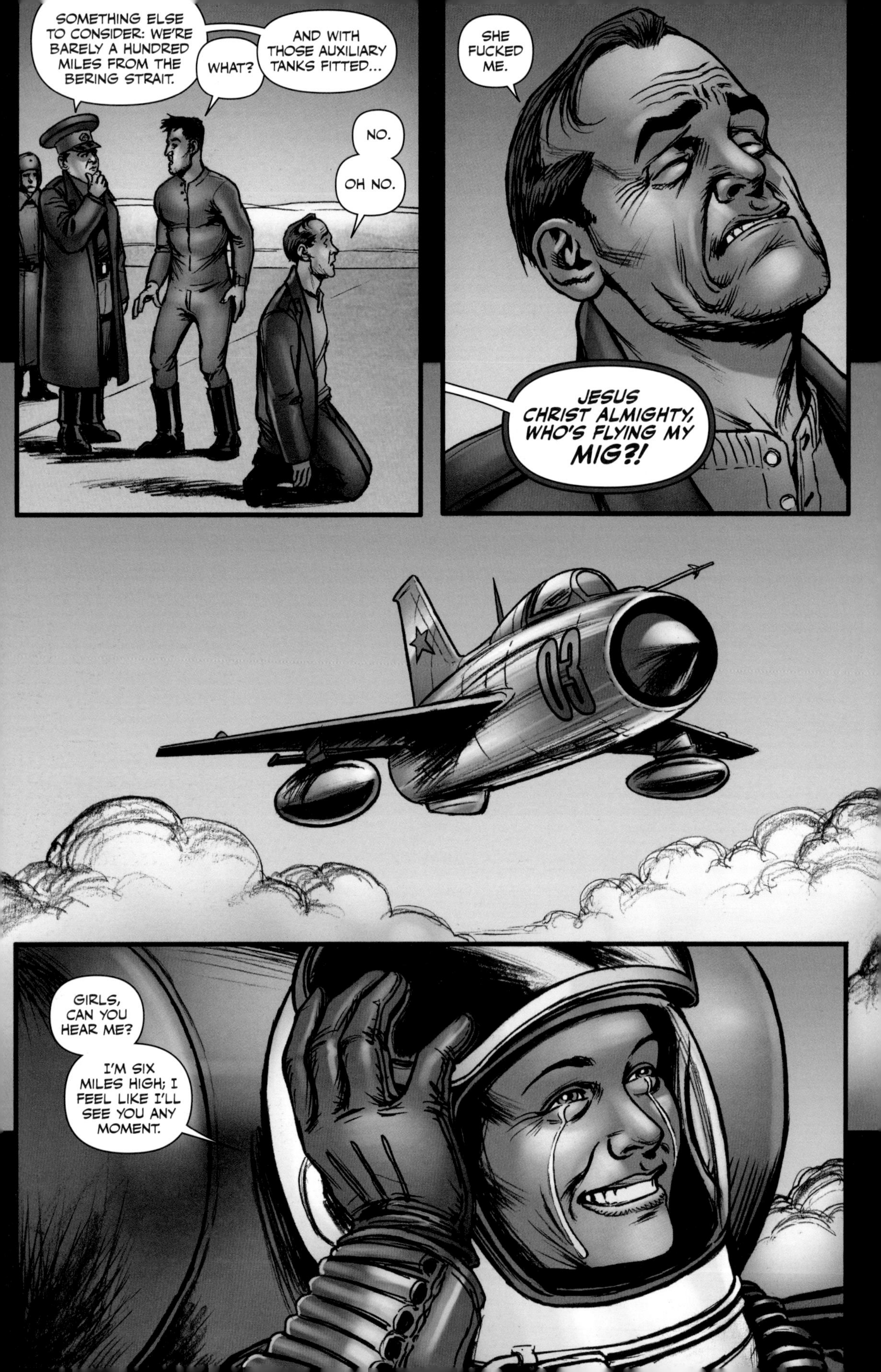
SOMETHING ELSE TO CONSIDER: WE'RE BARELY A HUNDRED MILES FROM THE BERING STRAIT.
WHAT?
AND WITH THOSE AUXILIARY TANKS FITTED...
NO.
OH NO.
SHE FUCKED ME.
JESUS CHRIST ALMIGHTY, WHO'S FLYING MY MIG?!
GIRLS, CAN YOU HEAR ME?
I'M SIX MILES HIGH; I FEEL LIKE I'LL SEE YOU ANY MOMENT.

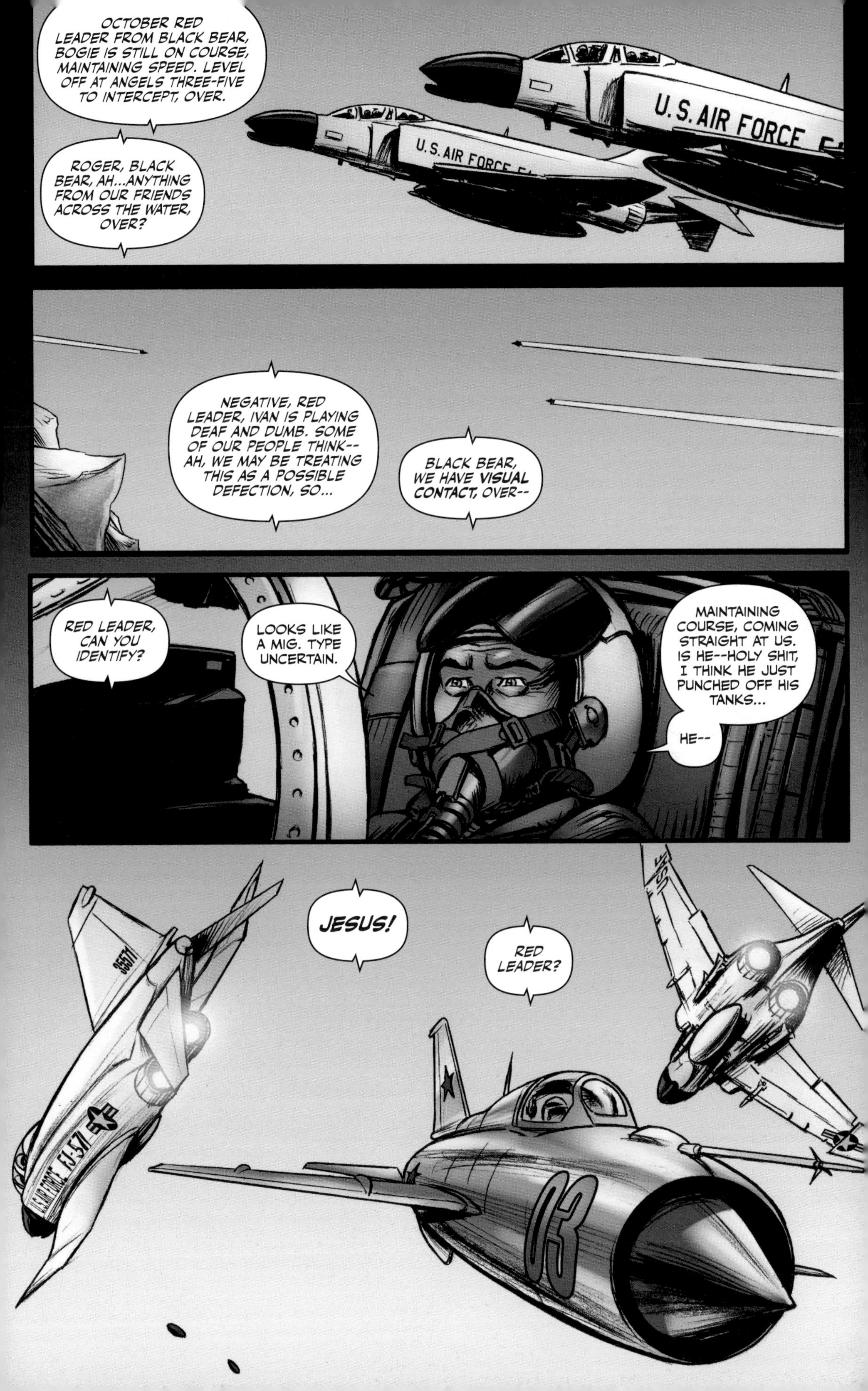
OCTOBER RED LEADER FROM BLACK BEAR, BOGIE IS STILL ON COURSE, MAINTAINING SPEED. LEVEL OFF AT ANGELS THREE-FIVE TO INTERCEPT, OVER.
ROGER, BLACK BEAR, AH...ANYTHING FROM OUR FRIENDS ACROSS THE WATER, OVER?
U.S. AIR FORCE
NEGATIVE, RED LEADER, IVAN IS PLAYING DEAF AND DUMB. SOME OF OUR PEOPLE THINK-- AH, WE MAY BE TREATING THIS AS A POSSIBLE DEFECTION, SO...
BLACK BEAR, WE HAVE **VISUAL CONTACT**, OVER--
RED LEADER, CAN YOU IDENTIFY?
LOOKS LIKE A MIG. TYPE UNCERTAIN.
MAINTAINING COURSE, COMING STRAIGHT AT US. IS HE--HOLY SHIT, I THINK HE JUST PUNCHED OFF HIS TANKS...
HE--
JESUS!
RED LEADER?

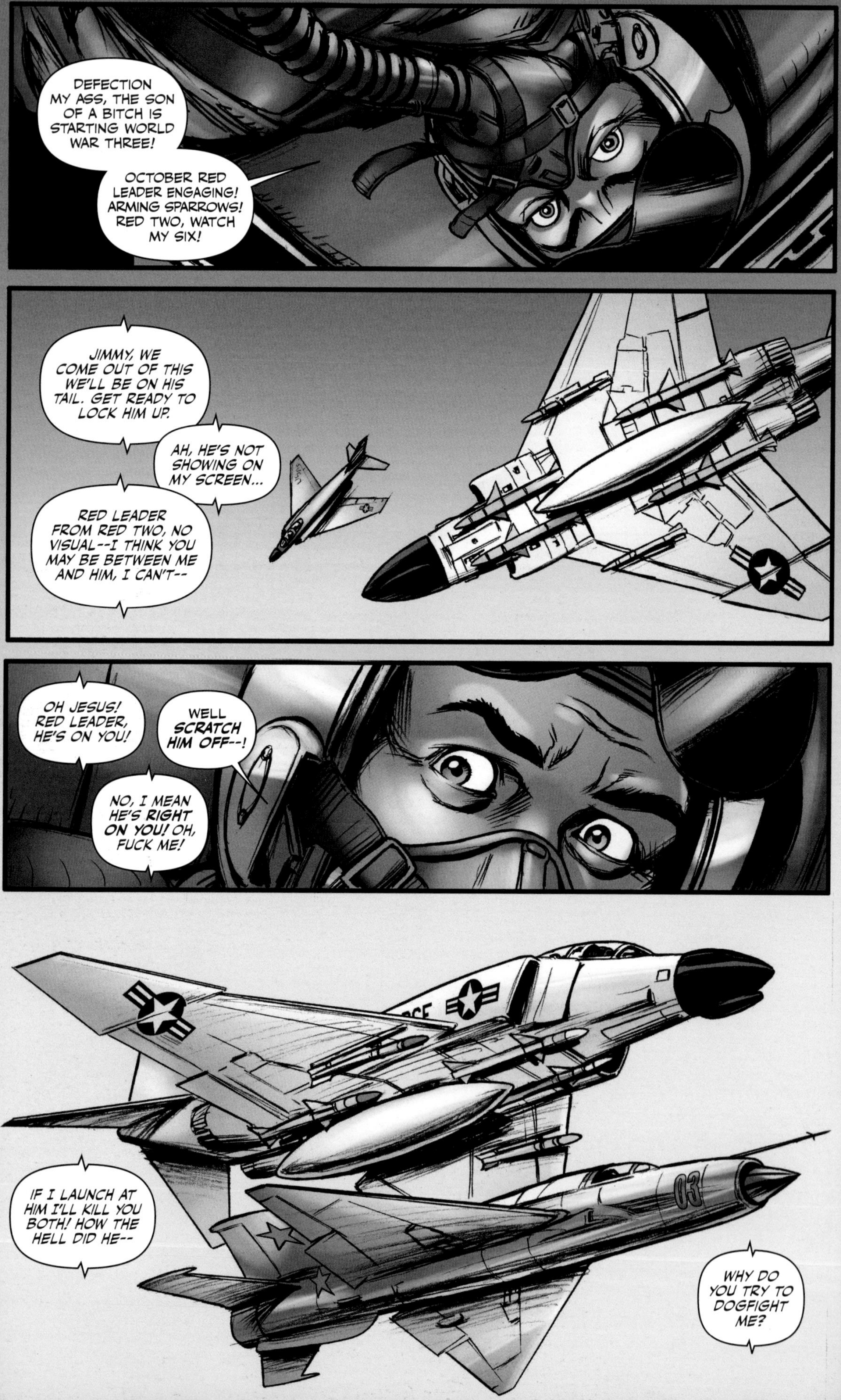
DEFECTION MY ASS, THE SON OF A BITCH IS STARTING WORLD WAR THREE!
OCTOBER RED LEADER ENGAGING! ARMING SPARROWS! RED TWO, WATCH MY SIX!
JIMMY, WE COME OUT OF THIS WE'LL BE ON HIS TAIL. GET READY TO LOCK HIM UP.
AH, HE'S NOT SHOWING ON MY SCREEN...
RED LEADER FROM RED TWO, NO VISUAL--I THINK YOU MAY BE BETWEEN ME AND HIM, I CAN'T--
OH JESUS! RED LEADER, HE'S ON YOU!
WELL SCRATCH HIM OFF--!
NO, I MEAN HE'S RIGHT ON YOU! OH, FUCK ME!
IF I LAUNCH AT HIM I'LL KILL YOU BOTH! HOW THE HELL DID HE--
WHY DO YOU TRY TO DOGFIGHT ME?

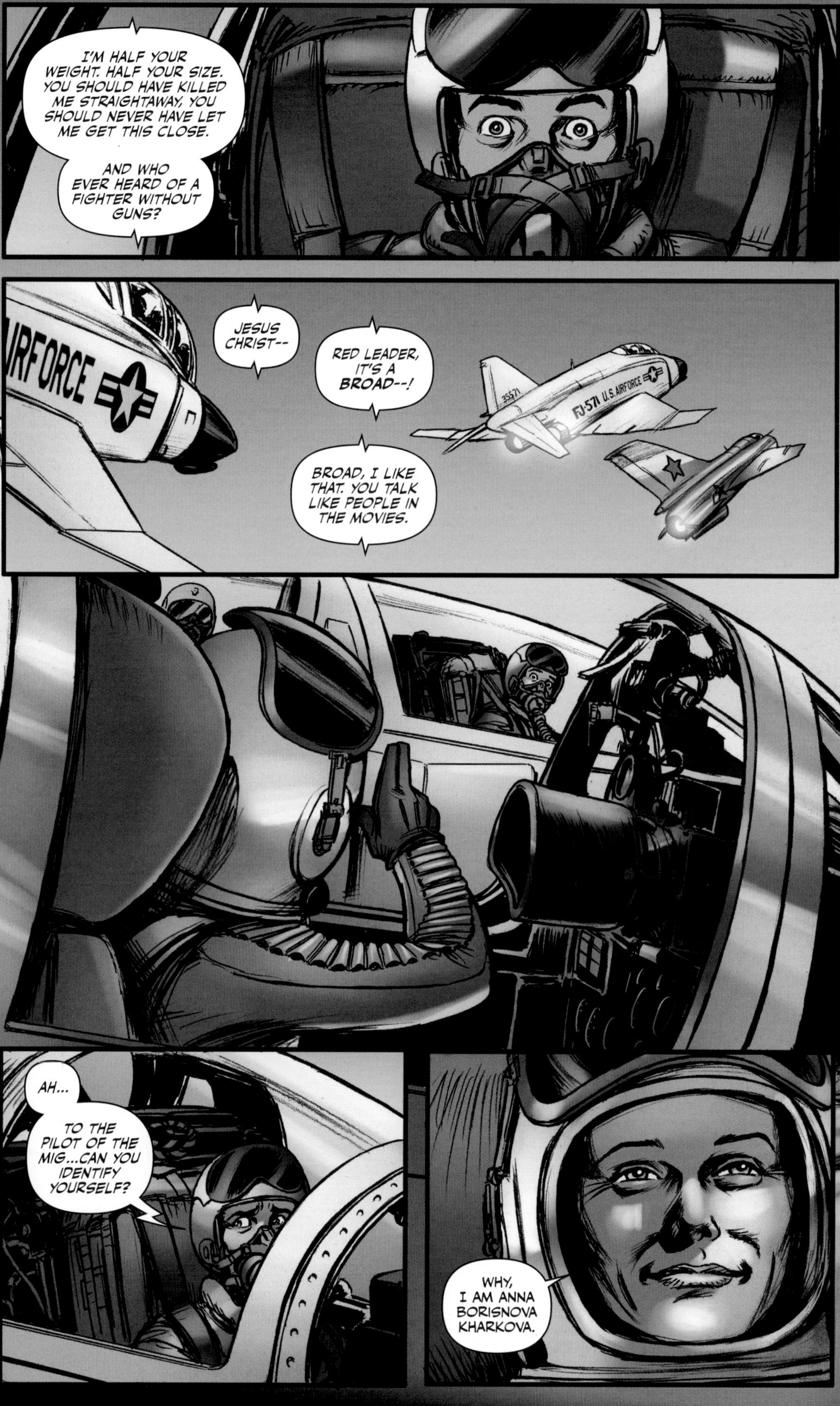
I'M HALF YOUR WEIGHT. HALF YOUR SIZE. YOU SHOULD HAVE KILLED ME STRAIGHTAWAY, YOU SHOULD NEVER HAVE LET ME GET THIS CLOSE.
AND WHO EVER HEARD OF A FIGHTER WITHOUT GUNS?
JESUS CHRIST--
RED LEADER, IT'S A BROAD--!
BROAD, I LIKE THAT. YOU TALK LIKE PEOPLE IN THE MOVIES.
AIRFORCE
35571
FJ-571 U.S. AIRFORCE
AH...
TO THE PILOT OF THE MIG...CAN YOU IDENTIFY YOURSELF?
WHY, I AM ANNA BORISNOVA KHARKOVA.

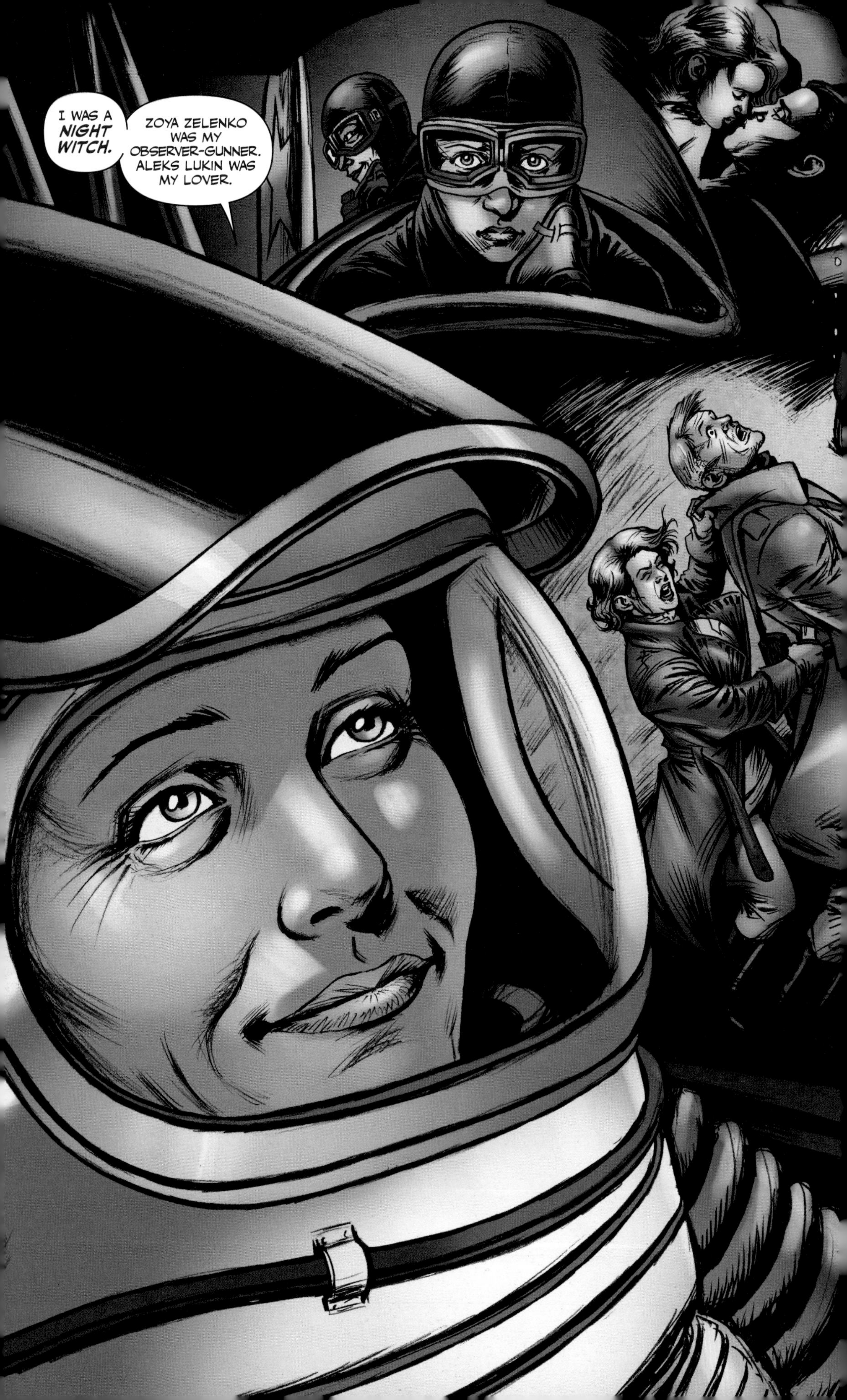
I WAS A NIGHT WITCH.
ZOYA ZELENKO WAS MY OBSERVER-GUNNER. ALEKS LUKIN WAS MY LOVER.

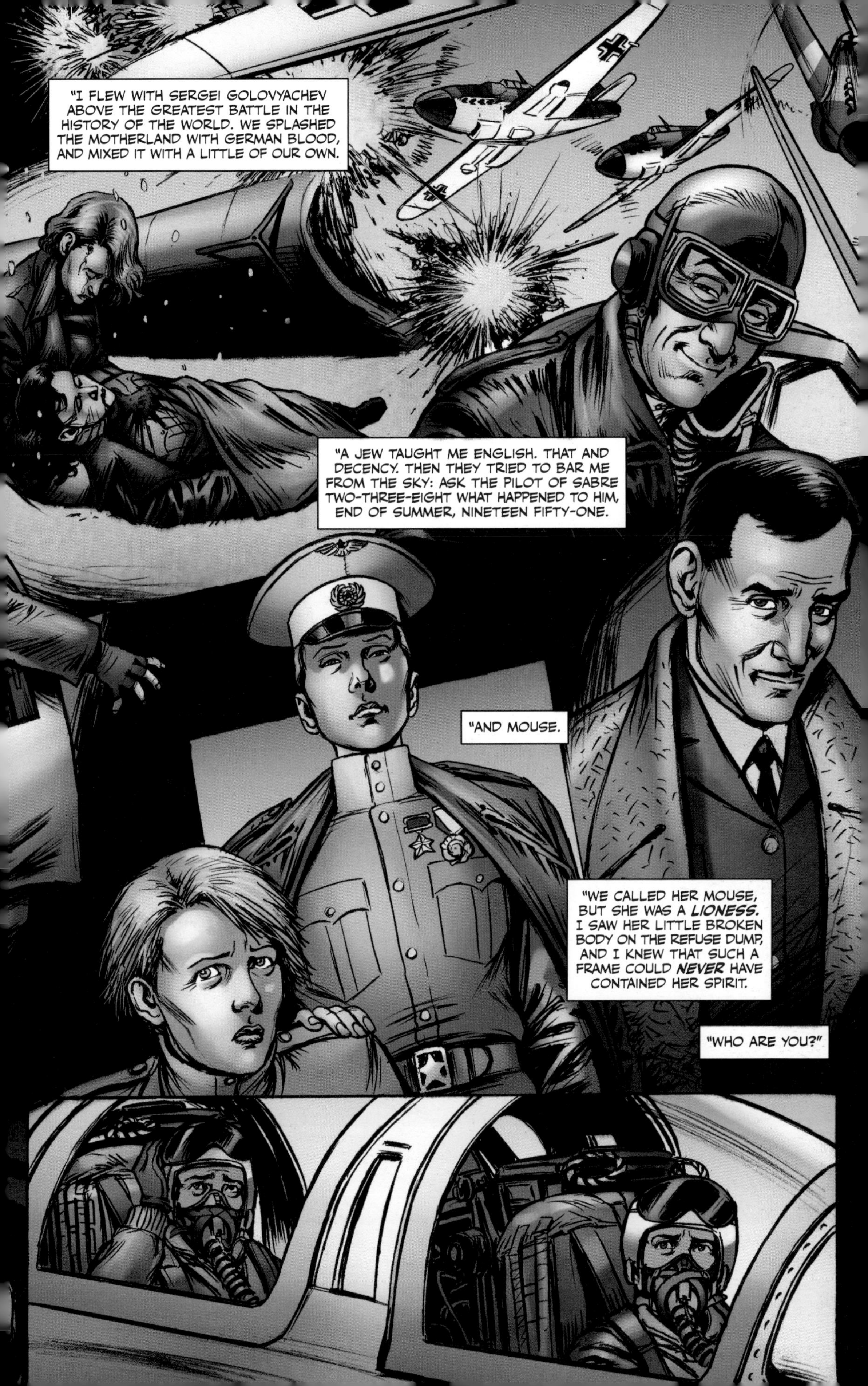
"I FLEW WITH SERGEI GOLOVYACHEV ABOVE THE GREATEST BATTLE IN THE HISTORY OF THE WORLD. WE SPLASHED THE MOTHERLAND WITH GERMAN BLOOD, AND MIXED IT WITH A LITTLE OF OUR OWN.
"A JEW TAUGHT ME ENGLISH. THAT AND DECENCY. THEN THEY TRIED TO BAR ME FROM THE SKY: ASK THE PILOT OF SABRE TWO-THREE-EIGHT WHAT HAPPENED TO HIM, END OF SUMMER, NINETEEN FIFTY-ONE.
"AND MOUSE.
"WE CALLED HER MOUSE, BUT SHE WAS A *LIONESS.* I SAW HER LITTLE BROKEN BODY ON THE REFUSE DUMP, AND I KNEW THAT SUCH A FRAME COULD *NEVER* HAVE CONTAINED HER SPIRIT.
"WHO ARE YOU?"

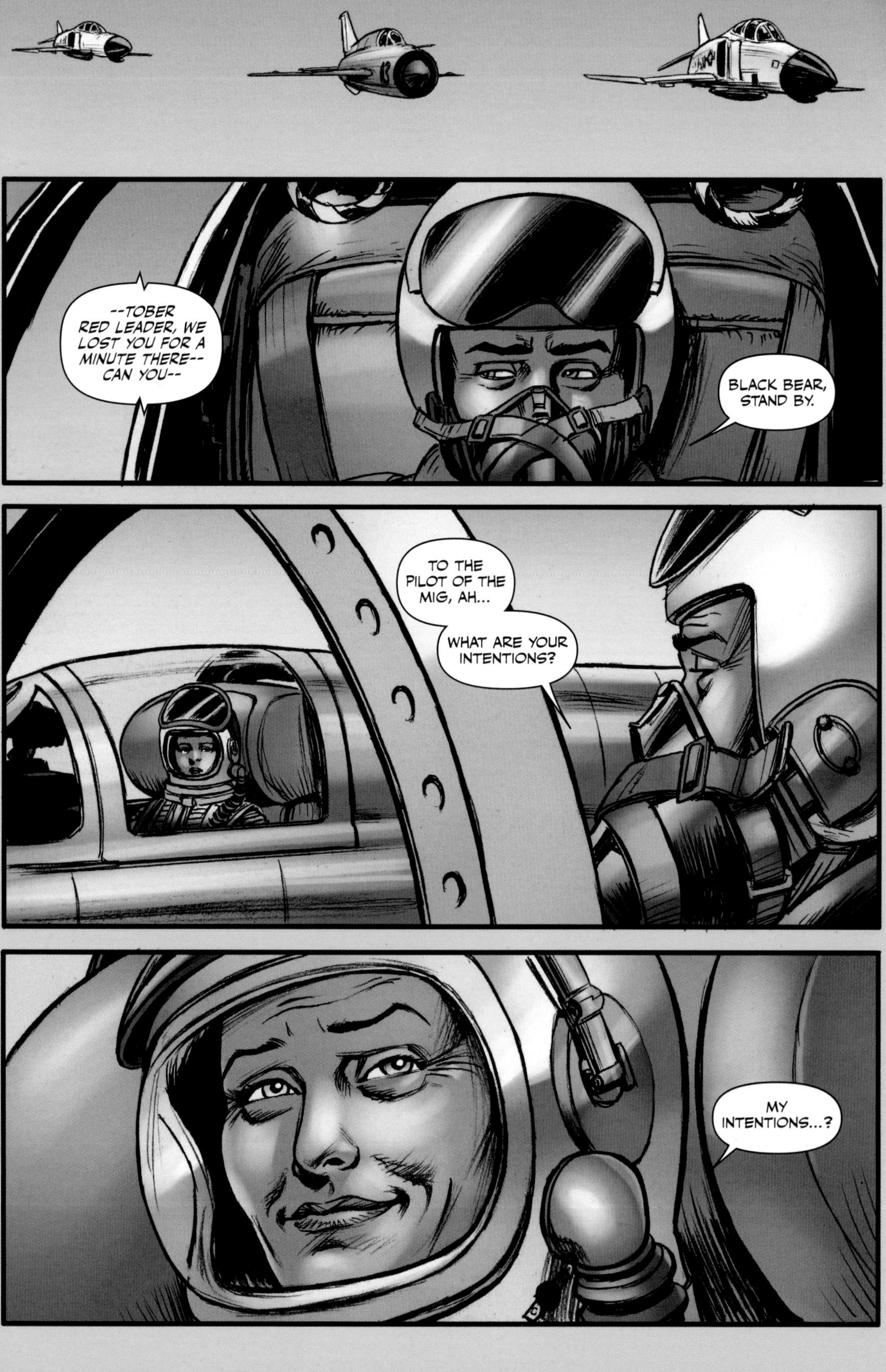
--TOBER RED LEADER, WE LOST YOU FOR A MINUTE THERE-- CAN YOU--
BLACK BEAR, STAND BY.
TO THE PILOT OF THE MIG, AH...
WHAT ARE YOUR INTENTIONS?
MY INTENTIONS...?

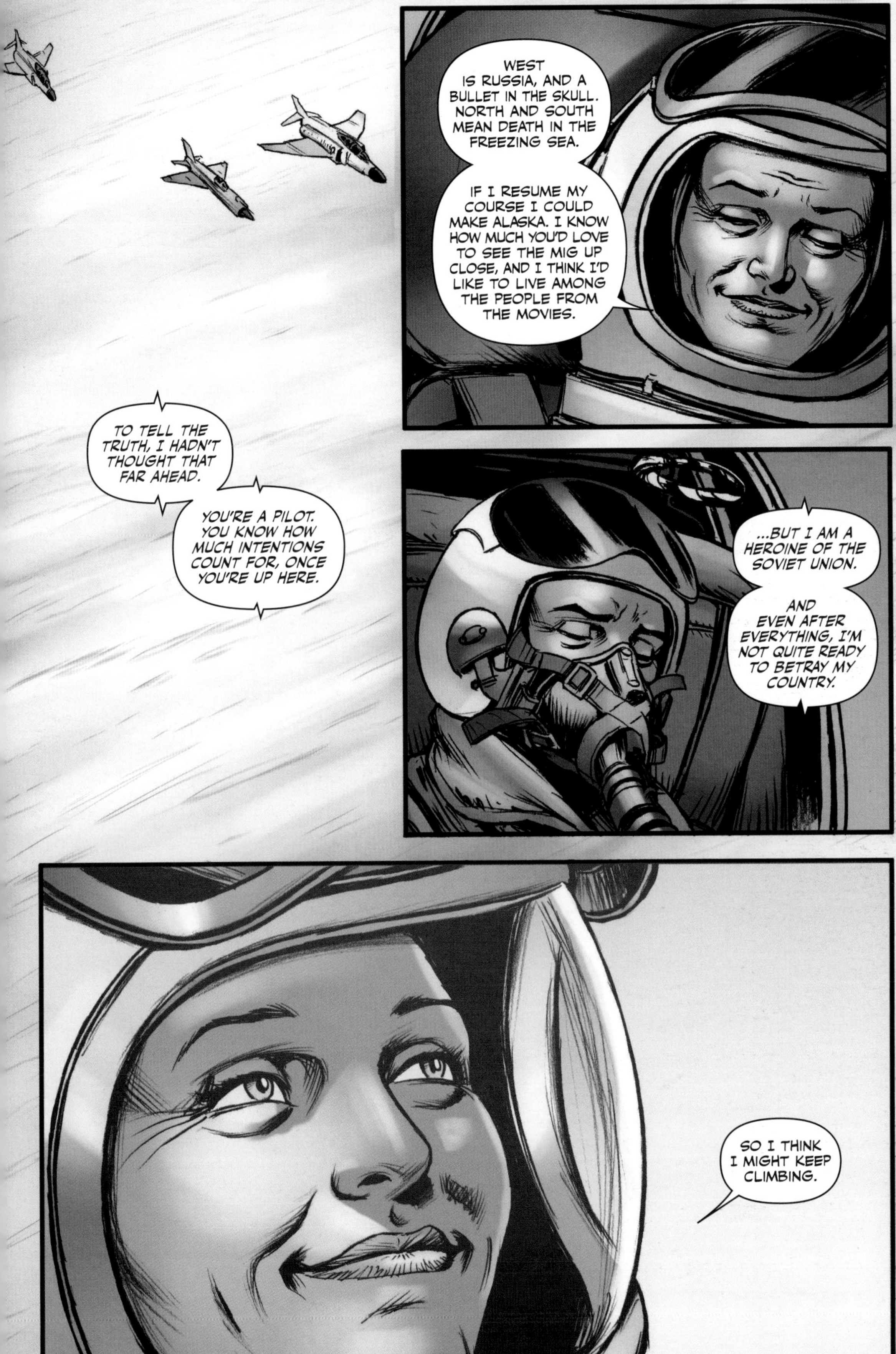
WEST IS RUSSIA, AND A BULLET IN THE SKULL. NORTH AND SOUTH MEAN DEATH IN THE FREEZING SEA.
IF I RESUME MY COURSE I COULD MAKE ALASKA. I KNOW HOW MUCH YOU'D LOVE TO SEE THE MIG UP CLOSE, AND I THINK I'D LIKE TO LIVE AMONG THE PEOPLE FROM THE MOVIES.
TO TELL THE TRUTH, I HADN'T THOUGHT THAT FAR AHEAD.
YOU'RE A PILOT. YOU KNOW HOW MUCH INTENTIONS COUNT FOR, ONCE YOU'RE UP HERE.
...BUT I AM A HEROINE OF THE SOVIET UNION.
AND EVEN AFTER EVERYTHING, I'M NOT QUITE READY TO BETRAY MY COUNTRY.
SO I THINK I MIGHT KEEP CLIMBING.

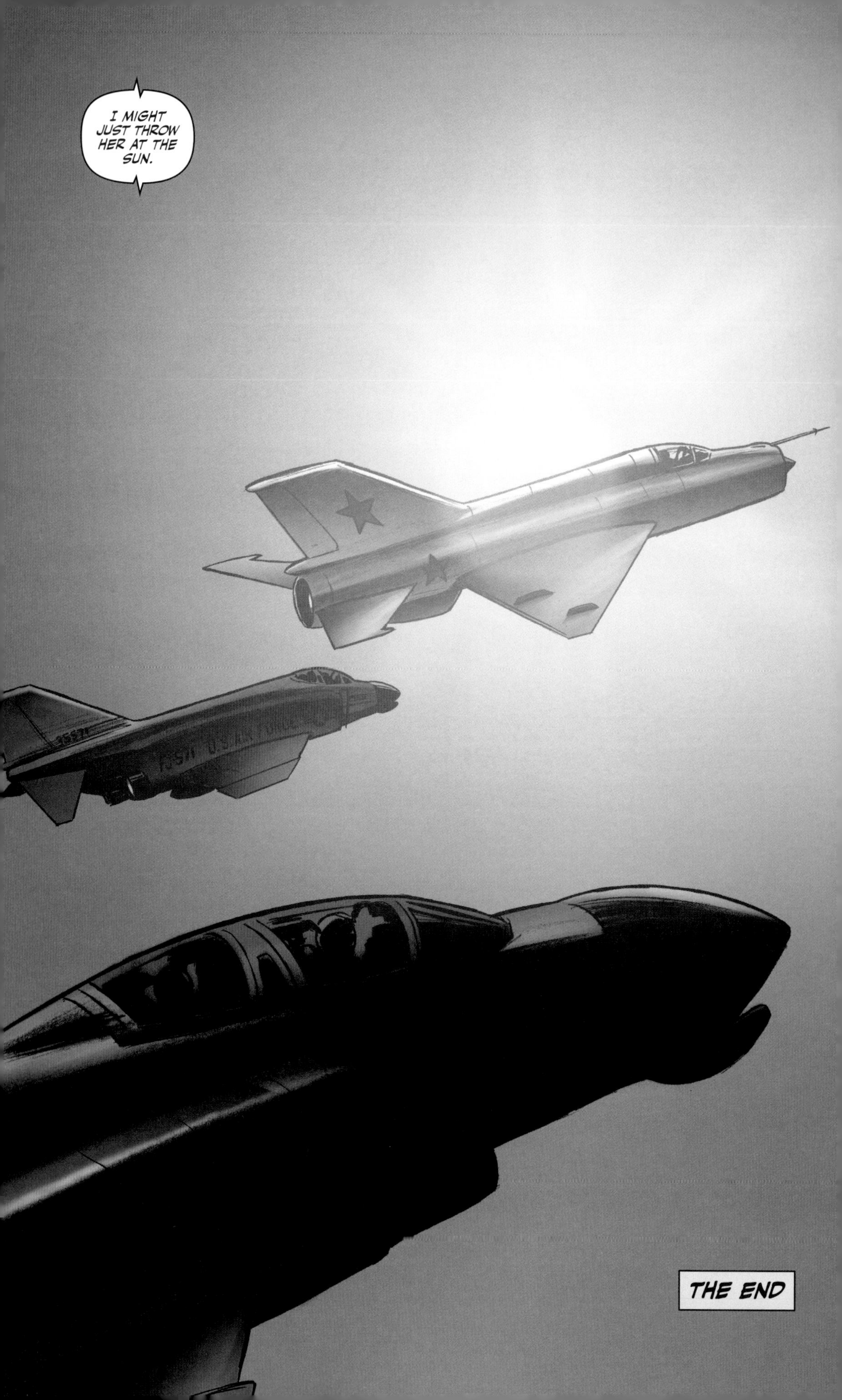
I MIGHT JUST THROW HER AT THE SUN.
THE END

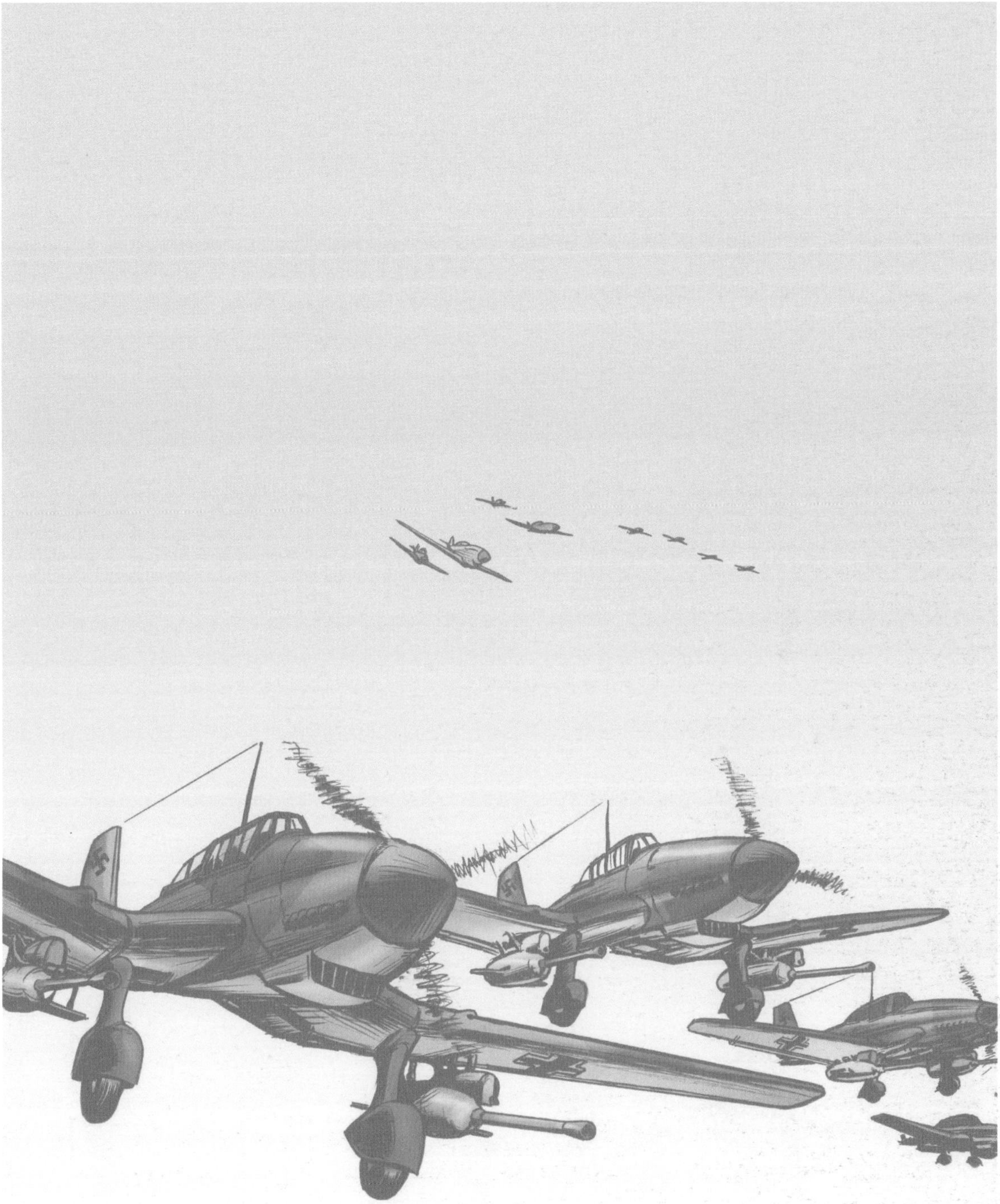

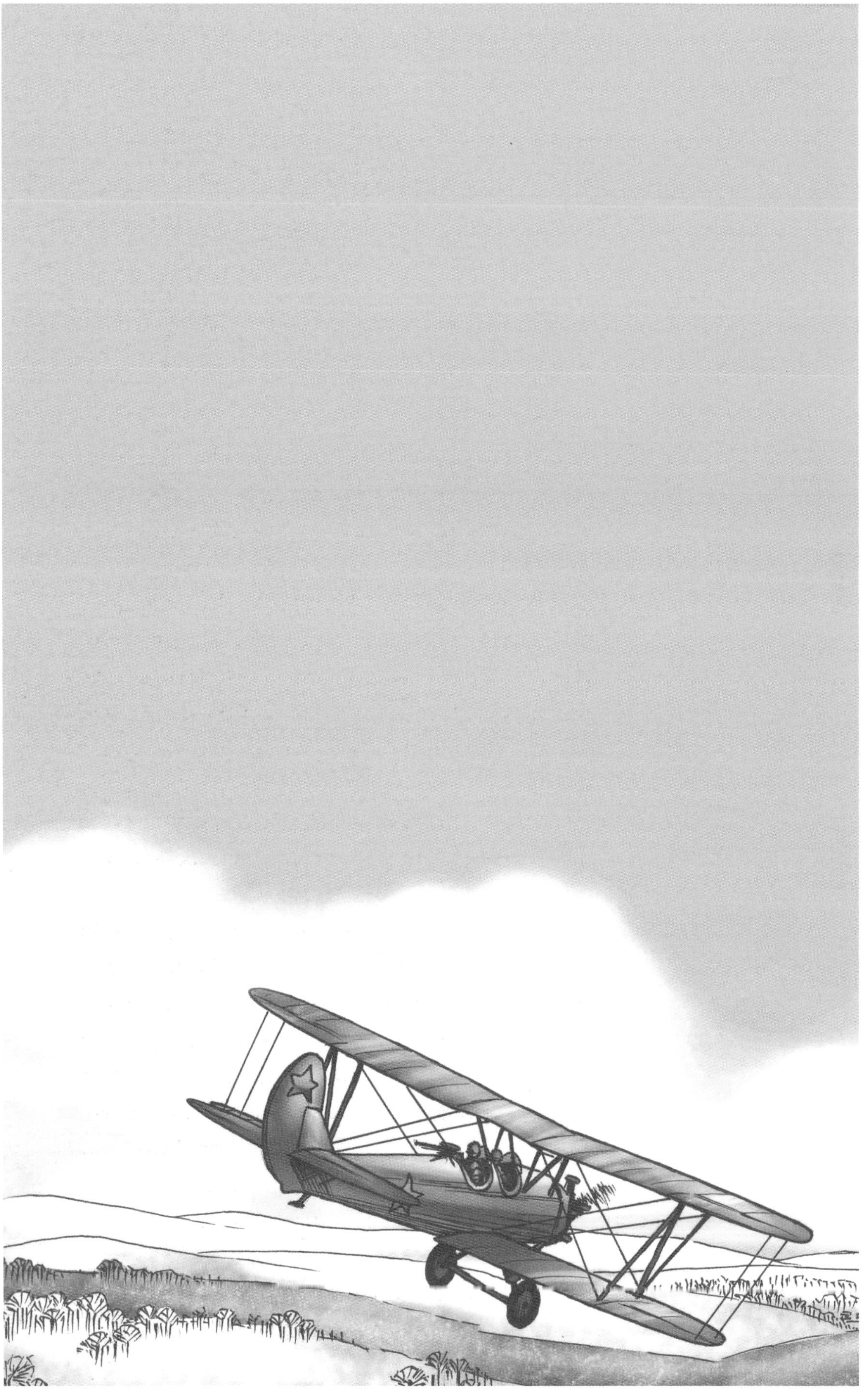

Afterword

The spark that began *The Night Witches* came from *Time to Kill*, a collection of essays on the theme "The Soldier's Experience of War, 1939–45". One of the most interesting is by Reina Pennington, "Offensive Women: Women in Combat in the Red Army in the Second World War," in which the writer takes exception to a statement by the British military historian John Keegan. In his *A History of Warfare*, Mr. Keegan claims that "Warfare is . . . the one human activity from which women, with the most insignificant exceptions, have always and everywhere stood apart," and that women "never, in any military sense, fight men." Such sweeping generalizations by a historian whose work I greatly admire gave me pause (as they did Ms. Pennington, who goes on to provide ample evidence to the contrary); how, I wondered, could he not have heard of the Night Witches?

Soviet Russia committed many thousands of women to combat in the Great Patriotic War, as Russians today still remember World War II. Women served as tank drivers, medics, machine-gunners, snipers, radio operators, fighter pilots, and bomber crew; the pilots and navigators of the 588th Night Bomber Regiment (later granted elite status as the 46th *Taman* Guards Night Bomber Regiment) are simply the best known. That their exploits are not more widely celebrated, outside the field of military history, may be due in part to the immediate post-war Soviet policy of downplaying the role of female personnel. A group of demobilized women was told, in July of 1945, ". . . do not give yourself airs in your future practical work. Do not talk about the services you rendered, let others do it for you. That will be better".

Yet there was a time when the services rendered by such women were very welcome, if not desperately needed. By the end of 1941, Nazi Germany's lightning invasion of Russia had brought the Panzers to the gates of Moscow; eight months later, Hitler's troops were on the Volga. Women were keen to serve, and the Soviet military was only too glad to have them. Inspired by the exploits of pre-war female aviators like Marina Roskova and Polina Osipenko, buoyed up by the proto-feminist principles contained within Marxist-Leninist doctrine, many hundreds of young Russian women had learned to fly during the 1930s. Now they were going to war, some crewing modern fighter and bomber aircraft, some assigned to fly the obsolete Polikarpov Po-2 as members of the 588th.

Anna Kharkova and Zoya Zelenko are fictional creations, both based only in the loosest sense on their real-life counterparts. The murderous rampage with which Anna ends the story is also invented. That said, I have tried to create a reasonably accurate snapshot of the night bomber crews' experiences; the pilots did indeed glide their aircraft into the attack, the Po-2's sputtering engine report having been quickly identified as a dead giveaway; initially, at least, the women struggled to gain the respect of their male comrades; and the number one fear expressed by nearly all female aircrew was what might occur if they were ever captured alive. Exactly how much material damage they did to the enemy remains open to question, given the dubious accuracy of dropping small bombs from a flimsy biplane in near-total darkness, and all of that without the aid of a bombsight. Their effect on German morale is less uncertain, however. The sudden arrival of high explosive from a silent night sky did little for the nerves of already exhausted soldiers, whose nickname for their tormentors was perhaps the ultimate compliment: *Nacht Hexen*.

Likewise, Kurt Graf and the men of Third Squad represent, I hope, a fairly realistic portrayal of a Wehrmacht unit engaged on the *Ostfront*. Particular incidents, such as the discovery of the child's homework and the two opposing units on different floors of the same building, are taken from published accounts. So too is the Russian medic and her drastic battlefield-expedient amputation (Reina Pennington relates the experience of Olga Omelchenko, who found herself treating a soldier whose smashed arm required immediate removal: "But I didn't have a knife or scissors. . . . What was I to do? I gnawed at the flesh with my teeth, gnawed it through and began to bandage the arm.").

Some readers may find the German characters' harsher actions difficult to accept, if only in terms of what the average *Landser* is believed to have done during his time on the Eastern Front. Certainly, my portrayal of a Wehrmacht unit in another war story, *Johann's Tiger*, drew criticism for its more general portrayal of similar incidents. Yet the central issues regarding Germany's war crimes—of who did what while who stood by, of who gave orders and who obeyed them, of looting, rape, brutality and murder, of whether certain acts were committed in the tens or tens of thousands—remain acutely relevant when considering the Third Reich's occupation of Soviet territory. The mass enslavement and deportation of both civilians and captured troops, reprisals committed against local populations as a result of partisan activity, massacres of Jews and other "undesirables"; all are now a matter of record. Whether through frustration, opportunism, official policy or simply as a by-product of Adolf Hitler's racial theorizing, the Germans' behavior in Russia was dreadful. While it seems unlikely that every single soldier was guilty of atrocity, the notion that any remained unaware of such activity is rather more difficult to believe.

In 1990, the American writer Anne Noggle traveled to the Soviet Union to interview a number of female air force veterans. The book she wrote to record their remarkable stories, *A Dance with Death*, includes a series of photographs depicting the interviewees (one is Nadezhda Popova, whose quotation closes out *The Night Witches*). The youngest must be in her late sixties, most are older. How many are still alive today is anybody's guess. Cheerful, sad, proud, serene, hopeful, mischievous, the personnel of the 588th/46th *Taman* regiment look no more warlike than any gathering of white-haired grandmothers, which of course most of them are. Some wear so many medals that it seems they can barely stand up straight. But they do.

★

If female personnel from Soviet night bomber units did go on to fly single-seat fighters I've found no record of them, so Anna's transfer at the beginning of *Motherland* may be regarded as invention for the sake of narrative. Her closest real-life counterpart would appear to be one Anna Timofeyeva-Yevgorova, who piloted the same Po-2 biplanes as the Night Witches but on artillery spotting flights during daylight hours. After several months of such hazardous duty she began flying the vastly more potent IL-2 Shturmovik on ground-attack missions. Changing squadrons and tasks was rare for these women warriors, but not completely beyond the bounds of possibility.

Our own Anna arrives at the front in time for the Battle of Kursk, which was every bit as epic in scope and dreadful in detail as the story suggests. Many would name the struggle for Stalingrad as the turning point for Hitler's fortunes on the Eastern Front, yet his forces managed to inflict a number of important setbacks on their enemy during the spring of 1943. Whether Kursk finally decided the matter, or merely confirmed the verdict handed down on the Volga, the exhausted Germans began their long and agonizing retreat from Russia in its immediate aftermath. They were left with little choice. For seven long weeks Waffen SS, Wehrmacht, and Luftwaffe units had wiped out Soviet tanks and aircraft by the hundreds, soldiers by the tens of thousands; and still the steppes were lined with T-34s, while Yaks and Petlyakovs darkened the skies above.

Life was always cheap on the Ostfront. For the period June 1941 to May 1945, to put the matter in appropriately brutal terms, some twenty-seven million Russians died killing four million Germans (compare this gruesome toll with the war in the west, where totals of British and American dead added together do not reach one million). Some estimates put the Russian figure much higher. Certainly, the Soviet war effort involved little in the way of sentimentality, with military incompetence, poor equipment, disregard for civilians, and savage reprisals for failure accounting for at least as many dead as German thoroughness. Stalin shared with Hitler a totalitarian disdain for the lives of his countrymen. Even when Russian soldiers and airmen became better trained and armed in the latter half of the conflict, even with more able generals directing their battles, their lives were still expended at a rate the modern observer will find staggering. When it came to blood, the Soviet leader seemed to suffer an embarrassment of riches.

This was as true in the air as anywhere else. The havoc wrought in the initial invasion of Russia is almost legendary, with so many Soviet aircraft shot down or destroyed on the ground that senior Luftwaffe officers initially refused to believe their pilots' claims. Only when ground forces overran Russian air bases could the skeptics see for themselves, witnessing the pitiful biplanes and other outdated relics lined up like so much scrap. Pilot quality was equally poor, many training officers and combat veterans having succumbed to Stalin's infamous purges in the 1930s. The Luftwaffe could not have provided a greater contrast. German fighter pilots began the conflict in the east with years of experience, having learned their trade over Spain, France, Britain, and North Africa. Their beloved Messerschmitt 109—as far as they were concerned—was still the king of the sky.

Things had improved a little for the Russians by the time of Kursk. More new pilots were arriving all the time. Older designs had given way to Yaks and Lavochkins, both capable aircraft in the right hands, and the Hurricanes and P-40s provided by Britain and the U.S. at least helped to make up the numbers. The Germans, unfortunately, had also acquired a new mount: the Focke-Wulf 190, thought by many to be the finest fighter of World War II. Worse still, their pilots had simply carried on getting better. One Luftwaffe unit, Jagdgeschwader 52, is reckoned to have destroyed over ten thousand aircraft (almost a quarter of total Soviet losses to fighter action) during less than four years on the Eastern Front. JG 52's combat strength would rarely have exceeded a hundred aircraft and pilots at any given time, and the wing was equipped with the older Messerschmitt—never the FW 190—throughout the war.

Very nearly one hundred German fighter pilots accumulated over 100 aerial kills during the war. Thirteen managed over 200. Two broke the 300 mark, top scorer being Erich Hartmann at 352 (Hartmann served ten years in a Siberian gulag after the war, his captors having charged him with destruction of Soviet property). By way of comparison, the reader may consider the scores of other air forces' leading pilots: Russia's Ivan Kozhedub (62), the American Richard Bong (40), and RAF Ace of Aces Marmaduke "Pat" Pattle (50). The odds of survival for someone like Anna Kharkova, facing the Luftwaffe at the controls of her Yak 1 in the summer of 1943, are not hard to calculate.

Motherland, I hope, paints a fairly accurate picture of a Russian fighter unit in action over the Kursk salient. Details like the dunking of medals in vodka and Mouse's performance on sentry duty are adapted from actual incidents, and the manner in which the battle develops— with the radar detection and subsequent ambush of Soviet formations over deserted German bases—reflects the actual historical events to a reasonable degree. Likewise, while several individual female pilots were indeed attached to male fighter regiments to gain valuable experience, the only all-female fighter regiment fulfilled Anna's suspicions and was relegated to rear defense duties. This is odd, as no such qualms were shown by senior officers about committing the women's bomber units to the savagery of frontline combat. Further, the few women who did see action with fighter regiments performed just as well as the men.

Some readers may look askance at Anna's achievements in the story; merely winging a handful of enemy aircraft might seem rather a desultory combat record for a fighter pilot. Yet very few of the great aces hit the ground running. It took most of them a while just to learn the tricks of survival, never mind success, and a while longer to learn to apply what they had learned. Erich Hartmann himself took several months to score his first kill, and was shot down over a dozen times. I was determined that Anna would not become an instant virtuoso of the kind found in B-movies or science fiction, particularly in light of the figure providing inspiration for this stage of her career: Lilya Litvyak, the White Rose of Stalingrad.

The highest-scoring female fighter pilot in history, Lieutenant Litvyak was something of a legend even in her own short lifetime. Attached to an all-male regiment in time for the Battle of Stalingrad, she flew a

Yak 1 marked with a white rose that soon became known to friend and foe alike. Her fame as the "White Rose" swiftly spread as her tally of kills increased, and in one remarkable incident her latest victim—the pilot of an ME 109—was brought before her, keen to meet the Russian who had bested him. Confronted by a diminutive girl barely out of her teens, the German ace simply refused to believe it. Only when "Lilly" described their combat in intimate detail did he give in and acknowledge that the unthinkable had happened: the Luftwaffe eagle had fallen to the guns of a woman.

If all of this sounds too good to be true, it should. There exists precious little evidence for many of the stories surrounding Lilya Litvyak. Her Yak was adorned with identification numbers like any other aircraft, either 32 or 44, depending on sources. "The White Rose of Stalingrad" was an invention of western writers, no doubt intrigued when Litvyak's story first appeared in English. "The White Lilly," a more obvious play on her name, was used by the Soviets—but only, it would seem, for propaganda purposes some time after the fact. As for the famous downed German, the thought of any Luftwaffe pilot surviving Russian captivity long enough to meet his victor seems dubious to begin with, even supposing his captors could identify which of the aircraft wheeling high above had done the job. One possible candidate, whose rank and Knight's Cross decoration seem to match the Russians' story, later turned out to have died two weeks before the alleged incident took place.

What we know for sure about this brave young woman's combat record can be summarized as follows: she first saw action over Stalingrad in the summer of 1942, she scored something in the region of 8–12 victories (again depending on sources), and she was shot down and killed approximately a year later. To me, such an account and the embellishments that surround it illustrate a maxim that must surely occur to any thoughtful reader of history, which is that the facts are usually inspiring enough. There is no need to add anything to stories like Lilya Litvyak's. She was one of the first female fighter pilots in the world, and overcame the prejudices of her male counterparts to join battle with a better-trained, better-equipped enemy, many of whom she shot out of the sky. She was wounded twice and eventually killed in action. "Lilly" died for her Motherland as well as did any man.

When it came to Anna Borisnova Kharkova, then, I decided that turning her into some kind of aerial killing machine would be less than appropriate. Having already enjoyed success flying night bombers, it seemed too much to hope that she would immediately shine as a fighter pilot—a very different job, requiring skills that were not simply transferable from one to the other. Anna remains a good pilot, a reasonable shot, and courageous beyond anything I can imagine. That will have to suffice.

★

Unlike its predecessors, *The Night Witches* and *Motherland*, the last chapter in Anna Kharkova's story lacks any direct historical equivalent. Some aspects of *The Fall and Rise of Anna Kharkova* bear passing resemblance to events that befell figures from real life—but only some. There was no one Soviet-era pilot, male or female, whose cumulative experience came close to matching Anna's: and at the risk of stating the obvious, the latter half of episode three very nearly qualifies as fantasy. In other words, some of these things happened to some people, and the rest I invented.

A number of Russian female pilots saw frontline service while attached to male fighter regiments, but all-female units were indeed assigned to flying more sedate patrols over friendly territory. Why this should be so remains unclear; Soviet authorities had no qualms about committing women to combat in both bomber and night interdiction squadrons, wherein casualties remained high throughout the war. Anna going freelancing seemed to me a reasonable piece of conjecture, given the naturally aggressive tendencies of any fighter pilot in pursuit of his or her raison d'être.

Her subsequent captivity is based loosely on the account of Heroine of the Soviet Union Anna Timofeyeva-Yegorova, whose Shturmovik fighter-bomber was shot down in flames near German-occupied

Warsaw in the summer of 1944. Badly burned, not expected to survive, Lieutenant Yegorova was held at a camp for Allied prisoners of war in western Poland, which was not overrun by Russian forces until some months afterward. Captured Soviet medical personnel not only tended the lieutenant's dreadful injuries, but also hid her medals and Communist Party ID card, lest the Nazi authorities seek retribution for her impressive combat record.

It should be noted that Flight-Lieutenant Cohen and the brutal female tank-driver are both inventions, although the latter is perhaps not much of a stretch. Life for Russian prisoners of the Germans was no picnic after their release, and many suffered interrogations far worse than Anna's in the hands of Soviet counterintelligence. As Stalin himself put it, withdrawing his nation from cooperation with the International Red Cross: "We don't have prisoners of war. We have traitors." Hauled before a tribunal in still-debilitated condition, Lieutenant Yegorova was once again saved only by her erstwhile POW medics—who testified in writing to her helpless condition on arrival at the camp, and her subsequent behavior in captivity.

To the best of my knowledge, no female pilots served as Soviet "advisors" during the Korean conflict—indeed, by 1950, most female aviators had left the service and joined the majority of their male comrades in civilian life. The line between wartime service and a lifelong military career is a broad one for most participants, and the women who fought in Russia's Great Patriotic War were no different. While many no doubt chafed at being urged not to talk about their exploits, the vast majority of Night Witches, fighter pilots, and bomber pilots—not to mention tank crew, snipers, medics, machine-gunners, and partisans—simply returned to the lives the war had interrupted.

The jet fighter encounters of the Korean War remain the only known instances of American and Russian pilots meeting in combat, and so provide some interesting pointers to the potential outcome of a wider conflict. It was believed, at least in Western military circles, that a major Cold War confrontation would see U.S. pilots and their allies heavily outnumbered by the air forces of Russia and the Eastern Bloc—but still holding the line, if only narrowly, due to superior equipment and training. Failure to do so would leave NATO troops without air cover in the face of massed Soviet armies, and the subsequent military collapse would force the West into employing atomic weapons on the battlefield—and possibly beyond it.

A healthy kill-to-loss ratio of 10:1 in favor of the U.S. Air Force seemed to validate such theories, as MiGs and Sabres dueled in the skies above Korea and reports filtered back to eager planners. No one was fooled by North Korean markings on the Soviet fighters, but the fiction was allowed to stand for purposes of public reassurance: neither Moscow nor Washington sought to escalate a provincial Asian conflict into World War III. The enemy pilots were Russian, American pilots were shooting them down by a comfortable margin, and that was good enough.

Only with the passage of time has a more complete picture of the aerial battles over Korea emerged, as conflicts waned and regimes crumbled, and archives yielded up their treasure. Today, researchers know much more about which Communist units met which American squadrons during 1950–53, and the 10:1 kill ratio is no longer seen as quite so clear-cut. Against those MiGs manned by Chinese or North Korean pilots, the USAF enjoyed a ratio of 9:1—but engaged with the very best of the Russians, the ratio could drop to as low as 1.2:1. Which, given the vast disparity in numbers of aircraft, may cast rather a shadow over NATO's chances of refraining from nuclear action.

Hundreds of Russian pilots, like their American opponents, emerged from the Second World War with a wealth of combat experience: something almost no Chinese or Korean had been granted the opportunity to gain. Tactical concepts could be practiced, applied, discussed, and refined until near-perfect, with the aces of 1939–45 on hand to guide the younger men. (Many American pilots learned to distinguish the Russians by talent alone, the MiG "honchos" being streets ahead of their Asian allies.) It is now generally accepted that most Soviet pilots of this era were more than worthy of the aircraft they flew.

And the MiG-15 was a very good aircraft. In North Vietnamese hands the later MiG-21 caused USAF and U.S. Navy pilots all manner of trouble, until the Americans developed appropriate tactics to cope with the agile Soviet fighter. By the time of the Vietnam War, U.S. aircraft designers seemed to have forgotten certain basic principles so tidily enshrined in the Sabre: as Anna demonstrates in the story's closing pages, the powerful but unwieldy F-4 Phantom could not survive a close-in dogfight with a carefully flown lighter aircraft. (One small point worth making is that very few USAF squadrons were flying the Phantom in 1964, and certainly none of those operating in the region of the Bering Strait. They were in fact stuck with fighters that the MiG-21 would have had for breakfast.)

Anna's twelve-year incarceration in a punishment camp may seem an unduly grim conclusion to an illustrious combat career; some readers have balked at the notion of so much heroism being rewarded with such wretched horror. And yet this was precisely the lot of far too many Russian veterans of World War II, whose exploits in battle were not enough to save them from their own nation's secret police. No totalitarian regime will stand much criticism from its people, war heroes or not, and millions of men and women disappeared into the Gulags. Many found themselves being worked to death alongside their former enemies, German POWs condemned to the same frozen hell.

The nature of the Soviet victory in the Second World War stood in stark contrast to that of the Western Allies. British and American forces returned the European nations they had liberated to their native populations; even the western portion of defeated Germany was carefully rebuilt as a democratic state. But East Germany, along with Hitler's allies such as Rumania and Hungary, was left at the mercy of the USSR. Puppet governments were soon installed, their loyalty to Moscow guaranteed, their people subject to the same harsh laws. Even poor martyred Poland, whose soldiers fought as hard as any to defeat the Germans, merely ended up exchanging the Nazi jackboot for a Soviet one.

The degree of sacrifice required to drive the German invader from Russian soil can scarcely be imagined by the modern observer. A death toll of twenty-seven million, the epics of Stalingrad and Leningrad, untold suffering and degradation: such things left little space for compromise in the minds of Soviet soldiers, and none at all in Josef Stalin's. To the victor went the spoils, which was hard luck on the people of Eastern Europe—and, perhaps, scant comfort to the men and women who had given so much for that victory. The ultimate reward for every Russian soldier's wartime service was life under Soviet Communism, which, while good enough for the many who kept their mouths shut, could be bleak indeed for those who failed to do so.

Such was Russia's tragedy. While the Gulag system ended officially in 1960, forced labor colonies were continued for at least another twenty years. Of the millions of inmates who suffered in the camps, many simply perished; the survivors eventually returned to civilian life, where they were monitored as political undesirables and denied certain forms of employment. None managed to escape in state-of-the-art jet fighters (although several dozen Communist pilots did defect to the West throughout the Cold War, bringing their high-performance aircraft with them). Any real life Anna Kharkova accused of sedition would have simply rotted in the camps like so many of her comrades, very likely succumbing to the harsh treatment and miserable conditions. But, in the end, I knew I couldn't do that to her.

—Garth Ennis

RUSS BRAUN
Sketchbook

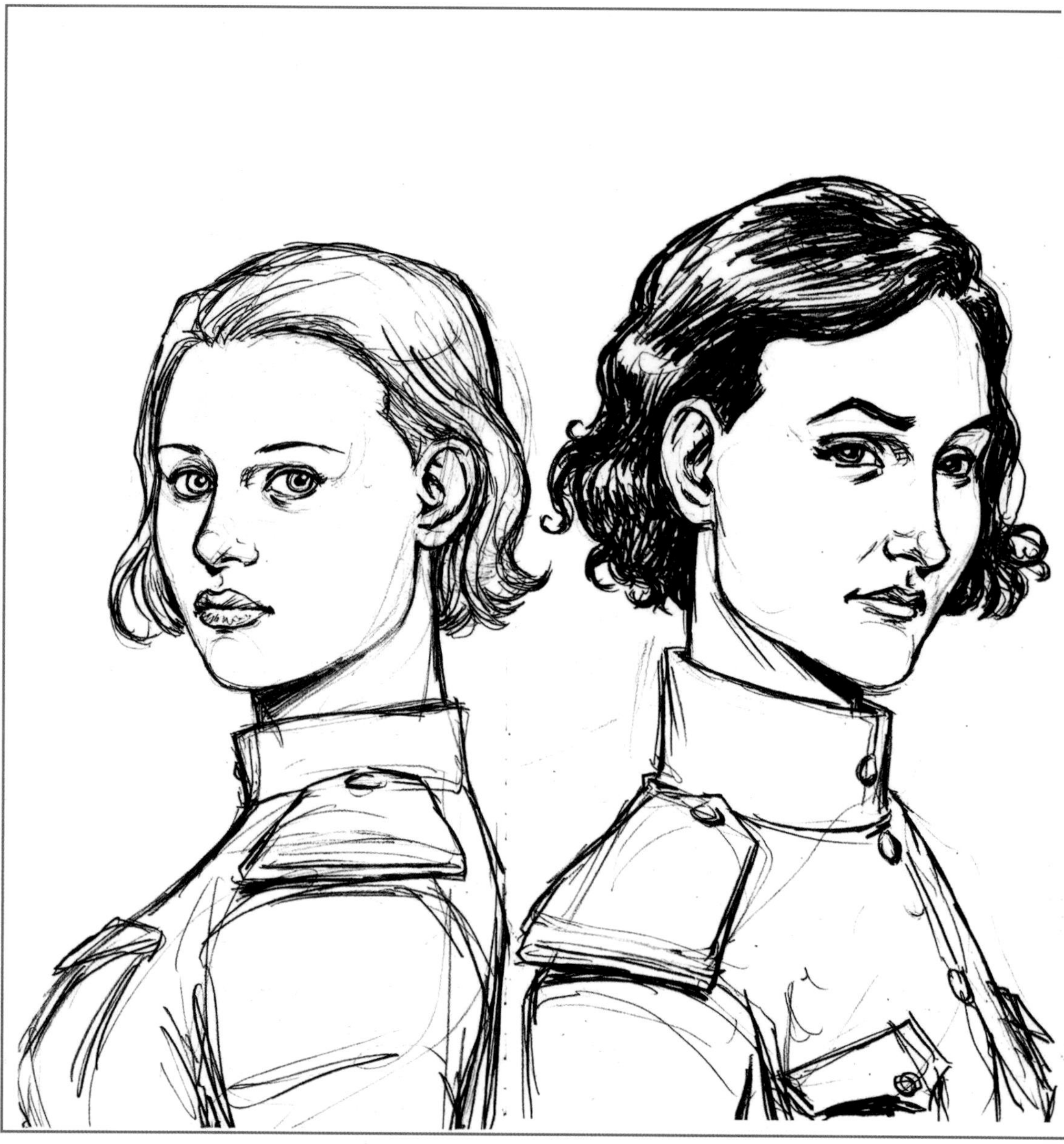

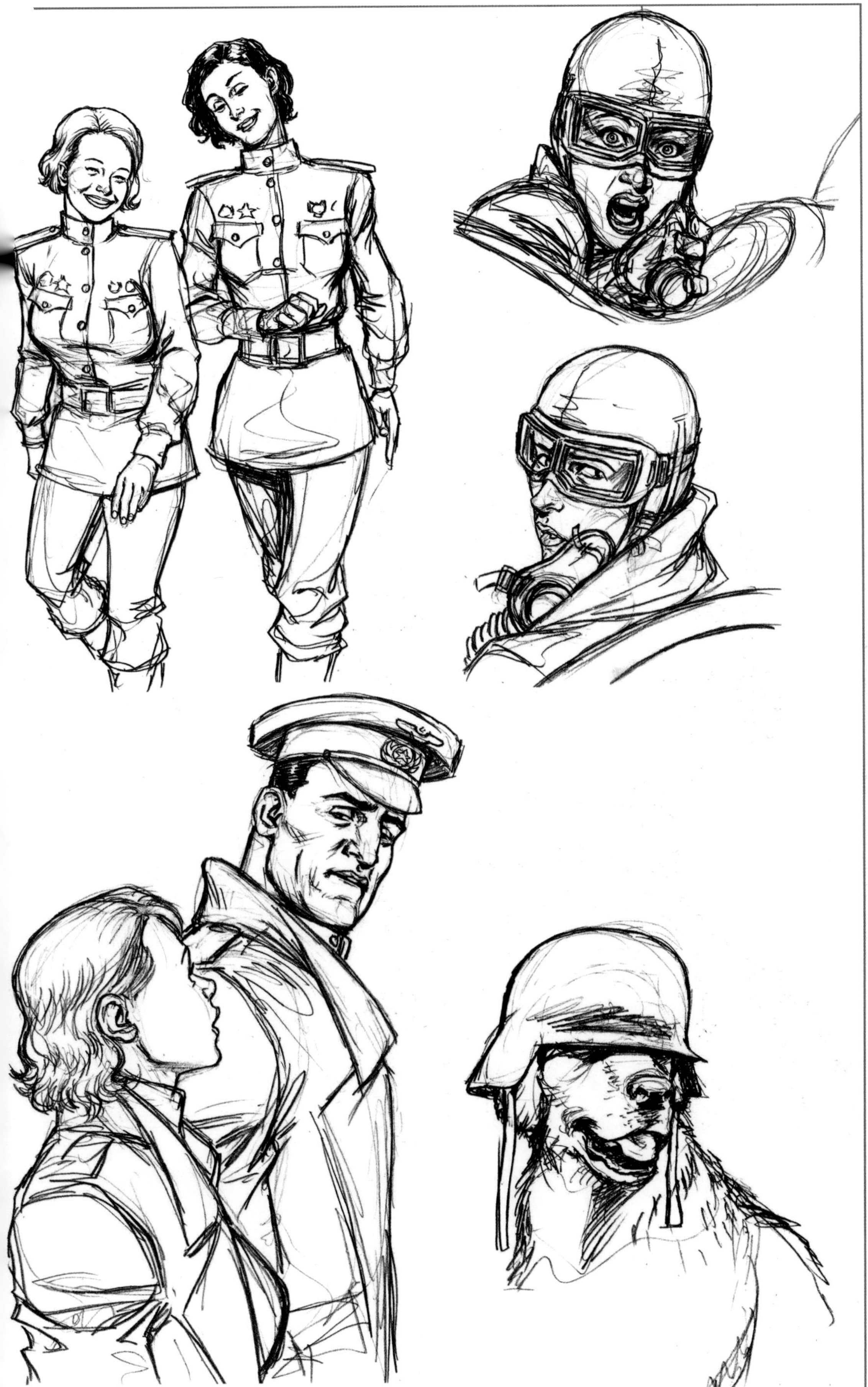

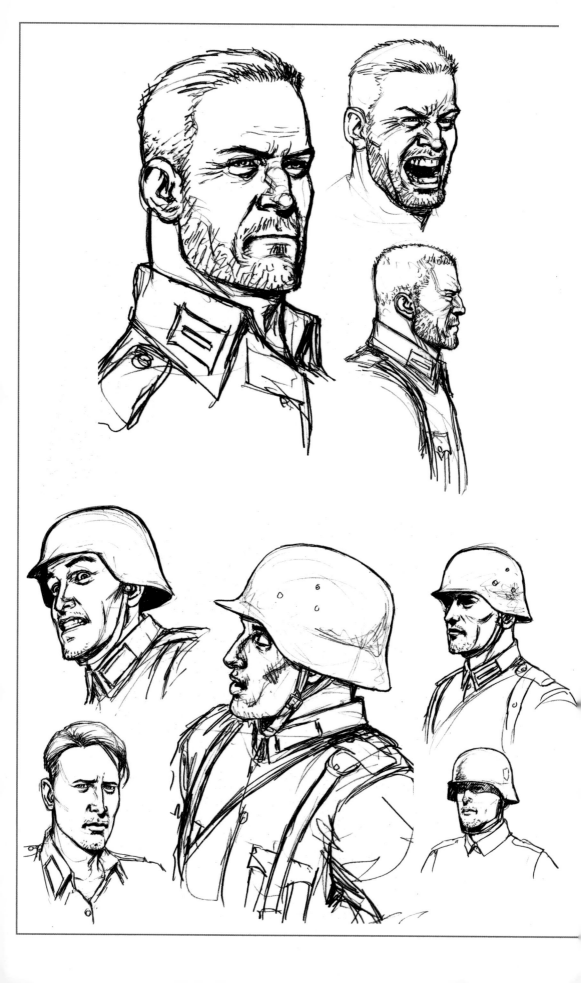

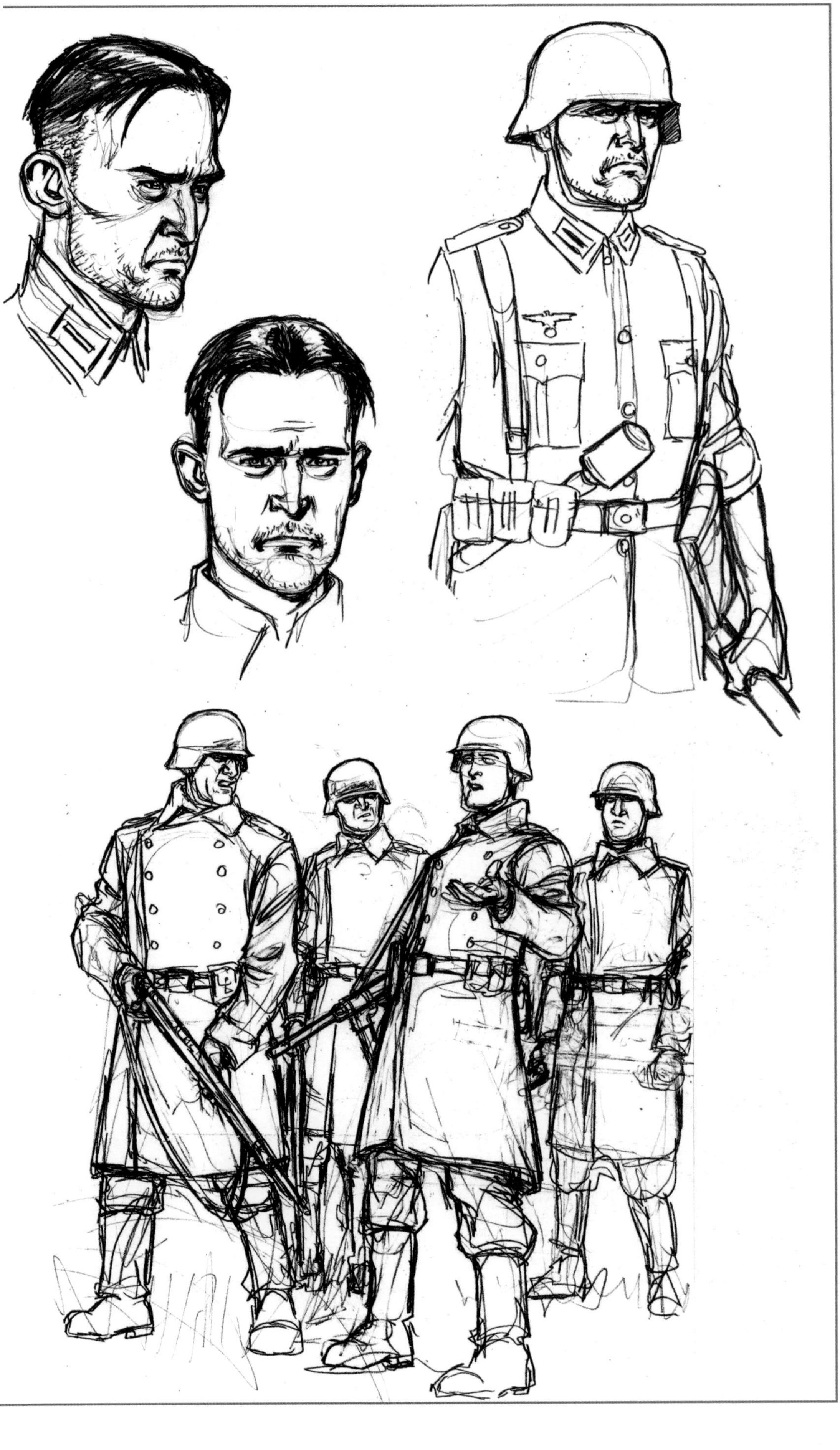

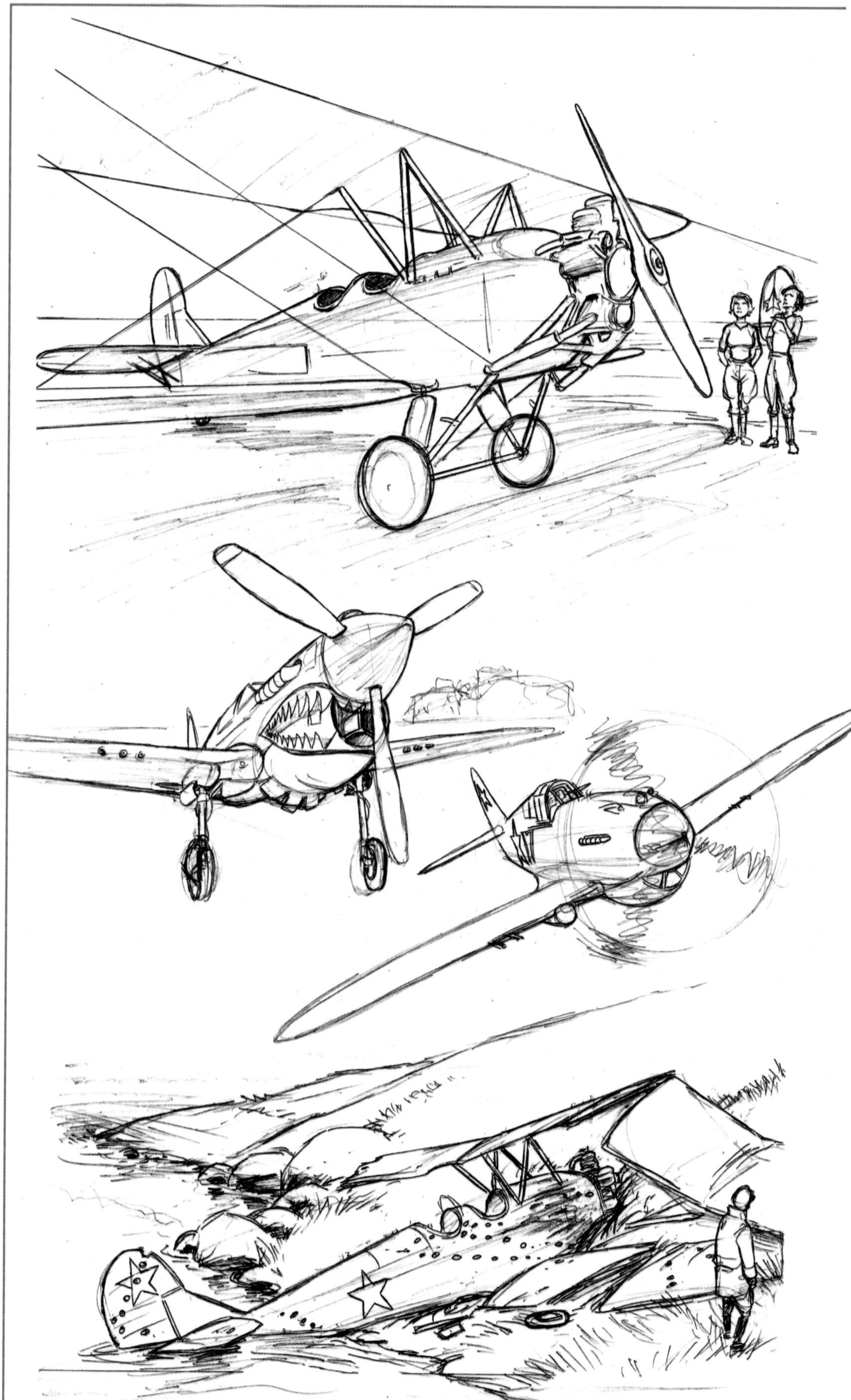

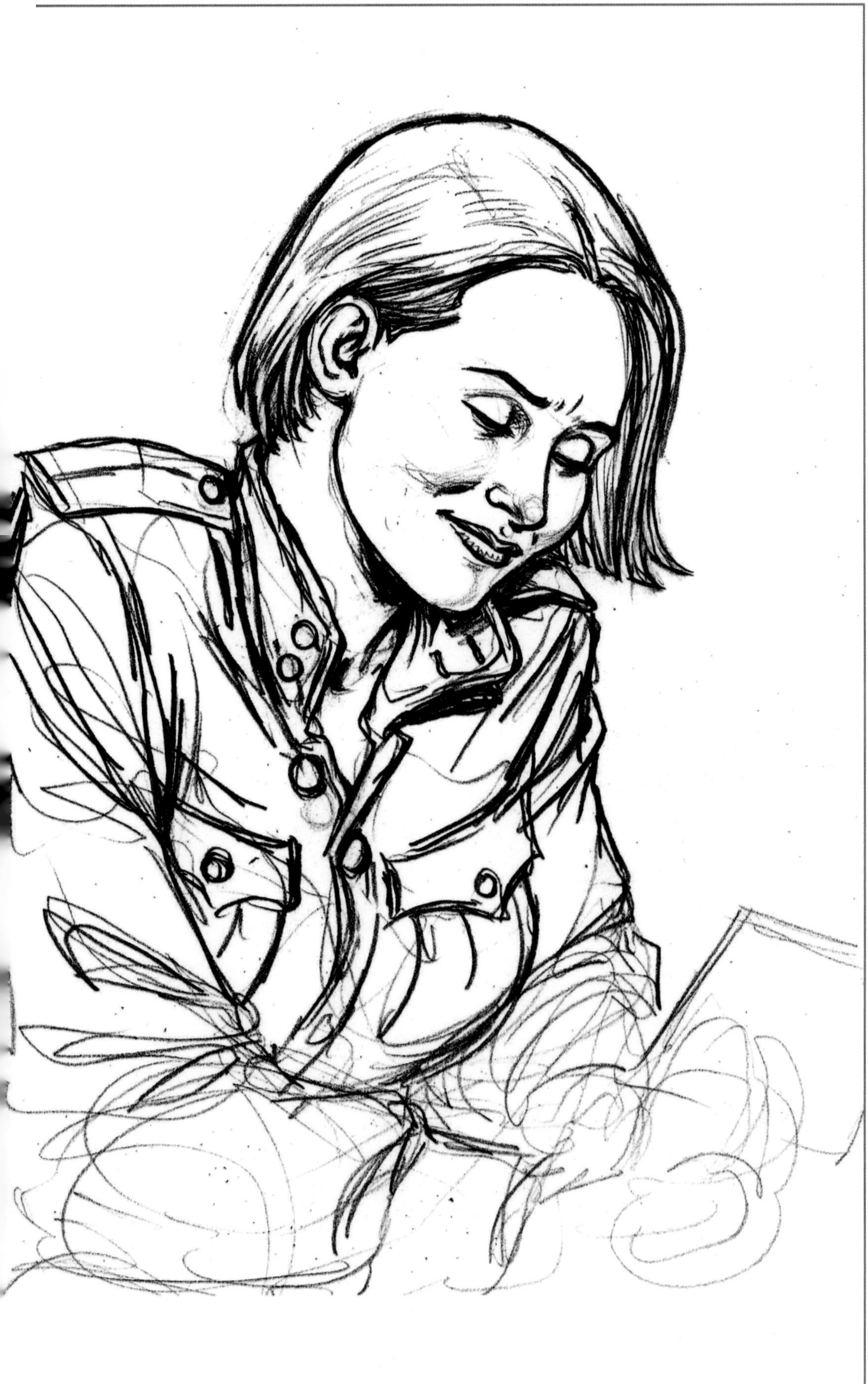

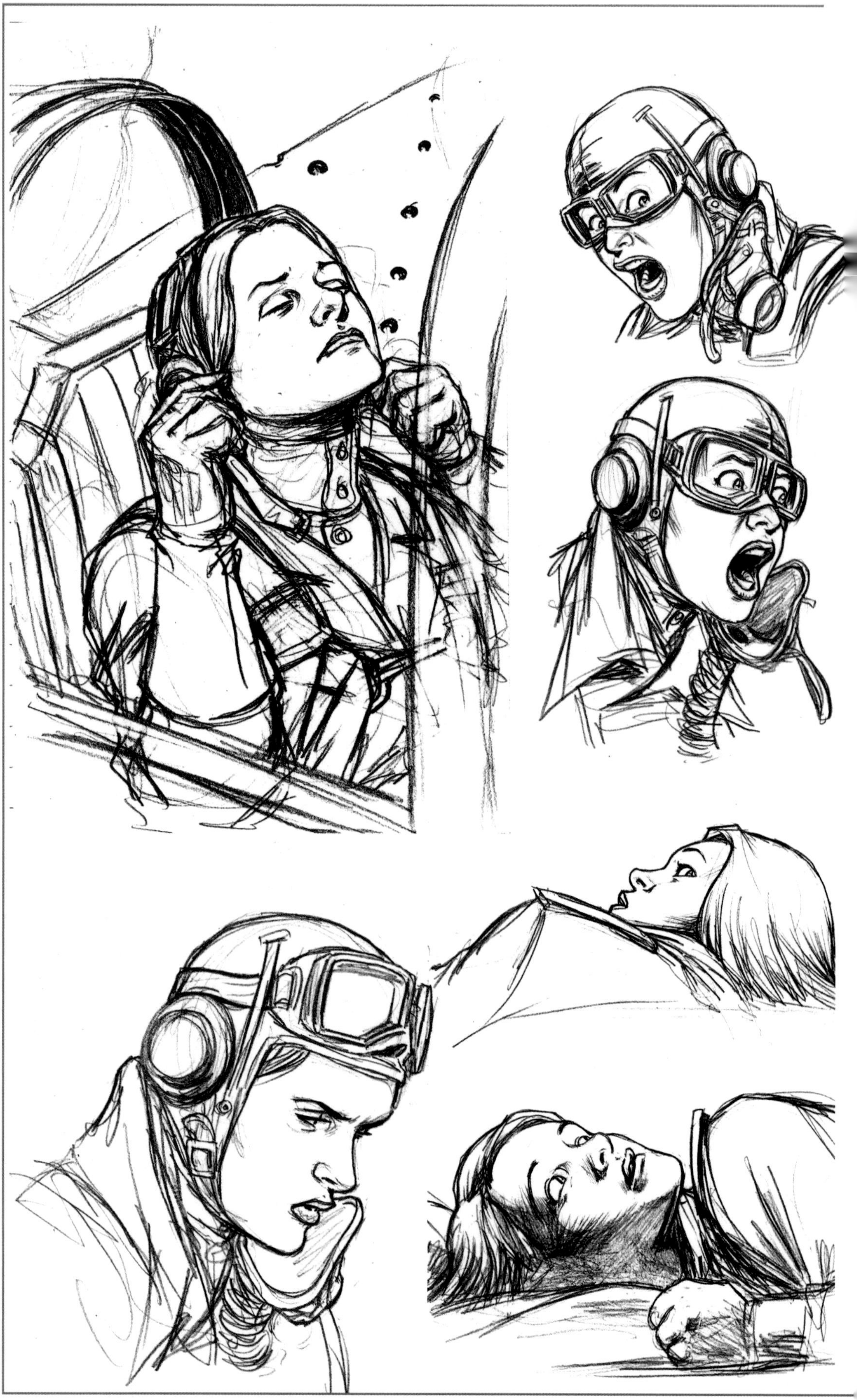

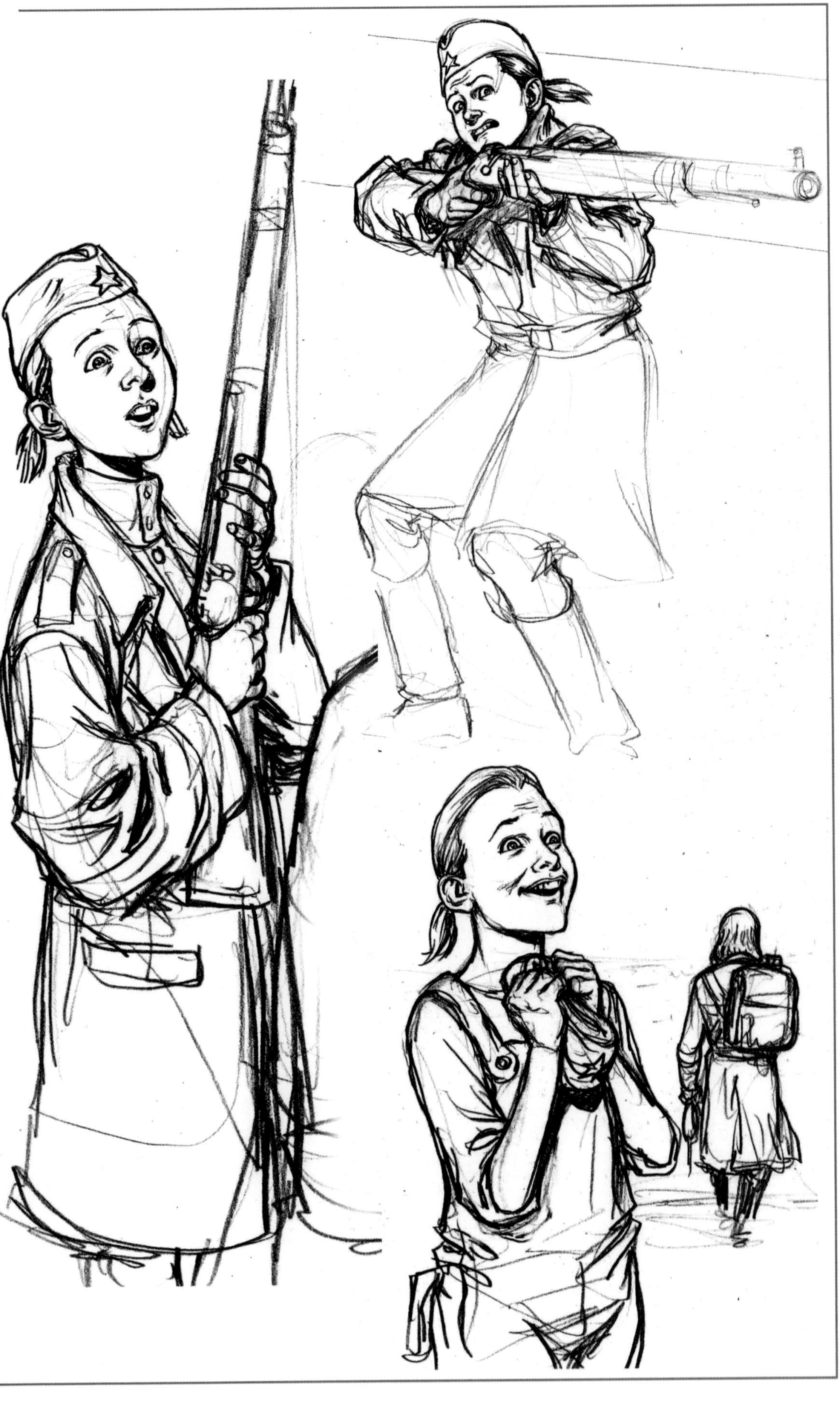

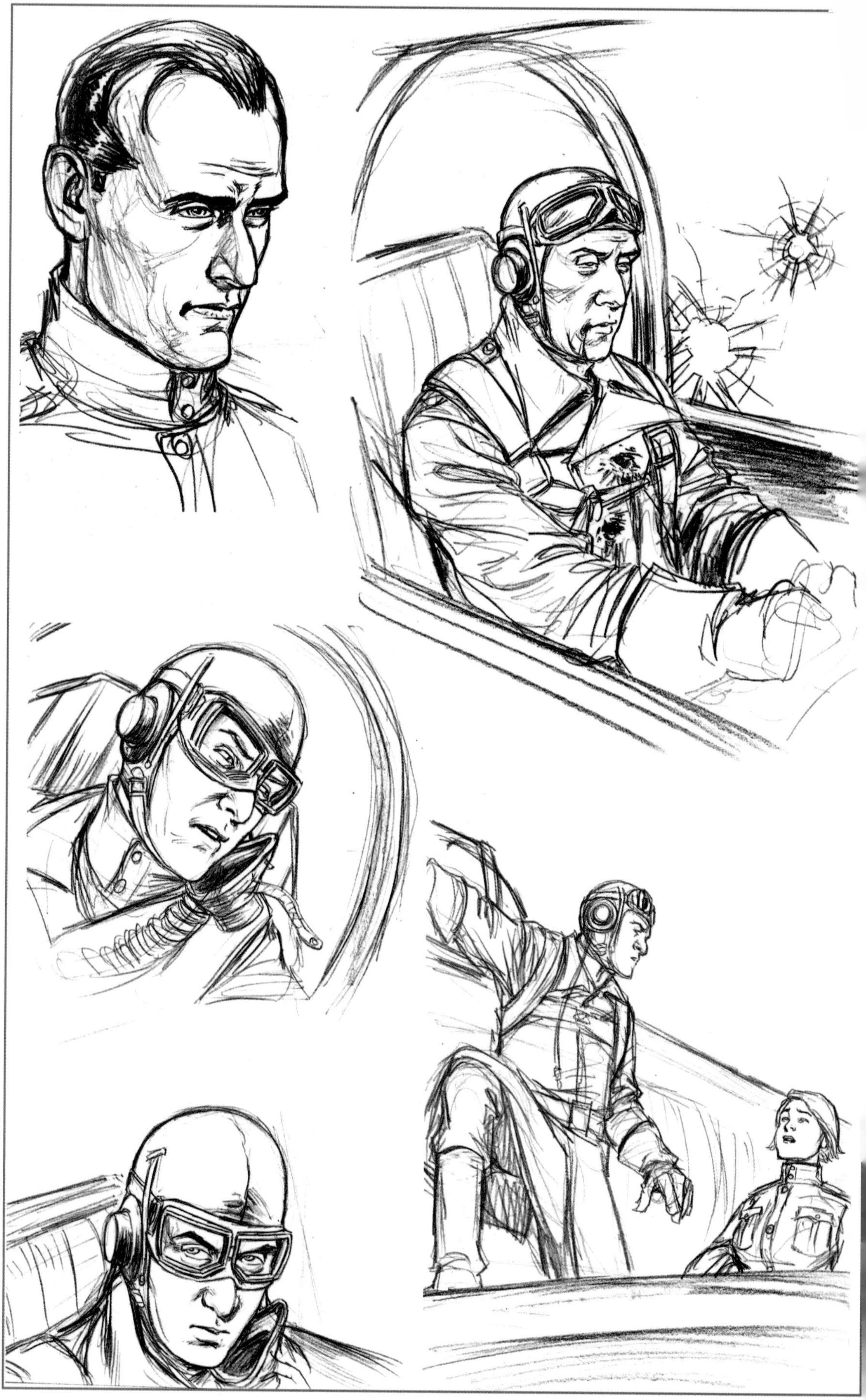

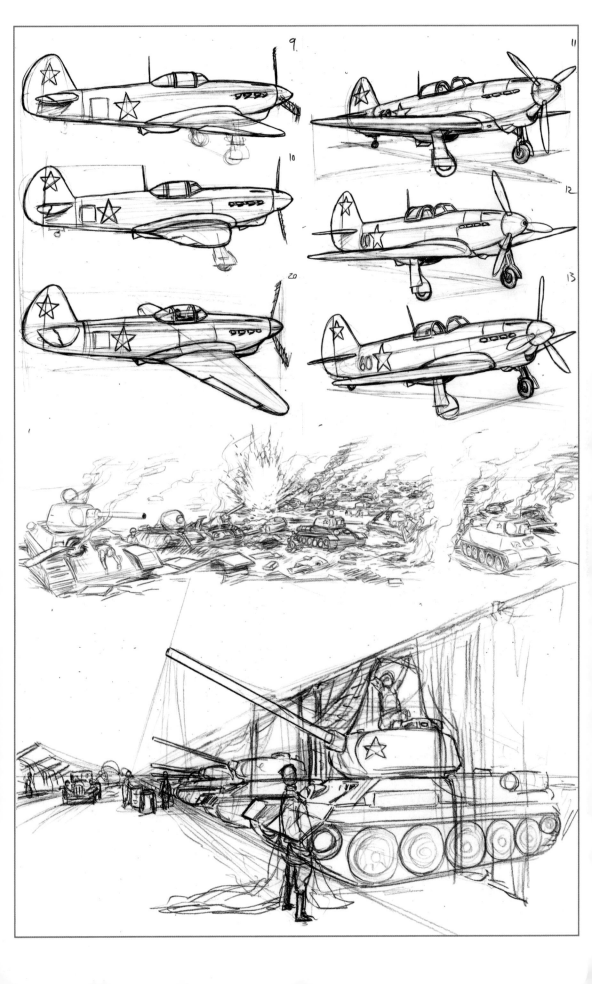

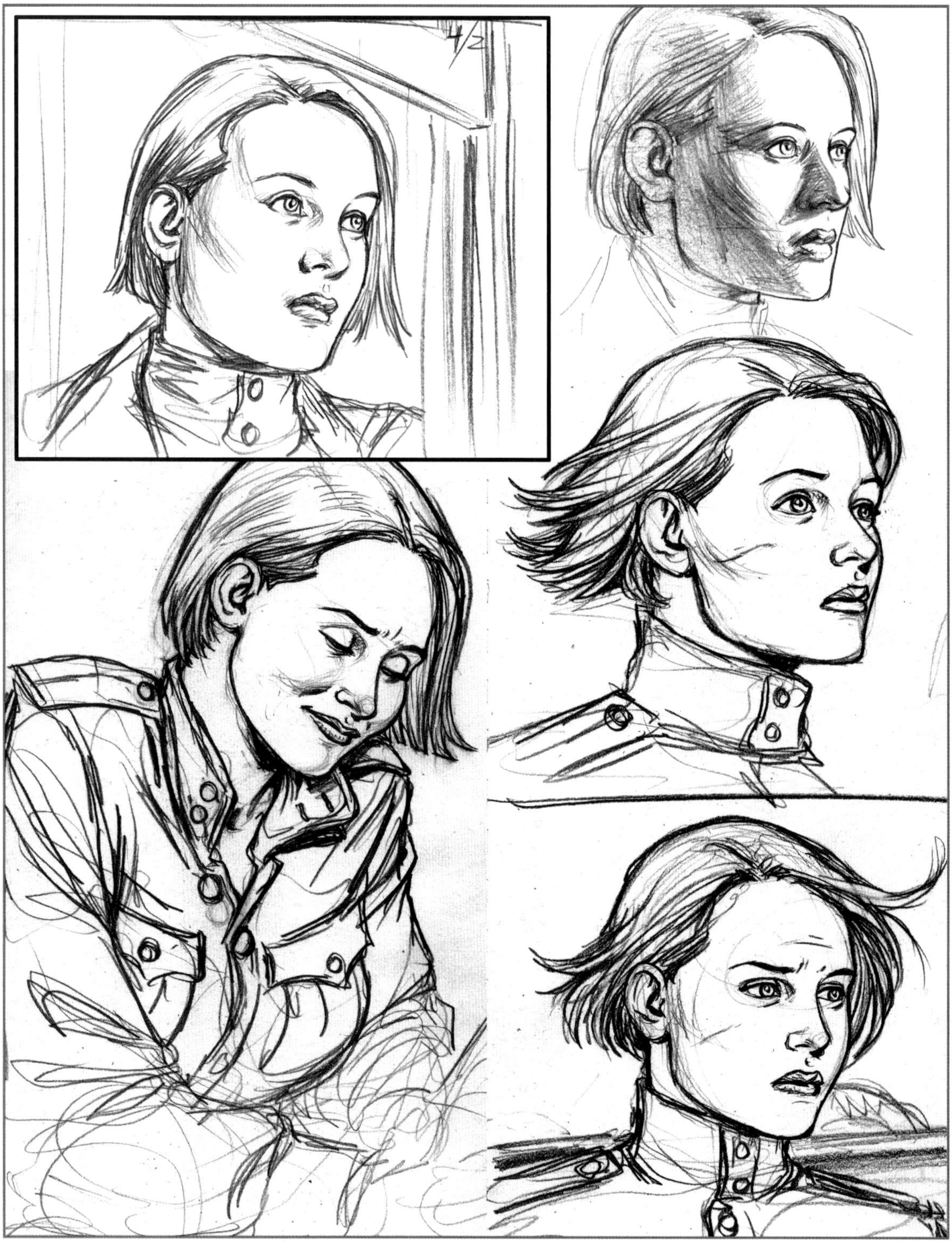

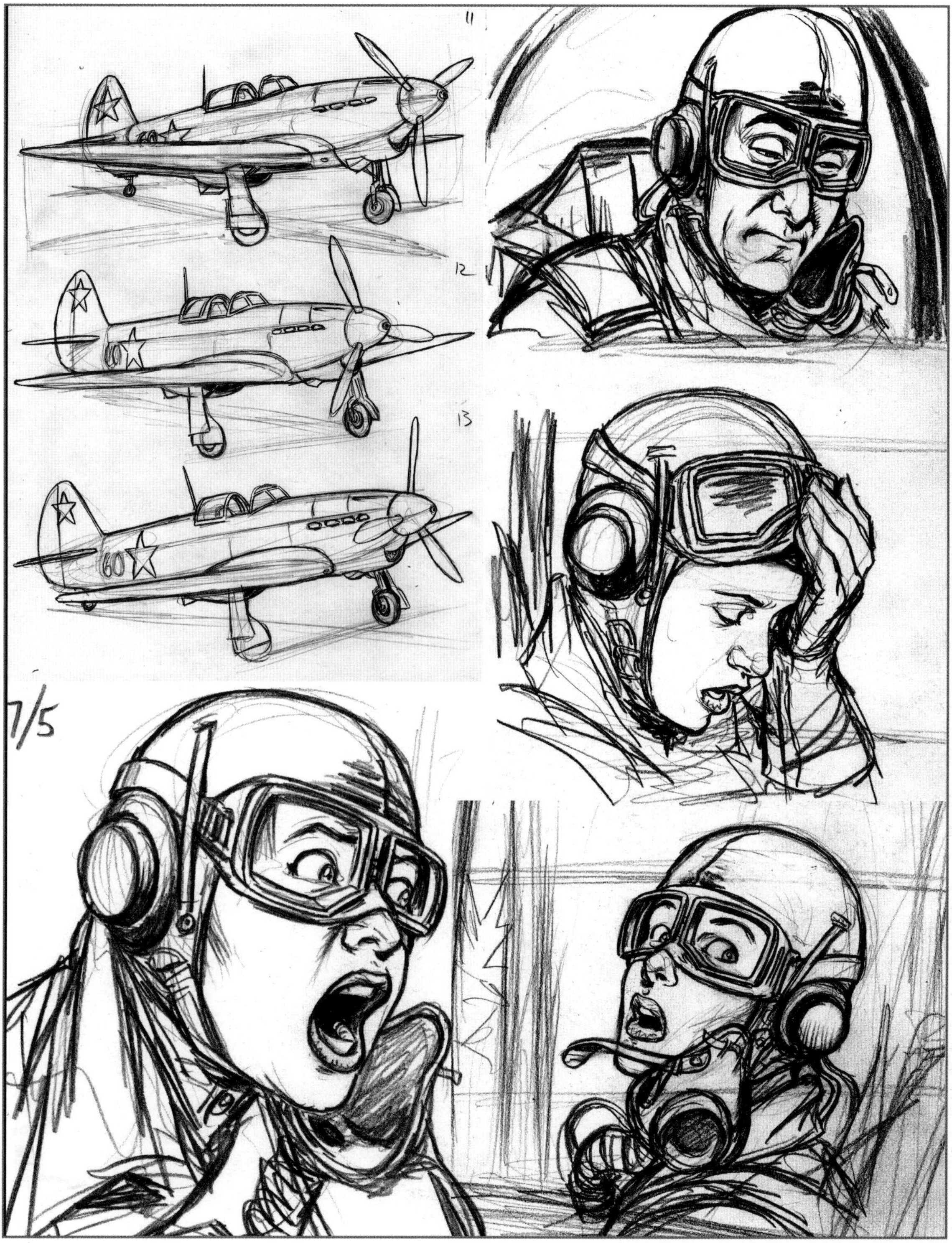
7/5

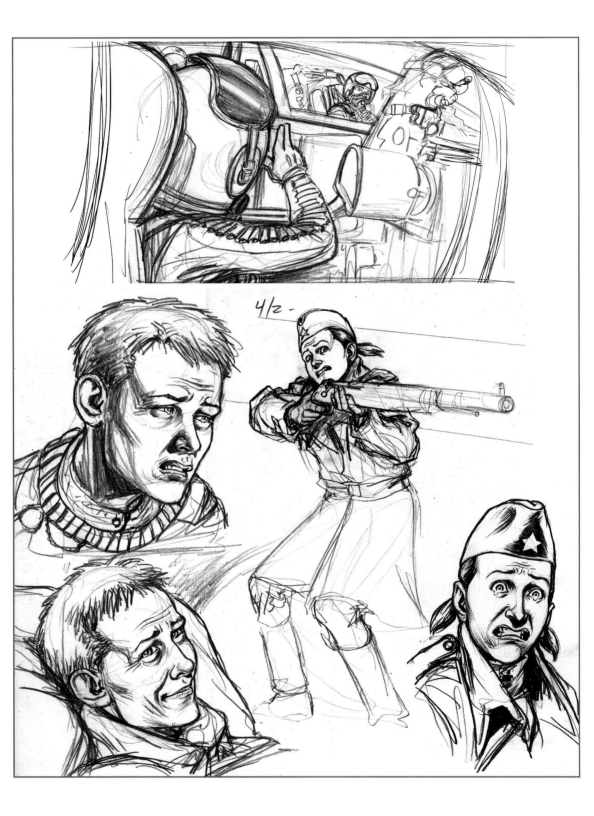

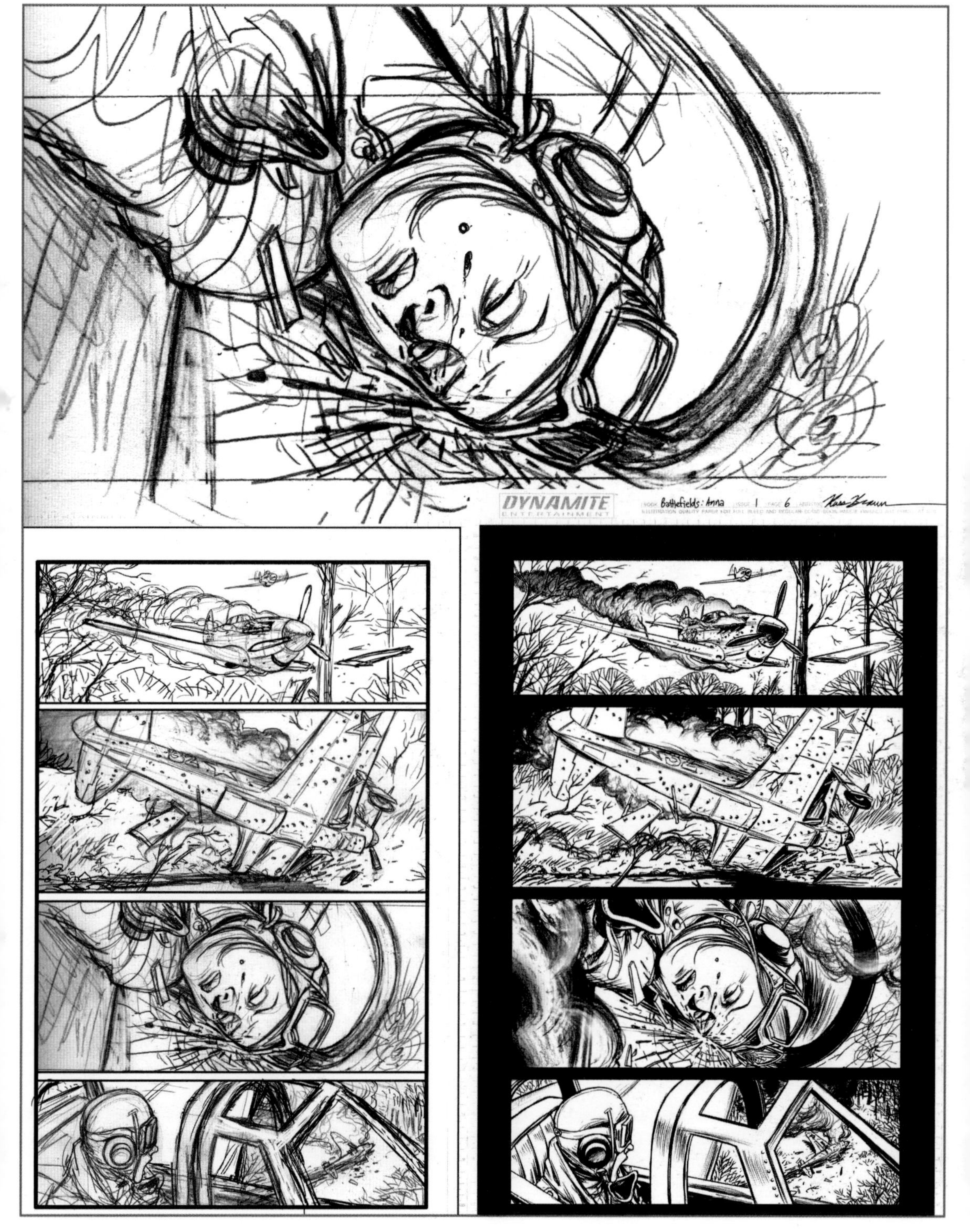
DYNAMITE
ENTERTAINMENT
BOOK Battlefields: Anna ISSUE 1 PAGE 6 ARTIST

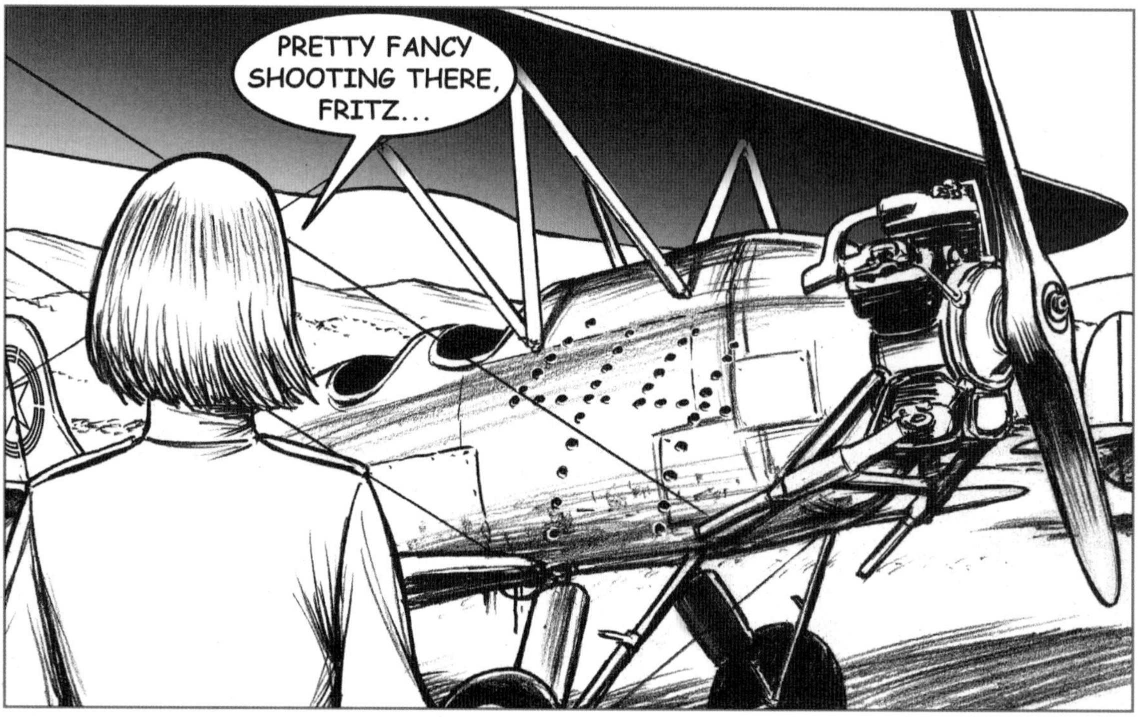
PRETTY FANCY SHOOTING THERE, FRITZ...

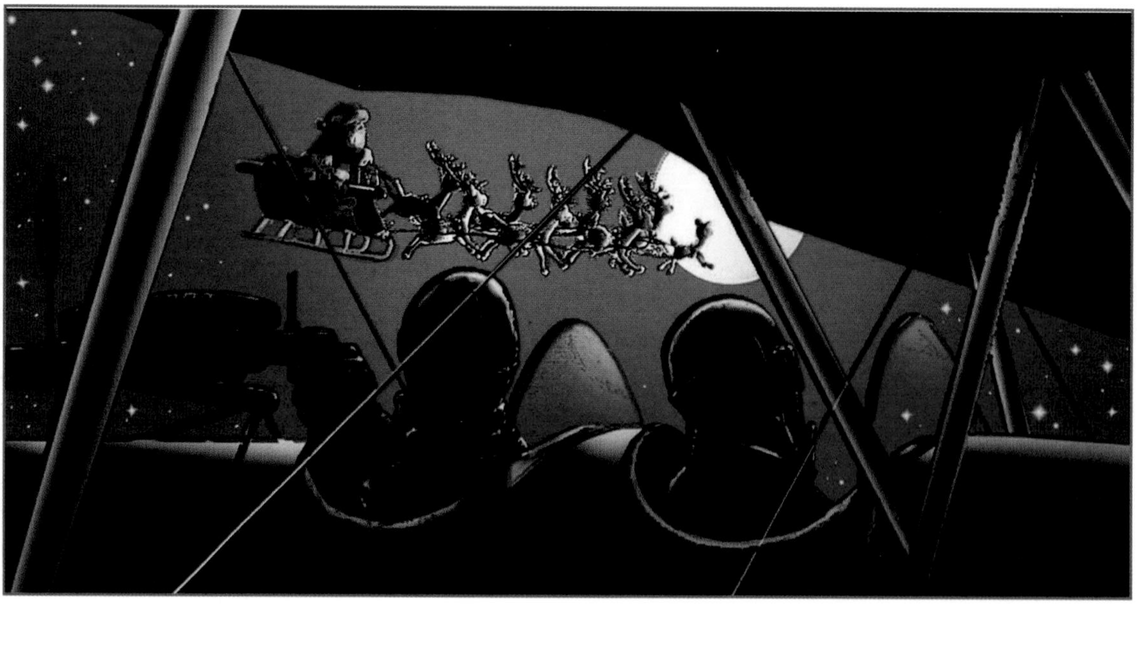

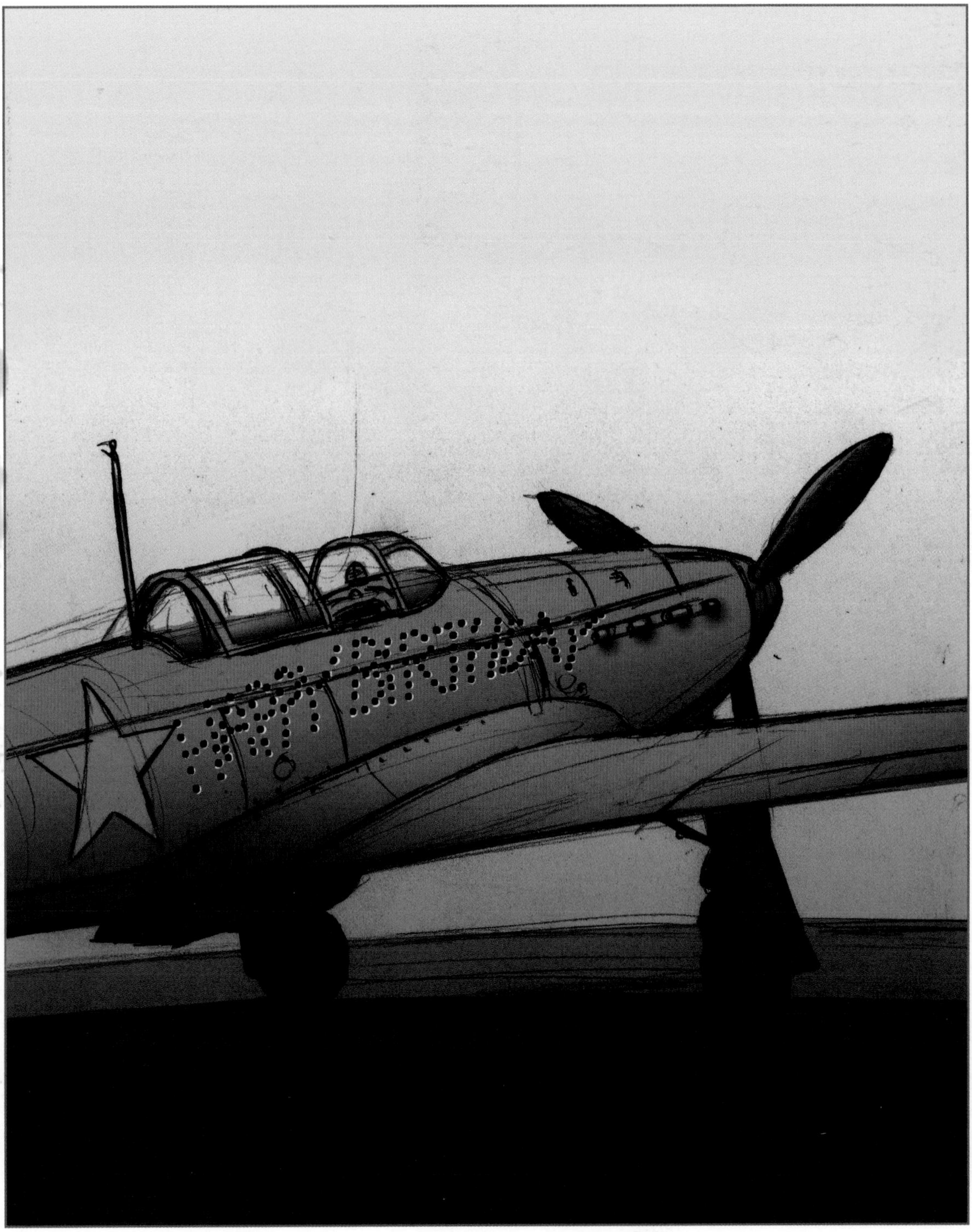

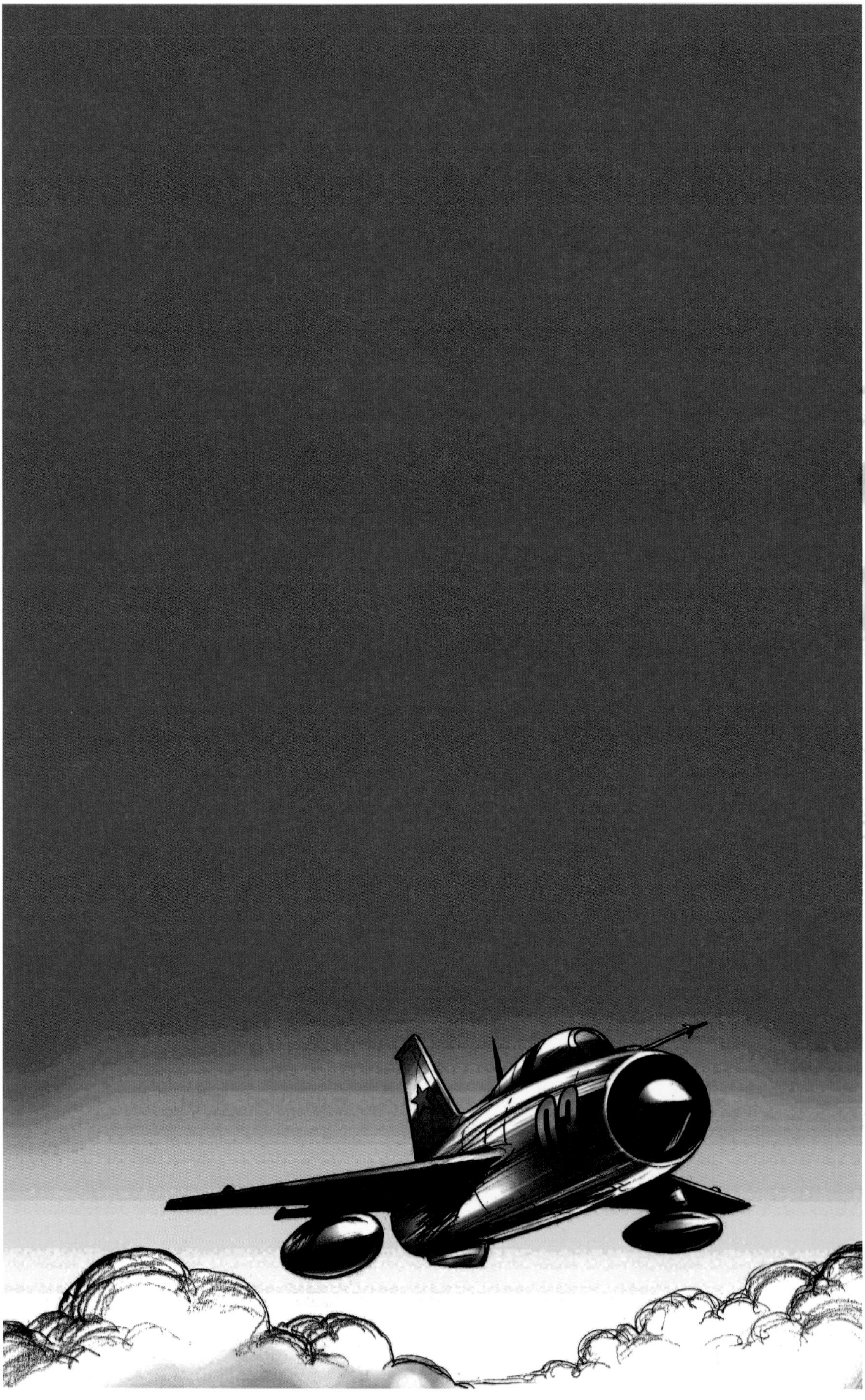

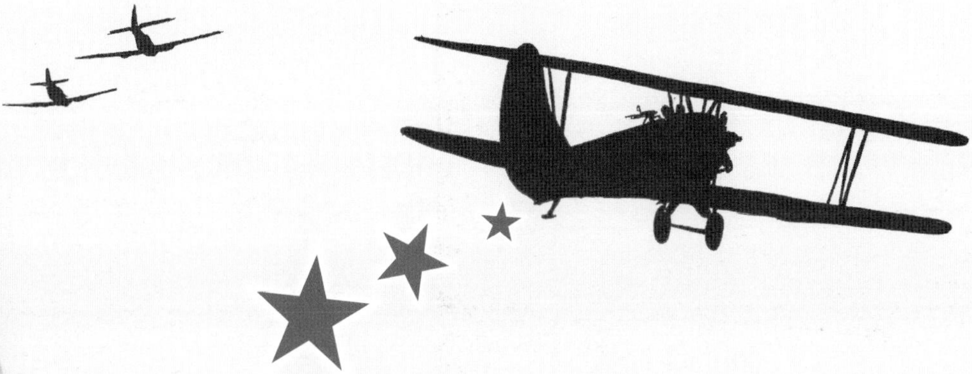

About the Creators

Garth Ennis has been writing comics since 1989. Credits include *Preacher, The Boys*, and *Hitman*, with successful runs on *The Punisher* and *Fury* for Marvel Comics. As well as his own war series *War Stories, Battlefields,* and *Dreaming Eagles*, he recently revived the classic British aviation character *Johnny Red* and has produced two series of *World of Tanks* for Wargaming.net. Originally from Northern Ireland, Ennis now resides in New York City with his wife, Ruth.

Russ Braun has been working in comics for almost thirty years, with a seven-year break for a stint with Disney Feature Animation. He is best known for his frequent collaborations with Garth Ennis on *The Boys, Battlefields, Where Monsters Dwell, Sixpack & Dogwelder,* and most recently *Jimmy's Bastards*.

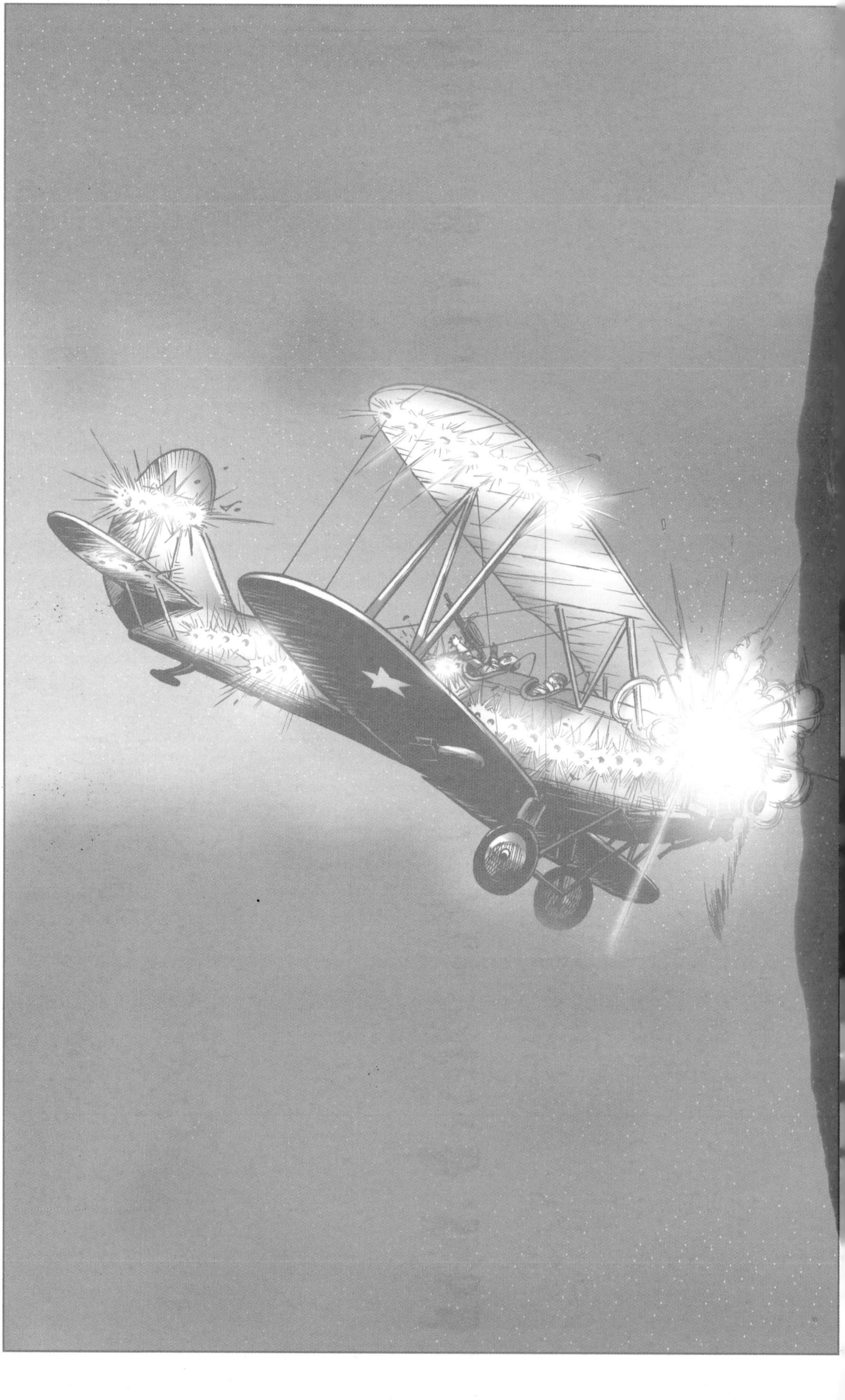